Harry Potter
AND THE DEATHLY HALLOWS

J.K. ROWLING

7

英汉对照版

哈利·波特与死亡圣器 [上]

〔英〕J.K. 罗琳／著

马爱农　马爱新／译

WIZARDING WORLD

人民文学出版社
PEOPLE'S LITERATURE PUBLISHING HOUSE

著作权合同登记号　图字　01-2024-1021

Harry Potter and the Deathly Hallows
First published in Great Britain in 2007 by Bloomsbury Publishing Plc.
Text © 2007 by J.K. Rowling
Interior illustrations by Mary GrandPré © 2007 by Warner Bros.
Wizarding World, Publishing and Theatrical Rights © J.K. Rowling
Wizarding World characters, names and related indicia are TM and © Warner Bros. Entertainment Inc.
Wizarding World TM & © Warner Bros. Entertainment Inc.
Cover illustrations by Mary GrandPré © 2007 by Warner Bros.

图书在版编目（CIP）数据

哈利·波特与死亡圣器：上下：英汉对照/（英）J.K.罗琳著；马爱农，马爱新译．—北京：人民文学出版社，2021（2025.6重印）
ISBN 978-7-02-015069-4

Ⅰ.①哈…　Ⅱ.①J…②马…③马…　Ⅲ.①儿童小说—长篇小说—英国—现代—汉、英　Ⅳ.①I561.84

中国版本图书馆CIP数据核字（2019）第042699号

责任编辑　翟　灿
美术编辑　刘　静
责任印制　苏文强

出版发行　人民文学出版社
社　　址　北京市朝内大街166号
邮政编码　100705

印　　刷　三河市龙林印务有限公司
经　　销　全国新华书店等
字　　数　1560千字
开　　本　640毫米×960毫米　1/16
印　　张　70.5　插页6
印　　数　90001—100000
版　　次　2021年2月北京第1版
印　　次　2025年6月第8次印刷
书　　号　978-7-02-015069-4
定　　价　158.00元（上下册）

如有印装质量问题，请与本社图书销售中心调换。电话：010-65233595

The
dedication
of this book
is split
seven ways:
to Neil,
to Jessica,
to David,
to Kenzie,
to Di,
to Anne,
and to you,
if you have
stuck
with Harry
until the
very
end.

本书
作为
献礼
分成
七份，
献给：
尼尔，
杰西卡，
戴维，
肯琦，
戴，
安妮，
还有你——
如果你
始终
忠于
哈利
直到
最后的
最后。

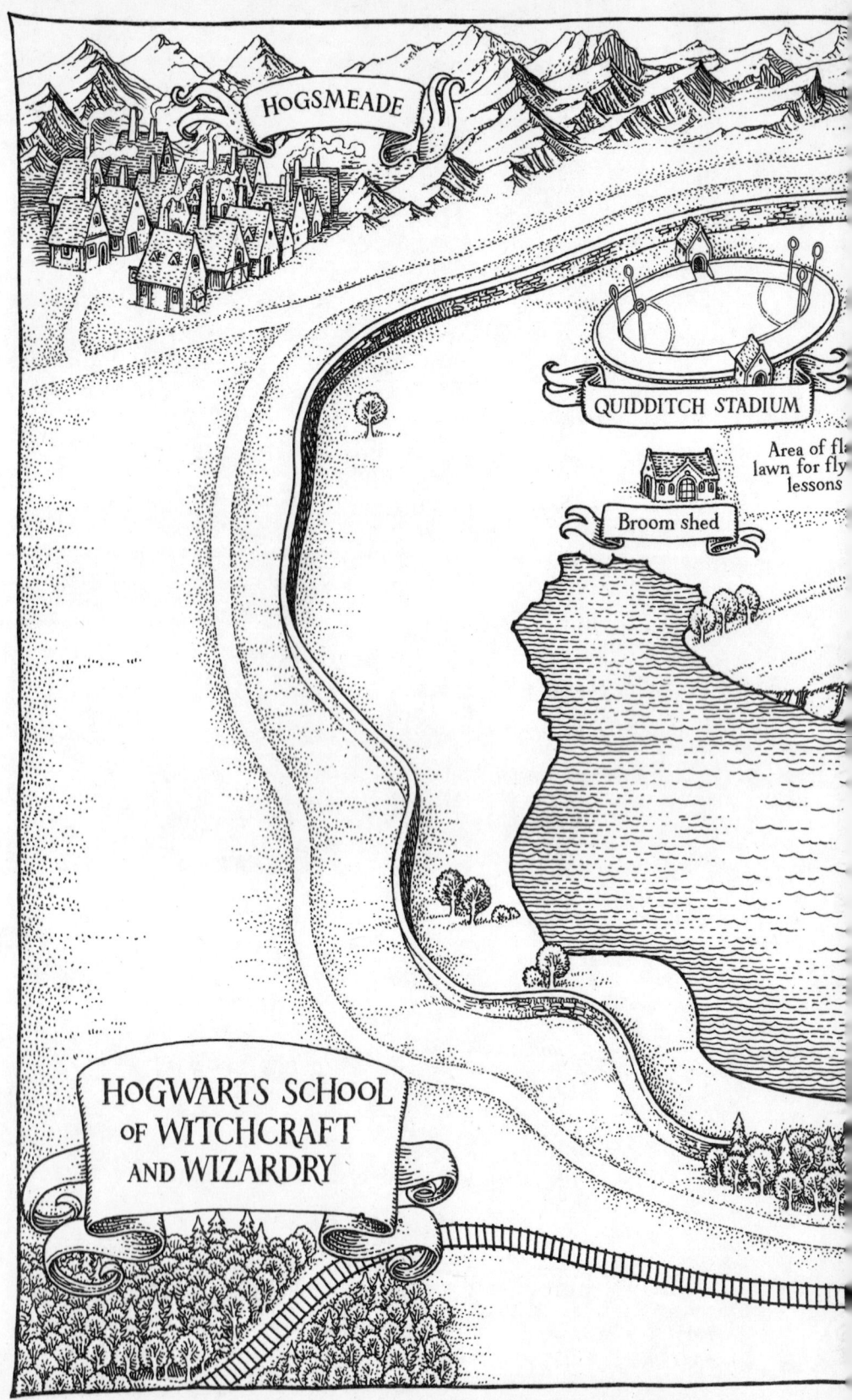

CONTENTS

CHAPTER ONE	The Dark Lord Ascending	010
CHAPTER TWO	In Memoriam	028
CHAPTER THREE	The Dursleys Departing	050
CHAPTER FOUR	The Seven Potters	070
CHAPTER FIVE	Fallen Warrior	100
CHAPTER SIX	The Ghoul in Pyjamas	136
CHAPTER SEVEN	The Will of Albus Dumbledore	172
CHAPTER EIGHT	The Wedding	212
CHAPTER NINE	A Place to Hide	248
CHAPTER TEN	Kreacher's Tale	272
CHAPTER ELEVEN	The Bribe	308
CHAPTER TWELVE	Magic is Might	340
CHAPTER THIRTEEN	The Muggle-Born Registration Commission	374
CHAPTER FOURTEEN	The Thief	406
CHAPTER FIFTEEN	The Goblin's Revenge	428
CHAPTER SIXTEEN	Godric's Hollow	468
CHAPTER SEVENTEEN	Bathilda's Secret	496
CHAPTER EIGHTEEN	The Life and Lies of Albus Dumbledore	526
CHAPTER NINETEEN	The Silver Doe	544
CHAPTER TWENTY	Xenophilius Lovegood	582
CHAPTER TWENTY-ONE	The Tale of the Three Brothers	608
CHAPTER TWENTY-TWO	The Deathly Hallows	636
CHAPTER TWENTY-THREE	Malfoy Manor	668

目 录

第 1 章	黑魔头崛起	011
第 2 章	回忆	029
第 3 章	德思礼一家离开	051
第 4 章	七个波特	071
第 5 章	坠落的勇士	101
第 6 章	穿睡衣的食尸鬼	137
第 7 章	阿不思·邓布利多的遗嘱	173
第 8 章	婚礼	213
第 9 章	藏身之处	249
第 10 章	克利切的故事	273
第 11 章	贿赂	309
第 12 章	魔法即强权	341
第 13 章	麻瓜出身登记委员会	375
第 14 章	小偷	407
第 15 章	妖精的报复	429
第 16 章	戈德里克山谷	469
第 17 章	巴希达的秘密	497
第 18 章	阿不思·邓布利多的生平和谎言	527
第 19 章	银色的牝鹿	545
第 20 章	谢诺菲留斯·洛夫古德	583
第 21 章	三兄弟的传说	609
第 22 章	死亡圣器	637
第 23 章	马尔福庄园	669

CHAPTER TWENTY-FOUR	The Wandmaker	714
CHAPTER TWENTY-FIVE	Shell Cottage	752
CHAPTER TWENTY-SIX	Gringotts	776
CHAPTER TWENTY-SEVEN	The Final Hiding Place	812
CHAPTER TWENTY-EIGHT	The Missing Mirror	826
CHAPTER TWENTY-NINE	The Lost Diadem	850
CHAPTER THIRTY	The Sacking of Severus Snape	876
CHAPTER THIRTY-ONE	The Battle of Hogwarts	906
CHAPTER THIRTY-TWO	The Elder Wand	952
CHAPTER THIRTY-THREE	The Prince's Tale	982
CHAPTER THIRTY-FOUR	The Forest Again	1030
CHAPTER THIRTY-FIVE	King's Cross	1050
CHAPTER THIRTY-SIX	The Flaw in the Plan	1078
Nineteen Years Later		1116

第 24 章	魔杖制作人	715
第 25 章	贝壳小屋	753
第 26 章	古灵阁	777
第 27 章	最后的隐藏之处	813
第 28 章	丢失的镜子	827
第 29 章	失踪的冠冕	851
第 30 章	西弗勒斯·斯内普被赶跑	877
第 31 章	霍格沃茨的战斗	907
第 32 章	老魔杖	953
第 33 章	"王子"的故事	983
第 34 章	又见禁林	1031
第 35 章	国王十字车站	1051
第 36 章	百密一疏	1079
尾　声	十九年后	1117

Oh, the torment bred in the race,
    the grinding scream of death
        and the stroke that hits the vein,
  the haemorrhage none can staunch, the grief,
the curse no man can bear.

But there is a cure in the house
    and not outside it, no,
        not from others but from *them,*
  their bloody strife. We sing to you,
dark gods beneath the earth.

Now hear, you blissful powers underground –
    answer the call, send help.
Bless the children, give them triumph now.

    Aeschylus, *The Libation Bearers*

Death is but crossing the world, as friends do the seas; they live in one another still. For they must needs be present, that love and live in that which is omnipresent. In this divine glass they see face to face; and their converse is free, as well as pure. This is the comfort of friends, that though they may be said to die, yet their friendship and society are, in the best sense, ever present, because immortal.

    William Penn, *More Fruits of Solitude*

哦，那与生俱来的痛苦和折磨，
　　那死亡之际刺耳的尖叫，
　　　　还有那正中血脉的一击，
　　那无法止住的鲜血流淌，那悲伤，
还有那无人能够承受的诅咒。

但是家里可以疗伤，
　　而不是家外的地方，不是，
　　　　无人能够相助，唯有他们，
　　他们的血泪奋争。我们向你们歌唱，
大地下的黑暗神祇。

听啊，你这大地下的极乐力量——
　　回应召唤，送来助襄。
庇佑孩子，赐他们以胜利和希望。

　　　　　　　　——《奠酒人》，埃斯库罗斯

死亡只是穿越世界，如同朋友远渡重洋。他们仍活在彼此的心中。他们必须存在，那份爱与生活无处不在。在这面神圣的镜子里，他们面对面相视，自由地交谈，坦诚而纯真。这就是朋友的安慰，尽管据说他们都要走向死亡，但他们的友谊和陪伴将因为不朽而永存。

　　　　　　　　——《再谈孤独的果实》，威廉·佩恩

CHAPTER ONE

The Dark Lord Ascending

The two men appeared out of nowhere, a few yards apart in the narrow, moonlit lane. For a second they stood quite still, wands directed at each other's chests; then, recognising each other, they stowed their wands beneath their cloaks and started walking briskly in the same direction.

'News?' asked the taller of the two.

'The best,' replied Severus Snape.

The lane was bordered on the left by wild, low-growing brambles, on the right by a high, neatly manicured hedge. The men's long cloaks flapped around their ankles as they marched.

'Thought I might be late,' said Yaxley, his blunt features sliding in and out of sight as the branches of overhanging trees broke the moonlight. 'It was a little trickier than I expected. But I hope he will be satisfied. You sound confident that your reception will be good?'

Snape nodded, but did not elaborate. They turned right, into a wide driveway that led off the lane. The high hedge curved with them, running off into the distance beyond the pair of impressive wrought-iron gates barring the men's way. Neither of them broke step: in silence both raised their left arms in a kind of salute and passed straight through as though the dark metal were smoke.

The yew hedges muffled the sound of the men's footsteps. There was a rustle somewhere to their right: Yaxley drew his wand again, pointing it over his companion's head, but the source of the noise proved to be nothing more than a pure white peacock, strutting majestically along the top of the hedge.

'He always did himself well, Lucius. *Peacocks* ...' Yaxley thrust his wand back under his cloak with a snort.

A handsome manor house grew out of the darkness at the end of the straight

第1章

黑魔头崛起

两个男人从虚空中突然现身,在月光映照的窄巷里相隔几米。他们一动不动地站立了一秒钟,用魔杖指着对方的胸口。接着,两人互相认了出来,便把魔杖塞进斗篷下面,朝同一方向快步走去。

"有消息吗?"个子高一些的那人问。

"再好不过了。"西弗勒斯·斯内普回答。

小巷左边是杂乱生长的低矮的荆棘丛,右边是修剪得整整齐齐的高高的树篱。两人大步行走,长长的斗篷拍打着他们的脚脖子。

"我还以为迟到了呢,"亚克斯利说,头顶上低悬的树枝不时地遮挡住月光,他轮廓不分明的脸显得忽明忽暗,"没想到事情这么棘手,不过我希望他会满意。听你的口气,你好像相信自己会受到欢迎?"

斯内普点点头,但没有细说。他们往右一转,离开小巷,进入一条宽宽的汽车道。高高的树篱也跟着拐了个弯,向远处延伸,两扇气派非凡的锻铁大门挡住了两人的去路。他们谁也没有停住脚步,而是像行礼一样默默地抬起左臂,径直穿了过去,就好像那黑色的锻铁不过是烟雾一般。

紫杉树篱使两人的脚步声听上去发闷。右边什么地方传来沙沙的响声,亚克斯利又抽出魔杖,举过同伴的头顶,结果发现弄出声音的是一只白孔雀,在树篱顶上仪态万方地走着。

"这个卢修斯,总是搞得这么讲究。孔雀……"亚克斯利哼了一声,把魔杖塞回斗篷下面。

笔直的车道尽头,一幢非常体面的宅邸赫然出现在黑暗中,底层

CHAPTER ONE   The Dark Lord Ascending

drive, lights glinting in the diamond-paned downstairs windows. Somewhere in the dark garden beyond the hedge, a fountain was playing. Gravel crackled beneath their feet as Snape and Yaxley sped towards the front door, which swung inwards at their approach, though nobody had visibly opened it.

The hallway was large, dimly lit and sumptuously decorated, with a magnificent carpet covering most of the stone floor. The eyes of the pale-faced portraits on the walls followed Snape and Yaxley as they strode past. The two men halted at a heavy wooden door leading into the next room, hesitated for the space of a heartbeat, then Snape turned the bronze handle.

The drawing room was full of silent people, sitting at a long and ornate table. The room's usual furniture had been pushed carelessly up against the walls. Illumination came from a roaring fire beneath a handsome marble mantelpiece surmounted by a gilded mirror. Snape and Yaxley lingered for a moment on the threshold. As their eyes grew accustomed to the lack of light they were drawn upwards to the strangest feature of the scene: an apparently unconscious human figure hanging upside-down over the table, revolving slowly as if suspended by an invisible rope, and reflected in the mirror and in the bare, polished surface of the table below. None of the people seated underneath this singular sight was looking at it except for a pale young man sitting almost directly below it. He seemed unable to prevent himself from glancing upwards every minute or so.

'Yaxley. Snape,' said a high, clear voice from the head of the table. 'You are very nearly late.'

The speaker was seated directly in front of the fireplace, so that it was difficult, at first, for the new arrivals to make out more than his silhouette. As they drew nearer, however, his face shone through the gloom, hairless, snake-like, with slits for nostrils and gleaming red eyes whose pupils were vertical. He was so pale that he seemed to emit a pearly glow.

'Severus, here,' said Voldemort, indicating the seat on his immediate right. 'Yaxley – beside Dolohov.'

The two men took their allotted places. Most of the eyes around the table followed Snape and it was to him that Voldemort spoke first.

'So?'

'My Lord, the Order of the Phoenix intends to move Harry Potter from his current place of safety on Saturday next, at nightfall.'

第1章 黑魔头崛起

窗户的菱形玻璃射出闪亮的灯光。在树篱后面黑黢黢的花园里，什么地方有个喷泉在喷水。斯内普和亚克斯利吱嘎吱嘎地踩着沙砾路朝正门走去，刚走到跟前，不见有人开门，门却自动朝里打开了。

门厅很大，光线昏暗，布置得十分豪华，一条华贵的地毯几乎覆盖了整个石头地面。斯内普和亚克斯利大步走过时，墙上那些脸色苍白的肖像用目光跟随着他们。两人在一扇通向另一房间的沉重木门前停下脚步，迟疑了一下，斯内普转动了青铜把手。

客厅里满是沉默不语的人，都坐在一张装潢考究的长桌旁边。房间里平常用的家具被胡乱地推到墙边。华丽的大理石壁炉里燃着熊熊旺火，火光照着屋子，壁炉上方是一面镀金的镜子。斯内普和亚克斯利在门口停留了一会儿，等适应了昏暗的光线后，他们的目光被长桌上方一幕最奇怪的景象吸引住了：一具神志明显不清的人体头朝下悬在桌子上方，像是被一根无形的绳子吊着，慢慢旋转，身影映在镜子里，映在空荡荡的、打磨得锃亮的桌面上。在座的那些人谁也没去看这奇异的景象，只有一个差不多正好位于它下方的脸色惨白的年轻人除外。他似乎无法克制自己，不时地往上扫一眼。

"亚克斯利，斯内普，"桌首响起一个高亢、清晰的声音，"你们差点就迟到了。"

说话的人坐在壁炉正前方，亚克斯利和斯内普一开始只能隐约分辨他的轮廓。等他们走近了，那人的脸才从阴影里闪现出来：没有头发，像蛇一样，两道细长的鼻孔，一双闪闪发亮的红眼睛，瞳孔是垂直的。他的肤色十分苍白，似乎发出一种珍珠般的光。

"西弗勒斯，坐在这里吧，"伏地魔指了指紧挨他右边的那个座位，"亚克斯利——坐在多洛霍夫旁边。"

两人在指定的位置上坐了下来。桌旁大多数人的目光都跟着斯内普，伏地魔也首先对他说话：

"怎么样？"

"主人，凤凰社打算下个星期六傍晚把哈利·波特从现在的安全住所转移出去。"

CHAPTER ONE The Dark Lord Ascending

The interest around the table sharpened palpably: some stiffened, others fidgeted, all gazing at Snape and Voldemort.

'Saturday ... at nightfall,' repeated Voldemort. His red eyes fastened upon Snape's black ones with such intensity that some of the watchers looked away, apparently fearful that they themselves would be scorched by the ferocity of the gaze. Snape, however, looked calmly back into Voldemort's face and, after a moment or two, Voldemort's lipless mouth curved into something like a smile.

'Good. Very good. And this information comes –'

'From the source we discussed,' said Snape.

'My Lord.'

Yaxley had leaned forward to look down the long table at Voldemort and Snape. All faces turned to him.

'My Lord, I have heard differently.'

Yaxley waited, but Voldemort did not speak, so he went on, 'Dawlish, the Auror, let slip that Potter will not be moved until the thirtieth, the night before the boy turns seventeen.'

Snape was smiling.

'My source told me that there are plans to lay a false trail; this must be it. No doubt a Confundus Charm has been placed upon Dawlish. It would not be the first time, he is known to be susceptible.'

'I assure you, my Lord, Dawlish seemed quite certain,' said Yaxley.

'If he has been Confunded, naturally he is certain,' said Snape. 'I assure *you*, Yaxley, the Auror Office will play no further part in the protection of Harry Potter. The Order believes that we have infiltrated the Ministry.'

'The Order's got one thing right, then, eh?' said a squat man sitting a short distance from Yaxley; he gave a wheezy giggle that was echoed here and there along the table.

Voldemort did not laugh. His gaze had wandered upwards, to the body revolving slowly overhead, and he seemed to be lost in thought.

'My Lord,' Yaxley went on, 'Dawlish believes an entire party of Aurors will be used to transfer the boy –'

第1章　黑魔头崛起

桌旁的人明显来了兴趣：有的挺直了身子，有的好像坐不住了，都用眼睛盯着斯内普和伏地魔。

"星期六……傍晚。"伏地魔重复了一句。他的红眼睛死死盯着斯内普的黑眼睛，目光如此锐利，旁边有几个人赶紧望向别处，似乎担心那凶残的目光会灼伤自己。斯内普却不动声色地望着伏地魔的脸，片刻之后，伏地魔那没有唇的嘴扭曲成一个古怪的笑容。

"好，很好。这个情报来自——"

"来自我们谈论过的那个出处。"斯内普说。

"主人。"

亚克斯利探身望着长桌那头的伏地魔和斯内普。大家都把脸转向了他。

"主人，我听到了不同的情报。"

亚克斯利等了等，但伏地魔没有说话，他就继续往下说道："德力士，就是那个傲罗，他无意中透露，波特要到三十号，也就是他满十七岁前的那个晚上才转移呢。"

斯内普微微一笑。

"向我提供消息的人告诉我，他们计划散布一些虚假情报，这肯定就是了。毫无疑问，德力士中了混淆咒。这不是第一次了，他意志薄弱是出了名的。"

"我向您保证，主人，德力士看上去很有把握。"亚克斯利说。

"如果中了混淆咒，他自然很有把握，"斯内普说，"我向你保证，亚克斯利，傲罗办公室在掩护哈利·波特的行动中不再起任何作用。凤凰社相信我们的人已经打入魔法部。"

"如此看来，凤凰社总算弄对了一件事，嗯？"坐在离亚克斯利不远处的一个矮胖男人说。他呼哧带喘地笑了几声，长桌旁有几个人也跟着笑了起来。

伏地魔没有笑。他将目光转向头顶上那具慢慢旋转的人体，似乎陷入了沉思。

"主人，"亚克斯利继续说，"德力士相信所有的傲罗都要参加转移那个男孩——"

CHAPTER ONE The Dark Lord Ascending

Voldemort held up a large, white hand and Yaxley subsided at once, watching resentfully as Voldemort turned back to Snape.

'Where are they going to hide the boy next?'

'At the home of one of the Order,' said Snape. 'The place, according to the source, has been given every protection that the Order and Ministry together could provide. I think that there is little chance of taking him once he is there, my Lord, unless, of course, the Ministry has fallen before next Saturday, which might give us the opportunity to discover and undo enough of the enchantments to break through the rest.'

'Well, Yaxley?' Voldemort called down the table, the firelight glinting strangely in his red eyes. '*Will* the Ministry have fallen by next Saturday?'

Once again, all heads turned. Yaxley squared his shoulders.

'My Lord, I have good news on that score. I have – with difficulty, and after great effort – succeeded in placing an Imperius Curse upon Pius Thicknesse.'

Many of those sitting around Yaxley looked impressed; his neighbour, Dolohov, a man with a long, twisted face, clapped him on the back.

'It is a start,' said Voldemort. 'But Thicknesse is only one man. Scrimgeour must be surrounded by our people before I act. One failed attempt on the Minister's life will set me back a long way.'

'Yes – my Lord, that is true – but you know, as Head of the Department of Magical Law Enforcement, Thicknesse has regular contact not only with the Minister himself, but also with the Heads of all the other Ministry departments. It will, I think, be easy, now that we have such a high-ranking official under our control, to subjugate the others, and then they can all work together to bring Scrimgeour down.'

'As long as our friend Thicknesse is not discovered before he has converted the rest,' said Voldemort. 'At any rate, it remains unlikely that the Ministry will be mine before next Saturday. If we cannot touch the boy at his destination, then it must be done while he travels.'

'We are at an advantage there, my Lord,' said Yaxley, who seemed determined to receive some portion of approval. 'We now have several people planted within the Department of Magical Transport. If Potter Apparates or uses the Floo Network, we shall know immediately.'

第1章　黑魔头崛起

伏地魔举起一只苍白的大手，亚克斯利立刻不作声了，怨恨地看着伏地魔把目光又转向了斯内普。

"接下来他们打算把那男孩藏在哪儿？"

"藏在某个凤凰社成员的家里。"斯内普说，"据情报说，那个地方已经采取了凤凰社和魔法部所能提供的各种保护措施。我认为，一旦他到了那里，就很难有机会抓住他了。当然啦，除非魔法部在下个星期六之前垮台，主人，那样我们或许有机会发现和解除一些魔咒，继而突破其他魔咒。"

"怎么样，亚克斯利？"伏地魔朝桌子那头大声问，火光在他的红眼睛里发出诡异的光芒，"魔法部到下个星期六会垮台吗？"

大家又一次把脑袋都转了过来。亚克斯利挺起胸膛。

"主人，这方面我有好消息。我——克服重重困难，经过种种努力——成功地给皮尔斯·辛克尼斯施了夺魂咒。"

亚克斯利周围的许多人露出钦佩的神情。坐在他旁边的多洛霍夫——一个长着一张扭曲的长脸的男人，拍了拍他的后背。

"算是个开始，"伏地魔说，"但辛克尼斯只是一个人。在我行动之前，斯克林杰周围必须全是我们的人。暗杀部长的努力一旦失败，我们就会前功尽弃。"

"是的——主人，的确如此——可是您知道，辛克尼斯是魔法法律执行司的司长，他不仅与部长本人，而且与魔法部各司的司长都有频繁接触。我想，我们要是把这样一位高级官员控制住了，再去制服别人就容易了，然后他们可以一起努力，把斯克林杰赶下台去。"

"但愿我们的朋友辛克尼斯在改造别人前不要暴露身份，"伏地魔说，"不管怎样，魔法部不可能在下个星期六之前就听命于我。既然不能在那男孩到达目的地以后抓他，我们就必须趁他在路上的时候动手。"

"主人，这方面我们有一个优势，"亚克斯利说，他似乎打定主意要得到一些夸奖，"我们已经在魔法交通司里安插了几个人。如果波特幻影移形或使用飞路网，我们立刻就会知道。"

CHAPTER ONE   The Dark Lord Ascending

'He will not do either,' said Snape. 'The Order is eschewing any form of transport that is controlled or regulated by the Ministry; they mistrust everything to do with the place.'

'All the better,' said Voldemort. 'He will have to move in the open. Easier to take, by far.'

Again, Voldemort looked up at the slowly revolving body as he went on, 'I shall attend to the boy in person. There have been too many mistakes where Harry Potter is concerned. Some of them have been my own. That Potter lives is due more to my errors, than to his triumphs.'

The company round the table watched Voldemort apprehensively, each of them, by his or her expression, afraid that they might be blamed for Harry Potter's continued existence. Voldemort, however, seemed to be speaking more to himself than to any of them, still addressing the unconscious body above him.

'I have been careless, and so have been thwarted by luck and chance, those wreckers of all but the best laid plans. But I know better now. I understand those things that I did not understand before. I must be the one to kill Harry Potter, and I shall be.'

At these words, seemingly in response to them, a sudden wail sounded, a terrible, drawn-out cry of misery and pain. Many of those at the table looked downwards, startled, for the sound had seemed to issue from below their feet.

'Wormtail,' said Voldemort, with no change in his quiet, thoughtful tone, and without removing his eyes from the revolving body above, 'have I not spoken to you about keeping our prisoner quiet?'

'Yes m – my Lord,' gasped a small man halfway down the table, who had been sitting so low in his chair that it had appeared, at first glance, to be unoccupied. Now he scrambled from his seat and scurried from the room, leaving nothing behind him but a curious gleam of silver.

'As I was saying,' continued Voldemort, looking again at the tense faces of his followers, 'I understand better now. I shall need, for instance, to borrow a wand from one of you before I go to kill Potter.'

The faces around him displayed nothing but shock; he might have announced that he wanted to borrow one of their arms.

'No volunteers?' said Voldemort. 'Let's see ... Lucius, I see no reason for you to have a wand any more.'

"他不会这么做的，"斯内普说，"凤凰社会避开任何受魔法部控制和管理的交通方式。凡是和魔法部有关的，他们都不相信。"

"这样更好，"伏地魔说，"他只好在露天转移，要抓住他就容易多了。"

伏地魔又抬起目光，望着那具慢慢旋转的人体，一边继续说道："我要亲自对付那个男孩。在哈利·波特的问题上，失误太多了。有些是我自己的失误。波特能活到今天，更多是由于我的失误，而不是他的成功。"

长桌旁的人战战兢兢地注视着伏地魔，从他们的表情看，似乎每个人都担心自己会因为哈利·波特仍然活着而受到责难。不过，伏地魔不像是针对他们某一个人，而更像是自言自语，他的目光仍然对着上方那具昏迷的人体。

"我过去太大意了，所以被糟糕的运气和偶然因素挫败，只有最周密的计划才不会被这些破坏。现在我明白多了。我明白了一些以前不明白的东西。杀死哈利·波特的必须是我，也必定是我。"

伏地魔的话音刚落，突然传来一声痛苦的哀号，拖得长长的，凄惨无比，像是在回答他的话。桌旁的许多人都大惊失色地往下看去，因为那声音似乎是从他们脚下发出来的。

"虫尾巴，"伏地魔那平静的、若有所思的声音毫无变化，目光也没有离开上面那具旋转的人体，"我没有跟你说过吗？让我们的俘虏保持安静！"

"是，主——主人。"桌子中间一个矮个子男人结结巴巴地说。他整个人缩在椅子上，猛一眼看去，还以为椅子上没有人。他慌慌张张地从椅子上爬下来，匆忙离开了房间，身后只留下一道奇怪的银光。

"我刚才说了，"伏地魔又看着自己的追随者们紧张的面孔，继续说道，"我现在明白多了。比如，我需要从你们某个人手里借一根魔杖，再去干掉波特。"

周围的人满脸惊愕，就好像他刚才宣布要借他们一条胳膊似的。

"没有人自愿？"伏地魔说，"让我想想……卢修斯，我看你没有理由再拿着魔杖了。"

CHAPTER ONE   The Dark Lord Ascending

Lucius Malfoy looked up. His skin appeared yellowish and waxy in the firelight and his eyes were sunken and shadowed. When he spoke, his voice was hoarse.

'My Lord?'

'Your wand, Lucius. I require your wand.'

'I ...'

Malfoy glanced sideways at his wife. She was staring straight ahead, quite as pale as he was, her long, blonde hair hanging down her back, but beneath the table her slim fingers closed briefly on his wrist. At her touch, Malfoy put his hand into his robes, withdrew a wand and passed it along to Voldemort, who held it up in front of his red eyes, examining it closely.

'What is it?'

'Elm, my Lord,' whispered Malfoy.

'And the core?'

'Dragon – dragon heartstring.'

'Good,' said Voldemort. He drew out his own wand and compared the lengths.

Lucius Malfoy made an involuntary movement; for a fraction of a second, it seemed he expected to receive Voldemort's wand in exchange for his own. The gesture was not missed by Voldemort, whose eyes widened maliciously.

'Give you my wand, Lucius? *My* wand?'

Some of the throng sniggered.

'I have given you your liberty, Lucius, is that not enough for you? But I have noticed that you and your family seem less than happy of late ... what is it about my presence in your home that displeases you, Lucius?'

'Nothing – nothing, my Lord!'

'Such *lies*, Lucius ...'

The soft voice seemed to hiss on even after the cruel mouth had stopped moving. One or two of the wizards barely repressed a shudder as the hissing grew louder; something heavy could be heard sliding across the floor beneath the table.

The huge snake emerged to climb slowly up Voldemort's chair. It rose, seemingly endlessly, and came to rest across Voldemort's shoulders: its neck

第1章 黑魔头崛起

卢修斯·马尔福抬起头。在火光的映照下，他的皮肤显得蜡黄蜡黄的，一双眼睛深陷下去，神色忧郁，说话声音沙哑。

"主人？"

"你的魔杖，卢修斯。我要你的魔杖。"

"我……"

马尔福侧眼望了望妻子。她呆呆地目视着前方，脸色和他一样苍白，长长的金黄色头发披散在背后，可是在桌子底下，她用细长的手指轻轻握了握马尔福的手腕。马尔福感觉到了她的触摸，便把手伸进长袍，抽出一根魔杖，递给了伏地魔。伏地魔把魔杖举到他的红眼睛前面，仔细端详。

"是什么做的？"

"榆木，主人。"马尔福小声说。

"杖芯呢？"

"火龙——火龙的心脏神经。"

"很好。"伏地魔说。他抽出自己的魔杖，比较着长短。

卢修斯·马尔福不由自主地动弹了一下，刹那间，他似乎指望伏地魔用自己的魔杖换他的那根。伏地魔注意到了他的表现，恶毒地睁大了眼睛。

"把我的魔杖给你，卢修斯？我的魔杖？"

有几个人发出了窃笑。

"我给了你自由，卢修斯，这对你来说还不够吗？但我注意到，你和你的家人最近好像不太高兴……我待在你家里，有什么让你们不愉快的吗，卢修斯？"

"没有——没有，主人！"

"全是撒谎，卢修斯……"

他冷酷的嘴已经不动了，但低低的咝咝声似乎还在响着。这声音越来越大，一两个巫师忍不住打了个寒战，只听见桌子底下的地板上有个沉重的东西在爬。

巨蛇探出身，慢慢爬上伏地魔的椅子。它越攀越高，似乎永无止境，然后把身子搭在伏地魔的肩膀上。它的身体和人的大腿一样粗，眼睛

CHAPTER ONE   The Dark Lord Ascending

the thickness of a man's thigh; its eyes, with their vertical slits for pupils, unblinking. Voldemort stroked the creature absently with long, thin fingers, still looking at Lucius Malfoy.

'Why do the Malfoys look so unhappy with their lot? Is my return, my rise to power, not the very thing they professed to desire for so many years?'

'Of course, my Lord,' said Lucius Malfoy. His hand shook as he wiped sweat from his upper lip. 'We did desire it – we do.'

To Malfoy's left, his wife made an odd, stiff nod, her eyes averted from Voldemort and the snake. To his right, his son Draco, who had been gazing up at the inert body overhead, glanced quickly at Voldemort and away again, terrified to make eye contact.

'My Lord,' said a dark woman halfway down the table, her voice constricted with emotion, 'it is an honour to have you here, in our family's house. There can be no higher pleasure.'

She sat beside her sister, as unlike her in looks, with her dark hair and heavily lidded eyes, as she was in bearing and demeanour; where Narcissa sat rigid and impassive, Bellatrix leaned towards Voldemort, for mere words could not demonstrate her longing for closeness.

'No higher pleasure,' repeated Voldemort, his head tilted a little to one side as he considered Bellatrix. 'That means a great deal, Bellatrix, from you.'

Her face flooded with colour; her eyes welled with tears of delight.

'My Lord knows I speak nothing but the truth!'

'No higher pleasure ... even compared with the happy event that, I hear, has taken place in your family this week?'

She stared at him, her lips parted, evidently confused.

'I don't know what you mean, my Lord.'

'I'm talking about your niece, Bellatrix. And yours, Lucius and Narcissa. She has just married the werewolf, Remus Lupin. You must be so proud.'

There was an eruption of jeering laughter from around the table. Many leaned forward to exchange gleeful looks; a few thumped the table with their fists. The great snake, disliking the disturbance, opened its mouth wide and hissed angrily, but the Death Eaters did not hear it, so jubilant were they at

第1章 黑魔头崛起

一眨不眨，瞳孔垂直。伏地魔用细长的手指漫不经心地抚摸着巨蛇，眼睛仍然望着卢修斯·马尔福。

"为什么马尔福一家对他们的境况表现得这么不高兴呢？这么多年来，他们不是一直口口声声地宣称希望我复出，希望我东山再起吗？"

"那是当然，主人。"卢修斯·马尔福说，他用颤抖的手擦去嘴唇上边的汗，"我们确实是这样——现在也是。"

在马尔福的左边，他的妻子纳西莎古怪而僵硬地点点头，眼睛躲避着伏地魔和那条蛇。他的右边是儿子德拉科，刚才一直盯着长桌上方那具毫无生气的人体，此刻迅速扫了一眼伏地魔，又赶紧移开目光，不敢跟他对视。

"主人，"说话的是坐在桌子中间的一个黑皮肤女人，她激动得声音发紧，"您待在我们家里是我们的荣幸，没有比这更令人高兴的了。"

贝拉特里克斯坐在她妹妹旁边。她黑头发，肿眼泡，模样不像她妹妹，举止神情也完全不同。纳西莎僵硬地坐在那里，面无表情，贝拉特里克斯则朝伏地魔探过身子，似乎语言不足以表达她渴望与他接近的意愿。

"没有比这更令人高兴的了。"伏地魔学着她的话，把脑袋微微偏向一边，打量着贝拉特里克斯，"这话从你嘴里说出来，可是意义非凡哪，贝拉特里克斯。"

贝拉特里克斯顿时脸涨得通红，眼睛里盈满喜悦的泪水。

"主人知道我说的都是真心话！"

"没有比这更令人高兴的了……跟我听说的你们家这星期发生的那件喜事相比呢？"

贝拉特里克斯呆呆地望着他，嘴唇微微张着，似乎被弄糊涂了。

"我不明白您的意思，主人。"

"我说的是你的外甥女，贝拉特里克斯。也是你们的外甥女，卢修斯和纳西莎。她刚刚嫁给了狼人莱姆斯·卢平。你们肯定骄傲得很吧？"

桌子周围爆发出一片讥笑声。许多人探身向前，互相交换着愉快的目光，有几个还用拳头擂起了桌子。巨蛇不喜欢这样的骚动，气呼呼地张大嘴巴，发出咝咝的声音。可是食死徒们没有听见，贝拉特里

Bellatrix and the Malfoys' humiliation. Bellatrix's face, so recently flushed with happiness, had turned an ugly, blotchy red.

'She is no niece of ours, my Lord,' she cried over the outpouring of mirth. 'We – Narcissa and I – have never set eyes on our sister since she married the Mudblood. This brat has nothing to do with either of us, nor any beast she marries.'

'What say you, Draco?' asked Voldemort, and though his voice was quiet, it carried clearly through the catcalls and jeers. 'Will you babysit the cubs?'

The hilarity mounted; Draco Malfoy looked in terror at his father, who was staring down into his own lap, then caught his mother's eye. She shook her head almost imperceptibly, then resumed her own deadpan stare at the opposite wall.

'Enough,' said Voldemort, stroking the angry snake. 'Enough.'

And the laughter died at once.

'Many of our oldest family trees become a little diseased over time,' he said, as Bellatrix gazed at him, breathless and imploring. 'You must prune yours, must you not, to keep it healthy? Cut away those parts that threaten the health of the rest.'

'Yes, my Lord,' whispered Bellatrix, and her eyes swam with tears of gratitude again. 'At the first chance!'

'You shall have it,' said Voldemort. 'And in your family, so in the world ... we shall cut away the canker that infects us until only those of the true blood remain ...'

Voldemort raised Lucius Malfoy's wand, pointed it directly at the slowly revolving figure suspended over the table and gave it a tiny flick. The figure came to life with a groan and began to struggle against invisible bonds.

'Do you recognise our guest, Severus?' asked Voldemort.

Snape raised his eyes to the upside-down face. All of the Death Eaters were looking up at the captive now, as though they had been given permission to show curiosity. As she revolved to face the firelight, the woman said, in a cracked and terrified voice, 'Severus! Help me!'

'Ah, yes,' said Snape, as the prisoner turned slowly away again.

'And you, Draco?' asked Voldemort, stroking the snake's snout with his

克斯和马尔福一家受到羞辱，这令他们太开心了。贝拉特里克斯刚才还幸福得满脸通红，可此刻脸上红一块、白一块的，难看极了。

"主人，她不是我们的外甥女。"她在闹哄哄的欢笑声中大声喊道，"自从我们的姐妹嫁给那个泥巴种之后，我们——纳西莎和我——从来都没有正眼瞧过她。那个孩子，还有她嫁的那个畜生，都跟我们没有任何关系。"

"德拉科，你说呢？"伏地魔问，他的声音虽然很轻，却清晰地盖过了尖叫声和嘲笑声，"你会去照料那些小狼崽子吗？"

场面更热闹了。德拉科·马尔福惊恐地望着父亲，他的父亲低头盯着自己的膝盖，接着他碰到了母亲的目光。他的母亲几乎不易察觉地摇摇头，然后又面无表情地盯着对面的墙壁。

"够了，"伏地魔抚摸着生气的巨蛇，说道，"够了。"

笑声立刻平息了。

"长期以来，我们的许多最古老的家族变得有点病态了。"他说。贝拉特里克斯屏住呼吸，恳切地盯着他。"你们必须修剪枝叶，让它保持健康，不是吗？砍掉那些威胁到整体健康的部分。"

"是的，主人，"贝拉特里克斯小声说，眼里又盈满了感激的泪水，"只要有机会！"

"会有机会的，"伏地魔说，"在你们家族里，在整个世界上……我们都要剜去那些侵害我们的烂疮，直到只剩下血统纯正的巫师……"

伏地魔举起卢修斯·马尔福的魔杖，对准悬在桌子上方微微旋转的人体，轻轻一挥。那人呻吟着醒了过来，开始拼命挣脱那些看不见的绳索。

"你认得出我们的客人吗，西弗勒斯？"伏地魔问。

斯内普抬起眼睛望着那张颠倒的脸。此刻，所有的食死徒都抬头看着这个被俘的人，好像他们得到批准，可以表现出自己的好奇心了。那女人旋转着面对炉火时，用沙哑而恐惧的声音说："西弗勒斯！救救我！"

"噢，认出来了。"斯内普说，俘虏又缓缓地转过去了。

"你呢，德拉科？"伏地魔用那只没拿魔杖的手抚摸着巨蛇的吻部，

CHAPTER ONE   The Dark Lord Ascending

wand-free hand. Draco shook his head jerkily. Now that the woman had woken, he seemed unable to look at her any more.

'But you would not have taken her classes,' said Voldemort. 'For those of you who do not know, we are joined here tonight by Charity Burbage who, until recently, taught at Hogwarts School of Witchcraft and Wizardry.'

There were small noises of comprehension around the table. A broad, hunched woman with pointed teeth cackled.

'Yes ... Professor Burbage taught the children of witches and wizards all about Muggles ... how they are not so different from us ...'

One of the Death Eaters spat on the floor. Charity Burbage revolved to face Snape again.

'Severus ... please ... please ...'

'Silence,' said Voldemort, with another twitch of Malfoy's wand, and Charity fell silent as if gagged. 'Not content with corrupting and polluting the minds of wizarding children, last week Professor Burbage wrote an impassioned defence of Mudbloods in the *Daily Prophet*. Wizards, she says, must accept these thieves of their knowledge and magic. The dwindling of the pure-bloods is, says Professor Burbage, a most desirable circumstance ... she would have us all mate with Muggles ... or, no doubt, werewolves ...'

Nobody laughed this time: there was no mistaking the anger and contempt in Voldemort's voice. For the third time, Charity Burbage revolved to face Snape. Tears were pouring from her eyes into her hair. Snape looked back at her, quite impassive, as she turned slowly away from him again.

'*Avada Kedavra.*'

The flash of green light illuminated every corner of the room. Charity fell, with a resounding crash, on to the table below, which trembled and creaked. Several of the Death Eaters leapt back in their chairs. Draco fell out of his on to the floor.

'Dinner, Nagini,' said Voldemort softly, and the great snake swayed and slithered from his shoulders on to the polished wood.

问道。德拉科猛地摇了一下脑袋。现在女人醒了,他倒似乎不敢再看她了。

"不过你大概没有上过她的课,"伏地魔说,"有些人可能不认识她,我来告诉你们吧,今晚光临我们这里的是凯瑞迪·布巴吉,她此前一直在霍格沃茨魔法学校教书。"

桌子周围发出轻轻的、恍然大悟的声音。一个宽肩膀、驼背、牙齿尖尖的女人咯咯地笑了起来。

"对……布巴吉教授教巫师们的孩子学习关于麻瓜的各种知识……说麻瓜和我们并没有多少差别……"

一个食死徒朝地下吐了口唾沫。凯瑞迪·布巴吉又转过来面对着斯内普。

"西弗勒斯……求求你……求求你……"

"安静。"伏地魔说着又轻轻一抖马尔福的魔杖,凯瑞迪像被堵住了嘴,立刻不作声了,"布巴吉教授不满足于腐蚀毒化巫师孩子的头脑,上个星期还在《预言家日报》上写了篇文章,慷慨激昂地为泥巴种辩护。她说,巫师必须容忍那些人盗窃他们的知识和魔法。布巴吉教授说,纯血统巫师人数的减少是一种极为可喜的现象……她希望我们都跟麻瓜……毫无疑问,还有狼人……通婚……"

这次没有人笑。毫无疑问,伏地魔的声音里透着愤怒和轻蔑。凯瑞迪·布巴吉第三次转过来面对着斯内普。泪水从她的眼睛涌出,流进了头发里。斯内普一脸冷漠地望着她,慢慢地,她又转了过去。

"阿瓦达索命。"

一道绿光照亮了房间的每个角落。轰隆一声,凯瑞迪落到桌面上,震得桌子颤抖着发出嘎吱声。几个食死徒惊得缩进椅子里。德拉科从座位滑到了地板上。

"用餐吧,纳吉尼。"伏地魔轻声说,巨蛇晃晃悠悠地离开了他的肩头,慢慢爬向光滑的木头桌面。

CHAPTER TWO

In Memoriam

Harry was bleeding. Clutching his right hand in his left and swearing under his breath, he shouldered open his bedroom door. There was a crunch of breaking china: he had trodden on a cup of cold tea that had been sitting on the floor outside his bedroom door.

'What the —?'

He looked around; the landing of number four, Privet Drive, was deserted. Possibly the cup of tea was Dudley's idea of a clever booby trap. Keeping his bleeding hand elevated, Harry scraped the fragments of cup together with the other hand and threw them into the already crammed bin just visible inside his bedroom door. Then he tramped across to the bathroom to run his finger under the tap.

It was stupid, pointless, irritating beyond belief, that he still had four days left of being unable to perform magic ... but he had to admit to himself that this jagged cut in his finger would have defeated him. He had never learned how to repair wounds and now he came to think of it — particularly in light of his immediate plans — this seemed a serious flaw in his magical education. Making a mental note to ask Hermione how it was done, he used a large wad of toilet paper to mop up as much of the tea as he could, before returning to his bedroom and slamming the door behind him.

Harry had spent the morning completely emptying his school trunk for the first time since he had packed it six years ago. At the start of the intervening school years, he had merely skimmed off the topmost three quarters of the contents and replaced or updated them, leaving a layer of general debris at the bottom — old quills, desiccated beetle eyes, single socks that no longer fitted. Minutes previously Harry had plunged his hand into this mulch, experienced a stabbing pain in the fourth finger of his right hand and withdrawn it to see a lot of blood.

第 2 章

回　忆

哈利在流血。他左手捏住右手，嘴里不出声地骂着，用肩膀推开卧室的门。脚下突然发出瓷器碎裂的嘎吱声：一杯凉茶放在他卧室门外的地上，他一脚踩了上去。

"怎么——？"

哈利四下张望，女贞路4号的楼梯平台上空无一人。这杯茶大概是达力自作聪明，想给他搞个恶作剧吧。哈利高举着流血的手，用另一只手捡起茶杯的碎片，扔进卧室门后那个已经满满当当的垃圾筒里。然后他穿过房间走进浴室，把手指放在水龙头下冲洗。

还有四天不能使用魔法，这真是荒唐，毫无道理，令人恼火……但他不得不承认，有了手指上这个锯齿状的伤口，他肯定不能得心应手。他从来没学会怎样修复创伤，现在想来——特别是想到他的下一步计划——这似乎是他魔法教育中的一个严重缺陷。他一边决定下次一定要向赫敏请教这个问题，一边拿一大团手纸尽量擦去地板上的茶渍，然后回到卧室，重重地关上了门。

早上，哈利彻底清空了他上学用的箱子，这是他六年前装箱以来的第一次。以前每次开学，他都是把箱子上面四分之三的东西替换、更新一下，箱底一直留着一层乱七八糟的杂物——旧的羽毛笔、枯干的甲虫眼睛、早已穿不下的配不成对的袜子。几分钟前，哈利把手伸进这层杂物，右手的无名指突然一阵钻心的剧痛，抽出来一看，已经血流如注。

CHAPTER TWO — In Memoriam

He now proceeded a little more cautiously. Kneeling down beside the trunk again, he groped around in the bottom and, after retrieving an old badge that flickered feebly between *Support CEDRIC DIGGORY* and *POTTER STINKS*, a cracked and worn-out Sneakoscope and a gold locket inside which a note signed 'R.A.B.' had been hidden, he finally discovered the sharp edge that had done the damage. He recognised it at once. It was a two-inch-long fragment of the enchanted mirror that his dead godfather, Sirius, had given him. Harry laid it aside and felt cautiously around the trunk for the rest, but nothing more remained of his godfather's last gift except powdered glass, which clung to the deepest layer of debris like glittering grit.

Harry sat up and examined the jagged piece on which he had cut himself, seeing nothing but his own bright green eye reflected back at him. Then he placed the fragment on top of that morning's *Daily Prophet*, which lay unread on the bed, and attempted to stem the sudden upsurge of bitter memories, the stabs of regret and of longing the discovery of the broken mirror had occasioned, by attacking the rest of the rubbish in the trunk.

It took another hour to empty it completely, throw away the useless items and sort the remainder in piles according to whether or not he would need them from now on. His school and Quidditch robes, cauldron, parchment, quills and most of his textbooks were piled in a corner, to be left behind. He wondered what his aunt and uncle would do with them; burn them in the dead of night, probably, as if they were the evidence of some dreadful crime. His Muggle clothing, Invisibility Cloak, potion-making kit, certain books, the photograph album Hagrid had once given him, a stack of letters and his wand had been repacked into an old rucksack. In a front pocket were the Marauder's Map and the locket with the note signed 'R.A.B.' inside it. The locket was accorded this place of honour not because it was valuable – in all usual senses it was worthless – but because of what it had cost to attain it.

This left a sizeable stack of newspapers sitting on his desk beside his snowy owl, Hedwig: one for each of the days Harry had spent at Privet Drive this summer.

He got up off the floor, stretched and moved across to his desk. Hedwig made no movement as he began to flick through the newspapers, throwing them on to the rubbish pile one by one; the owl was asleep, or else faking; she was angry with Harry about the limited amount of time she was allowed out of her cage at the moment.

第 2 章 回　忆

　　现在他的动作比较谨慎了。他重新跪在箱子旁边,在箱底小心摸索,掏出一个破旧的徽章,上面交替闪烁着支持**塞德里克·迪戈里**和**波特臭大粪**的淡淡字样；接着他又掏出一个破旧开裂的窥镜和一个金挂坠盒,盒里藏着一张签名为 R.A.B. 的字条,最后发现了划伤他手指的利刃。他立刻认了出来,是已故教父小天狼星送给他的魔镜碎片,有两英寸长。哈利把它放在一边,小心翼翼地在箱子里寻找其他残片,可是教父的最后一件礼物只剩下了星星点点的玻璃碎屑,粘在箱子的最底层,像亮晶晶的粗沙粒。

　　哈利直起身子,仔细端详着那块划伤他手指、边缘不齐的碎片,在里面只看见自己的一双明亮的绿眼睛。他把破镜片放在床上那份早晨刚送到、还没有看过的《预言家日报》上,转身去对付箱子里剩下的垃圾,想以此遏制突然涌上心头的痛苦回忆,那些由破碎的镜片引起的揪心的悔恨和思念。

　　他又花了一小时才把箱子彻底清空,扔掉没用的东西,剩下的根据以后是否需要分成了几堆。校袍、魁地奇队服、坩埚、羊皮纸、羽毛笔以及大多数课本都堆在一个墙角,准备留在这里。不知道姨妈姨父会怎么处理它们,没准是半夜三更一把火烧掉,就好像它们是某种滔天大罪的证据。他的麻瓜衣服、隐形衣、配制魔药的用具、几本书,还有海格以前送给他的那本相册、一沓信件和魔杖则放进了一只旧背包里。背包的前兜里塞着活点地图和装着 R.A.B. 签名字条的金挂坠盒。把挂坠盒放在这么重要的位置,不是因为它有多么珍贵——按常理说,它毫无价值——而是因为获取它所付出的代价。

　　现在,只剩下桌上他的雪鸮海德薇旁边那一大堆报纸了：哈利在女贞路过暑假,每天都有一份。

　　他从地上站起来,伸了个懒腰,朝书桌走去。他飞快地翻看着报纸,把它们一份份扔到那堆垃圾上,海德薇在旁边一动不动。猫头鹰睡着了,也许是在装睡。它在生哈利的气,因为这段时间让它出笼的时间太少了。

CHAPTER TWO In Memoriam

As he neared the bottom of the pile of newspapers, Harry slowed down, searching for one particular edition which he knew had arrived shortly after he had returned to Privet Drive for the summer; he remembered that there had been a small mention on the front about the resignation of Charity Burbage, the Muggle Studies teacher at Hogwarts. At last he found it. Turning to page ten, he sank into his desk chair and reread the article he had been looking for.

ALBUS DUMBLEDORE REMEMBERED
by Elphias Doge

I met Albus Dumbledore at the age of eleven, on our first day at Hogwarts. Our mutual attraction was undoubtedly due to the fact that we both felt ourselves to be outsiders. I had contracted dragon pox shortly before arriving at school, and while I was no longer contagious, my pockmarked visage and greenish hue did not encourage many to approach me. For his part, Albus had arrived at Hogwarts under the burden of unwanted notoriety. Scarcely a year previously, his father, Percival, had been convicted of a savage and well-publicised attack upon three young Muggles.

Albus never attempted to deny that his father (who was to die in Azkaban) had committed this crime; on the contrary, when I plucked up courage to ask him, he assured me that he knew his father to be guilty. Beyond that, Dumbledore refused to speak of the sad business, though many attempted to make him do so. Some, indeed, were disposed to praise his father's action and assumed that Albus, too, was a Muggle-hater. They could not have been more mistaken: as anybody who knew Albus would attest, he never revealed the remotest anti-Muggle tendency. Indeed, his determined support for Muggle rights gained him many enemies in subsequent years.

In a matter of months, however, Albus's own fame had begun to eclipse that of his father. By the end of his first year, he would never again be known as the son of a Muggle-hater, but as nothing more or less than the most brilliant student ever seen at the school. Those of us who were privileged to be his friends benefited from his example, not to mention his help and encouragement, with which he was always generous. He confessed to me in later life that he knew even then that his greatest pleasure lay in teaching.

第2章 回　忆

　　那堆报纸快要见底的时候，哈利的速度慢了下来，他在寻找他回女贞路过暑假后不久送来的某一期报纸。他记得头版有一小条关于霍格沃茨学校的麻瓜研究课教师凯瑞迪·布巴吉辞职的消息。好，终于找到了。他翻到第10版，坐在书桌前的椅子上，再次阅读他一直在寻找的那篇文章。

怀念阿不思·邓布利多

埃非亚斯·多吉

　　我是进入霍格沃茨的那天认识阿不思·邓布利多的，当时我十一岁。我们之所以相互吸引，无疑是因为都觉得自己不太合群。我入学前不久染上了龙痘疮，虽然不再传染，但满脸痘痕，肤色发青，没有多少人愿意接近我。阿不思呢，他是顶着恶名的压力来到霍格沃茨的。就在不到一年前，他父亲珀西瓦尔凶残地袭击了三个年轻麻瓜，事情闹得沸沸扬扬。

　　阿不思从不试图否认他父亲（在阿兹卡班终身监禁）犯有这桩罪行。相反，当我鼓起勇气问他时，他向我明确表示他知道父亲有罪。除此之外，邓布利多拒绝谈论这件令人伤心的事，虽然有许多人想套他的话，有人甚至津津乐道地赞扬他父亲的行为，并断定阿不思也是个仇视麻瓜的人。但是他们大错特错了。凡是认识阿不思的人都可以证明，他从未表露出丝毫反麻瓜倾向。事实上，他日后坚决维护麻瓜权益的做法为他树敌不少。

　　几个月后，阿不思的名声就开始超过他父亲。第一学年快结束时，人们不再把他看作一个仇视麻瓜者的儿子，而是看作学校里一个前所未有的最聪明的学生。我们有幸成为他朋友的人，以他为榜样获益匪浅，更不用说他总是毫不吝啬地给我们以帮助和鼓励。他多年之后向我坦言，他当时就知道他最大的乐趣在教书上。

CHAPTER TWO   In Memoriam

He not only won every prize of note that the school offered, he was soon in regular correspondence with the most notable magical names of the day, including Nicolas Flamel, the celebrated alchemist, Bathilda Bagshot, the noted historian, and Adalbert Waffling, the magical theoretician. Several of his papers found their way into learned publications such as *Transfiguration Today, Challenges in Charming* and *The Practical Potioneer*. Dumbledore's future career seemed likely to be meteoric, and the only question that remained was when he would become Minister for Magic. Though it was often predicted in later years that he was on the point of taking the job, however, he never had Ministerial ambitions.

Three years after we had started at Hogwarts Albus's brother, Aberforth, arrived at school. They were not alike; Aberforth was never bookish and, unlike Albus, preferred to settle arguments by duelling rather than through reasoned discussion. However, it is quite wrong to suggest, as some have, that the brothers were not friends. They rubbed along as comfortably as two such different boys could do. In fairness to Aberforth, it must be admitted that living in Albus's shadow cannot have been an altogether comfortable experience. Being continually outshone was an occupational hazard of being his friend and cannot have been any more pleasurable as a brother.

When Albus and I left Hogwarts, we intended to take the then traditional tour of the world together, visiting and observing foreign wizards, before pursuing our separate careers. However, tragedy intervened. On the very eve of our trip, Albus's mother, Kendra, died, leaving Albus the head, and sole breadwinner, of the family. I postponed my departure long enough to pay my respects at Kendra's funeral, then left for what was now to be a solitary journey. With a younger brother and sister to care for, and little gold left to them, there could no longer be any question of Albus accompanying me.

That was the period of our lives when we had least contact. I wrote to Albus, describing, perhaps insensitively, the wonders of my journey from narrow escapes from Chimaeras in Greece to the experiments of the Egyptian alchemists. His letters told me little of his day-to-day life, which I guessed to be frustratingly dull for such a brilliant wizard. Immersed in my own experiences, it was with horror that I heard, towards the end of my year's travels, that yet another

第2章 回 忆

　　他不仅赢得了学校颁发的各种重要奖项，而且很快就和当时最有名的魔法大师保持频繁的通信联系，包括著名炼金术士尼克·勒梅，知名历史学家巴希达·巴沙特，以及魔法理论家阿德贝·沃夫林。他的几篇论文刊登在《今日变形术》《魔咒创新》和《实用魔药大师》等学术刊物上。邓布利多的前途似乎一片辉煌，唯一的问题就是他什么时候出任魔法部长。在后来的日子里，虽然经常有人预言他将要担任这个职务，他却从未有当部长的野心。

　　我们入学三年后，阿不思的弟弟阿不福思也来到了霍格沃茨。兄弟两个不像。阿不福思从来不爱读书，而且，他喜欢决斗，不喜欢通过理性的协商来解决问题，这点也不像阿不思。不过，有人说兄弟俩关系不好，这也不符合事实。他们虽然性格迥异，相处还算和睦。替阿不福思说句公道话，必须承认生活在阿不思的阴影里不是件特别舒服的事。作为他的朋友，总是被他比得黯然失色，实在有伤士气；作为一个弟弟，肯定也不会愉快多少。

　　阿不思和我离开霍格沃茨后，打算按当时的传统结伴周游世界，拜访和观察国外的巫师，然后再追求各自的事业。然而，悲剧从天而降。就在我们出发的前一天，阿不思的母亲坎德拉过世，阿不思成了一家之主，成了挣钱养家的顶梁柱。我推迟动身，参加了坎德拉的葬礼，然后一个人踏上了孤独的旅途。阿不思要照顾一对年幼的弟妹，家里生活拮据，他不可能和我结伴旅行了。

　　在我们的一生中，那段时间接触最少。我给阿不思写信，描绘旅途中的奇特见闻，从侥幸逃脱希腊的客迈拉，到参观埃及炼金术士们的实验。我这么做也许太不善解人意了。他的信里很少提及他的日常生活，我猜想对于他这样一位出色的巫师来说，那肯定乏味得令人沮丧。我沉浸在自己的游历中，一年的旅行快要

CHAPTER TWO In Memoriam

tragedy had struck the Dumbledores: the death of his sister, Ariana.

Though Ariana had been in poor health for a long time, the blow, coming so soon after the loss of their mother, had a profound effect on both of her brothers. All those closest to Albus – and I count myself one of that lucky number – agree that Ariana's death and Albus's feeling of personal responsibility for it (though, of course, he was guiltless) left their mark upon him forever more.

I returned home to find a young man who had experienced a much older person's suffering. Albus was more reserved than before, and much less light-hearted. To add to his misery, the loss of Ariana had led, not to a renewed closeness between Albus and Aberforth, but to an estrangement. (In time this would lift – in later years they re-established, if not a close relationship, then certainly a cordial one.) However, he rarely spoke of his parents or of Ariana from then on, and his friends learned not to mention them.

Other quills will describe the triumphs of the following years. Dumbledore's innumerable contributions to the store of wizarding knowledge, including his discovery of the twelve uses of dragon's blood, will benefit generations to come, as will the wisdom he displayed in the many judgements he made while Chief Warlock of the Wizengamot. They say, still, that no wizarding duel ever matched that between Dumbledore and Grindelwald in 1945. Those who witnessed it have written of the terror and the awe they felt as they watched these two extraordinary wizards do battle. Dumbledore's triumph and its consequences for the wizarding world, are considered a turning point in magical history to match the introduction of the International Statute of Secrecy or the downfall of He Who Must Not Be Named.

Albus Dumbledore was never proud or vain; he could find something to value in anyone, however apparently insignificant or wretched, and I believe that his early losses endowed him with great humanity and sympathy. I shall miss his friendship more than I can say, but my loss is as nothing compared to the wizarding world's. That he was the most inspiring and the best loved of all Hogwarts headmasters cannot be in question. He died as he lived: working

第2章 回 忆

结束时，悲剧再次降临邓布利多家中：他的妹妹阿利安娜死了。我听了万分震惊。

虽说阿利安娜长期体弱多病，但母亲刚去世不久又遭此打击，阿利安娜的两个哥哥久久难以释怀。所有与阿不思亲近的人——我自己也有幸算在内——一致认为，阿利安娜的死，以及阿不思觉得自己对此事所负的责任（当然了，他实际上并无罪责），成为了他终生无法摆脱的阴影。

我回国后，看到的是一个年轻人经历了与他年龄不相称的痛苦。阿不思比以前更加沉默寡言，心思也重了许多。更令他痛苦的是，阿利安娜的死不仅没有使阿不思和阿不福思的关系更加紧密，反而使他们变得疏远了。（这种疏远逐渐改善——后来他们重新建立了关系，即使不算亲密，无疑还算友好。）然而，从那以后，阿不思很少谈及他的父母和阿利安娜，他的朋友们也避免谈论他们。

此后那些年，他的辉煌成就自会有人去描述。邓布利多对巫术知识宝库所做的巨大贡献，包括发现火龙血的十二种用途，还有他担任威森加摩首席魔法师时在许多判决中所展示的智慧，都会使后人受益。人们还说，没有一场巫师决斗能比得上一九四五年邓布利多与格林德沃之间的较量。很多目睹过这两位非凡巫师展开决战的人都曾撰文描述他们当时所感受到的恐惧和敬畏。邓布利多的胜利，及其对巫师界产生的影响，被看作是魔法历史上的一个转折点，堪与《国际保密法》的出台和神秘人的垮台相提并论。

阿不思·邓布利多从不恃才傲物，追求虚荣。他总能发现别人身上值得珍视的东西，不管那个人表面看去多么落魄和不起眼。我相信，是他早年痛失亲人的经历，赋予了他博大的仁慈和悲悯之心。我将无比怀念他的友情，然而，跟整个巫师界相比，我个人的损失实在不算什么。毫无疑问，他是霍格沃茨历届校长中最有影响力、最受人爱戴的一位，无论活着时还是死去时，总是在

CHAPTER TWO In Memoriam

always for the greater good and, to his last hour, as willing to stretch out a hand to a small boy with dragon pox as he was on the day that I met him.

Harry finished reading but continued to gaze at the picture accompanying the obituary. Dumbledore was wearing his familiar, kindly smile, but as he peered over the top of his half-moon spectacles he gave the impression, even in newsprint, of X-raying Harry, whose sadness mingled with a sense of humiliation.

He had thought he knew Dumbledore quite well, but ever since reading this obituary he had been forced to recognise that he had barely known him at all. Never once had he imagined Dumbledore's childhood or youth; it was as though he had sprung into being as Harry had known him, venerable and silver-haired and old. The idea of a teenage Dumbledore was simply odd, like trying to imagine a stupid Hermione or a friendly Blast-Ended Skrewt.

He had never thought to ask Dumbledore about his past. No doubt it would have felt strange, impertinent even, but after all, it had been common knowledge that Dumbledore had taken part in that legendary duel with Grindelwald, and Harry had not thought to ask Dumbledore what that had been like, nor about any of his other famous achievements. No, they had always discussed Harry, Harry's past, Harry's future, Harry's plans ... and it seemed to Harry now, despite the fact that his future was so dangerous and so uncertain, that he had missed irreplaceable opportunities when he had failed to ask Dumbledore more about himself, even though the only personal question he had ever asked his Headmaster was also the only one he suspected that Dumbledore had not answered honestly:

'What do you see when you look in the Mirror?'

'I? I see myself holding a pair of thick, woollen socks.'

After several minutes' thought, Harry tore the obituary out of the *Prophet*, folded it carefully and tucked it inside the first volume of *Practical Defensive Magic and its Use Against the Dark Arts*. Then he threw the rest of the newspaper on to the rubbish pile and turned to face the room. It was much tidier. The only things left out of place were today's *Daily Prophet*, still lying on the bed and, on top of it, the piece of broken mirror.

Harry moved across the room, slid the mirror fragment off today's *Prophet*

第2章 回　忆

为更崇高的利益而工作，直到生命的最后一刻；就像我第一次见到他的那天，他向一个患龙痘疮的小男孩友好地伸出了手。

哈利读完了，但仍然凝视着讣文旁的那张照片。邓布利多脸上带着那种熟悉的、慈祥的微笑，但从半月形镜片上望过来的目光——虽然是印在报纸上的，却仿佛正用 X 光审视着哈利，使哈利觉得又伤心，又有一种羞愧感。

他曾经以为自己很了解邓布利多，可是读了这篇讣文，他不得不承认他对邓布利多几乎一无所知。他从来没有想象过邓布利多的童年和青年时代，似乎邓布利多一下子就变成了哈利认识他的那个样子，年高德劭，须发银白。想到少年时期的邓布利多，总使人感觉很怪异，就如同要想象一个头脑迟钝的赫敏，或想象一只待人友善的炸尾螺。

他从来没想过问问邓布利多的过去。当然啦，那么做会显得有点别扭，甚至冒昧，但是邓布利多参加了与格林德沃的那场传奇般的决斗，这是尽人皆知的事实，而哈利居然没有想到向邓布利多问问当时的情景，也没有向他问问他的其他著名成就。没有，他们总是在谈论哈利，哈利的过去，哈利的未来，哈利的计划……而现在哈利感觉到，尽管他的未来确实危机四伏，前途未卜，但他失去的机会再也无法挽回：他没有向邓布利多询问有关他自己的更多情况，而他向校长提出的唯一一个私人问题，也是他怀疑邓布利多唯一没有诚实回答的问题：

"你照魔镜的时候，看见了什么？"

"我？我看见自己拿着一双厚厚的羊毛袜。"

哈利沉思了几分钟，把讣文从《预言家日报》上撕下来，仔细折叠，夹在了《实用防御魔法及其对抗黑魔法的应用》第一册里。他把剩下来的报纸扔在垃圾堆上，转身望着房间。房间里整洁多了。唯一放得不是地方的是当天的《预言家日报》，仍然摊在床上，上面压着那块破碎的镜片。

哈利走过去，把碎镜片从当天的《预言家日报》上抖落，然后展

CHAPTER TWO   In Memoriam

and unfolded the newspaper. He had merely glanced at the headline when he had taken the rolled-up paper from the delivery owl early that morning and thrown it aside, after noting that it said nothing about Voldemort. Harry was sure that the Ministry was leaning on the *Prophet* to suppress news about Voldemort. It was only now, therefore, that he saw what he had missed.

Across the bottom half of the front page, a smaller headline was set over a picture of Dumbledore striding along looking harried:

DUMBLEDORE: THE TRUTH AT LAST?

Coming next week, the shocking story of the flawed genius considered by many to be the greatest wizard of his generation. Stripping away the popular image of serene, silver-bearded wisdom, Rita Skeeter reveals the disturbed childhood, the lawless youth, the lifelong feuds and the guilty secrets that Dumbledore carried to his grave. WHY was the man tipped to be Minister for Magic content to remain a mere headmaster? WHAT was the real purpose of the secret organisation known as the Order of the Phoenix? HOW did Dumbledore really meet his end?

The answers to these, and many more questions are explored in the explosive new biography *The Life and Lies of Albus Dumbledore*, by Rita Skeeter, exclusively interviewed by Betty Braithwaite, page 13, inside.

Harry ripped open the paper and found page thirteen. The article was topped with a picture showing another familiar face: a woman wearing jewelled glasses with elaborately curled, blonde hair, her teeth bared in what was clearly supposed to be a winning smile, wiggling her fingers up at him. Doing his best to ignore this nauseating image, Harry read on.

In person, Rita Skeeter is much warmer and softer than her famously ferocious quill-portraits might suggest. Greeting me in the hallway of her cosy home, she leads me straight into the kitchen for a cup of tea, a slice of pound cake and, it goes without saying, a steaming vat of freshest gossip.

'Well, of course, Dumbledore is a biographer's dream,' says

开了报纸。早晨他从猫头鹰邮差那里接过卷成筒状的报纸时,匆匆扫了一眼标题,发现没有伏地魔的消息,就把它扔到了一边。哈利相信是魔法部给《预言家日报》施加了压力,要求封锁关于伏地魔的消息。直到这时,他才发现自己漏掉了什么。

在报纸头版的下半页,有一幅邓布利多神色匆匆、大步行走的照片,上面略小一点的标题是:

邓布利多——终于真相大白?

一部令人震惊的传记下周问世,主角是那位有缺陷的天才,许多人认为他是他所属的时代最伟大的巫师。丽塔·斯基特剥去那个深受大家喜爱的须发银白、神色安详的智者形象的外衣,揭露了邓布利多动荡的童年和混乱的青春时代、他终生的仇敌,以及他带入坟墓的那些罪恶的秘密。**为什么**这个有望成为魔法部部长的人仅满足于当一名校长?那个名为凤凰社的秘密组织的真正目的是**什么**?邓布利多究竟是**怎么**死的?

这些以及更多问题的答案,都在丽塔·斯基特最新出版的爆炸性传记《阿不思·邓布利多的生平与谎言》中做了探究,贝蒂·布雷思韦特对传记作者做了独家采访,见本报第13版。

哈利扯开报纸,找到第13版。文章上面有幅照片,又是一张熟悉的脸:一个女人戴着一副镶着珠宝的眼镜,一头金发弄成精致的大卷儿,牙齿露着,绽开一个显然自以为很迷人的笑容,手指张开朝哈利摆动。哈利尽量不去看这令人恶心的照片,继续往下读。

丽塔·斯基特的文笔以犀利著称,但她本人却热情随和得多。在她那温暖舒适的家中,她在门厅里迎接了我,把我直接领进厨房,享用一杯茶、一片重奶油蛋糕,当然啦,还有刚出锅的、热气腾腾的八卦秘闻。

"不用说,邓布利多是一个传记作家梦寐以求的人物,"斯基

CHAPTER TWO   In Memoriam

Skeeter. 'Such a long, full life. I'm sure my book will be the first of very, very many.'

Skeeter was certainly quick off the mark. Her nine-hundred-page book was completed a mere four weeks after Dumbledore's mysterious death in June. I ask her how she managed this super-fast feat.

'Oh, when you've been a journalist as long as I have, working to a deadline is second nature. I knew that the wizarding world was clamouring for the full story and I wanted to be the first to meet that need.'

I mention the recent, widely publicised remarks of Elphias Doge, Special Advisor to the Wizengamot and long-standing friend of Albus Dumbledore's, that 'Skeeter's book contains less fact than a Chocolate Frog Card.'

Skeeter throws back her head and laughs.

'Darling Dodgy! I remember interviewing him a few years back about merpeople rights, bless him. Completely gaga, seemed to think we were sitting at the bottom of Lake Windermere, kept telling me to watch out for trout.'

And yet Elphias Doge's accusations of inaccuracy have been echoed in many places. Does Skeeter really feel that four short weeks have been enough to gain a full picture of Dumbledore's long and extraordinary life?

'Oh, my dear,' beams Skeeter, rapping me affectionately across the knuckles, 'you know as well as I do how much information can be generated by a fat bag of Galleons, a refusal to hear the word "no" and a nice sharp Quick-Quotes Quill! People were queuing to dish the dirt on Dumbledore, anyway. Not everyone thought he was so wonderful, you know – he trod on an awful lot of important toes. But old Dodgy Doge can get off his high Hippogriff, because I've had access to a source most journalists would swap their wands for, one who has never spoken in public before and who was close to Dumbledore during the most turbulent and disturbing phase of his youth.'

The advance publicity for Skeeter's biography has certainly suggested that there will be shocks in store for those who believe Dumbledore to have led a blameless life. What were the biggest

第2章 回　忆

特说，"这么漫长而丰富的一生。我的书是第一本，我相信后面会有许多许多。"

斯基特无疑是个快手。这本长达九百页的传记仅在邓布利多六月份神秘死亡的四个星期后就完成了。我问她是怎么做到如此神速的。

"噢，如果你像我一样做了这么多年的记者，抢时间就成了第二天性。我知道巫师界如饥似渴地想要一本完整的传记，我希望第一个满足这种需要。"

我提到最近广为流传的埃非亚斯·多吉的评论，他是威森加摩的特别顾问，也是阿不思·邓布利多长期的朋友，他说"斯基特书里所包含的事实，还不如一张巧克力蛙画片"。

斯基特仰天大笑。

"可爱的老滑头！我记得我几年前为了人鱼权益的问题采访过他，老天保佑他吧。整个儿一个老糊涂，他好像以为我们坐在温德米尔湖的湖底，不停地叫我提防鲑鱼。"

可是，许多人都在附和埃非亚斯·多吉指责传记错误百出的话。难道斯基特真的觉得短短四个星期就足以充分描绘邓布利多漫长而极不平凡的一生吗？

"哦，亲爱的，"斯基特笑容满面地说，一边亲切地拍拍我的手，"你和我一样清楚，有了一袋沉甸甸的金加隆，一股打破砂锅问到底的劲头，还有一支漂亮而锋利的速记羽毛笔，就能套出多少情报来呀！而且，人们都排着队要说邓布利多的闲话呢。你知道，并不是人人都认为他有那么出色——他得罪了太多的重要人物。不过，老滑头多吉可以从他高高在上的鹰头马身有翼兽上下来了，因为我找到了大多数记者愿意用魔杖交换的消息来源，此人以前从未当众发表过讲话，却在邓布利多极其动荡不安的青年时代与他关系密切。"

斯基特这部传记的新书广告明确提出，对于那些相信邓布利多一生白璧无瑕的人们来说，等待他们的将是强烈的震惊。那么，

CHAPTER TWO In Memoriam

surprises she uncovered, I ask.

'Now, come off it, Betty, I'm not giving away all the highlights before anybody's bought the book!' laughs Skeeter. 'But I can promise that anybody who still thinks Dumbledore was white as his beard is in for a rude awakening! Let's just say that nobody hearing him rage against You-Know-Who would have dreamed that he dabbled in the Dark Arts himself in his youth! And for a wizard who spent his later years pleading for tolerance, he wasn't exactly broad-minded when he was younger! Yes, Albus Dumbledore had an extremely murky past, not to mention that very fishy family, which he worked so hard to keep hushed up.'

I ask whether Skeeter is referring to Dumbledore's brother, Aberforth, whose conviction by the Wizengamot for misuse of magic caused a minor scandal fifteen years ago.

'Oh, Aberforth is just the tip of the dungheap,' laughs Skeeter. 'No, no, I'm talking about much worse than a brother with a fondness for fiddling about with goats, worse even than the Muggle-maiming father – Dumbledore couldn't keep either of them quiet, anyway, they were both charged by the Wizengamot. No, it's the mother and the sister that intrigued me, and a little digging uncovered a positive nest of nastiness – but, as I say, you'll have to wait for chapters nine to twelve for full details. All I can say now is, it's no wonder Dumbledore never talked about how his nose got broken.'

Family skeletons notwithstanding, does Skeeter deny the brilliance that led to Dumbledore's many magical discoveries?

'He had brains,' she concedes, 'although many now question whether he could really take full credit for all of his supposed achievements. As I reveal in chapter sixteen, Ivor Dillonsby claims he had already discovered eight uses of dragon's blood when Dumbledore "borrowed" his papers.'

But the importance of some of Dumbledore's achievements cannot, I venture, be denied. What of his famous defeat of Grindelwald?

'Oh, now, I'm glad you mentioned Grindelwald,' says Skeeter, with a tantalising smile. 'I'm afraid those who go dewy-eyed over

第2章 回 忆

她发现的最令人惊诧的秘密是什么呢?

"行啦,别说了,贝蒂,在大家买到书前,我是不会把最精彩的内容透露出来的!"斯基特大笑着说,"不过我可以保证,凡是仍然认为邓布利多像他的胡须一样清白的人,都会猛然从梦中惊醒!比如,那些听说他对神秘人义愤填膺的人,做梦也不会想到他本人年轻时就曾涉足黑魔法!他晚年呼吁宽容,年轻时却心胸狭隘!是的,阿不思·邓布利多有一个极其不可告人的过去,更不用说他那个非常可疑的家庭,对此他想尽办法,百般遮掩。"

我问斯基特是不是指邓布利多的弟弟阿不福思,十五年前他因滥用魔法被威森加摩定罪,成为当时的一个小小的丑闻。

"噢,阿不福思只是粪堆的一角。"斯基特笑着说,"不是,不是,我谈论的事情比一个喜欢捉弄山羊的弟弟严重得多,甚至比那个残害麻瓜的父亲还要严重——他们都受到过威森加摩的指控,所以邓布利多不可能把这两件事遮掩住。不,激起我好奇心的是他的母亲和妹妹,我稍加挖掘,发现了一连串肮脏的往事——不过,我说过了,欲知详情,你需要阅读第九章到第十二章。我现在所能说的是,怪不得邓布利多从来闭口不谈他的鼻子是怎么断的。"

尽管有这些家丑,难道斯基特能够否认邓布利多做出重大魔法发现的出色才华吗?

"他脑子不笨,"斯基特承认,"不过现在许多人提出质疑:他的那些所谓成就是否真的都归功于他。我在第十六章中透露,伊凡·迪隆斯比声称,当时邓布利多把他的论文'借走'时,他已经发现了火龙血的八种用途。"

可是邓布利多某些成就的重要性是无法否认的,我冒昧提出。他战胜格林德沃的那场著名的较量呢?

"噢,我真高兴你提到了格林德沃,"斯基特露出一个意味深长的微笑说,"那些轻信邓布利多取得辉煌胜利的人们恐怕要做好准

CHAPTER TWO In Memoriam

Dumbledore's spectacular victory must brace themselves for a bombshell – or perhaps a Dungbomb. Very dirty business indeed. All I'll say is, don't be so sure that there really was the spectacular duel of legend. After they've read my book, people may be forced to conclude that Grindelwald simply conjured a white handkerchief from the end of his wand and came quietly!'

Skeeter refuses to give any more away on this intriguing subject, so we turn instead to the relationship that will undoubtedly fascinate her readers more than any other.

'Oh yes,' says Skeeter, nodding briskly, 'I devote an entire chapter to the whole Potter–Dumbledore relationship. It's been called unhealthy, even sinister. Again, your readers will have to buy my book for the whole story, but there is no question that Dumbledore took an unnatural interest in Potter from the word go. Whether that was really in the boy's best interests – well, we'll see. It's certainly an open secret that Potter has had a most troubled adolescence.'

I ask whether Skeeter is still in touch with Harry Potter, whom she so famously interviewed last year: a breakthrough piece in which Potter spoke exclusively of his conviction that You-Know-Who had returned.

'Oh, yes, we've developed a close bond,' says Skeeter. 'Poor Potter has few real friends, and we met at one of the most testing moments of his life – the Triwizard Tournament. I am probably one of the only people alive who can say that they know the real Harry Potter.'

Which leads us neatly to the many rumours still circulating about Dumbledore's final hours. Does Skeeter believe that Potter was there when Dumbledore died?

'Well, I don't want to say too much – it's all in the book – but eye witnesses inside Hogwarts Castle saw Potter running away from the scene moments after Dumbledore fell, jumped or was pushed. Potter later gave evidence against Severus Snape, a man against whom he has a notorious grudge. Is everything as it seems? That is for the wizardiing community to decide – once they've read my book.'

On that intriguing note I take my leave. There can be no doubt that Skeeter has quilled an instant bestseller. Dumbledore's legions

第2章 回 忆

备,迎接一个炸弹——说不定是个粪弹呢。非常肮脏的交易。我只想说,千万别相信真有那场传奇般的惊人决斗。人们读了我的书,便不得不认定格林德沃只是从魔杖尖上变出一块白手帕,就偃旗息鼓了!"

关于这个令人感兴趣的话题,斯基特不肯透露更多的内容,于是我们转向那个无疑最能吸引读者的二人关系。

"噢,没错,"斯基特连连点头说,"我用整整一章详细描写了波特和邓布利多之间的关系。这种关系可以说是不健康的,甚至是邪恶的。读者也需要购买我的书才能知道全部故事,但是毫无疑问,邓布利多从一开始就对波特有一种不正常的兴趣。究竟是不是真的为了那个男孩考虑——咳,等着瞧吧。波特的青春期极为混乱动荡,这无疑已是一个公开的秘密。"

我问斯基特是否还跟哈利·波特有联系,她去年对哈利·波特的采访尽人皆知:一篇突破性的文章,独家披露了波特宣称他确信神秘人已经回来。

"噢,是的,我们建立了很密切的关系。"斯基特说,"可怜的波特没有几个真正的朋友,我和他是在他人生最艰难的时刻——三强争霸赛期间相识的。我可以说是世上仅有的几个堪称真正了解哈利·波特的人之一吧。"

话题自然而然地转向了围绕邓布利多最后时刻的许多传言。斯基特相信邓布利多死的时候波特在场吗?

"哦,我不想说得太多——书里都写着呢——可是霍格沃茨城堡里的目击者看到,在邓布利多或失足跌落,或自己跳楼,或被人推下去的片刻之后,波特匆匆从现场逃离。波特后来做证说西弗勒斯·斯内普是凶手,众所周知,他对此人一直怀恨在心。一切都像表面上那样吗?且让巫师界自己做出判断吧——在读完我的书后。"

她说完这句吊人胃口的话,我就告辞了。毫无疑问,斯基特的书立刻就会畅销。而邓布利多的大批崇拜者大概会怕得发抖,

CHAPTER TWO In Memoriam

of admirers, meanwhile, may well be trembling at what is soon to emerge about their hero.

Harry reached the bottom of the article, but continued to stare blankly at the page. Revulsion and fury rose in him like vomit; he balled up the newspaper and threw it, with all his force, at the wall, where it joined the rest of the rubbish heaped around his overflowing bin.

He began to stride blindly around the room, opening empty drawers and picking up books only to replace them on the same piles, barely conscious of what he was doing, as random phrases from Rita's article echoed in his head: *an entire chapter to the whole Potter–Dumbledore relationship ... it's been called unhealthy, even sinister ... he dabbled in the Dark Arts himself in his youth ... I've had access to a source most journalists would swap their wands for ...*

'Lies!' Harry bellowed, and through the window he saw the next-door neighbour, who had paused to restart his lawnmower, look up nervously.

Harry sat down hard on the bed. The broken bit of mirror danced away from him; he picked it up and turned it over in his fingers, thinking, thinking of Dumbledore and the lies with which Rita Skeeter was defaming him ...

A flash of brightest blue. Harry froze, his cut finger slipping on the jagged edge of the mirror again. He had imagined it, he must have done. He glanced over his shoulder, but the wall was a sickly peach colour of Aunt Petunia's choosing: there was nothing blue there for the mirror to reflect. He peered into the mirror fragment again, and saw nothing but his own bright green eye looking back at him.

He had imagined it, there was no other explanation; imagined it, because he had been thinking of his dead Headmaster. If anything was certain, it was that the bright blue eyes of Albus Dumbledore would never pierce him again.

第2章 回 忆

不知他们心目中的英雄会有什么事将被披露出来。

哈利看完文章,眼睛仍然呆呆地望着报纸,心头的厌恶和愤怒直往上翻。他把报纸揉成一团,使劲往墙上砸去,报纸落在满得溢出来的垃圾筒周围的废物堆里。

他开始漫无目的地在房间里走来走去,拉开空抽屉,拿起几本书看看,又把它们放回原处,几乎不知道自己在做什么,丽塔文章里的片言只语在他脑海里回响:用整整一章详细描写了波特和邓布利多之间的关系……这种关系可以说是不健康的,甚至是邪恶的。……他本人年轻时就曾涉足黑魔法……我找到了大多数记者愿意用魔杖交换的消息来源……

"谎言!"哈利吼道,窗外,他看见停下来发动割草机的隔壁邻居不安地抬头张望。

哈利一屁股坐在床上,破碎的镜片从他身边弹开。他拿起镜片,捏在手指间翻看,陷入了沉思,他想到了邓布利多,想到了丽塔·斯基特诽谤他的那些不实之词……

一道明亮的蓝光一闪。哈利怔住了,受伤的手指又滑过不齐的镜片边缘。错觉,肯定是错觉。他扭头看看,墙纸是佩妮姨妈挑选的令人恶心的桃色,并没有蓝色的东西让镜片反射蓝光。他又朝碎镜片里望去,只看见自己的一双亮晶晶的绿眼睛。

准是错觉,没有别的解释。因为他一直想着已故的校长,才产生了这样的错觉。要说有一点是肯定的,那就是阿不思·邓布利多那双明亮的蓝眼睛再也不会犀利地盯着他了。

CHAPTER THREE

The Dursleys Departing

The sound of the front door slamming echoed up the stairs and a voice yelled, 'Oi! You!'

Sixteen years of being addressed thus left Harry in no doubt whom his uncle was calling; nevertheless, he did not immediately respond. He was still gazing at the mirror fragment in which, for a split second, he had thought he saw Dumbledore's eye. It was not until his uncle bellowed 'BOY!' that Harry got slowly to his feet and headed for the bedroom door, pausing to add the piece of broken mirror to the rucksack filled with things he would be taking with him.

'You took your time!' roared Vernon Dursley when Harry appeared at the top of the stairs. 'Get down here, I want a word!'

Harry strolled downstairs, his hands deep in his jeans pockets. When he reached the living room, he found all three Dursleys. They were dressed for travelling: Uncle Vernon in a fawn zip-up jacket, Aunt Petunia in a neat, salmon-coloured coat and Dudley, Harry's large, blond, muscular cousin, in his leather jacket.

'Yes?' asked Harry.

'Sit down!' said Uncle Vernon. Harry raised his eyebrows. 'Please!' added Uncle Vernon, wincing slightly as though the word was sharp in his throat.

Harry sat. He thought he knew what was coming. His uncle began to pace up and down, Aunt Petunia and Dudley following his movements with anxious expressions. Finally, his large, purple face crumpled with concentration, Uncle Vernon stopped in front of Harry and spoke.

'I've changed my mind,' he said.

'What a surprise,' said Harry.

'Don't you take that tone –' began Aunt Petunia in a shrill voice, but

第 3 章

德思礼一家离开

前门重重关上的声音传到楼上，一个人高喊道："喂！你！"哈利十六年来都被这样呼来喝去。他知道姨父在喊谁，但他没有立刻回答。他仍然凝视着破碎的镜片，刚才一刹那间，他恍惚在里面看见了邓布利多的眼睛。直到姨父怒吼一声"小子！"哈利才慢吞吞地站起身，朝卧室门口走去，半路停下来把破碎的镜片塞进背包，那里面已经装满了他打算带走的东西。

"磨蹭什么？"弗农·德思礼看到哈利出现在楼梯口，又气呼呼地吼道，"快下来，我有话要说！"

哈利双手插在牛仔裤的口袋里，慢慢地走下楼梯。他来到客厅，发现德思礼一家三口都在。他们一副出远门的打扮：弗农姨父穿着浅黄褐色的拉链夹克，佩妮姨妈穿着一件式样简洁的浅橙色外套，哈利那位大块头、金头发、肌肉发达的表哥达力，穿着皮夹克。

"有事吗？"哈利问。

"坐下！"弗农姨父说。哈利扬起眉毛。"请！"弗农姨父赶紧找补道，一边皱了皱眉头，似乎这个字刺着了他的喉咙。

哈利坐下了。他似乎猜到了是什么事。姨父开始在房间里踱来踱去，佩妮姨妈和达力用目光追随着姨父，一副忧心忡忡的样子。最后，弗农姨父在哈利面前停下脚步，绛紫色的大脸膛皱成一团，开口说话了。

"我改主意了。"他说。

"真让人吃惊。"哈利说。

"不许用那种口气——"佩妮姨妈尖声嚷了起来，弗农姨父挥挥手

CHAPTER THREE   The Dursleys Departing

Vernon Dursley waved her down.

'It's all a lot of claptrap,' said Uncle Vernon, glaring at Harry with piggy little eyes. 'I've decided I don't believe a word of it. We're staying put, we're not going anywhere.'

Harry looked up at his uncle and felt a mixture of exasperation and amusement. Vernon Dursley had been changing his mind every twenty-four hours for the past four weeks, packing and unpacking and repacking the car with every change of heart. Harry's favourite moment had been the one when Uncle Vernon, unaware that Dudley had added his dumb-bells to his case since the last time it had been unpacked, had attempted to hoist it back into the boot and collapsed with roars of pain and much swearing.

'According to you,' Vernon Dursley said now, resuming his pacing up and down the living room, 'we – Petunia, Dudley and I – are in danger. From – from –'

'Some of "my lot", right,' said Harry.

'Well, I don't believe it,' repeated Uncle Vernon, coming to a halt in front of Harry again. 'I was awake half the night thinking it all over, and I believe it's a plot to get the house.'

'The house?' repeated Harry. 'What house?'

'*This* house!' shrieked Uncle Vernon, the vein in his forehead starting to pulse. '*Our* house! House prices are sky-rocketing round here! You want us out of the way and then you're going to do a bit of hocuspocus and before we know it the deeds will be in your name and –'

'Are you out of your mind?' demanded Harry. 'A plot to get this house? Are you actually as stupid as you look?'

'Don't you dare –!' squealed Aunt Petunia, but again, Vernon waved her down: slights on his personal appearance were, it seemed, as nothing to the danger he had spotted.

'Just in case you've forgotten,' said Harry, 'I've already got a house, my godfather left me one. So why would I want this one? All the happy memories?'

There was silence. Harry thought he had rather impressed his uncle with this argument.

'You claim,' said Uncle Vernon, starting to pace yet again, 'that this Lord Thing –'

'Voldemort,' said Harry impatiently, 'and we've been through this about a hundred times already. This isn't a claim, it's fact, Dumbledore told you last year, and Kingsley and Mr Weasley –'

叫她闭嘴。

"都是些骗人的鬼话，"弗农姨父用一双小猪眼睛盯着哈利，"我决定一个字也不相信。我们不走，哪儿也不去。"

哈利抬头看着姨父，觉得又气恼又好笑。在过去的四个星期里，弗农·德思礼每二十四小时改变一次主意，每次改变主意都要折腾一番，把行李搬上车、搬下车、再搬上车。哈利觉得最可笑的是有一回弗农姨父想把行李重新拎进汽车后备厢，却不知道达力这次把哑铃装进了行李，结果被坠得摔倒在地，又气又疼，破口大骂。

"照你说来，"这会儿弗农·德思礼说着，又在客厅里踱起步来，"我们——佩妮、达力和我——都有危险。危险来自——来自——"

"'我们那类'里的一些人，没错。"哈利说。

"哼，我不相信。"弗农姨父又说了一遍，再次在哈利面前停住脚步，"我昨天半夜没睡，盘算着这个事情，肯定是阴谋，想霸占房子。"

"房子？"哈利问，"什么房子？"

"这所房子！"弗农姨父尖声叫道，额头上的血管开始突突地跳动，"我们的房子！这附近的房价涨得厉害！你想把我们支走，然后搞点儿鬼把戏，不等我们明白过来，房契上的名字就成了你的——"

"你糊涂了吗？"哈利问，"密谋霸占这所房子？难道你真像你的模样一样傻吗？"

"你怎么敢——！"佩妮姨妈尖叫起来，弗农又一次挥手叫她闭嘴，似乎跟他所识破的危险相比，相貌遭到一些侮辱算不得什么。

"恐怕你是忘了，"哈利说，"我已经有了一所房子，我教父留给我的。我还要这所房子干什么？为了所有那些愉快的往事？"

沉默。哈利认为这番话把姨父给镇住了。

"你声称，"弗农姨父说着，又开始踱步，"这个魔王——"

"——伏地魔，"哈利不耐烦地说，"这件事我们已经讨论过一百遍了。不是声称，是事实，邓布利多去年就告诉过你，金斯莱和韦斯莱先生——"

CHAPTER THREE   The Dursleys Departing

Vernon Dursley hunched his shoulders angrily, and Harry guessed that his uncle was attempting to ward off recollections of the unannounced visit, a few days into Harry's summer holidays, of two fully grown wizards. The arrival on the doorstep of Kingsley Shacklebolt and Arthur Weasley had come as a most unpleasant shock to the Dursleys. Harry had to admit, however, that as Mr Weasley had once demolished half of the living room, his reappearance could not have been expected to delight Uncle Vernon.

'– Kingsley and Mr Weasley explained it all as well,' Harry pressed on remorselessly. 'Once I'm seventeen, the protective charm that keeps me safe will break, and that exposes you as well as me. The Order is sure Voldemort will target you, whether to torture you to try and find out where I am, or because he thinks by holding you hostage I'd come and try to rescue you.'

Uncle Vernon's and Harry's eyes met. Harry was sure that in that instant they were both wondering the same thing. Then Uncle Vernon walked on and Harry resumed, 'You've got to go into hiding and the Order wants to help. You're being offered serious protection, the best there is.'

Uncle Vernon said nothing, but continued to pace up and down. Outside, the sun hung low over the privet hedges. The next-door neighbour's lawnmower stalled again.

'I thought there was a Ministry of Magic?' asked Vernon Dursley abruptly.

'There is,' said Harry, surprised.

'Well, then, why can't they protect us? It seems to me that, as innocent victims, guilty of nothing more than harbouring a marked man, we ought to qualify for government protection!'

Harry laughed; he could not help himself. It was so very typical of his uncle to put his hopes in the establishment, even within this world that he despised and mistrusted.

'You heard what Mr Weasley and Kingsley said,' Harry replied. 'We think the Ministry has been infiltrated.'

Uncle Vernon strode to the fireplace and back, breathing so heavily that his great, black moustache rippled, his face still purple with concentration.

'All right,' he said, stopping in front of Harry yet again. 'All right, let's say, for the sake of argument, we accept this protection. I still don't see why we can't have that Kingsley bloke.'

第3章 德思礼一家离开

弗农·德思礼气呼呼地弓起肩膀，哈利猜想姨父是想摆脱那段回忆。当时哈利刚放暑假没几天，两位成年巫师突然来访。金斯莱·沙克尔和亚瑟·韦斯莱出现在门口，给德思礼一家带来了极不愉快的惊吓。哈利不得不承认，韦斯莱先生曾经把半个客厅捣成了废墟，他的再次露面肯定不会让弗农姨父感到高兴。

"——金斯莱和韦斯莱先生也解释过了，"哈利不为所动地继续说道，"我一满十七岁，保护我安全的咒语就会解除，我和你们就会暴露。凤凰社相信伏地魔会把目标锁定你们，或者折磨你们，拷问我的下落，或者以为把你们扣为人质我就会赶去援救。"

弗农姨父和哈利的目光相遇了。这一刻，哈利相信两人心里产生了同样的疑问。然后，弗农姨父又开始踱步，哈利接着说道："你们必须躲起来，凤凰社愿意帮忙，给你们提供最好的、最严密的保护。"

弗农姨父没说话，继续踱来踱去。外面，太阳低低地悬在女贞树篱上。隔壁邻居家的割草机又熄火了。

"不是有个魔法部吗？"弗农·德思礼突然问道。

"不错。"哈利感到意外。

"那么，他们为什么不能保护我们？在我看来，我们作为无辜的受害者，除了收养了一个被盯上的人外，没干过任何坏事，应该得到政府的保护！"

哈利笑出了声。他忍不住要笑。姨父就是这样，总是把希望寄托于权势部门，即使在那个他敌视和不信任的世界里也不例外。

"你听见了韦斯莱先生和金斯莱说的话，"哈利回答，"我们认为魔法部混进了坏人。"

弗农姨父大步踱到壁炉前又返回来，呼哧呼哧地喘着粗气，浓密的黑色八字胡也跟着波动起伏，大脸膛仍然涨成紫红色。

"好吧，"他说，再次停在了哈利面前，"好吧，姑且这么说吧，我们接受这种保护。但我还是不明白为什么不能让那个大个子金斯莱保护我们。"

CHAPTER THREE   The Dursleys Departing

Harry managed not to roll his eyes, but with difficulty. This question had also been addressed half a dozen times.

'As I've told you,' he said, through gritted teeth, 'Kingsley is protecting the Mug – I mean, your Prime Minister.'

'Exactly – he's the best!' said Uncle Vernon, pointing at the blank television screen. The Dursleys had spotted Kingsley on the news, walking along discreetly behind the Muggle Prime Minister as he visited a hospital. This, and the fact that Kingsley had mastered the knack of dressing like a Muggle, not to mention a certain reassuring something in his slow, deep voice, had caused the Dursleys to take to Kingsley in a way that they had certainly not done with any other wizard, although it was true that they had never seen him with his earring in.

'Well, he's taken,' said Harry. 'But Hestia Jones and Dedalus Diggle are more than up to the job –'

'If we'd even seen CVs ...' began Uncle Vernon, but Harry lost patience. Getting to his feet, he advanced on his uncle, now pointing at the TV set himself.

'These accidents aren't accidents – the crashes and explosions and derailments and whatever else has happened since we last watched the news. People are disappearing and dying and he's behind it – Voldemort. I've told you this over and over again, he kills Muggles for fun. Even the fogs – they're caused by Dementors, and if you can't remember what they are, ask your son!'

Dudley's hands jerked upwards to cover his mouth. With his parents' and Harry's eyes upon him, he slowly lowered them again and asked, 'There are ... more of them?'

'More?' laughed Harry. 'More than the two that attacked us, you mean? Of course there are, there are hundreds, maybe thousands by this time, seeing as they feed off fear and despair –'

'All right, all right,' blustered Vernon Dursley. 'You've made your point–'

'I hope so,' said Harry, 'because once I'm seventeen, all of them – Death Eaters, Dementors, maybe even Inferi, which means dead bodies enchanted by a Dark wizard – will be able to find you and will certainly attack you. And if you remember the last time you tried to outrun wizards, I think you'll agree you need help.'

There was a brief silence in which the distant echo of Hagrid smashing

哈利使劲忍了忍,才没有翻白眼。这个问题也已经提过六七遍了。

"我告诉过你,"哈利咬着牙说,"金斯莱在保护麻——我是说你们的首相。"

"这就对了——他是最棒的!"弗农姨父指着空白的电视屏幕说。德思礼一家在新闻里见过金斯莱,他在麻瓜首相访问医院时悄悄地跟在后面。凭这一点,还有金斯莱掌握了麻瓜的穿衣窍门,更重要的是他那低沉、缓慢的声音里有某种令人宽慰的东西,使德思礼一家在巫师中独独对金斯莱另眼相看。不过呢,他们从来没见过金斯莱戴耳环的样子。

"他已经有任务了,"哈利说,"海丝佳·琼斯和德达洛·迪歌完全能够胜任这项工作——"

"哪怕让我们看看简历……"弗农姨父话没说完,哈利就失去了耐心。他腾地站起来,走到姨父面前,也用手指着电视机。

"这些事故都不是事故——爆炸、飞机坠毁、火车出轨,还有我们上次看新闻之后发生的所有事情。有人失踪、死亡,这一切的背后都是他——伏地魔。我跟你说过不知多少遍了,他以屠杀麻瓜为乐。就连那大雾——也是摄魂怪弄出来的,如果你想不起摄魂怪是什么,就问问你儿子吧!"

达力猛地抬手捂住嘴巴。看到父母和哈利都盯着他,他慢慢把手放下,问道:"它们……还有更多?"

"还有更多?"哈利笑了起来,"你是说,除了上次攻击我们的那两个之外?当然有,有好几百,现在说不定有好几千了,因为它们靠恐惧和绝望活着——"

"行了,行了,"弗农·德思礼咆哮道,"你已经说清楚了——"

"希望如此,"哈利说,"因为我一满十七岁,所有那些家伙——食死徒、摄魂怪,说不定还有阴尸——就是被黑巫师施了魔法的死尸——都能够找到你们,而且肯定会对你们下手。如果你还记得你上次跟巫师较量的情景,我想你会承认你们需要帮助。"

片刻的沉默,海格打烂一扇木门的声音,似乎隔着这么多年的岁

CHAPTER THREE The Dursleys Departing

down a wooden front door seemed to reverberate through the intervening years. Aunt Petunia was looking at Uncle Vernon; Dudley was staring at Harry. Finally Uncle Vernon blurted out, 'But what about my work? What about Dudley's school? I don't suppose those things matter to a bunch of layabout wizards –'

'Don't you understand?' shouted Harry. '*They will torture and kill you like they did my parents!*'

'Dad,' said Dudley in a loud voice, 'Dad – I'm going with these Order people.'

'Dudley,' said Harry, 'for the first time in your life, you're talking sense.'

He knew that the battle was won. If Dudley was frightened enough to accept the Order's help, his parents would accompany him: there could be no question of being separated from their Diddykins. Harry glanced at the carriage clock on the mantelpiece.

'They'll be here in about five minutes,' he said, and when none of the Dursleys replied, he left the room. The prospect of parting – probably forever – from his aunt, uncle and cousin was one that he was able to contemplate quite cheerfully, but there was nevertheless a certain awkwardness in the air. What did you say to one another at the end of sixteen years' solid dislike?

Back in his bedroom, Harry fiddled aimlessly with his rucksack, then poked a couple of owl nuts through the bars of Hedwig's cage. They fell with dull thuds to the bottom, where she ignored them.

'We're leaving soon, really soon,' Harry told her. 'And then you'll be able to fly again.'

The doorbell rang. Harry hesitated, then headed back out of his room and downstairs: it was too much to expect Hestia and Dedalus to cope with the Dursleys on their own.

'Harry Potter!' squeaked an excited voice, the moment Harry had opened the door; a small man in a mauve top hat was sweeping him a deep bow. 'An honour, as ever!'

'Thanks, Dedalus,' said Harry, bestowing a small and embarrassed smile upon the dark-haired Hestia. 'It's really good of you to do this ... they're through here, my aunt and uncle and cousin ...'

'Good day to you, Harry Potter's relatives!' said Dedalus happily, striding into the living room. The Dursleys did not look at all happy to be addressed thus; Harry half expected another change of mind. Dudley shrank nearer to his mother at the sight of the witch and wizard.

第3章 德思礼一家离开

月远远传来。佩妮姨妈看着弗农姨父；达力瞪着哈利。最后，弗农姨父突然说道："可是我的工作怎么办？达力的学校怎么办？我想，一帮游手好闲的巫师是不会管这些事情的——"

"你还不明白吗？"哈利喊道，"他们会折磨你们，杀死你们，就像对我的父母那样！"

"爸爸，"达力大声说，"爸爸——我要跟凤凰社的那些人走。"

"达力，"哈利说，"你这辈子第一次说了句明白话。"

他知道胜局已定。既然达力吓得愿意接受凤凰社的帮助，他的父母肯定会陪着他：他们怎么可能离开他们的小宝贝达达呢？哈利看了看壁炉台上的旅行钟。

"再有五分钟左右他们就来了。"他说，德思礼一家谁也没有回答，他便离开了客厅。想到他和姨妈、姨父、表哥就此分离——也许永不再见——他的心头不无欢喜，但气氛还是有些尴尬。在十六年的极度厌恶之后，互相之间还能说什么呢？

回到卧室，哈利漫无目的地摆弄着他的背包，又往海德薇的笼子里塞了几粒猫头鹰食。它们噗噗落在笼子底部，海德薇没有理睬。

"我们很快就要离开了，真的很快，"哈利告诉它，"那时你就又可以飞了。"

门铃响了。哈利犹豫了一下，离开房间，走下楼来。要指望海丝佳和德达洛单独对付德思礼一家，恐怕有点不切实际。

"哈利·波特！"哈利刚打开门，一个激动的声音就尖叫起来。一位头戴淡紫色高顶礼帽的小个子男人朝他深深鞠了一躬。"不胜荣幸！"

"谢谢，德达洛，"哈利说着，朝黑头发的海丝佳尴尬地微微一笑，"你们能来真是太好了……他们就在这儿，我的姨妈、姨父和表哥……"

"你们好，哈利·波特的亲戚们！"德达洛一边大步走进客厅，一边乐呵呵地说。德思礼一家听到这样的称呼似乎一点儿也不高兴。哈利隐约担心他们又要改变主意。达力看到这两个男女巫师，吓得又往妈妈跟前缩了缩。

CHAPTER THREE   The Dursleys Departing

'I see you are packed and ready. Excellent! The plan, as Harry has told you, is a simple one,' said Dedalus, pulling an immense pocket watch out of his waistcoat and examining it. 'We shall be leaving before Harry does. Due to the danger of using magic in your house – Harry being still under-age, it could provide the Ministry with an excuse to arrest him – we shall be driving, say ten miles or so, before Disapparating to the safe location we have picked out for you. You know how to drive, I take it?' he asked Uncle Vernon politely.

'Know how to –? Of course I ruddy well know how to drive!' spluttered Uncle Vernon.

'Very clever of you, sir, very clever, I personally would be utterly bamboozled by all those buttons and knobs,' said Dedalus. He was clearly under the impression that he was flattering Vernon Dursley, who was visibly losing confidence in the plan with every word Dedalus spoke.

'Can't even drive,' he muttered under his breath, his moustache rippling indignantly, but fortunately neither Dedalus nor Hestia seemed to hear him.

'You, Harry,' Dedalus continued, 'will wait here for your guard. There has been a little change in the arrangements –'

'What d'you mean?' said Harry at once. 'I thought Mad-Eye was going to come and take me by Side-Along-Apparition?'

'Can't do it,' said Hestia tersely. 'Mad-Eye will explain.'

The Dursleys, who had listened to all of this with looks of utter incomprehension on their faces, jumped as a loud voice screeched: '*Hurry up!*' Harry looked all around the room before realising that the voice had issued from Dedalus's pocket watch.

'Quite right, we're operating to a very tight schedule,' said Dedalus, nodding at his watch and tucking it back into his waistcoat. 'We are attempting to time your departure from the house with your family's Disapparition, Harry; thus, the charm breaks at the moment you all head for safety.' He turned to the Dursleys. 'Well, are we all packed and ready to go?'

None of them answered him: Uncle Vernon was still staring, appalled, at the bulge in Dedalus's waistcoat pocket.

'Perhaps we should wait outside in the hall, Dedalus,' murmured Hestia: she clearly felt that it would be tactless for them to remain in the room while Harry and the Dursleys exchanged loving, possibly tearful farewells.

第3章 德思礼一家离开

"你们收拾了东西,做好了准备。太好了!计划很简单,就像哈利告诉你们的一样,"德达洛说着,从马甲里掏出一块巨大的怀表看了看,"我们先走,哈利后走。由于在你们家里使用魔法有危险——哈利还没成年,这会使魔法部有借口逮捕他——我们先把车开出去大概十英里左右,然后再幻影移形,到我们为你们选择的安全地方去。我想,您会开车吧?"他很有礼貌地问弗农姨父。

"会开——?我当然会他妈的开车!"弗农姨父急吼吼地说。

"您真聪明,先生,真聪明,我一看到那么多按键和旋钮就彻底糊涂了。"德达洛说。他显然以为是在恭维弗农·德思礼,而德思礼对计划的信心,显然随着德达洛说的每一句话而逐渐丧失。

"连车都不会开。"他低声嘟囔,气得胡子直抖,幸好德达洛和海丝佳好像都没听见。

"你,哈利,"德达洛继续说,"在这里等你的警卫。安排上有了点小小的变化——"

"你说什么?"哈利立刻说,"我记得疯眼汉要来带我随从显形的呀。"

"不成了,"海丝佳生硬地说,"疯眼汉会解释的。"

德思礼一家满脸疑惑地听着这些对话,突然一个声音尖叫起来:"快点!"他们吓了一跳。哈利在客厅里左右张望,才发现声音是德达洛的怀表发出来的。

"不错,我们时间很紧,"德达洛朝他的怀表点点头,又把它塞进马甲里,"我们打算,哈利,你在你的家人幻影移形的同时离开这所房子。这样,咒语破除时,你们都奔向了安全的地方。"他转向德思礼一家,"怎么样,行李都收拾好了吗?我们准备走吧?"

没人回答。弗农姨父仍然胆战心惊地盯着德达洛马甲口袋里的那个鼓包。

"也许我们应该在外面厅里等,德达洛。"海丝佳低声说。她显然觉得哈利和德思礼一家要温情脉脉,说不定还要热泪盈眶地互相告别,他们留在屋里不合适。

CHAPTER THREE   The Dursleys Departing

'There's no need,' Harry muttered, but Uncle Vernon made any further explanation unnecessary by saying loudly, 'Well, this is goodbye, then, boy.'

He swung his right arm upwards to shake Harry's hand, but at the last moment seemed unable to face it, and merely closed his fist and began swinging it backwards and forwards like a metronome.

'Ready, Diddy?' asked Aunt Petunia, fussily checking the clasp of her handbag so as to avoid looking at Harry altogether.

Dudley did not answer, but stood there with his mouth slightly ajar, reminding Harry a little of the giant, Grawp.

'Come along, then,' said Uncle Vernon.

He had already reached the living-room door when Dudley mumbled, 'I don't understand.'

'What don't you understand, Popkin?' asked Aunt Petunia, looking up at her son.

Dudley raised a large, ham-like hand to point at Harry.

'Why isn't he coming with us?'

Uncle Vernon and Aunt Petunia froze where they stood, staring at Dudley as though he had just expressed a desire to become a ballerina.

'What?' said Uncle Vernon loudly.

'Why isn't he coming too?' asked Dudley.

'Well, he – he doesn't want to,' said Uncle Vernon, turning to glare at Harry and adding, 'you don't want to, do you?'

'Not in the slightest,' said Harry.

'There you are,' Uncle Vernon told Dudley. 'Now come on, we're off.'

He marched out of the room: they heard the front door open, but Dudley did not move and after a few faltering steps Aunt Petunia stopped too.

'What now?' barked Uncle Vernon, reappearing in the doorway.

It seemed that Dudley was struggling with concepts too difficult to put into words. After several moments of apparently painful internal struggle, he said, 'But where's he going to go?'

Aunt Petunia and Uncle Vernon looked at each other. It was clear that Dudley was frightening them. Hestia Jones broke the silence.

'But ... surely you know where your nephew is going?' she asked, looking bewildered.

第3章 德思礼一家离开

"不必了。"哈利嘟囔道。弗农姨父的话使更多的解释变得没有必要，他大声说道："得，这就告别了，小子。"

他把右胳膊往前一伸，想跟哈利握手，但在最后一刻似乎无法面对，便把手握成拳头，像节拍器一样前后摆动。

"准备好了，达达？"佩妮姨妈问，一边没事找事地检查手包的搭扣，为的是根本不看哈利。

达力没有回答，他站在那里，嘴巴微微张着，这使哈利隐约想起了巨人格洛普。

"快走吧。"弗农姨父说。

他已经走到客厅门口了，忽听达力嘟囔道："我不明白。"

"有什么不明白的，宝贝？"佩妮姨妈抬头看着儿子问。

达力举起一只火腿般粗胖的手指着哈利。

"他为什么不跟我们一起走？"

弗农姨父和佩妮姨妈怔在原地，呆呆地望着达力，就好像达力刚刚表示想当一名芭蕾舞演员。

"什么？"弗农姨父大声问。

"他为什么不一起走？"达力问。

"噢，他——他不想走，"弗农姨父说完，转脸瞪着哈利问道，"你不想走，对不对？"

"一点儿也不想。"哈利说。

"这下行了吧，"弗农姨父对达力说，"好了，我们走吧。"

弗农姨父大步走出客厅。屋里的人听见前门打开的声音，可是达力没有动弹，佩妮姨妈跟跟跄跄地走了几步，也停下了。

"又怎么啦？"弗农姨父又出现在门口，咆哮着问。

达力好像在努力对付一些难以用语言表达的思想。经过片刻看似很痛苦的内心挣扎之后，他说："可是他去哪儿呢？"

佩妮姨妈和弗农姨父面面相觑。显然，达力把他们吓坏了。海丝佳·琼斯打破了沉默。

"可是……你们当然知道你们的外甥要去哪儿，不是吗？"她一脸迷惑地问。

063

CHAPTER THREE The Dursleys Departing

'Certainly we know,' said Vernon Dursley. 'He's off with some of your lot, isn't he? Right, Dudley, let's get in the car, you heard the man, we're in a hurry.'

Again, Vernon Dursley marched as far as the front door, but Dudley did not follow.

'Off with some of *our* lot?'

Hestia looked outraged. Harry had met this attitude before: witches and wizards seemed stunned that his closest living relatives took so little interest in the famous Harry Potter.

'It's fine,' Harry assured her. 'It doesn't matter, honestly.'

'Doesn't matter?' repeated Hestia, her voice rising ominously. 'Don't these people realise what you've been through? What danger you are in? The unique position you hold in the hearts of the anti-Voldemort movement?'

'Er – no, they don't,' said Harry. 'They think I'm a waste of space, actually, but I'm used to –'

'I don't think you're a waste of space.'

If Harry had not seen Dudley's lips move, he might not have believed it. As it was, he stared at Dudley for several seconds before accepting that it must have been his cousin who had spoken; for one thing, Dudley had turned red. Harry was embarrassed and astonished himself.

'Well ... er ... thanks, Dudley.'

Again, Dudley appeared to grapple with thoughts too unwieldy for expression before mumbling, 'You saved my life.'

'Not really,' said Harry. 'It was your soul the Dementor would have taken ...'

He looked curiously at his cousin. They had had virtually no contact during this summer or last, as Harry had come back to Privet Drive so briefly and kept to his room so much. It now dawned on Harry, however, that the cup of cold tea on which he had trodden that morning might not have been a booby trap at all. Although rather touched, he was nevertheless quite relieved that Dudley appeared to have exhausted his ability to express his feelings. After opening his mouth once or twice more, Dudley subsided into scarlet-faced silence.

Aunt Petunia burst into tears. Hestia Jones gave her an approving look which changed to outrage as Aunt Petunia ran forwards and embraced Dudley rather than Harry.

第3章 德思礼一家离开

"我们当然知道。"弗农·德思礼说,"他跟你们那类的几个人走,不是吗?好了,达力,我们快上车吧,你听见那个人说了,时间很紧。"

弗农·德思礼又一次大步流星地走到前门,可是达力并没有跟上去。

"跟我们这类的几个人走?"

海丝佳好像被惹恼了。哈利以前也碰到过这种态度。巫师们看到与大名鼎鼎的哈利·波特关系最近的亲戚对他这样漠不关心,似乎都很震惊。

"算了,"哈利劝解道,"没什么,真的没什么。"

"没什么?"海丝佳跟着说了一句,声音提得很高,透着不祥,"这些人知不知道你经历了什么?知不知道你面临着什么危险?知不知道你在反伏地魔运动的核心中所处的独特位置?"

"呃——不知道,他们不知道。"哈利说,"实际上,他们以为我是废物一个,不过我也习惯了——"

"我不认为你是废物。"

如果不是看到达力的嘴唇在动,哈利大概不会相信。他瞪了达力几秒钟,才终于承认刚才是达力在说话,至少他看见达力的脸涨得通红。哈利自己也是又尴尬又诧异。

"噢……嗯……谢谢你,达力。"

达力似乎又在对付一些难以表达的思想,最后喃喃地说:"你救过我的命。"

"不能这么说,"哈利说,"摄魂怪要掳走的是你的灵魂……"

他好奇地打量着表哥。这个暑假和上个暑假,他们几乎没有什么接触,哈利回到女贞路的时间很短,而且总是待在自己的房间里。哈利这才隐约明白过来,那天早晨他踩到的那杯凉茶也许根本不是什么恶作剧。他虽然很感动,但看到达力表达感情的能力似乎已经消耗殆尽,他还是感到松了口气。达力张了张嘴,满脸通红,没再说话。

佩妮姨妈哭了起来。海丝佳·琼斯赞许地看着她,没想到佩妮姨妈冲过来搂抱的不是哈利,而是达力,海丝佳顿时怒容满面。

CHAPTER THREE   The Dursleys Departing

'S – So sweet, Dudders ...' she sobbed into his massive chest, 's – such a lovely b – boy ... s – saying thank you ...'

'But he hasn't said thank you at all!' said Hestia indignantly. 'He only said he didn't think Harry was a waste of space!'

'Yeah, but coming from Dudley that's like "I love you",' said Harry, torn between annoyance and a desire to laugh as Aunt Petunia continued to clutch at Dudley as if he had just saved Harry from a burning building.

'Are we going or not?' roared Uncle Vernon, reappearing yet again at the living-room door. 'I thought we were on a tight schedule!'

'Yes – yes, we are,' said Dedalus Diggle, who had been watching these exchanges with an air of bemusement and now seemed to pull himself together. 'We really must be off. Harry –'

He tripped forwards and wrung Harry's hand with both of his own.

'– good luck. I hope we meet again. The hopes of the wizarding world rest upon your shoulders.'

'Oh,' said Harry, 'right. Thanks.'

'Farewell, Harry,' said Hestia, also clasping his hand. 'Our thoughts go with you.'

'I hope everything's OK,' said Harry, with a glance towards Aunt Petunia and Dudley.

'Oh, I'm sure we shall end up the best of chums,' said Diggle brightly, waving his hat as he left the room. Hestia followed him.

Dudley gently released himself from his mother's clutches and walked towards Harry, who had to repress an urge to threaten him with magic. Then Dudley held out his large, pink hand.

'Blimey, Dudley,' said Harry, over Aunt Petunia's renewed sobs, 'did the Dementors blow a different personality into you?'

'Dunno,' muttered Dudley. 'See you, Harry.'

'Yeah ...' said Harry, taking Dudley's hand and shaking it. 'Maybe. Take care, Big D.'

Dudley nearly smiled, then lumbered from the room. Harry heard his heavy footfalls on the gravelled drive, and then a car door slammed.

Aunt Petunia, whose face had been buried in her handkerchief, looked round at the sound. She did not seem to have expected to find herself alone

"真——真乖,达达……"她贴着达力宽阔的胸脯哭起来,"多——多么可爱的孩——孩子……会——会说谢谢……"

"他根本没说谢谢!"海丝佳气愤地说,"他只说了他认为哈利不是废物!"

"是啊,不过这话从达力嘴里说出来,就像'我爱你'一样了。"哈利说,佩妮姨妈继续紧紧地搂住达力,好像达力刚把哈利从一座着火的房子里救出来一样,哈利看着不禁又气恼又好笑。

"我们还走不走啊?"弗农姨父又一次出现在客厅门口,粗声吼道,"不是时间很紧吗!"

"对——对,"德达洛·迪歌说,他刚才一头雾水地看着这些场景,这会儿才似乎回过神来,"我们真的得走了。哈利——"

他匆匆上前,用两只手紧紧攥住哈利的手。

"——祝你好运。希望我们后会有期。巫师界的希望就落在你的肩上了。"

"噢,"哈利说,"好的,谢谢了。"

"再见,哈利,"海丝佳也紧紧地拉住他的手说,"我们会挂念你的。"

"希望一切顺利。"哈利说着,看了一眼佩妮姨妈和达力。

"哦,我相信我们会成为好朋友的。"迪歌愉快地说,挥挥帽子,离开了客厅。海丝佳也跟了出去。

达力轻轻挣脱母亲的搂抱,朝哈利走来。哈利不得不克制住想用魔法威胁他的冲动。达力伸出他那只肥大的、粉红色的手。

"天哪,达力,"哈利的声音盖过佩妮姨妈重新响起的啜泣,"难道摄魂怪给你灌输了另一种性格吗?"

"不知道。"达力低声说,"再见,哈利。"

"好的……"哈利说着握了握达力的手,"也许吧。保重,D 哥。"

达力几乎是笑了笑,然后蹒跚地走出客厅。哈利听见他沉重的脚步踏在砾石车道上,然后砰的一声,车门关上了。

听见这声音,一直把脸埋在手帕里的佩妮姨妈抬头张望。她似乎没有料到自己会和哈利单独待在一起。她匆匆把湿漉漉的手帕塞进口

CHAPTER THREE   The Dursleys Departing

with Harry. Hastily stowing her wet handkerchief into her pocket she said, 'Well – goodbye,' and marched towards the door without looking at him.

'Goodbye,' said Harry.

She stopped and looked back. For a moment Harry had the strangest feeling that she wanted to say something to him: she gave him an odd, tremulous look and seemed to teeter on the edge of speech, but then, with a little jerk of her head, she bustled out of the room after her husband and son.

袋,说了声:"好了——再见吧。"然后看也不看哈利,就大步朝门口走去。

"再见。"哈利说。

佩妮姨妈停住脚步,回过头来。一时间,哈利有一种特别奇怪的感觉,好像佩妮姨妈想对他说点什么:她用古怪而胆怯的目光看看他,似乎迟疑着想说话,可随即猛地把头一摆,冲出房门,追她的丈夫和儿子去了。

CHAPTER FOUR

The Seven Potters

Harry ran back upstairs to his bedroom, arriving at the window just in time to see the Dursleys' car swinging out of the drive and off up the road. Dedalus's top hat was visible between Aunt Petunia and Dudley in the back seat. The car turned right at the end of Privet Drive, its windows burned scarlet for a moment in the now setting sun, and then it was gone.

Harry picked up Hedwig's cage, his Firebolt and his rucksack, gave his unnaturally tidy bedroom one last sweeping look and then made his ungainly way back downstairs to the hall, where he deposited cage, broomstick and bag near the foot of the stairs. The light was fading rapidly now, the hall full of shadows in the evening light. It felt most strange to stand here in the silence and know that he was about to leave the house for the last time. Long ago, when he had been left alone while the Dursleys went out to enjoy themselves, the hours of solitude had been a rare treat: pausing only to sneak something tasty from the fridge he had rushed upstairs to play on Dudley's computer, or put on the television and flicked through the channels to his heart's content. It gave him an odd, empty feeling to remember those times; it was like remembering a younger brother whom he had lost.

'Don't you want to take a last look at the place?' he asked Hedwig, who was still sulking with her head under her wing. 'We'll never be here again. Don't you want to remember all the good times? I mean, look at this doormat. What memories ... Dudley puked on it after I saved him from the Dementors ... Turns out he was grateful after all, can you believe it? ... And last summer, Dumbledore walked through that front door ...'

Harry lost the thread of his thoughts for a moment and Hedwig did nothing to help him retrieve it, but continued to sit with her head under her wing. Harry turned his back on the front door.

第 4 章

七个波特

哈利跑回楼上自己的卧室，冲到窗前，正好看见德思礼家的汽车拐过车道，上了马路，后座上德达洛的高顶礼帽位于佩妮姨妈和达力中间。汽车到了女贞路尽头往右一拐，车窗在西斜的太阳照耀下射出火一般的红光，然后就不见了。

哈利拎起海德薇的笼子，拿起他的火弩箭和背包，最后扫了一眼整洁得有些反常的卧室，然后歪歪斜斜地下楼来到客厅，把鸟笼、扫帚和背包放在楼梯脚旁。光线很快变暗，客厅在暮色中显得阴影重重。四下里一片寂静，哈利站在这里，知道自己将要永远离开这所房子，感觉真是特别异样。很久以前，德思礼一家出去玩乐，把他一个人留在家里，那几个小时独处的时光是一种难得的享受：从冰箱里快速偷些好吃的东西，然后冲到楼上，玩玩达力的电脑，或打开电视，随心所欲地选择频道。想起那些时光，他内心里泛起一种莫名的惆怅，如同想起一个已经失去的小弟弟。

"你不想最后一次看看这个地方吗？"他问海德薇。猫头鹰仍然把脑袋藏在翅膀底下生闷气。"我们再也不会到这里来了。你不想回忆回忆所有那些快乐的时光吗？我是说，看看门口这块擦鞋垫。想想往事……我把达力从摄魂怪手里救出来后，他在这块垫子上吐了……想不到他还是知道感恩的，你相信吗？……还有去年夏天，邓布利多穿过那道前门……"

哈利的思路断了，海德薇并没有帮他找回，仍把脑袋藏在翅膀底下不动。哈利从前门那儿转过身来。

CHAPTER FOUR   The Seven Potters

'And under here, Hedwig –' Harry pulled open a door under the stairs '– is where I used to sleep! You never knew me then – blimey, it's small, I'd forgotten ...'

Harry looked around at the stacked shoes and umbrellas, remembering how he used to wake every morning looking up at the underside of the staircase, which was more often than not adorned with a spider or two. Those had been the days before he had known anything about his true identity; before he had found out how his parents had died or why such strange things often happened around him. But Harry could still remember the dreams that had dogged him, even in those days: confused dreams involving flashes of green light and, once – Uncle Vernon had nearly crashed the car when Harry had recounted it – a flying motorbike ...

There was a sudden, deafening roar from somewhere nearby. Harry straightened up with a jerk and smacked the top of his head on the low door frame. Pausing only to employ a few of Uncle Vernon's choicest swear words, he staggered back into the kitchen, clutching his head and staring out of the window into the back garden.

The darkness seemed to be rippling, the air itself quivering. Then, one by one, figures began to pop into sight as their Disillusionment Charms lifted. Dominating the scene was Hagrid, wearing a helmet and goggles and sitting astride an enormous motorbike with a black sidecar attached. All around him other people were dismounting from brooms and, in two cases, skeletal, black winged horses.

Wrenching open the back door, Harry hurtled into their midst. There was a general cry of greeting as Hermione flung her arms around him, Ron clapped him on the back and Hagrid said, 'All righ', Harry? Ready fer the off?'

'Definitely,' said Harry, beaming around at them all. 'But I wasn't expecting this many of you!'

'Change of plan,' growled Mad-Eye, who was holding two enormous, bulging sacks and whose magical eye was spinning from darkening sky to house to garden with dizzying rapidity. 'Let's get undercover before we talk you through it.'

Harry led them all back into the kitchen where, laughing and chattering, they settled on chairs, sat themselves upon Aunt Petunia's gleaming work-surfaces or leaned up against her spotless appliances: Ron, long and lanky; Hermione, her bushy hair tied back in a long plait; Fred and George, grinning identically; Bill, badly scarred and long-haired; Mr Weasley, kind-faced,

第4章 七个波特

"在这下面,海德薇——"哈利拉开楼梯下面的一扇门,"——就是我以前睡觉的地方!那时你还不认识我呢——天哪,真小啊,我都不记得了……"

哈利看看那一堆堆的鞋子和雨伞,想起当年每天早晨醒来,抬眼看着楼梯底侧,那里总会吊着一两只蜘蛛。那些日子,他还对自己的真实身份一无所知,还没有弄清父母是怎么死的,也不明白为什么经常会有那些奇怪的事情在他周围发生。哈利仍然记得那些当年就纠缠着他的梦境:乱梦颠倒,绿光闪烁,还有一次——哈利说起这个梦时,弗农姨父差点儿撞了车——居然梦见一辆会飞的摩托车……

突然,附近什么地方传来震耳欲聋的吼声。哈利猛地直起身,头顶砰的一声撞在低矮的门框上。他顿了顿,用弗农姨父最喜欢的粗话骂了几句,然后跌跌撞撞地走回厨房,手捂着脑袋,朝窗外的后花园望去。

黑暗似乎泛起了涟漪,空气本身也在颤动。接着,随着幻身咒的解除,一个个人影开始显现出来。最显眼的是海格,戴着头盔和护目镜,骑在一辆巨大的、带黑色挎斗的摩托车上。在他周围,其他人纷纷从飞天扫帚上下来,还有两个是从瘦骨嶙峋的、带翅膀的黑马身上下来的。

哈利打开后门,一下子蹿到他们中间。四下里一片问候声,赫敏张开双臂把他搂住,罗恩拍着他的后背。海格说:"怎么样,哈利?准备离开了?"

"当然,"哈利说,笑眯眯地看着大家,"没想到你们来了这么多人!"

"计划变了。"疯眼汉粗声粗气地说,他提着两个鼓鼓囊囊的巨大口袋,那只魔眼嗖嗖地扫视着逐渐变暗的天空、房屋和花园,速度快得令人眩晕,"我们先掩护起来,再跟你细说。"

哈利把他们都领进厨房,大家嘻嘻哈哈、谈笑风生地坐在椅子上,坐在佩妮姨妈光洁锃亮的厨房操作台上,或靠在她一尘不染的各种电器上。罗恩,又瘦又高;赫敏,浓密的头发在脑后编成了一根长辫子;弗雷德和乔治,一模一样地咧嘴笑着;比尔,满脸伤痕,留着长发;

CHAPTER FOUR The Seven Potters

balding, his spectacles a little awry; Mad-Eye, battle-worn, one-legged, his bright blue magical eye whizzing in its socket; Tonks, whose short hair was her favourite shade of bright pink; Lupin, greyer, more lined; Fleur, slender and beautiful, with her long, silvery blonde hair; Kingsley, bald, black, broad-shouldered; Hagrid, with his wild hair and beard, standing hunchbacked to avoid hitting his head on the ceiling, and Mundungus Fletcher, small, dirty and hangdog, with his droopy, basset hound's eyes and matted hair. Harry's heart seemed to expand and glow at the sight: he felt incredibly fond of all of them, even Mundungus, whom he had tried to strangle the last time they had met.

'Kingsley, I thought you were looking after the Muggle Prime Minister?' he called across the room.

'He can get along without me for one night,' said Kingsley. 'You're more important.'

'Harry, guess what?' said Tonks from her perch on top of the washing machine, and she wiggled her left hand at him; a ring glittered there.

'You got married?' Harry yelped, looking from her to Lupin.

'I'm sorry you couldn't be there, Harry, it was very quiet.'

'That's brilliant, congrat–'

'All right, all right, we'll have time for a cosy catch-up later!' roared Moody over the hubbub, and silence fell in the kitchen. Moody dropped the sacks at his feet and turned to Harry. 'As Dedalus probably told you, we had to abandon Plan A. Pius Thicknesse has gone over, which gives us a big problem. He's made it an imprisonable offence to connect this house to the Floo Network, place a Portkey here or Apparate in or out. All done in the name of your protection, to prevent You-Know-Who getting in at you. Absolutely pointless, seeing as your mother's charm does that already. What he's really done is to stop you getting out of here safely.

'Second problem: you're under-age, which means you've still got the Trace on you.'

'I don't –'

'The Trace, the Trace!' said Mad-Eye impatiently. 'The charm that detects magical activity around under-seventeens, the way the Ministry finds out about under-age magic! If you, or anyone around you, casts a spell to get you out of here, Thicknesse is going to know about it, and so will the Death Eaters.

第4章 七个波特

韦斯莱先生，慈眉善目，秃顶，眼镜戴得有点儿歪；疯眼汉，久经沙场，只有一条腿，那只亮晶晶的蓝色魔眼在眼窝里嗖嗖地转个不停；唐克斯，一头短发是她最喜欢的亮粉色；卢平，更加憔悴、瘦削；芙蓉，美丽苗条，长长的银白色秀发；金斯莱，秃头，宽肩膀，皮肤黝黑；海格，头发胡子蓬乱茂密，弓着腰站在那里，生怕脑袋撞到天花板；蒙顿格斯·弗莱奇，小个子，邋里邋遢，一副猥琐样，眼皮像短腿猎狗那样耷拉着，头发蓬乱纠结。此情此景，令哈利心花怒放，开心极了：他真喜欢他们大家啊，就连蒙顿格斯他也喜欢上了，而上次见面时，哈利还想掐死他呢。

"金斯莱，你不是在照顾麻瓜首相吗？"他朝屋子那头喊道。

"一个晚上没有我，他对付得了，"金斯莱说，"你更重要啊。"

"哈利，你猜怎么着？"唐克斯坐在洗衣机上，朝哈利晃动着她的左手：一枚戒指闪闪发光。

"你们结婚了？"哈利叫道，看看她，又看看卢平。

"对不起，你没能参加，哈利，我们没怎么声张。"

"太棒了，祝贺——"

"好了，好了，以后有时间好好聊个痛快！"穆迪在一片喧闹声中吼道，厨房里顿时安静下来。穆迪把口袋扔在脚下，转向哈利："德达洛大概已经跟你说了，我们不得不放弃第一套计划。皮尔斯·辛克尼斯叛变了，给我们带来了很大麻烦。他把许多做法都归为犯法行为，抓住就要坐牢，比如：让这所房子跟飞路网连接，在这里放一个门钥匙，或者幻影显形进进出出。还说这么做都是为了保护你，为了不让神秘人抓住你。纯属无稽之谈，你母亲的咒语已经做到了这点。辛克尼斯所做的实际上是阻止你安全地离开这里。

"第二个难题：你还没有成年，这意味着你身上仍然带有踪丝。"

"我不明白——"

"踪丝，踪丝！"疯眼汉不耐烦地说，"探测十七岁以下的巫师进行魔法活动的咒语，魔法部通过它来发现未成年者使用魔法！如果你，或者你周围的什么人，念一个咒语让你离开这里，辛克尼斯就会知道，食死徒也会知道。

CHAPTER FOUR The Seven Potters

'We can't wait for the Trace to break, because the moment you turn seventeen you'll lose all the protection your mother gave you. In short: Pius Thicknesse thinks he's got you cornered good and proper.'

Harry could not help but agree with the unknown Thicknesse.

'So what are we going to do?'

'We're going to use the only means of transport left to us, the only ones the Trace can't detect, because we don't need to cast spells to use them: brooms, Thestrals and Hagrid's motorbike.'

Harry could see flaws in this plan; however, he held his tongue to give Mad-Eye the chance to address them.

'Now, your mother's charm will only break under two conditions: when you come of age, or –' Moody gestured around the pristine kitchen '– you no longer call this place home. You and your aunt and uncle are going your separate ways tonight, in the full understanding that you're never going to live together again, correct?'

Harry nodded.

'So this time, when you leave, there'll be no going back, and the charm will break the moment you get outside its range. We're choosing to break it early, because the alternative is waiting for You-Know-Who to come and seize you the moment you turn seventeen.

'The one thing we've got on our side is that You-Know-Who doesn't know we're moving you tonight. We've leaked a fake trail to the Ministry: they think you're not leaving until the thirtieth. However, this is You-Know-Who we're dealing with, so we can't just rely on him getting the date wrong; he's bound to have a couple of Death Eaters patrolling the skies in this general area, just in case. So, we've given a dozen different houses every protection we can throw at them. They all look like they could be the place we're going to hide you, they've all got some connection with the Order: my house, Kingsley's place, Molly's Auntie Muriel's – you get the idea.'

'Yeah,' said Harry, not entirely truthfully, because he could still spot a gaping hole in the plan.

'You'll be going to Tonks's parents'. Once you're within the boundaries of the protective enchantments we've put on their house, you'll be able to use a Portkey to The Burrow. Any questions?'

第4章　七个波特

"我们不能等踪丝消失,因为你一满十七岁,就会失去你母亲给你的全部保护。简单地说:皮尔斯·辛克尼斯认为你已经彻底走投无路了。"

哈利忍不住赞同这位素不相识的辛克尼斯。

"那我们怎么办呢?"

"我们只能使用这几种交通工具:飞天扫帚、夜骐和海格的摩托,只有它们是踪丝无法探测的,因为不需要念咒语。"

哈利看到了这个计划里的漏洞,但他忍住没说,让疯眼汉自己有机会处理。

"你母亲的咒语在两种条件下会破除:你成年了,或者——"穆迪指了指一尘不染的厨房,"——你不再管这个地方叫家。今晚,你和你的姨妈姨父分道扬镳,彼此都明白你们今后再也不会共同生活了,对不对?"

哈利点点头。

"所以,这次你一离开就再也不会回来,咒语会在你走出它的范围时破除。我们选择提早打破它,因为神秘人很可能会在你满十七岁时过来抓你。

"我们有一个优势,就是神秘人不知道我们今晚要来转移你。我们给魔法部透露了一个假情报:他们以为你三十号才会离开。不过,我们的对手是神秘人,光指望他把日子搞错是不够的;他肯定会让两个食死徒在这个地区的上空巡视,以防万一。所以,我们对整整一打房屋采取了最好的保护措施。它们看上去都像是我们准备藏你的地方,都和凤凰社有某种联系:我的房子、金斯莱家、莫丽的穆丽尔姨妈家——你明白这意思吧?"

"明白。"哈利没有完全说实话,他仍然看出计划里有个很大的漏洞。

"你去唐克斯的父母家。一旦进入我们给房子设置的保护魔咒的范围,你就可以利用一个门钥匙转移到陋居去。有问题吗?"

CHAPTER FOUR The Seven Potters

'Er – yes,' said Harry. 'Maybe they won't know which of the twelve secure houses I'm heading for at first, but won't it be sort of obvious once –' he performed a quick headcount '– fourteen of us fly off towards Tonks's parents'?'

'Ah,' said Moody, 'I forgot to mention the key point. Fourteen of us won't be flying to Tonks's parents'. There will be seven Harry Potters moving through the skies tonight, each of them with a companion, each pair heading for a different safe house.'

From inside his cloak Moody now withdrew a flask of what looked like mud. There was no need for him to say another word; Harry understood the rest of the plan immediately.

'No!' he said loudly, his voice ringing through the kitchen. 'No way!'

'I told them you'd take it like this,' said Hermione, with a hint of complacency.

'If you think I'm going to let six people risk their lives –!'

'– because it's the first time for all of us,' said Ron.

'This is different, pretending to be me –'

'Well, none of us really fancy it, Harry,' said Fred earnestly. 'Imagine if something went wrong and we were stuck as specky, scrawny gits forever.'

Harry did not smile.

'You can't do it if I don't cooperate, you need me to give you some hair.'

'Well, that's that plan scuppered,' said George. 'Obviously there's no chance at all of us getting a bit of your hair unless you cooperate.'

'Yeah, thirteen of us against one bloke who's not allowed to use magic; we've got no chance,' said Fred.

'Funny,' said Harry. 'Really amusing.'

'If it has to come to force, then it will,' growled Moody, his magical eye now quivering a little in its socket as he glared at Harry. 'Everyone here's over-age, Potter, and they're all prepared to take the risk.'

Mundungus shrugged and grimaced; the magical eye swerved sideways to glare at him out of the side of Moody's head.

'Let's have no more arguments. Time's wearing on. I want a few of your hairs, boy, now.'

第4章 七个波特

"呃——有，"哈利说，"也许他们一开始并不知道我要去那十二处安全房子中的哪一处，可是——"他快速清点了一下人数，"——我们十四个人飞向唐克斯的父母家，这不一下子就完全暴露了吗？"

"啊，"穆迪说，"关键的一点我忘记说了。我们十四个人并不都飞往唐克斯的父母家。今晚将有七个哈利·波特在天上飞，每个都有人陪伴，每一组都飞往一处不同的安全房屋。"

穆迪从斗篷里掏出一瓶泥浆般的东西。不用他再说一个字，哈利立刻明白了整个计划。

"不！"他大声说，声音在厨房里回荡，"不行！"

"我告诉过你们他会是这种反应吧。"赫敏有点儿得意地说。

"如果你们认为我会让六个人冒着生命危险——！"

"——因为这对我们来说都是第一次呢。"罗恩说。

"这次不一样，假装成我——"

"咳，其实我们谁都不喜欢，哈利。"弗雷德一本正经地说，"想象一下吧，如果出了故障，我们变不回去，就要永远成为戴着眼镜、皮包骨头的小笨蛋了。"

哈利没有笑。

"如果我不配合，你们就办不成，你们需要我贡献几根头发。"

"是啊，这么一来，整个计划可就泡汤了。"乔治说，"如果你不配合，我们显然根本不可能弄到你的一点儿头发。"

"没错，十三个对付一个，而那一个还不能使用魔法。我们真是一点胜算也没有啊。"弗雷德说。

"荒唐，"哈利说，"真是太可笑了。"

"如果需要动用武力，那就来吧。"穆迪吼道，他瞪着哈利，魔眼在眼窝里微微颤抖，"这里的每个人都到了法定年龄，波特，他们都准备冒此风险。"

蒙顿格斯耸耸肩膀，做了个鬼脸。穆迪的魔眼嗖地一转，从脑袋一侧狠狠瞪着他。

"别再争执了，时间有限。我需要你几根头发，孩子，快。"

CHAPTER FOUR The Seven Potters

'But this is mad, there's no need –'

'No need!' snarled Moody. 'With You-Know-Who out there and half the Ministry on his side? Potter, if we're lucky, he'll have swallowed the fake bait and he'll be planning to ambush you on the thirtieth, but he'd be mad not to have a Death Eater or two keeping an eye out, it's what I'd do. They might not be able to get at you or this house while your mother's charm holds, but it's about to break and they know the rough position of the place. Our only chance is to use decoys. Even You-Know-Who can't split himself into seven.'

Harry caught Hermione's eye and looked away at once.

'So, Potter – some of your hair, if you please.'

Harry glanced at Ron, who grimaced at him in a just-do-it sort of way.

'Now!' barked Moody.

With all of their eyes upon him, Harry reached up to the top of his head, grabbed a hank of hair and pulled.

'Good,' said Moody, limping forwards as he pulled the stopper out of the flask of Potion. 'Straight in here, if you please.'

Harry dropped the hair into the mud-like liquid. The moment it made contact with its surface the Potion began to froth and smoke then, all at once, it turned a clear, bright gold.

'Ooh, you look much tastier than Crabbe and Goyle, Harry,' said Hermione, before catching sight of Ron's raised eyebrows, blushing slightly and saying, 'oh, you know what I mean – Goyle's Potion looked like bogies.'

'Right then, fake Potters line up over here, please,' said Moody.

Ron, Hermione, Fred, George and Fleur lined up in front of Aunt Petunia's gleaming sink.

'We're one short,' said Lupin.

'Here,' said Hagrid gruffly, and he lifted Mundungus by the scruff of the neck and dropped him down beside Fleur, who wrinkled her nose pointedly and moved along to stand between Fred and George instead.

'I've toldjer, I'd sooner be a protector,' said Mundungus.

'Shut it,' growled Moody. 'As I've already told you, you spineless worm, any Death Eaters we run into will be aiming to capture Potter, not kill him. Dumbledore always said You-Know-Who would want to finish Potter in

第4章 七个波特

"可是这太荒唐了，没有必要——"

"没有必要！"穆迪厉声吼道，"外面有神秘人，还有半个魔法部都和他站在一边！波特，如果我们运气好，他会相信那个假情报，计划在三十号打你一个埋伏，但他肯定会安排一两个食死徒监视你，除非他脑子坏了，换了我也会这么做。有你母亲的咒语在，他们大概还不能拿你或这所房子怎么样，但咒语很快就要失效，而他们知道房子的大致位置。我们唯一的机会就是使用替身。就连神秘人也不可能把自己分成七份。"

哈利碰到赫敏的目光，赶紧望向别处。

"所以，波特——劳驾，给几根头发。"

哈利看了看罗恩，罗恩朝他做了个鬼脸，仿佛是说"你就照办吧"。

"快！"穆迪咆哮道。

在众目睽睽之下，哈利伸手揪住头顶的一撮头发，拔了几根下来。

"很好，"穆迪说着一瘸一拐地走上前，一边拔出魔药瓶的塞子，"劳驾，放在这里面。"

哈利把头发丢进泥浆般的液体中。头发刚一接触液体表面，魔药就开始起泡、冒烟，一眨眼就变成了清澈的金黄色。

"哟，哈利，你的味道看上去比克拉布和高尔好多了。"赫敏说，她看见罗恩扬起眉毛，微微红了红脸又说，"噢，你知道我的意思——高尔的药剂活像干鼻屎。"

"好了好了，劳驾，假波特在这里排队。"穆迪说。

罗恩、赫敏、弗雷德、乔治和芙蓉在佩妮姨妈那闪闪发亮的洗涤槽前站成一排。

"还少一个。"卢平说。

"这儿。"海格粗声粗气地说，提着蒙顿格斯的后颈把他扔在芙蓉身边。芙蓉明显皱了皱鼻子，走过去站在弗雷德和乔治中间。

"我告诉过你，我宁愿当保镖。"蒙顿格斯说。

"闭嘴，"穆迪吼道，"你这个没有骨头的爬虫，我对你说过，不管我们碰到的是哪些食死徒，他们的目标都是抓住波特，而不是杀死他。

person. It'll be the protectors who have got the most to worry about, the Death Eaters'll want to kill them.'

Mundungus did not look particularly reassured, but Moody was already pulling half a dozen egg-cup-sized glasses from inside his cloak, which he handed out, before pouring a little Polyjuice Potion into each one.

'Altogether, then ...'

Ron, Hermione, Fred, George, Fleur and Mundungus drank. All of them gasped and grimaced as the Potion hit their throats: at once, their features began to bubble and distort like hot wax. Hermione and Mundungus were shooting upwards; Ron, Fred and George were shrinking; their hair was darkening, Hermione's and Fleur's appearing to shoot backwards into their skulls.

Moody, quite unconcerned, was now loosening the ties of the large sacks he had brought with him: when he straightened up again, there were six Harry Potters gasping and panting in front of him.

Fred and George turned to each other and said together, 'Wow – we're identical!'

'I dunno, though, I think I'm still better-looking,' said Fred, examining his reflection in the kettle.

'Bah,' said Fleur, checking herself in the microwave door, 'Bill, don't look at me – I'm 'ideous.'

'Those whose clothes are a bit roomy, I've got smaller here,' said Moody, indicating the first sack, 'and vice versa. Don't forget the glasses, there's six pairs in the side pocket. And when you're dressed, there's luggage in the other sack.'

The real Harry thought that this might just be the most bizarre thing he had ever seen, and he had seen some extremely odd things. He watched as his six doppelgängers rummaged in the sacks, pulling out sets of clothes, putting on glasses, stuffing their own things away. He felt like asking them to show a little more respect for his privacy as they all began stripping off with impunity, clearly much more at ease with displaying his body than they would have been with their own.

'I knew Ginny was lying about that tattoo,' said Ron, looking down at his bare chest.

'Harry, your eyesight really is awful,' said Hermione, as she put on glasses.

第4章 七个波特

邓布利多总是说神秘人想要亲手结果波特。最需要担心的是保镖，食死徒见了保镖不留活口。"

蒙顿格斯似乎并没有完全放心，但穆迪已经从斗篷里掏出六只蛋杯大小的玻璃杯，分给大家，然后往每个杯子里倒了一点儿复方汤剂。

"预备——喝……"

罗恩、赫敏、弗雷德、乔治、芙蓉和蒙顿格斯同时喝下。魔药刚一咽下，一个个便立刻大口喘气，龇牙咧嘴。顿时，他们的五官像烤热的蜡一样开始蠕动、变形。赫敏和蒙顿格斯噌噌往上长，罗恩、弗雷德和乔治则越缩越矮。他们的头发变黑了，赫敏和芙蓉的头发似乎在迅速蹿回头皮里。

穆迪对这一幕漠不关心，正在解开他带来的两个大口袋的带子。等他直起身来时，面前是呼哧呼哧喘粗气的六个哈利·波特。

弗雷德和乔治转脸看着对方，同时说道："哇——我们一模一样！"

"难说，我觉得还是我更好看一点儿。"弗雷德拿烧水壶当镜子照了照，说道。

"哎哟，"芙蓉对着微波炉门打量着自己，"比尔，别看我——我丑死了。"

"谁的衣服嫌大，我这里有小的，"穆迪指指第一个口袋说，"嫌小的，我这里有大的。别忘记眼镜，侧面口袋里有六副眼镜。等你们穿戴好了，另一个口袋里有行李。"

真哈利觉得，虽然他见识过一些极其古怪的事情，但眼前这一幕大概是他见过的最怪异的了。他注视着自己的六个替身在口袋里翻找，掏出一套套衣服，戴上眼镜，把他们自己的东西塞到一边。他真想请求他们略微尊重一点他的隐私，因为他们都开始毫无顾忌地脱衣服，显然是满不在乎地展示他的身体，他们对待自己的身体肯定不会这样。

"我就知道金妮说你有文身是在说谎。"罗恩低头看着赤裸的胸脯说。

"哈利，你的视力真是糟糕透了。"赫敏戴上眼镜说。

CHAPTER FOUR The Seven Potters

Once dressed, the fake Harrys took rucksacks and owl cages, each containing a stuffed snowy owl, from the second sack.

'Good,' said Moody, as at last seven dressed, bespectacled and luggage-laden Harrys faced him. 'The pairs will be as follows: Mundungus will be travelling with me, by broom –'

'Why'm I with you?' grunted the Harry nearest the back door.

'Because you're the one that needs watching,' growled Moody, and sure enough, his magical eye did not waver from Mundungus as he continued, 'Arthur and Fred –'

'I'm George,' said the twin at whom Moody was pointing. 'Can't you even tell us apart when we're Harry?'

'Sorry, George –'

'I'm only yanking your wand, I'm Fred really –'

'Enough messing around!' snarled Moody. 'The other one – George or Fred or whoever you are – you're with Remus. Miss Delacour –'

'I'm taking Fleur on a Thestral,' said Bill. 'She's not that fond of brooms.'

Fleur walked over to stand beside him, giving him a soppy, slavish look that Harry hoped with all his heart would never appear on his face again.

'Miss Granger with Kingsley, again by Thestral –'

Hermione looked reassured as she answered Kingsley's smile; Harry knew that Hermione, too, lacked confidence on a broomstick.

'Which leaves you and me, Ron!' said Tonks brightly, knocking over a mug-tree as she waved at him.

Ron did not look quite as pleased as Hermione.

'An' you're with me, Harry. That all righ'?' said Hagrid, looking a little anxious. 'We'll be on the bike, brooms an' Thestrals can't take me weight, see. 'Not a lot o' room on the seat with me on it, though, so you'll be in the sidecar.'

'That's great,' said Harry, not altogether truthfully.

'We think the Death Eaters will expect you to be on a broom,' said Moody, who seemed to guess how Harry was feeling. 'Snape's had plenty of time to tell them everything about you he's never mentioned before, so if we do run into any Death Eaters, we're betting they'll choose one of the Potters who

第4章 七个波特

假哈利们穿戴好了，又从第二个口袋里掏出背包和猫头鹰笼子，每个笼子里都有一只剥制的雪鸮标本。

"很好，"穆迪看到面前终于站着七个衣冠整齐、戴着眼镜、提着行李的哈利，便说，"分组的情况是这样的：蒙顿格斯和我一起，骑扫帚——"

"我为什么和你一起？"离后门最近的那个哈利嘟囔道。

"因为只有你需要监视。"穆迪吼道，确实，他接着说话时那只魔眼一直没有离开蒙顿格斯，"亚瑟和弗雷德——"

"我是乔治，"双胞胎中穆迪所指的那个说道，"怎么我们变成哈利了，你还分不出我们谁是谁呀？"

"对不起，乔治——"

"跟你开个玩笑，其实我是弗雷德——"

"别再胡闹了！"穆迪气恼地咆哮道，"另一个——弗雷德，乔治，不管是谁——跟莱姆斯走。德拉库尔小姐——"

"我带芙蓉骑夜骐，"比尔说，"她不太喜欢飞天扫帚。"

芙蓉走过去站在比尔身边，用含情脉脉、小鸟依人的目光看着他，哈利从心底里希望这种眼神以后永远别在他脸上出现。

"格兰杰小姐和金斯莱，也骑夜骐——"

赫敏向笑眯眯的金斯莱回以微笑，似乎心里很踏实。哈利知道赫敏也对骑飞天扫帚缺乏信心。

"就剩下你和我了，罗恩！"唐克斯愉快地说，她朝罗恩一挥手，打翻了一个杯子架。

罗恩看上去可不像赫敏那样高兴。

"你跟着我，哈利。行吗？"海格显得有点担心地说，"我们骑摩托车，扫帚和夜骐都吃不住我的重量。可是我往摩托车上一坐，就没有多少地方了，所以你坐在挎斗里。"

"太好了。"哈利并没有完全说心里话。

"我们推测，食死徒会以为你是骑扫帚的。"穆迪似乎猜到了哈利的感觉，说道，"斯内普有大量的时间把他以前没有提起的你的情况都

CHAPTER FOUR   The Seven Potters

look at home on a broomstick. All right then,' he went on, tying up the sack with the fake Potters' clothes in it and leading the way back to the door, 'I make it three minutes until we're supposed to leave. No point locking the back door, it won't keep the Death Eaters out when they come looking ... Come on ...'

Harry hurried into the hall to fetch his rucksack, Firebolt and Hedwig's cage before joining the others in the dark back garden. On every side broomsticks were leaping into hands; Hermione had already been helped up on to a great, black Thestral by Kingsley; Fleur on to the other by Bill. Hagrid was standing ready beside the motorbike, goggles on.

'Is this it? Is this Sirius's bike?'

'The very same,' said Hagrid, beaming down at Harry. 'An' the last time you was on it, Harry, I could fit yeh in one hand!'

Harry could not help but feel a little humiliated as he got into the sidecar. It placed him several feet below everybody else: Ron smirked at the sight of him sitting there like a child in a bumper car. Harry stuffed his rucksack and broomstick down by his feet and rammed Hedwig's cage between his knees. It was extremely uncomfortable.

'Arthur's done a bit o' tinkerin',' said Hagrid, quite oblivious to Harry's discomfort. He settled himself astride the motorcycle, which creaked slightly and sank inches into the ground. 'It's got a few tricks up its handlebars now. Tha' one was my idea.'

He pointed a thick finger at a purple button near the speedometer.

'Please be careful, Hagrid,' said Mr Weasley, who was standing beside them, holding his broomstick. 'I'm still not sure that was advisable and it's certainly only to be used in emergencies.'

'All right then,' said Moody. 'Everyone ready, please; I want us all to leave at exactly the same time or the whole point of the diversion's lost.'

Everybody mounted their brooms.

'Hold tight, now, Ron,' said Tonks, and Harry saw Ron throw a furtive, guilty look at Lupin before placing his hands on either side of her waist. Hagrid kicked the motorbike into life: it roared like a dragon and the sidecar began to vibrate.

'Good luck, everyone,' shouted Moody. 'See you all in about an hour at

第4章 七个波特

告诉他们，所以，万一碰到食死徒，我们估计他们肯定会选择那个骑扫帚特别熟练的波特。好了，"他把装着假波特衣服的口袋系紧，领着大家朝门口走去，一边继续说道，"我们三分钟内离开。后门不用锁，食死徒要过来搜查，锁是挡不住他们的……来吧……"

哈利赶紧跑到门厅里去拿他的背包、火弩箭和海德薇的笼子，然后跟大家一起来到黑魆魆的后花园里。在他身边，一把把扫帚跳到人的手中，赫敏已经在金斯莱的搀扶下坐到一匹巨大的黑色夜骐的背上，比尔扶着芙蓉骑上了另一匹夜骐。海格戴着护目镜，站在摩托车旁，准备出发。

"就是它吗？这就是小天狼星的摩托车？"

"就是这辆，"海格笑眯眯地低头看着哈利说，"哈利，你上次坐它的时候，我一个巴掌就能把你托起来！"

哈利钻进挎斗，忍不住觉得有点儿丢脸。这样一来，他就比别人矮了好几头：罗恩看到哈利像小孩子坐在碰碰车里一样，不禁笑了起来。哈利把背包和扫帚塞在脚边，又把海德薇的笼子夹在双膝间。这真是太不舒服了。

"亚瑟做了些修修补补。"海格似乎没有注意到哈利的不适，只管说道，他跨上摩托车，摩托车发出吱吱嘎嘎的响声，往地里陷了几寸，"现在它的把手上有几个机关。这玩意儿是我的主意。"

他用粗粗的手指点着仪表盘旁边的一个紫色按钮。

"千万留神，海格，"韦斯莱先生抓着他的扫帚站在他们身边，说道，"我仍然拿不准这是不是明智，必须万不得已的时候才用。"

"好了好了，"穆迪说，"每个人都做好准备。我要求大家在同一时间离开，不然整个牵制战术就失败了。"

每个人都骑上了扫帚。

"抱紧点儿，罗恩。"唐克斯说，哈利看见罗恩心虚地偷偷瞥了卢平一眼，然后双手搂住唐克斯的腰。海格用脚一踢，发动了摩托车。车子像火龙一样吼叫起来，挎斗也跟着抖动。

"祝大家好运！"穆迪喊道，"一小时左右在陋居见。我数到三。"

CHAPTER FOUR The Seven Potters

The Burrow. On the count of three. One ... two ... THREE.'

There was a great roar from the motorbike and Harry felt the sidecar give a nasty lurch: he was rising through the air fast, his eyes watering slightly, hair whipped back off his face. Around him brooms were soaring upwards too: the long, black tail of a Thestral flicked past. His legs, jammed into the sidecar by Hedwig's cage and his rucksack, were already sore and starting to go numb. So great was his discomfort that he almost forgot to take a last glimpse of number four, Privet Drive; by the time he looked over the edge of the sidecar, he could no longer tell which one it was. Higher and higher they climbed into the sky –

And then, out of nowhere, out of nothing, they were surrounded. At least thirty hooded figures, suspended in mid-air, formed a vast circle in the midst of which the Order members had risen, oblivious –

Screams, a blaze of green light on every side: Hagrid gave a yell and the motorbike rolled over. Harry lost any sense of where they were: street lights above him, yells around him, he was clinging to the sidecar for dear life. Hedwig's cage, the Firebolt and his rucksack slipped from beneath his knees –

'No – HEDWIG!'

The broomstick spun to earth, but he just managed to seize the strap of his rucksack and the top of the cage as the motorbike swung the right way up again. A second's relief, and then another burst of green light. The owl screeched and fell to the floor of the cage.

'No – NO!'

The motorbike zoomed forwards; Harry glimpsed hooded Death Eaters scattering as Hagrid blasted through their circle.

'Hedwig – *Hedwig* –'

But the owl lay motionless and pathetic as a toy on the floor of her cage. He could not take it in, and his terror for the others was paramount. He glanced over his shoulder and saw a mass of people moving, flares of green light, two pairs of people on brooms soaring off into the distance, but he could not tell who they were –

'Hagrid, we've got to go back, we've got to go back!' he yelled over the thunderous roar of the engine, pulling out his wand, ramming Hedwig's cage on to the floor, refusing to believe that she was dead. 'Hagrid, TURN ROUND!'

'My job's ter get you there safe, Harry!' bellowed Hagrid, and he opened the throttle.

第4章 七个波特

"一……二……三。"

摩托车发出惊天动地的吼声,哈利感到挎斗危险地倾向一侧。他在夜空中飞速穿行,眼睛微微流泪,头发被吹向脑后。在他周围,一把把扫帚也腾空升起,一匹夜骐的黑色长尾巴嗖地掠过。挎斗里,他的两条腿被海德薇的笼子和他的背包挤着,已经隐隐作痛,开始发麻。他太难受了,几乎忘了最后再看一眼女贞路4号。等他从挎斗边缘放眼望去,已经辨认不出是哪座房子了。他们在空中越飞越高——

然后,神不知鬼不觉地,他们被包围了。至少三十个戴兜帽的人影悬在空中,组成一个巨大的圆圈,凤凰社的成员们浑然不觉地飞入了他们的包围圈——

到处都是尖叫声和耀眼的绿光。海格大吼一声,摩托车翻了个身。哈利不知道自己身在何处:头顶上是街灯,周围是喊叫声。他死死地抓住挎斗,海德薇的笼子、火弩箭和他的背包从他的膝盖底下滑落——

"不——**海德薇!**"

飞天扫帚打着旋儿往地面落去,就在摩托车重新扳正过来的一刹那,哈利及时抓住了背包带子和鸟笼顶部。他刚松一口气,又是一道绿光射来,猫头鹰尖叫一声,倒在笼底。

"不——不!"

摩托车隆隆地往前驶去。海格迅疾地冲破包围圈,哈利看见戴兜帽的食死徒们四散逃开。

"海德薇——海德薇——"

然而猫头鹰像个玩具一样,可怜巴巴地躺在鸟笼底部一动不动。哈利无法接受这个现实,心里更加担忧其他人的安危。他扭头望去,看见一大群人在移动,一道道绿光来回发射,两组骑扫帚的人迅速飞向远处,但看不清他们是谁——

"海格,我们得回去,我们得回去!"他喊道,盖过了马达的轰鸣声,一边抽出魔杖,把海德薇的笼子胡乱塞到挎斗底部,不愿意相信它已经死了,"海格,**转回去!**"

"我的任务是把你安全送到,哈利!"海格大吼一声,加大了油门。

CHAPTER FOUR   The Seven Potters

'Stop – STOP!' Harry shouted. But as he looked back again two jets of green light flew past his left ear: four Death Eaters had broken away from the circle and were pursuing them, aiming for Hagrid's broad back. Hagrid swerved, but the Death Eaters were keeping up with the bike; more curses shot after them, and Harry had to sink low into the sidecar to avoid them. Wriggling round, he cried, '*Stupefy!*' and a red bolt of light shot from his own wand, cleaving a gap between the four pursuing Death Eaters as they scattered to avoid it.

'Hold on, Harry, this'll do for 'em!' roared Hagrid, and Harry looked up just in time to see Hagrid slamming a thick finger into a green button near the fuel gauge.

A wall, a solid brick wall, erupted out of the exhaust pipe. Craning his neck, Harry saw it expand into being in mid-air. Three of the Death Eaters swerved and avoided it, but the fourth was not so lucky: he vanished from view and then dropped like a boulder from behind it, his broomstick broken into pieces. One of his fellows slowed up to save him, but they and the airborne wall were swallowed by darkness as Hagrid leaned low over the handlebars and sped up.

More Killing Curses flew past Harry's head from the two remaining Death Eaters' wands; they were aiming for Hagrid. Harry responded with further Stunning Spells: red and green collided in mid-air in a shower of multi-coloured sparks and Harry thought wildly of fireworks, and the Muggles below who would have no idea what was happening –

'Here we go again, Harry, hold on!' yelled Hagrid, and he jabbed at a second button. This time a great net burst from the bike's exhaust, but the Death Eaters were ready for it. Not only did they swerve to avoid it, but the companion who had slowed to save their unconscious friend had caught up: he bloomed suddenly out of the darkness and now three of them were pursuing the motorbike, all shooting curses after it.

'This'll do it, Harry, hold on tight!' yelled Hagrid, and Harry saw him slam his whole hand on to the purple button beside the speedometer.

With an unmistakeable bellowing roar, dragon fire burst from the exhaust, white-hot and blue, and the motorbike shot forwards like a bullet with a sound of wrenching metal. Harry saw the Death Eaters swerve out of sight to avoid the deadly trail of flame, and at the same time felt the sidecar sway ominously: its metal connections to the bike had splintered with the force of acceleration.

第4章 七个波特

"停下——**停下**！"哈利喊道，他再次回头的时候，两道绿光从他左耳边嗖嗖掠过：四个食死徒离开包围圈，对着海格宽阔的后背施恶咒。海格突然转向，但是食死徒跟着摩托车紧追不放。后面又有魔咒射来，哈利不得不把身子缩进挎斗里躲避。他扭过身喊道："昏昏倒地！"一道红光从他自己的魔杖里射出，那四个追来的食死徒急忙躲避，闪出一个空当。

"坐稳了，哈利，这一下准叫他们完蛋！"海格咆哮道，哈利一抬头，正好看见海格用粗粗的手指使劲一摁燃油表旁边的一个绿色按钮。

一道墙，一道结结实实的砖墙，从排气管里喷了出来。哈利扭过脖子，看见砖墙在空中延伸、成形。三个食死徒急忙转身躲开，第四个就没那么幸运了。他消失不见了，然后像大石头一样从砖墙后面掉下去，扫帚散成了碎片。他的一个同伙放慢脚步去救他，海格弯腰伏在把手上加速前进，那两个食死徒和空中砖墙就都被黑暗吞没了。

剩下两个食死徒的魔杖里继续射出杀戮咒，嗖嗖地从哈利头顶掠过。它们是冲着海格来的。哈利又用昏迷咒去反击。红光、绿光在空中相撞，喷射出五颜六色的火星，哈利不着边际地想到了烟花，想到了下面不知道怎么回事的麻瓜们——

"我们又来了，哈利，坐稳了！"海格嚷道，猛地一戳第二个按钮。这次摩托车排气管里喷出的是一张巨大的网，可是食死徒早有防备。他们不仅闪身避开了，而且刚才那个放慢脚步去救不省人事的同伙的食死徒，此刻也赶了上来。他突然从黑暗中现身，现在他们三个都在追赶摩托车，都在不停地射出魔咒。

"这下他们准完蛋，哈利，坐稳了！"海格大吼，哈利看见他把整个手掌拍向仪表盘旁边的紫色按钮。

随着一阵绝对震耳欲聋的轰鸣，排气管中喷出了白热的蓝色龙火，摩托车像子弹一样冲向前去，发出金属扭曲的声音。哈利看见食死徒为了躲避致命的火焰，闪身不见了，同时他感到挎斗不祥地摇晃起来：在加速的冲力下，挎斗和摩托车的金属连接断裂了。

CHAPTER FOUR   The Seven Potters

'It's all righ', Harry!' bellowed Hagrid, now thrown flat on to his back by the surge of speed; nobody was steering now, and the sidecar was starting to twist violently in the bike's slipstream.

'I'm on it, Harry, don' worry!' Hagrid yelled, and from inside his jacket pocket he pulled his flowery pink umbrella.

'Hagrid! No! Let me!'

'*REPARO!*'

There was a deafening bang and the sidecar broke away from the bike completely: Harry sped forwards, propelled by the impetus of the bike's flight, then the sidecar began to lose height –

In desperation Harry pointed his wand at the sidecar and shouted, '*Wingardium Leviosa!*'

The sidecar rose like a cork, unsteerable but at least still airborne: he had but a split second's relief, however, as more curses streaked past him: the three Death Eaters were closing in.

'I'm comin', Harry!' Hagrid yelled from out of the darkness, but Harry could feel the sidecar beginning to sink again: crouching as low as he could, he pointed at the middle of the oncoming figures and yelled, '*Impedimenta!*'

The jinx hit the middle Death Eater in the chest: for a moment the man was absurdly spread-eagled in mid-air as though he had hit an invisible barrier: one of his fellows almost collided with him –

Then the sidecar began to fall in earnest, and the remaining Death Eater shot a curse so close to Harry that he had to duck below the rim of the car, knocking out a tooth on the edge of his seat –

'I'm comin', Harry, I'm comin'!'

A huge hand seized the back of Harry's robes and hoisted him out of the plummeting sidecar; Harry pulled his rucksack with him as he dragged himself on to the motorbike's seat and found himself back to back with Hagrid. As they soared upwards, away from the two remaining Death Eaters, Harry spat blood out of his mouth, pointed his wand at the falling sidecar, and yelled, '*Confringo!*'

He knew a dreadful, gut-wrenching pang for Hedwig as it exploded; the Death Eater nearest it was blasted off his broom and fell from sight; his companion fell back and vanished.

第4章 七个波特

"没关系，哈利！"海格咆哮道，速度太快，他被迫仰身躺倒。此刻已经无人驾驶，挎斗在气流的冲击下开始剧烈扭动。

"有我呢，哈利，别担心！"海格喊道，从外衣口袋里抽出他那把粉红色的花伞。

"海格！不！让我来！"

"恢复如初！"

一声震耳欲聋的巨响，挎斗彻底跟摩托车脱开了：哈利在飞驰的摩托车的冲力下急速向前飞去，然后，挎斗开始往下降落——

绝望中，哈利用魔杖指着挎斗，大喊一声："羽加迪姆 勒维奥萨！"

挎斗像瓶塞一样蹿了上去，虽然无法操控，但至少还悬在空中。哈利刚松口气，又有魔咒嗖嗖地从他身边飞过：三个食死徒围了上来。

"我来了，哈利！"海格在黑暗中喊道，但哈利感觉到挎斗又开始下沉。他尽量把身子缩得低低的，瞄准那几个追过来的身影，大声喊道："障碍重重！"

魔咒击中了中间那个食死徒的胸口，顿时，那人怪模怪样地张开四肢悬在空中，就像撞上了一道看不见的屏障，他的一个伙伴差点撞在他身上——

这时，挎斗真的开始下降了，剩下的那个食死徒射出的一个魔咒离哈利太近，他只好赶紧低头，躲到挎斗边缘的下面，结果一颗牙齿在座位上磕掉了——

"我来了，哈利，我来了！"

一只大手揪住哈利长袍的后背，把他拽出了急速下降的挎斗。哈利拖着背包，奋力骑上摩托车的座位，发现自己与海格背靠着背。他们越飞越高，甩掉了剩下的两个食死徒。哈利吐出嘴里的血，用魔杖指着下落的挎斗，喊了声："霹雳爆炸！"

挎斗爆炸时，他为海德薇感到一阵剧烈的、撕心裂肺般的痛苦。靠近挎斗的那个食死徒被炸得从扫帚上摔下去，不见了踪影。他的同伙落在后面，也消失了。

CHAPTER FOUR   The Seven Potters

'Harry, I'm sorry, I'm sorry,' moaned Hagrid, 'I shouldn'ta tried ter repair it meself – yeh've got no room –'

'It's not a problem, just keep flying!' Harry shouted back, as two more Death Eaters emerged out of the darkness, drawing closer.

As the curses came shooting across the intervening space again, Hagrid swerved and zigzagged: Harry knew that Hagrid did not dare use the dragon-fire button again, with Harry seated so insecurely. Harry sent Stunning Spell after Stunning Spell back at their pursuers, barely holding them off. He shot another blocking jinx at them: the closest Death Eater swerved to avoid it and his hood slipped, and by the red light of his next Stunning Spell, Harry saw the strangely blank face of Stanley Shunpike – Stan –

'*Expelliarmus!*' Harry yelled.

'That's him, it's him, it's the real one!'

The hooded Death Eater's shout reached Harry even above the thunder of the motorbike's engine: next moment, both pursuers had fallen back and disappeared from view.

'Harry, what's happened?' bellowed Hagrid. 'Where've they gone?'

'I don't know!'

But Harry was afraid: the hooded Death Eater had shouted 'it's the real one'; how had he known? He gazed around at the apparently empty darkness and felt its menace. Where were they?

He clambered round on the seat to face forwards and seized hold of the back of Hagrid's jacket.

'Hagrid, do the dragon fire thing again, let's get out of here!'

'Hold on tight, then, Harry!'

There was a deafening, screeching roar again and the white-blue fire shot from the exhaust: Harry felt himself slipping backwards off what little of the seat he had, Hagrid flung backwards upon him, barely maintaining his grip on the handlebars –

'I think we've lost 'em Harry, I think we've done it!' yelled Hagrid.

But Harry was not convinced: fear lapped at him as he looked left and right for pursuers he was sure would come ... why had they fallen back? One of them had still had a wand ... *It's him, it's the real one* ... they had said it right after he had tried to Disarm Stan ...

第4章 七个波特

"哈利,对不起,对不起,"海格难过地低声说,"我不应该自己修补挎斗——现在你没有地方坐了——"

"没关系,尽管飞吧!"哈利大声回答,这时又有两个食死徒从黑暗中冒了出来,越逼越近。

魔咒又隔着夜空发射过来。海格不停地左转右拐,绕来绕去,哈利知道海格不敢再使用那个龙火按钮了,因为哈利坐得很不稳当。哈利朝追逐者们射出一个又一个昏迷咒,却没能把他们击退。哈利又对他们发出一个阻挡咒语:最近的那个食死徒闪身躲避,他的兜帽滑了下来,在下一个昏迷咒的红光映照下,哈利看到了斯坦·桑帕克那张古怪的、毫无表情的脸——斯坦——

"除你武器!"哈利大喊一声。

"是他,是他,这个是真的!"

戴兜帽的食死徒的喊声甚至盖过摩托车马达的轰鸣,传到了哈利耳朵里。接着,两个追逐者落到后面,消失不见了。

"哈利,怎么回事?"海格粗声大气地问,"他们哪儿去啦?"

"不知道!"

可是哈利很担心:刚才那个戴兜帽的食死徒喊了声"这个是真的!"他怎么会知道的?哈利凝视着看上去空无一人的黑夜,感觉到了威胁。他们在哪儿呢?

他费力地在座位上转过身,面朝前方,抓住海格的上衣后襟。

"海格,再来一遍那个龙火,我们赶紧离开这儿!"

"那你可坐稳了,哈利!"

又是一阵震耳欲聋的尖锐的轰鸣,蓝白色的火焰从排气管喷射出来:哈利挤在那逼仄得可怜的座位上,感到自己向后滑去,海格仰倒在他身上,勉强抓住把手——

"我想我们甩掉他们了,哈利,我想我们成功了!"海格喊道。

可是哈利不能确信。他左右张望寻找追逐者,知道他们肯定会来,他心里泛起一阵阵的恐惧……他们为什么退回去?其中一个还拿着魔杖呢……是他……这个是真的……他刚想给斯坦施缴械咒,他们就说了这话……

CHAPTER FOUR   The Seven Potters

'We're nearly there, Harry, we've nearly made it!' shouted Hagrid.

Harry felt the bike drop a little, though the lights down on the ground still seemed remote as stars.

Then the scar on his forehead burned like fire: as a Death Eater appeared on either side of the bike, two Killing Curses missed Harry by millimetres, cast from behind –

And then Harry saw him. Voldemort was flying like smoke on the wind, without broomstick or Thestral to hold him, his snake-like face gleaming out of the blackness, his white fingers raising his wand again –

Hagrid let out a bellow of fear and steered the motorbike into a vertical dive. Clinging on for dear life, Harry sent Stunning Spells flying at random into the whirling night. He saw a body fly past him and knew he had hit one of them, but then he heard a bang and saw sparks from the engine; the motorbike spiralled through the air, completely out of control –

Green jets of light shot past them again. Harry had no idea which way was up, which down: his scar was still burning; he expected to die at any second. A hooded figure on a broomstick was feet from him, he saw it raise its arm –

'NO!'

With a shout of fury, Hagrid launched himself off the bike at the Death Eater; to his horror, Harry saw both Hagrid and the Death Eater falling out of sight, their combined weight too much for the broomstick –

Barely gripping the plummeting bike with his knees, Harry heard Voldemort scream, '*Mine!*'

It was over: he could not see or hear where Voldemort was; he glimpsed another Death Eater swooping out of the way and heard '*Avada* –'

As the pain from Harry's scar forced his eyes shut, his wand acted of its own accord. He felt it drag his hand round like some great magnet, saw a spurt of golden fire through his half-closed eyelids, heard a *crack* and a scream of fury. The remaining Death Eater yelled; Voldemort screamed, '*No!* ': somehow, Harry found his nose an inch from the dragon-fire button: he punched it with his wand-free hand and the bike shot more flames into the air, hurtling straight towards the ground.

'Hagrid!' Harry called, holding on to the bike for dear life, 'Hagrid – *accio Hagrid!*'

第4章 七个波特

"快到了,哈利,我们就要成功了!"海格大声嚷。

哈利觉得摩托车下降了一些,但地面的灯光看上去仍然像星星一样遥远。

突然,哈利额头上的伤疤火烧火燎地痛了起来。摩托车两边各出现了一个食死徒,两个杀戮咒从后面射来,只差一毫米就击中了哈利——

接着,哈利看见了他。伏地魔像烟一样乘风飞翔,没有扫帚,也没有夜骐,那张蛇脸在黑暗中闪着亮光,苍白的手指又举起了魔杖——

海格惊恐地大吼一声,驾驶摩托车垂直降落。哈利一边拼命稳住身子,一边对着旋转的黑夜胡乱发射昏迷咒。他看见一个身体从旁边飞过,知道自己击中了一个,可是接着听见一声巨响,看见马达迸出火花。摩托车在空中打着旋儿,完全失控——

又是一道道绿光射过。哈利已经分辨不出上下左右。伤疤仍然火辣辣地疼。他以为自己随时都会死去。一个戴兜帽的身影骑在扫帚上,离他只有几步远,哈利看见他举起了手臂——

"不!"

海格怒吼一声,纵身跳出摩托车,朝那个食死徒扑去。哈利惊恐地看见海格和食死徒都坠落下去,不见了踪影,飞天扫帚吃不住他们两个加起来的重量——

哈利用膝盖勉强钩住急速下降的摩托车,只听伏地魔叫道:"我的!"

完了!他看不见也听不到伏地魔在哪里。他只瞥见另一个食死徒突然闪到一边,然后听见:"阿瓦达——"

伤疤的剧痛逼得哈利闭上眼睛,他的魔杖自己采取了行动。哈利感觉魔杖像有某种巨大的磁力般把他的手拽向一边,他半闭着的眼睛看见一道金色的火焰喷射出来,接着听见一声爆响和一声愤怒的尖叫。剩下的那个食死徒在大嚷,伏地魔在尖叫:"不!"不知怎么一来,哈利发现自己的鼻子离那个龙火按钮只有一寸。他用没拿魔杖的那只手使劲一砸按钮,摩托车又朝空中喷射出火焰,同时径直朝地面坠落下去。

"海格!"哈利死死抓住摩托车,大声喊道,"海格——海格飞来!"

CHAPTER FOUR   The Seven Potters

The motorbike sped up, sucked towards the earth. Face level with the handlebars, Harry could see nothing but distant lights growing nearer and nearer: he was going to crash and there was nothing he could do about it. Behind him came another scream —

'*Your wand, Selwyn, give me your wand!*'

He felt Voldemort before he saw him. Looking sideways, he stared into the red eyes and was sure they would be the last thing he ever saw: Voldemort preparing to curse him once more —

And then Voldemort vanished. Harry looked down and saw Hagrid spread-eagled on the ground below him: he pulled hard at the handlebars to avoid hitting him, groped for the brake, but with an ear-splitting, ground-trembling crash, he smashed into a muddy pond.

第 4 章 七个波特

摩托车在加速，似乎是被吸引着坠向地面。哈利的脸与把手平行，只能看见远处的灯光越来越近。他肯定要摔死了，可是除了坐以待毙之外没别的办法。身后又传来一声喊叫：

"你的魔杖，塞尔温，把你的魔杖给我！"

他还没有看见伏地魔就已经感觉到了他。哈利往旁边一看，正撞上那双红红的眼睛，它们肯定是他这辈子看到的最后一样东西了：伏地魔正准备再次对他念咒——

突然，伏地魔消失了。哈利低头一看，海格四仰八叉地躺在下面的地上。哈利使劲拉动把手以免撞到海格，然后摸索着去踩刹车，可是随着一声震耳欲聋、惊天动地的巨响，他一头栽进了一个泥潭。

CHAPTER FIVE

Fallen Warrior

'Hagrid?'

Harry struggled to raise himself out of the debris of metal and leather that surrounded him; his hands sank into inches of muddy water as he tried to stand. He could not understand where Voldemort had gone and expected him to swoop out of the darkness at any moment. Something hot and wet was trickling down his chin and from his forehead. He crawled out of the pond and stumbled towards the great, dark mass on the ground that was Hagrid.

'Hagrid? Hagrid, talk to me —'

But the dark mass did not stir.

'Who's there? Is it Potter? Are you Harry Potter?'

Harry did not recognise the man's voice. Then a woman shouted, 'They've crashed, Ted! Crashed in the garden!'

Harry's head was swimming.

'Hagrid,' he repeated stupidly, and his knees buckled.

The next thing he knew, he was lying on his back on what felt like cushions, with a burning sensation in his ribs and right arm. His missing tooth had been regrown. The scar on his forehead was still throbbing.

'Hagrid?'

He opened his eyes and saw that he was lying on a sofa in an unfamiliar, lamplit sitting room. His rucksack lay on the floor a short distance away, wet and muddy. A fair-haired, big-bellied man was watching Harry anxiously.

'Hagrid's fine, son,' said the man, 'the wife's seeing to him now. How are you feeling? Anything else broken? I've fixed your ribs, your tooth and your

第 5 章

坠落的勇士

"海格?"

哈利费力地从一堆金属和皮革碎片中挣脱出来；他使劲想站起身，可双手在泥潭里又陷了几寸。他不明白伏地魔上哪儿去了，以为他随时会从黑暗中突然冲出来。一股热热的、湿湿的东西从他的下巴和额头上流淌下来。他爬出泥潭，跌跌撞撞地走向躺在地上的那个黑乎乎的庞然大物——海格。

"海格？海格，跟我说话——"

可是黑乎乎的庞然大物一动不动。

"谁在那儿？是波特？你是哈利·波特吗？"

哈利没有听出那个男人是谁。接着一个女人喊道："他们掉下来了，泰德！掉在花园里了！"

哈利脑袋发晕。

"海格。"他愣愣地又喊了一声，便双膝一软。

哈利苏醒过来时，感到自己仰面躺在一堆靠垫般的东西上，肋骨和右臂有一种火烧火燎的感觉，那颗撞掉的牙齿已经长出来了，额头上的伤疤仍然一跳一跳地疼。

"海格？"

哈利睁开眼睛，发现自己躺在一间陌生的、点着灯的客厅的沙发上。他的背包放在不远处的地板上，湿漉漉的，沾满泥浆。一个金色头发、大肚子的男人正担忧地注视着他。

"海格没事儿，孩子，"那人说，"我妻子在照顾他呢。你感觉怎么样？还有什么地方断了吗？我给你修补好了肋骨、牙齿和胳膊。对了，

CHAPTER FIVE   Fallen Warrior

arm. I'm Ted, by the way, Ted Tonks – Dora's father.'

Harry sat up too quickly: lights popped in front of his eyes and he felt sick and giddy.

'Voldemort –'

'Easy, now,' said Ted Tonks, placing a hand on Harry's shoulder and pushing him back against the cushions. 'That was a nasty crash you just had. What happened, anyway? Something go wrong with the bike? Arthur Weasley overstretch himself again, him and his Muggle contraptions?'

'No,' said Harry, as his scar pulsed like an open wound. 'Death Eaters, loads of them – we were chased –'

'Death Eaters?' said Ted sharply. 'What d'you mean, Death Eaters? I thought they didn't know you were being moved tonight, I thought –'

'They knew,' said Harry.

Ted Tonks looked up at the ceiling as though he could see through it to the sky above.

'Well, we know our protective charms hold, then, don't we? They shouldn't be able to get within a hundred yards of the place in any direction.'

Now Harry understood why Voldemort had vanished; it had been at the point when the motorbike crossed the barrier of the Order's charms. He only hoped they would continue to work: he imagined Voldemort, a hundred yards above them as they spoke, looking for a way to penetrate what Harry visualised as a great, transparent bubble.

He swung his legs off the sofa; he needed to see Hagrid with his own eyes before he would believe that he was alive. He had barely stood up, however, when a door opened and Hagrid squeezed through it, his face covered in mud and blood, limping a little but miraculously alive.

'Harry!'

Knocking over two delicate tables and an aspidistra, he covered the floor between them in two strides and pulled Harry into a hug that nearly cracked his newly repaired ribs. 'Blimey, Harry, how did yeh get out o' that? I thought we were both goners.'

'Yeah, me too. I can't believe –'

Harry broke off: he had just noticed the woman who had entered the room behind Hagrid.

第5章　坠落的勇士

我是泰德，泰德·唐克斯——朵拉的父亲。"

哈利猛地坐起来，眼前直冒金星，觉得恶心、眩晕。

"伏地魔——"

"别着急。"泰德·唐克斯说着，一只手放在哈利的肩头把他推回到靠垫上，"你们刚才摔得可够惨的。到底怎么回事？摩托车出故障了？亚瑟·韦斯莱又做过头了吧？他倒腾的那些麻瓜新奇玩意儿？"

"不是，"哈利说，伤疤像裸露的伤口一样疼，突突直跳，"食死徒，一大群食死徒——他们追赶我们——"

"食死徒？"泰德警惕地说，"你说什么，食死徒？我还以为他们不知道你今晚转移，我还以为——"

"他们知道。"哈利说。

泰德·唐克斯抬头望着天花板，似乎能透过天花板望到上面的天空。

"不过，这下我们就知道防护咒是有效的，对吗？他们从任何方向都不能进入这方圆一百米以内。"

哈利这才明白伏地魔为什么消失了。当时摩托车正好穿过凤凰社魔咒的屏障。但愿这些魔咒能继续生效。他想象着，就在他们此刻说话的当儿，伏地魔正在他们头顶一百米的上空，绞尽脑汁地想穿透哈利幻想中的那个透明的大肥皂泡。

哈利两腿一甩离开了沙发，他需要亲眼看看海格，才能相信他还活着。他刚起身，门就开了，海格挤了进来，满脸都是泥浆和血污，腿有点儿瘸，却还奇迹般地活着。

"哈利！"

海格撞倒了两张精致的桌子和一棵蜘蛛抱蛋，两步就冲了过来，把哈利紧紧搂在怀里，差点挤断了哈利刚刚修复的肋骨，"天哪，哈利，你是怎么死里逃生的？我还以为我们都完蛋了呢。"

"是啊，我也是。真不敢相信——"

哈利突然住了口：他刚注意到那个跟在海格身后走进房间的女人。

CHAPTER FIVE   Fallen Warrior

'You!' he shouted, and he thrust his hand into his pocket, but it was empty.

'Your wand's here, son,' said Ted, tapping it on Harry's arm. 'It fell right beside you, I picked it up. And that's my wife you're shouting at.'

'Oh, I'm – I'm sorry.'

As she moved forwards into the room, Mrs Tonks's resemblance to her sister Bellatrix became much less pronounced: her hair was a light, soft brown and her eyes were wider and kinder. Nevertheless, she looked a little haughty after Harry's exclamation.

'What happened to our daughter?' she asked. 'Hagrid said you were ambushed; where is Nymphadora?'

'I don't know,' said Harry. 'We don't know what happened to anyone else.'

She and Ted exchanged looks. A mixture of fear and guilt gripped Harry at the sight of their expressions; if any of the others had died, it was his fault, all his fault. He had consented to the plan, given them his hair ...

'The Portkey,' he said, remembering all of a sudden. 'We've got to get back to The Burrow and find out – then we'll be able to send you word, or – or Tonks will, once she's –'

'Dora'll be OK, 'Dromeda,' said Ted. 'She knows her stuff, she's been in plenty of tight spots with the Aurors. The Portkey's through here,' he added to Harry. 'It's supposed to leave in three minutes, if you want to take it.'

'Yeah, we do,' said Harry. He seized his rucksack, swung it on to his shoulders. 'I –'

He looked at Mrs Tonks, wanting to apologise for the state of fear in which he left her and for which he felt so terribly responsible, but no words occurred to him that did not seem hollow and insincere.

'I'll tell Tonks – Dora – to send word, when she ... thanks for patching us up, thanks for everything. I –'

He was glad to leave the room and follow Ted Tonks along a short hallway and into a bedroom. Hagrid came after them, bending low to avoid hitting his head on the door lintel.

'There you go, son. That's the Portkey.'

Mr Tonks was pointing to a small, silver-backed hairbrush lying on the dressing table.

第5章 坠落的勇士

"你！"他大喊一声，伸手到口袋里去掏魔杖，但口袋是空的。

"你的魔杖在这儿，孩子，"泰德说着，用魔杖轻轻敲了敲哈利的胳膊，"正好落在你身边，我就捡起来了。你是在冲我妻子嚷嚷呢。"

"噢，我——我很抱歉。"

唐克斯夫人又往屋里走了几步，模样就不那么像她姐姐贝拉特里克斯了。她的头发是柔和的浅褐色，眼睛更大、更慈祥。不过，听到哈利的惊叫，她显得有点儿矜持。

"我们的女儿怎么样了？"她问，"海格说你们遭了埋伏。尼法朵拉呢？"

"不知道，"哈利说，"我们也不知道其他人怎么样了。"

她和泰德交换了一下目光。哈利看到他们的表情，心里又是担忧又是内疚。如果其他人中间有谁死了，那便是他的错，全是他的错。是他同意了那个计划，给出了自己的头发……

"门钥匙。"他说，一下子全想起来了，"我们必须回陋居弄清情况——然后就能给你们捎信，或者——或者唐克斯自己给你们捎信，一旦她——"

"朵拉不会有事的，多米达，"泰德说，"她能力足够，她和傲罗们一起经历了许多危险的场面。门钥匙就在这儿，"他又对哈利说，"如果你们想用它，应该是三分钟内出发。"

"好的，我们用它。"哈利说，他抓起背包，背到肩上，"我——"

他看着唐克斯夫人，想说一句道歉的话，因为是他让她处于这种忧心忡忡的状态，他认为自己负有不可推卸的责任，可是他又觉得说什么都显得空洞、虚伪。

"我会叫唐克斯——朵拉——给你们送信，等她……感谢你们救了我们，感谢一切。我——"

他离开房间后才松了口气，跟着泰德·唐克斯穿过一条短短的过道，进入了一间卧室。海格也跟来了，身子弯得低低的，以免脑袋撞到门框。

"你们走吧，孩子。那是门钥匙。"

唐克斯先生指着梳妆台上一把小小的银背发刷。

CHAPTER FIVE   Fallen Warrior

'Thanks,' said Harry, reaching out to place a finger on it, ready to leave.

'Wait a moment,' said Hagrid, looking around. 'Harry, where's Hedwig?'

'She ... she got hit,' said Harry.

The realisation crashed over him: he felt ashamed of himself as the tears stung his eyes. The owl had been his companion, his one great link with the magical world whenever he had been forced to return to the Dursleys.

Hagrid reached out a great hand and patted him painfully on the shoulder. 'Never mind,' he said gruffly. 'Never mind. She had a great old life –'

'Hagrid!' said Ted Tonks warningly, as the hairbrush glowed bright blue, and Hagrid only just got his forefinger to it in time.

With a jerk behind the navel as though an invisible hook and line had dragged him forwards, Harry was pulled into nothingness, spinning uncontrollably, his finger glued to the Portkey as he and Hagrid hurtled away from Mr Tonks: seconds later Harry's feet slammed on to hard ground and he fell on his hands and knees in the yard of The Burrow. He heard screams. Throwing aside the no longer glowing hairbrush, Harry stood up, swaying slightly, and saw Mrs Weasley and Ginny running down the steps by the back door as Hagrid, who had also collapsed on landing, clambered laboriously to his feet.

'Harry? You are the real Harry? What happened? Where are the others?' cried Mrs Weasley.

'What d'you mean? Isn't anyone else back?' Harry panted.

The answer was clearly etched in Mrs Weasley's pale face.

'The Death Eaters were waiting for us,' Harry told her. 'We were surrounded the moment we took off – they knew it was tonight – I don't know what happened to anyone else. Four of them chased us, it was all we could do to get away, and then Voldemort caught up with us –'

He could hear the self-justifying note in his voice, the plea for her to understand why he did not know what had happened to her sons, but –

'Thank goodness you're all right,' she said, pulling him into a hug he did not feel he deserved.

'Haven't go' any brandy, have yeh, Molly?' asked Hagrid a little shakily. 'Fer medicinal purposes?'

第5章 坠落的勇士

"谢谢。"哈利探身把一个手指放在上面,准备离开。

"等等,"海格四处张望着说,"哈利,海德薇呢?"

"它……它被击中了。"哈利说。

哈利猛然认清了这个事实,他为自己感到羞愧,泪水火辣辣地刺痛了他的眼睛。猫头鹰是他的伴侣,是他每次被迫返回德思礼家后与魔法世界的一个重要联系。

海格伸出一只大手,沉痛地拍了拍他的肩膀。

"别难过,"他用粗哑的声音说,"别难过。它这辈子过得可不平凡——"

"海格!"泰德·唐克斯提醒道,发刷已经放射出耀眼的蓝光,海格赶紧把食指按在它上面,差一点就来不及了——

说时迟那时快,似乎肚脐眼后面有一个无形的钩子猛地向前一钩,哈利和海格忽地一下离开了唐克斯先生,被拽着飞入虚空。哈利无法控制地旋转着,手指紧紧粘在门钥匙上。几秒钟后,哈利的双脚重重地砸在坚硬的地面上,四肢着地摔在了陋居的院子里。他听见了尖叫声。他把不再闪光的发刷扔到一边,晃晃悠悠地站起身,看见韦斯莱夫人和金妮从后门跑下台阶。海格也摔得瘫倒在地,正十分吃力地爬起来。

"哈利?你是真的哈利?出什么事了?其他人呢?"韦斯莱夫人大声问。

"你说什么?别人都没回来吗?"哈利喘着粗气问。

答案清清楚楚地刻在韦斯莱夫人苍白的脸上。

"食死徒就等着我们呢,"哈利告诉她,"我们一出发就被包围了——他们知道是今晚——我不知道别人怎么样了,有四个食死徒追我们,我们只能拼命摆脱,后来伏地魔追上来了——"

哈利听出自己的口气里有替自己辩解的意思,似乎在恳求韦斯莱夫人理解他为什么不知道她儿子们的情况,可是——

"谢天谢地,你平安就好。"韦斯莱夫人说着,把哈利拉到怀里搂了一下,哈利觉得十分羞愧。

"莫丽,有白兰地吗?"海格声音有点发抖地问,"当药用的?"

CHAPTER FIVE Fallen Warrior

She could have summoned it by magic, but as she hurried back towards the crooked house Harry knew that she wanted to hide her face. He turned to Ginny and she answered his unspoken plea for information at once.

'Ron and Tonks should have been back first, but they missed their Portkey, it came back without them,' she said, pointing at a rusty oilcan lying on the ground nearby. 'And that one,' she pointed at an ancient plimsoll, 'should have been Dad and Fred's, they were supposed to be second. You and Hagrid were third and,' she checked her watch, 'if they made it, George and Lupin ought to be back in about a minute.'

Mrs Weasley reappeared carrying a bottle of brandy, which she handed to Hagrid. He uncorked it and drank it straight down in one.

'Mum!' shouted Ginny, pointing to a spot several feet away.

A blue light had appeared in the darkness: it grew larger and brighter, and Lupin and George appeared, spinning and then falling. Harry knew immediately that there was something wrong: Lupin was supporting George, who was unconscious and whose face was covered in blood.

Harry ran forwards and seized George's legs. Together, he and Lupin carried George into the house and through the kitchen to the sitting room, where they laid him on the sofa. As the lamplight fell across George's head, Ginny gasped and Harry's stomach lurched: one of George's ears was missing. The side of his head and neck were drenched in wet, shockingly scarlet blood.

No sooner had Mrs Weasley bent over her son than Lupin grabbed Harry by the upper arm and dragged him, none too gently, back into the kitchen, where Hagrid was still attempting to ease his bulk through the back door.

'Oi!' said Hagrid indignantly. 'Le' go of him! Le' go of Harry!'

Lupin ignored him.

'What creature sat in the corner, the first time that Harry Potter visited my office at Hogwarts?' he said, giving Harry a small shake. 'Answer me!'

'A – a Grindylow in a tank, wasn't it?'

Lupin released Harry and fell back against a kitchen cupboard.

'Wha' was tha' about?' roared Hagrid.

'I'm sorry, Harry, but I had to check,' said Lupin tersely. 'We've been betrayed. Voldemort knew that you were being moved tonight and the only

第5章 坠落的勇士

韦斯莱夫人完全可以用魔法把酒召来,但她匆匆地朝歪歪斜斜的房子走去。哈利知道她是不想让别人看见她的脸。哈利转向金妮,金妮立刻回答了他没有说出口的询问。

"罗恩和唐克斯应该第一批回来的,但他们错过了门钥匙,门钥匙自己回来了。"金妮说着,指了指旁边地上一个锈迹斑斑的油罐,"还有那个,"她又指了指一只破旧的运动鞋,"是爸爸和弗雷德的,他们应该第二批到达。你和海格是第三批,然后,"她看了看表,"如果不出意外,乔治和卢平应该在一分钟内回来。"

韦斯莱夫人拿着一瓶白兰地回来了,她把酒递给海格。海格拔出瓶塞,一口就喝干了。

"妈妈!"金妮指着几步开外的一个地方喊道。

黑暗中突然有了一点蓝光:越来越大,越来越亮,接着卢平和乔治出现了,嗖嗖旋转着落到地上。哈利立刻知道出事了:卢平架着乔治,乔治满脸是血,不省人事。

哈利跑过去抓住乔治的腿。他和卢平一起抬着乔治走进房子,穿过厨房来到客厅,把他放在沙发上。灯光照在乔治的脑袋上,金妮倒吸了一口冷气,哈利心里猛地抽了一下。乔治的一只耳朵不见了。他脑袋一侧和脖子里满是殷红的、触目惊心的鲜血。

韦斯莱夫人刚俯下身去查看儿子,卢平就一把抓住哈利的胳膊,颇为粗暴地把他拉进厨房,海格还在努力把他那庞大的身躯挤进后门。

"喂!"海格气愤地说,"放开他!放开哈利!"

卢平没理睬他。

"哈利·波特第一次到我在霍格沃茨的办公室时,墙角那里有个什么动物?"他轻轻摇晃了一下哈利说,"快回答!"

"是——一个格林迪洛,关在水箱里,对吗?"

卢平松开了哈利,仰身靠在厨房的碗柜上。

"这是搞什么鬼?"海格吼道。

"对不起,哈利,但我得核实一下。"卢平生硬地说,"有人叛变了。伏地魔知道我们今晚转移,只有直接参与制订计划的人才会向他通风

people who could have told him were directly involved in the plan. You might have been an impostor.'

'So why aren' you checkin' me?' panted Hagrid, still struggling to fit through the door.

'You're half-giant,' said Lupin, looking up at Hagrid. 'The Polyjuice Potion is designed for human use only.'

'None of the Order would have told Voldemort we were moving tonight,' said Harry: the idea was dreadful to him, he could not believe it of any of them. 'Voldemort only caught up with me towards the end, he didn't know which one I was in the beginning. If he'd been in on the plan, he'd have known from the start I was the one with Hagrid.'

'Voldemort caught up with you?' said Lupin sharply. 'What happened? How did you escape?'

Harry explained, briefly, how the Death Eaters pursuing them had seemed to recognise him as the true Harry, how they had abandoned the chase, how they must have summoned Voldemort, who had appeared just before he and Hagrid had reached the sanctuary of Tonks's parents'.

'They recognised you? But how? What had you done?'

'I ...' Harry tried to remember; the whole journey seemed like a blur of panic and confusion. 'I saw Stan Shunpike ... you know, the bloke who was the conductor on the Knight Bus? And I tried to Disarm him instead of – well, he doesn't know what he's doing, does he? He must be Imperiused!'

Lupin looked aghast.

'Harry, the time for Disarming is past! These people are trying to capture and kill you! At least Stun if you aren't prepared to kill!'

'We were hundreds of feet up! Stan's not himself, and if I Stunned him and he'd fallen he'd have died the same as if I'd used *Avada Kedavra*! *Expelliarmus* saved me from Voldemort two years ago,' Harry added defiantly. Lupin was reminding him of the sneering Hufflepuff Zacharias Smith, who had jeered at Harry for wanting to teach Dumbledore's Army how to Disarm.

'Yes, Harry,' said Lupin with painful restraint, 'and a great number of Death Eaters witnessed that happening! Forgive me, but it was a very unusual move then, under imminent threat of death. Repeating it tonight in front of

报信。你很可能是个冒牌货。"

"那你干吗不来核实我？"海格气喘吁吁地问，仍然挣扎着想把身子挤进门框。

"你是混血巨人，"卢平抬头看着海格说，"复方汤剂只是给普通人用的。"

"凤凰社的人谁也不会告诉伏地魔我们今晚转移。"哈利说。这种想法太可怕了，他不能相信他们中间的任何人会这么做。"伏地魔是最后才来追我的，他一开始并不知道哪个是我。如果他掌握了整个计划，一上来就会知道跟着海格的那个是我。"

"伏地魔追上你们了？"卢平警惕地问，"后来呢？你们是怎么逃脱的？"

哈利简单解释了一下，说追赶他们的食死徒认出了他是真哈利，他们突然放弃追赶，准是去向伏地魔报告了，伏地魔刚一出现，他和海格就到达了唐克斯父母家的安全区。

"他们认出了你？怎么会呢？你做了什么？"

"我……"哈利努力回忆着，整个旅程都是一片模糊不清的紧张和混乱，"我看见了斯坦·桑帕克……你知道吧？就是骑士公共汽车上的那个售票员。我想给他施个缴械咒，而不是——唉，他根本不知道自己在做什么，是不是？他肯定中了夺魂咒！"

卢平一脸惊愕。

"哈利，缴械咒的时代已经过去了！这些人想要抓住你、干掉你！即使你没有准备好杀人，至少也得用昏迷咒啊！"

"我们当时在几百米的高空！斯坦又是糊涂状态，如果我把他击昏，他肯定会掉下去，就像我对他施了阿瓦达索命咒一样必死无疑！两年前，缴你武器曾让我从伏地魔手里死里逃生。"哈利倔强地说。卢平使他想起了赫奇帕奇学院那个爱讥笑人的扎卡赖斯·史密斯，他当时就嘲笑哈利想教邓布利多军的成员学习缴械咒。

"是啊，哈利，"卢平努力克制着自己说，"有一大批食死徒目睹了当时的情景！请原谅，但是在生死攸关的紧急关头，这种举动是十分

Death Eaters who either witnessed or heard about the first occasion was close to suicidal!'

'So you think I should have killed Stan Shunpike?' said Harry angrily.

'Of course not,' said Lupin, 'but the Death Eaters – frankly, most people! – would have expected you to attack back! *Expelliarmus* is a useful spell, Harry, but the Death Eaters seem to think it is your signature move, and I urge you not to let it become so!'

Lupin was making Harry feel idiotic, and yet there was still a grain of defiance inside him.

'I won't blast people out of my way just because they're there,' said Harry. 'That's Voldemort's job.'

Lupin's retort was lost: finally succeeding in squeezing through the door, Hagrid staggered to a chair and sat down; it collapsed beneath him. Ignoring his mingled oaths and apologies, Harry addressed Lupin again.

'Will George be OK?'

All Lupin's frustration with Harry seemed to drain away at the question.

'I think so, although there's no chance of replacing his ear, not when it's been cursed off –'

There was a scuffling from outside. Lupin dived for the back door; Harry leapt over Hagrid's legs, and sprinted into the yard.

Two figures had appeared in the yard and as Harry ran towards them he realised they were Hermione, now returning to her normal appearance, and Kingsley, both clutching a bent coat hanger. Hermione flung herself into Harry's arms, but Kingsley showed no pleasure at the sight of any of them. Over Hermione's shoulder Harry saw him raise his wand and point it at Lupin's chest.

'The last words Albus Dumbledore spoke to the pair of us?'

'"*Harry is the best hope we have. Trust him,*"' said Lupin calmly.

Kingsley turned his wand on Harry, but Lupin said, 'It's him, I've checked!'

'All right, all right!' said Kingsley, stowing his wand back beneath his cloak. 'But somebody betrayed us! They knew, they knew it was tonight!'

'So it seems,' replied Lupin, 'but apparently they did not realise that there would be seven Harrys.'

第 5 章　坠落的勇士

反常的。食死徒都目睹或听说过你的那次行为，今晚你在他们面前故伎重演，简直等于自杀！"

"那你认为我应该杀死斯坦·桑帕克？"哈利气愤地说。

"当然不是，"卢平说，"但是食死徒——坦白地说，大多数人！——都以为你会出手反击！除你武器是一个很有用的咒语，哈利，但食死徒似乎把它看成你的标志性行为，我强烈要求你别让这种印象成真！"

卢平的话使哈利觉得自己像个傻瓜，但是他心里仍有点儿不服气。

"我不能无缘无故地把挡我路的人咒死，"哈利说，"那是伏地魔的做法。"

卢平无言以对。海格终于成功地挤进门来，跌跌撞撞地走到椅子前坐下。椅子在他的重压下坍塌了。哈利没有理睬海格的咒骂和道歉，又对卢平说：

"乔治不会有事吧？"

听到这话，卢平对哈利的恼怒似乎顿时烟消云散。

"我想不会，但他的耳朵不可能修复了，是被咒语击掉的——"

外面传来一阵乱哄哄的声音。卢平立刻朝后门口冲去，哈利跳过海格的腿，迅速奔到院子里。

院子里出现了两个人影，哈利飞跑过去，认出是赫敏——正在恢复她自己的相貌——和金斯莱，两人都抓着一只弯了的挂衣架。赫敏一头扑进哈利怀里，金斯莱看见他们却没有露出一丝喜悦。哈利从赫敏肩头上看见他举起魔杖，对准卢平的胸口。

"阿不思·邓布利多对我们俩说的最后一句话？"

"'哈利是我们最宝贵的希望。相信他。'"卢平平静地说。

金斯莱又把魔杖转向哈利，卢平说："是他，我检查过了！"

"好吧，好吧！"金斯莱说着把魔杖重新塞进长袍，"但是有人叛变了！他们知道了，他们知道是今晚！"

"好像是的，"卢平回答，"但看来他们不知道会有七个哈利。"

CHAPTER FIVE   Fallen Warrior

'Small comfort!' snarled Kingsley. 'Who else is back?'

'Only Harry, Hagrid, George and me.'

Hermione stifled a little moan behind her hand.

'What happened to you?' Lupin asked Kingsley.

'Followed by five, injured two, might've killed one,' Kingsley reeled off, 'and we saw You-Know-Who as well, he joined the chase halfway through, but vanished pretty quickly. Remus, he can –'

'Fly,' supplied Harry. 'I saw him too, he came after Hagrid and me.'

'So that's why he left – to follow you!' said Kingsley. 'I couldn't understand why he'd vanished. But what made him change targets?'

'Harry behaved a little too kindly to Stan Shunpike,' said Lupin.

'Stan?' repeated Hermione. 'But I thought he was in Azkaban?'

Kingsley let out a mirthless laugh.

'Hermione, there's obviously been a mass breakout which the Ministry has hushed up. Travers's hood fell off when I cursed him, he's supposed to be inside too. But what happened to you, Remus? Where's George?'

'He lost an ear,' said Lupin.

'Lost an –?' repeated Hermione in a high voice.

'Snape's work,' said Lupin.

'*Snape?*' shouted Harry. 'You didn't say –'

'He lost his hood during the chase. *Sectumsempra* was always a speciality of Snape's. I wish I could say I'd paid him back in kind, but it was all I could do to keep George on the broom after he was injured, he was losing so much blood.'

Silence fell between the four of them as they looked up at the sky. There was no sign of movement; the stars stared back, unblinking, indifferent, unobscured by flying friends. Where was Ron? Where were Fred and Mr Weasley? Where were Bill, Fleur, Tonks, Mad-Eye and Mundungus?

'Harry, give us a hand!' called Hagrid hoarsely from the door, in which he was stuck again. Glad of something to do, Harry pulled him free, then headed through the empty kitchen and back into the sitting room, where Mrs Weasley and Ginny were still tending to George. Mrs Weasley had staunched

"那也好不了多少。"金斯莱恶声恶气地说,"还有谁回来了?"

"只有哈利、海格、乔治和我。"

赫敏用手捂着嘴,低低地呜咽了一声。

"你们怎么样?"卢平问金斯莱。

"五个人追,伤了两个,大概死了一个。"金斯莱一口气地说,"我们也看见神秘人了,他在一半的时候加入进来,可是很快就消失了。莱姆斯,他会——"

"会飞,"哈利插嘴道,"我也看见了,他来追海格和我。"

"怪不得他跑了,原来是去追你们了!"金斯莱说,"我还想不通他为什么消失呢。可是他为什么会改变目标呢?"

"哈利对斯坦·桑帕克表现得太仁慈了点儿。"卢平说。

"斯坦?"赫敏重复了一次,"他不是在阿兹卡班吗?"

金斯莱悲哀地笑了一声。

"赫敏,显然发生了集体越狱,但魔法部封锁了消息。我给特拉弗斯念咒时,他的兜帽掉了。他也应该关在牢里的。你们怎么样,莱姆斯?乔治呢?"

"他丢了一只耳朵。"卢平说。

"丢了一只——?"赫敏尖声重复。

"斯内普干的。"卢平说。

"斯内普?"哈利叫了起来,"你不会是说——"

"他在追赶中兜帽滑掉了。神锋无影咒一直是斯内普的拿手功夫。我真希望当时以牙还牙地报复他,可是乔治受伤后,我只能尽力扶着他待在扫帚上,他失血太多了。"

沉默中,四个人抬头望着天空。四下里没有一点儿动静。星星瞪着一眨不眨的眼睛,那样冷漠,没有被朋友们飞翔的身影遮掩。罗恩在哪里?弗雷德和韦斯莱先生在哪里?比尔、芙蓉、唐克斯、疯眼汉和蒙顿格斯又在哪里?

"哈利,帮我一把!"海格又卡在门框里了,粗声喊道。哈利巴不得有点事情做做,就过去把他拉了出来,然后穿过空无一人的厨房回

CHAPTER FIVE Fallen Warrior

his bleeding now, and by the lamplight Harry saw a clean, gaping hole where George's ear had been.

'How is he?'

Mrs Weasley looked round and said, 'I can't make it grow back, not when it's been removed by Dark Magic. But it could have been so much worse ... he's alive.'

'Yeah,' said Harry. 'Thank God.'

'Did I hear someone else in the yard?' Ginny asked.

'Hermione and Kingsley,' said Harry.

'Thank goodness,' Ginny whispered. They looked at each other; Harry wanted to hug her, hold on to her; he did not even care much that Mrs Weasley was there, but before he could act on the impulse there was a great crash from the kitchen.

'I'll prove who I am, Kingsley, after I've seen my son, now back off if you know what's good for you!'

Harry had never heard Mr Weasley shout like that before. He burst into the living room, his bald patch gleaming with sweat, his spectacles askew, Fred right behind him, both pale but uninjured.

'Arthur!' sobbed Mrs Weasley. 'Oh thank goodness!'

'How is he?'

Mr Weasley dropped to his knees beside George. For the first time since Harry had known him, Fred seemed to be lost for words. He gaped over the back of the sofa at his twin's wound as if he could not believe what he was seeing.

Perhaps roused by the sound of Fred and their father's arrival, George stirred.

'How do you feel, Georgie?' whispered Mrs Weasley.

George's fingers groped for the side of his head.

'Saint-like,' he murmured.

'What's wrong with him?' croaked Fred, looking terrified. 'Is his mind affected?'

'Saint-like,' repeated George, opening his eyes and looking up at his brother. 'You see ... I'm holy. *Holey*, Fred, geddit?'

Mrs Weasley sobbed harder than ever. Colour flooded Fred's pale face.

第5章 坠落的勇士

到客厅。韦斯莱夫人和金妮还在照料乔治。韦斯莱夫人已经给他止住了血,哈利就着灯光,看见乔治的耳朵不见了,只留下一个裂开的大洞。

"他怎么样?"

韦斯莱夫人转过头来说道:"我没法让它重新长出来,是被黑魔法弄掉的。但是不幸中的大幸……他还活着。"

"是啊,"哈利说,"感谢上帝。"

"我好像听见院子里还有别人?"金妮问。

"赫敏和金斯莱。"哈利说。

"谢天谢地。"金妮小声说。他们互相望着对方。哈利真想搂住她,搂得紧紧的不松手,他甚至不在乎韦斯莱夫人就在旁边。可是没等他一时冲动做出什么,厨房里突然传来哗啦一声巨响。

"我会证明我是谁的,金斯莱,但我要先看看我的儿子,你要知趣就赶紧闪开!"

哈利从没听见韦斯莱先生这样喊叫过。只见韦斯莱先生冲进客厅,秃脑袋上汗珠闪亮,眼镜歪斜着,弗雷德跟在他身后,两人都脸色苍白,但并未受伤。

"亚瑟!"韦斯莱夫人啜泣着说,"哦,感谢上天!"

"他怎么样?"

韦斯莱先生扑通一声跪倒在乔治身边。哈利认识弗雷德到现在,第一次看到他说不出话来。弗雷德从沙发背后目瞪口呆地望着双胞胎兄弟的伤口,似乎不敢相信自己的眼睛。

也许是听见了弗雷德和父亲到来的声音,乔治动了动。

"你感觉怎么样,乔治?"韦斯莱夫人轻声问道。

乔治用手指摸索着脑袋的一侧。

"动听啊。"他喃喃地说。

"他怎么啦?"弗雷德惊恐地哑声问道,"他脑子也受伤了?"

"动听啊,"乔治又说了一遍,抬眼望着他的兄弟,"你看……我有个洞。洞听啊,弗雷德,明白了吗?"

韦斯莱夫人哭得更伤心了。弗雷德苍白的脸上顿时泛出血色。

117

CHAPTER FIVE   Fallen Warrior

'Pathetic,' he told George. 'Pathetic! With the whole wide world of ear-related humour before you, you go for *holey*?'

'Ah well,' said George, grinning at his tear-soaked mother. 'You'll be able to tell us apart now, anyway, Mum.'

He looked round.

'Hi Harry – you are Harry, right?'

'Yeah, I am,' said Harry, moving closer to the sofa.

'Well, at least we got you back OK,' said George. 'Why aren't Ron and Bill huddled round my sickbed?'

'They're not back yet, George,' said Mrs Weasley. George's grin faded. Harry glanced at Ginny and motioned to her to accompany him back outside. As they walked through the kitchen, she said in a low voice, 'Ron and Tonks should be back by now. They didn't have a long journey; Auntie Muriel's not that far from here.'

Harry said nothing. He had been trying to keep fear at bay ever since reaching The Burrow, but now it enveloped him, seeming to crawl over his skin, throbbing in his chest, clogging his throat. As they walked down the back steps into the dark yard, Ginny took his hand.

Kingsley was striding backwards and forwards, glancing up at the sky every time he turned. Harry was reminded of Uncle Vernon pacing the living room a million years ago. Hagrid, Hermione and Lupin stood shoulder to shoulder, gazing upwards in silence. None of them looked round when Harry and Ginny joined their silent vigil.

The minutes stretched into what might as well have been years. The slightest breath of wind made them all jump and turn towards the whispering bush or tree in the hope that one of the missing Order members might leap unscathed from its leaves –

And then a broom materialised directly above them and streaked towards the ground –

'It's them!' screamed Hermione.

Tonks landed in a long skid that sent earth and pebbles everywhere.

'Remus!' Tonks cried as she staggered off the broom into Lupin's arms. His face was set and white: he seemed unable to speak. Ron tripped dazedly towards Harry and Hermione.

第5章 坠落的勇士

"差劲，"他对乔治说，"真差劲！整个大千世界跟耳朵有关的幽默都摆在你面前，你就挑了个'洞听'？"

"这下好了，"乔治笑着对泪流满面的母亲说，"妈妈，你总算可以把我们俩分出来了。"

他看看四周。

"嘿，哈利——你是哈利吧？"

"对，我是。"哈利说着挪到沙发跟前。

"嘿，至少我们把你平安弄回来了。"乔治说，"罗恩和比尔怎么没有挤在我的病榻周围？"

"他们还没回来呢，乔治。"韦斯莱夫人说。乔治脸上的笑容不见了。哈利看了看金妮，示意她跟他到外面去。穿过厨房时，金妮压低声音说："罗恩和唐克斯现在应该回来了。他们路不远。穆丽尔姨婆家离这里挺近的。"

哈利什么也没说。来到陋居后，他一直拼命控制内心的恐惧，此刻却完全被恐惧包围。恐惧似乎在他的皮肤上蠕动，在他的胸膛里跳动，并且哽住了他的咽喉。他们走下屋后的台阶进入黑漆漆的后院时，金妮抓住了他的手。

金斯莱大踏步地踱来踱去，每次转身时都抬头扫一眼天空。这使哈利想起弗农姨父在客厅里踱步的情景，那仿佛是一百万年前的事了。海格、赫敏和卢平并肩站在那里，默不作声地抬头凝视。哈利和金妮走过去和他们一起默默守候，他们谁也没有转头望一望。

时间一分一秒地过去，感觉有许多年那么漫长。稍有风吹草动，大家就惊跳起来，转向沙沙作响的树丛和灌木丛，希望能看到某个失踪的凤凰社成员安然无恙地从树叶间一跃而出——

突然，一把扫帚在他们头顶上显出形状，朝地面疾驰而来——

"是他们！"赫敏叫道。

唐克斯落地时滑出很远，蹭得泥土和卵石四处飞溅。

"莱姆斯！"随着一声喊叫，唐克斯跌跌撞撞地下了扫帚，扑进卢平怀里。卢平神情严峻，脸色苍白，似乎说不出话来。罗恩晕头晕脑地朝哈利和赫敏跑过来。

'You're OK,' he mumbled, before Hermione flew at him and hugged him tightly.

'I thought – I thought –'

''M all right,' said Ron, patting her on the back. ''M fine.'

'Ron was great,' said Tonks warmly, relinquishing her hold on Lupin. 'Wonderful. Stunned one of the Death Eaters, straight to the head, and when you're aiming at a moving target from a flying broom –'

'You did?' said Hermione, gazing up at Ron with her arms still around his neck.

'Always the tone of surprise,' he said a little grumpily, breaking free. 'Are we the last back?'

'No,' said Ginny, 'we're still waiting for Bill and Fleur and Mad-Eye and Mundungus. I'm going to tell Mum and Dad you're OK, Ron –'

She ran back inside.

'So what kept you? What happened?' Lupin sounded almost angry at Tonks.

'Bellatrix,' said Tonks. 'She wants me quite as much as she wants Harry, Remus, she tried very hard to kill me. I just wish I'd got her, I owe Bellatrix. But we definitely injured Rodolphus ... then we got to Ron's Auntie Muriel's and we'd missed our Portkey and she was fussing over us –'

A muscle was jumping in Lupin's jaw. He nodded, but seemed unable to say anything else.

'So what happened to you lot?' Tonks asked, turning to Harry, Hermione and Kingsley.

They recounted the stories of their own journeys, but all the time the continued absence of Bill, Fleur, Mad-Eye and Mundungus seemed to lie upon them like a frost, its icy bite harder and harder to ignore.

'I'm going to have to get back to Downing Street. I should have been there an hour ago,' said Kingsley finally, after a last sweeping gaze at the sky. 'Let me know when they're back.'

Lupin nodded. With a wave to the others, Kingsley walked away into the darkness towards the gate. Harry thought he heard the faintest *pop* as Kingsley Disapparated just beyond The Burrow's boundaries.

Mr and Mrs Weasley came racing down the back steps, Ginny behind them. Both parents hugged Ron before turning to Lupin and Tonks.

第5章 坠落的勇士

"你们都没事吧。"罗恩喃喃地说,赫敏奔过去紧紧搂住了他。

"我还以为——我还以为——"

"我没事儿,"罗恩拍着赫敏的后背说,"我挺好。"

"罗恩真了不起,"唐克斯不情不愿地松开卢平,兴奋地说,"太棒了。击昏了一个食死徒,正好击中脑袋;要从飞行的扫帚上瞄准一个移动目标——"

"真的?"赫敏说,仍用双臂搂着罗恩的脖子,一边抬头看着他。

"老是用这种惊讶的口吻。"罗恩有点气呼呼地说,挣脱了赫敏,"我们是最后回来的?"

"不是,"金妮说,"我们还在等比尔、芙蓉、疯眼汉和蒙顿格斯。罗恩,我去告诉爸爸妈妈你没事儿——"

她跑进了屋里。

"你们怎么耽搁了?出什么事了?"卢平听起来简直在生唐克斯的气。

"贝拉特里克斯,"唐克斯说,"她不顾一切地想抓我,就像想抓哈利一样,莱姆斯。她千方百计想要我的命。我真希望当时击中她,我应该击中贝拉特里克斯的。不过我们肯定击伤了罗道夫斯……后来到了罗恩的穆丽尔姨婆家,却错过了门钥匙,她把我们好一顿埋怨——"

卢平下巴上的一块肌肉在跳动。他点点头,但似乎再也说不出话来。

"你们大家情况怎么样?"唐克斯转向哈利、赫敏和金斯莱问。

他们各自讲述了旅途上的遭遇,可是比尔、芙蓉、疯眼汉和蒙顿格斯一直没有回来,这事实像严霜一样压在他们心头,冰冷的寒意越来越叫人无法忍受。

"我得回唐宁街了,一小时前就应该到那儿的。"金斯莱最后扫了一眼天空,说道,"他们一回来就告诉我。"

卢平点点头。金斯莱朝大家挥了挥手,穿过黑暗朝大门口走去。哈利隐约听见噗的一声轻响,金斯莱一出陋居的范围就幻影移形了。

韦斯莱夫妇快速奔下后门台阶,后面跟着金妮。夫妇俩搂了搂罗恩,又转向卢平和唐克斯。

CHAPTER FIVE Fallen Warrior

'Thank you,' said Mrs Weasley, 'for our sons.'

'Don't be silly, Molly,' said Tonks at once.

'How's George?' asked Lupin.

'What's wrong with him?' piped up Ron.

'He's lost –'

But the end of Mrs Weasley's sentence was drowned in a general outcry: a Thestral had just soared into sight and landed a few feet from them. Bill and Fleur slid from its back, windswept but unhurt.

'Bill! Thank God, thank God –'

Mrs Weasley ran forwards, but the hug Bill bestowed upon her was perfunctory. Looking directly at his father, he said, 'Mad-Eye's dead.'

Nobody spoke, nobody moved. Harry felt as though something inside him was falling, falling through the earth, leaving him forever.

'We saw it,' said Bill; Fleur nodded, tear tracks glittering on her cheeks in the light from the kitchen window. 'It happened just after we broke out of the circle: Mad-Eye and Dung were close by us, they were heading north too. Voldemort – he can fly – went straight for them. Dung panicked, I heard him cry out, Mad-Eye tried to stop him, but he Disapparated. Voldemort's curse hit Mad-Eye full in the face, he fell backwards off his broom and – there was nothing we could do, nothing, we had half a dozen of them on our own tail –'

Bill's voice broke.

'Of course you couldn't have done anything,' said Lupin.

They all stood looking at each other. Harry could not quite comprehend it. Mad-Eye dead; it could not be … Mad-Eye, so tough, so brave, the consummate survivor …

At last it seemed to dawn on everyone, though nobody said it, that there was no point waiting in the yard any more, and in silence they followed Mr and Mrs Weasley back into The Burrow, and into the living room, where Fred and George were laughing together.

'What's wrong?' said Fred, scanning their faces, as they entered. 'What's happened? Who's –?'

第5章 坠落的勇士

"谢谢你们,"韦斯莱夫人说,"为了我们的儿子,谢谢你们。"

"别说傻话了,莫丽。"唐克斯立刻说。

"乔治怎么样?"卢平问。

"他怎么啦?"罗恩尖声问。

"他失去了——"

韦斯莱夫人后面的话被一片高喊声淹没了。一匹夜骐赫然出现在天空,降落在离他们几步远的地方。比尔和芙蓉从夜骐背上滑下来,头发被风吹得乱蓬蓬的,但并没有受伤。

"比尔!谢天谢地,谢天谢地——"

韦斯莱夫人跑上前去,但比尔只是草草地搂了她一下,便直视着父亲说:"疯眼汉死了。"

没有人说话,没有人动弹。哈利觉得内心的某种东西在坠落、坠落,坠入地下,永远地离他而去。

"我们看见了。"比尔说,芙蓉点点头,在厨房窗口的灯光映照下,她面颊上的泪痕闪闪发亮,"我们刚刚突破包围圈,事情就发生了。疯眼汉和顿格就在我们近旁,也是在往北飞。伏地魔——他会飞——直接就去追他们了。顿格吓坏了,我听见他高声大叫,疯眼汉想让他住嘴,没想到他幻影移形了。伏地魔的咒语不偏不倚地击中了疯眼汉的脸,疯眼汉朝后一倒,从扫帚上摔了下去——我们在一旁眼睁睁地看着,毫无办法,有六七个人在后面追我们——"

比尔说不下去了。

"你们当然没有办法。"卢平说。

大家站在那里面面相觑。哈利不能完全理解。疯眼汉死了,这不可能……疯眼汉,那么强悍,那么勇敢,久经死亡的考验……

最后,大家虽然没有说出口,但也明白再在院子里等待已经毫无意义,于是都默默地跟着韦斯莱夫妇返回陋居,走进客厅,弗雷德和乔治正在那里哈哈大笑。

"怎么啦?"弗雷德在他们进去时看了看他们的脸,问道,"出什么事了?谁——?"

CHAPTER FIVE Fallen Warrior

'Mad-Eye,' said Mr Weasley. 'Dead.'

The twins' grins turned to grimaces of shock. Nobody seemed to know what to do. Tonks was crying silently into a handkerchief: she had been close to Mad-Eye, Harry knew, his favourite and his protégée at the Ministry of Magic. Hagrid, who had sat down on the floor in the corner where he had most space, was dabbing at his eyes with his tablecloth-sized handkerchief.

Bill walked over to the sideboard and pulled out a bottle of Firewhisky and some glasses.

'Here,' he said, and with a wave of his wand he sent twelve full glasses soaring through the room to each of them, holding the thirteenth aloft. 'Mad-Eye.'

'Mad-Eye,' they all said, and drank.

'Mad-Eye,' echoed Hagrid, a little late, with a hiccough.

The Firewhisky seared Harry's throat: it seemed to burn feeling back into him, dispelling the numbness and sense of unreality, firing him with something that was like courage.

'So Mundungus disappeared?' said Lupin, who had drained his own glass in one.

The atmosphere changed at once: everybody looked tense, watching Lupin, both wanting him to go on, it seemed to Harry, and slightly afraid of what they might hear.

'I know what you're thinking,' said Bill, 'and I wondered that too, on the way back here, because they seemed to be expecting us, didn't they? But Mundungus can't have betrayed us. They didn't know there would be seven Harrys, that confused them the moment we appeared, and in case you've forgotten, it was Mundungus who suggested that little bit of skullduggery. Why wouldn't he have told them the essential point? I think Dung panicked, it's as simple as that. He didn't want to come in the first place, but Mad-Eye made him, and You-Know-Who went straight for them: it was enough to make anyone panic.'

'You-Know-Who acted exactly as Mad-Eye expected him to,' sniffed Tonks. 'Mad-Eye said he'd expect the real Harry to be with the toughest, most skilled Aurors. He chased Mad-Eye first, and when Mundungus gave them away he switched to Kingsley ...'

'Yes, and zat eez all very good,' snapped Fleur, 'but still eet does not explain 'ow zey knew we were moving 'Arry tonight, does eet? Somebody must 'ave been careless. Somebody let slip ze date to an outsider. Eet eez ze

第5章 坠落的勇士

"疯眼汉，"韦斯莱先生说，"死了。"

双胞胎兄弟脸上的笑容变成了惊愕。一时间似乎谁也不知道该怎么办。唐克斯用手帕捂着脸默默哭泣。哈利知道她跟疯眼汉一直很亲密，是疯眼汉在魔法部里最好的朋友，深受疯眼汉的关照。海格席地坐在几乎被他占满的墙角，用他桌布那么大的手帕擦着眼泪。

比尔走到餐具柜前，拿出一瓶火焰威士忌和几个玻璃杯。

"来，"他一挥魔杖，让十二个斟满酒的玻璃杯飞到屋里每个人手中，然后自己高举起第十三个杯子，"敬疯眼汉。"

"敬疯眼汉。"大家齐声说道，举杯饮酒。

"敬疯眼汉。"海格打了个嗝儿，比别人慢了一拍，像是回声。

火焰威士忌灼痛了哈利的喉咙，似乎驱散了麻木和不真实感，使他在烧灼中重新有了感觉，有了某种类似于勇气的东西。

"这么说，蒙顿格斯消失了？"卢平一口喝干他杯里的酒，说道。

气氛立刻变了。每个人都神色紧张地望着卢平。在哈利看来，大家既希望他说下去，又有点害怕将会听到的话。

"我知道你在想什么，"比尔说，"在回这里的路上，我也有过那样的怀疑，因为他们似乎知道我们要来，不是吗？但告密的不可能是蒙顿格斯。他们不知道会有七个哈利，我们一出现，就把他们搞糊涂了。也许你已经忘了，这个替身的点子就是蒙顿格斯提出来的，他为什么不把最关键的一点告诉他们呢？我认为顿格当时是紧张了，仅此而已。他本来就不想来，是疯眼汉强迫他的，神秘人直接朝他们追去，换了谁都会惊慌失措。"

"神秘人的做法跟疯眼汉预料的完全一样。"唐克斯抽噎着说，"疯眼汉说，神秘人肯定以为真的哈利会跟最强悍、最有经验的傲罗在一起。他首先去追疯眼汉，等蒙顿格斯露了馅，他才回身去追金斯莱……"

"是啊，那都没有问题，"芙蓉毫不客气地说，"可是仍然无法解释他们怎么知道我们今晚转移哈利，不是吗？肯定有人大意了。有人不小心把日期透露给了外人。这样才能解释他们只知道日期但不知道整

only explanation for zem knowing ze date but not ze 'ole plan.'

She glared around at them all, tear tracks still etched on her beautiful face, silently daring any of them to contradict her. Nobody did. The only sound to break the silence was that of Hagrid hiccoughing from behind his handkerchief. Harry glanced at Hagrid, who had just risked his own life to save Harry's – Hagrid, whom he loved, whom he trusted, who had once been tricked into giving Voldemort crucial information in exchange for a dragon's egg …

'No,' Harry said aloud, and they all looked at him, surprised: the Firewhisky seemed to have amplified his voice. 'I mean … if somebody made a mistake,' Harry went on, 'and let something slip, I know they didn't mean to do it. It's not their fault,' he repeated, again a little louder than he would usually have spoken. 'We've got to trust each other. I trust all of you, I don't think anyone in this room would ever sell me to Voldemort.'

More silence followed his words. They were all looking at him; Harry felt a little hot again, and drank some more Firewhisky for something to do. As he drank, he thought of Mad-Eye. Mad-Eye had always been scathing about Dumbledore's willingness to trust people.

'Well said, Harry,' said Fred unexpectedly.

'Yeah, 'ear, 'ear,' said George, with half a glance at Fred, the corner of whose mouth twitched.

Lupin was wearing an odd expression as he looked at Harry: it was close to pitying.

'You think I'm a fool?' demanded Harry.

'No, I think you're like James,' said Lupin, 'who would have regarded it as the height of dishonour to mistrust his friends.'

Harry knew what Lupin was getting at: that his father had been betrayed by his friend, Peter Pettigrew. He felt irrationally angry. He wanted to argue, but Lupin had turned away from him, set down his glass upon a side table and addressed Bill, 'There's work to do. I can ask Kingsley whether –'

'No,' said Bill at once, 'I'll do it, I'll come.'

'Where are you going?' said Tonks and Fleur together.

'Mad-Eye's body,' said Lupin. 'We need to recover it.'

'Can't it –?' began Mrs Weasley, with an appealing look at Bill.

'Wait?' said Bill. 'Not unless you'd rather the Death Eaters took it?'

个计划。"

她默默地瞪着大家，看有谁提出反驳，她美丽的脸上仍然印着泪痕。没有人说话，只有海格大手帕后面的打嗝儿声打破沉默。哈利看着刚才冒着生命危险救了自己的海格——海格，他爱戴和信任的海格，曾经为了换取一个火龙蛋，受人哄骗，把重要情报泄露给了伏地魔……

"不会。"哈利大声说道，大家都吃惊地望着他。火焰威士忌似乎使他的声音放大了。"我的意思是……即使有人不小心犯了错误，"哈利继续说，"泄露了消息，我知道他们肯定不是故意的，不能怪他们。"他说话的声音还是比平常大一些，"我们必须彼此信任。我信任你们大家，我认为这个房间里的人谁也不会把我出卖给伏地魔。"

他说完后又是一阵沉默。大家都看着他。哈利又觉得有点儿燥热，为了找点事做，他又喝了几口火焰威士忌，一边喝，一边想着疯眼汉。疯眼汉以前总是责骂邓布利多轻易相信别人。

"说得好，哈利。"弗雷德出人意料地说。

"没错，说得好，说得好。"乔治瞥了瞥弗雷德，弗雷德的嘴角在抽动。

卢平看着哈利，脸上的表情很古怪，简直近乎怜悯。

"你认为我是个傻瓜？"哈利质问道。

"不，我看你真像詹姆，"卢平说，"他认为不信任朋友是最最可耻的事情。"

哈利知道卢平指的是什么。父亲就是被他的朋友小矮星彼得出卖的。哈利觉得又气又恼。他想反驳，可是卢平已经转过身，把杯子放在靠墙的一张桌子上，对比尔说："还有活儿要干呢。我可以问问金斯莱——"

"不，"比尔立刻说道，"我来，我来干。"

"你们去哪儿？"唐克斯和芙蓉异口同声地问。

"疯眼汉的遗体，"卢平说，"我们必须把它找到。"

"就不能——？"韦斯莱夫人恳求地望着比尔，问道。

"等一等？"比尔打断了她，"除非你想让它落到食死徒手里。"

Nobody spoke. Lupin and Bill said goodbye and left.

The rest of them now dropped into chairs, all except for Harry, who remained standing. The suddenness and completeness of death was with them like a presence.

'I've got to go too,' said Harry.

Ten pairs of startled eyes looked at him.

'Don't be silly, Harry,' said Mrs Weasley. 'What are you talking about?'

'I can't stay here.'

He rubbed his forehead: it was prickling again; it had not hurt like this for more than a year.

'You're all in danger while I'm here. I don't want –'

'But don't be so silly!' said Mrs Weasley. 'The whole point of tonight was to get you here safely, and thank goodness it worked. And Fleur's agreed to get married here rather than in France, we've arranged everything so that we can all stay together and look after you –'

She did not understand; she was making him feel worse, not better.

'If Voldemort finds out I'm here –'

'But why should he?' asked Mrs Weasley.

'There are a dozen places you might be now, Harry,' said Mr Weasley. 'He's got no way of knowing which safe house you're in.'

'It's not me I'm worried for!' said Harry.

'We know that,' said Mr Weasley quietly, 'but it would make our efforts tonight seem rather pointless if you left.'

'Yer not goin' anywhere,' growled Hagrid. 'Blimey, Harry, after all we wen' through ter get you here?'

'Yeah, what about my bleeding ear?' said George, hoisting himself up on his cushions.

'I know that –'

'Mad-Eye wouldn't want –'

'I KNOW!' Harry bellowed.

He felt beleaguered and blackmailed: did they think he did not know what they had done for him, didn't they understand that it was for precisely that reason that he wanted to go now, before they had to suffer any more on his behalf? There was a long and awkward silence in which his scar continued to

第5章 坠落的勇士

谁也没有说话。卢平和比尔告辞离开了。

其他人纷纷坐到椅子上，只有哈利还站着。突如其来的、真真切切的死亡，像看得见的东西一样陪伴着他们，挥之不去。

"我也得走。"哈利说。

十双惊愕的眼睛齐刷刷地看着他。

"别傻了，哈利，"韦斯莱夫人说，"你在说什么呀？"

"我不能待在这儿。"

他揉了揉前额。那里又在刺痛，已经有一年多没有这么痛过了。

"我在这儿，你们都有危险。我不想——"

"别说这种傻话！"韦斯莱夫人说，"今晚唯一关键的就是把你安全地转移到这里，谢天谢地我们成功了。芙蓉同意不在法国而在这里结婚，我们一切都安排好了，好让大家都可以聚在一起来照顾你——"

她不理解。哈利听了她的话反而更难受了。

"如果伏地魔发现我在这儿——"

"但他怎么会发现呢？"韦斯莱夫人问。

"你现在有可能在十几个地方呢，哈利，"韦斯莱先生说，"他不可能知道你到底藏在哪座安全的房子里。"

"我不是为自己担心！"哈利说。

"我们知道，"韦斯莱先生轻声说，"但如果你离开，我们今晚的努力就毫无意义了。"

"你哪儿也不能去。"海格粗暴地嘟囔道，"天哪，哈利，我们经历了千辛万苦才把你弄到这儿，你还要走？"

"是啊，我那只倒霉的耳朵怎么办？"乔治从靠垫上支起身子说。

"我知道——"

"疯眼汉也不会愿意——"

"**我知道！**"哈利大吼一声。

他觉得大家都在围攻他、逼迫他。难道他们以为他不知道他们为他做的一切吗？难道他们不理解他正是因为这个才打算现在离开，免得他们为了他遭受更多的灾难吗？一阵漫长而令人尴尬的沉默，他的

CHAPTER FIVE   Fallen Warrior

prickle and throb, and which was broken at last by Mrs Weasley.

'Where's Hedwig, Harry?' she said coaxingly. 'We can put her up with Pigwidgeon and give her something to eat.'

His insides clenched like a fist. He could not tell her the truth. He drank the last of his Firewhisky to avoid answering.

'Wait 'til it gets out yeh did it again, Harry,' said Hagrid. 'Escaped him, fought him off when he was right on top of yeh!'

'It wasn't me,' said Harry flatly. 'It was my wand. My wand acted of its own accord.'

After a few moments, Hermione said gently, 'But that's impossible, Harry. You mean that you did magic without meaning to; you reacted instinctively.'

'No,' said Harry. 'The bike was falling, I couldn't have told you where Voldemort was, but my wand spun in my hand and found him and shot a spell at him, and it wasn't even a spell I recognised. I've never made gold flames appear before.'

'Often,' said Mr Weasley, 'when you're in a pressured situation you can produce magic you never dreamed of. Small children often find, before they're trained —'

'It wasn't like that,' said Harry through gritted teeth. His scar was burning: he felt angry and frustrated; he hated the idea that they were all imagining him to have power to match Voldemort's.

No one said anything. He knew that they did not believe him. Now that he came to think of it, he had never heard of a wand performing magic on its own before.

His scar seared with pain; it was all he could do not to moan aloud. Muttering about fresh air, he set down his glass and left the room.

As he crossed the dark yard, the great, skeletal Thestral looked up, rustled its enormous bat-like wings, then resumed its grazing. Harry stopped at the gate into the garden, staring out at its overgrown plants, rubbing his pounding forehead and thinking of Dumbledore.

Dumbledore would have believed him, he knew it. Dumbledore would have known how and why Harry's wand had acted independently, because Dumbledore always had the answers; he had known about wands, had explained to Harry the strange connection that existed between his wand and

伤疤仍在刺痛、跳动。最后韦斯莱夫人打破了沉默。

"海德薇呢，哈利？"她柔声问道，"我们可以让它跟小猪待在一起，喂它点儿吃的。"

哈利的五脏六腑像拳头一样攥紧了。他没办法把实情告诉她。为了逃避回答，他喝光了最后一点儿火焰威士忌。

"哈利，等消息传出去，让他们瞧瞧，你又一次大难不死，"海格说，"逃脱了他的魔爪。当时他就在你上面，你却把他击退了！"

"不是我，"哈利淡淡地说，"是我的魔杖。我的魔杖自己采取了行动。"

过了片刻，赫敏委婉地说："但那是不可能的，哈利。其实你的意思是你在无意识中施了魔法，你本能地做出了反应。"

"不，"哈利说，"当时摩托车在坠落，我也弄不清伏地魔在哪儿，但我的魔杖在我手里转了个圈，对准了他，朝他射出一个魔咒，我连那是什么魔咒都不知道。我以前从没弄出过金色的火焰。"

"形势紧急的时候，"韦斯莱先生说，"一个人经常会施出他做梦也没想到过的魔法。没受过训练的小孩子经常发现——"

"不是那样的。"哈利咬着牙说。伤疤火辣辣地疼，他觉得又生气又沮丧。他不愿意他们都想象他有力量对抗伏地魔。

谁也没有吭声。哈利知道他们不相信他的话。现在想来，他确实没听说过一根魔杖会自己施魔法。

伤疤火烧火燎地疼起来。他用全部力气克制着不要大声呻吟。他嘟囔着说要呼吸点新鲜空气，就放下杯子离开了房间。

穿过黑漆漆的院子时，那匹巨大而消瘦的夜骐抬头看看他，将蝙蝠般的大翅膀哗啦啦地扑扇几下，就又埋头吃草了。哈利在通向花园的门口停住脚步，望着那些疯长的植物，揉着一阵阵剧痛的额头，想起了邓布利多。

他知道邓布利多一定会相信他。邓布利多肯定理解哈利的魔杖会自己采取行动，而且明白是为什么，因为邓布利多总是知道答案。他精通魔杖，曾向哈利解释过哈利的魔杖和伏地魔的魔杖之间存在的奇

CHAPTER FIVE   Fallen Warrior

Voldemort's ... but Dumbledore, like Mad-Eye, like Sirius, like his parents, like his poor owl, all were gone where Harry could never talk to them again. He felt a burning in his throat that had nothing to do with Firewhisky ...

And then, out of nowhere, the pain in his scar peaked. As he clutched his forehead and closed his eyes, a voice screamed inside his head.

'*You told me the problem would be solved by using another's wand!*'

And into his mind burst the vision of an emaciated old man lying in rags upon a stone floor, screaming, a horrible, drawn-out scream, a scream of unendurable agony ...

'No! No! I beg you, I beg you ...'

'You lied to Lord Voldemort, Ollivander!'

'I did not ... I swear I did not ...'

'You sought to help Potter, to help him escape me!'

'I swear I did not ... I believed a different wand would work ...'

'Explain, then, what happened. Lucius's wand is destroyed!'

'I cannot understand ... the connection ... exists only ... between your two wands ...'

'*Lies!*'

'Please ... I beg you ...'

And Harry saw the white hand raise its wand and felt Voldemort's surge of vicious anger, saw the frail old man on the floor writhe in agony –

'Harry?'

It was over as quickly as it had come: Harry stood shaking in the darkness, clutching the gate into the garden, his heart racing, his scar still tingling. It was several moments before he realised that Ron and Hermione were at his side.

'Harry, come back in the house,' Hermione whispered. 'You aren't still thinking of leaving?'

'Yeah, you've got to stay, mate,' said Ron, thumping Harry on the back.

'Are you all right?' Hermione asked, close enough now to look into Harry's face. 'You look awful!'

'Well,' said Harry shakily, 'I probably look better than Ollivander ...'

第5章 坠落的勇士

特联系……可是邓布利多像疯眼汉,像小天狼星,像他的父母,像他可怜的猫头鹰一样,都去了一个哈利永远不能与他们交谈的地方。他觉得嗓子眼儿里火辣辣的,却与火焰威士忌没有关系……

就在这时,突如其来地,伤疤的疼痛达到了顶峰。他抓住前额,闭上眼睛,一个声音在他脑海里尖叫:

"你告诉过我,只要用了别人的魔杖,问题就解决了!"

哈利脑海里突然浮现出一个瘦弱憔悴的老头儿,衣衫褴褛,躺在石头地面上,发出一声可怕的、长长的尖叫,声音里透着无法忍受的痛苦……

"不!不!我求求您,我求求您……"

"你竟敢欺骗伏地魔,奥利凡德!"

"我没有……我发誓我没有……"

"你想帮助波特,你想帮助波特从我手里逃走!"

"我发誓我没有……我以为换一根魔杖就会管用……"

"那你就解释解释这件事吧。卢修斯的魔杖被毁掉了!"

"我不明白……那种联系……只存在于……你们的两根魔杖之间……"

"撒谎!"

"求求您……我求求您……"

哈利看到那只白色的手举起魔杖,感觉到伏地魔狂暴的怒火,看见那个虚弱的老头儿在地上痛苦地蠕动——

"哈利?"

一切又突然消失了。哈利站在黑暗中瑟瑟发抖,双手攥着花园的门,心脏怦怦狂跳。伤疤仍然一刺一刺地疼。过了片刻,他才意识到罗恩和赫敏在他身边。

"哈利,回屋里去吧。"赫敏小声说,"你不会还在想着离开吧?"

"是啊,你一定要留下来,伙计。"罗恩用拳头擂着哈利的后背说。

"你没事儿吧?"赫敏凑近了,端详着哈利的脸,"你的脸色好可怕!"

"没事儿,"哈利声音发抖地说,"我的脸色大概要比奥利凡德的好些……"

CHAPTER FIVE   Fallen Warrior

When he had finished telling them what he had seen, Ron looked appalled, but Hermione downright terrified.

'But it was supposed to have stopped! Your scar – it wasn't supposed to do this any more! You mustn't let that connection open up again – Dumbledore wanted you to close your mind!'

When he did not reply, she gripped his arm.

'Harry, he's taking over the Ministry and the newspapers and half the wizarding world! Don't let him inside your head too!'

第5章 坠落的勇士

他把刚才看到的一幕原原本本告诉了他们,罗恩显得十分惊恐,赫敏则完全吓坏了。

"可是这应该停止了!你的伤疤——它不应该再这样了!你绝不能让那种联系再接通——邓布利多希望你封闭你的大脑!"

看到哈利没有回答,赫敏抓住了他的胳膊。

"哈利,他已经占领了魔法部、报纸和半个魔法界!别让他再占领你的大脑了!"

CHAPTER SIX

The Ghoul in Pyjamas

The shock of losing Mad-Eye hung over the house in the days that followed; Harry kept expecting to see him stumping in through the back door like the other Order members, who passed in and out to relay news. Harry felt that nothing but action would assuage his feelings of guilt and grief and that he ought to set out on his mission to find and destroy Horcruxes as soon as possible.

'Well, you can't do anything about the –' Ron mouthed the word *Horcruxes*, '"til you're seventeen. You've still got the Trace on you. And we can plan here as well as anywhere, can't we? Or,' he dropped his voice to a whisper, 'd'you reckon you already know where the you-know-whats are?'

'No,' Harry admitted.

'I think Hermione's been doing a bit of research,' said Ron. 'She said she was saving it for when you got here.'

They were sitting at the breakfast table; Mr Weasley and Bill had just left for work, Mrs Weasley had gone upstairs to wake Hermione and Ginny, while Fleur had drifted off to take a bath.

'The Trace'll break on the thirty-first,' said Harry. 'That means I only need to stay here four days. Then I can –'

'Five days,' Ron corrected him firmly. 'We've got to stay for the wedding. They'll kill us if we miss it.'

Harry understood 'they' to mean Fleur and Mrs Weasley.

'It's one extra day,' said Ron, when Harry looked mutinous.

'Don't they realise how important –?'

"Course they don't,' said Ron. 'They haven't got a clue. And now you mention it, I wanted to talk to you about that.'

第6章

穿睡衣的食尸鬼

接下来的几天里,失去疯眼汉的震惊依然在整座房子里停留不去。哈利总忍不住期待疯眼汉会像那些进进出出、传递消息的其他凤凰社成员一样,迈着沉重的脚步从后门走进来。哈利觉得只有行动才能减轻他的悲伤和负罪感,他觉得自己应该出发去完成使命,去尽快找到和摧毁魂器。

"唉,你还不满十七岁,不能去对付——"罗恩用口型说出魂器这个词,"——你身上还带着踪丝呢。我们完全可以在这里制订计划嘛,是不是?或者,"他把声音压得低低的,"你是不是已经知道那些东西在哪儿了?"

"不知道。"哈利老老实实地承认。

"赫敏好像在做一些研究,"罗恩说,"她说要等你来了再说。"

这会儿他们正坐在桌旁吃早饭,韦斯莱先生和比尔刚刚上班去了。韦斯莱夫人上楼去叫赫敏和金妮起床,芙蓉迈着轻盈的步子去洗澡了。

"三十一号那天踪丝就消失了,"哈利说,"也就是说,我只需要在这里待四天,然后就可以——"

"五天,"罗恩认真地纠正他,"我们还得留下来参加婚礼呢。不然她们准会杀了我们。"

哈利明白"她们"指的是芙蓉和韦斯莱夫人。

"只多一天嘛。"罗恩看到哈利要发脾气,赶紧说道。

"她们难道不知道这有多重要——?"

"当然不知道,"罗恩说,"她们什么都不知道。既然你提到这点,我一直想跟你好好谈谈。"

CHAPTER SIX   The Ghoul in Pyjamas

Ron glanced towards the door into the hall to check that Mrs Weasley was not returning yet, then leaned in closer to Harry.

'Mum's been trying to get it out of Hermione and me. What we're off to do. She'll try you next, so brace yourself. Dad and Lupin've both asked as well, but when we said Dumbledore told you not to tell anyone except us, they dropped it. Not Mum, though. She's determined.'

Ron's prediction came true within hours. Shortly before lunch, Mrs Weasley detached Harry from the others by asking him to help identify a lone man's sock that she thought might have come out of his rucksack. Once she had him cornered in the tiny scullery off the kitchen, she started.

'Ron and Hermione seem to think that the three of you are dropping out of Hogwarts,' she began in a light, casual tone.

'Oh,' said Harry. 'Well, yeah. We are.'

The mangle turned of its own accord in a corner, wringing out what looked like one of Mr Weasley's vests.

'May I ask *why* you are abandoning your education?' said Mrs Weasley.

'Well, Dumbledore left me ... stuff to do,' mumbled Harry. 'Ron and Hermione know about it, and they want to come too.'

'What sort of "stuff"?'

'I'm sorry, I can't –'

'Well, frankly, I think Arthur and I have a right to know, and I'm sure Mr and Mrs Granger would agree!' said Mrs Weasley. Harry had been afraid of the 'concerned parent' attack. He forced himself to look directly into her eyes, noticing as he did so that they were precisely the same shade of brown as Ginny's. This did not help.

'Dumbledore didn't want anyone else to know, Mrs Weasley. I'm sorry. Ron and Hermione don't have to come, it's their choice –'

'I don't see that you have to go, either!' she snapped, dropping all pretence now. 'You're barely of age, any of you! It's utter nonsense, if Dumbledore needed work doing, he had the whole Order at his command! Harry, you must have misunderstood him. Probably he was telling you something he *wanted* done, and you took it to mean that he wanted *you* –'

第6章 穿睡衣的食尸鬼

罗恩透过房门朝大厅扫了一眼,确认韦斯莱夫人还没有回来,便凑到哈利跟前说:

"妈妈一直想套赫敏和我的话,想弄清我们要做什么。她接下来就会找你了,做好准备吧。爸爸和卢平也问过我们,但我们说邓布利多叫你除了我们不告诉任何人,他们就不再问了。但妈妈不同,她是不会罢休的。"

不出几个小时,罗恩的预言就变成了现实。快要吃午饭了,韦斯莱夫人把哈利从别人身边支走,叫他帮着辨认一只配不成对的男袜,她猜想可能是从他背包里掉出来的。韦斯莱夫人刚把哈利堵在厨房那头的小洗涤室里,审问就开始了。

"罗恩和赫敏说,你们三个好像打算从霍格沃茨退学?"她用轻松随意的口气问道。

"哦,"哈利说,"是啊,没错。"

墙角的绞干机自己转动起来,绞干了一件衣服,看着像是韦斯莱先生的马甲。

"我可以问问你们为什么要放弃学业吗?"韦斯莱夫人说。

"是这样,邓布利多留给我……一些事情要做,"哈利含混地说,"罗恩和赫敏知道了,他们也想去。"

"什么样的'事情'?"

"对不起,我不能——"

"好吧,坦白地说,我认为亚瑟和我有权知道,而且我相信格兰杰夫妇也会赞同!"韦斯莱夫人说。哈利早就担心"家长"的杀手锏。他强迫自己直盯着韦斯莱夫人的眼睛,却发现它们是和金妮的眼睛完全一样的褐色。这让他更感到心慌。

"邓布利多不想让别的任何人知道,韦斯莱夫人。对不起。罗恩和赫敏用不着去的,那是他们自己的选择——"

"我认为你也用不着去!"她厉声说道,一下子卸掉了所有的伪装,"你们还不够年龄呢,你们谁也不够!全是一派胡言,如果邓布利多有工作需要完成,整个凤凰社都由他随意调遣!哈利,你肯定弄错他的意思了。他大概是告诉你他希望完成的事情,结果你就以为他是想让你——"

CHAPTER SIX

The Ghoul in Pyjamas

'I didn't misunderstand,' said Harry flatly. 'It's got to be me.'

He handed her back the single sock he was supposed to be identifying, which was patterned with golden bulrushes.

'And that's not mine, I don't support Puddlemere United.'

'Oh, of course not,' said Mrs Weasley, with a sudden and rather unnerving return to her casual tone. 'I should have realised. Well, Harry, while we've still got you here, you won't mind helping with the preparations for Bill and Fleur's wedding, will you? There's still so much to do.'

'No – I – of course not,' said Harry, disconcerted by this sudden change of subject.

'Sweet of you,' she replied, and she smiled as she left the scullery.

From that moment on, Mrs Weasley kept Harry, Ron and Hermione so busy with preparations for the wedding that they hardly had time to think. The kindest explanation of this behaviour would have been that Mrs Weasley wanted to distract them all from thoughts of Mad-Eye, and the terrors of their recent journey. After two days of non-stop cutlery cleaning, of colour-matching favours, ribbons and flowers, of de-gnoming the garden and helping Mrs Weasley cook vast batches of canapés, however, Harry started to suspect her of a different motive. All the jobs she handed out seemed to keep him, Ron and Hermione away from one another; he had not had a chance to speak to the two of them, alone, since the first night, when he had told them about Voldemort torturing Ollivander.

'I think Mum thinks that if she can stop the three of you getting together and planning, she'll be able to delay you leaving,' Ginny told Harry in an undertone, as they laid the table for dinner on the third night of his stay.

'And then what does she think's going to happen?' Harry muttered. 'Someone else might kill off Voldemort while she's holding us here making vol-au-vents?'

He had spoken without thinking, and saw Ginny's face whiten.

'So it's true?' she said. 'That's what you're trying to do?'

'I – not – I was joking,' said Harry evasively.

They stared at each other, and there was something more than shock in Ginny's expression. Suddenly Harry became aware that this was the first time that he had been alone with her since those stolen hours in secluded corners

第6章 穿睡衣的食尸鬼

"我没有弄错他的意思,"哈利面无表情地说,"肯定是我。"

他把要他辨认的那只袜子递还给韦斯莱夫人,上面的图案是金色的宽叶香蒲。

"这不是我的,我不是普德米尔联队的球迷。"

"噢,当然不是,"韦斯莱夫人突然又恢复了她那轻松随意的口气,令哈利感到不知所措,"我应该想到的。好了,哈利,既然你还待在我们这里,你不会反对帮着操办一下比尔和芙蓉的婚礼吧?要做的事情还很多呢。"

"行——我——当然没问题。"哈利说,韦斯莱夫人突然改变话题使他有些慌乱。

"真懂事。"她回答,然后笑眯眯地离开了洗涤室。

从那时候起,韦斯莱夫人就让哈利、罗恩和赫敏为筹备婚礼忙得团团转,几乎没有时间想事情。对这种行为最宽容的解释是,韦斯莱夫人想分散他们的注意力,不让他们想着疯眼汉和最近那次恐怖的旅行。经过两天没完没了地擦洗餐具,给礼品、丝带和鲜花搭配颜色,清除花园里的地精,又帮韦斯莱夫人做了一大堆开胃薄饼,哈利开始怀疑她另有动机。她分派的活计似乎都让他、罗恩和赫敏互相分开。自从第一天夜里哈利告诉罗恩和赫敏伏地魔在折磨奥利凡德之后,便再也没有机会与他们俩单独说话。

"我想,妈妈以为只要不让你们三个凑在一起商量计划,就能推迟你们离开的时间。"金妮压低声音对哈利说,这已经是哈利待在这里的第三天晚上,他们正摆桌子准备吃晚饭。

"那她认为会怎么样呢?"哈利小声嘟囔道,"她把我们拴在这里做酥皮馅饼时,会有另外的人去干掉伏地魔吗?"

他不假思索地说出这句话,便看见金妮的脸白了。

"这么说是真的喽?"她问,"这就是你们打算做的事情?"

"我——不是——我开玩笑呢。"哈利闪烁其词地说。

他们互相望着对方,金妮的表情里除了惊愕,还有些别的东西。突然,哈利意识到自从他们在霍格沃茨操场的僻静角落里偷偷约会以后,

CHAPTER SIX   The Ghoul in Pyjamas

of the Hogwarts grounds. He was sure she was remembering them too. Both of them jumped as the door opened, and Mr Weasley, Kingsley and Bill walked in.

They were often joined by other Order members for dinner now, because The Burrow had replaced number twelve, Grimmauld Place as the Headquarters. Mr Weasley had explained that after the death of Dumbledore, their Secret Keeper, each of the people to whom Dumbledore had confided Grimmauld Place's location had become a Secret Keeper in turn.

'And as there are around twenty of us, that greatly dilutes the power of the Fidelius Charm. Twenty times as many opportunities for the Death Eaters to get the secret out of somebody. We can't expect it to hold much longer.'

'But surely Snape will have told the Death Eaters the address by now?' asked Harry.

'Well, Mad-Eye set up a couple of curses against Snape in case he turns up there again. We hope they'll be strong enough both to keep him out and to bind his tongue if he tries to talk about the place, but we can't be sure. It would have been insane to keep using the place as Headquarters now that its protection has become so shaky.'

The kitchen was so crowded that evening it was difficult to manoeuvre knives and forks. Harry found himself crammed beside Ginny; the unsaid things that had just passed between them made him wish they had been separated by a few more people. He was trying so hard to avoid brushing her arm he could barely cut his chicken.

'No news about Mad-Eye?' Harry asked Bill.

'Nothing,' replied Bill.

They had not been able to hold a funeral for Moody, because Bill and Lupin had failed to recover his body. It had been difficult to know where he might have fallen, given the darkness and the confusion of the battle.

'The *Daily Prophet* hasn't said a word about him dying, or about finding the body,' Bill went on. 'But that doesn't mean much. It's keeping a lot quiet these days.'

'And they still haven't called a hearing about all the under-age magic I used escaping the Death Eaters?' Harry called across the table to Mr Weasley, who shook his head. 'Because they know I had no choice or because they don't want me to tell the world Voldemort attacked me?'

第6章 穿睡衣的食尸鬼

这还是他第一次和她单独在一起。他可以肯定金妮也想起了那些时光。就在这时,门开了,韦斯莱先生、金斯莱和比尔走了进来,把他们俩吓了一跳。

现在,经常有凤凰社的其他成员来吃晚饭,因为陋居已经取代格里莫广场12号成了总部。韦斯莱先生解释说,自从保密人邓布利多死后,凡是邓布利多向其透露过格里莫广场位置的人,统统都变成了保密人。

"我们大概有二十个人,这就大大削弱了赤胆忠心咒的力量。食死徒就有二十倍的机会从某人嘴里套出秘密。所以我们不能指望这个秘密能保持多久。"

"可是斯内普肯定已经把地址告诉食死徒了呀?"哈利问。

"噢,疯眼汉给斯内普预备了几个魔咒,以防他再在那里露面。我们希望这些咒语很厉害,既能把斯内普挡在门外,又能捆住他的舌头,使他不能说起那个地方,但我们没有把握。现在那里的防范措施这么不稳定,再把它当成总部可就太不明智了。"

那天晚上,厨房里挤满了人,使用刀叉都很困难。哈利发现自己挤在金妮旁边。刚才两人之间欲言又止的话,使他希望能有几个人坐在中间把他们俩隔开。他特别当心不要碰到金妮的胳膊,简直都没法切鸡肉了。

"有疯眼汉的消息吗?"哈利问比尔。

"没有。"比尔回答。

他们没能为穆迪举行葬礼,因为比尔和卢平没有找到他的遗体。当时天很黑,双方一场混战,很难弄清他坠落到什么地方了。

"《预言家日报》只字没提他的死,也没提找到遗体,"比尔继续说,"不过这也说明不了什么。最近报纸对许多事情都保持沉默。"

"他们还没有因为我在逃脱食死徒时使用的那些未成年魔法传我受审吗?"哈利隔着桌子大声问韦斯莱先生,韦斯莱先生摇了摇头。"他们是知道我别无选择,还是不想让我告诉大家伏地魔袭击了我?"

CHAPTER SIX The Ghoul in Pyjamas

'The latter, I think. Scrimgeour doesn't want to admit that You-Know-Who is as powerful as he is, nor that Azkaban's seen a mass breakout.'

'Yeah, why tell the public the truth?' said Harry, clenching his knife so tightly that the faint scars on the back of his right hand stood out, white against his skin: *I must not tell lies.*

'Isn't anyone at the Ministry prepared to stand up to him?' asked Ron angrily.

'Of course, Ron, but people are terrified,' Mr Weasley replied, 'terrified that they will be next to disappear, their children the next to be attacked! There are nasty rumours going round; I, for one, don't believe the Muggle Studies professor at Hogwarts resigned. She hasn't been seen for weeks now. Meanwhile, Scrimgeour remains shut up in his office all day: I just hope he's working on a plan.'

There was a pause in which Mrs Weasley magicked the empty plates on to the side, and served apple tart.

'We must decide 'ow you will be disguised, 'Arry,' said Fleur, once everyone had pudding. 'For ze wedding,' she added, when he looked confused. 'Of course, none of our guests are Death Eaters, but we cannot guarantee zat zey will not let something slip after zey 'ave 'ad champagne.'

From this, Harry gathered that she still suspected Hagrid.

'Yes, good point,' said Mrs Weasley from the top of the table, where she sat, spectacles perched on the end of her nose, scanning an immense list of jobs that she had scribbled on a very long piece of parchment. 'Now, Ron, have you cleaned out your room yet?'

'*Why?*' exclaimed Ron, slamming his spoon down and glaring at his mother. 'Why does my room have to be cleaned out? Harry and I are fine with it the way it is!'

'We are holding your brother's wedding here in a few days' time, young man –'

'And are they getting married in my bedroom?' asked Ron furiously. 'No! So why in the name of Merlin's saggy left –'

'Don't talk to your mother like that,' said Mr Weasley firmly. 'And do as you're told.'

Ron scowled at both his parents, then picked up his spoon and attacked the last few mouthfuls of his apple tart.

第6章 穿睡衣的食尸鬼

"我认为是后一种。斯克林杰不愿意承认神秘人已经和他势均力敌，也不愿意承认阿兹卡班发生了集体越狱。"

"就是，何必对公众说实话呢？"哈利说，他紧紧攥住手里的餐刀，右手背上淡淡的伤痕在皮肤上白得那么显眼：我不可以说谎。

"魔法部就没有人准备抵抗他吗？"罗恩生气地说。

"当然有，罗恩，但是人们很害怕，"韦斯莱先生回答，"害怕自己成为下一个失踪者，害怕下一个遭到袭击的就是自己的孩子！可怕的谣言四处流传。比如，我就不相信霍格沃茨的麻瓜研究课教师是辞职了。她已经好几个星期不见踪影。这段时间，斯克林杰整天把自己关在办公室里，我真希望他在制订方案。"

一时间没有人说话，韦斯莱夫人用魔法把空盘子收到一边，然后端出了苹果馅饼。

"我们必须决定一下你化装成什么样儿，哈利，"芙蓉在大家都分到馅饼后说，"参加婚礼。"看到哈利一脸迷惑，她又说道，"当然啦，我们的客人里可没有食死徒，但不能保证他们喝了香槟酒之后不走漏消息啊。"

听了这话，哈利猜想她仍在怀疑海格。

"对，有道理。"韦斯莱夫人坐在桌首说，她的眼镜架在鼻子尖上，正在浏览她草草记在一张很长的羊皮纸上的一大堆工作，"我说，罗恩，你的屋子打扫了没有？"

"干吗？"罗恩叫了起来，重重地放下勺子，气呼呼地瞪着母亲，"我的屋子干吗要打扫？哈利和我在里面待得很舒服！"

"再过几天，我们这里就要举办你哥哥的婚礼了，年轻人——"

"难道他们是在我的卧室里结婚吗？"罗恩气愤地问道，"不是！那么看在梅林那老鬼——"

"不许对你妈妈这么说话。"韦斯莱先生不容置疑地说，"照她说的去做。"

罗恩气恼地瞪着父母，然后拿起勺子，朝他的最后几口苹果馅饼发起了进攻。

CHAPTER SIX   The Ghoul in Pyjamas

'I can help, some of it's my mess,' Harry told Ron, but Mrs Weasley cut across him.

'No, Harry, dear, I'd much rather you helped Arthur muck out the chickens, and Hermione, I'd be ever so grateful if you'd change the sheets for Monsieur and Madame Delacour, you know they're arriving at eleven tomorrow morning.'

But as it turned out, there was very little to do for the chickens.

'There's no need to, er, mention it to Molly,' Mr Weasley told Harry, blocking his access to the coop, 'but, er, Ted Tonks sent me most of what was left of Sirius's bike and, er, I'm hiding — that's to say, keeping — it in here. Fantastic stuff: there's an exhaust gaskin, as I believe it's called, the most magnificent battery, and it'll be a great opportunity to find out how brakes work. I'm going to try and put it all back together again when Molly's not — I mean, when I've got time.'

When they returned to the house, Mrs Weasley was nowhere to be seen, so Harry slipped upstairs to Ron's attic bedroom.

'I'm doing it, I'm doing —! Oh, it's you,' said Ron in relief, as Harry entered the room. Ron lay back down on the bed, which he had evidently just vacated. The room was just as messy as it had been all week; the only change was that Hermione was now sitting in the far corner, her fluffy ginger cat Crookshanks at her feet, sorting books, some of which Harry recognised as his own, into two enormous piles.

'Hi, Harry,' she said, as he sat down on his camp bed.

'And how did you manage to get away?'

'Oh, Ron's mum forgot that she asked Ginny and me to change the sheets yesterday,' said Hermione. She threw *Numerology and Grammatica* on to one pile and *The Rise and Fall of the Dark Arts* on to the other.

'We were just talking about Mad-Eye,' Ron told Harry. 'I reckon he might have survived.'

'But Bill saw him hit by the Killing Curse,' said Harry.

'Yeah, but Bill was under attack too,' said Ron. 'How can he be sure what he saw?'

'Even if the Killing Curse missed, Mad-Eye still fell about a thousand feet,' said Hermione, now weighing *Quidditch Teams of Britain and Ireland* in her hand.

第6章 穿睡衣的食尸鬼

"我可以帮忙,有些东西是我的。"哈利对罗恩说,可是韦斯莱夫人打断了他。

"不,哈利,亲爱的,我希望你去帮亚瑟打扫鸡棚;赫敏,劳驾你去给德拉库尔夫妇换一下床单,你知道他们明天上午十一点就到了。"

结果,鸡棚里并没有多少事情可做。

"你用不着,嗯,用不着告诉莫丽,"韦斯莱先生挡住正向鸡笼走去的哈利,说道,"就是,嗯,泰德·唐克斯把小天狼星那辆摩托车的大部分残骸给我送来了,嗯,我把它藏在——我是说收在这里了。这东西太奇妙了:有一个排气垫,我相信是叫这个名字,有威力无比的电瓶,而且给了我一个难得的机会弄清刹车是怎么工作的。趁莫丽不在——我是说趁我有时间,我要试着把它重新组装起来。"

他们回到家里,没有看见韦斯莱夫人,哈利就偷偷爬到阁楼上罗恩的房间里。

"我在打扫,在打扫呢——!噢,是你啊。"罗恩看见哈利走进房间,松了口气说。罗恩重新躺到床上,看样子他是刚从床上起来。房间里还和整个星期以来一样乱糟糟的。唯一的变化是赫敏坐在那边的墙角里,把图书分成了两大堆,其中有几本书哈利认出是他的。赫敏那只毛茸茸的姜黄色猫克鲁克山蹲在她的脚边。

"你好,哈利。"哈利在他的行军床上坐下时,赫敏说道。

"你是怎么溜号的?"

"噢,罗恩的妈妈忘记她昨天已经叫金妮和我换过床单了。"赫敏说,她把《数字占卜与图形》扔到一堆书上,《黑魔法的兴衰》扔到另一堆上。

"我们刚才在谈疯眼汉,"罗恩对哈利说,"我猜想他大概没有死。"

"可是比尔亲眼看见他中了杀戮咒。"哈利说。

"没错,但比尔当时也正遭到袭击,"罗恩说,"他怎么能肯定没有看错?"

"即使杀戮咒没有击中疯眼汉,他也从几百米的高处摔了下去啊。"赫敏说,她在掂量手里那本《不列颠和爱尔兰的魁地奇球队》。

CHAPTER SIX   The Ghoul in Pyjamas

'He could have used a Shield Charm –'

'Fleur said his wand was blasted out of his hand,' said Harry.

'Well, all right, if you want him to be dead,' said Ron grumpily, punching his pillow into a more comfortable shape.

'Of course we don't want him to be dead!' said Hermione, looking shocked. 'It's dreadful that he's dead! But we're being realistic!'

For the first time, Harry imagined Mad-Eye's body, broken as Dumbledore's had been, yet with that one eye still whizzing in its socket. He felt a stab of revulsion mixed with a bizarre desire to laugh.

'The Death Eaters probably tidied up after themselves, that's why no one's found him,' said Ron wisely.

'Yeah,' said Harry. 'Like Barty crouch, turned into a bone and buried in Hagrid's front garden. They probably Transfigured Moody and stuffed him –'

'Don't!' squealed Hermione. Startled, Harry looked over just in time to see her burst into tears over her copy of *Spellman's Syllabary*.

'Oh, no,' said Harry, struggling to get up from the old camp bed. 'Hermione, I wasn't trying to upset –'

But with a great creaking of rusty bedsprings Ron bounded off the bed and got there first. One arm around Hermione, he fished in his jeans pocket and withdrew a revolting-looking handkerchief that he had used to clean out the oven earlier. Hastily pulling out his wand, he pointed it at the rag and said, '*Tergeo*.'

The wand siphoned off most of the grease. Looking rather pleased with himself, Ron handed the slightly smoking handkerchief to Hermione.

'Oh … thanks, Ron … I'm sorry …' She blew her nose and hiccoughed. 'It's just so awf – ful, isn't it? R – right after Dumbledore … I j – just n – never imagined Mad-Eye dying, somehow, he seemed so tough!'

'Yeah, I know,' said Ron, giving her a squeeze. 'But you know what he'd say to us if he was here?'

'"C – Constant vigilance",' said Hermione, mopping her eyes.

'That's right,' said Ron, nodding. 'He'd tell us to learn from what happened to him. And what I've learned is not to trust that cowardly little

第6章 穿睡衣的食尸鬼

"他可以使用铁甲咒啊——"

"芙蓉说他的魔杖从手里炸飞了。"哈利说。

"好吧,好吧,既然你们偏要让他死。"罗恩没好气地说,一边把他的枕头拍成更舒服的形状。

"我们当然不希望他死!"赫敏一脸惊愕地说,"他的死太可怕了!但我们要面对现实!"

哈利第一次想象疯眼汉的遗体,它像邓布利多的遗体一样残缺不全,但那只眼睛仍然在眼窝里嗖嗖地转个不停。哈利感到一阵恶心,又有一种莫名其妙的想笑的感觉。

"食死徒们大概清理过战场了,所以谁也找不到他。"罗恩挺明智地说。

"是啊,"哈利说,"就像巴蒂·克劳奇,变成了一块骨头,埋在海格屋前的院子里。他们大概给穆迪变了形,把他塞在——"

"别说了!"赫敏尖叫起来。哈利惊讶地抬起眼,正好看见她对着她那本《魔法字音表》哭了起来。

"哦,不,"哈利说,一边挣扎着想从旧行军床上爬起来,"赫敏,我不想让你难过——"

但是随着生锈的弹簧床吱嘎吱嘎一阵乱响,罗恩从床上一跃而起,抢先赶了过去。他用胳膊搂住赫敏,从牛仔裤口袋里掏出一条看着脏兮兮的手帕,他先前曾用它擦过烤炉。他匆匆抽出魔杖,指着那块破布说了句:"旋风扫净。"

魔杖吸走了大部分油渍。罗恩似乎对自己很满意,把微微冒烟的手帕递给了赫敏。

"哦……谢谢,罗恩……真对不起……"赫敏擤擤鼻子,抽噎着说,"只是太——太可怕了,不是吗?邓——邓布利多刚死不久……我真——真想象不到疯眼汉会死,他看上去那么强大!"

"是啊,我知道,"罗恩搂了搂她,说道,"如果他在这儿,你知道他会对我们说什么吗?"

"'时——时刻保持警惕。'"赫敏擦着眼泪说。

"对,"罗恩点点头说,"他会告诉我们要从他的遭遇中吸取教训。

CHAPTER SIX   The Ghoul in Pyjamas

squit Mundungus.'

Hermione gave a shaky laugh and leaned forwards to pick up two more books. A second later, Ron had snatched his arm back from around her shoulders; she had dropped *The Monster Book of Monsters* on his foot. The book had broken free from its restraining belt and snapped viciously at Ron's ankle.

'I'm sorry, I'm sorry!' Hermione cried, as Harry wrenched the book from Ron's leg and retied it shut.

'What are you doing with all those books, anyway?' Ron asked, limping back to his bed.

'Just trying to decide which ones to take with us,' said Hermione. 'When we're looking for the Horcruxes.'

'Oh, of course,' said Ron, clapping a hand to his forehead. 'I forgot we'll be hunting down Voldemort in a mobile library.'

'Ha ha,' said Hermione, looking down at *Spellman's Syllabary*. 'I wonder ... will we need to translate runes? It's possible ... I think we'd better take it, to be safe.'

She dropped the syllabary on to the larger of the two piles and picked up *Hogwarts: A History*.

'Listen,' said Harry.

He had sat up straight. Ron and Hermione looked at him with similar mixtures of resignation and defiance.

'I know you said, after Dumbledore's funeral, that you wanted to come with me,' Harry began.

'Here he goes,' Ron said to Hermione, rolling his eyes.

'As we knew he would,' she sighed, turning back to the books. 'You know, I think I *will* take *Hogwarts: A History*. Even if we're not going back there, I don't think I'd feel right if I didn't have it with –'

'Listen!' said Harry again.

'No, Harry, *you* listen,' said Hermione. 'We're coming with you. That was decided months ago – years, really.'

'But –'

'Shut up,' Ron advised him.

'– are you sure you've thought this through?' Harry persisted.

'Let's see,' said Hermione, slamming *Travels with Trolls* on to the discarded

第6章 穿睡衣的食尸鬼

我得到的教训是，千万不要相信那个胆小如鼠的废物，蒙顿格斯。"

赫敏声音颤抖地笑了笑，又探身捡起两本书。一秒钟后，罗恩猛地从赫敏肩膀上抽回了胳膊；赫敏把《妖怪们的妖怪书》掉在他脚上了。书挣脱了捆住它的皮带，凶狠地咬着罗恩的脚脖子。

"对不起，对不起！"赫敏喊道，哈利赶紧把书从罗恩腿上拽过来，重新捆好。

"你倒腾这些书干什么呀？"罗恩一瘸一拐地走回他的床边，问道。

"决定一下我们出去找魂器时要带哪些书。"赫敏说。

"噢，对了，"罗恩用手一拍脑门说，"我忘了我们是在流动图书馆里追踪伏地魔呢。"

"哈哈，"赫敏低头看着《魔法字音表》说，"我拿不准了……我们会需要翻译如尼文吗？有可能……为了保险起见，还是带着它吧。"

她把字音表扔到那较大的一堆书上，又拿起《霍格沃茨：一段校史》。

"听我说。"哈利说。

他坐直了身子。罗恩和赫敏望着他，脸上的表情一模一样，既有无奈的顺从，又有些不以为然。

"我知道，邓布利多的葬礼之后，你们说过要跟我一起去。"哈利这么说道。

"他这就开始了。"罗恩翻着眼珠对赫敏说。

"早就知道他会这样，"赫敏叹了口气，转身面对着那些书，"你们知道，我想我还是带着《霍格沃茨：一段校史》吧。虽说我们不再回去上学了，但如果不带上它，我恐怕会觉得不适应——"

"听我说！"哈利又说。

"不，哈利，你听我说，"赫敏说，"我们要和你一起去。这是几个月前——确切地说是几年前就决定了的。"

"可是——"

"你就闭嘴吧。"罗恩打断了他的话。

"——你们真的仔细考虑过了？"哈利追问道。

"怎么说呢，"赫敏说着，一边狠狠地把《与巨怪同行》扔到那堆

CHAPTER SIX   The Ghoul in Pyjamas

pile with a rather fierce look. 'I've been packing for days, so we're ready to leave at a moment's notice, which for your information has included doing some pretty difficult magic, not to mention smuggling Mad-Eye's whole stock of Polyjuice Potion right under Ron's mum's nose.

'I've also modified my parents' memories so that they're convinced they're really called Wendell and Monica Wilkins, and that their life's ambition is to move to Australia, which they have now done. That's to make it more difficult for Voldemort to track them down and interrogate them about me – or you, because unfortunately, I've told them quite a bit about you.

'Assuming I survive our hunt for the Horcruxes, I'll find Mum and Dad and lift the enchantment. If I don't – well, I think I've cast a good enough charm to keep them safe and happy. Wendell and Monica Wilkins don't know that they've got a daughter, you see.'

Hermione's eyes were swimming with tears again. Ron got back off the bed, put his arm around her once more and frowned at Harry as though reproaching him for lack of tact. Harry could not think of anything to say, not least because it was highly unusual for Ron to be teaching anyone else tact.

'I – Hermione, I'm sorry – I didn't –'

'Didn't realise that Ron and I know perfectly well what might happen if we come with you? Well, we do. Ron, show Harry what you've done.'

'Nah, he's just eaten,' said Ron.

'Go on, he needs to know!'

'Oh, all right. Harry, come here.'

For the second time, Ron withdrew his arm from around Hermione and stumped over to the door.

'C'mon.'

'Why?' Harry asked, following Ron out of the room on to the tiny landing.

'*Descendo*,' muttered Ron, pointing his wand at the low ceiling. A hatch opened right over their heads and a ladder slid down to their feet. A horrible half-sucking, half-moaning sound came out of the square hole, along with an unpleasant smell like open drains.

'That's your ghoul, isn't it?' asked Harry, who had never actually met the creature that sometimes disrupted the nightly silence.

不要的书上,"这些天来我一直在收拾行李,随时准备说走就走。告诉你吧,为此我施了几个蛮有难度的魔法,更不用说在罗恩妈妈鼻子底下把疯眼汉储藏的那些复方汤剂都偷了出来。

"我还修改了我父母的记忆,让他们相信他们实际上名叫温德尔和莫尼卡·威尔金斯,平生最大的愿望是移居澳大利亚,现在他们已经去了。这样伏地魔就不太容易找到他们,向他们盘问我——或者你的下落,因为很不幸,我跟他们谈过不少你的情况。

"假如我们找到魂器之后我还活着,我就找到爸爸妈妈,给他们解除魔法。如果我不在了——唉,我想我已经给他们施了足够强大的魔法,保证他们一辈子平安、快乐。温德尔和莫尼卡·威尔金斯不知道他们曾经有个女儿,明白了吧。"

赫敏的眼睛里又盈满了泪水。罗恩赶紧从床上下来,再次用胳膊搂住赫敏,并朝哈利皱着眉头,似乎在责怪他不注意策略。哈利不知道该说什么,居然由罗恩来教别人注意策略,这简直太不真实了。

"我——赫敏,对不起——我没——"

"你没想到罗恩和我完全清楚跟着你会有什么结果?告诉你吧,我们清楚。罗恩,让哈利看看你干的事情。"

"别,他刚吃过饭。"罗恩说。

"快去,他需要知道!"

"噢,好吧。哈利,过来。"

罗恩第二次把胳膊从赫敏肩头抽回来,脚步笨重地朝门口走去。

"快来。"

"干吗?"哈利问,他跟着罗恩走出房门,来到小小的楼梯平台上。

"应声落地。"罗恩用魔杖指着低矮的天花板低声念道。一个活板门在他们头顶上打开了,一把梯子滑到他们脚下,方方的洞口里传来一种可怕的、半是吮吸半是呻吟的声音,还伴随着类似阴沟里散发的难闻气味。

"那是你们家的食尸鬼,对吗?"哈利问,他实际上从没碰见过这个有时在静夜里搅扰人们的家伙。

CHAPTER SIX   The Ghoul in Pyjamas

'Yeah, it is,' said Ron, climbing the ladder. 'Come and have a look at him.'

Harry followed Ron up the few short steps into the tiny attic space. His head and shoulders were in the room before he caught sight of the creature curled up a few feet from him, fast asleep in the gloom with its large mouth wide open.

'But it ... it looks ... Do ghouls normally wear pyjamas?'

'No,' said Ron. 'Nor have they usually got red hair or that number of pustules.'

Harry contemplated the thing, slightly revolted. It was human in shape and size, and was wearing what, now Harry's eyes became used to the darkness, was clearly an old pair of Ron's pyjamas. He was also sure that ghouls were generally rather slimy and bald, rather than distinctly hairy and covered in angry purple blisters.

'He's me, see?' said Ron.

'No,' said Harry. 'I don't.'

'I'll explain it back in my room, the smell's getting to me,' said Ron. They climbed back down the ladder, which Ron returned to the ceiling, and rejoined Hermione, who was still sorting books.

'Once we've left, the ghoul's going to come and live down here in my room,' said Ron. 'I think he's really looking forward to it – well, it's hard to tell, because all he can do is moan and drool – but he nods a lot when you mention it. Anyway, he's going to be me with spattergroit. Good, eh?'

Harry merely looked his confusion.

'It is!' said Ron, clearly frustrated that Harry had not grasped the brilliance of the plan. 'Look, when we three don't turn up at Hogwarts again, everyone's going to think Hermione and I must be with you, right? Which means the Death Eaters will go straight for our families to see if they've got information on where you are.'

'But hopefully it'll look like I've gone away with Mum and Dad; a lot of Muggle-borns are talking about going into hiding at the moment,' said Hermione.

'We can't hide my whole family, it'll look too fishy and they can't all leave their jobs,' said Ron. 'So we're going to put out the story that I'm seriously ill with spattergroit, which is why I can't go back to school. If anyone comes calling to investigate, Mum or Dad can show them the ghoul in my bed, covered in pustules. Spattergroit's really contagious, so they're not going to want to go near him. It won't matter that he can't say anything, either,

第6章 穿睡衣的食尸鬼

"对,没错,"罗恩一边说,一边顺着梯子往上爬,"来看看吧。"

哈利跟着罗恩爬了几级,把身子探进了狭小的阁楼里。他的脑袋和肩膀进入阁楼后,便看见那家伙蜷缩在离他几步远的地方,张着大嘴,正在阴影里呼呼大睡。

"可是……可是它的样子……食尸鬼一般都穿着睡衣吗?"

"不是,"罗恩说,"它们一般也不长着红头发和那么多脓疱。"

哈利注视着那个家伙,觉得有点儿恶心。它的形状、大小都和人类一样,现在哈利的眼睛已经适应了这里昏暗的光线,看清它身上穿的显然是罗恩的一套旧睡衣。而且,哈利相信食尸鬼一般都是黏糊糊的、没有毛发,绝不是这样头发浓密,身上布满红得发紫的水疱。

"它是我,明白吗?"罗恩说。

"不,"哈利说,"不明白。"

"我回屋再跟你解释,这气味真让我受不了。"罗恩说。他们顺着梯子下来,然后罗恩把梯子放回天花板上,他们回到仍在挑书的赫敏身边。

"我们一走,这个食尸鬼就下来住在我的房间里,"罗恩说,"我想它正巴不得呢——不容易确定,因为它只会哼哼、流口水——不过听到这个建议就不停点头。反正,它就是患了散花痘的我。怎么样,嗯?"

哈利只是一脸茫然。

"很棒啊!"罗恩说,显然对哈利没能理解这个绝妙的计划而感到失望,"你看,我们三个不再出现在霍格沃茨,每个人都会认为赫敏和我肯定跟你在一起,对吧?这就意味着食死徒会直接来找我们的家人,看他们是不是知道你的下落。"

"但愿他们会以为我和爸爸妈妈一起走了。目前许多麻瓜出身的人都在谈论避难呢。"赫敏说。

"我们全家不可能都藏起来,那样太可疑,而且他们不可能都不工作呀,"罗恩说,"所以我们要放出风去,说我患了严重的散花痘,不能回学校了。如果有人上门调查,爸爸或妈妈可以让他们看我床上满脸脓疱的食尸鬼。散花痘传染性很强,他们肯定不愿意靠近它。它不

because apparently you can't once the fungus has spread to your uvula.'

'And your mum and dad are in on this plan?' asked Harry.

'Dad is. He helped Fred and George transform the ghoul. Mum ... well, you've seen what she's like. She won't accept we're going 'til we've gone.'

There was silence in the room, broken only by gentle thuds, as Hermione continued to throw books on to one pile or the other. Ron sat watching her, and Harry looked from one to the other, unable to say anything. The measures they had taken to protect their families made him realise, more than anything else could have done, that they really were going to come with him and that they knew exactly how dangerous that would be. He wanted to tell them what that meant to him, but he simply could not find words important enough.

Through the silence came the muffled sounds of Mrs Weasley shouting from four floors below.

'Ginny's probably left a speck of dust on a poxy napkin ring,' said Ron. 'I dunno why the Delacours have got to come two days before the wedding.'

'Fleur's sister's a bridesmaid, she needs to be here for the rehearsal and she's too young to come on her own,' said Hermione, as she pored indecisively over *Break with a Banshee*.

'Well, guests aren't going to help Mum's stress levels,' said Ron.

'What we really need to decide,' said Hermione, tossing *Defensive Magical Theory* into the bin without a second glance and picking up *An Appraisal of Magical Education in Europe*, 'is where we're going after we leave here. I know you said you wanted to go to Godric's Hollow first, Harry, and I understand why, but ... well ... shouldn't we make the Horcruxes our priority?'

'If we knew where any of the Horcruxes were, I'd agree with you,' said Harry, who did not believe that Hermione really understood his desire to return to Godric's Hollow. His parents' graves were only part of the attraction: he had a strong, though inexplicable, feeling that the place held answers for him. Perhaps it was simply because it was there that he had survived Voldemort's Killing Curse; now that he was facing the challenge of repeating the feat, Harry was drawn to the place where it had happened, wanting to understand.

'Don't you think there's a possibility that Voldemort's keeping a watch on Godric's Hollow?' Hermione asked. 'He might expect you to go back and visit your parents' graves once you're free to go wherever you like?'

第6章 穿睡衣的食尸鬼

会说话也不要紧,因为真菌蔓延到了小舌头上,肯定说不出话来。"

"你爸爸妈妈知道这个计划吗?"哈利问。

"爸爸知道。他帮弗雷德和乔治给食尸鬼变了形。妈妈……唉,你见过她是什么样儿。不到我们走了,她是不会接受的。"

屋里一片沉默,只有赫敏把一本本书扔到这堆或那堆上,发出啪啪的轻响。罗恩坐在那里望着她,哈利轮番望着他们两个,什么话也说不出来。他们采取的这些保护家人的措施,使他格外强烈地意识到他们真的要和他一起去,而且他们清楚地知道将会有怎样的危险。他想告诉他们这对他意味着什么,但他就是想不出够分量的话来。

沉默中,隐隐传来四层楼以下韦斯莱夫人的喊叫声。

"大概金妮在一个该死的餐巾环上留了点灰尘。"罗恩说,"真不明白德拉库尔一家干吗要在婚礼前两天就来。"

"芙蓉的妹妹是伴娘,她需要来排演一下,可她年纪太小,自己一个人来不了。"赫敏说,一边对着《与女鬼决裂》拿不定主意。

"唉,客人来了也缓解不了妈妈的压力指数。"罗恩说。

"我们真正需要决定的,"赫敏说着,不假思索地把《魔法防御理论》扔进垃圾箱里,拿起《欧洲魔法教育评估》,"是我们离开这里之后到哪里去。哈利,我知道你说过你想先去戈德里克山谷,我也明白是为什么,可是……我是说……我们不是应该首先考虑魂器吗?"

"如果我们知道某个魂器的下落,我也会同意你的意见。"哈利说,他相信赫敏并不真的理解他想回戈德里克山谷的意愿。父母的坟墓对他的吸引只占一部分。他有一种虽然无法解释却很强烈的感觉,似乎那个地方有答案在等待着他。也许只是因为那里是他从伏地魔的杀戮咒下死里逃生的地方,现在他又面临挑战,需要重复这一壮举,哈利被那个地方吸引着,想去弄个究竟。

"你难道不认为伏地魔可能派人监视戈德里克山谷吗?"赫敏问,"他大概猜得到你一旦行动自由,首先就会去祭拜父母的坟墓,不是吗?"

CHAPTER SIX   The Ghoul in Pyjamas

This had not occurred to Harry. While he struggled to find a counter-argument, Ron spoke up, evidently following his own train of thought.

'This R.A.B. person,' he said. 'You know, the one who stole the real locket?'

Hermione nodded.

'He said in his note he was going to destroy it, didn't he?'

Harry dragged his rucksack towards him and pulled out the fake Horcrux in which R.A.B.'s note was still folded.

'"*I have stolen the real Horcrux and intend to destroy it as soon as I can*",' Harry read out.

'Well, what if he did finish it off?' said Ron.

'Or she,' interposed Hermione.

'Whichever,' said Ron, 'it'd be one less for us to do!'

'Yes, but we're still going to have to try and trace the real locket, aren't we?' said Hermione. 'To find out whether or not it's destroyed.'

'And once we get hold of it, how *do* you destroy a Horcrux?' asked Ron.

'Well,' said Hermione, 'I've been researching that.'

'How?' asked Harry. 'I didn't think there were any books on Horcruxes in the library?'

'There weren't,' said Hermione, who had turned pink. 'Dumbledore removed them all, but he – he didn't destroy them.'

Ron sat up straight, wide-eyed.

'How in the name of Merlin's pants have you managed to get your hands on those Horcrux books?'

'It – it wasn't stealing!' said Hermione, looking from Harry to Ron with a kind of desperation. 'They were still library books, even if Dumbledore had taken them off the shelves. Anyway, if he *really* didn't want anyone to get at them, I'm sure he would have made it much harder to –'

'Get to the point!' said Ron.

'Well ... it was easy,' said Hermione in a small voice. 'I just did a Summoning Charm. You know – *accio*. And – they zoomed out of Dumbledore's study window right into the girls' dormitory.'

'But when did you do this?' Harry asked, regarding Hermione with a mixture of admiration and incredulity.

第6章 穿睡衣的食尸鬼

这倒是哈利没想到的。他努力想找话反驳时，罗恩说话了，显然是循着自己的思路。

"这个叫R.A.B.的人，"他说，"知道吗，就是偷了真挂坠盒的那个人？"

赫敏点点头。

"他在字条里说要把它毁掉，对吗？"

哈利拉过背包，掏出那个假魂器，R.A.B.的那张字条仍然叠放在里面。

"我偷走了真正的魂器，并打算尽快销毁它。"哈利大声念道。

"是啊，如果他已经把它毁了呢？"罗恩说。

"说不定这人是个女的呢。"赫敏插嘴说。

"不管是谁，"罗恩说，"我们的任务都少了一个！"

"是啊，但我们还是要争取找到真正的挂坠盒，不是吗？"赫敏说，"弄清它是不是真的被毁掉了。"

"那么，如果我们弄到了一个魂器，怎么把它毁掉呢？"罗恩问。

"这个嘛，"赫敏说，"我一直在研究。"

"怎么研究？"哈利问，"我记得图书馆里好像没有关于魂器的书啊？"

"确实没有，"赫敏微微红了红脸，说道，"邓布利多把这些书都转移走了，但他——他并没有把它们销毁。"

罗恩腾地坐直身子，睁大了眼睛。

"看在梅林裤子的分儿上，你是怎么弄到那些魂器书的？"

"我——我没有偷！"赫敏说着，恳求般地看看哈利又看看罗恩，"它们还是图书馆的书，虽然邓布利多把它们从架子上拿走了。如果他真的不想让人得到它们，我相信他会设置更大的障碍——"

"说重点！"罗恩说。

"其实……其实挺简单的，"赫敏声音小小地说，"我只施了一个召唤咒。你们知道——就是飞来飞去。然后——它们就从邓布利多书房的窗户直接飞进了女生宿舍。"

"你是什么时候做这件事的？"哈利既钦佩又不敢相信地看着赫敏，问道。

CHAPTER SIX   The Ghoul in Pyjamas

'Just after his – Dumbledore's – funeral,' said Hermione, in an even smaller voice. 'Right after we agreed we'd leave school and go and look for the Horcruxes. When I went back upstairs to get my things, it – it just occurred to me that the more we knew about them, the better it would be ... and I was alone in there ... so I tried ... and it worked. They flew straight in through the open window and I – I packed them.'

She swallowed and then said imploringly, 'I can't believe Dumbledore would have been angry, it's not as though we're going to use the information to make a Horcrux, is it?'

'Can you hear us complaining?' said Ron. 'Where are these books, anyway?'

Hermione rummaged for a moment and then extracted from the pile a large volume, bound in faded, black leather. She looked a little nauseated and held it as gingerly as if it were something recently dead.

'This is the one that gives explicit instructions on how to make a Horcrux. *Secrets of the Darkest Art* – it's a horrible book, really awful, full of evil magic. I wonder when Dumbledore removed it from the library ... if he didn't do it until he was Headmaster, I bet Voldemort got all the instruction he needed from here.'

'Why did he have to ask Slughorn how to make a Horcrux, then, if he'd already read that?' asked Ron.

'He only approached Slughorn to find out what would happen if you split your soul into seven,' said Harry. 'Dumbledore was sure Riddle already knew how to make a Horcrux by the time he asked Slughorn about them. I think you're right, Hermione, that could easily have been where he got the information.'

'And the more I've read about them,' said Hermione, 'the more horrible they seem, and the less I can believe that he actually made six. It warns in this book how unstable you make the rest of your soul by ripping it, and that's just by making one Horcrux!'

Harry remembered what Dumbledore had said, about Voldemort moving beyond 'usual evil'.

'Isn't there any way of putting yourself back together?' Ron asked.

'Yes,' said Hermione, with a hollow smile, 'but it would be excruciatingly painful.'

'Why? How do you do it?' asked Harry.

第6章 穿睡衣的食尸鬼

"就在他——邓布利多——的葬礼后不久,"赫敏的声音更小了,"就在我们决定离开学校去找魂器之后。我上楼拿我的东西,我——我突然想到,我们对魂器了解得越多就越有利……当时宿舍里就我一个人……我试了试……没想到竟然成了。它们直接从敞开的窗口飞了进来,我——我就把它们收进了行李。"

她咽了口唾沫,又恳求地说:"我相信邓布利多不会生气的,我们又不是要利用这些知识去制造魂器,不是吗?"

"你听到我们怪你了吗?"罗恩说,"好啦好啦,那些书究竟在哪儿?"

赫敏翻找了一会儿,从那堆书里抽出一本褪色的黑皮面大部头。她露出厌恶的神情,小心翼翼地把书递过来,就好像那是某种刚刚死去的东西。

"这本书里详细讲述了如何制造魂器。《尖端黑魔法揭秘》——是一本很吓人的书,非常可怕,里面全是邪恶的魔法。我不知道邓布利多是什么时候把它从图书馆里拿走的……如果是在他当了校长之后,我敢说伏地魔已经从里面得到了他需要的所有知识。"

"如果他已经读过这本书,他为什么还要问斯拉格霍恩怎么制造魂器呢?"罗恩问。

"他接近斯拉格霍恩只是为了弄清把灵魂分裂成七份后会怎么样。"哈利说,"邓布利多相信,里德尔向斯拉格霍恩打听这些的时候已经知道怎么制造魂器。我想你是对的,赫敏,他很可能就是从这里得到的知识。"

"关于魂器的内容,"赫敏说,"我越读越觉得可怕,真不敢相信他居然弄了六个。这本书里警告说,分裂灵魂会使你的灵魂变得很不稳定,而那还只是制造一个魂器!"

哈利想起邓布利多曾经说过伏地魔已经超出了"一般邪恶"的范围。

"还有办法让自己重新变得完整吗?"罗恩问。

"有,"赫敏干巴巴地笑了笑说,"但那是极其痛苦的。"

"为什么?要怎么做呢?"哈利问。

CHAPTER SIX   The Ghoul in Pyjamas

'Remorse,' said Hermione. 'You've got to really feel what you've done. There's a footnote. Apparently the pain of it can destroy you. I can't see Voldemort attempting it, somehow, can you?'

'No,' said Ron, before Harry could answer. 'So does it say how to destroy Horcruxes in that book?'

'Yes,' said Hermione, now turning the fragile pages as if examining rotting entrails, 'because it warns Dark wizards how strong they have to make the enchantments on them. From all that I've read, what Harry did to Riddle's diary was one of the few really foolproof ways of destroying a Horcrux.'

'What, stabbing it with a Basilisk fang?' asked Harry.

'Oh, well, lucky we've got such a large supply of Basilisk fangs, then,' said Ron. 'I was wondering what we were going to do with them.'

'It doesn't have to be a Basilisk fang,' said Hermione patiently. 'It has to be something so destructive that the Horcrux can't repair itself. Basilisk venom only has one antidote, and it's incredibly rare –'

'– phoenix tears,' said Harry, nodding.

'Exactly,' said Hermione. 'Our problem is that there are very few substances as destructive as Basilisk venom, and they're all dangerous to carry around with you. That's a problem we're going to have to solve, though, because ripping, smashing or crushing a Horcrux won't do the trick. You've got to put it beyond magical repair.'

'But even if we wreck the thing it lives in,' said Ron, 'why can't the bit of soul in it just go and live in something else?'

'Because a Horcrux is the complete opposite of a human being.'

Seeing that Harry and Ron looked thoroughly confused, Hermione hurried on, 'Look, if I picked up a sword right now, Ron, and ran you through with it, I wouldn't damage your soul at all.'

'Which would be a real comfort to me, I'm sure,' said Ron.

Harry laughed.

'It should be, actually! But my point is that whatever happens to your body, your soul will survive, untouched,' said Hermione. 'But it's the other way round with a Horcrux. The fragment of soul inside it depends on its container, its enchanted body, for survival. It can't exist without it.'

第6章 穿睡衣的食尸鬼

"忏悔，"赫敏说，"必须真正感受你的所作所为。书里有个注解，显然这种痛苦就能把你摧毁。我看伏地魔并没有打算这么做，你们说呢？"

"对。"罗恩抢在哈利前面说，"那么书里有没有说怎么毁掉魂器呢？"

"说了。"赫敏一边说，一边翻动松脆的书页，就像在检查腐烂的内脏似的，"因为书里提醒了黑巫师，他们必须让魂器上的魔咒多么强大才行。从我读到的内容看，哈利对付里德尔那本日记的做法，就是少数几种绝对可靠的摧毁魂器的方式。"

"什么，用蛇怪的毒牙刺它？"哈利问。

"嘀，好啊，幸亏我们有这么多蛇怪的毒牙，"罗恩说，"我还发愁拿它们怎么办呢。"

"并不一定是蛇怪的毒牙，"赫敏耐心地说，"必须是破坏力极强的东西，使魂器再也不能修复。蛇怪的毒牙只有一种解药，是极为稀罕的——"

"——凤凰的眼泪。"哈利点着头说。

"对极了。"赫敏说，"我们的问题是，像蛇怪毒牙那样破坏性极强的东西很少，而且带在身边十分危险。这个问题必须解决，因为把魂器撕碎、砸烂、碾成粉末都不管用。你必须使它再也无法用魔法修复。"

"可是，就算我们毁掉了它寄居的东西，"罗恩说，"它里面的灵魂碎片就不能跑出来住到别的东西里吗？"

"因为魂器和人的灵魂正好相反。"

看到哈利和罗恩脸上不解的神情，赫敏急忙继续说道："比如，罗恩，我现在拿起一把宝剑，刺穿你的身体，你的灵魂还是安然无恙。"

"那可真是不幸中的万幸。"罗恩说。

哈利笑了起来。

"确实，应该是！但我想说的是，不管你的身体发生了什么事，你的灵魂都会毫无损伤地继续活着。"赫敏说，"但是魂器正好相反。它里面的灵魂碎片之所以存活，完全依赖于它的容器，依赖于它那施了魔法的载体，不然它就无法生存。"

CHAPTER SIX The Ghoul in Pyjamas

'That diary sort of died when I stabbed it,' said Harry, remembering ink pouring like blood from the punctured pages, and the screams of the piece of Voldemort's soul as it vanished.

'And once the diary was properly destroyed, the bit of soul trapped in it could no longer exist. Ginny tried to get rid of the diary before you did, flushing it away, but, obviously, it came back good as new.'

'Hang on,' said Ron, frowning. 'The bit of soul in that diary was possessing Ginny, wasn't it? How does that work, then?'

'While the magical container is still intact, the bit of soul inside it can flit in and out of someone if they get too close to the object. I don't mean holding it for too long, it's nothing to do with touching it,' she added, before Ron could speak. 'I mean close emotionally. Ginny poured her heart out into that diary, she made herself incredibly vulnerable. You're in trouble if you get too fond of or dependent on the Horcrux.'

'I wonder how Dumbledore destroyed the ring?' said Harry. 'Why didn't I ask him? I never really ...'

His voice tailed away: he was thinking of all the things he should have asked Dumbledore, and of how, since the Headmaster had died, it seemed to Harry that he had wasted so many opportunities, when Dumbledore had been alive, to find out more ... to find out everything ...

The silence was shattered as the bedroom door flew open with a wall-shaking crash. Hermione shrieked and dropped *Secrets of the Darkest Art*; Crookshanks streaked under the bed, hissing indignantly; Ron jumped off the bed, skidded on a discarded Chocolate Frog wrapper and smacked his head on the opposite wall, and Harry instinctively dived for his wand before realising that he was looking up at Mrs Weasley, whose hair was dishevelled and whose face was contorted with rage.

'I'm so sorry to break up this cosy little gathering,' she said, her voice trembling. 'I'm sure you all need your rest ... but there are wedding presents stacked in my room that need sorting out and I was under the impression that you had agreed to help.'

'Oh, yes,' said Hermione, looking terrified as she leapt to her feet, sending books flying in every direction, 'we will ... we're sorry ...'

With an anguished look at Harry and Ron, Hermione hurried out of the room after Mrs Weasley.

第6章 穿睡衣的食尸鬼

"我刺中那本日记,它好像就死去了。"哈利想起墨水像鲜血一样从被刺穿的书页里喷出来,还有伏地魔的灵魂碎片消失时的尖叫。

"日记一旦被彻底毁掉,关在里面的灵魂碎片也就不能继续存活。在你之前,金妮也试过摆脱这本日记,把它扔在马桶里冲掉,但显然它又完好无损地回来了。"

"且慢,"罗恩皱着眉头说,"那本日记里的灵魂碎片把金妮控制住了,对吗?那又是怎么回事呢?"

"只要魔法容器完好,它里面的灵魂碎片就能在接近容器的某个人的体内飞进飞出。我指的不是把它拿在手里很长时间,这跟身体接触没有关系,"她不等罗恩开口就继续说道,"我指的是感情上的接近。金妮把她的情感全部倾注于那本日记,就使自己变得非常容易受到支配。如果你过于喜欢或依赖魂器,就有麻烦了。"

"真不知道邓布利多是怎么毁掉那枚戒指的,"哈利说,"我为什么没有问问他呢?我从来没有真正……"

他的声音低了下去。他想起了有那么多事情应该问邓布利多,想起了自从校长死后,他觉得自己在邓布利多活着时浪费了那么多机会,没有弄清更多的事情……弄清一切……

沉默突然被打得粉碎,卧室的门被猛地撞开,震得墙壁发抖。赫敏尖叫一声,《尖端黑魔法揭秘》掉在地上。克鲁克山噼溜蹿到床底下,气咻咻地嘶嘶叫着。罗恩从床上猛跳起来,脚踩在一张巧克力蛙糖纸上一滑,脑袋重重地撞在对面墙上。哈利本能地去拔魔杖,随即发现站在他面前的是韦斯莱夫人,她头发凌乱,脸都气歪了。

"真抱歉,打搅了这场亲密的小聚会。"她声音发抖地说,"我相信你们都需要休息……可是我房间里堆着婚礼用的礼品需要分类,我好像记得你们答应要来帮忙的。"

"噢,是的,"赫敏惊慌失措地一下子站起来,书散落得到处都是,"我们会的……真对不起……"

赫敏痛苦地看了一眼哈利和罗恩,跟着韦斯莱夫人匆匆离开了房间。

CHAPTER SIX   The Ghoul in Pyjamas

'It's like being a house-elf,' complained Ron in an undertone, still massaging his head as he and Harry followed. 'Except without the job-satisfaction. The sooner this wedding's over, the happier I'll be.'

'Yeah,' said Harry, 'then we'll have nothing to do except find Horcruxes ... it'll be like a holiday, won't it?'

Ron started to laugh, but at the sight of the enormous pile of wedding presents waiting for them in Mrs Weasley's room, stopped quite abruptly.

The Delacours arrived the following morning at eleven o'clock. Harry, Ron, Hermione and Ginny were feeling quite resentful towards Fleur's family by this time, and it was with an ill grace that Ron stumped back upstairs to put on matching socks, and Harry attempted to flatten his hair. Once they had all been deemed smart enough, they trooped out into the sunny backyard to await the visitors.

Harry had never seen the place looking so tidy. The rusty cauldrons and old wellington boots that usually littered the steps by the back door were gone, replaced by two new Flutterby Bushes standing either side of the door in large pots; though there was no breeze, the leaves waved lazily, giving an attractive rippling effect. The chickens had been shut away, the yard had been swept and the nearby garden had been pruned, plucked and generally spruced up, although Harry, who liked it in its overgrown state, thought that it looked rather forlorn without its usual contingent of capering gnomes.

He had lost track of how many security enchantments had been placed upon The Burrow by both the Order and the Ministry; all he knew was that it was no longer possible for anybody to travel by magic directly into the place. Mr Weasley had therefore gone to meet the Delacours on top of a nearby hill, where they were to arrive by Portkey. The first sound of their approach was an unusually high-pitched laugh, which turned out to be coming from Mr Weasley, who appeared at the gate moments later, laden with luggage and leading a beautiful, blonde woman in long, leaf-green robes, who could only be Fleur's mother.

'*Maman!*' cried Fleur, rushing forwards to embrace her. '*Papa!*'

Monsieur Delacour was nowhere near as attractive as his wife; he was a head shorter and extremely plump, with a little, pointed, black beard. However, he looked good-natured. Bouncing towards Mrs Weasley on high-heeled boots, he kissed her twice on each cheek, leaving her flustered.

第6章 穿睡衣的食尸鬼

"简直像个家养小精灵了，"罗恩压低声音说，一边揉着脑袋，和哈利一起跟了出去，"只是没有工作成就感。我真巴不得这场婚礼赶快结束。"

"是啊，"哈利说，"然后我们就什么也不用做，专门去找魂器了……听着简直像过节一样呢，是不是？"

罗恩刚想大笑，突然看见在韦斯莱夫人的房间里，等着他们分类的结婚礼品堆积如山，他立刻不笑了。

第二天上午十一点，德拉库尔一家三口来了。到这时候，哈利、罗恩、赫敏和金妮对芙蓉的家人已经是一肚子怨气了。罗恩满不情愿地嘟嘟囔囔走上楼去穿上配对的袜子，哈利很不乐意地试图把头发压平。好了，终于认为打扮得够体面了，他们排着队来到阳光照耀的院子里，迎候客人。

哈利从没见过院子显得这么整洁。平常散落在后门台阶上的锈坩埚和旧雨靴都不见了，取而代之的是两株新栽在大盆里的振翅灌木，门的两边各放一盆。虽然没有风，但叶子懒洋洋地舞动着，形成一种迷人的、微波涟漪的效果。鸡都关起来了，院子也清扫过了，近旁的花园都修剪装扮一新。其实哈利还是喜欢它蓬勃疯长的状态，觉得少了平常那些跳来跳去的地精，显得怪冷清的。

他已经弄不清凤凰社和魔法部究竟给陋居施了多少安全魔咒，只知道任何人都不可能再凭借魔法直接来到这里。所以，韦斯莱先生到附近一座山顶上去迎接通过门钥匙到达那里的德拉库尔一家。客人到来时，人们首先听到的是一声尖得反常的大笑，原来却是韦斯莱先生发出来的。片刻之后他出现在门口，提着沉重的行李，领着一位穿着叶绿色长袍的美丽的金发女人，她无疑便是芙蓉的母亲。

"妈妈！"芙蓉大喊一声，冲过去拥抱她，"爸爸！"

德拉库尔先生远不及妻子那么迷人。他比妻子矮一头，胖墩墩的，留着尖尖的小黑胡子。不过，看上去他脾气倒是很好。他踩着高跟靴子快步走到韦斯莱夫人跟前，在她两边腮帮子上各吻了两下，韦斯莱夫人受宠若惊。

CHAPTER SIX The Ghoul in Pyjamas

'You 'ave been to much trouble,' he said in a deep voice. 'Fleur tells us you 'ave been working very 'ard.'

'Oh, it's been nothing, nothing!' trilled Mrs Weasley. 'No trouble at all!'

Ron relieved his feelings by aiming a kick at a gnome who was peering out from behind one of the new Flutterby Bushes.

'Dear lady!' said Monsieur Delacour, still holding Mrs Weasley's hand between his own two plump ones and beaming. 'We are most honoured at the approaching union of our two families! Let me present my wife, Apolline.'

Madame Delacour glided forwards and stooped to kiss Mrs Weasley too.

'*Enchantée*,' she said. 'Your 'usband 'as been telling us such amusing stories!'

Mr Weasley gave a maniacal laugh; Mrs Weasley threw him a look, upon which he became immediately silent and assumed an expression appropriate to the sickbed of a close friend.

'And, of course, you 'ave met my leetle daughter, Gabrielle!' said Monsieur Delacour. Gabrielle was Fleur in miniature; eleven years old, with waist-length hair of pure, silvery blonde, she gave Mrs Weasley a dazzling smile and hugged her, then threw Harry a glowing look, batting her eyelashes. Ginny cleared her throat loudly.

'Well, come in, do!' said Mrs Weasley brightly, and she ushered the Delacours into the house, with many 'No, please!'s and 'After you!'s and 'Not at all!'s.

The Delacours, it soon transpired, were helpful, pleasant guests. They were pleased with everything and keen to assist with the preparations for the wedding. Monsieur Delacour pronounced everything from the seating plan to the bridesmaids' shoes '*charmant!*' Madame Delacour was most accomplished at household spells and had the oven properly cleaned in a trice; Gabrielle followed her elder sister around, trying to assist in any way she could and jabbering away in rapid French.

On the downside, The Burrow was not built to accommodate so many people. Mr and Mrs Weasley were now sleeping in the sitting room, having shouted down Monsieur and Madame Delacour's protests and insisted they take their bedroom. Gabrielle was sleeping with Fleur in Percy's old room and Bill would be sharing with Charlie, his best man, once Charlie arrived from Romania. Opportunities to make plans together became virtually non-

第6章 穿睡衣的食尸鬼

"真是太麻烦你们了,"他用低沉的声音说,"芙蓉告诉我们,你们一直在辛苦忙碌。"

"哦,那没什么,没什么!"韦斯莱夫人声音颤颤地说,"一点儿也不麻烦!"

罗恩为了解恨,对准一个在一盆新栽的振翅灌木后面探头探脑的地精踢了一脚。

"亲爱的夫人!"德拉库尔先生说,他满脸带笑,两只胖乎乎的手仍然握着韦斯莱夫人的手,"对于我们两家即将联姻,我们感到万分荣幸!请允许我介绍一下我的妻子,阿波琳。"

德拉库尔夫人脚步轻盈地走上去,也俯身亲吻了韦斯莱夫人。

"您好,"她说,"您丈夫给我们讲的故事真有趣!"

韦斯莱先生发出神经质的笑声,韦斯莱夫人朝他横了一眼,他立刻不吭声了,脸上露出像是坐在好友病床边的表情。

"不用说,你们已经见过我的小女儿加布丽了!"德拉库尔先生说。加布丽是芙蓉的小型翻版,十一岁,一头齐腰的纯银色长发,她朝韦斯莱夫人露出一个灿烂的笑容,拥抱了她一下,然后用放电的眼睛看着哈利,眼睫毛扑闪扑闪。金妮大声清了清嗓子。

"好了,进来吧!"韦斯莱夫人愉快地说,把德拉库尔一家让进房间,嘴里不停地说着"不,您请!""您在前!"和"没有什么!"

大家很快发现,德拉库尔一家是令人愉快的客人,非常乐于助人。他们对一切都很满意,而且积极帮忙筹备婚礼。从座次安排,到伴娘的鞋子,德拉库尔先生一概表示"太可爱了!"德拉库尔夫人在家务咒语方面真是一把好手,一眨眼工夫就把烤炉擦得干干净净。加布丽像小尾巴一样跟着姐姐,一边尽力帮点儿忙,一边用法语叽叽喳喳地说个不停。

美中不足的是,陋居的结构容纳不了这么多人。韦斯莱夫妇用大声嚷嚷压倒德拉库尔夫妇的反对,坚持让客人睡在他们的卧室,他们自己则睡客厅。加布丽和芙蓉一起睡在珀西以前的房间里,伴郎查理从罗马尼亚回来后,将和比尔合住一屋。这样一来,哈利、罗恩和赫

CHAPTER SIX The Ghoul in Pyjamas

existent, and it was in desperation that Harry, Ron and Hermione took to volunteering to feed the chickens just to escape the overcrowded house.

'But she *still* won't leave us alone!' snarled Ron, as their second attempt at a meeting in the yard was foiled by the appearance of Mrs Weasley carrying a large basket of laundry in her arms.

'Oh, good, you've fed the chickens,' she called as she approached them. 'We'd better shut them away again before the men arrive tomorrow ... to put up the tent for the wedding,' she explained, pausing to lean against the hen house. She looked exhausted. 'Millamant's Magic Marquees ... they're very good. Bill's escorting them ... you'd better stay inside while they're here, Harry. I must say it does complicate organising a wedding, having all these security spells around the place.'

'I'm sorry,' said Harry humbly.

'Oh, don't be silly, dear!' said Mrs Weasley at once. 'I didn't mean – well, your safety's much more important! Actually, I've been wanting to ask you how you want to celebrate your birthday, Harry. Seventeen, after all, it's an important day ...'

'I don't want a fuss,' said Harry quickly, envisaging the additional strain this would put on them all. 'Really, Mrs Weasley, just a normal dinner would be fine ... it's the day before the wedding ...'

'Oh, well, if you're sure, dear. I'll invite Remus and Tonks, shall I? And how about Hagrid?'

'That'd be great,' said Harry. 'But please don't go to loads of trouble.'

'Not at all, not at all ... it's no trouble ...'

She looked at him, a long, searching look, then smiled a little sadly, straightened up and walked away. Harry watched as she waved her wand near the washing line, and the damp clothes rose into the air to hang themselves up, and suddenly he felt a great wave of remorse for the inconvenience and the pain he was giving her.

第6章 穿睡衣的食尸鬼

敏根本就不可能凑在一起商量计划了。情急之下，他们为了避开过分拥挤的房子，主动跑去喂鸡。

"她还是不让我们单独待着！"罗恩咆哮道，刚才他们第二次想在院子里碰头，韦斯莱夫人提着一大篮洗好的衣服出现了，挫败了他们的计划。

"噢，很好，你们喂了鸡，"她走过来大声说，"我们最好把鸡再关起来，明天有人要来……为婚礼搭帐篷。"她停下来靠在鸡棚上解释说，神情显得很疲惫，"米拉芒的魔法帐篷……美妙极了，比尔陪他们一起过来……哈利，他们在这里的时候，你最好待在屋里。唉，周围弄了这么多安全魔咒，办一场婚礼变得真复杂啊。"

"对不起。"哈利过意不去地说。

"哦，别说傻话，亲爱的！"韦斯莱夫人立刻说道，"我不是那个意思——唉，你的安全才是顶顶重要的！对了，我一直想问你希望怎么庆祝你的生日，哈利。十七岁啊，这毕竟是个重要的日子……"

"我不想兴师动众，"哈利设想这事会给他们增加压力，赶紧说道，"真的，韦斯莱夫人，一顿平平常常的晚餐就行了……就在婚礼的前一天……"

"哦，好吧，亲爱的，如果你真这样想。我邀请莱姆斯和唐克斯，好吗？海格呢？"

"那太棒了，"哈利说，"可是千万别太麻烦了。"

"没有，没有……一点儿也不麻烦……"

她用探究的目光久久地望着哈利，然后有点凄楚地笑笑，直起身子走开了。哈利注视着她在晾衣绳旁挥舞魔杖，那些湿衣服自动飞到空中挂了起来。他突然感到一阵强烈的悔恨，他给韦斯莱夫人带来的麻烦和痛苦太多了。

CHAPTER SEVEN

The Will of Albus Dumbledore

He was walking along a mountain road in the cool, blue light of dawn. Far below, swathed in mist, was the shadow of a small town. Was the man he sought down there? The man he needed so badly he could think of little else, the man who held the answer, the answer to his problem ...

'Oi, wake up.'

Harry opened his eyes. He was lying again on the camp bed in Ron's dingy attic room. The sun had not yet risen and the room was still shadowy. Pigwidgeon was asleep with his head under his tiny wing. The scar on Harry's forehead was prickling.

'You were muttering in your sleep.'

'Was I?'

'Yeah. "Gregorovitch." You kept saying "Gregorovitch".'

Harry was not wearing his glasses; Ron's face appeared slightly blurred.

'Who's Gregorovitch?'

'I dunno, do I? You were the one saying it.'

Harry rubbed his forehead, thinking. He had a vague idea he had heard the name before, but he could not think where.

'I think Voldemort's looking for him.'

'Poor bloke,' said Ron fervently.

Harry sat up, still rubbing his scar, now wide awake. He tried to remember exactly what he had seen in the dream, but all that came back was a mountainous horizon and the outline of the little village cradled in a deep valley.

第7章

阿不思·邓布利多的遗嘱

拂晓时空气凉爽，晨光熹微，哈利走在一条山路上。下面裹在浓雾里的是一座朦朦胧胧的小镇。他寻找的那个人在下面吗？他迫切地、不顾一切地需要那个人，那个人知道答案，知道他那个问题的答案……

"喂，醒醒。"

哈利睁开眼睛。他还是躺在罗恩昏暗脏乱的阁楼间的行军床上。太阳还没有升起，屋里仍然很暗。小猪把脑袋埋在小翅膀底下睡得正香。哈利额头上的伤疤一刺一刺地疼。

"你说梦话了。"

"是吗？"

"是啊。'格里戈维奇。'你一直在说'格里戈维奇'。"

哈利没戴眼镜，罗恩的脸看上去模糊不清。

"谁是格里戈维奇？"

"我怎么知道？说梦话的是你啊。"

哈利揉着额头，陷入了沉思。他隐约觉得以前听过这个名字，但想不起来是在什么地方。

"我想伏地魔是在找他。"

"可怜的家伙。"罗恩激动地说。

哈利坐起身子，仍然揉着伤疤，现在完全清醒了。他努力回忆刚才梦中见到的情景，却只能想起一片连绵的群山和位于深深峡谷里的小村庄的轮廓。

CHAPTER SEVEN   The Will of Albus Dumbledore

'I think he's abroad.'

'Who, Gregorovitch?'

'Voldemort. I think he's somewhere abroad, looking for Gregorovitch. It didn't look like anywhere in Britain.'

'You reckon you were seeing into his mind again?'

Ron sounded worried.

'Do me a favour and don't tell Hermione,' said Harry. 'Although how she expects me to stop seeing stuff in my sleep ...'

He gazed up at little Pigwidgeon's cage, thinking ... why was the name 'Gregorovitch' familiar?

'I think,' he said slowly, 'he's got something to do with Quidditch. There's some connection, but I can't – I can't think what it is.'

'Quidditch?' said Ron. 'Sure you're not thinking of Gorgovitch?'

'Who?'

'Dragomir Gorgovitch, Chaser, transferred to the Chudley Cannons for a record fee two years ago. Record-holder for most Quaffle drops in a season.'

'No,' said Harry. 'I'm definitely not thinking of Gorgovitch.'

'I try not to, either,' said Ron. 'Well, happy birthday, anyway.'

'Wow – that's right, I forgot! I'm seventeen!'

Harry seized the wand lying beside his camp bed, pointed it at the cluttered desk where he had left his glasses and said, '*Accio glasses!*' Although they were only around a foot away, there was something immensely satisfying about seeing them zoom towards him, at least until they poked him in the eye.

'Slick,' snorted Ron.

Revelling in the removal of his Trace, Harry sent Ron's possessions flying around the room, causing Pigwidgeon to wake up and flutter excitedly around his cage. Harry also tried tying the laces of his trainers by magic (the resultant knot took several minutes to untie by hand) and, purely for the pleasure of it, turned the orange robes on Ron's Chudley Cannons posters bright blue.

'I'd do your flies by hand, though,' Ron advised Harry, sniggering when

第7章 阿不思·邓布利多的遗嘱

"我想他是在国外。"

"谁?格里戈维奇?"

"伏地魔。我想他是在国外某个地方寻找格里戈维奇。看样子不像是在英国。"

"你认为你又在窥探他的思想?"

罗恩的声音里透着担忧。

"行行好,别告诉赫敏,"哈利说,"她那么希望我别在梦里再看到那些东西……"

他抬头望着小猪的笼子,继续思索……为什么"格里戈维奇"这个名字听着耳熟呢?

"我想,"他慢悠悠地说,"他大概跟魁地奇有关。这中间有某种联系,但我——我想不起来是什么了。"

"魁地奇?"罗恩问,"你该不会是想到高尔格维奇了吧?"

"谁?"

"德拉戈米尔·高尔格维奇,追球手,两年前转到查德里火炮队,转会费破了纪录。他保持了单赛季里投鬼飞球最多的纪录。"

"不是,"哈利说,"我想的肯定不是高尔格维奇。"

"我也尽量不想他。"罗恩说,"好了,祝你生日快乐吧。"

"哇——对了,我怎么忘了!我十七岁了!"

哈利抓起行军床旁边的魔杖,指着他放眼镜的乱糟糟的书桌,说了声:"眼镜飞来!"虽然眼镜离他只有一尺来远,但看着它嗖地朝他飞来,还是给他带来了巨大的满足。不过好景不长:眼镜飞过来戳了他的眼睛。

"真不赖。"罗恩哼了一声。

哈利陶醉在踪丝消失的喜悦中,他让罗恩的东西在房间里到处乱飞,让小猪醒来在笼子里兴奋地扑扇翅膀。哈利还试着用魔法给运动鞋系鞋带(结果用手花了好几分钟才把那个疙瘩解开),然后,纯粹是为了取乐,他把罗恩那些查德里火炮队海报上的橘黄色队服变成了鲜蓝色。

"我要空手对付你的裤子拉链。"罗恩警告哈利,哈利赶紧查看,

CHAPTER SEVEN The Will of Albus Dumbledore

Harry immediately checked them. 'Here's your present. Unwrap it up here, it's not for my mother's eyes.'

'A book?' said Harry, as he took the rectangular parcel. 'Bit of a departure from tradition, isn't it?'

'This isn't your average book,' said Ron. 'It's pure gold: *Twelve Fail-Safe Ways to Charm Witches*. Explains everything you need to know about girls. If only I'd had this last year, I'd have known exactly how to get rid of Lavender and I would've known how to get going with ... well, Fred and George gave me a copy, and I've learned a lot. You'd be surprised, it's not all about wandwork, either.'

When they arrived in the kitchen, they found a pile of presents waiting on the table. Bill and Monsieur Delacour were finishing their breakfast, while Mrs Weasley stood chatting to them over the frying pan.

'Arthur told me to wish you a happy seventeenth, Harry,' said Mrs Weasley, beaming at him. 'He had to leave early for work, but he'll be back for dinner. That's our present on top.'

Harry sat down, took the square parcel she had indicated and unwrapped it. Inside was a watch very like the one Mr and Mrs Weasley had given Ron for his seventeenth; it was gold, with stars circling round the face instead of hands.

'It's traditional to give a wizard a watch when he comes of age,' said Mrs Weasley, watching him anxiously from beside the cooker. 'I'm afraid that one isn't new like Ron's, it was actually my brother Fabian's and he wasn't terribly careful with his possessions, it's a bit dented on the back, but –'

The rest of her speech was lost; Harry had got up and hugged her. He tried to put a lot of unsaid things into the hug and perhaps she understood them, because she patted his cheek clumsily when he released her, then waved her wand in a slightly random way, causing half a pack of bacon to flop out of the frying pan on to the floor.

'Happy birthday, Harry!' said Hermione, hurrying into the kitchen and adding her own present to the top of the pile. 'It's not much, but I hope you like it. What did you get him?' she added to Ron, who seemed not to hear her.

'Come on, then, open Hermione's!' said Ron.

第 7 章 阿不思·邓布利多的遗嘱

罗恩在一旁咯咯笑出了声,"这是给你的礼物,就在这儿拆吧。可不能给我妈妈看见。"

"一本书?"哈利接过那个长方形的包裹,说道,"有点告别传统了,是不是?"

"这可不是一般的书,"罗恩说,"是沉甸甸的金子啊:《迷倒女巫的十二个制胜法宝》,解释了你需要知道的关于女孩子的所有事情。我去年要是有这本书就好了,我就会知道怎么甩掉拉文德,也会知道怎么接近……咳,弗雷德和乔治给了我一本,我弄懂了许多东西。你会大吃一惊的,而且并不都需要使用魔杖。"

他们来到厨房,发现桌上有一大堆礼物在等哈利。比尔和德拉库尔先生快吃完早饭了,韦斯莱夫人站在煎锅前跟他们聊天。

"哈利,亚瑟叫我祝你十七岁生日快乐。"韦斯莱夫人笑眯眯地看着他说,"他必须早早地去上班,但会赶回来吃晚饭的。我们的礼物在最顶上。"

哈利坐下来,拿起韦斯莱夫人指的那个方形包裹,拆了开来。里面是一块手表,跟罗恩十七岁时韦斯莱夫妇送给他的那块很像。质地是金的,表盘上没有指针,只有几颗星星在跑动。

"巫师成年时送他一块手表,这是一种传统。"韦斯莱夫人说着,在厨灶旁不安地注视着哈利,"这块手表恐怕不如罗恩的那块那么新,实际上它以前是我哥哥费比安的,他用东西不太仔细,表的背面有点不平了,但——"

她的话没说完,哈利已经站起来紧紧搂住了她。哈利想把许多没有说出口的意思都倾注在这个拥抱里,韦斯莱夫人大概理解了。哈利松开她时,她不自然地拍拍哈利的面颊,然后有点杂乱无章地挥舞她的魔杖,弄得一半熏咸肉都从煎锅里跳出来,掉在地板上。

"生日快乐,哈利!"赫敏匆匆走进厨房说道,把她的一份礼物放在那堆礼物的最上面,"不是很贵重,但愿你会喜欢。你给他准备了什么?"她又问罗恩,罗恩假装没有听见。

"来吧,快打开赫敏的!"罗恩说。

CHAPTER SEVEN The Will of Albus Dumbledore

She had bought him a new Sneakoscope. The other packages contained an enchanted razor from Bill and Fleur ('Ah yes, zis will give you ze smoothest shave you will ever 'ave,' Monsieur Delacour assured him, 'but you must tell it clearly what you want ... ozzerwise you might find you 'ave a leetle less hair zan you would like ...'), chocolates from the Delacours and an enormous box of the latest Weasleys' Wizard Wheezes merchandise from Fred and George.

Harry, Ron and Hermione did not linger at the table, as the arrival of Madame Delacour, Fleur and Gabrielle made the kitchen uncomfortably crowded.

'I'll pack these for you,' Hermione said brightly, taking Harry's presents out of his arms as the three of them headed back upstairs. 'I'm nearly done, I'm just waiting for the rest of your pants to come out of the wash, Ron –'

Ron's splutter was interrupted by the opening of a door on the first-floor landing.

'Harry, will you come in here a moment?'

It was Ginny. Ron came to an abrupt halt, but Hermione took him by the elbow and tugged him on up the stairs. Feeling nervous, Harry followed Ginny into her room.

He had never been inside it before. It was small, but bright. There was a large poster of the wizarding band the Weird Sisters on one wall, and a picture of Gwenog Jones, captain of the all-witch Quidditch team the Holyhead Harpies, on the other. A desk stood facing the open window, which looked out over the orchard where he and Ginny had once played two-a-side Quidditch with Ron and Hermione, and which now housed a large, pearly-white marquee. The golden flag on top was level with Ginny's window.

Ginny looked up into Harry's face, took a deep breath and said, 'Happy seventeenth.'

'Yeah ... thanks.'

She was looking at him steadily; he, however, found it difficult to look back at her; it was like gazing into a brilliant light.

'Nice view,' he said feebly, pointing towards the window.

She ignored this. He could not blame her.

'I couldn't think what to get you,' she said.

'You didn't have to get me anything.'

第7章　阿不思·邓布利多的遗嘱

赫敏给他买了个新的窥镜。另外几个包裹里有比尔和芙蓉送的一把魔术剃须刀（"没错，这会让你剃须时感到前所未有的光滑舒服，"德拉库尔先生向他保证，"但你必须把你的想法清清楚楚地告诉它……不然你可能会发现你的头发有点太少了……"），有德拉库尔夫妇送的巧克力，还有弗雷德和乔治送的一大盒韦斯莱魔法把戏坊的最新商品。

哈利、罗恩和赫敏没有在桌边逗留，因为德拉库尔夫人、芙蓉和加布丽来了，厨房里显得拥挤不堪。

"我帮你把它们收拾起来。"赫敏愉快地说，从哈利怀里接过那些礼物，三人一起朝楼上走去，"我差不多快整理完了，罗恩，就等你的另外几条内裤洗出来——"

二楼平台上的一扇门突然打开，打断了罗恩急赤白脸的抗议。

"哈利，你能进来一下吗？"

是金妮。罗恩猛地停住脚步，但赫敏抓住他的胳膊肘，拉着他继续往楼上走。哈利有点忐忑不安地跟着金妮走进她的房间。

他以前从没有进来过。房间不大，但很明亮，一面墙上贴着古怪姐妹演唱组的大幅海报，另一面墙上贴着女巫魁地奇球队霍利黑德哈比队的队长格韦诺格·琼斯的照片，一张书桌对着敞开的窗户。窗外是果园，他和金妮曾在那里跟罗恩和赫敏玩过两人对两人的魁地奇，现在那里扎了个很大的、乳白色的帐篷。帐篷顶上的金色旗子正好跟金妮的窗户一样高。

金妮抬头望着哈利的脸，深深吸了口气，说："十七岁快乐。"

"嗯……谢谢。"

她目不转睛地盯着他，他却觉得很难与她的目光对视，就像不敢凝视耀眼的亮光一样。

"风景不错。"他指着窗外，小声地说。

金妮没有接话。他不能怪她。

"我想不好送给你什么。"金妮说。

"你用不着送我什么。"

CHAPTER SEVEN The Will of Albus Dumbledore

She disregarded this too.

'I didn't know what would be useful. Nothing too big, because you wouldn't be able to take it with you.'

He chanced a glance at her. She was not tearful; that was one of the many wonderful things about Ginny, she was rarely weepy. He had sometimes thought that having six brothers must have toughened her up.

She took a step closer to him.

'So then I thought, I'd like you to have something to remember me by, you know, if you meet some Veela when you're off doing whatever you're doing.'

'I think dating opportunities are going to be pretty thin on the ground, to be honest.'

'There's the silver lining I've been looking for,' she whispered, and then she was kissing him as she had never kissed him before, and Harry was kissing her back, and it was blissful oblivion, better than Firewhisky; she was the only real thing in the world, Ginny, the feel of her, one hand at her back and one in her long, sweet-smelling hair –

The door banged open behind them and they jumped apart.

'Oh,' said Ron pointedly. 'Sorry.'

'Ron!' Hermione was just behind him, slightly out of breath. There was a strained silence, then Ginny said in a flat little voice, 'Well, happy birthday anyway, Harry.'

Ron's ears were scarlet; Hermione looked nervous. Harry wanted to slam the door in their faces, but it felt as though a cold draught had entered the room when the door opened and his shining moment had popped like a soap bubble. All the reasons for ending his relationship with Ginny, for staying well away from her, seemed to have slunk inside the room with Ron, and all happy forgetfulness was gone.

He looked at Ginny, wanting to say something, though he hardly knew what, but she had turned her back on him. He thought that she might have succumbed, for once, to tears. He could not do anything to comfort her in front of Ron.

'I'll see you later,' he said, and followed the other two out of the bedroom.

Ron marched downstairs, through the still crowded kitchen and into the yard, and Harry kept pace with him all the way, Hermione trotting along behind them looking scared.

第7章 阿不思·邓布利多的遗嘱

金妮还是没有接话。

"我不知道什么东西有用。不能太大,不然你没法随身带着。"

哈利鼓足勇气看了她一眼。她没有哭,这是金妮许多了不起的地方之一,她很少哭。哈利有时候想,上面有六个哥哥肯定把她磨炼得坚强了。

金妮朝他走近一步。

"所以,我希望你有一件能够想起我的东西,我是说,万一你在外面做事的时候碰到了某个媚娃。"

"说句实话,我认为那时候谈情说爱的机会很少很少。"

"我正希望能有这么点儿安慰。"她低声说,然后她吻住了他,以前所未有的方式吻住了他,哈利也回吻着她。他飘飘欲仙,脑子里一片空白,比火焰威士忌的感觉还好。她是世界上唯一真实的东西,金妮,她给他的感觉。他一只手搂在她的背上,一只手抚着她长长的、散发着淡淡香味的秀发——

身后的门突然被撞开,两人赶紧分开。

"噢,"罗恩尖刻地说,"对不起。"

"罗恩!"赫敏跟在他后面,跑得上气不接下气。沉默中气氛紧张,然后金妮用平淡的口气小声说:"好了,哈利,祝你生日快乐吧。"

罗恩耳朵通红,赫敏显得忐忑不安。哈利真想对着他们把门砰地关上,可是刚才门一打开,仿佛有一股冷风刮进屋来,使他那辉煌的瞬间像肥皂泡一样爆裂了。与金妮断绝关系、尽量疏远金妮的种种理由,似乎跟着罗恩一起钻进屋来,使所有忘怀一切的幸福都消失了。

他看着金妮,想说几句话——其实并不知道说什么好,但是金妮已经把身子转过去了。哈利心想这次她大概终于忍不住哭了。当着罗恩的面,他没有任何办法安慰她。

"待会儿见。"他说,便跟着罗恩和赫敏走出了卧室。

罗恩大步走下楼梯,穿过仍然拥挤的厨房走进院子,哈利一路尾随着他,赫敏小跑着跟在他们后面,神色惊慌。

CHAPTER SEVEN   The Will of Albus Dumbledore

Once he reached the seclusion of the freshly mown lawn, Ron rounded on Harry.

'You ditched her. What are you doing now, messing her around?'

'I'm not messing her around,' said Harry, as Hermione caught up with them.

'Ron –'

But Ron held up a hand to silence her.

'She was really cut up when you ended it –'

'So was I. You know why I stopped it, and it wasn't because I wanted to.'

'Yeah, but you go snogging her now and she's just going to get her hopes up again –'

'She's not an idiot, she knows it can't happen, she's not expecting us to – to end up married, or –'

As he said it, a vivid picture formed in Harry's mind of Ginny in a white dress, marrying a tall, faceless and unpleasant stranger. In one spiralling moment it seemed to hit him: her future was free and unencumbered, whereas his ... he could see nothing but Voldemort ahead.

'If you keep groping her every chance you get –'

'It won't happen again,' said Harry harshly. The day was cloudless, but he felt as though the sun had gone in. 'OK?'

Ron looked half resentful, half sheepish; he rocked backwards and forwards on his feet for a moment, then said, 'Right then, well, that's ... yeah.'

Ginny did not seek another one-to-one meeting with Harry for the rest of the day, nor by any look or gesture did she show that they had shared more than polite conversation in her room. Nevertheless, Charlie's arrival came as a relief to Harry. It provided a distraction, watching Mrs Weasley force Charlie into a chair, raise her wand threateningly and announce that he was about to get a proper haircut.

As Harry's birthday dinner would have stretched The Burrow's kitchen to breaking point even before the arrival of Charlie, Lupin, Tonks and Hagrid, several tables were placed end to end in the garden. Fred and George bewitched a number of purple lanterns, all emblazoned with a large number '17', to hang in mid-air over the guests. Thanks to Mrs Weasley's

第 7 章 阿不思·邓布利多的遗嘱

刚来到新剪过的草坪的僻静处，罗恩就转身朝哈利发难了。

"你把她给甩了，现在又想干什么，勾引她？"

"我没有勾引她。"哈利说，这时赫敏也赶了上来。

"罗恩——"

罗恩举起一只手让她闭嘴。

"当初你提出一刀两断，她心都碎了——"

"我也是。你知道我为什么要终止，我也不想那么做。"

"是啊，可是现在你跟她勾勾搭搭，又让她重新燃起希望——"

"她不是傻瓜，她知道这不可能，她并不指望我们——最后结婚，或者——"

哈利说着，脑海里浮现出一幅逼真的画面：金妮一袭白衣，嫁给一个面目不清、不招人喜欢的高个子陌生男子。在这一瞬间，他仿佛被击中了：金妮的未来自由自在、无牵无挂，而他……他的前面除了伏地魔什么也没有。

"如果你一逮住机会就跟她调情——"

"再也不会了。"哈利生硬地说。天空蔚蓝无云，他却似乎觉得太阳被乌云遮住了。"满意了吗？"

罗恩看上去又是愤恨又有点局促不安，他把身子前后摇晃了一会儿，说："好吧，那就……好吧。"

在这天剩下来的时间里，金妮没有再找机会跟哈利单独在一起。从她的神情举止上，也看不出他们曾在她房间里有过超越礼貌的交谈。不过,查理的到来给了哈利些许安慰。韦斯莱夫人逼着查理坐在椅子上，气势汹汹地举起魔杖，大声说要给他好好剪剪头发，哈利在一旁看着，忘记了自己的烦恼。

查理、卢平、唐克斯和海格还没到来之前，哈利的生日宴就把陋居厨房挤得快要爆炸了，于是大家就在花园里拼了几张桌子。弗雷德和乔治用魔法变出一大批紫色的灯笼，悬挂在客人们的头顶上。灯笼上闪着耀眼醒目的数字："17"。多亏韦斯莱夫人的精心照料，乔治的伤口已变得光滑平整，但哈利还是不习惯他脑袋侧面那个黑乎乎的洞

CHAPTER SEVEN The Will of Albus Dumbledore

ministrations, George's wound was neat and clean, but Harry was not yet used to the dark hole in the side of his head, despite the twins' many jokes about it.

Hermione made purple and gold streamers erupt from the end of her wand and drape themselves artistically over the trees and bushes.

'Nice,' said Ron, as with one final flourish of her wand, Hermione turned the leaves on the crab-apple tree to gold. 'You've really got an eye for that sort of thing.'

'Thank you, Ron!' said Hermione, looking both pleased and a little confused. Harry turned away, smiling to himself. He had a funny notion that he would find a chapter on compliments when he found time to peruse his copy of *Twelve Fail-Safe Ways to Charm Witches*; he caught Ginny's eye and grinned at her, before remembering his promise to Ron and hurriedly striking up a conversation with Monsieur Delacour.

'Out of the way, out of the way!' sang Mrs Weasley, coming through the gate with what appeared to be a giant, beach-ball-sized Snitch floating in front of her. Seconds later Harry realised that it was his birthday cake, which Mrs Weasley was suspending with her wand rather than risk carrying it over the uneven ground. When the cake had finally landed in the middle of the table, Harry said, 'That looks amazing, Mrs Weasley.'

'Oh, it's nothing, dear,' she said fondly. Over her shoulder, Ron gave Harry the thumbs up and mouthed, *Good one*.

By seven o'clock, all the guests had arrived, led into the house by Fred and George, who had waited for them at the end of the lane. Hagrid had honoured the occasion by wearing his best, and horrible, hairy brown suit. Although Lupin smiled as he shook Harry's hand, Harry thought he looked rather unhappy. It was all very odd; Tonks, beside him, looked simply radiant.

'Happy birthday, Harry,' she said, hugging him tightly.

'Seventeen, eh!' said Hagrid, as he accepted a bucket-sized glass of wine from Fred. 'Six years ter the day since we met, Harry, d'yeh remember it?'

'Vaguely,' said Harry, grinning up at him. 'Didn't you smash down the front door, give Dudley a pig's tail and tell me I was a wizard?'

'I forge' the details,' Hagrid chortled. 'All righ', Ron, Hermione?'

'We're fine,' said Hermione. 'How are you?'

第7章 阿不思·邓布利多的遗嘱

口,尽管双胞胎兄弟拿它开了许多玩笑。

赫敏从她的魔杖顶上喷出紫色和金色的横幅,很有艺术性地悬挂在树上和灌木丛上。

"真好,"罗恩看着赫敏最后一挥魔杖,把沙果树的树叶变成了金色,不禁赞叹道,"你在这方面真有品位。"

"谢谢你,罗恩!"赫敏说,显得既高兴又有点困惑。哈利转过身暗自发笑。他有一种奇怪的想法:等他有时间浏览那本《迷倒女巫的十二个制胜法宝》,准会发现有一章是专门讲如何奉承人的。他碰到了金妮的目光,对她报以微笑,却突然想起自己对罗恩的承诺,便赶紧跟德拉库尔先生聊起天来。

"让开,让开!"韦斯莱夫人用唱歌般的语调说着走进了花园的门,一个沙滩球那么大的金色飞贼在她面前飘浮。几秒钟后,哈利才意识到那是他的生日蛋糕。韦斯莱夫人用魔杖让蛋糕悬在半空,而不是冒险端着它走过坑洼不平的地面。蛋糕终于落到桌子中央,哈利说道:"真是太棒了,韦斯莱夫人。"

"哦,没什么,亲爱的。"韦斯莱夫人慈爱地说。罗恩在她身后朝哈利竖起两个大拇指,用口型说:好样的。

七点钟,客人们都来了,弗雷德和乔治站在小路尽头迎候,把他们领进屋子。海格为了表示重视,穿上了他最好的那件毛茸茸的褐色西服,难看极了。卢平跟哈利握手时虽然面带微笑,但哈利却觉得他似乎很不高兴。这可真奇怪。他身边的唐克斯看上去简直光彩照人。

"生日快乐,哈利。"唐克斯说着,紧紧地搂抱了他一下。

"十七了,是不?"海格一边从弗雷德手里接过小桶那么大的一杯酒,一边说,"六年前的今天我们俩相见,哈利,你还记得吗?"

"有点印象,"哈利笑嘻嘻地抬头看着他说,"你是不是撞烂了大门,给了达力一条猪尾巴,还对我说我是个巫师?"

"具体细节我记不清了。"海格咯咯笑着,"怎么样啊,罗恩,赫敏?"

"挺好的。"赫敏说,"你呢?"

CHAPTER SEVEN   The Will of Albus Dumbledore

'Ar, not bad. Bin busy, we got some newborn unicorns, I'll show yeh when yeh get back –' Harry avoided Ron and Hermione's gaze as Hagrid rummaged in his pocket. 'Here, Harry – couldn' think what ter get yeh, but then I remembered this.' He pulled out a small, slightly furry drawstring pouch with a long string, evidently intended to be worn around the neck. 'Mokeskin. Hide anythin' in there an' no one but the owner can get it out. They're rare, them.'

'Hagrid, thanks!'

''S'nothin',' said Hagrid, with a wave of a dustbin-lid-sized hand. 'An' there's Charlie! Always liked him – hey! Charlie!'

Charlie approached, running his hand slightly ruefully over his new, brutally short haircut. He was shorter than Ron, thickset, with a number of burns and scratches up his muscly arms.

'Hi, Hagrid, how's it going?'

'Bin meanin' ter write fer ages. How's Norbert doin'?'

'Norbert?' Charlie laughed. 'The Norwegian Ridgeback? We call her Norberta now.'

'Wha – Norbert's a girl?'

'Oh yeah,' said Charlie.

'How can you tell?' asked Hermione.

'They're a lot more vicious,' said Charlie. He looked over his shoulder and dropped his voice. 'Wish Dad would hurry up and get here. Mum's getting edgy.'

They all looked over at Mrs Weasley. She was trying to talk to Madame Delacour while glancing repeatedly at the gate.

'I think we'd better start without Arthur,' she called to the garden at large after a moment or two. 'He must have been held up at – oh!'

They all saw it at the same time: a streak of light that came flying across the yard and on to the table, where it resolved itself into a bright silver weasel, which stood on its hind legs and spoke with Mr Weasley's voice.

'Minister for Magic coming with me.'

The Patronus dissolved into thin air, leaving Fleur's family peering in astonishment at the place where it had vanished.

第7章 阿不思·邓布利多的遗嘱

"哦,还行。忙着呢,我们有了几只刚生下来的独角兽,等你们回去了我让你们看——"哈利躲避着罗恩和赫敏的目光。海格在他的口袋里翻找着什么。"给,哈利——想不出送你什么好,后来我想起了这个。"他掏出一个有点毛茸茸的拉绳小袋子,袋子上拴着一根长长的带子,显然是为了挂在脖子上的。"驴皮的。不管把什么东西藏在里面,只有主人自己才拿得出来。挺稀罕的,这玩意儿。"

"海格,太谢谢了!"

"没什么。"海格挥了挥垃圾桶盖那么大的手,"哟,查理来了!我一向喜欢他——喂!查理!"

查理一边走过来,一边无可奈何地摸着自己新剪的、短得惨不忍睹的头发。他个子比罗恩矮,体格粗壮,肌肉结实的胳膊上满是灼伤和挠伤的痕迹。

"你好,海格,一切都好吧?"

"早就想给你写信。诺伯怎么样了?"

"诺伯?"查理笑了起来,"那条挪威脊背龙?我们现在叫它诺贝塔了。"

"什么——诺伯是个姑娘?"

"是啊。"查理说。

"怎么能看出来呢?"赫敏问。

"母的要凶恶得多。"查理说。他扭头看看,压低了声音:"真希望爸爸赶紧回来,妈妈开始烦躁了。"

他们都朝韦斯莱夫人望去,只见她一边打起精神跟德拉库尔夫人说话,一边不住地朝大门口张望。

过了片刻,她对着花园大声说:"我想,我们最好别等亚瑟了,现在就开始吧,他准是有事耽搁了——哦!"

大家同时看到:一道光掠过院子,蹿到桌上,变成了一只明亮的银色鼬鼠,它后腿直立,用韦斯莱先生的声音说话了。

"魔法部部长和我一起来了。"

守护神突然不见了踪影,芙蓉一家人惊愕地盯着它消失的地方。

CHAPTER SEVEN The Will of Albus Dumbledore

'We shouldn't be here,' said Lupin at once. 'Harry – I'm sorry – I'll explain another time –'

He seized Tonks's wrist and pulled her away; they reached the fence, climbed over it and vanished from sight. Mrs Weasley looked bewildered.

'The Minister – but why –? I don't understand –'

But there was no time to discuss the matter; a second later, Mr Weasley had appeared out of thin air at the gate, accompanied by Rufus Scrimgeour, instantly recognisable by his mane of grizzled hair.

The two newcomers marched across the yard towards the garden and the lantern-lit table, where everybody sat in silence, watching them draw closer. As Scrimgeour came within range of the lantern light, Harry saw that he looked much older than the last time they had met, scraggy and grim.

'Sorry to intrude,' said Scrimgeour, as he limped to a halt before the table. 'Especially as I can see that I am gatecrashing a party.'

His eyes lingered for a moment on the giant Snitch cake.

'Many happy returns.'

'Thanks,' said Harry.

'I require a private word with you,' Scrimgeour went on. 'Also with Mr Ronald Weasley and Miss Hermione Granger.'

'Us?' said Ron, sounding surprised. 'Why us?'

'I shall tell you that when we are somewhere more private,' said Scrimgeour. 'Is there such a place?' he demanded of Mr Weasley.

'Yes, of course,' said Mr Weasley, who looked nervous. 'The, er, sitting room, why don't you use that?'

'You can lead the way,' Scrimgeour said to Ron. 'There will be no need for you to accompany us, Arthur.'

Harry saw Mr Weasley exchange a worried look with Mrs Weasley as he, Ron and Hermione stood up. As they led the way back to the house in silence, Harry knew that the other two were thinking the same as he was: Scrimgeour must, somehow, have learned that the three of them were planning to drop out of Hogwarts.

Scrimgeour did not speak as they all passed through the messy kitchen and into The Burrow's sitting room. Although the garden had been full of

第7章 阿不思·邓布利多的遗嘱

"我们不应该在这儿,"卢平立刻说道,"哈利——抱歉了——我下次再解释——"

他抓住唐克斯的手腕把她拉走。他们跑到栅栏前,翻过去不见了。韦斯莱夫人一脸迷惑。

"部长——可是为什么——? 我不明白——"

没有时间讨论这个问题了,一秒钟后,韦斯莱先生在大门口突然出现,身边跟着鲁弗斯·斯克林杰,他那头花白浓密的长发使人一眼就能认出来。

刚到的两个人大步穿过院子,朝花园和点着灯笼的桌子走来,桌旁的每个人都默默无语,看着他们一步步走近。斯克林杰走到灯笼的亮光里,哈利发现他比他们上次见面时苍老了许多,消瘦憔悴,神色严峻。

"抱歉,打扰了,"斯克林杰一瘸一拐地走到桌旁停下,说道,"而且我发现我擅自闯入了一个晚会。"

他的目光在巨大的飞贼蛋糕上停留了片刻。

"祝你长命百岁。"

"谢谢。"哈利说。

"我想和你单独谈谈,"斯克林杰继续说,"还有罗恩·韦斯莱先生和赫敏·格兰杰小姐。"

"我们? "罗恩说,声音里透着惊讶,"叫我们干吗? "

"等我们找到更隐蔽的地方,我会告诉你们的。"斯克林杰说,"有这样的地方吗? "他问韦斯莱先生。

"有,当然有。"韦斯莱先生说,显得有点紧张,"嗯,客厅,客厅不就可以嘛。"

"你在前面走。"斯克林杰对罗恩说,"亚瑟,你就不用陪着我们了。"

同罗恩和赫敏站起来的时候,哈利看见韦斯莱先生和韦斯莱夫人交换了一个不安的眼神。三个人一声不吭地向房子里走去,哈利知道另外两个人心里的想法和他一样:斯克林杰肯定不知从哪儿得知他们三个打算从霍格沃茨退学了。

四个人穿过杂乱的厨房,进入陋居的客厅,斯克林杰一直没有说

CHAPTER SEVEN The Will of Albus Dumbledore

soft, golden evening light, it was already dark in here: Harry flicked his wand at the oil lamps as he entered and they illuminated the shabby but cosy room. Scrimgeour sat himself in the sagging armchair that Mr Weasley normally occupied, leaving Harry, Ron and Hermione to squeeze side by side on the sofa. Once they had done so, Scrimgeour spoke.

'I have some questions for the three of you, and I think it will be best if we do it individually. If you two,' he pointed at Harry and Hermione, 'can wait upstairs, I will start with Ronald.'

'We're not going anywhere,' said Harry, while Hermione nodded vigorously. 'You can speak to us together, or not at all.'

Scrimgeour gave Harry a cold, appraising look. Harry had the impression that the Minister was wondering whether it was worthwhile opening hostilities this early.

'Very well, then, together,' he said, shrugging. He cleared his throat. 'I am here, as I'm sure you know, because of Albus Dumbledore's will.'

Harry, Ron and Hermione looked at one another.

'A surprise, apparently! You were not aware, then, that Dumbledore had left you anything?'

'A – all of us?' said Ron. 'Me and Hermione too?'

'Yes, all of –'

But Harry interrupted.

'Dumbledore died over a month ago. Why has it taken this long to give us what he left us?'

'Isn't it obvious?' said Hermione, before Scrimgeour could answer. 'They wanted to examine whatever he's left us. You had no right to do that!' she said, and her voice trembled slightly.

'I had every right,' said Scrimgeour dismissively. 'The Decree for Justifiable Confiscation gives the Ministry the power to confiscate the contents of a will –'

'That law was created to stop wizards passing on Dark artefacts,' said Hermione, 'and the Ministry is supposed to have powerful evidence that the deceased's possessions are illegal before seizing them! Are you telling me that you thought Dumbledore was trying to pass us something cursed?'

'Are you planning to follow a career in Magical Law, Miss Granger?' asked Scrimgeour.

第7章 阿不思·邓布利多的遗嘱

话。花园里映着柔和的金色晚霞，但客厅里已经很暗了。哈利进屋时朝那些油灯挥了挥魔杖，它们便放出光来，照亮了这个破旧但舒适的房间。斯克林杰在韦斯莱先生平常坐的那把松软凹陷的扶手椅上坐了下来，哈利、罗恩和赫敏只好一个挨一个挤坐在沙发上。他们刚一坐定，斯克林杰就说话了。

"我有几个问题要问你们三个，我想最好一个一个地问。你们俩——"他指着哈利和赫敏，"——到楼上去等着，我先跟罗恩谈谈。"

"我们哪儿也不去。"哈利说，赫敏也在一旁拼命点头，"要么跟我们三个谈，要么一个也别谈。"

斯克林杰用冷冷的、审视的目光看着哈利。哈利觉得部长似乎在考虑是否值得这么早就把敌意公开。

"好吧，那就一起谈。"他耸耸肩说，然后清了清嗓子，"我相信你们知道，我是为了阿不思·邓布利多的遗嘱来的。"

哈利、罗恩和赫敏面面相觑。

"看来很意外啊！难道你们没有意识到邓布利多给你们留了东西？"

"我——我们都有？"罗恩说，"我和赫敏也有？"

"对，你们都有——"

但哈利打断了他的话。

"邓布利多死了一个多月了，为什么这么长时间才把他留给我们的东西给我们？"

"这还用说吗？"没等斯克林杰回答，赫敏就说道，"他们要检查他留给我们的东西。你没有权利这么做！"她说，声音微微有点发抖。

"我当然有权利，"斯克林杰轻蔑地说，"根据《正当没收物资法》，魔法部有权没收遗嘱所涉及的东西——"

"那个法律是为了阻止巫师转移黑魔法用品才制定的，"赫敏说，"魔法部必须有确凿证据证明死者的东西是非法的才能没收它们！难道你是说你认为邓布利多想留给我们一些邪恶的东西？"

"你打算将来从事魔法法律的职业吗，格兰杰小姐？"斯克林杰问。

CHAPTER SEVEN   The Will of Albus Dumbledore

'No I'm not,' retorted Hermione. 'I'm hoping to do some good in the world!'

Ron laughed. Scrimgeour's eyes flickered towards him and away again as Harry spoke.

'So why have you decided to let us have our things now? Can't think of a pretext to keep them?'

'No, it'll be because the thirty-one days are up,' said Hermione at once. 'They can't keep the objects longer than that unless they can prove they're dangerous. Right?'

'Would you say you were close to Dumbledore, Ronald?' asked Scrimgeour, ignoring Hermione. Ron looked startled.

'Me? Not – not really ... it was always Harry who ...'

Ron looked round at Harry and Hermione, to see Hermione giving him a *stop-talking-now!* Sort of look, but the damage was done: Scrimgeour looked as though he had heard exactly what he had expected, and wanted, to hear. He swooped like a bird of prey upon Ron's answer.

'If you were not very close to Dumbledore, how do you account for the fact that he remembered you in his will? He made exceptionally few personal bequests. The vast majority of his possessions – his private library, his magical instruments and other personal effects – were left to Hogwarts. Why do you think you were singled out?'

'I ... dunno,' said Ron. 'I ... when I say we weren't close ... I mean, I think he liked me ...'

'You're being modest, Ron,' said Hermione. 'Dumbledore was very fond of you.'

This was stretching the truth to breaking point; as far as Harry knew, Ron and Dumbledore had never been alone together, and direct contact between them had been negligible. However, Scrimgeour did not seem to be listening. He put his hand inside his cloak and drew out a drawstring pouch much larger than the one Hagrid had given Harry. From it he removed a scroll of parchment, which he unrolled and read aloud.

'"*The Last Will and Testament of Albus Percival Wulfric Brian Dumbledore*" ... yes, here we are ... "*to Ronald Bilius Weasley, I leave my Deluminator, in the hope that he will remember me when he uses it.*"'

Scrimgeour took from the bag an object that Harry had seen before: it

第7章 阿不思·邓布利多的遗嘱

"不是,"赫敏反唇相讥,"我希望在世上做些好事!"

罗恩笑出声来。斯克林杰的目光朝他扫了一下,又挪开了,因为哈利说话了。

"现在你怎么又决定让我们拿到我们的东西了?找不到借口扣留它们了?"

"不,是因为三十一天的期限到了,"赫敏立刻说道,"他们扣留的时间不能超过这个期限,除非能证明东西是危险的。对吗?"

"你能说你和邓布利多很亲密吗,罗恩?"斯克林杰没有理睬赫敏,说道。罗恩显得很吃惊。

"我?不——不太亲密……一向都是哈利……"

罗恩转脸看看哈利和赫敏,却见赫敏朝他丢了个"赶紧闭嘴!"的眼神,但是危害已经造成:斯克林杰似乎听到了他所期待和需要的话。他像猛禽扑食似的扑向罗恩的回答。

"如果你和邓布利多并不十分亲密,又怎么解释他在遗嘱里给你留下礼物呢?他专门给几个人遗赠了东西。他的大部分财物——他的私人藏书室、他的魔法仪器和其他个人财产——都留给了霍格沃茨。你认为他为什么对你另眼相看呢?"

"我……不知道,"罗恩说,"我……我刚才说我们不太亲密……其实我是说我觉得他挺喜欢我……"

"你太谦虚了,罗恩,"赫敏说,"邓布利多非常喜欢你。"

这其实是夸大事实了。据哈利所知,罗恩和邓布利多从来没有单独在一起待过,他们之间的直接接触少得可怜。然而,斯克林杰似乎并没在听。他把手伸进斗篷里掏出一个拉绳小袋,比海格送给哈利的那个大得多。他从里面抽出一卷羊皮纸,展开来大声读道:

"阿不思·珀西瓦尔·伍尔弗里克·布赖恩·邓布利多的遗嘱……对,在这里……我的熄灯器留给罗恩·比利尔斯·韦斯莱,希望他使用时能想起我。"

斯克林杰从袋子里掏出一个哈利以前见过的东西:看上去像银质

CHAPTER SEVEN   The Will of Albus Dumbledore

looked something like a silver cigarette lighter but it had, he knew, the power to suck all light from a place, and restore it, with a simple click. Scrimgeour leaned forward and passed the Deluminator to Ron, who took it and turned it over in his fingers, looking stunned.

'That is a valuable object,' said Scrimgeour, watching Ron. 'It may even be unique. Certainly it is of Dumbledore's own design. Why would he have left you an item so rare?'

Ron shook his head, looking bewildered.

'Dumbledore must have taught thousands of students,' Scrimgeour persevered. 'Yet the only ones he remembered in his will are you three. Why is that? To what use did he think you would put his Deluminator, Mr Weasley?'

'Put out lights, I s'pose,' mumbled Ron. 'What else could I do with it?'

Evidently Scrimgeour had no suggestions. After squinting at Ron for a moment or two, he turned back to Dumbledore's will.

'"*To Miss Hermione Jean Granger, I leave my copy of* The Tales of Beedle the Bard, *in the hope that she will find it entertaining and instructive.*"'

Scrimgeour now pulled out of the bag a small book that looked as ancient as the copy of *Secrets of the Darkest Art* upstairs. Its binding was stained and peeling in places. Hermione took it from Scrimgeour without a word. She held the book in her lap and gazed at it. Harry saw that the title was in runes; he had never learned to read them. As he looked, a tear splashed on to the embossed symbols.

'Why do you think Dumbledore left you that book, Miss Granger?' asked Scrimgeour.

'He ... he knew I liked books,' said Hermione in a thick voice, mopping her eyes with her sleeve.

'But why that particular book?'

'I don't know. He must have thought I'd enjoy it.'

'Did you ever discuss codes, or any means of passing secret messages, with Dumbledore?'

'No, I didn't,' said Hermione, still wiping her eyes on her sleeve. 'And if the Ministry hasn't found any hidden codes in this book in thirty-one days, I doubt that I will.'

第7章 阿不思·邓布利多的遗嘱

的打火机，但哈利知道只要轻轻一弹，它就能把一个地方的所有灯光都吸走，然后再重新点亮。斯克林杰探身把熄灯器递给罗恩，罗恩接过来拿在手里翻看着，一副目瞪口呆的样子。

"这是一件很有价值的东西，"斯克林杰注视着罗恩说，"甚至可能是独一无二的。肯定是邓布利多自己设计的。他为什么要把这么稀罕的东西留给你呢？"

罗恩摇摇头，一脸茫然。

"邓布利多教过的学生准有好几千，"斯克林杰固执地追问，"但他在遗嘱里只给你们三个留了礼物，这是为什么呢？韦斯莱先生，他认为你会拿他的熄灯器做什么用呢？"

"大概是把灯熄灭吧。"罗恩喃喃地说，"我还能拿它做什么用？"

斯克林杰显然也提不出什么想法。他眯着眼睛看了罗恩一会儿，又转向邓布利多的遗嘱。

"我的《诗翁彼豆故事集》留给赫敏·简·格兰杰小姐，希望她会觉得这本书有趣而有教益。"

斯克林杰又从袋子里掏出一本小书，看上去跟楼上那本《尖端黑魔法揭秘》一样破旧，封皮上斑斑点点，好几处都剥落了。赫敏一言不发地从斯克林杰手里接过书，放在膝盖上，低头望着。哈利看见书名是用如尼文写的，他从来没学会认如尼文。他看着看着，一颗泪珠啪地落在那些凸出的符号上。

"你认为邓布利多为什么要把这本书留给你，格兰杰小姐？"斯克林杰问。

"他……他知道我喜欢书。"赫敏声音嘶哑地说，用袖子擦了擦眼睛。

"但为什么是这本书呢？"

"不知道，他肯定认为我会喜欢。"

"你跟邓布利多谈论过密码和其他传递秘密情报的方式吗？"

"没有，"赫敏仍然用袖子擦着眼睛说，"如果魔法部三十一天都没能发现这本书里藏着密码，恐怕我也不能。"

CHAPTER SEVEN   The Will of Albus Dumbledore

She suppressed a sob. They were wedged together so tightly that Ron had difficulty extracting his arm to put it around Hermione's shoulders. Scrimgeour turned back to the will.

'"*To Harry James Potter,*"'he read, and Harry's insides contracted with a sudden excitement, '"*I leave the Snitch he caught in his first Quidditch match at Hogwarts, as a reminder of the rewards of perseverance and skill.*"'

As Scrimgeour pulled out the tiny, walnut-sized golden ball, its silver wings fluttered rather feebly and Harry could not help feeling a definite sense of anticlimax.

'Why did Dumbledore leave you this Snitch?' asked Scrimgeour.

'No idea,' said Harry. 'For the reasons you just read out, I suppose ... to remind me what you can get if you ... persevere and whatever it was.'

'You think this a mere symbolic keepsake, then?'

'I suppose so,' said Harry. 'What else could it be?'

'I'm asking the questions,' said Scrimgeour, shifting his chair a little closer to the sofa. Dusk was really falling outside, now; the marquee beyond the windows towered ghostly white over the hedge.

'I notice that your birthday cake is in the shape of a Snitch,' Scrimgeour said to Harry. 'Why is that?'

Hermione laughed derisively.

'Oh, it can't be a reference to the fact Harry's a great Seeker, that's way too obvious,' she said. 'There must be a secret message from Dumbledore hidden in the icing!'

'I don't think there's anything hidden in the icing,' said Scrimgeour, 'but a Snitch would be a very good hiding place for a small object. You know why, I'm sure?'

Harry shrugged. Hermione, however, answered: Harry thought that answering questions correctly was such a deeply ingrained habit she could not suppress the urge.

'Because Snitches have flesh memories,' she said.

'What?' said Harry and Ron together; both considered Hermione's Quidditch knowledge negligible.

'Correct,' said Scrimgeour. 'A Snitch is not touched by bare skin before it is released, not even by the maker, who wears gloves. It carries an enchantment by which it can identify the first human to lay hands upon it, in

第7章 阿不思·邓布利多的遗嘱

她忍住一声啜泣。三个人挤坐得太紧了，罗恩很难把胳膊抽出来搂住赫敏的肩膀。斯克林杰又转向遗嘱。

"我留给哈利·詹姆·波特的，"他念道，哈利一下子兴奋得五脏六腑都抽紧了，"是他在霍格沃茨第一次参加魁地奇比赛时抓到的金色飞贼，以提醒他记住毅力和技巧的报偿。"

斯克林杰掏出那个胡桃大的小小金球，它的一对银翅膀有气无力地扇动着，哈利看了不禁一阵扫兴。

"邓布利多为什么要把这个飞贼留给你呢？"斯克林杰问。

"不知道，"哈利说，"大概是为了你刚才念的那些理由吧……提醒我只要有毅力，还有那什么……就能得到怎样的收获。"

"这么说，你认为这只是一个有象征意义的纪念品？"

"我想是吧，"哈利说，"还会是什么呢？"

"我在问你呢。"斯克林杰把椅子挪得离沙发更近了一点儿。外面暮色真的降临了，窗外的大帐篷高耸在树篱上方，白得令人害怕。

"我注意到你的生日蛋糕是一个飞贼的形状，"斯克林杰对哈利说，"为什么？"

赫敏大声发出嘲笑。

"哦，不可能是指哈利是个出色的找球手，那太明显了。"她说，"但糖霜里肯定藏着邓布利多的一条秘密情报！"

"我倒不认为糖霜里藏着什么东西，"斯克林杰说，"飞贼本身就是个藏小东西的绝妙所在。我相信你们知道为什么吧？"

哈利耸耸肩膀，赫敏却做出了回答。哈利觉得，正确回答问题是赫敏的一种根深蒂固的习惯，她无法克制这种欲望。

"因为飞贼有肉体记忆。"她说。

"什么？"哈利和罗恩同时问。他们都以为赫敏的魁地奇知识少得可怜。

"正确，"斯克林杰说，"飞贼被放出来前，没有被裸露的皮肤触摸过，就连制造者也没有摸过，他们都戴着手套。飞贼身上带有一种魔法，它能辨认第一个用手触摸它的人，以防抓球时产生争议。这个飞贼——"

CHAPTER SEVEN   The Will of Albus Dumbledore

case of a disputed capture. This Snitch,' he held up the tiny golden ball, 'will remember your touch, Potter. It occurs to me that Dumbledore, who had prodigious magical skill, whatever his other faults, might have enchanted this Snitch so that it will open only for you.'

Harry's heart was beating rather fast. He was sure that Scrimgeour was right. How could he avoid taking the Snitch with his bare hand in front of the Minister?

'You don't say anything,' said Scrimgeour. 'Perhaps you already know what the Snitch contains?'

'No,' said Harry, still wondering how he could appear to touch the Snitch without really doing so. If only he knew Legilimency, really knew it, and could read Hermione's mind; he could practically hear her brain whirring beside him.

'Take it,' said Scrimgeour quietly.

Harry met the Minister's yellow eyes and knew he had no option but to obey. He held out his hand and Scrimgeour leaned forwards again and placed the Snitch, slowly and deliberately, into Harry's palm.

Nothing happened. As Harry's fingers closed around the Snitch, its tired wings fluttered and were still. Scrimgeour, Ron and Hermione continued to gaze avidly at the now partially concealed ball, as if still hoping it might transform in some way.

'That was dramatic,' said Harry coolly. Both Ron and Hermione laughed.

'That's all, then, is it?' asked Hermione, making to prise herself off the sofa.

'Not quite,' said Scrimgeour, who looked bad-tempered now. 'Dumbledore left you a second bequest, Potter.'

'What is it?' asked Harry, excitement rekindling.

Scrimgeour did not bother to read from the will this time.

'The sword of Godric Gryffindor,' he said.

Hermione and Ron both stiffened. Harry looked around for a sign of the ruby-encrusted hilt, but Scrimgeour did not pull the sword from the leather pouch which, in any case, looked much too small to contain it.

'So where is it?' Harry asked suspiciously.

'Unfortunately,' said Scrimgeour, 'that sword was not Dumbledore's to give away. The sword of Godric Gryffindor is an important historical

第 7 章 阿不思·邓布利多的遗嘱

他举起小小的金球,"——会记得你的触摸,波特。我突然想起,邓布利多虽然有这样那样的缺点,但魔法技艺却十分高超,他大概给这个飞贼施了魔法,只有你才能打开。"

哈利的心怦怦狂跳。他相信斯克林杰的分析是对的。他怎么能避免当着部长的面徒手接过飞贼呢?

"你什么话也不说,"斯克林杰说,"难道你已经知道飞贼里藏着什么了?"

"不知道。"哈利说,仍然在想怎样才能假装碰到飞贼、实际上并不真的接触它。如果他知道并且精通摄神取念咒就好了,就能读到赫敏的思想。他简直可以听见赫敏的大脑在他旁边呼呼旋转。

"拿着。"斯克林杰轻声说。

哈利碰上了部长的一双黄眼睛,知道除了服从别无选择。他伸出手去,斯克林杰又俯身向前,把飞贼慢慢地、慎重地放在哈利的手心里。

什么也没发生。哈利用手指团住飞贼,飞贼疲倦的翅膀扑扇几下,就不动了。斯克林杰、罗恩和赫敏继续用急切的目光盯着被哈利握住的金球,似乎仍然希望它会有所变化。

"很有戏剧性。"哈利冷冷地说。罗恩和赫敏都笑了起来。

"完事儿了吧?"赫敏问,挣扎着想从沙发上站起来。

"还没完呢,"斯克林杰说,他此刻显得有点烦躁了,"邓布利多还遗赠给你一件东西,波特。"

"是什么?"哈利问,心情再一次激动起来。

斯克林杰这次没有去看遗嘱。

"戈德里克·格兰芬多的宝剑。"他说。

赫敏和罗恩都呆住了。哈利扭头寻找那镶着红宝石的剑柄,但斯克林杰并没有从皮袋里抽出宝剑,而且皮袋子太小,根本不可能装得下宝剑。

"在哪儿呢?"哈利怀疑地问。

"很不幸,"斯克林杰说,"邓布利多没有权利把宝剑赠送给他人。

CHAPTER SEVEN   The Will of Albus Dumbledore

artefact, and as such, belongs –'

'It belongs to Harry!' said Hermione hotly. 'It chose him, he was the one who found it, it came to him out of the Sorting Hat –'

'According to reliable historical sources, the sword may present itself to any worthy Gryffindor,' said Scrimgeour. 'That does not make it the exclusive property of Mr Potter, whatever Dumbledore may have decided.' Scrimgeour scratched his badly shaven cheek, scrutinising Harry. 'Why do you think –?'

'Dumbledore wanted to give me the sword?' said Harry, struggling to keep his temper. 'Maybe he thought it would look nice on my wall.'

'This is not a joke, Potter!' growled Scrimgeour. 'Was it because Dumbledore believed that only the sword of Godric Gryffindor could defeat the Heir of Slytherin? Did he wish to give you that sword, Potter, because he believed, as do many, that you are the one destined to destroy He Who Must Not Be Named?'

'Interesting theory,' said Harry. 'Has anyone ever tried sticking a sword in Voldemort? Maybe the Ministry should put some people on to that, instead of wasting their time stripping down Deluminators, or covering up breakouts from Azkaban. So is this what you've been doing, Minister, shut up in your office, trying to break open a Snitch? People are dying, I was nearly one of them, Voldemort chased me across three counties, he killed Mad-Eye Moody, but there's been no word about any of that from the Ministry, has there? And you still expect us to cooperate with you!'

'You go too far!' shouted Scrimgeour, standing up; Harry jumped to his feet too. Scrimgeour limped towards Harry and jabbed him hard in the chest with the point of his wand: it singed a hole in Harry's T-shirt like a lit cigarette.

'Oi!' said Ron, jumping up and raising his own wand, but Harry said, 'No! D'you want to give him an excuse to arrest us?'

'Remembered you're not at school, have you?' said Scrimgeour, breathing hard into Harry's face. 'Remembered that I am not Dumbledore, who forgave your insolence and insubordination? You may wear that scar like a crown, Potter, but it is not up to a seventeen-year-old boy to tell me how to do my job! It's time you learned some respect!'

'It's time you earned it,' said Harry.

第7章 阿不思·邓布利多的遗嘱

戈德里克·格兰芬多的宝剑是一件重要的历史文物,它属于——"

"它属于哈利!"赫敏激动地说,"它选择了哈利,是哈利发现了它,它从分院帽里出来找哈利——"

"根据可靠的历史资料,"斯克林杰说,"宝剑会呈现在每一个出色的格兰芬多学生面前。"斯克林杰说,"那并不能使它成为波特先生的个人财产,不管邓布利多怎么决定。"斯克林杰挠了挠没剃干净的面颊,审视着哈利,"你说为什么——"

"——邓布利多想把宝剑给我?"哈利说,拼命克制着自己的火气,"他大概认为宝剑挂在我的墙上会很好看吧。"

"这不是开玩笑,波特!"斯克林杰咆哮道,"是不是邓布利多相信只有戈德里克·格兰芬多的宝剑才能打败斯莱特林的继承人?波特,他希望把宝剑给你,是不是因为他像许多人一样,相信你注定要消灭那个连名字都不能提的人?"

"有趣的理论,"哈利说,"有人试过用宝剑去刺伏地魔吗?也许魔法部应该安排一些人去做这件事,而不是整天把时间浪费在拆熄灯器和封锁阿兹卡班越狱的消息上。原来你是在干这个,部长,把自己关在办公室里,绞尽脑汁想打开一个飞贼?到处都在死人——我差点儿也死了——伏地魔追着我过了三个郡,他杀死了疯眼汉,可是魔法部对这些事情只字不提,不是吗?你还指望我们跟你合作?!"

"你太过分了!"斯克林杰大喊一声站了起来。哈利也一跃而起。斯克林杰一瘸一拐地跳到哈利跟前,用他的魔杖尖狠狠戳了戳哈利的胸口:魔杖像点燃的香烟一样在哈利的T恤衫上烧了个洞。

"嘿!"罗恩大叫,跳起来举起自己的魔杖,可是哈利说:"别!你想让他有借口逮捕我们吗?"

"你想起了不是在学校,对吗?"斯克林杰说,他粗重的呼吸喷到哈利的脸上,"想起了我不是邓布利多,不会原谅你的无礼和放肆,对吗?你可以把那道伤疤当成王冠,波特,但是还轮不到一个十七岁的毛孩子来告诉我怎么干我的工作!你应该学会尊重别人!"

"你应该学会赢得别人的尊重!"哈利说。

CHAPTER SEVEN   The Will of Albus Dumbledore

The floor trembled; there was a sound of running footsteps, then the door to the sitting room burst open and Mr and Mrs Weasley ran in.

'We – we thought we heard –' began Mr Weasley, looking thoroughly alarmed at the sight of Harry and the Minister virtually nose to nose.

'– raised voices,' panted Mrs Weasley.

Scrimgeour took a couple of steps back from Harry, glancing at the hole he had made in Harry's T-shirt. He seemed to regret his loss of temper.

'It – it was nothing,' he growled. 'I ... regret your attitude,' he said, looking Harry full in the face once more. 'You seem to think that the Ministry does not desire what you – what Dumbledore – desired. We ought to be working together.'

'I don't like your methods, Minister,' said Harry. 'Remember?'

For the second time, he raised his right fist, and displayed to Scrimgeour the scars that still showed white on the back of it, spelling *I must not tell lies*. Scrimgeour's expression hardened. He turned away without another word and limped from the room. Mrs Weasley hurried after him; Harry heard her stop at the back door. After a minute or so, she called, 'He's gone!'

'What did he want?' Mr Weasley asked, looking around at Harry, Ron and Hermione, as Mrs Weasley came hurrying back to them.

'To give us what Dumbledore left us,' said Harry. 'They've only just released the contents of his will.'

Outside in the garden, over the dinner tables, the three objects Scrimgeour had given them were passed from hand to hand. Everyone exclaimed over the Deluminator and *The Tales of Beedle the Bard* and lamented the fact that Scrimgeour had refused to pass on the sword, but none of them could offer any suggestion as to why Dumbledore would have left Harry an old Snitch. As Mr Weasley examined the Deluminator for the third or fourth time, Mrs Weasley said tentatively, 'Harry, dear, everyone's awfully hungry, we didn't like to start without you ... shall I serve dinner now?'

They all ate rather hurriedly and then, after a hasty chorus of 'Happy Birthday' and much gulping of cake, the party broke up. Hagrid, who was invited to the wedding the following day, but was far too bulky to sleep in the overstretched Burrow, left to set up a tent for himself in a neighbouring field.

第7章 阿不思·邓布利多的遗嘱

地板在颤抖,传来了奔跑的脚步声,接着客厅的门突然打开,韦斯莱夫妇冲了进来。

"我们——我们好像听见——"韦斯莱先生看到哈利和部长几乎鼻尖碰着鼻尖,一下子惊呆了。

"——听见高声喧哗。"韦斯莱夫人气喘吁吁地说。

斯克林杰从哈利面前退后几步,扫了一眼他在哈利T恤衫上烧出的那个小洞,似乎为自己的失态感到懊悔。

"没——没什么,"他粗声粗气地说,"我……我为你的态度感到遗憾。"他又一次盯着哈利的脸说道,"你好像以为魔法部的愿望和你的——邓布利多的——愿望不一样。我们应该共同合作。"

"我不喜欢你的方式,部长,"哈利说,"记得吗?"

他第二次举起右手,给斯克林杰看他手背上那些泛白的伤痕:我不可以说谎。斯克林杰的表情僵住了。他一言不发地转过身,一瘸一拐地走出了房间。韦斯莱夫人急忙跟了过去。哈利听见她在后门口停住脚步。过了一分钟左右,她喊道:"他走了!"

"他想做什么?"韦斯莱先生问,转头看着哈利、罗恩和赫敏,这时韦斯莱夫人又匆匆回到他们身边。

"把邓布利多留给我们的东西交给我们。"哈利说,"他们刚把他遗赠的东西拿出来。"

来到外面的花园里,在晚餐桌上,斯克林杰给他们的那三样东西从一人手里递到另一个人手里。每个人都为熄灯器和《诗翁彼豆故事集》发出惊叫,都为斯克林杰不肯把宝剑传给哈利而感到遗憾,但是,至于邓布利多为什么要送给哈利一个旧的飞贼,谁也说不出所以然来。韦斯莱先生三番五次地仔细端详熄灯器时,韦斯莱夫人试探地说:"哈利,亲爱的,大家都饿坏了,我们不愿意在你缺席的时候开始……现在我可以上菜了吗?"

大家都吃得很匆忙,然后草草唱了一首《祝你生日快乐》,三口两口地吃完了蛋糕,晚会就散了。海格被邀请参加第二天的婚礼,但他块头实在太大,在已经挤得满满当当的陋居里睡不下,只好自己在旁边的田地里搭了个帐篷。

CHAPTER SEVEN The Will of Albus Dumbledore

'Meet us upstairs,' Harry whispered to Hermione, while they helped Mrs Weasley restore the garden to its normal state. 'After everyone's gone to bed.'

Up in the attic room, Ron examined his Deluminator and Harry filled Hagrid's Mokeskin purse, not with gold, but with those items he most prized, apparently worthless though some of them were: the Marauder's Map, the shard of Sirius's enchanted mirror and R.A.B.'s locket. He pulled the strings tight and slipped the purse around his neck, then sat holding the old Snitch and watching its wings flutter feebly. At last, Hermione tapped on the door and tiptoed inside.

'*Muffliato*,' she whispered, waving her wand in the direction of the stairs.

'Thought you didn't approve of that spell?' said Ron.

'Times change,' said Hermione. 'Now, show us that Deluminator.'

Ron obliged at once. Holding it up in front of him, he clicked it. The solitary lamp they had lit went out at once.

'The thing is,' whispered Hermione through the dark, 'we could have achieved that with Peruvian Instant Darkness Powder.'

There was a small *click*, and the ball of light from the lamp flew back to the ceiling and illuminated them all once more.

'Still, it's cool,' said Ron, a little defensively. 'And from what they said, Dumbledore invented it himself!'

'I know, but surely he wouldn't have singled you out in his will just to help us turn out the lights!'

'D'you think he knew the Ministry would confiscate his will and examine everything he'd left us?' asked Harry.

'Definitely,' said Hermione. 'He couldn't tell us in the will why he was leaving us these things, but that still doesn't explain ...'

'... why he couldn't have given us a hint when he was alive?' asked Ron.

'Well, exactly,' said Hermione, now flicking through *The Tales of Beedle the Bard*. 'If these things are important enough to pass on right under the nose of the Ministry, you'd think he'd have let us know why ... unless he thought it was obvious?'

'Thought wrong, then, didn't he?' said Ron. 'I always said he was mental. Brilliant, and everything, but cracked. Leaving Harry an old Snitch – what the hell was that about?'

第7章 阿不思·邓布利多的遗嘱

"到楼上找我们，"他们帮韦斯莱夫人把花园恢复原样时，哈利小声对赫敏说，"等大家都睡了以后。"

在阁楼间里，罗恩研究着他的熄灯器，哈利把海格送给他的那个驴皮袋装满，装的不是金子，而是他最珍贵的几样东西，虽然有些看上去没有什么价值：活点地图、小天狼星魔镜的碎片、R.A.B.的挂坠盒。他扎紧带子，把皮袋挂在脖子上，然后拿着旧飞贼坐了下来，注视着飞贼有气无力地扑扇翅膀。终于，赫敏在门上敲了敲，踮着脚尖走了进来。

"闭耳塞听。"她用魔杖朝楼梯的方向挥了挥，小声说道。

"你好像不赞成那个咒语的呀？"罗恩说。

"此一时彼一时嘛。"赫敏说，"来，给我们看看熄灯器。"

罗恩立刻照办。他把熄灯器举在面前，咔嗒一声，他们刚才点亮的那盏孤灯立刻熄灭了。

"问题是，"赫敏在黑暗中小声说，"我们用秘鲁隐身烟幕弹也能办到。"

随着轻微的咔嗒一声，那盏灯里的光球飞到天花板上，一下子把他们都照亮了。

"它还是挺酷的，"罗恩有点替自己辩护，"而且他们说这是邓布利多自己发明的！"

"我知道，但他在遗嘱里单独把你挑出来，肯定不会就为了让你帮我们灭灯吧！"

"你们说，他是不是知道魔法部会没收他的遗嘱，检查他留给我们的每一样东西？"哈利问。

"肯定知道，"赫敏说，"他不能在遗嘱里告诉我们为什么留给我们这些东西，但那仍然不能解释……"

"……他为什么没在活着的时候给我们一点暗示，对吗？"罗恩问。

"对啊，"赫敏翻着《诗翁彼豆故事集》说，"如果这些东西非常重要，必须在魔法部的鼻子底下传给我们，至少他应该让我们知道为什么呀……除非他认为这是明摆着的？"

"他的认为错了，不是吗？"罗恩说，"我总说他脑子坏了。聪明智慧，那没说的，但疯疯癫癫。留给哈利一个旧飞贼——这到底是怎么回事儿呀？"

CHAPTER SEVEN   The Will of Albus Dumbledore

'I've no idea,' said Hermione. 'When Scrimgeour made you take it, Harry, I was so sure that something was going to happen!'

'Yeah, well,' said Harry, his pulse quickening as he raised the Snitch in his fingers. 'I wasn't going to try too hard in front of Scrimgeour, was I?'

'What do you mean?' asked Hermione.

'The Snitch I caught in my first ever Quidditch match?' said Harry. 'Don't you remember?'

Hermione looked simply bemused. Ron, however, gasped, pointing frantically from Harry to the Snitch and back again until he found his voice.

'That was the one you nearly swallowed!'

'Exactly,' said Harry, and with his heart beating fast, he pressed his mouth to the Snitch.

It did not open. Frustration and bitter disappointment welled up inside him: he lowered the golden sphere, but then Hermione cried out.

'Writing! There's writing on it, quick, look!'

He nearly dropped the Snitch in surprise and excitement. Hermione was quite right. Engraved upon the smooth golden surface, where seconds before there had been nothing, were five words written in the thin slanting handwriting that Harry recognised as Dumbledore's:

I open at the close.

He had barely read them when the words vanished again.

'"*I open at the close* ..." What's that supposed to mean?'

Hermione and Ron shook their heads, looking blank.

'I open at the close ... at the *close* ... I open at the close ...'

But no matter how often they repeated the words, with many different inflections, they were unable to wring any more meaning from them.

'And the sword,' said Ron finally, when they had at last abandoned their attempts to divine meaning in the Snitch's inscription. 'Why did he want Harry to have the sword?'

'And why couldn't he just have told me?' Harry said quietly. 'It was *there*, it was right there on the wall of his office during all our talks last year! If he wanted me to have it, why didn't he just give it to me then?'

第7章 阿不思·邓布利多的遗嘱

"不知道。"赫敏说,"哈利,斯克林杰叫你接过它时,我以为肯定会发生什么事情呢!"

"是啊,不过,"哈利说,他用手指托起飞贼,脉搏突然加快了,"当着斯克林杰的面,我可不能太使劲尝试,对不?"

"什么意思?"赫敏问。

"我第一次参加魁地奇比赛抓住的飞贼?"哈利说,"你们不记得了吗?"

赫敏看上去一头雾水。罗恩激动得喘不过气来,他胡乱地指指哈利,指指飞贼,又指指哈利,然后才说出话来。

"就是你差点吞下去的那个!"

"正是。"哈利说,他把嘴贴向飞贼,心怦怦地狂跳。

飞贼没有打开。哈利内心一阵失望和沮丧。他放下金球,赫敏却突然叫了起来。

"有字!球上有字,快,快看!"

哈利既惊讶又激动,差点把球掉在地上。赫敏说得对。光溜溜的金球表面刻着几个刚才还没有的字,细细的,歪向一边,哈利认出是邓布利多的笔迹:

我在结束时打开。

他刚念完,字迹又消失了。

"我在结束时打开……这是什么意思呢?"

赫敏和罗恩都摇摇头,一脸茫然。

"我在结束时打开……结束时……结束时打开……"

他们变着各种腔调把这几个字念了许多遍,还是琢磨不出更多的意思。

"还有那把宝剑,"当他们终于放弃了猜测飞贼上文字的意思时,罗恩说道,"他为什么希望哈利得到宝剑呢?"

"他为什么不能直接告诉我呢?"哈利轻声地说,"我们去年有过那么多次谈话,宝剑就在那儿,挂在他办公室的墙上!如果他想让我得到它,为什么当时不直接给我呢?"

CHAPTER SEVEN   The Will of Albus Dumbledore

He felt as though he were sitting in an examination with a question he ought to have been able to answer in front of him, his brain slow and unresponsive. Was there something he had missed in the long talks with Dumbledore last year? Ought he to know what it all meant? Had Dumbledore expected him to understand?

'And as for this book,' said Hermione, '*The Tales of Beedle the Bard* ... I've never even heard of them!'

'You've never heard of *The Tales of Beedle the Bard?*' said Ron incredulously. 'You're kidding, right?'

'No, I'm not!' said Hermione in surprise. 'Do you know them, then?'

'Well, of course I do!'

Harry looked up, diverted. The circumstance of Ron having read a book that Hermione had not was unprecedented. Ron, however, looked bemused by their surprise.

'Oh, come on! All the old kids' stories are supposed to be Beedle's, aren't they? *The Fountain of Fair Fortune* ... *The Wizard and the Hopping Pot* ... *Babbitty Rabbitty and her Cackling Stump* ...'

'Excuse me?' said Hermione, giggling. 'What was that last one?'

'Come off it!' said Ron, looking in disbelief from Harry to Hermione. 'You must've heard of Babbitty Rabbitty –'

'Ron, you know full well Harry and I were brought up by Muggles!' said Hermione. 'We didn't hear stories like that when we were little, we heard *Snow White and the Seven Dwarves* and *Cinderella* –'

'What's that, an illness?' asked Ron.

'So these are children's stories?' asked Hermione, bending again over the runes.

'Yeah,' said Ron uncertainly, 'I mean, that's just what you hear, you know, that all these old stories came from Beedle. I dunno what they're like in the original versions.'

'But I wonder why Dumbledore thought I should read them?'

Something creaked downstairs.

'Probably just Charlie, now Mum's asleep, sneaking off to regrow his hair,' said Ron nervously.

'All the same, we should get to bed,' whispered Hermione. 'It wouldn't do to oversleep tomorrow.'

第7章 阿不思·邓布利多的遗嘱

哈利觉得自己像在进行考试,面对一个他应该能够回答的问题,而他的大脑却反应迟钝。他是否忽略了去年与邓布利多几次长谈中的什么内容?他是否应该知道所有这一切的意思?邓布利多是否指望他能够理解?

"还有这本书,"赫敏说,"《诗翁彼豆故事集》……我连听都没听说过!"

"你没听说过《诗翁彼豆故事集》?"罗恩不敢相信地说,"你是在开玩笑吧?"

"没有啊!"赫敏吃惊地说,"难道你知道?"

"嘿,我当然知道!"

哈利被吸引住了,抬起头来。罗恩居然读过一本赫敏没读过的书,这真是前所未有的稀罕事儿。罗恩却被他们的惊讶弄糊涂了。

"哦,别逗了!小孩子听的老故事据说都是彼豆写的,不是吗?《好运泉》……《巫师和跳跳埚》……《兔子巴比蒂和她的呱呱树桩》……"

"对不起,"赫敏咯咯笑着说,"最后一个是什么?"

"得了得了!"罗恩说,他不相信地看看哈利又看看赫敏,"你们肯定听过兔子巴比蒂——"

"罗恩,你完全清楚哈利和我都是由麻瓜带大的!"赫敏说,"小时候没听过那样的故事,我们听的是《白雪公主》和《灰姑娘》——"

"那是什么,一种病吗?"罗恩问。

"这么说,这些都是儿童故事?"赫敏问,又埋头研究那些如尼文。

"是啊,"罗恩不能肯定地说,"反正我听说所有的老故事都是彼豆写的,但我不知道它们最初的版本是什么样的。"

"可我不明白为什么邓布利多认为我应该读这些故事呢?"

楼下传来吱吱嘎嘎的声音。

"大概是查理,趁妈妈睡着了偷偷摸摸地让头发再长出来。"罗恩紧张地说。

"不管怎样,我们应该睡觉了。"赫敏小声说,"明天可不能睡过头。"

CHAPTER SEVEN The Will of Albus Dumbledore

'No,' agreed Ron. 'A brutal triple murder by the bridegroom's mother might put a bit of a damper on the wedding. I'll get the lights.'

And he clicked the Deluminator once more as Hermione left the room.

第7章　阿不思·邓布利多的遗嘱

"绝对不能，"罗恩同意道，"新郎的母亲残忍杀死三人，会使整个婚礼有点煞风景的。我来关灯。"

赫敏离开房间时，他又咔嗒按下了熄灯器。

CHAPTER EIGHT

The Wedding

Three o'clock on the following afternoon found Harry, Ron, Fred and George standing outside the great, white marquee in the orchard, awaiting the arrival of the wedding guests. Harry had taken a large dose of Polyjuice Potion and was now the double of a redheaded Muggle boy from the local village, Ottery St Catchpole, from whom Fred had stolen hairs using a Summoning Charm The plan was to introduce Harry as 'Cousin Barny' and trust to the great number of Weasley relatives to camouflage him.

All four of them were clutching seating plans, so that they could help show people to the right seats. A host of white-robed waiters had arrived an hour earlier, along with a golden-jacketed band, and all of these wizards were currently sitting a short distance away under a tree; Harry could see a blue haze of pipe smoke issuing from the spot.

Behind Harry, the entrance to the marquee revealed rows and rows of fragile golden chairs set either side of a long, purple carpet. The supporting poles were entwined with white and gold flowers. Fred and George had fastened an enormous bunch of golden balloons over the exact point where Bill and Fleur would shortly become husband and wife. Outside, butterflies and bees were hovering lazily over the grass and hedgerow. Harry was rather uncomfortable. The Muggle boy whose appearance he was affecting was slightly fatter than him, and his dress robes felt hot and tight in the full glare of a summer's day.

'When I get married,' said Fred, tugging at the collar of his own robes, 'I won't be bothering with any of this nonsense. You can all wear what you like, and I'll put a full Body-Bind Curse on Mum until it's all over.'

'She wasn't too bad this morning, considering,' said George. 'Cried a bit about Percy not being here, but who wants him? Oh blimey, brace yourselves – here they come, look.'

第 8 章

婚　礼

第二天下午三点，哈利、罗恩、弗雷德、乔治站在果园里巨大的白色帐篷外，恭候前来参加婚礼的客人们。哈利喝了大剂量的复方汤剂，现在成了当地奥特里·圣卡奇波尔村里一个红头发麻瓜男孩的模样，弗雷德用召唤咒偷了那个男孩的几根头发。他们计划向客人介绍哈利是"堂弟巴尼"，反正韦斯莱家亲戚众多，但愿能把他掩护住。

四个人手里都捏着座次表，可以帮着指点客人坐到合适的座位上。一小时前，来了一群穿白色长袍的侍者和一支穿金黄色上衣的乐队，此刻这些巫师都坐在不远处的一棵树下，抽着烟斗。哈利可以看见那里袅袅升起一片青色的烟雾。

在哈利身后，大帐篷的入口里面铺着一条长长的紫色地毯，两边放着一排排精致纤巧的金色椅子。柱子上缠绕着白色和金色的鲜花。弗雷德和乔治把一大串金色气球拴在比尔和芙蓉即将举行结婚仪式的地点上空。外面，蜜蜂和蝴蝶懒洋洋地在草丛和灌木树篱上飞舞。哈利感到很不舒服。他冒充的那个麻瓜男孩比他稍胖一些，在夏天火辣辣的太阳底下，他感觉他的礼服长袍又热又紧。

"等我结婚的时候，"弗雷德一边扯着他长袍的领子，一边说道，"我才不搞这些讨厌的名堂呢。你们爱穿什么就穿什么，我要给妈妈来一个全身束缚咒，一直到事情办完。"

"不过，她今天上午表现还可以，"乔治说，"为珀西不能来哭了一鼻子，其实谁稀罕他来呢？哦，天哪，做好准备——他们来了，看。"

CHAPTER EIGHT   The Wedding

Brightly coloured figures were appearing, one by one, out of nowhere at the distant boundary of the yard. Within minutes a procession had formed, which began to snake its way up through the garden towards the marquee. Exotic flowers and bewitched birds fluttered on the witches' hats, while precious gems glittered from many of the wizards' cravats; a hum of excited chatter grew louder and louder, drowning the sound of the bees as the crowd approached the tent.

'Excellent, I think I see a few Veela cousins,' said George, craning his neck for a better look. 'They'll need help understanding our English customs, I'll look after them ...'

'Not so fast, Lugless,' said Fred, and darting past the gaggle of middle-aged witches heading the procession he said, 'Here – *permettezmoi to assister vous*,' to a pair of pretty French girls, who giggled and allowed him to escort them inside. George was left to deal with the middle-aged witches and Ron took charge of Mr Weasley's old Ministry colleague, Perkins, while a rather deaf old couple fell to Harry's lot.

'Wotcher,' said a familiar voice as he came out of the marquee again and found Tonks and Lupin at the front of the queue. She had turned blonde for the occasion. 'Arthur told us you were the one with the curly hair. Sorry about last night,' she added in a whisper, as Harry led them up the aisle. 'The Ministry's being very anti-werewolf at the moment and we thought our presence might not do you any favours.'

'It's fine, I understand,' said Harry, speaking more to Lupin than Tonks. Lupin gave him a swift smile, but as they turned away, Harry saw Lupin's face fall again into lines of misery. He did not understand it, but there was no time to dwell on the matter: Hagrid was causing a certain amount of disruption. Having misunderstood Fred's directions, he had sat himself, not upon the magically enlarged and reinforced seat set aside for him in the back row, but on five seats that now resembled a large pile of golden matchsticks.

While Mr Weasley repaired the damage and Hagrid shouted apologies to anybody who would listen, Harry hurried back to the entrance to find Ron face to face with a most eccentric-looking wizard. Slightly cross-eyed, with shoulder-length white hair the texture of candyfloss, he wore a cap whose tassel dangled in front of his nose and robes of an eye-watering shade of egg-yolk yellow. An odd symbol, rather like a triangular eye, glistened from a golden chain around his neck.

第8章 婚　礼

在院子的最远端，一个又一个色彩鲜艳的身影凭空出现。几分钟后就形成了一支队伍，开始蜿蜒穿过花园，朝大帐篷走来。奇异的花朵和带魔法的小鸟在女巫们的帽子上颤动，珍贵的宝石在许多巫师的领结上闪闪发光。这群人离帐篷越来越近，兴奋的、喊喊喳喳的说话声越来越响，淹没了蜜蜂的嗡嗡声。

"太棒了，我好像看见了几个媚娃表妹。"乔治说，伸长脖子想看得更清楚些，"需要有人帮助她们了解英国习俗，我去照应她们……"

"不用这么着急嘛，洞听。"弗雷德说着，冲过队伍前面那群吵闹的中年女巫，抢先对两个漂亮的法国姑娘说道，"嘿——请允许我为你们服务。"法国姑娘咯咯笑着，让他陪她们进去了。剩下乔治去对付那些中年女巫，罗恩负责招呼韦斯莱先生在魔法部的老同事珀金斯，而落到哈利手里的，是一对耳朵很背的老夫妻。

"你好哇。"他刚走出帐篷就听到一个熟悉的声音，接着看见唐克斯和卢平站在队伍前面。唐克斯专门把头发变成了金黄色。"亚瑟告诉我说你是卷头发的那个。昨晚真是抱歉，"哈利领他们走过通道时，她压低声音说，"魔法部目前对狼人镇压得很厉害，我们认为我们在场恐怕会给你们惹麻烦。"

"没关系，我理解。"哈利更多是对卢平说的。卢平迅速朝他笑了笑，但他们转过身去时，哈利看见卢平的脸又变得阴郁愁苦起来。哈利很不理解，但没有时间琢磨这件事了：海格制造了一场大混乱。他把弗雷德指点的位置搞错了，没有坐在后排专门给他用魔法增大、加固的那个座位上，而是一屁股坐在了五把椅子上，现在那些散了架的椅子就像一大堆金色的火柴棍儿。

韦斯莱先生在修复那些破烂，海格大声对每个肯听他说话的人道歉，哈利匆匆回到入口处，发现罗恩正与一个模样十分古怪的巫师面对面站着。那人有点对眼儿，棉花糖一般的白发蓬在肩头，帽子上的穗儿直垂到鼻子前面，身上穿着一件蛋黄色长袍，颜色耀眼刺目。他脖子上挂着一根金链子，上面闪着一个古怪的符号，很像一只三角形的眼睛。

CHAPTER EIGHT The Wedding

'Xenophilius Lovegood,' he said, extending a hand to Harry, 'my daughter and I live just over the hill, so kind of the good Weasleys to invite us. But I think you know my Luna?' he added to Ron.

'Yes,' said Ron. 'Isn't she with you?'

'She lingered in that charming little garden to say hello to the gnomes, such a glorious infestation! How few wizards realise just how much we can learn from the wise little gnomes – or, to give them their correct name, the *Gernumbli gardensi.*'

'Ours do know a lot of excellent swear words,' said Ron, 'but I think Fred and George taught them those.'

He led a party of warlocks into the marquee as Luna rushed up.

'Hello, Harry!' she said.

'Er – my name's Barny,' said Harry, flummoxed.

'Oh, have you changed that too?' she asked brightly.

'How did you know –?'

'Oh, just your expression,' she said.

Like her father, Luna was wearing bright yellow robes, which she had accessorised with a large sunflower in her hair. Once you got over the brightness of it all, the general effect was quite pleasant. At least there were no radishes dangling from her ears.

Xenophilius, who was deep in conversation with an acquaintance, had missed the exchange between Luna and Harry. Bidding the wizard farewell, he turned to his daughter, who held up her finger and said, 'Daddy, look – one of the gnomes actually bit me!'

'How wonderful! Gnome saliva is enormously beneficial!' said Mr Lovegood, seizing Luna's outstretched finger and examining the bleeding puncture marks. 'Luna, my love, if you should feel any burgeoning talent today – perhaps an unexpected urge to sing opera or to declaim in Mermish – do not repress it! You may have been gifted by the *Gernumblies!*'

Ron, passing them in the opposite direction, let out a loud snort.

'Ron can laugh,' said Luna serenely, as Harry led her and Xenophilius towards their seats, 'but my father has done a lot of research on *Gernumbli* magic.'

'Really?' said Harry, who had long since decided not to challenge Luna or

第8章 婚 礼

"我是谢诺菲留斯·洛夫古德。"他朝哈利伸出一只手说,"我和我女儿就住在山那边,善良的韦斯莱夫妇好心邀请了我们。我想你认识我们家卢娜吧?"后面这句话是对罗恩说的。

"认识,"罗恩说,"她没跟你一起来吗?"

"她在那个迷人的小花园里,跟地精们打招呼呢,它们遍地都是,真是讨人喜欢哪!很少有巫师明白我们能从聪明的小地精那儿学到多少东西——哦,它们准确的名字是,花园工兵精。"

"我们的地精知道许多绝妙的骂人话,"罗恩说,"但我想是弗雷德和乔治教它们的。"

哈利领着一群男巫走进大帐篷,这时卢娜跑了过来。

"你好,哈利!"她说。

"呃——我叫巴尼。"哈利慌乱地说。

"哦,你连名字也变了?"卢娜愉快地问。

"你怎么知道——?"

"噢,从你的表情看出来的。"她说。

卢娜像她父亲一样,穿着鲜艳的黄色长袍,头发上还配了一朵大大的向日葵。一旦适应了这些明亮的色彩,你会觉得整体效果其实还是挺赏心悦目的,至少她耳朵上没再挂着小萝卜。

谢诺菲留斯正和一个熟人谈得投机,没有听见卢娜和哈利之间的对话。他跟那个巫师道了别,转脸看着女儿,卢娜举起一根手指说:"爸爸,看——一只地精居然咬了我!"

"太棒了!地精的唾液特别有用!"洛夫古德先生说着,抓住卢娜伸出的手指,仔细打量那个出血点,"卢娜,我亲爱的,如果你今天觉得有什么才华冒头——也许是一种突如其来的冲动,想唱歌剧,想用人鱼的语言朗诵——千万不要抑制它!那可能是工兵精赠予你的才华!"

罗恩与他们擦肩而过,从鼻子里响亮地哼了一声。

"罗恩尽管笑吧,"卢娜平静地说,这时哈利领着她和谢诺菲留斯走向他们的座位,"但我父亲在工兵精魔法方面做了大量研究。"

"真的?"哈利说,他早就决定不要对卢娜和她父亲的奇特观点提

CHAPTER EIGHT The Wedding

her father's peculiar views. 'Are you sure you don't want to put anything on that bite, though?'

'Oh, it's fine,' said Luna, sucking her finger in a dreamy fashion and looking Harry up and down. 'You look smart. I told Daddy most people would probably wear dress robes, but he believes you ought to wear sun colours to a wedding, for luck, you know.'

As she drifted off after her father, Ron reappeared with an elderly witch clutching his arm. Her beaky nose, red-rimmed eyes, and feathery pink hat gave her the look of a bad-tempered flamingo.

'... and your hair's much too long, Ronald, for a moment I thought you were Ginevra. Merlin's beard, what is Xenophilius Lovegood wearing? He looks like an omelette. And who are you?' she barked at Harry.

'Oh yeah, Auntie Muriel, this is our Cousin Barny.'

'Another Weasley? You breed like gnomes. Isn't Harry Potter here? I was hoping to meet him. I thought he was a friend of yours, Ronald, or have you merely been boasting?'

'No – he couldn't come –'

'Hmm. Made an excuse, did he? Not as gormless as he looks in press photographs, then. I've just been instructing the bride on how best to wear my tiara,' she shouted at Harry. 'Goblin-made, you know, and been in my family for centuries. She's a good-looking girl, but still – *French*. Well, well, find me a good seat, Ronald, I am a hundred and seven and I ought not to be on my feet too long.'

Ron gave Harry a meaningful look as he passed and did not reappear for some time: when next they met at the entrance Harry had shown a dozen more people to their places. The marquee was nearly full now, and for the first time there was no queue outside.

'Nightmare, Muriel is,' said Ron, mopping his forehead on his sleeve. 'She used to come for Christmas every year, then, thank God, she took offence because Fred and George set off a Dungbomb under her chair at dinner. Dad always says she'll have written them out of her will – like they care, they're going to end up richer than anyone in the family, rate they're going ... wow,' he added, blinking rather rapidly as Hermione came hurrying towards them. 'You look great!'

第8章 婚 礼

出质疑,"可是,你真的不需要在那伤口上涂点什么吗?"

"哦,没关系。"卢娜说,她像做梦一样吮着手指,上上下下地打量着哈利,"你看着真精神。我对爸爸说大多数人可能都会穿礼服长袍,但他相信出席婚礼应该穿太阳色的衣服,为了讨个彩头,你知道的。"

她飘飘然地跟着父亲走了。罗恩又出现了,一个年迈的女巫紧紧抓着他的胳膊。老女巫鹰钩鼻,红眼圈,还戴着一顶粉红色的羽毛帽子,看上去活像一只坏脾气的火烈鸟。

"……你的头发太长了,罗恩,刚才我还以为你是金妮呢。我的老天,谢诺菲留斯·洛夫古德穿的那是什么呀?他看着真像一块煎蛋饼。你是谁呀?"她朝哈利大声问。

"哦,穆丽尔姨婆,这是我们的堂弟巴尼。"

"又是韦斯莱家的?你们繁殖得像地精一样快。哈利·波特不在这儿吗?我还以为能见到他呢。罗恩,我好像记得他是你的朋友,那也许只是你自己吹牛吧?"

"不——他不能来——"

"唔,找借口,是吗?看来他倒不像报纸照片上那样没头脑。我刚才一直在教新娘怎么戴我的头饰才最好看。"她嚷嚷着对哈利说,"妖精做的,知道吗,在我们家流传了好几个世纪。她倒是个漂亮姑娘,不过到底是个——法国人。好了,好了,快给我找个好座位,罗恩,我都一百零七岁了,最好别站得太久。"

罗恩意味深长地看了哈利一眼,走了过去,很长时间没再露面。当他们在入口处再次碰见时,哈利已经又领十几个客人找到座位。帐篷里差不多坐满了,外面总算不再排队。

"穆丽尔简直是个噩梦,"罗恩用袖子擦着脑门说,"她以前每年都来过圣诞节,后来,谢天谢地,她生气了,因为吃饭时弗雷德和乔治在她椅子底下放了个粪弹。爸爸总说她在遗嘱里不会赠给他们俩任何东西——他们才不稀罕呢,以后家里谁也赶不上他们俩有钱,估计他们会……哇,"他快速地眨巴眼睛,看着赫敏匆匆朝他们走来,"你的样子太棒了!"

CHAPTER EIGHT The Wedding

'Always the tone of surprise,' said Hermione, though she smiled. She was wearing a floaty, lilac-coloured dress with matching high heels; her hair was sleek and shiny. 'Your Great Aunt Muriel doesn't agree, I just met her upstairs while she was giving Fleur the tiara. She said "Oh dear, is this the Muggle-born?" and then "bad posture and skinny ankles".'

'Don't take it personally, she's rude to everyone,' said Ron.

'Talking about Muriel?' enquired George, reemerging from the marquee with Fred. 'Yeah, she's just told me my ears are lopsided. Old bat. I wish old Uncle Bilius was still with us, though; he was a right laugh at weddings.'

'Wasn't he the one who saw a Grim and died twenty-four hours later?' asked Hermione.

'Well, yeah, he went a bit odd towards the end,' conceded George.

'But before he went loopy he was the life and soul of the party,' said Fred. 'He used to down an entire bottle of Firewhisky, then run on to the dance floor, hoist up his robes and start pulling bunches of flowers out of his–'

'Yes, he sounds a real charmer,' said Hermione, while Harry roared with laughter.

'Never married, for some reason,' said Ron.

'You amaze me,' said Hermione.

They were all laughing so much that none of them noticed the late-comer, a dark-haired young man with a large, curved nose and thick, black eyebrows, until he held out his invitation to Ron and said, with his eyes on Hermione, 'You look vunderful.'

'Viktor!' she shrieked, and dropped her small beaded bag, which made a loud thump quite disproportionate to its size. As she scrambled, blushing, to pick it up, she said, 'I didn't know you were – goodness – it's lovely to see – how are you?'

Ron's ears had turned bright red again. After glancing at Krum's invitation as if he did not believe a word of it, he said, much too loudly, 'How come you're here?'

'Fleur invited me,' said Krum, eyebrows raised.

Harry, who had no grudge against Krum, shook hands; then, feeling that it would be prudent to remove Krum from Ron's vicinity, offered to show him his seat.

第8章 婚 礼

"总是这副吃惊的口气。"赫敏说，不过脸上还是笑着。她穿着一件飘逸的丁香紫色长裙，脚下是配套的高跟鞋，头发光滑、柔顺。"你的姨婆穆丽尔可不这么认为，刚才我在楼上碰到她在给芙蓉送头饰。她说：'噢，天哪，这就是那个麻瓜出身的？'然后又说，'姿势不美，踝骨太突出。'"

"别往心里去，她对谁都不客气。"罗恩说。

"是说穆丽尔吗？"乔治和弗雷德一起从大帐篷里钻出来，问道，"是啊，她刚才还说我的耳朵不对称，这个老太婆！唉，我真希望比利尔斯叔叔还在。他在婚礼上可是个活宝。"

"就是看到'不祥'后二十四小时就死掉的那个？"赫敏问。

"是啊，他最后变得有点古怪。"乔治承认。

"但他在发疯前，可是每次聚会的生命和灵魂哪。"弗雷德说，"他经常一气灌下整整一瓶火焰威士忌，然后跑到舞池里，撩起长袍，掏出一束又一束鲜花，就从他的——"

"是啊，听上去他真是个可爱的人。"赫敏说，哈利哈哈大笑起来。

"一辈子没结婚，不知为什么。"罗恩说。

"真让我吃惊。"赫敏说。

他们笑得太厉害了，谁也没有注意到新来的人，那是个黑头发的年轻人，大鹰钩鼻子，两道黑黑的浓眉。最后他把请柬递到罗恩面前，眼睛盯着赫敏，说道："你看上去太美了。"

"威克多尔！"赫敏尖叫一声，砰，她的串珠小包掉在地上，发出与它的体积不相称的一声巨响。她红着脸慌乱地捡起包，说道："我不知道你也——天哪——见到你真是太好了——你怎么样？"

罗恩的耳朵又变得通红。他扫了一眼克鲁姆的请柬，似乎对上面的字一个也不相信，然后粗声大气地问："你怎么会来这儿？"

"芙蓉邀请我的。"克鲁姆扬起眉毛说。

哈利对克鲁姆并无恶感，跟他握了握手。他觉得还是让克鲁姆离开罗恩身边比较明智，就主动领他去找座位。

CHAPTER EIGHT The Wedding

'Your friend is not pleased to see me,' said Krum, as they entered the now packed marquee. 'Or is he a relative?' he added, with a glance at Harry's red, curly hair.

'Cousin,' Harry muttered, but Krum was not really listening. His appearance was causing a stir, particularly amongst the Veela cousins: he was, after all, a famous Quidditch player. While people were still craning their necks to get a good look at him, Ron, Hermione, Fred and George came hurrying down the aisle.

'Time to sit down,' Fred told Harry, 'or we're going to get run over by the bride.'

Harry, Ron and Hermione took their seats in the second row behind Fred and George. Hermione looked rather pink and Ron's ears were still scarlet. After a few moments, he muttered to Harry, 'Did you see he's grown a stupid little beard?'

Harry gave a non-committal grunt.

A sense of jittery anticipation had filled the warm tent, the general murmuring broken by occasional spurts of excited laughter. Mr and Mrs Weasley strolled up the aisle, smiling and waving at relatives; Mrs Weasley was wearing a brand new set of amethyst-coloured robes with a matching hat.

A moment later Bill and Charlie stood up at the front of the marquee, both wearing dress robes, with large, white roses in their button-holes; Fred wolf-whistled and there was an outbreak of giggling from the Veela cousins. Then the crowd fell silent as music swelled, from what seemed to be the golden balloons.

'Ooooh!' said Hermione, swivelling round in her seat to look at the entrance.

A great collective sigh issued from the assembled witches and wizards as Monsieur Delacour and Fleur came walking up the aisle, Fleur gliding, Monsieur Delacour bouncing and beaming. Fleur was wearing a very simple white dress and seemed to be emitting a strong, silvery glow. While her radiance usually dimmed everyone else by comparison, today it beautified everybody it fell upon. Ginny and Gabrielle, both wearing golden dresses, looked even prettier than usual, and once Fleur had reached him, Bill did not look as though he had ever met Fenrir Greyback.

'Ladies and gentlemen,' said a slightly sing-song voice, and with a slight shock Harry saw the same small, tufty-haired wizard who had presided

第8章 婚　礼

"你的朋友看到我不太高兴嘛。"他们走进已经挤满了人的大帐篷时，克鲁姆说，"还是说，他是你的亲戚？"他扫了一眼哈利的红色鬈发，又问了一句。

"堂哥。"哈利嘟囔了一句，但克鲁姆并没有听。他的出现引起了一片骚动，特别是在那些媚娃表姐妹当中：他毕竟是一位赫赫有名的魁地奇球星呀。就在人们还伸着脖子看他时，罗恩、赫敏、弗雷德和乔治匆匆从过道上走来。

"该坐下了，"弗雷德对哈利说，"不然就要被新娘撞上了。"

哈利、罗恩和赫敏在弗雷德和乔治后面的第二排落座。赫敏脸色绯红，罗恩的耳朵仍然红得耀眼。过了一会儿，他小声对哈利说："你有没有看见，他留了个傻乎乎的小胡子？"

哈利不置可否地嘟囔了一声。

温暖的帐篷里充满了紧张不安的期待，嗡嗡的说话声不时被兴奋的大笑声打断。韦斯莱夫妇顺着通道慢慢走来，笑吟吟地朝亲戚们招手致意。韦斯莱夫人穿了件崭新的紫色长袍，戴着配套的帽子。

片刻之后，比尔和查理站在了大帐篷的前面，两人都穿着礼服长袍，纽扣眼里插着大朵的白玫瑰。弗雷德挑逗地吹起了口哨，那群媚娃表姐妹们顿时咯咯笑成一片。接着响起了音乐，似乎是从那些金色气球里飘出来的。人群安静下来。

"噢！"赫敏在座位里转过身看着入口处说。

德拉库尔先生和芙蓉顺着通道走来时，聚集在帐篷里的巫师们异口同声地发出叹息。芙蓉步态轻盈，德拉库尔先生连蹦带跳，满脸笑容。芙蓉穿着一件非常简单的白色连衣裙，周身似乎散发出一种强烈的银光。平常，光彩照人的她总是把别人比得黯然失色，但今天这银光却把每个人照得更加美丽。金妮和加布丽都穿着金黄色的连衣裙，看上去比平常还要漂亮。芙蓉走到比尔面前，顿时，比尔看上去就像从未遭到芬里尔·格雷伯克的毒手似的。

"女士们先生们，"一个抑扬顿挫的声音说，哈利微微吃惊地看到主持邓布利多葬礼的那个头发浓密的小个子巫师，此刻站在了比尔和

CHAPTER EIGHT   The Wedding

at Dumbledore's funeral, now standing in front of Bill and Fleur. 'We are gathered here today to celebrate the union of two faithful souls ...'

'Yes, my tiara sets off the whole thing nicely,' said Auntie Muriel in a rather carrying whisper. 'But I must say, Ginevra's dress is far too low-cut.'

Ginny glanced round, grinning, winked at Harry, then quickly faced the front again. Harry's mind wandered a long way from the marquee, back to afternoons spent alone with Ginny in lonely parts of the school grounds. They seemed so long ago; they had always seemed too good to be true, as though he had been stealing shining hours from a normal person's life, a person without a lightning-shaped scar on his forehead ...

'Do you, William Arthur, take Fleur Isabelle ...?'

In the front row, Mrs Weasley and Madame Delacour were both sobbing quietly into scraps of lace. Trumpet-like sounds from the back of the marquee told everyone that Hagrid had taken out one of his own tablecloth-sized handkerchiefs. Hermione turned and beamed at Harry; her eyes, too, were full of tears.

'... then I declare you bonded for life.'

The tufty-haired wizard raised his wand high over the heads of Bill and Fleur and a shower of silver stars fell upon them, spiralling around their now entwined figures. As Fred and George led a round of applause, the golden balloons overhead burst: birds of paradise and tiny, golden bells flew and floated out of them, adding their songs and chimes to the din.

'Ladies and gentlemen!' called the tufty-haired wizard. 'If you would please stand up!'

They all did so, Auntie Muriel grumbling audibly; he waved his wand. The seats on which they had been sitting rose gracefully into the air as the canvas walls of the marquee vanished, so that they stood beneath a canopy supported by golden poles, with a glorious view of the sunlit orchard and surrounding countryside. Next, a pool of molten gold spread from the centre of the tent to form a gleaming dance floor; the hovering chairs grouped themselves around small, white-clothed tables, which all floated gracefully back to earth around it, and the golden-jacketed band trooped towards a podium.

'Smooth,' said Ron approvingly, as the waiters popped up on all sides, some bearing silver trays of pumpkin juice, Butterbeer and Firewhisky, others tottering piles of tarts and sandwiches.

芙蓉面前,"今天我们聚集在这里,庆祝两个忠贞的灵魂彼此结合……"

"没错,我的头饰使她整个人更漂亮了,"穆丽尔姨婆用传得很远的低语声说,"可是我得说一句,金妮的裙子开口太低了。"

金妮扭过脸笑笑,朝哈利眨了眨眼睛,又赶紧面朝前方。哈利的思绪飘离了帐篷,回到他和金妮在学校操场上独处的那些下午。那似乎是很久很久以前的事了。他总是觉得那些下午太过美好,不像是真的,就好像他从一个普通人——一个额头上没有闪电形伤疤的人的生命里偷来了一些幸福时光……

"威廉姆·亚瑟,你愿意娶芙蓉·伊萨贝尔……?"

坐在前排的韦斯莱夫人和德拉库尔夫人都用花边帕子捂着脸小声哭泣。大帐篷后面传来了吹喇叭似的声音,大家便知道海格掏出了他的桌布大的手帕。赫敏转脸微笑地看着哈利,眼里也满是泪水。

"……我宣布你们结为终身伴侣。"

头发浓密的巫师在比尔和芙蓉头顶上高高挥舞魔杖,一大片银色的星星落在他们身上,绕着他们此刻紧紧相拥的身体旋转。弗雷德和乔治领头鼓掌喝彩,头顶上金色的气球炸开了:极乐鸟和小金铃铛从里面飞出来,飘浮在半空,于是,全场的喧闹声中又增添了鸟叫声和铃铛声。

"女士们先生们!"头发浓密的巫师大声说,"请起立!"

大家都站了起来,穆丽尔姨婆嘟嘟囔囔地大声抱怨了几句。巫师又挥起了魔杖。所有的座位都轻盈优雅地升到半空,大帐篷的帆布消失了,他们站在由金柱子支撑的天棚下面,放眼看去是阳光灿烂的果园和环绕的乡村,景致美丽极了。接着,一摊熔化的金子从帐篷中央铺散开来,形成了一个金光闪闪的舞池。那些飘浮在半空的椅子自动聚集在铺着白桌布的小桌子旁边,一同轻盈优雅地飘回舞池周围的地面上,穿金黄色上衣的乐队齐步走向演出台。

"绝了。"罗恩赞叹道。侍者从四面八方冒出来,有的托着银色托盘,上面是南瓜汁、黄油啤酒和火焰威士忌;有的托着一大堆摇摇欲坠的馅饼和三明治。

CHAPTER EIGHT   The Wedding

'We should go and congratulate them!' said Hermione, standing on tiptoe to see the place where Bill and Fleur had vanished amid a crowd of well-wishers.

'We'll have time later,' shrugged Ron, snatching three Butterbeers from a passing tray and handing one to Harry. 'Hermione, cop hold, let's grab a table ... not there! Nowhere near Muriel –'

Ron led the way across the empty dance floor, glancing left and right as he went: Harry felt sure that he was keeping an eye out for Krum. By the time they had reached the other side of the marquee, most of the tables were occupied: the emptiest was the one where Luna sat alone.

'All right if we join you?' asked Ron.

'Oh yes,' she said happily. 'Daddy's just gone to give Bill and Fleur our present.'

'What is it, a lifetime's supply of Gurdyroots?' asked Ron.

Hermione aimed a kick at him under the table, but caught Harry instead. Eyes watering in pain, Harry lost track of the conversation for a few moments.

The band had begun to play. Bill and Fleur took to the dance floor first, to great applause; after a while, Mr Weasley led Madame Delacour on to the floor, followed by Mrs Weasley and Fleur's father.

'I like this song,' said Luna, swaying in time to the waltz-like tune, and a few seconds later she stood up and glided on to the dance floor, where she revolved on the spot, quite alone, eyes closed and waving her arms.

'She's great, isn't she?' said Ron admiringly. 'Always good value.'

But the smile vanished from his face at once: Viktor Krum had dropped into Luna's vacant seat. Hermione looked pleasurably flustered, but this time Krum had not come to compliment her. With a scowl on his face he said, 'Who is that man in the yellow?'

'That's Xenophilius Lovegood, he's the father of a friend of ours,' said Ron. His pugnacious tone indicated that they were not about to laugh at Xenophilius, despite the clear provocation. 'Come and dance,' he added abruptly to Hermione.

She looked taken aback, but pleased too, and got up: they vanished together into the growing throng on the dance floor.

'Ah, they are together now?' asked Krum, momentarily distracted.

第8章 婚 礼

"我们应该过去向他们表示祝贺!"赫敏说着,踮着脚尖看向比尔和芙蓉,他们已被祝福的人群淹没。

"待会儿会有时间的。"罗恩耸耸肩膀说,从旁边经过的一个托盘上抓了三杯黄油啤酒,递了一杯给哈利,"赫敏,拿着,我们先去找一张桌子……别在那儿!离穆丽尔远点儿——"

罗恩打头走过空荡荡的舞池,边走边左右张望。哈利知道他肯定是在提防克鲁姆。他们来到大帐篷的另一边,发现大多数桌子旁都坐满了人,最空的就数卢娜独坐的那张桌子了。

"我们和你坐在一起好吗?"罗恩问。

"好啊,"卢娜高兴地说,"爸爸刚去把我们的礼物送给比尔和芙蓉。"

"是什么?向他们终身提供戈迪根?"罗恩问。

赫敏在桌子底下踢他一脚,不料却踢到了哈利。哈利疼得眼泪直流,一时间都听不见他们在说什么了。

乐队开始演奏。比尔和芙蓉首先步入舞池,赢得大家的热烈喝彩。过了一会儿,韦斯莱先生领着德拉库尔夫人走向舞池,后面跟着韦斯莱夫人和芙蓉的父亲。

"我喜欢这首歌。"卢娜说,她和着类似华尔兹乐曲的节奏轻轻摇摆。几秒钟后,她站起身,脚步轻盈地滑向舞池,在那里独自一人原地旋转,闭着眼睛,摆着双臂。

"她可真棒,是不是?"罗恩赞叹地说,"总是很有趣。"

可是他脸上的笑容突然隐去了:威克多尔·克鲁姆坐在了卢娜空出来的座位上。赫敏看上去既高兴又慌乱,但这次克鲁姆可不是来恭维她的。他皱着眉头说:"穿黄衣服的那个男人是谁?"

"谢诺菲留斯·洛夫古德,是我们一个朋友的父亲。"罗恩说。他口气里火药味很浓,表明他们并不打算嘲笑谢诺菲留斯,尽管克鲁姆明显语带挑衅。"跳舞去吧。"他很突兀地对赫敏说。

赫敏显得很吃惊但也很高兴,立刻站了起来。他们一起消失在舞池里越来越拥挤的人群中。

"啊,他们俩好上了?"克鲁姆问,一时有点走神。

227

CHAPTER EIGHT The Wedding

'Er – sort of,' said Harry.

'Who are you?' Krum asked.

'Barny Weasley.'

They shook hands.

'You, Barny – you know this man Lovegood vell?'

'No, I only met him today. Why?'

Krum glowered over the top of his drink, watching Xenophilius, who was chatting to several warlocks on the other side of the dance floor.

'Because,' said Krum, 'if he vos not a guest of Fleur's, I vould duel him, here and now, for vearing that filthy sign upon his chest.'

'Sign?' said Harry, looking over at Xenophilius too. The strange, triangular eye was gleaming on his chest. 'Why? What's wrong with it?'

'Grindelvald. That is Grindelvald's sign.'

'Grindelwald ... the Dark wizard Dumbledore defeated?'

'Exactly.'

Krum's jaw muscles worked as if he were chewing, then he said, 'Grindelvald killed many people, my grandfather, for instance. Of course, he vos never poverful in this country, they said he feared Dumbledore – and rightly, seeing how he vos finished. But this –' He pointed a finger at Xenophilius. 'This is his symbol, I recognised it at vunce: Grindelvald carved it into a vall at Durmstrang ven he vos a pupil there. Some idiots copied it on to their books and clothes, thinking to shock, make themselves impressive – until those of us who had lost family members to Grindelvald taught them better.'

Krum cracked his knuckles menacingly and glowered at Xenophilius. Harry felt perplexed. It seemed incredibly unlikely that Luna's father was a supporter of the Dark Arts, and nobody else in the tent seemed to have recognised the triangular, rune-like shape.

'Are you – er – quite sure it's Grindelwald's –?'

'I am not mistaken,' said Krum coldly. 'I valked past that sign for several years, I know it vell.'

'Well, there's a chance,' said Harry, 'that Xenophilius doesn't actually know what the symbol means. The Lovegoods are quite ... unusual. He

第8章 婚 礼

"嗯——就算是吧。"哈利说。

"你是谁?"

"巴尼·韦斯莱。"

他们握了握手。

"巴尼——你熟悉这个姓洛夫古德的人吗?"

"不熟悉,我今天第一次见到他。怎么啦?"

克鲁姆端着酒杯,怒气冲冲地盯着谢诺菲留斯在舞池另一边跟几个男巫聊天。

"因为,"克鲁姆说,"他要不是芙蓉请来的客人,我就要跟他当场决斗,他居然在胸口戴着那个邪恶的标志。"

"标志?"哈利说着,也朝谢诺菲留斯望去。那个奇怪的三角形眼睛在他胸口闪闪发亮。"怎么啦?有什么不对吗?"

"格林德沃。那是格林德沃的标志。"

"格林德沃……就是邓布利多打败的那个黑巫师?"

"没错。"

克鲁姆下巴上肌肉蠕动,好像在咀嚼什么东西,然后他说:"格林德沃杀害了许多人,我祖父就是其中一个。当然,他在这个国家一直没什么势力,他们说他害怕邓布利多——说得不错,看他最后的下场!可是,这个——"他用手指指着谢诺菲留斯,"——是他的符号,我一眼就认出来了。格林德沃在德姆斯特朗读书时,把它刻在了一面墙上。有些傻瓜把这符号复制在课本上、衣服上,想用它吓唬别人,使自己显得了不起——后来,我们这些因格林德沃而失去亲人的人给了他们一些教训。"

克鲁姆气势汹汹地把指关节按得啪啪响,狠狠地瞪着谢诺菲留斯。哈利觉得很不理解。卢娜的父亲是黑魔法的支持者?这实在令人难以置信,而且,帐篷里的其他人似乎都没认出那个如尼文般的三角形标志。

"你——嗯——你真的肯定那是格林德沃的——?"

"我不会弄错的,"克鲁姆冷冷地说,"几年来我几乎天天经过那个标志,对它了如指掌。"

"嗯,"哈利说,"说不定谢诺菲留斯并不知道那个符号的意思。洛

CHAPTER EIGHT The Wedding

could easily have picked it up somewhere and think it's a cross-section of the head of a Crumple-Horned Snorkack or something.'

'The cross-section of a vot?'

'Well, I don't know what they are, but apparently he and his daughter go on holiday looking for them ...'

Harry felt he was doing a bad job explaining Luna and her father.

'That's her,' he said, pointing at Luna, who was still dancing alone, waving her arms around her head like someone attempting to beat off midges.

'Vy is she doing that?' asked Krum.

'Probably trying to get rid of a Wrackspurt,' said Harry, who recognised the symptoms.

Krum did not seem to know whether or not Harry was making fun of him. He drew his wand from inside his robes and tapped it menacingly on his thigh; sparks flew out of the end.

'Gregorovitch!' said Harry loudly, and Krum started, but Harry was too excited to care: the memory had come back to him at the sight of Krum's wand: Ollivander taking it and examining it carefully before the Triwizard Tournament.

'Vot about him?' asked Krum suspiciously.

'He's a wandmaker!'

'I know that,' said Krum.

'He made your wand! That's why I thought – Quidditch ...'

Krum was looking more and more suspicious.

'How do you know Gregorovitch made my vand?'

'I ... I read it somewhere, I think,' said Harry. 'In a – a fan magazine,' he improvised wildly and Krum looked mollified.

'I had not realised I ever discussed my vand vith fans,' he said.

'So ... er ... where is Gregorovitch these days?'

Krum looked puzzled.

'He retired several years ago. I vos one of the last to purchase a Gregorovitch vand. They are the best – although I know, of course, that you Britons set much store by Ollivander.'

Harry did not answer. He pretended to watch the dancers, like Krum, but

夫古德家的人都很……不同寻常。他可能无意中在什么地方看见了它，以为是弯角鼾兽之类的横切面图。"

"什么的横切面图？"

"咳，我也不知道是什么，但他和他女儿放假时好像在找这东西……"

哈利觉得自己没把卢娜和她父亲介绍清楚。

"那就是他女儿。"他指着卢娜说。卢娜还在独自跳舞，双臂在脑袋周围舞动，就像试图赶走蚊虫一样。

"她干吗那样？"克鲁姆问。

"大概想摆脱一只骚扰虻吧。"哈利认出了这种表现，说道。

克鲁姆似乎弄不清哈利是不是在捉弄他。他从长袍里抽出魔杖，恶狠狠地用它敲着大腿，杖尖冒出金星。

"格里戈维奇！"哈利大声说，克鲁姆一惊，但哈利太兴奋了，没有注意到。看到克鲁姆的魔杖，他想起了过去的一幕：在三强争霸赛前，奥利凡德曾接过这根魔杖仔细端详。

"他怎么啦？"克鲁姆怀疑地问。

"他是个制作魔杖的人！"

"这我知道。"克鲁姆说。

"你的魔杖就是他做的！所以我想——魁地奇——"

克鲁姆似乎越来越疑心了。

"你怎么知道我的魔杖是格里戈维奇做的？"

"我……我大概是从什么地方看来的，"哈利说，"在——在球迷杂志上吧。"他信口胡编，克鲁姆的怒容似乎缓和了。

"我不记得我跟球迷谈过我的魔杖。"他说。

"那么……嗯……格里戈维奇最近在哪儿？"

克鲁姆一脸困惑。

"他几年前就退休了。我是最后一批购买格里戈维奇魔杖的人之一。它们是最棒的——不过我知道，你们英国人看重的是奥利凡德的魔杖。"

哈利没有回答。他假装像克鲁姆一样看别人跳舞，心里却在苦苦

CHAPTER EIGHT   The Wedding

he was thinking hard. So Voldemort was looking for a celebrated wandmaker, and Harry did not have to search far for a reason: it was surely because of what Harry's wand had done on the night that Voldemort had pursued him across the skies. The holly and phoenix feather wand had conquered the borrowed wand, something that Ollivander had not anticipated or understood. Would Gregorovitch know better? Was he truly more skilled than Ollivander, did he know secrets of wands that Ollivander did not?

'This girl is very nice-looking,' Krum said, recalling Harry to his surroundings. Krum was pointing at Ginny, who had just joined Luna. 'She is also a relative of yours?'

'Yeah,' said Harry, suddenly irritated, 'and she's seeing someone. Jealous type. Big bloke. You wouldn't want to cross him.'

Krum grunted.

'Vot,' he said, draining his goblet and getting to his feet again, 'is the point of being an international Quidditch player if all the good-looking girls are taken?'

And he strode off, leaving Harry to take a sandwich from a passing waiter and make his way round the edge of the crowded dance floor. He wanted to find Ron, to tell him about Gregorovitch, but Ron was dancing with Hermione out in the middle of the floor. Harry leaned up against one of the golden pillars and watched Ginny, who was now dancing with Fred and George's friend Lee Jordan, trying not to feel resentful about the promise he had given Ron.

He had never been to a wedding before, so he could not judge how wizarding celebrations differed from Muggle ones, though he was pretty sure that the latter would not involve a wedding cake topped with two model phoenixes that took flight when the cake was cut, or bottles of champagne that floated unsupported through the crowd. As evening drew in and moths began to swoop under the canopy, now lit with floating golden lanterns, the revelry became more and more uncontained. Fred and George had long since disappeared into the darkness with a pair of Fleur's cousins; Charlie, Hagrid and a squat wizard in a purple pork-pie hat were singing 'Odo the Hero' in a corner.

Wandering through the crowd so as to escape a drunken uncle of Ron's who seemed unsure whether or not Harry was his son, Harry spotted an old wizard sitting alone at a table. His cloud of white hair made him look

第8章 婚 礼

思索。这么说伏地魔寻找的是一位著名的魔杖制作人,哈利觉得这个原因倒不难理解:肯定是因为伏地魔在空中追他的那天夜里哈利魔杖的所作所为。冬青木和凤凰羽毛的魔杖征服了那根借来的魔杖,这是奥利凡德没有料到和不能理解的。格里戈维奇是不是知道更多?他真的比奥利凡德技术高明,他真的知道奥利凡德不知道的魔杖秘密吗?

"这姑娘很漂亮。"克鲁姆的话把哈利拉回到眼前的场景中,克鲁姆指的是金妮,她来到卢娜身边和她一起跳舞,"她也是你们家亲戚?"

"对,"哈利说,心头突然烦躁起来,"她有男朋友了。那家伙块头挺大,爱吃醋。你可千万别惹他。"

克鲁姆不满地嘟哝着。

"唉,"他喝干杯里的酒,重又站起身来,"所有的漂亮姑娘都名花有主,做一个国际球星又有什么用呢?"

他大步走开了,哈利从旁边走过的侍者手里拿过一块三明治,在拥挤的舞池边缘穿行。他想找到罗恩,跟他说说格里戈维奇的事,可是罗恩正在舞池中央跟赫敏跳舞呢。哈利靠在一根金柱子上注视着金妮,她现在正跟弗雷德和乔治的朋友李·乔丹一起翩翩起舞,哈利努力不让自己因为对罗恩许了诺言而心生怨恨。

他以前从没参加过婚礼,所以没法判断巫师的仪式和麻瓜们有什么不同,不过他知道麻瓜婚礼上肯定不会有一瓶瓶香槟酒在人群中悬空飘浮,也不会有这样的结婚蛋糕:顶上有两只凤凰模型,蛋糕一切开它们就展翅起飞。夜幕降临,浮在半空的金色灯笼照亮了天棚,蛾子开始在天棚下成群飞舞,狂欢的气氛越来越浓,越来越没有节制。弗雷德和乔治早就跟芙蓉的一对表姐妹消失在了黑暗里。查理、海格和一个戴紫色馅饼式男帽的矮胖巫师在墙角高唱《英雄奥多》。

罗恩的一个叔叔喝醉了酒,弄不清哈利到底是不是他儿子。哈利为了躲避他,在人群里胡乱地穿行,突然看见一个老巫师独自坐在一张桌子旁。他的白头发毛茸茸的,使他看上去活像一个年迈的蒲公英

CHAPTER EIGHT The Wedding

rather like an aged dandelion clock, and was topped by a moth-eaten fez. He was vaguely familiar: racking his brains Harry suddenly realised that this was Elphias Doge, member of the Order of the Phoenix, and the writer of Dumbledore's obituary.

Harry approached him.

'May I sit down?'

'Of course, of course,' said Doge; he had a rather high-pitched, wheezy voice.

Harry leaned in.

'Mr Doge, I'm Harry Potter.'

Doge gasped.

'My dear boy! Arthur told me you were here, disguised ... I am so glad, so honoured!'

In a flutter of nervous pleasure Doge poured Harry a goblet of champagne.

'I thought of writing to you,' he whispered, 'after Dumbledore ... the shock ... and for you, I am sure ...'

Doge's tiny eyes filled with sudden tears.

'I saw the obituary you wrote for the *Daily Prophet*,' said Harry. 'I didn't realise you knew Professor Dumbledore so well.'

'As well as anyone,' said Doge, dabbing his eyes with a napkin. 'Certainly I knew him longest, if you don't count Aberforth – and somehow, people never *do* seem to count Aberforth.'

'Speaking of the *Daily Prophet* ... I don't know whether you saw, Mr Doge –?'

'Oh, please call me Elphias, dear boy.'

'Elphias, I don't know whether you saw the interview Rita Skeeter gave about Dumbledore?'

Doge's face flooded with angry colour.

'Oh, yes, Harry, I saw it. That woman, or vulture might be a more accurate term, positively pestered me to talk to her. I am ashamed to say that I became rather rude, called her an interfering trout, which resulted, as you may have seen, in aspersions cast upon my sanity.'

茸毛头，头顶上还戴着一顶被虫蛀了的土耳其帽。哈利觉得他有点眼熟，使劲儿想了想，突然想起这是埃非亚斯·多吉，凤凰社成员，邓布利多那篇讣文的作者。

哈利朝他走去。

"我可以坐下吗？"

"当然，当然。"多吉说，他的声音非常尖细，呼哧带喘。

哈利探过身去。

"多吉先生，我是哈利·波特。"

多吉倒抽了口冷气。

"我亲爱的孩子！亚瑟告诉我说你在这儿，化了装……我太高兴了，太荣幸了！"

多吉又是紧张又是高兴，手忙脚乱地给哈利倒了杯香槟。

"我早就想给你写信，"他小声说，"邓布利多死后……那种震惊……我相信对你来说……"

多吉的小眼睛里突然充满泪水。

"我看了你给《预言家日报》写的那篇讣文，"哈利说，"没想到你对邓布利多教授这么熟悉。"

"并不比别人更熟悉。"多吉说着，用一块餐巾擦了擦眼睛，"当然啦，我认识他的时间最长，如果不算阿不福思——不知怎么，人们好像确实从不算上阿不福思。"

"说到《预言家日报》……多吉先生，我不知道你有没有看到——？"

"哦，就叫我埃非亚斯吧，亲爱的孩子。"

"埃非亚斯，不知道你有没有看到丽塔·斯基特关于邓布利多的那篇专访？"

多吉的脸顿时气得通红。

"看到了，哈利，我看到了。那个女人，叫她秃老雕恐怕更合适些，她竟然缠着我跟她说话。说来惭愧，我当时态度也很粗野，骂她是爱管闲事的讨厌婆娘，结果，你大概也看到了，她给我泼脏水，诽谤我神志不清。"

CHAPTER EIGHT The Wedding

'Well, in that interview,' Harry went on, 'Rita Skeeter hinted that Professor Dumbledore was involved in the Dark Arts when he was young.'

'Don't believe a word of it!' said Doge at once. 'Not a word, Harry! Let nothing tarnish your memories of Albus Dumbledore!'

Harry looked into Doge's earnest, pained face and felt not reassured, but frustrated. Did Doge really think it was that easy, that Harry could simply *choose* not to believe? Didn't Doge understand Harry's need to be sure, to know *everything*?

Perhaps Doge suspected Harry's feelings, for he looked concerned and hurried on, 'Harry, Rita Skeeter is a dreadful –'

But he was interrupted by a shrill cackle.

'Rita Skeeter? Oh, I love her, always read her!'

Harry and Doge looked up to see Auntie Muriel standing there, the plumes dancing on her hat, a goblet of champagne in her hand. 'She's written a book about Dumbledore, you know!'

'Hello, Muriel,' said Doge. 'Yes, we were just discussing –'

'You there! Give me your chair, I'm a hundred and seven!'

Another redheaded Weasley cousin jumped off his seat, looking alarmed, and Auntie Muriel swung it round with surprising strength and plopped herself down upon it between Doge and Harry.

'Hello again, Barry, or whatever your name is,' she said to Harry. 'Now, what were you saying about Rita Skeeter, Elphias? You know she's written a biography of Dumbledore? I can't wait to read it, I must remember to place an order at Flourish and Blotts!'

Doge looked stiff and solemn at this, but Auntie Muriel drained her goblet and clicked her bony fingers at a passing waiter for a replacement. She took another large gulp of champagne, belched and then said, 'There's no need to look like a pair of stuffed frogs! Before he became so respected and respectable and all that tosh, there were some mighty funny rumours about Albus!'

'Ill-informed sniping,' said Doge, turning radish-coloured again.

'You would say that, Elphias,' cackled Auntie Muriel. 'I noticed how you skated over the sticky patches in that obituary of yours!'

第8章 婚 礼

"嗯,在那篇专访里,"哈利继续说,"丽塔·斯基特暗示说邓布利多教授年轻时接触过黑魔法。"

"一个字儿也别信!"多吉立刻说道,"一个字儿也别信,哈利!别让任何东西玷污你记忆中的阿不思·邓布利多!"

哈利凝视着多吉那张真诚而痛苦的脸,心里并没有得到安慰,反而觉得失望。难道多吉真的以为事情那么简单,哈利只要选择不去相信就行了吗?难道多吉不明白哈利需要弄个水落石出,需要知道一切?

多吉大概觉察到了哈利的感受,他露出担忧的神情,急忙又说道:"哈利,丽塔·斯基特是个非常讨厌的——"

一声刺耳的嘎嘎尖笑打断了他的话。

"丽塔·斯基特?哦,我喜欢她,总是读她写的东西!"

哈利和多吉抬头一看,面前站着穆丽尔姨婆,她帽子上的羽毛上下翻飞,手里端着一杯香槟。"知道吗,她写了一本关于邓布利多的书!"

"你好,穆丽尔,"多吉说,"是啊,我们正在谈论——"

"那边的!把你的椅子给我,我都一百零七岁了!"

韦斯莱家的另一个红头发堂哥惊慌失措地从椅子上跳起来,穆丽尔姨婆用惊人的力气把椅子转了个圈,放在多吉和哈利中间,然后扑通坐了下去。

"又见到你了,巴利,不管你叫什么名字吧。"她对哈利说,"好了,埃非亚斯,你们刚才在说丽塔·斯基特什么?知道她写了一本邓布利多的传记吗?我迫不及待地想读呢,我得记着在丽痕书店订购一本。"

听了这话,多吉沉下脸,表情僵硬,可是穆丽尔姨婆一口喝干杯里的酒,用瘦骨嶙峋的手朝旁边一位侍者打了个响指,要求斟满。她又喝下一大口香槟,打了个响嗝儿,才说道:"没必要看上去像两只青蛙标本似的!阿不思在变得这么德高望重、受人尊敬之前,曾经有过一些非常滑稽的谣传呢!"

"无中生有的诽谤。"多吉说,脸又变得像萝卜一样通红。

"随你怎么说吧,埃非亚斯,"穆丽尔姨婆咯咯笑着说,"我注意到你那篇讣文把不好处理的地方一带而过!"

CHAPTER EIGHT The Wedding

'I'm sorry you think so,' said Doge, more coldly still. 'I assure you I was writing from the heart.'

'Oh, we all know you worshipped Dumbledore; I daresay you'll still think he was a saint even if it does turn out that he did away with his Squib sister!'

'*Muriel!*' exclaimed Doge.

A chill that had nothing to do with the iced champagne was stealing through Harry's chest.

'What do you mean?' he asked Muriel. 'Who said his sister was a Squib? I thought she was ill?'

'Thought wrong, then, didn't you, Barry!' said Auntie Muriel, looking delighted at the effect she had produced. 'Anyway, how could you expect to know anything about it? It all happened years and years before you were even thought of, my dear, and the truth is that those of us who were alive then never knew what really happened. That's why I can't wait to find out what Skeeter's unearthed! Dumbledore kept that sister of his quiet for a long time!'

'Untrue!' wheezed Doge. 'Absolutely untrue!'

'He never told me his sister was a Squib,' said Harry, without thinking, still cold inside.

'And why on earth would he tell you?' screeched Muriel, swaying a little in her seat as she attempted to focus upon Harry.

'The reason Albus never spoke about Ariana,' began Elphias, in a voice stiff with emotion, 'is, I should have thought, quite clear. He was so devastated by her death –'

'Why did nobody ever see her, Elphias?' squawked Muriel. 'Why did half of us never even know she existed, until they carried the coffin out of the house and held a funeral for her? Where was saintly Albus, while Ariana was locked in the cellar? Off being brilliant at Hogwarts, and never mind what was going on in his own house!'

'What d'you mean "locked in the cellar"?' asked Harry. 'What is this?'

Doge looked wretched. Auntie Muriel cackled again and answered Harry.

'Dumbledore's mother was a terrifying woman, simply terrifying. Muggle-born, though I heard she pretended otherwise –'

第8章 婚 礼

"很遗憾你这么想。"多吉口气更加冷淡地说,"我向你保证,我写的都是发自内心的话。"

"噢,我们都知道你崇拜邓布利多。我敢说你一直都把他看成圣人,即使后来发现他真的杀死了他的哑炮妹妹!"

"穆丽尔!"多吉惊叫。

一股与冰镇香槟酒无关的寒意穿过哈利的胸膛。

"你说什么?"他问穆丽尔,"谁说他妹妹是个哑炮?她不是身体有病吗?"

"那你可就错了,巴利!"穆丽尔姨婆说,似乎对她制造的效果非常满意,"是啊,你怎么可能知道这件事呢?亲爱的,事情发生的时候,你连影子都没有呢,事实上,我们这些当时活着的人也根本不清楚到底是怎么回事。所以我才等不及要看看斯基特挖掘出了什么!邓布利多很长时间都只字不提他那个妹妹!"

"不实之词!"多吉气呼呼地说,"纯粹是不实之词!"

"他从没对我说过他妹妹是个哑炮。"哈利的话脱口而出,心里仍然充满寒意。

"他凭什么要对你说?"穆丽尔尖声说道,在椅子上摇晃着身子,想把目光对准哈利的脸。

"阿不思从来不提阿利安娜,"埃非亚斯用激动得发紧的声音说,"其中的原因我想是很明显的。妹妹的死让他伤心欲绝——"

"为什么从来没有人见过阿利安娜,埃非亚斯?"穆丽尔粗声大气地问,"为什么我们一半的人甚至都不知道有她这个人存在,直到他们从房子里抬出棺材,为她举行葬礼?阿利安娜被关在地窖里的时候,圣人阿不思在哪儿呢?他在霍格沃茨大出风头呢,根本不关心自己家里发生的事儿!"

"你说什么,'关在地窖里'?"哈利问,"这是怎么回事?"

多吉显出痛苦的样子。穆丽尔姨婆又咯咯大笑一阵,然后回答了哈利。

"邓布利多的母亲是个可怕的女人,非常可怕,麻瓜出身,但我听说她谎称自己不是——"

CHAPTER EIGHT   The Wedding

'She never pretended anything of the sort! Kendra was a fine woman,' whispered Doge miserably, but Auntie Muriel ignored him.

'– proud and very domineering, the sort of witch who would have been mortified to produce a Squib –'

'Ariana was not a Squib!' wheezed Doge.

'So you say, Elphias, but explain, then, why she never attended Hogwarts!' said Auntie Muriel. She turned back to Harry. 'In our day Squibs were often hushed up. Though to take it to the extreme of actually imprisoning a little girl in the house and pretending she didn't exist –'

'I tell you, that's not what happened!' said Doge, but Auntie Muriel steamrollered on, still addressing Harry.

'Squibs were usually shipped off to Muggle schools and encouraged to integrate into the Muggle community ... much kinder than trying to find them a place in the wizarding world, where they must always be second class; but naturally Kendra Dumbledore wouldn't have dreamed of letting her daughter go to a Muggle school –'

'Ariana was delicate!' said Doge desperately. 'Her health was always too poor to permit her –'

'To permit her to leave the house?' cackled Muriel. 'And yet she was never taken to St Mungo's and no healer was ever summoned to see her!'

'Really, Muriel, how you can possibly know whether –'

'For your information, Elphias, my cousin Lancelot was a healer at St Mungo's at the time, and he told my family in strictest confidence that Ariana had never been seen there. All most suspicious, Lancelot thought!'

Doge looked to be on the verge of tears. Auntie Muriel, who seemed to be enjoying herself hugely, snapped her fingers for more champagne. Numbly Harry thought of how the Dursleys had once shut him up, locked him away, kept him out of sight, all for the crime of being a wizard. Had Dumbledore's sister suffered the same fate in reverse: imprisoned for her lack of magic? And had Dumbledore truly left her to her fate while he went off to Hogwarts, to prove himself brilliant and talented?

'Now, if Kendra hadn't died first,' Muriel resumed, 'I'd have said that it was she who finished off Ariana –'

第8章 婚　礼

"她从来没有谎称过那样的事！坎德拉是个很好的女人。"多吉可怜巴巴地小声说，但穆丽尔姨婆根本不理他。

"——非常骄傲，盛气凌人，那种女巫生下一个哑炮，肯定觉得大丢面子——"

"阿利安娜不是哑炮！"多吉喘着气说。

"这是你的看法，埃非亚斯，那请你解释一下，她为什么一直没上霍格沃茨？"穆丽尔姨婆说，然后她又转向哈利，"在我们那个年代，家里有个哑炮经常要遮掩起来，但是做得那么过分，竟然把一个小姑娘囚禁在家里，假装她不存在——"

"我告诉你，根本就没有那回事！"多吉说，但穆丽尔姨婆继续势不可挡地往下说，仍然冲着哈利。

"一般是把哑炮送到麻瓜学校，鼓励他们融入麻瓜社会……这要比给他们在巫师界找个位置仁慈得多，因为他们在巫师界永远只能是二等公民。可是，当然啦，坎德拉·邓布利多做梦也不想把女儿送进一所麻瓜学校——"

"阿利安娜身体不好！"多吉绝望地说，"她健康状况很差，不能——"

"——不能离开家门？"穆丽尔咯咯笑着说，"她从来不去圣芒戈医院，也没有请治疗师上门看她！"

"说真的，穆丽尔，你怎么可能知道是不是——"

"告诉你吧，埃非亚斯，我的亲戚兰斯洛特当时就是圣芒戈医院的治疗师，他非常机密地告诉我们家人，他们从没看见阿利安娜去过医院。兰斯洛特认为这十分可疑！"

多吉看上去快要哭了。穆丽尔姨婆似乎开心极了，又打着响指要香槟。哈利呆呆地想着德思礼一家曾经把他关起来、锁起来、不让别人看见他，就因为他是个巫师。难道邓布利多的妹妹由于相反的原因遭受过同样的命运：因为不会魔法而被囚禁？难道邓布利多真的对她的命运不闻不问，只管在霍格沃茨证明自己有多么优秀，多么才华横溢？

"咳，要不是坎德拉死在前面，"穆丽尔又说道，"我都怀疑是她干掉了阿利安娜——"

CHAPTER EIGHT   The Wedding

'How can you, Muriel?' groaned Doge. 'A mother kill her own daughter? Think what you are saying!'

'If the mother in question was capable of imprisoning her daughter for years on end, why not?' shrugged Auntie Muriel. 'But as I say, it doesn't fit, because Kendra died before Ariana – of what, nobody ever seemed sure –'

'Oh, no doubt Ariana murdered her,' said Doge, with a brave attempt at scorn. 'Why not?'

'Yes, Ariana might have made a desperate bid for freedom and killed Kendra in the struggle,' said Auntie Muriel thoughtfully. 'Shake your head all you like, Elphias! You were at Ariana's funeral, were you not?'

'Yes, I was,' said Doge, through trembling lips. 'And a more desperately sad occasion I cannot remember. Albus was heartbroken –'

'His heart wasn't the only thing. Didn't Aberforth break Albus's nose halfway through the service?'

If Doge had looked horrified before this, it was nothing to how he looked now. Muriel might have stabbed him. She cackled loudly and took another swig of champagne, which dribbled down her chin.

'How do you –?' croaked Doge.

'My mother was friendly with old Bathilda Bagshot,' said Auntie Muriel happily. 'Bathilda described the whole thing to Mother while I was listening at the door. A coffin-side brawl! The way Bathilda told it, Aberforth shouted that it was all Albus's fault that Ariana was dead and then punched him in the face. According to Bathilda, Albus did not even defend himself, and that's odd enough in itself, Albus could have destroyed Aberforth in a duel with both hands tied behind his back.'

Muriel swigged yet more champagne. The recitation of these old scandals seemed to elate her as much as they horrified Doge. Harry did not know what to think, what to believe: he wanted the truth, and yet all Doge did was sit there and bleat feebly that Ariana had been ill. Harry could hardly believe that Dumbledore would not have intervened if such cruelty was happening inside his own house, and yet there was undoubtedly something odd about the story.

'And I'll tell you something else,' Muriel said, hiccoughing slightly as she

第 8 章 婚　礼

"你怎么能这么说，穆丽尔？"多吉哀叹着说，"一个母亲杀死自己的亲生女儿？你想想你都在说些什么！"

"如果这位母亲能够多年囚禁自己的女儿，还有什么做不出来的？"穆丽尔姨婆耸耸肩膀说，"不过我说了，这不成立，因为坎德拉死在阿利安娜之前——怎么死的，似乎谁都说不准——"

"哦，肯定是阿利安娜谋杀了她，"多吉勇敢地做出讥笑的神情说，"有什么做不出来的？"

"对，阿利安娜可能为了自由拼死反抗，在搏斗中杀死了坎德拉。"穆丽尔姨婆若有所思地说，"你就尽管摇头吧，埃非亚斯！你当时也参加了阿利安娜的葬礼，不是吗？"

"是啊，"多吉嘴唇颤抖地说，"这是我记忆中最最令人伤心的场面。阿不思的心都碎了——"

"碎的不只是他的心。葬礼举行到一半的时候，阿不福思是不是打断了阿不思的鼻子？"

如果说刚才多吉显出的神情是惊恐，那跟他此刻的神情相比简直不算什么，他就好像被穆丽尔一刀刺中了似的。穆丽尔姨婆哈哈大笑，又喝了一大口香槟，酒顺着下巴滴滴答答地流下来。

"你怎么——？"多吉哑着嗓子问。

"我母亲跟老巴希达·巴沙特关系很好，"穆丽尔姨婆兴高采烈地说，"巴希达跟我母亲讲述了整个事情，我在门口听见了。棺材边的争斗！巴希达说，阿不福思大声嚷嚷说阿利安娜的死都怪阿不思，然后一拳砸在阿不思脸上。巴希达说，阿不思甚至都没有抵挡一下，这本身就够奇怪的，阿不思即使两只手捆在背后跟阿不福思决斗，也能把他干掉。"

穆丽尔又大口喝了一些香槟。讲述这些昔日的丑闻把多吉吓得不轻，她自己却兴致盎然。哈利不知道该怎么想，该相信什么：他希望了解事实，可多吉只是坐在那里用颤抖的声音有气无力地说阿利安娜体弱多病。如果邓布利多家里真的发生了这样惨无人道的事，哈利相信他绝不会听之任之，然而这故事里无疑存在着一些蹊跷之处。

"我再告诉你一件事吧，"穆丽尔姨婆放下酒杯，轻轻打着嗝儿说，

lowered her goblet. 'I think Bathilda has spilled the beans to Rita Skeeter. All those hints in Skeeter's interview about an important source close to the Dumbledores – goodness knows she was there all through the Ariana business and it would fit!'

'Bathilda would never talk to Rita Skeeter!' whispered Doge.

'Bathilda Bagshot?' Harry said. 'The author of *A History of Magic*?'

The name was printed on the front of one of Harry's textbooks, though admittedly not one of the ones he had read most attentively.

'Yes,' said Doge, clutching at Harry's question like a drowning man at a lifebelt. 'A most gifted magical historian and an old friend of Albus's.'

'Quite gaga these days, I've heard,' said Auntie Muriel cheerfully.

'If that is so, it is even more dishonourable for Skeeter to have taken advantage of her,' said Doge, 'and no reliance can be placed on anything Bathilda may have said!'

'Oh, there are ways of bringing back memories, and I'm sure Rita Skeeter knows them all,' said Auntie Muriel. 'But even if Bathilda's completely cuckoo, I'm sure she'd still have old photographs, maybe even letters. She knew the Dumbledores for years … well worth a trip to Godric's Hollow, I'd have thought.'

Harry, who had been taking a sip of Butterbeer, choked. Doge banged him on the back as Harry coughed, looking at Auntie Muriel through streaming eyes. Once he had control of his voice again, he asked, 'Bathilda Bagshot lives in Godric's Hollow?'

'Oh yes, she's been there forever! The Dumbledores moved there after Percival was imprisoned, and she was their neighbour.'

'The Dumbledores lived in Godric's Hollow?'

'Yes, Barry, that's what I just said,' said Auntie Muriel testily.

Harry felt drained, empty. Never once, in six years, had Dumbledore told Harry that they had both lived and lost loved ones in Godric's Hollow. Why? Were Lily and James buried close to Dumbledore's mother and sister? Had Dumbledore visited their graves, perhaps walked past Lily and James's to do so? And he had never once told Harry … never bothered to say …

第8章 婚 礼

"我猜想是巴希达向丽塔·斯基特透露了秘密。斯基特的那篇专访暗示说,有一位与邓布利多一家关系密切的人提供了重要消息——老天做证,巴希达从头到尾目睹了阿利安娜的事情,肯定是她!"

"巴希达绝不会跟丽塔·斯基特说话!"多吉低声说。

"巴希达·巴沙特?"哈利说,"《魔法史》的作者?"

这个名字印在哈利一本教科书的封面上,不过必须承认,那本书他读得并不认真。

"是啊,"多吉说,他一把抓住哈利的问题,就像一个快要淹死的人抓住救生带一样,"一位非常有天分的魔法历史学家,也是阿不思的老朋友。"

"听说最近糊涂得厉害。"穆丽尔姨婆开心地说。

"如果是这样,斯基特利用她就更可耻了。"多吉说,"巴希达说的任何东西都不可信!"

"哦,有许多办法可以唤回记忆,我相信丽塔·斯基特对它们都很精通。"穆丽尔姨婆说,"就算巴希达成了彻头彻尾的老傻瓜,她肯定还会有老照片,甚至以前的信件。她认识邓布利多一家好多年……没错,完全值得去一趟戈德里克山谷。"

哈利正在喝黄油啤酒,突然呛住了,多吉使劲拍他的后背。哈利一边咳嗽,一边用泪汪汪的眼睛看着穆丽尔姨婆。他刚找回自己的声音就问道:"巴希达·巴沙特住在戈德里克山谷?"

"是啊,一直住在那儿!邓布利多一家在珀西瓦尔坐牢后搬到了那儿,巴希达是他们的邻居。"

"邓布利多一家住在戈德里克山谷?"

"是啊,巴利,我刚才已经说了。"穆丽尔姨婆不耐烦地说。

哈利觉得心里一下子被抽空了。六年来,邓布利多一次也没有告诉过哈利,他们都曾在戈德里克山谷生活过,都在那里失去过自己的亲人。为什么?莉莉和詹姆是不是就埋在邓布利多的母亲和妹妹旁边?邓布利多扫墓时,是不是要经过莉莉和詹姆的坟墓?而他一次也没有告诉过哈利……从来没说过……

CHAPTER EIGHT The Wedding

And why it was so important, Harry could not explain, even to himself, yet he felt it had been tantamount to a lie not to tell him that they had this place, and these experiences, in common. He stared ahead of him, barely noticing what was going on around him, and did not realise that Hermione had appeared out of the crowd until she drew up a chair beside him.

'I simply can't dance any more,' she panted, slipping off one of her shoes and rubbing the sole of her foot. 'Ron's gone looking to find more Butterbeers. It's a bit odd, I've just seen Viktor storming away from Luna's father, it looked like they'd been arguing –' She dropped her voice, staring at him. 'Harry, are you OK?'

Harry did not know where to begin, but it did not matter. At that moment, something large and silver came falling through the canopy over the dance floor. Graceful and gleaming, the lynx landed lightly in the middle of the astonished dancers. Heads turned, as those nearest it froze, absurdly, in mid-dance. Then the Patronus's mouth opened wide and it spoke in the loud, deep, slow voice of Kingsley Shacklebolt.

'The Ministry has fallen. Scrimgeour is dead. They are coming.'

第8章 婚　礼

　　为什么这一点如此重要，哈利自己也无法解释，但他觉得，邓布利多对他只字不提他们共同拥有这个地方和这些经历，就等于是在欺骗。他呆呆地望着前面，几乎没有注意到周围的动静，直到赫敏搬了把椅子坐到他身边，他才发现她已经从人群里出来了。

　　"我实在不能再跳了。"赫敏喘着气说，她脱掉一只鞋子，揉着脚底，"罗恩去找黄油啤酒了。真是怪事，我刚才看见威克多尔怒气冲冲地从卢娜父亲的身边走开，好像他们吵架了——"她放低声音，望着哈利，"哈利，你没事吧？"

　　哈利不知从何说起，但已经没有关系了。就在这时，一个银色的大家伙穿透舞池上方的天棚掉了下来。这只猞猁姿态优雅、闪闪发光，轻盈地落在大惊失色的跳舞者中间。人们纷纷扭过头，离它最近的一些人滑稽地僵住了，还保持着跳舞的动作。守护神把嘴张得大大的，用金斯莱·沙克尔那响亮、浑厚而缓慢的声音说话了。

　　"魔法部垮台了。斯克林杰死了。他们来了。"

CHAPTER NINE

A Place to Hide

Everything seemed fuzzy, slow. Harry and Hermione jumped to their feet and drew their wands. Many people were only just realising that something strange had happened; heads were still turning towards the silver cat as it vanished. Silence spread outwards in cold ripples from the place where the Patronus had landed. Then somebody screamed.

Harry and Hermione threw themselves into the panicking crowd. Guests were sprinting in all directions; many were Disapparating; the protective enchantments around The Burrow had broken.

Ron!' Hermione cried. 'Ron, where are you?'

As they pushed their way across the dance floor, Harry saw cloaked and masked figures appearing in the crowd; then he saw Lupin and Tonks, their wands raised, and heard both of them shout '*Protego!* ', a cry that was echoed on all sides –

'Ron! Ron!' Hermione called, half sobbing as she and Harry were buffeted by terrified guests: Harry seized her hand to make sure they weren't separated as a streak of light whizzed over their heads, whether a protective charm or something more sinister he did not know –

And then Ron was there. He caught hold of Hermione's free arm and Harry felt her turn on the spot; sight and sound were extinguished as darkness pressed in upon him; all he could feel was Hermione's hand as he was squeezed through space and time, away from The Burrow, away from the descending Death Eaters, away, perhaps, from Voldemort himself …

'Where are we?' said Ron's voice.

Harry opened his eyes. For a moment he thought they had not left the wedding after all: they still seemed to be surrounded by people.

第 9 章

藏身之处

一切都显得那么缓慢、模糊不清。哈利和赫敏一跃而起，抽出魔杖。许多人刚意识到发生了变故；银色的猞猁消失了，人们仍然扭头望着那里。沉默像冰冷的河水，从守护神降落的地方一波一波向外扩展。接着有人尖叫起来。

哈利和赫敏冲进惊慌失措的人群。宾客向四面八方逃窜，许多人在幻影移形。陋居周围的保护魔咒已被破坏。

"罗恩！"赫敏叫道，"罗恩，你在哪儿？"

他们穿过拥挤的舞池时，哈利看见人群里出现了一些穿斗篷、戴面具的身影。然后他发现了卢平和唐克斯，两人都举着魔杖，还听见他们同时大喊："盔甲护身！"声音在四处回荡——

"罗恩！罗恩！"赫敏带着哭腔喊，她和哈利被惊恐的宾客撞得东倒西歪。哈利抓住她的手，确保两人不被冲散，这时他们的头顶上嗖地掠过一道光，不知是防护咒，还是某种更加凶险的东西——

罗恩出现了。他抓住赫敏的另一只胳膊，哈利感觉到赫敏原地转了个身。黑暗向他袭来，眼前一片模糊，声音也听不见了，唯一感觉到的就是赫敏的手，他被挤压着穿越时空，离开了陋居，离开了那些从天而降的食死徒，或许还有伏地魔本人……

"我们在哪儿？"罗恩的声音问。

哈利睁开眼睛，恍惚间以为他们并没有离开婚礼现场：周围似乎还是挤满了人。

CHAPTER NINE A Place to Hide

'Tottenham Court Road,' panted Hermione. 'Walk, just walk, we need to find somewhere for you to change.'

Harry did as she asked. They half walked, half ran up the wide, dark street thronged with late-night revellers and lined with closed shops, stars twinkling above them. A double-decker bus rumbled by and a group of merry pub-goers ogled them as they passed; Harry and Ron were still wearing dress robes.

'Hermione, we haven't got anything to change into,' Ron told her, as a young woman burst into raucous giggles at the sight of him.

'Why didn't I make sure I had the Invisibility Cloak with me?' said Harry, inwardly cursing his own stupidity. 'All last year I kept it on me and –'

'It's OK, I've got the Cloak, I've got clothes for both of you,' said Hermione. 'Just try and act naturally until – this will do.'

She led them down a side street, then into the shelter of a shadowy alleyway.

'When you say you've got the Cloak, and clothes ...' said Harry, frowning at Hermione, who was carrying nothing except her small beaded handbag, in which she was now rummaging.

'Yes, they're here,' said Hermione, and to Harry and Ron's utter astonishment, she pulled out a pair of jeans, a sweatshirt, some maroon socks and, finally, the silvery Invisibility Cloak.

'How the ruddy hell –?'

'Undetectable Extension Charm,' said Hermione. 'Tricky, but I think I've done it OK; anyway, I managed to fit everything we need in here.' She gave the fragile-looking bag a little shake and it echoed like a cargo hold as a number of heavy objects rolled around inside it. 'Oh, damn, that'll be the books,' she said, peering into it, 'and I had them all stacked by subject ... oh well ... Harry, you'd better take the Invisibility Cloak. Ron, hurry up and change ...'

'When did you do all this?' Harry asked, as Ron stripped off his robes.

'I told you at The Burrow, I've had the essentials packed for days, you know, in case we needed to make a quick getaway. I packed your rucksack this morning, Harry, after you changed, and put it in here ... I just had a feeling ...'

'You're amazing, you are,' said Ron, handing her his bundled-up robes.

'Thank you,' said Hermione, managing a small smile as she pushed the

第9章 藏身之处

"托腾汉宫路。"赫敏喘着气说,"走,快走,需要找个地方让你们换换衣服。"

哈利照她说的做了。他们在黑黢黢的宽阔街道上连走带跑,街上满是深夜纵酒狂欢的人,两边是打烊的店铺,头顶上群星闪烁。一辆双层公共汽车隆隆驶过,一群饮酒作乐的人走过时直盯着他们看。哈利和罗恩身上仍然穿着礼服长袍。

"赫敏,我们没有带替换的衣服。"罗恩对赫敏说。这时,一个年轻女人看见他的样子,发出粗野的大笑。

"我为什么不检查一下,把隐形衣带上呢?"哈利暗自责备自己的愚蠢,"去年我一直带在身上的——"

"没关系,隐形衣我拿着了,我还给你们俩都带了衣服。"赫敏说,"表现得自然一点,等我们——这里就行。"

她把他们领进一条小街,又领进一条阴影里的僻静窄巷。

"你说你带了隐形衣,还带了衣服……"哈利皱着眉头对赫敏说,赫敏只带着她那只串珠小包,此刻正在里面翻找。

"有了,在这儿。"赫敏说着掏出一条牛仔裤、一件运动衫、几只酱紫色的袜子,最后是那件银色的隐形衣,哈利和罗恩看得目瞪口呆。

"真是活见鬼了!你怎么——"

"无痕伸展咒,"赫敏说,"很不好弄,但我相信我是弄成了,反正我把我们需要的东西都放了进去。"她拎起那只看上去很精巧的小包抖了抖,里面发出很大的动静,就好像一大堆沉重的东西在货舱里滚动。"哟,该死,肯定是书。"赫敏朝小包里看了看,"我把它们分门别类归成几堆……好了……哈利,你最好穿上隐形衣。罗恩,快换衣服……"

"这是你什么时候干的?"哈利问,罗恩在一旁脱去长袍。

"我在陋居就告诉过你们,这些天来我一直在收拾必需用品,以备我们说走就走。哈利,今天早晨你换好衣服后,我整理了你的背包,把它放了进去……我当时就有种预感……"

"你真是太了不起了。"罗恩说着,把卷成一团的长袍递给赫敏。

"谢谢。"赫敏说,脸上勉强挤出一点笑容,把长袍塞进了包里,"哈

CHAPTER NINE A Place to Hide

robes into the bag. 'Please, Harry, get that Cloak on!'

Harry threw the Invisibility Cloak around his shoulders and pulled it up over his head, vanishing from sight. He was only just beginning to appreciate what had happened.

'The others – everyone at the wedding –'

'We can't worry about that now,' whispered Hermione. 'It's you they're after, Harry, and we'll just put everyone in even more danger by going back.'

'She's right,' said Ron, who seemed to know that Harry was about to argue, even if he could not see his face. 'Most of the Order was there, they'll look after everyone.'

Harry nodded, then remembered that they could not see him, and said, 'Yeah.' But he thought of Ginny and fear bubbled like acid in his stomach.

'Come on, I think we ought to keep moving,' said Hermione.

They moved back up the side street and on to the main road again, where a group of men on the opposite side was singing and weaving across the pavement.

'Just as a matter of interest, why Tottenham Court Road?' Ron asked Hermione.

'I've no idea, it just popped into my head, but I'm sure we're safer out in the Muggle world, it's not where they'll expect us to be.'

'True,' said Ron, looking around, 'but don't you feel a bit – exposed?'

'Where else is there?' asked Hermione, cringing as the men on the other side of the road started wolf-whistling at her. 'We can hardly book rooms at the Leaky Cauldron, can we? And Grimmauld Place is out if Snape can get in there ... I suppose we could try my parents' house, though I think there's a chance they might check there ... oh, I wish they'd shut up!'

'All right, darling?' the drunkest of the men on the other pavement was yelling. 'Fancy a drink? Ditch ginger and come and have a pint!'

'Let's sit down somewhere,' Hermione said hastily, as Ron opened his mouth to shout back across the road. 'Look, this will do, in here!'

It was a small and shabby all-night café. A light layer of grease lay on all the formica-topped tables, but it was at least empty. Harry slipped into a booth first and Ron sat next to him opposite Hermione, who had her back to the entrance and did not like it: she glanced over her shoulder so frequently

第9章 藏身之处

利,快把隐形衣穿上!"

哈利把隐形衣披在肩头,从后面拉上来盖住脑袋,整个人便消失不见了。他这才开始反应过来刚才发生的一切。

"其他人——参加婚礼的每个人——"

"现在顾不上那么多了。"赫敏小声说,"他们追的是你,哈利,如果我们回去,只会让大家的处境更危险。"

"她说得对,"罗恩虽然看不见哈利的脸,但似乎知道哈利要反驳,"大多数凤凰社成员都在那儿,他们会照顾大家的。"

哈利点点头,接着才想起他们看不见他,于是说:"是啊。"可一想起金妮,他立刻感到一种揪心的恐惧。

"快走,我认为我们不应该停下。"赫敏说。

他们重新走过那条小街,回到大马路上,对面一群男人唱着歌在人行道上歪歪扭扭地走着。

"我只是觉得有趣,为什么是托腾汉宫路呢?"罗恩问赫敏。

"不知道,脑子里突然冒出这个地名,但我相信我们在麻瓜世界里更安全些,他们想不到我们会在这儿。"

"不错,"罗恩说着看了看四周,"但你不觉得有点儿——太暴露了吗?"

"除了这儿还有哪儿?"赫敏问,这时马路对面的男人开始吹口哨挑逗她,她吓得缩成一团,"总不能在破釜酒吧订几个房间吧?至于格里莫广场,如果斯内普能进得去,肯定也不行……我想我们可以到我父母家去试试,不过他们恐怕也会去那里搜查的……哦,我真希望这帮人能闭嘴!"

"怎么样,宝贝儿?"对面人行道上一个醉得最厉害的男人喊道,"想喝点儿吗?甩了那个红头发的,过来喝一杯吧!"

"我们找个地方坐下来吧。"赫敏看到罗恩张嘴要冲马路对面嚷嚷,赶紧说道,"看,这儿就行,进去吧!"

这是一间昼夜营业的破破烂烂的小咖啡馆。塑料贴面的桌子上粘着一层薄薄的油腻,但至少还算清静。哈利首先坐进一个卡座,罗恩

CHAPTER NINE   A Place to Hide

she appeared to have a twitch. Harry did not like being stationary; walking had given the illusion that they had a goal. Beneath the Cloak he could feel the last vestiges of the Polyjuice Potion leaving him, his hands returning to their usual length and shape. He pulled his glasses out of his pocket and put them on again.

After a minute or two, Ron said, 'You know, we're not far from the Leaky Cauldron here, it's only in Charing Cross –'

'Ron, we can't!' said Hermione at once.

'Not to stay there, but to find out what's going on!'

'We know what's going on! Voldemort's taken over the Ministry, what else do we need to know?'

'OK, OK, it was just an idea!'

They relapsed into a prickly silence. The gum-chewing waitress shuffled over and Hermione ordered two cappuccinos: as Harry was invisible, it would have looked odd to order him one. A pair of burly workmen entered the café and squeezed into the next booth. Hermione dropped her voice to a whisper.

'I say we find a quiet place to Disapparate and head for the countryside. Once we're there, we could send a message to the Order.'

'Can you do that talking Patronus thing, then?' asked Ron.

'I've been practising and I think so,' said Hermione.

'Well, as long as it doesn't get them into trouble, though they might've been arrested already. God, that's revolting,' Ron added, after one sip of the foamy, greyish coffee. The waitress had heard; she shot Ron a nasty look as she shuffled off to take the new customers' orders. The larger of the two workmen, who was blond and quite huge, now that Harry came to look at him, waved her away. She stared, affronted.

'Let's get going, then, I don't want to drink this muck,' said Ron. 'Hermione, have you got Muggle money to pay for this?'

'Yes, I took out all my building society savings before I came to The Burrow. I'll bet all the change is at the bottom,' sighed Hermione, reaching for her beaded bag.

The two workmen made identical movements and Harry mirrored them without conscious thought: all three of them drew their wands. Ron, a few

第9章 藏身之处

坐在他旁边面对赫敏。赫敏背朝门口，很不自在，不时地扭头看看，像害了抽动症似的。哈利不喜欢坐着不动，刚才走路给了他一个错觉，好像他们有个目标。隐形衣下，他感到复方汤剂的最后一点效果也在消失，他的手恢复了正常的大小和形状。他从口袋里掏出眼镜戴上。

过了一两分钟，罗恩说："其实，我们离破釜酒吧并不远，它就在查令十字——"

"罗恩，我们不能！"赫敏立刻说。

"不是要住在那里，是去弄清发生了什么事！"

"我们知道发生了什么事！伏地魔占领了魔法部，还有什么需要知道的呢？"

"好了，好了，我只是那么一想！"

他们气呼呼地重新陷入了沉默。嚼着口香糖的女侍者懒洋洋地走过来，赫敏要了两杯卡布奇诺。哈利是隐形的，如果给他要一杯会显得很反常。这时，两个膀大腰圆的工人走进咖啡馆，挤进了旁边的卡座里。赫敏把声音压得低低的。

"要我说，我们找个安静的地方幻影移形到乡村去，然后可以给凤凰社送个信。"

"你也能变出那种会说话的守护神？"罗恩问。

"我一直在练习，应该没问题。"赫敏说。

"好吧，只要不给他们惹麻烦，不过他们大概都已经被抓起来了。天哪，真恶心。"罗恩喝了口泛着泡沫的灰乎乎的咖啡，说了一句。女侍者听见了，朝罗恩狠狠瞪了一眼，懒洋洋地走过去招待新来的顾客。现在哈利看清了，两个工人里块头较大的那个一头金发，身材魁梧，他挥挥手叫女侍者走开。女侍者瞪着他，像是受了冒犯。

"我们走吧，我不想喝这垃圾。"罗恩说，"赫敏，你有麻瓜钱付账吗？"

"有，我到陋居去之前把我建房互助会的所有存款都取出来了。零钱肯定都放在包底。"赫敏叹了口气，伸手去拿她的串珠小包。

突然，两个工人不约而同地行动起来，哈利不假思索地迅速做出反应：三个人都拔出了魔杖。罗恩几秒钟后才明白发生了什么事，隔

CHAPTER NINE A Place to Hide

seconds late in realising what was going on, lunged across the table, pushing Hermione sideways on to her bench. The force of the Death Eaters' spells shattered the tiled wall where Ron's head had just been, as Harry, still invisible, yelled, '*Stupefy!*'

The great, blond Death Eater was hit in the face by a jet of red light: he slumped sideways, unconscious. His companion, unable to see who had cast the spell, fired another at Ron: shining black ropes flew from his wand-tip and bound Ron head to foot – the waitress screamed and ran for the door – Harry sent another Stunning Spell at the Death Eater with the twisted face who had tied up Ron, but the spell missed, rebounded on the window and hit the waitress, who collapsed in front of the door.

'*Expulso!*' bellowed the Death Eater, and the table behind which Harry was standing blew up: the force of the explosion slammed him into the wall and he felt his wand leave his hand as the Cloak slipped off him.

'*Petrificus Totalus!*' screamed Hermione from out of sight, and the Death Eater fell forwards like a statue to land with a crunching thud on the mess of broken china, table and coffee. Hermione crawled out from underneath the bench, shaking bits of glass ashtray out of her hair and trembling all over.

'D – *Diffindo*,' she said, pointing her wand at Ron, who roared in pain as she slashed open the knee of his jeans, leaving a deep cut. 'Oh, I'm so sorry, Ron, my hand's shaking! *Diffindo!*'

The severed ropes fell away. Ron got to his feet, shaking his arms to regain feeling in them. Harry picked up his wand and climbed over all the debris to where the large, blond Death Eater was sprawled across the bench.

'I should've recognised him, he was there the night Dumbledore died,' he said. He turned over the darker Death Eater with his foot; the man's eyes moved rapidly between Harry, Ron and Hermione.

'That's Dolohov,' said Ron. 'I recognise him from the old wanted posters. I think the big one's Thorfinn Rowle.'

'Never mind what they're called!' said Hermione a little hysterically. 'How did they find us? What are we going to do?'

Somehow her panic seemed to clear Harry's head.

'Lock the door,' he told her, 'and Ron, turn out the lights.'

第9章 藏身之处

着桌子扑过去，把赫敏推倒在她的座位上。食死徒咒语的力量震碎了砖墙，真悬，罗恩的脑袋刚才就在那里。仍然隐身的哈利大喊一声："昏昏倒地！"

一道红光闪过，击中了那个金发大块头食死徒的脸：他往旁边一倒，昏了过去。他的同伴看不见是谁念的咒语，又朝罗恩射出一咒：杖尖飞出亮闪闪的黑绳子，把罗恩从头到脚捆得结结实实——女侍者尖叫着跑向门口——哈利又朝那个捆绑罗恩的歪脸食死徒发了个昏迷咒，可是偏了，弹到窗户上，击中了女侍者，她立刻瘫倒在门口。

"飞沙走石！"食死徒大吼一声，哈利面前的一张桌子突然炸飞，爆炸的冲力把他推到墙上，他觉得魔杖脱了手，隐形衣也从身上滑落。

"统统石化！"赫敏在看不见的地方尖叫一声。食死徒向前一扑，像雕塑一样重重摔在瓷器、桌子和咖啡的残渣碎片上，发出嘎吱吱的响声。赫敏从座位底下钻出来，抖掉头发里烟灰缸的玻璃碎片，浑身发抖。

"四——四分五裂。"她用魔杖指着罗恩说，不料划破了罗恩牛仔裤的膝部，留下一道深深的伤口，罗恩痛得大叫起来。"哎哟，对不起，罗恩，我的手在发抖！四分五裂！"

割断的绳索掉了下来，罗恩站起身，晃晃胳膊恢复知觉。哈利捡起自己的魔杖，在一片狼藉中爬向那个瘫倒在座位上的金发大块头食死徒。

"我应该认出他来的，邓布利多死的那天夜里他也在。"哈利说完，用脚把那个皮肤较黑的食死徒踢得翻过身来，那人的目光在哈利、罗恩、赫敏之间来回移动。

"是多洛霍夫，"罗恩说，"我以前在通缉布告上见过他。我想这个大个子准是多尔芬·罗尔。"

"别管他们叫什么名字了！"赫敏有点儿歇斯底里地说，"他们怎么会找到我们的？我们怎么办呢？"

不知怎的，她的紧张倒使哈利头脑清醒了。

"把门锁上。"他对赫敏说，"罗恩，把灯灭了。"

CHAPTER NINE   A Place to Hide

He looked down at the paralysed Dolohov, thinking fast as the lock clicked and Ron used the Deluminator to plunge the café into darkness. Harry could hear the men who had jeered at Hermione earlier, yelling at another girl in the distance.

'What are we going to do with them?' Ron whispered to Harry through the dark; then, even more quietly, 'Kill them? They'd kill us. They had a good go just now.'

Hermione shuddered and took a step backwards. Harry shook his head.

'We just need to wipe their memories,' said Harry. 'It's better like that, it'll throw them off the scent. If we killed them, it'd be obvious we were here.'

'You're the boss,' said Ron, sounding profoundly relieved. 'But I've never done a Memory Charm.'

'Nor have I,' said Hermione, 'but I know the theory.'

She took a deep, calming breath, then pointed her wand at Dolohov's forehead and said, '*Obliviate.*'

At once, Dolohov's eyes became unfocused and dreamy.

'Brilliant!' said Harry, clapping her on the back. 'Take care of the other one and the waitress while Ron and I clear up.'

'Clear up?' said Ron, looking around at the partly destroyed café. 'Why?'

'Don't you think they might wonder what's happened if they wake up and find themselves in a place that looks like it's just been bombed?'

'Oh right, yeah …'

Ron struggled for a moment before managing to extract his wand from his pocket.

'It's no wonder I can't get it out, Hermione, you packed my old jeans, they're tight.'

'Oh, I'm so sorry,' hissed Hermione, and as she dragged the waitress out of sight of the windows Harry heard her mutter a suggestion as to where Ron could stick his wand instead.

Once the café was restored to its previous condition, they heaved the Death Eaters back into their booth and propped them up facing each other.

'But how did they find us?' Hermione asked, looking from one inert man to the other. 'How did they know where we were?'

第9章 藏身之处

他低头看着全身瘫痪的多洛霍夫，脑子飞快地思索着。门咔嗒一声锁上了，罗恩用熄灯器使整个咖啡馆陷入了黑暗。哈利听见刚才挑逗赫敏的那帮人在远处冲另一个姑娘叫嚷着。

"我们拿他们怎么办呢？"罗恩在黑暗中小声问哈利，然后又把声音压得更低地说，"把他们干掉？不然他们会杀死我们的。刚才就差点得手了。"

赫敏打了个寒战，朝后退了一步。哈利摇了摇头。

"我们只需要抹去他们的记忆，"哈利说，"这样更好，这样他们就没有线索了。如果把他们杀死，会暴露我们来过这里。"

"还是你厉害。"罗恩说，显然松了口气，"可是我从来没学过遗忘咒。"

"我也没有，"赫敏说，"但我知道原理。"

她深吸一口气，让自己平静下来，然后用魔杖指着多洛霍夫的脑门说："一忘皆空！"

多洛霍夫的眼睛立刻就变得茫然、呆滞了。

"太棒了！"哈利拍拍赫敏的后背说，"另一个家伙和女侍者也交给你了，我和罗恩清理战场。"

"清理战场？"罗恩望着几乎被毁掉一半的咖啡馆说，"为什么要清理？"

"你想，他们醒过来，发现自己待在一个像被炮弹轰炸过的地方，不会感到纳闷吗？"

"噢，是啊……"

罗恩费了好大劲儿，才从口袋里抽出魔杖。

"怪不得拔不出来呢，赫敏，你带的是我的旧牛仔裤，太紧了。"

"噢，对不起。"赫敏咬着牙说，她把女侍者从窗户边拖开时，哈利听见她低声建议罗恩把魔杖插在另外一个地方。

咖啡馆又恢复了先前的模样，他们把两个食死徒扶回到卡座上，让他们面对面坐在那里。

"他们是怎么发现我们的？"赫敏轮流看着这两个傻呆呆的人，问道，"他们怎么会知道我们在哪儿呢？"

CHAPTER NINE A Place to Hide

She turned to Harry.

'You – you don't think you've still got your Trace on you, do you, Harry?'

'He can't have,' said Ron. 'The Trace breaks at seventeen, that's wizarding law, you can't put it on an adult.'

'As far as you know,' said Hermione. 'What if the Death Eaters have found a way to put it on a seventeen-year-old?'

'But Harry hasn't been near a Death Eater in the last twenty-four hours. Who's supposed to have put a Trace back on him?'

Hermione did not reply. Harry felt contaminated, tainted: was that really how the Death Eaters had found them?

'If I can't use magic, and you can't use magic near me, without us giving away our position ...' he began.

'We're not splitting up!' said Hermione firmly.

'We need a safe place to hide,' said Ron. 'Give us time to think things through.'

'Grimmauld Place,' said Harry.

The other two gaped.

'Don't be silly, Harry, Snape can get in there!'

'Ron's dad said they've put up jinxes against him – and even if they haven't worked,' he pressed on, as Hermione began to argue, 'so what? I swear, I'd like nothing better than to meet Snape!'

'But –'

'Hermione, where else is there? It's the best chance we've got. Snape's only one Death Eater. If I've still got the Trace on me, we'll have whole crowds of them on us wherever else we go.'

She could not argue, though she looked as if she would have liked to. While she unlocked the café door, Ron clicked the Deluminator to release the café's light. Then, on Harry's count of three, they reversed the spells upon their three victims and before the waitress or either of the Death Eaters could do more than stir sleepily, Harry, Ron and Hermione had turned on the spot and vanished into the compressing darkness once more.

第9章 藏身之处

她转向哈利。

"你——你说,你身上是不是还带着踪丝呢,哈利?"

"不可能,"罗恩说,"十七岁踪丝就消失了,这是巫师法规定的,成年人不可能有踪丝。"

"那只是你了解的信息。"赫敏说,"如果食死徒有办法让十七岁的人还保留踪丝怎么办呢?"

"可是在过去的二十四小时里,哈利并没有靠近过一个食死徒。谁会把踪丝放回他身上呢?"

赫敏没有回答,哈利却觉得自己被玷污了,不纯净了:难道食死徒真是通过这个发现他们的?

"我不能用魔法,你们在我身边也不能用魔法,不然就会暴露我们的位置——"他说。

"我们不能分开!"赫敏坚决地打断了他。

"需要一个安全的藏身之处,"罗恩说,"让我们有时间把事情想想清楚。"

"格里莫广场。"哈利说。

另外两人惊讶得瞪大眼睛。

"别说傻话了,哈利,斯内普也能进得去!"

"罗恩的爸爸说他们弄了些恶咒专门对付他——即使不管用,"他看到赫敏要张嘴反驳,便赶紧往下说,"那又怎么样?我发誓,我还巴不得会一会斯内普呢!"

"可是——"

"赫敏,除此之外还有哪儿?这是我们最好的去处了。斯内普只是一个食死徒。如果我身上还带着踪丝,不管我们走到哪儿,都会有一大群食死徒把我们包围。"

赫敏无言以对,但看上去心里并不服气。她打开咖啡馆的锁,罗恩咔嗒一按熄灯器,把咖啡馆里的灯光释放出来。然后,哈利数到三,他们给那三个人解除了魔咒。女侍者和两个食死徒迷迷糊糊地刚开始动弹,哈利、罗恩和赫敏就原地转了个身,再次消失在压迫得人喘不过气来的黑暗中。

CHAPTER NINE   A Place to Hide

Seconds later Harry's lungs expanded gratefully and he opened his eyes: they were now standing in the middle of a familiar small and shabby square. Tall, dilapidated houses looked down on them from every side. Number twelve was visible to them, for they had been told of its existence by Dumbledore, its Secret Keeper, and they rushed towards it, checking every few yards that they were not being followed or observed. They raced up the stone steps and Harry tapped the front door once, with his wand. They heard a series of metallic clicks and the clatter of a chain, then the door swung open with a creak and they hurried over the threshold.

As Harry closed the door behind them, the old-fashioned gas lamps sprang into life, casting flickering light along the length of the hallway. It looked just as Harry remembered it: eerie, cobwebbed, the outlines of the house-elf heads on the wall throwing odd shadows up the staircase. Long, dark curtains concealed the portrait of Sirius's mother. The only thing that was out of place was the troll's leg umbrella stand, which was lying on its side as if Tonks had just knocked it over again.

'I think somebody's been in here,' Hermione whispered, pointing towards it.

'That could've happened as the Order left,' Ron murmured back.

'So where are these jinxes they put up against Snape?' Harry asked.

'Maybe they're only activated if he shows up?' suggested Ron.

Yet they remained close together on the doormat, backs against the door, scared to move further into the house.

'Well, we can't stay here forever,' said Harry, and he took a step forwards.

'*Severus Snape?*'

Mad-Eye Moody's voice whispered out of the darkness, making all three of them jump back in fright. 'We're not Snape!' croaked Harry, before something whooshed over him like cold air and his tongue curled backwards on itself, making it impossible to speak. Before he had time to feel inside his mouth, however, his tongue had unravelled again.

The other two seemed to have experienced the same unpleasant sensation. Ron was making retching noises; Hermione stammered, 'That m – must have b – been the T – Tongue-Tying Curse Mad-Eye set up for Snape!'

Gingerly, Harry took another step forwards. Something shifted in the shadows at the end of the hall, and before any of them could say another

第9章　藏身之处

几秒钟后，哈利的肺终于得到舒展，他睁开眼睛。他们站在一个熟悉的、破败的小广场中央。四面都是高高的摇摇欲坠的破旧房屋。他们三个人都能看见12号，因为保密人邓布利多把它的存在告诉过他们。他们朝那幢房子跑去，每跑几码就检查一下是否有人跟踪或监视。跑上石头台阶，哈利用魔杖敲了一下前门，只听见一连串响亮的金属撞击声，还有像链条发出的哗啦哗啦声，然后门吱吱呀呀地开了，他们赶紧跨过门槛。

哈利关上身后的门，老式的汽灯一下子都亮了起来，闪烁不定的灯光照着长长的门厅。门厅还是哈利记忆中的样子：诡谲怪异，蛛网密布，墙上那些家养小精灵的脑袋在楼梯上投下古怪的阴影，长长的深色帷幔遮住了小天狼星母亲的肖像。唯一不对劲儿的是那个用巨怪断腿做成的大伞架，它倒在地上，好像唐克斯又把它撞倒了似的。

"我认为有人来过这里。"赫敏指着它小声说。

"可能是凤凰社离开时弄倒的。"罗恩喃喃地回答。

"他们搞的那些专门对付斯内普的恶咒呢？"哈利问。

"大概只有他露面时才起作用？"罗恩猜测道。

但他们还是靠拢了站在门垫上，背靠着门，不敢再往房子里走。

"我说，我们不能永远站在这儿啊。"哈利说着，往前迈了一步。

"西弗勒斯·斯内普？"

黑暗中轻轻传来疯眼汉的声音，吓得他们三个人都往后一跳。"我们不是斯内普！"哈利用沙哑的嗓音说，紧接着什么东西像冷风一样朝他扑来，他舌头向后卷缩，再也说不出话来。没等他来得及用手去嘴里掏摸，他的舌头又舒展开了。

另外两个人似乎也经历了这种令人不快的遭遇。罗恩嘴里发出干呕的声音，赫敏说起话来结结巴巴："那——那准是疯——疯眼汉为斯——斯内普准备的结舌咒！"

哈利小心翼翼地又往前迈了一步。门厅尽头的阴影里有什么东西在动。没等他们说出话来，地毯上突然蹿起一个身影，高高的，土灰色，模样狰狞。赫敏惊叫起来，布莱克夫人也尖声大叫：她的帷幔掀起来了。

CHAPTER NINE   A Place to Hide

word, a figure had risen up out of the carpet, tall, dust-coloured and terrible: Hermione screamed and so did Mrs Black, her curtains flying open; the grey figure was gliding towards them, faster and faster, its waist-length hair and beard streaming behind it, its face sunken, fleshless, with empty eye sockets: horribly familiar, dreadfully altered, it raised a wasted arm, pointing at Harry.

'No!' Harry shouted, and though he had raised his wand no spell occurred to him. 'No! It wasn't us! We didn't kill you –'

On the word 'kill' the figure exploded in a great cloud of dust: coughing, his eyes watering, Harry looked round to see Hermione crouched on the floor by the door with her arms over her head and Ron, who was shaking from head to foot, patting her clumsily on the shoulder and saying, 'It's all r – right ... it's g – gone ...'

Dust swirled around Harry like mist, catching the blue gaslight, as Mrs Black continued to scream.

'*Mudbloods, filth, stains of dishonour, taint of shame on the house of my fathers –*'

'SHUT UP!' Harry bellowed, directing his wand at her, and with a bang and a burst of red sparks the curtains swung shut again, silencing her.

'That ... that was ...' Hermione whimpered, as Ron helped her to her feet.

'Yeah,' said Harry, 'but it wasn't really him, was it? Just something to scare Snape.'

Had it worked, Harry wondered, or had Snape already blasted the horror-figure aside as casually as he had killed the real Dumbledore? Nerves still tingling, he led the other two up the hall, half expecting some new terror to reveal itself, but nothing moved except for a mouse skittering along the skirting board.

'Before we go any further, I think we'd better check,' whispered Hermione, and she raised her wand and said, '*Homenum revelio.*'

Nothing happened.

'Well, you've just had a big shock,' said Ron kindly. 'What was that supposed to do?'

'It did what I meant it to do!' said Hermione rather crossly. 'That was a spell to reveal human presence, and there's nobody here except us!'

'And old Dusty,' said Ron, glancing at the patch of carpet from which the corpse-figure had risen.

第9章 藏身之处

那个灰色身影朝他们飘来,越来越快,拖到腰部的头发和胡须在身后飘飘荡荡,脸颊凹陷,瘦骨嶙峋,眼窝里空洞洞的。这身影熟悉得可怕,又有令人恐怖的变化,它举起一只枯槁的手指着哈利。

"不!"哈利大喊,他虽然举起了魔杖,却想不出一个咒语,"不!不是我们!我们没有杀死你——"

听到"杀死"这个词,那身影突然爆炸,腾起一大团尘雾。哈利连连咳嗽,泪眼模糊。他回头看见赫敏蹲在门边的地上,用胳膊捂着脑袋,罗恩从头到脚都在发抖,笨拙地拍着赫敏的肩膀,说道:"没——没事了……它——它不见了……"

在汽灯的蓝光下,灰尘像烟雾一样在哈利周围旋舞。布莱克夫人还在那里尖叫。

"泥巴种,脏货,败类,竟敢玷污我祖上的家宅——"

"**闭嘴**!"哈利大吼一声,用魔杖朝她一指,砰的一声,魔杖迸出红色的火星,帷幔忽地合拢,她不作声了。

"那……那是……"赫敏呜咽着说,罗恩扶她站了起来。

"对,"哈利说,"但并不真的是他,对不?只是为了吓唬斯内普的。"

它起作用了吗,或者斯内普满不在乎地炸开了那个可怕的身影,就像他杀死真正的邓布利多那样简单?哈利暗自思索。他惊魂未定地领着另外两个人走过门厅,随时提防着还有新的恐怖出现,但是除了一只老鼠沿着壁脚板一蹿而过,什么动静也没有。

"我想,我们最好检查一下再往前走。"赫敏说,她举起魔杖,念了声:"人形显身!"

没有动静。

"没关系,你刚才受的惊吓不轻。"罗恩好意地说,"这本来应该起什么作用?"

"该起的作用已经起了!"赫敏没好气地说,"这是个让人显形的咒语,这里除了我们没有别人!"

"还有灰尘老鬼。"罗恩说着,扫了一眼地毯上冒出骷髅的地方。

CHAPTER NINE   A Place to Hide

'Let's go up,' said Hermione, with a frightened look at the same spot, and she led the way up the creaking stairs to the drawing room on the first floor.

Hermione waved her wand to ignite the old gas lamps, then, shivering slightly in the draughty room, she perched on the sofa, her arms wrapped tightly around her. Ron crossed to the window and moved the heavy velvet curtain aside an inch.

'Can't see anyone out there,' he reported. 'And you'd think, if Harry still had a Trace on him, they'd have followed us here. I know they can't get in the house, but – what's up, Harry?'

Harry had given a cry of pain: his scar had burned again as something flashed across his mind like a bright light on water. He saw a large shadow and felt a fury that was not his own pound through his body, violent and brief as an electric shock.

'What did you see?' Ron asked, advancing on Harry. 'Did you see him at my place?'

'No, I just felt anger – he's really angry –'

'But that could be at The Burrow,' said Ron loudly. 'What else? Didn't you see anything? Was he cursing someone?'

'No, I just felt anger – I couldn't tell –'

Harry felt badgered, confused, and Hermione did not help as she said in a frightened voice, 'Your scar, again? But what's going on? I thought that connection had closed!'

'It did, for a while,' muttered Harry; his scar was still painful, which made it hard to concentrate. 'I – I think it's started opening again whenever he loses control, that's how it used to –'

'But then, you've got to close your mind!' said Hermione shrilly. 'Harry, Dumbledore didn't want you to use that connection, he wanted you to shut it down, that's why you were supposed to use Occlumency! Otherwise Voldemort can plant false images in your mind, remember –'

'Yeah, I do remember, thanks,' said Harry through gritted teeth; he did not need Hermione to tell him that Voldemort had once used this selfsame connection between them to lead him into a trap, nor that it had resulted in Sirius's death. He wished that he had not told them what he had seen and felt; it made Voldemort more threatening, as though he were pressing against

第 9 章 藏身之处

"我们上去吧。"赫敏心有余悸地也看了看那个地方,领头踩着吱嘎作响的楼梯走向二楼的客厅。

赫敏一挥魔杖,点亮了老式的汽灯,屋里有穿堂风,她微微发抖地在沙发上坐下,双臂紧紧地抱住身子。罗恩走到窗户前,把厚重的天鹅绒窗帘拉开了一条缝。

"外面一个人也看不见。"他报告说,"如果哈利身上仍然有踪丝,他们肯定会跟踪到这里来的,对吧?我知道他们进不了房子,可是——怎么啦,哈利?"

哈利痛苦地叫了一声:什么东西闪过他的脑海,就像一道强光掠过水面,他的伤疤又剧烈地灼痛起来。他看见一片很大的阴影,并感到一种不属于他的怒火在心头腾腾烧过,像电击一样强烈,转瞬即逝。

"你看见什么了?"罗恩朝哈利走去,问道,"是不是看见他在我家里?"

"不,我只是感到生气——他气得要命——"

"但很可能是在陋居。"罗恩大声说,"还有什么?你看见什么没有?他是不是在给人施咒?"

"不,我只是感到生气——我不清楚——"

哈利觉得烦躁,不知所措,赫敏的话也没给他多少帮助。赫敏战战兢兢地说:"你的伤疤?又疼了?怎么回事呀?我还以为那种联系已经断了呢!"

"确实断过一阵子,"哈利低声说,伤疤仍然在疼,他无法集中思想,"我——我想,他一失去自控就又连接上了,以前就是这样——"

"那你必须封闭你的大脑!"赫敏尖声说道,"哈利,邓布利多不希望你使用那种联系,他希望你把它断掉,所以才让你用大脑封闭术!不然伏地魔就会把虚假的想法放进你的头脑,你还记得——"

"我记得,多谢你了。"哈利咬紧牙关说。他不需要赫敏提醒他伏地魔曾利用他们之间的这种联系,把他诱入一个陷阱,最后导致了小天狼星的死亡。他真希望自己没有把他看到的和感觉到的东西告诉他们俩,因为这样一来,伏地魔的威胁显得更逼近了,似乎他就在这个

CHAPTER NINE A Place to Hide

the window of the room, and still the pain in his scar was building and he fought it: it was like resisting the urge to be sick.

He turned his back on Ron and Hermione, pretending to examine the old tapestry of the Black family tree on the wall. Then Hermione shrieked: Harry drew his wand again and spun round to see a silver Patronus soar through the drawing-room window and land upon the floor in front of them, where it solidified into the weasel that spoke with the voice of Ron's father.

'Family safe, do not reply, we are being watched.'

The Patronus dissolved into nothingness. Ron let out a noise between a whimper and a groan and dropped on to the sofa: Hermione joined him, gripping his arm.

'They're all right, they're all right!' she whispered, and Ron half laughed and hugged her.

'Harry,' he said over Hermione's shoulder, 'I –'

'It's not a problem,' said Harry, sickened by the pain in his head. 'It's your family, 'course you're worried. I'd feel the same way.' He thought of Ginny. 'I *do* feel the same way.'

The pain in his scar was reaching a peak, burning as it had done in the garden of The Burrow. Faintly, he heard Hermione say, 'I don't want to be on my own. Could we use the sleeping bags I've brought and camp in here tonight?'

He heard Ron agree. He could not fight the pain much longer: he had to succumb.

'Bathroom,' he muttered, and he left the room as fast as he could without running.

He barely made it: bolting the door behind him with trembling hands, he grasped his pounding head and fell to the floor, then, in an explosion of agony, he felt the rage that did not belong to him possess his soul, saw a long room, lit only by firelight, and the great, blond Death Eater on the floor, screaming and writhing, and a slighter figure standing over him, wand outstretched, while Harry spoke in a high, cold, merciless voice.

'More, Rowle, or shall we end it and feed you to Nagini? Lord Voldemort is not sure that he will forgive this time ... You called me back for this, to tell me that Harry Potter has escaped again? Draco, give Rowle another taste of our displeasure ... do it, or feel my wrath yourself!'

第9章 藏身之处

房间的窗外虎视眈眈。伤疤的疼痛还在加剧，哈利拼命忍着，就像拼命忍着恶心的感觉。

他转过去背朝罗恩和赫敏，假装端详墙上绘着布莱克家谱图的旧挂毯。突然赫敏尖叫起来，哈利又拔出魔杖，急忙转过身来，却见一个银色的守护神穿过客厅的窗户，落到他们面前的地板上，变成了银色的鼬鼠，用罗恩父亲的声音说话了。

"家人平安，不用回复，我们被监视了。"

守护神消失得无影无踪。罗恩发出又像呜咽又像呻吟的声音，跌坐在沙发上，赫敏靠过去抓住他的胳膊。

"他们都没事儿，他们都没事儿！"赫敏小声说，罗恩似笑非笑了一声，紧紧地搂了搂她。

"哈利，"他从赫敏的肩头说，"我——"

"没关系，"哈利说，脑袋的疼痛使他一阵阵恶心，"是你的家人，你当然要担心。换了我也会担心，"他想起了金妮，"我确实也很担心。"

伤疤的疼痛达到了顶峰，就像那天在陋居花园里一样火烧火燎。他隐隐约约听见赫敏说："我不想一个人待着。我们今晚能不能用我带来的睡袋就睡在这里？"

他听见罗恩同意了。他再也抵挡不住剧痛，不得不缴械投降。

"去趟卫生间。"他嘟囔一句，尽快走出了房间。

他刚用颤抖的手把身后的门插上，就一把掐住突突剧痛的脑袋，摔倒在地。在压倒一切的痛楚中，他感到那种不属于他的愤怒占据了他的灵魂。他看见一个仅由火光照亮的长长的房间，那个大块头金发食死徒在地板上惨叫、挣扎，一个较为瘦弱的身影举着魔杖站在他旁边，哈利用高亢的、冷漠无情的声音说话了。

"罗尔，是再来一些，还是到此为止，拿你去喂纳吉尼？伏地魔不能保证这次是不是原谅你……你把我召回来就为了这个，就为了告诉我哈利·波特又逃跑了？德拉科，再让罗尔感受一下我们的不满……快，不然就让你尝尝我的愤怒！"

CHAPTER NINE A Place to Hide

A log fell in the fire: flames reared, their light darting across a terrified, pointed white face – with a sense of emerging from deep water Harry drew heaving breaths and opened his eyes.

He was spread-eagled on the cold black marble floor, his nose inches from one of the silver serpent tails that supported the large bathtub. He sat up. Malfoy's gaunt, petrified face seemed branded on the inside of his eyes. Harry felt sickened by what he had seen, by the use to which Draco was now being put by Voldemort.

There was a sharp rap on the door and Harry jumped as Hermione's voice rang out.

'Harry, do you want your toothbrush? I've got it here.'

'Yeah, great, thanks,' he said, fighting to keep his voice casual as he stood up to let her in.

第9章 藏身之处

一段木头落在炉火里,烈焰腾起,火光照着一张惊恐万状的、苍白的尖脸——哈利如同从深水里浮出来一样,大口喘着粗气,睁开了眼睛。

他四肢摊开躺在冰冷的黑色大理石地面上,鼻子离支撑大浴缸的银蛇尾巴只有几寸。他坐起身来。马尔福那张憔悴、惊恐的脸似乎深深刻在了他的脑海里。刚才看到的一幕,以及伏地魔现在让德拉科充当的角色,都使哈利感到恶心。

突然有人重重地敲门,哈利猛吃一惊,只听赫敏的声音响亮地传来。

"哈利,你要牙刷吗?我带着呢。"

"要,太好了,谢谢。"哈利努力使自己的声音听上去若无其事,起身开门让赫敏进来。

CHAPTER TEN

Kreacher's Tale

Harry woke early next morning, wrapped in a sleeping bag on the drawing-room floor. A chink of sky was visible between the heavy curtains: it was the cool, clear blue of watered ink, somewhere between night and dawn, and everything was quiet except for Ron and Hermione's slow, deep breathing. Harry glanced over at the dark shapes they made on the floor beside him. Ron had had a fit of gallantry and insisted that Hermione sleep on the cushions from the sofa, so that her silhouette was raised above his. Her arm curved to the floor, her fingers inches from Ron's. Harry wondered whether they had fallen asleep holding hands. The idea made him feel strangely lonely.

He looked up at the shadowy ceiling, the cobwebbed chandelier. Less than twenty-four hours ago he had been standing in the sunlight at the entrance to the marquee, waiting to show in wedding guests. It seemed a lifetime away. What was going to happen now? He lay on the floor and he thought of the Horcruxes, of the daunting, complex mission Dumbledore had left him ... Dumbledore ...

The grief that had possessed him since Dumbledore's death felt different now. The accusations he had heard from Muriel at the wedding seemed to have nested in his brain, like diseased things, infecting his memories of the wizard he had idolised. Could Dumbledore have let such things happen? Had he been like Dudley, content to watch neglect and abuse as long as it did not affect him? Could he have turned his back on a sister who was being imprisoned and hidden?

Harry thought of Godric's Hollow, of graves Dumbledore had never mentioned there; he thought of mysterious objects left, without explanation, in Dumbledore's will, and resentment swelled in the darkness. Why hadn't Dumbledore told him? Why hadn't he explained? Had Dumbledore actually cared about Harry at all? Or had Harry been nothing more than a tool to be polished and honed, but not trusted, never confided in?

第 10 章

克利切的故事

哈利第二天清晨醒来，裹着睡袋躺在客厅地板上。厚厚的窗帘间漏出一线天空，像冲淡的蓝墨水一般凉爽清澈，是那种介于夜晚与黎明之间的颜色。周围静悄悄的，只听到罗恩和赫敏缓慢深长的呼吸。哈利望着他们在他旁边地板上的身影。罗恩昨晚一时大显绅士风度，坚持让赫敏睡在沙发垫子上，所以她的身影比罗恩的高，胳膊弯着搭在地板上，手指离罗恩的只有几英寸。哈利猜测他们或许是手拉手睡着的，这想法让他感到莫名的孤独。

他仰望着昏暗的天花板、结着蛛网的枝形吊灯。不到二十四小时前，他还站在阳光下，在大帐篷门口接待参加婚礼的嘉宾，这会儿想起来恍若隔世。现在会发生什么呢？他躺在地板上，想着魂器，想着邓布利多留给他的艰难而复杂的使命……邓布利多……

邓布利多死后一直笼罩在他心头的那种悲伤现在感觉不同了。婚礼上穆丽尔姨婆的非议仿佛病菌寄生在他脑子里，侵蚀着他原来心目中的偶像。邓布利多会让那种事发生吗？他会像达力那样，只要不影响到自己，就对冷落和虐待袖手旁观吗？他会对一个被禁闭、被隐藏的亲妹妹置之不理吗？

哈利又想到戈德里克山谷，想到邓布利多从没提过的坟墓，想到邓布利多遗嘱中那些未加解释的神秘赠物。怨恨在黑暗中翻涌。邓布利多为什么不告诉他？为什么没有解释？邓布利多真正关心哈利吗？还是只把哈利当成一个需要磨砺的工具，但不信任他，从来不会向他倾吐秘密？

CHAPTER TEN   Kreacher's Tale

Harry could not stand lying there with nothing but bitter thoughts for company. Desperate for something to do, for distraction, he slipped out of his sleeping bag, picked up his wand and crept out of the room. On the landing he whispered, '*Lumos*,' and started to climb the stairs by wandlight.

On the second landing was the bedroom in which he and Ron had slept last time they had been here; he glanced into it. The wardrobe doors stood open and the bedclothes had been ripped back. Harry remembered the overturned troll leg downstairs. Somebody had searched the house since the Order had left. Snape? Or perhaps Mundungus, who had pilfered plenty from this house both before and after Sirius died? Harry's gaze wandered to the portrait that sometimes contained Phineas Nigellus Black, Sirius's great-great-grandfather, but it was empty, showing nothing but a stretch of muddy backdrop. Phineas Nigellus was evidently spending the night in the Headmaster's study at Hogwarts.

Harry continued up the stairs until he reached the topmost landing, where there were only two doors. The one facing him bore a nameplate reading *Sirius*. Harry had never entered his godfather's bedroom before. He pushed open the door, holding his wand high to cast light as widely as possible.

The room was spacious and must, once, have been handsome. There was a large bed with a carved wooden headboard, a tall window obscured by long velvet curtains and a chandelier thickly coated in dust, with candle stubs still resting in its sockets, solid wax hanging in frost-like drips. A fine film of dust covered the pictures on the walls and the bed's headboard; a spider's web stretched between the chandelier and the top of the large wooden wardrobe and as Harry moved deeper into the room, he heard a scurrying of disturbed mice.

The teenaged Sirius had plastered the walls with so many posters and pictures that little of the walls' silvery-grey silk was visible. Harry could only assume that Sirius's parents had been unable to remove the Permanent Sticking Charm that kept them on the wall, because he was sure they would not have appreciated their eldest son's taste in decoration. Sirius seemed to have gone out of his way to annoy his parents. There were several large Gryffindor banners, faded scarlet and gold, just to underline his difference from all the rest of the Slytherin family. There were many pictures of Muggle motorcycles, and also (Harry had to admire Sirius's nerve) several posters of bikini-clad Muggle girls; Harry could tell that they were Muggles because they remained quite stationary within their pictures, faded smiles and glazed eyes frozen on the paper. This was in contrast to the only wizarding photograph on the walls, which was a picture of four Hogwarts students standing arm in arm, laughing at the camera.

第10章 克利切的故事

哈利再也无法忍受躺在那里,只有怨恨的念头相伴。必须找点事情做,分分心。他钻出睡袋,捡起自己的魔杖,蹑手蹑脚地走出房间。到了楼梯口,他悄悄说了声"荧光闪烁",用魔杖照着上楼。

第二个楼梯口是他和罗恩上次住过的那间卧室,他往里看了一眼,衣柜敞着,床单也拉开了。哈利想起楼下翻倒的巨怪断腿。凤凰社离开后有人搜查过这个房间。是斯内普吗?还是蒙顿格斯?那家伙在小天狼星生前和死后从这所宅子里偷走了许多东西。哈利的目光移到那幅有时可看到菲尼亚斯·奈杰勒斯·布莱克的肖像上,然而此时相框中空空荡荡,只有一片浑浊的背景。小天狼星的这位高祖显然是在霍格沃茨的校长书房里过夜了。

哈利继续往楼上走,一直走到最高层楼梯口,那里只有两扇门,正对着他的那扇门上有块牌子写着小天狼星。哈利以前从未进过他教父的卧室。他推开门,高举魔杖,尽量照得远一点。

屋里很宽敞,以前肯定是相当漂亮的。有一张床头雕花的大床,高窗上遮着长长的天鹅绒帷幔,枝形吊灯上积着厚厚的灰尘,蜡烛头还留在插座里,凝固的烛泪像冰晶一样滴垂下。墙上的图画和床头板上也蒙着一层薄灰,一张蜘蛛网从枝形吊灯拉到木质的大衣柜顶部。哈利往屋子中间走时,听到有老鼠逃窜的声音。

少年小天狼星在墙上贴了这么多的招贴画和照片,原来银灰色的缎面墙壁几乎全被遮住了。哈利只能猜测小天狼星的父母无法消除墙上的永久粘贴咒,他相信他们不会欣赏大儿子的装饰品位。小天狼星似乎想方设法要惹父母生气,屋里有几面大大的格兰芬多旗帜,已经褪了色,强调他与这个斯莱特林家族中的其他人有多么不同,金红的旗子已经褪色。还有许多麻瓜摩托车的图片,甚至有几张身着比基尼的麻瓜女孩招贴画(哈利不得不佩服小天狼星的勇气)。之所以看出是麻瓜女孩,是因为她们在画上一动不动,褪色的笑容和凝固在纸上的目光,与墙上唯一的一张巫师照片形成对比,那是四个霍格沃茨学生挽着手臂站在一起,冲着镜头呵呵地笑。

CHAPTER TEN — Kreacher's Tale

With a leap of pleasure, Harry recognised his father; his untidy, black hair stuck up at the back like Harry's and he, too, wore glasses. Beside him was Sirius, carelessly handsome, his slightly arrogant face so much younger and happier than Harry had ever seen it alive. To Sirius's right stood Pettigrew, more than a head shorter, plump and watery-eyed, flushed with pleasure at his inclusion in this coolest of gangs, with the much admired rebels that James and Sirius had been. On James's left was Lupin, even then a little shabby-looking, but he had the same air of delighted surprise at finding himself liked and included ... or was it simply because Harry knew how it had been, that he saw these things in the picture? He tried to take it from the wall; it was his, now, after all – Sirius had left him everything – but it would not budge. Sirius had taken no chances in preventing his parents from redecorating his room.

Harry looked around at the floor. The sky outside was growing brighter: a shaft of light revealed bits of paper, books and small objects scattered over the carpet. Evidently Sirius's bedroom had been searched too, although its contents seemed to have been judged mostly, if not entirely, worthless. A few of the books had been shaken roughly enough to part company with their covers, and sundry pages littered the floor.

Harry bent down, picked up a few of the pieces of paper and examined them. He recognised one as part of an old edition of *A History of Magic*, by Bathilda Bagshot, and another as belonging to a motorcycle maintenance manual. The third was handwritten and crumpled: he smoothed it out.

Dear Padfoot,

Thank you, thank you, for Harry's birthday present! It was his favourite by far. One year old and already zooming along on a toy broomstick, he looked so pleased with himself, I'm enclosing a picture so you can see. You know it only rises about two feet off the ground, but he nearly killed the cat and he smashed a horrible vase Petunia sent me for Christmas (no complaints there). Of course, James thought it was so funny, says he's going to be a great Quidditch player, but we've had to pack away all the ornaments and make sure we don't take our eyes off him when he gets going.

We had a very quiet birthday tea, just us and old Bathilda, who has always been sweet to us and who dotes on Harry. We were so

第10章 克利切的故事

哈利的心欢跳起来,他认出了自己的父亲,不服帖的黑发像哈利的一样在脑后支棱着,而且也戴着眼镜。他旁边是小天狼星,英俊而洒脱不羁,稍带高傲的面庞比哈利见过的任何时候都更加年轻快乐。小天狼星的右边站着小矮星,比他矮一个头还多,胖乎乎的,眼睛湿润,为自己能加入这最拉风的一群,与詹姆和小天狼星这样受人钦佩的叛逆者结交而兴奋不已。詹姆的左边是卢平,他甚至那时候就显得有一点邋遢,但也带着那种惊讶而快乐的神情,发现自己被喜欢、被接纳……莫非只是因为哈利知道了内情,才会在照片中看出这些东西?他想把它从墙上摘下来,反正这照片属于他了——小天狼星把一切都留给了他。可是他拿不下来,小天狼星为了不让自己的父母改变这间屋子的装饰,真是无所不用其极。

哈利扫视地面,外面天色亮了起来,一道光线照出地毯上凌乱的纸片、书籍和零碎物品。显然小天狼星的卧室也被搜过了,不过里面的东西似乎被认为大都无用——或全部无用。有几本书被粗暴地抖过,封皮都掉了,书页散落在地上。

哈利弯下腰,捡起几张纸看了看,认出有一张是巴希达·巴沙特所著《魔法史》的老版本散页,还有一张是摩托车维修手册里的;第三张是手写的字条,揉皱了,他把它抹平来看。

亲爱的大脚板:

谢谢你,谢谢你送给哈利的生日礼物!这是他最喜欢的玩具了。才一岁就已经能骑着玩具扫帚飞来飞去,他看上去多得意啊。我附上一张照片给你看看。你知道小扫帚只能离地两英尺,但哈利差点撞死了小猫,还差点打碎了一只难看的花瓶,那是佩妮送给我的圣诞礼物(不是抱怨)。当然,詹姆觉得非常好玩,说这孩子会成为一个魁地奇明星,但我们不得不把所有的装饰品都收起来,并且在他飞的时候一直看着他。

我们搞了一个很低调的生日茶会,只有老巴希达在场,她一直对我们很好,也特别宠爱哈利。很遗憾你不能来,但凤凰社是

CHAPTER TEN Kreacher's Tale

sorry you couldn't come, but the Order's got to come first and Harry's not old enough to know it's his birthday anyway! James is getting a bit frustrated shut up here, he tries not to show it but I can tell — also, Dumbledore's still got his Invisibility Cloak, so no chance of little excursions. If you could visit, it would cheer him up so much. Wormy was here last weekend, I thought he seemed down, but that was probably the news about the McKinnons; I cried all evening when I heard.

Bathilda drops in most days, she's a fascinating old thing with the most amazing stories about Dumbledore, I'm not sure he'd be pleased if he knew! I don't know how much to believe, actually, because it seems incredible that Dumbledore

Harry's extremities seemed to have gone numb. He stood quite still, holding the miraculous paper in his nerveless fingers while inside him a kind of quiet eruption sent joy and grief thundering in equal measure through his veins. Lurching to the bed, he sat down.

He read the letter again, but could not take in any more meaning than he had done the first time, and was reduced to staring at the handwriting itself. She had made her g's the same way he did: he searched through the letter for every one of them, and each felt like a friendly little wave glimpsed from behind a veil. The letter was an incredible treasure, proof that Lily Potter had lived, really lived, that her warm hand had once moved across this parchment, tracing ink into these letters, these words, words about him, Harry, her son.

Impatiently brushing away the wetness in his eyes, he reread the letter, this time concentrating on the meaning. It was like listening to a half-remembered voice.

They had had a cat ... perhaps it had perished, like his parents, at Godric's Hollow ... or else fled when there was nobody left to feed it ... Sirius had bought him his first broomstick ... his parents had known Bathilda Bagshot; had Dumbledore introduced them? *Dumbledore's still got his Invisibility Cloak ...* there was something funny there ...

Harry paused, pondering his mother's words. Why had Dumbledore taken James's Invisibility Cloak? Harry distinctly remembered his Headmaster telling him, years before, '*I don't need a cloak to become invisible.*' Perhaps some less gifted Order member had needed its assistance, and Dumbledore had acted as carrier? Harry passed on ...

第10章 克利切的故事

第一位的,再说哈利这么小也不懂过生日的事!关在这里詹姆有些憋闷,他尽量不表现出来,可是我看得出——隐形衣还在邓布利多那里,所以没有机会出去。如果你能来,他会多么高兴啊。小虫上周末来过了,我觉得他情绪低落,但也许是因为麦金农夫妇的消息吧。我听到后也哭了一夜。

巴希达经常过来,她是个有趣的老太太,讲了好些邓布利多的故事,真是想象不到。我不知道他本人听到会不会高兴!说实在的,我不知道该相信多少,很难相信邓布利多

哈利的四肢似乎麻木了,他静立在那里,失去知觉的手指举着那张神奇的纸片,心里却像经历了一场无声的火山喷发。喜悦与悲伤等量地在血管中涌动。他摇摇晃晃地走到床边,坐了下来。

他又读了一遍信,却不能比第一次读懂更多的含义,于是便只是盯着纸上的笔迹。母亲写字母 g 的方式与他一样。他在信中寻找每一个这样的字母,每一个都像透过面纱看到的温柔的挥手。这封信是一件不可思议的珍宝,证明莉莉·波特存在过,真正存在过。她温暖的手曾经在这张羊皮纸上移动,将墨水注入这些字母,这些词句,写的是他,哈利,她的儿子。

他急切地抹去眼中的泪花,重新读起信来,这次专心体会含义,就像聆听一个似曾相识的声音。

他们有一只猫……它也许像他父母一样,死在戈德里克山谷……也可能因为没人喂养而离开了……小天狼星给他买了第一把飞天扫帚……他父母认识巴希达·巴沙特,是邓布利多介绍的吗?隐形衣还在邓布利多那里……这儿有点蹊跷……

哈利停下来,琢磨着母亲的话。邓布利多为什么拿走詹姆的隐形衣呢?哈利清楚地记得校长多年前对他说过:"我不用隐形衣就能隐身。"也许某个法力较弱的凤凰社成员需要用它,邓布利多帮着借一下?哈利又往下读……

CHAPTER TEN   Kreacher's Tale

Wormy was here ... Pettigrew, the traitor, had seemed 'down', had he? Was he aware that he was seeing James and Lily alive for the last time?

And finally Bathilda again, who told incredible stories about Dumbledore: *it seems incredible that Dumbledore –*

That Dumbledore what? But there were any number of things that would seem incredible about Dumbledore; that he had once received bottom marks in a Transfiguration test, for instance, or had taken up goat-charming like Aberforth ...

Harry got to his feet and scanned the floor: perhaps the rest of the letter was here somewhere. He seized papers, treating them, in his eagerness, with as little consideration as the original searcher; he pulled open drawers, shook out books, stood on a chair to run his hand over the top of the wardrobe and crawled under the bed and armchair.

At last, lying face down on the floor he spotted what looked like a torn piece of paper under the chest of drawers. When he pulled it out, it proved to be most of the photograph Lily had described in her letter. A black-haired baby was zooming in and out of the picture on a tiny broom, roaring with laughter, and a pair of legs that must have belonged to James were chasing after him. Harry tucked the photograph into his pocket with Lily's letter and continued to look for the second sheet.

After another quarter of an hour, however, he was forced to conclude that the rest of his mother's letter was gone. Had it simply been lost in the sixteen years that had elapsed since it had been written, or had it been taken by whoever had searched the room? Harry read the first sheet again, this time looking for clues as to what might have made the second sheet valuable. His toy broomstick could hardly be considered interesting to the Death Eaters ... the only potentially useful thing he could see here was possible information on Dumbledore. *It seems incredible that Dumbledore –* what?

'Harry? Harry! *Harry!*'

'I'm here!' he called. 'What's happened?'

There was a clatter of footsteps outside the door, and Hermione burst inside.

'We woke up and didn't know where you were!' she said breathlessly. She turned and shouted over her shoulder, 'Ron! I've found him!'

Ron's annoyed voice echoed distantly from several floors below.

'Good! Tell him from me he's a git!'

'Harry, don't just disappear, please, we were terrified! Why did you come up here, anyway?' She gazed around the ransacked room. 'What have you been doing?'

第10章 克利切的故事

小虫来过……小矮星，那个叛徒，显得"情绪低落"？他是否知道这是最后一次见到詹姆和莉莉？

最后又是巴希达，讲了关于邓布利多的惊人故事：很难相信邓布利多——

很难相信邓布利多什么呢？可是邓布利多的许多事情都会令人难以相信呀：比如，他有一次在变形课上得了最低分，还有像阿不福思一样对山羊念咒……

哈利站起来在地面搜寻：也许缺失的信纸还在屋里。他抓起一张张纸片，性急之中，像前一位搜索者那样不顾一切，翻抽屉，抖书页，站在椅子上摸衣柜顶部，钻到床肚里和扶手椅下寻找。

终于，他趴在地上，在一个五斗橱底下看到了一张破纸，抽出来之后，发现是莉莉信中提到的那张照片的大部分。一个黑头发的婴儿骑着小扫帚飞进飞出，咯咯欢笑，还有两条腿（想必是詹姆的）在追他。哈利把照片和莉莉的信一起塞进衣袋，继续寻找第二页信纸。

又过了一刻钟，他不得不承认母亲这封信的后面部分不在了。它是在从那时到现在这十六年中遗失的，还是被搜屋子的人拿走的呢？哈利又读了读第一页，这次仔细寻找着能使第二页有价值的线索。他的玩具扫帚不大会引起食死徒的兴趣……唯一可能有用的就是关于邓布利多的内容，很难相信邓布利多——什么呢？

"哈利？哈利！哈利！"

"我在这儿！"他喊道，"什么事？"

门外一阵急促的脚步声，赫敏冲了进来。

"我们醒来不知道你去哪儿了！"她气喘吁吁地说，又扭头叫道，"罗恩！我找到他了！"

罗恩恼火的声音从几层楼下面远远传来。

"好！告诉他，我骂他是混蛋！"

"哈利，求求你不要失踪，我们都吓坏了！你上这儿来干什么？"她打量着翻得乱糟糟的房间，"你在做什么？"

CHAPTER TEN Kreacher's Tale

'Look what I've just found.'

He held out his mother's letter. Hermione took it and read it while Harry watched her. When she reached the end of the page, she looked up at him.

'Oh, Harry ...'

'And there's this, too.'

He handed her the torn photograph, and Hermione smiled at the baby zooming in and out of sight on the toy broom.

'I've been looking for the rest of the letter,' Harry said, 'but it's not here.'

Hermione glanced around.

'Did you make all this mess, or was some of it done when you got here?'

'Someone had searched before me,' said Harry.

'I thought so. Every room I looked into on the way up had been disturbed. What were they after, do you think?'

'Information on the Order, if it was Snape.'

'But you'd think he'd already have all he needed, I mean, he was in the Order, wasn't he?'

'Well then,' said Harry, keen to discuss his theory, 'what about information on Dumbledore? The second page of this letter, for instance. You know this Bathilda my mum mentions, you know who she is?'

'Who?'

'Bathilda Bagshot, the author of –'

'*A History of Magic*,' said Hermione, looking interested. 'So your parents knew her? She was an incredible magical historian.'

'And she's still alive,' said Harry, 'and she lives in Godric's Hollow, Ron's Auntie Muriel was talking about her at the wedding. She knew Dumbledore's family too. Be pretty interesting to talk to, wouldn't she?'

There was a little too much understanding in the smile Hermione gave him for Harry's liking. He took back the letter and the photograph and tucked them inside the pouch around his neck, so as not to have to look at her and give himself away.

'I understand why you'd love to talk to her about your mum and dad, and Dumbledore too,' said Hermione. 'But, that wouldn't really help us in our search for the Horcruxes, would it?' Harry did not answer, and she rushed on, 'Harry, I know you really want to go to Godric's Hollow, but I'm scared ...

第10章 克利切的故事

"瞧，我找到了什么。"

他举起母亲的信。赫敏接过去读了起来，哈利注视着她。读到末尾，赫敏抬起头看着哈利。

"哦，哈利……"

"还有这个。"

他又递过撕破的照片，赫敏冲着那个骑玩具扫帚飞出飞进的婴儿微笑。

"我在找缺掉的信纸，"哈利说，"可是找不到。"

赫敏环顾四周。

"这全是你翻乱的吗，还是你进来时就已经乱了？"

"有人在我之前翻过了。"哈利说。

"我猜也是。我上来时看到每间屋子都有点乱，你认为他们在找什么呢？"

"关于凤凰社的消息，如果是斯内普的话。"

"但他不是都已经知道了吗，我是说，他曾经是凤凰社成员，不是吗？"

"那么，"哈利急于讨论他的推想，"关于邓布利多的消息呢？比如这封信的第二页。我妈妈提到的这个巴希达，你知道她是谁吗？"

"谁？"

"巴希达·巴沙特，写过——"

"《魔法史》。"赫敏说，看上去来了兴趣，"你爸爸妈妈认识她？她是一位了不起的魔法史专家。"

"她还活着，"哈利说，"住在戈德里克山谷。罗恩的穆丽尔姨婆在婚礼上讲到过她。她还认识邓布利多一家，跟她聊聊会很有意思，是不是？"

赫敏的笑容中包含着过多的理解和同情，哈利觉得不大自在。他收回信纸和照片，塞进挂在脖子上的袋子里，避免与她对视，泄露自己的心思。

"我明白你为什么想跟她聊聊你的爸爸妈妈，还有邓布利多，"赫敏说，"可这对我们寻找魂器没多大帮助，是不是？"哈利没有回答，她

'I'm scared at how easily those Death Eaters found us yesterday. It just makes me feel more than ever that we ought to avoid the place where your parents are buried, I'm sure they'd be expecting you to visit it.'

'It's not just that,' Harry said, still avoiding looking at her. 'Muriel said stuff about Dumbledore at the wedding. I want to know the truth ...'

He told Hermione everything that Muriel had told him. When he had finished, Hermione said, 'Of course, I can see why that's upset you, Harry –'

'– I'm not upset,' he lied, 'I'd just like to know whether or not it's true or –'

'Harry, do you really think you'll get the truth from a malicious old woman like Muriel, or from Rita Skeeter? How can you believe them? You knew Dumbledore!'

'I thought I did,' he muttered.

'But you know how much truth there was in everything Rita wrote about you! Doge is right, how can you let these people tarnish your memories of Dumbledore?'

He looked away, trying not to betray the resentment he felt. There it was again: choose what to believe. He wanted the truth. Why was everybody so determined that he should not get it?

'Shall we go down to the kitchen?' Hermione suggested after a little pause. 'Find something for breakfast?'

He agreed, but grudgingly, and followed her out on to the landing and past the second door that led off it. There were deep scratch marks in the paintwork below a small sign that he had not noticed in the dark. He paused at the top of the stairs to read it. It was a pompous, little sign, neatly lettered by hand, the sort of thing that Percy Weasley might have stuck on his bedroom door:

Do Not Enter
Without the Express Permission of
Regulus Arcturus Black

Excitement trickled through Harry, but he was not immediately sure why. He read the sign again. Hermione was already a flight of stairs below him.

'Hermione,' he said, and he was surprised that his voice was so calm. 'Come back up here.'

第10章 克利切的故事

一口气说下去，"哈利，我知道你真的想去戈德里克山谷，可我害怕……昨天食死徒那么容易就发现了我们，我很害怕。这让我更觉得应该避开你父母长眠的地方，我相信他们会猜到你要去的。"

"不光是那样，"哈利说，仍然不敢看她，"穆丽尔在婚礼上提到了邓布利多的一些事，我想知道真相……"

他把穆丽尔讲的事全部告诉了赫敏，赫敏听完后说："当然，我能理解这为什么让你心烦意乱，哈利——"

"——我没有心烦意乱，"他撒了个谎，"只是想知道真假——"

"哈利，你真以为能从穆丽尔这样恶毒的老太婆和丽塔·斯基特那里得到真相吗？你怎么能相信她们呢？你了解邓布利多！"

"我以为我了解。"他嘟囔道。

"可是你知道丽塔写你的那些文章里有多少真实性！多吉说得对，你怎么能让这些人玷污你对邓布利多的记忆呢？"

他看着别处，努力不泄露内心的恼恨。又是这样：选择相信什么。他要的是真相。为什么所有的人都坚决不让他了解呢？

"下楼到厨房去吧？"赫敏沉默片刻后说道，"弄点早饭吃？"

他同意了，但很不情愿，跟着她走到楼梯口，从另一扇门前经过。刚才在黑暗中没注意到，门上有块小牌子，下面的油漆有深深的划痕。他停在楼梯口细看，这是一块气派十足的小牌子，工整的手写字母，很像珀西·韦斯莱会钉在卧室门上的东西：

未经本人明示允许
禁止入内
雷古勒斯·阿克图勒斯·布莱克

一阵兴奋传遍哈利的全身，可他并没有马上意识到为什么。他又读了一遍牌子，赫敏已经下了一段楼梯。

"赫敏，"哈利说，他为自己的声音如此平静而感到惊讶，"上来。"

CHAPTER TEN Kreacher's Tale

'What's the matter?'

'R.A.B. I think I've found him.'

There was a gasp and then Hermione ran back up the stairs.

'In your mum's letter? But I didn't see –'

Harry shook his head, pointing at Regulus's sign. She read it, then clutched Harry's arm so tightly that he winced.

'Sirius's brother?' she whispered.

'He was a Death Eater,' said Harry, 'Sirius told me about him, he joined up when he was really young and then got cold feet and tried to leave – so they killed him.'

'That fits!' gasped Hermione. 'If he was a Death Eater, he had access to Voldemort, and if he became disenchanted then he would have wanted to bring Voldemort down!'

She released Harry, leaned over the banister and screamed, 'Ron! RON! Get up here, quick!'

Ron appeared, panting, a minute later, his wand ready in his hand.

'What's up? If it's massive spiders again, I want breakfast before I –'

He frowned at the sign on Regulus's door, to which Hermione was silently pointing.

'What? That was Sirius's brother, wasn't it? Regulus Arcturus ... Regulus ... R.A.B.! The locket – you don't reckon –?'

'Let's find out,' said Harry. He pushed the door: it was locked. Hermione pointed her wand at the handle and said, '*Alohomora.*' There was a click, and the door swung open.

They moved over the threshold together, gazing around. Regulus's bedroom was slightly smaller than Sirius's, though it had the same sense of former grandeur. Whereas Sirius had sought to advertise his difference from the rest of the family, Regulus had striven to emphasise the opposite. The Slytherin colours of emerald and silver were everywhere, draping the bed, the walls and the windows. The Black family crest was painstakingly painted over the bed, along with its motto, *Toujours Pur*. Beneath this was a collection of yellow newspaper cuttings, all stuck together to make a ragged collage. Hermione crossed the room to examine them.

'They're all about Voldemort,' she said. 'Regulus seems to have been a fan for a few years before he joined the Death Eaters ...'

"怎么啦？"

"R.A.B.，我想我找到他了。"

一声惊叫，赫敏奔上楼梯。

"在你妈妈的信里？可我没看见——"

哈利摇摇头，指着雷古勒斯的牌子。赫敏看后紧紧抓住哈利的胳膊，疼得他直咧嘴。

"小天狼星的弟弟？"她低声问。

"是个食死徒，"哈利说，"小天狼星跟我说过，年轻时候加入的，后来害怕了，想要退出——他们就杀死了他。"

"对得上啊！"赫敏叫道，"如果他是食死徒，就能接触伏地魔，他后来悔悟了，就有可能想打败伏地魔！"

她放开哈利，伏在栏杆上尖叫道："罗恩！**罗恩！快来啊！**"

一分钟后，罗恩出现了，举着魔杖，气喘吁吁。

"搞什么名堂？如果又是巨蜘蛛，我可要先吃早饭——"

赫敏静静地指着门上雷古勒斯的牌子，罗恩皱眉端详着。

"什么呀？这是小天狼星的弟弟，对不对？雷古勒斯·阿克图勒斯……雷古勒斯……R.A.B.！挂坠盒——你们不会认为——？"

"我们来查个明白。"哈利说。他推了推门，是锁着的。赫敏用魔杖指着门把手说："阿拉霍洞开。"咔嗒一声，门开了。

三人跨过门槛，打量四周，雷古勒斯的卧室比小天狼星的小一点儿，但也同样可以感受到先前的富丽。小天狼星希望表现自己与家中其他成员不同，雷古勒斯强调的则正好相反。斯莱特林的银色和绿色随处可见，覆盖着床、墙壁和窗户。布莱克家族饰章和永远纯洁的格言精心描绘在床头上方，下面有许多泛黄的剪报，粘成不规则的拼贴画。赫敏走过去看了看。

"都是关于伏地魔的。"她说，"雷古勒斯似乎是当了几年崇拜者之后成为食死徒的……"

CHAPTER TEN   Kreacher's Tale

A little puff of dust rose from the bedcovers as she sat down to read the clippings. Harry, meanwhile, had noticed another photograph; a Hogwarts Quidditch team was smiling and waving out of the frame. He moved closer and saw the snakes emblazoned on their chests: Slytherins. Regulus was instantly recognisable as the boy sitting in the middle of the front row: he had the same dark hair and slightly haughty look of his brother, though he was smaller, slighter and rather less handsome than Sirius had been.

'He played Seeker,' said Harry.

'What?' said Hermione vaguely; she was still immersed in Voldemort's press clippings.

'He's sitting in the middle of the front row, that's where the Seeker ... never mind,' said Harry, realising that nobody was listening: Ron was on his hands and knees, searching under the wardrobe. Harry looked around the room for likely hiding places and approached the desk. Yet again, somebody had searched before them. The drawers' contents had been turned over recently, the dust disturbed, but there was nothing of value there: old quills, out of date textbooks that bore evidence of being roughly handled, a recently smashed ink bottle, its sticky residue covering the contents of the drawer.

'There's an easier way,' said Hermione, as Harry wiped his inky fingers on his jeans. She raised her wand and said, '*Accio locket!*'

Nothing happened. Ron, who had been searching the folds of the faded curtains, looked disappointed.

'Is that it, then? It's not here?'

'Oh, it could still be here, but under counter-enchantments,' said Hermione. 'Charms to prevent it being summoned magically, you know.'

'Like Voldemort put on the stone basin in the cave,' said Harry, remembering how he had been unable to Summon the fake locket.

'How are we supposed to find it, then?' asked Ron.

'We search manually,' said Hermione.

'That's a good idea,' said Ron, rolling his eyes, and he resumed his examination of the curtains.

They combed every inch of the room for over an hour, but were forced, finally, to conclude that the locket was not there.

The sun had risen now; its light dazzled them even through the grimy landing windows.

第 10 章 克利切的故事

她坐下来读剪报,床罩上扬起一小股灰尘。哈利则注意到一张照片,一支霍格沃茨魁地奇球队在相框中微笑挥手。他凑近一些,看到了球员胸前的蛇形图案,是斯莱特林队。他一眼就找到了雷古勒斯,坐在前排中间:黑头发和略带高傲的表情,和他哥哥一样,但体型瘦小一些,不如小天狼星那么英俊。

"他是找球手。"哈利说。

"什么?"赫敏茫然地问,还沉浸在伏地魔的剪报中。

"他坐在前排中间,那是找球手的……没什么。"哈利意识到没人在听:罗恩趴在地上查看衣柜底下。哈利环顾房间寻找着可能藏东西的地方,走到桌边。然而,这里也有人搜过了,抽屉里的东西不久前被翻动过,灰尘被搅乱了。可是看不到什么有价值的东西,旧羽毛笔、看上去被粗鲁翻动过的老课本,还有一只不久前打破的墨水瓶,黏稠的墨汁沾得抽屉里到处都是。

"有个轻巧的办法,"看见哈利把沾了墨汁的手往牛仔裤上擦,赫敏说。她举起魔杖念道:"挂坠盒飞来!"

没有动静。罗恩刚才在褪色的窗帘褶缝中搜寻,见状一脸失望。

"那就完了?不在这儿?"

"哦,它可能还在这儿,但被施了抵御咒,"赫敏说,"防止被咒语召出,你知道。"

"就像伏地魔对岩洞中的石盆施的那种。"哈利说,想起了他无法召出假挂坠盒。

"那我们怎么能找到它呢?"罗恩问。

"用手搜。"赫敏说。

"好主意。"罗恩翻了翻白眼,继续检查他的窗帘。

他们花了一个多小时,找遍了屋里的每一寸角落,最后被迫得出结论:挂坠盒不在这里。

太阳已经升起,隔着楼梯口污浊的窗玻璃仍然光芒刺眼。

CHAPTER TEN

Kreacher's Tale

'It could be somewhere else in the house, though,' said Hermione in a rallying tone as they walked back downstairs: as Harry and Ron had become more discouraged, she seemed to have become more determined. 'Whether he'd managed to destroy it or not, he'd want to keep it hidden from Voldemort, wouldn't he? Remember all those awful things we had to get rid of when we were here last time? That clock that shot bolts at everyone and those old robes that tried to strangle Ron; Regulus might have put them there to protect the locket's hiding place, even though we didn't realise it at … at …'

Harry and Ron looked at her. She was standing with one foot in mid-air, with the dumbstruck look of one who had just been Obliviated; her eyes had even drifted out of focus.

'… at the time,' she finished in a whisper.

'Something wrong?' asked Ron.

'There was a locket.'

'What?' said Harry and Ron together.

'In the cabinet in the drawing room. Nobody could open it. And we … we …'

Harry felt as though a brick had slid down through his chest into his stomach. He remembered: he had even handled the thing as they passed it round, each trying in turn to prise it open. It had been tossed into a sack of rubbish, along with the snuffbox of Wartcap powder and the music box that had made everyone sleepy …

'Kreacher nicked loads of things back from us,' said Harry. It was the only chance, the only slender hope left to them, and he was going to cling to it until forced to let go. 'He had a whole stash of stuff in his cupboard in the kitchen. C'mon.'

He ran down the stairs taking two steps at a time, the other two thundering along in his wake. They made so much noise that they woke the portrait of Sirius's mother as they passed through the hall.

'*Filth! Mudbloods! Scum!*' she screamed after them as they dashed down into the basement kitchen and slammed the door behind them.

Harry ran the length of the room, skidded to a halt at the door of Kreacher's cupboard and wrenched it open. There was the nest of dirty, old blankets in which the house-elf had once slept, but they were no longer glittering with the trinkets Kreacher had salvaged. The only thing there was an old copy of *Nature's Nobility: A Wizarding Genealogy*. Refusing to believe his

第10章 克利切的故事

"不过,它有可能在宅子里的其他地方。"下楼时,赫敏用鼓劲的语气说。哈利和罗恩有些气馁,她却似乎更坚定了。"那个人不管是否摧毁了挂坠盒,都不会希望伏地魔发现它,是不是?记得我们上次来的时候有那么多可怕的机关吗?朝每个人发射螺栓的老爷钟,还有要把罗恩勒死的旧袍子。也许都是雷古勒斯用来掩护挂坠盒的,尽管我们当时没有意……意……"

哈利和罗恩都望着赫敏,她一只脚悬在空中,表情好像刚刚被施了消除记忆咒,连眼神都散了。

"……意识到。"她耳语般地说。

"怎么回事?"罗恩问。

"确实有个挂坠盒。"

"什么?"哈利和罗恩齐声叫道。

"在客厅的柜子里,没人打得开,我们……我们……"

哈利感到一块砖头从胸口坠到肚子里。他记起来了:他还摸过一下呢,当时大家传看那个东西,轮流尝试想把它撬开。后来它被丢进了一个垃圾袋,那里面还有装着肉瘤粉的鼻烟盒和让每个人打瞌睡的音乐盒……

"克利切从我们这里偷走了许多东西。"哈利说,这是最后的可能性,他们的最后一线希望,他要紧紧抓住,直到不得不放手,"他在厨房碗柜里藏了一大堆宝贝。来吧。"

他一步两级地跑下楼梯,两个朋友噔噔噔地跟在后面。声音那么大,跑过走廊时,把小天狼星母亲的肖像都吵醒了。

"脏货!泥巴种!渣滓!"她在后面尖叫。三个人冲进地下的厨房,把门重重地关上。

哈利冲过房间,在克利切的碗柜前打着滑刹住脚,拽开了柜门。家养小精灵睡过的那堆肮脏的旧毯子还在,可是不再闪闪发光地缀满克利切救回来的小摆设。只有一本旧版的《生而高贵:巫师家谱》。哈

eyes, Harry snatched up the blankets and shook them. A dead mouse fell out and rolled dismally across the floor. Ron groaned as he threw himself into a kitchen chair; Hermione closed her eyes.

'It's not over yet,' said Harry, and he raised his voice and called, '*Kreacher!*'

There was a loud *crack* and the house-elf that Harry had so reluctantly inherited from Sirius appeared out of nowhere in front of the cold and empty fireplace: tiny, half-human-sized, his pale skin hanging off him in folds, white hair sprouting copiously from his bat-like ears. He was still wearing the filthy rag in which they had first met him, and the contemptuous look he bent upon Harry showed that his attitude to his change of ownership had altered no more than his outfit.

'Master,' croaked Kreacher in his bullfrog's voice, and he bowed low, muttering to his knees, 'back in my mistress's old house with the blood traitor Weasley and the Mudblood —'

'I forbid you to call anyone "blood traitor" or "Mudblood",' growled Harry. He would have found Kreacher, with his snout-like nose and bloodshot eyes, a distinctly unloveable object even if the elf had not betrayed Sirius to Voldemort.

'I've got a question for you,' said Harry, his heart beating rather fast as he looked down at the elf, 'and I order you to answer it truthfully. Understand?'

'Yes, Master,' said Kreacher, bowing low again: Harry saw his lips moving soundlessly, undoubtedly framing the insults he was now forbidden to utter.

'Two years ago,' said Harry, his heart now hammering against his ribs, 'there was a big gold locket in the drawing room upstairs. We threw it out. Did you steal it back?'

There was a moment's silence, during which Kreacher straightened up to look Harry full in the face. Then he said, 'Yes.'

'Where is it now?' asked Harry jubilantly, as Ron and Hermione looked gleeful.

Kreacher closed his eyes as though he could not bear to see their reactions to his next word.

'Gone.'

'Gone?' echoed Harry, elation flooding out of him. 'What do you mean, it's gone?'

The elf shivered. He swayed.

利不愿相信自己的眼睛，抓起毯子抖了又抖。一只死老鼠掉了出来，惨兮兮地滚到了一边。罗恩呻吟了一声，倒在一把椅子上。赫敏闭上了眼睛。

"还没有完。"哈利说，他提高嗓门叫道，"克利切！"

啪的一声，哈利极不情愿地从小天狼星名下继承的家养小精灵出现了。他站在冷冰冰、空荡荡的壁炉前：瘦瘦小小，只有半人高，苍白的皮肤打着褶垂下来，蝙蝠般的耳朵里冒出大量白毛。他仍穿着他们第一次见他时穿的那块肮脏的抹布，投向哈利的轻蔑眼神表明，他对换主人的态度也和穿衣风格一样没有改变。

"主人，"克利切牛蛙般的嗓子嘶哑地说，他低低地鞠了一躬，对着膝盖嘀咕，"回到我女主人的老宅，带着败类韦斯莱和泥巴种——"

"我禁止你叫任何人'败类'或'泥巴种'。"哈利吼道，就算这家养小精灵没有把小天狼星出卖给伏地魔，他也会觉得克利切那难看的大鼻子和充血的眼睛讨厌之极。

"我有话问你，"哈利说，他低头望着小精灵，心跳加快了，"我命令你如实回答，明白吗？"

"是，主人。"克利切说，又低低地鞠了一躬。哈利看到他的嘴唇在无声地蠕动，无疑是在默念现在禁止他说的侮辱性的话语。

"两年前，"哈利说道，心脏咚咚地撞击着肋骨，"楼上客厅里有一个挺大的金挂坠盒，被我们扔掉了，你有没有把它捡回来？"

片刻的沉默，克利切直起身子注视着哈利的面庞，然后说："捡回来了。"

"它现在在哪儿？"哈利高兴地问道，罗恩和赫敏也露出了喜色。

克利切闭上眼睛，似乎不敢看到他们对他下一个词的反应。

"没了。"

"没了？"哈利失声叫道，喜悦一下子退去，"你说什么，挂坠盒没了？"

小精灵哆嗦着，摇摇晃晃。

CHAPTER TEN   Kreacher's Tale

'Kreacher,' said Harry fiercely, 'I order you –'

'Mundungus Fletcher,' croaked the elf, his eyes still tight shut. 'Mundungus Fletcher stole it all: Miss Bella and Miss cissy's pictures, my mistress's gloves, the Order of Merlin, First Class, the goblets with the family crest, and, and –'

Kreacher was gulping for air: his hollow chest was rising and falling rapidly, then his eyes flew open and he uttered a blood-curdling scream.

'– *and the locket, Master Regulus's locket, Kreacher did wrong, Kreacher failed in his orders!*'

Harry reacted instinctively: as Kreacher lunged for the poker standing in the grate, he launched himself upon the elf, flattening him. Hermione's scream mingled with Kreacher's, but Harry bellowed louder than both of them: 'Kreacher, I order you to stay still!'

He felt the elf freeze and released him. Kreacher lay flat on the cold stone floor, tears gushing from his sagging eyes.

'Harry, let him up!' Hermione whispered.

'So he can beat himself up with the poker?' snorted Harry, kneeling beside the elf. 'I don't think so. Right, Kreacher, I want the truth: how do you know Mundungus Fletcher stole the locket?'

'Kreacher saw him!' gasped the elf, as tears poured over his snout and into his mouth full of greying teeth. 'Kreacher saw him coming out of Kreacher's cupboard with his hands full of Kreacher's treasures. Kreacher told the sneakthief to stop, but Mundungus Fletcher laughed and r – ran …'

'You called the locket "Master Regulus's",' said Harry. 'Why? Where did it come from? What did Regulus have to do with it? Kreacher, sit up and tell me everything you know about that locket, and everything Regulus had to do with it!'

The elf sat up, curled into a ball, placed his wet face between his knees and began to rock backwards and forwards. When he spoke, his voice was muffled but quite distinct in the silent, echoing kitchen.

'Master Sirius ran away, good riddance, for he was a bad boy and broke my mistress's heart with his lawless ways. But Master Regulus had proper pride; he knew what was due to the name of Black and the dignity of his pure blood. For years he talked of the Dark Lord, who was going to bring

"克利切,"哈利厉声说,"我命令你——"

"蒙顿格斯·弗莱奇,"小精灵嘶声说,仍然紧闭双眼,"都被蒙顿格斯·弗莱奇偷走了:贝拉小姐和西茜小姐的照片、我女主人的手套、一级梅林勋章、有家族饰章的高脚杯,还有,还有——"

克利切大口喘气,干瘪的胸脯急剧起伏,然后他睁开眼睛,发出一声令人血液凝固的尖叫。

"——还有挂坠盒,雷古勒斯少爷的挂坠盒,克利切犯了错误,克利切没能执行少爷的命令!"

哈利本能地做出反应:当克利切冲向立在炉边的拨火棍时,他扑到小精灵身上,把他压住。赫敏的尖叫和克利切的哭喊混在一起,但哈利的吼声比它们都响:"克利切,我命令你不许动!"

他感到小精灵僵住了,才放开手。克利切直挺挺地躺在冰冷的石板地上,泪水从凹陷的眼窝里哗哗涌出。

"哈利,让他起来!"赫敏悄声说。

"好让他用拨火棍痛打自己?"哈利不以为然地说,在小精灵旁边跪坐起来,"我可不想。好了,克利切,我要听真话:你怎么知道蒙顿格斯·弗莱奇偷走了挂坠盒?"

"克利切看到的!"小精灵抽噎地说,泪水顺着他的长鼻子流进咧开的嘴巴里,可以看到一口发灰的牙齿,"克利切看到他从克利切的碗柜里钻出来,捧的全是克利切的宝贝,克利切叫那个窃贼站住,可是蒙顿格斯·弗莱奇哈哈大笑,跑——跑……"

"你说那挂坠盒是'雷古勒斯少爷的',"哈利说,"为什么?它是哪儿来的?雷古勒斯跟它有什么关系?克利切,坐起来,把你所知道的一切告诉我,关于那个挂坠盒,还有雷古勒斯跟它的关系!"

小精灵坐了起来,蜷成一团,把潮湿的面孔夹在膝盖之间,开始前后摇晃。他开口说话时,声音低沉发闷,但在安静的、有回音的厨房里听得相当清楚。

"小天狼星少爷逃走了,走了倒好,因为他是个坏孩子,他那些不上规矩的行为让我的女主人伤透了心。但雷古勒斯少爷有自尊心,他

the wizards out of hiding to rule the Muggles and the Muggle-borns ... and when he was sixteen years old, Master Regulus joined the Dark Lord. So proud, so proud, so happy to serve ...

'And one day, a year after he had joined, Master Regulus came down to the kitchen to see Kreacher. Master Regulus always liked Kreacher. And Master Regulus said ... he said ...'

The old elf rocked faster than ever.

'... he said that the Dark Lord required an elf.'

'Voldemort needed an *elf?*' Harry repeated, looking round at Ron and Hermione, who looked just as puzzled as he did.

'Oh yes,' moaned Kreacher. 'And Master Regulus had volunteered Kreacher. It was an honour, said Master Regulus, an honour for him and for Kreacher, who must be sure to do whatever the Dark Lord ordered him to do ... and then to c – come home.'

Kreacher rocked still faster, his breath coming in sobs.

'So Kreacher went to the Dark Lord. The Dark Lord did not tell Kreacher what they were to do, but took Kreacher with him to a cave beside the sea. And beyond the cave there was a cavern, and in the cavern was a great, black lake ...'

The hairs on the back of Harry's neck stood up. Kreacher's croaking voice seemed to come to him from across that dark water. He saw what had happened as clearly as though he had been present.

'... there was a boat ...'

Of course there had been a boat; Harry knew the boat, ghostly green and tiny, bewitched so as to carry one wizard and one victim towards the island in the centre. This, then, was how Voldemort had tested the defences surrounding the Horcrux: by borrowing a disposable creature, a house-elf ...

'There was a b – basin full of potion on the island. The D – Dark Lord made Kreacher drink it ...'

The elf quaked from head to foot.

'Kreacher drank, and as he drank, he saw terrible things ... Kreacher's insides burned ... Kreacher cried for Master Regulus to save him, he cried for his Mistress Black, but the Dark Lord only laughed ... he made Kreacher drink all the potion ... he dropped a locket into the empty basin ... he filled it with more potion.

第 10 章 克利切的故事

知道布莱克这个姓氏和他纯正的血统意味着什么。许多年里他经常谈到黑魔王，黑魔王要让巫师不必再躲躲藏藏，而能出来统治麻瓜和麻瓜出身的巫师……雷古勒斯少爷十六岁时，加入了黑魔王的组织，他那么自豪，那么自豪，那么快乐，能够效力于……

"一年之后，有一天，雷古勒斯少爷到厨房里来看望克利切。雷古勒斯少爷一直都喜欢克利切。雷古勒斯少爷说……他说……"

年迈的小精灵摇晃得更快了。

"……他说黑魔王要一个小精灵。"

"伏地魔要一个小精灵？"哈利问道，回头看看罗恩和赫敏，他们俩也和他一样困惑。

"哦，是的，"克利切痛苦地说，"雷古勒斯少爷贡献了克利切。这是一种荣耀，雷古勒斯少爷说，是他本人和克利切的荣耀。克利切必须去做黑魔王要他做的一切事情……然后回——回家。"

克利切摇晃得更快了，呼吸变成了抽泣。

"于是克利切到了黑魔王那里。黑魔王没有告诉克利切要干什么，而是把克利切带到海边的一个山洞里。那是个大岩洞，洞中有一片黑色的大湖……"

哈利颈后的汗毛竖了起来，克利切嘶哑的声音似乎是从那黑色的水面上传来的。他看到了当时的情景，就像亲身经历的一样。

"……有一条船……"

当然有一条船，哈利知道那条船，幽灵般的绿色小船，被施了魔法，只能带一名巫师和一个牺牲品到湖心小岛。那么，伏地魔就是这样测试魂器的保护措施的：借助一个无足轻重的生命，一个家养小精灵……

"岛上有一个石——石盆，盛满魔药。黑——黑魔王让克利切喝……"

小精灵浑身发抖。

"克利切喝了，喝的时候看到好多恐怖的景象……克利切的五脏六腑都着火了……克利切喊雷古勒斯少爷救救他，喊女主人，可是黑魔王只是大笑……他逼克利切喝光了魔药……他把一个挂坠盒丢进空盆……又在盆里加满魔药。

CHAPTER TEN   Kreacher's Tale

'And then the Dark Lord sailed away, leaving Kreacher on the island ...'

Harry could see it happening. He watched Voldemort's white, snake-like face vanishing into darkness, those red eyes fixed pitilessly on the thrashing elf whose death would occur within minutes, whenever he succumbed to the desperate thirst that the burning potion caused its victim ... but here, Harry's imagination could go no further, for he could not see how Kreacher had escaped.

'Kreacher needed water, he crawled to the island's edge and he drank from the black lake ... and hands, dead hands, came out of the water and dragged Kreacher under the surface ...'

'How did you get away?' Harry asked, and he was not surprised to hear himself whispering.

Kreacher raised his ugly head and looked at Harry with his great, bloodshot eyes.

'Master Regulus told Kreacher to come back,' he said.

'I know – but how did you escape the Inferi?'

Kreacher did not seem to understand.

'Master Regulus told Kreacher to come back,' he repeated.

'I know, but –'

'Well, it's obvious, isn't it, Harry?' said Ron. 'He Disapparated!'

'But ... you couldn't Apparate in and out of that cave,' said Harry, 'otherwise Dumbledore –'

'Elf magic isn't like wizard's magic, is it?' said Ron. 'I mean, they can Apparate and Disapparate in and out of Hogwarts when we can't.'

There was silence as Harry digested this. How could Voldemort have made such a mistake? But even as he thought this, Hermione spoke, and her voice was icy.

'Of course, Voldemort would have considered the ways of house-elves far beneath his notice, just like all the pure-bloods who treat them like animals ... it would never have occurred to him that they might have magic that he didn't.'

'The house-elf's highest law is his master's bidding,' intoned Kreacher. 'Kreacher was told to come home, so Kreacher came home ...'

'Well, then, you did what you were told, didn't you?' said Hermione kindly. 'You didn't disobey orders at all!'

第10章 克利切的故事

"然后黑魔王上船走了,把克利切留在岛上……"

哈利能看到那一幕。他看到伏地魔苍白的蛇脸消失在黑暗中,红红的眼睛冷酷地盯着那个痛苦打滚的小精灵。小精灵几分钟后就会死亡,他抵抗不住那魔药烧心造成的极度干渴……但是到了这里,哈利的想象进行不下去了,因为他想不通克利切是怎么逃出来的。

"克利切需要水,他爬到小岛边缘,去喝黑湖里的水……许多手,死人的手,从水里伸出来把克利切拖了下去……"

"你是怎么逃脱的?"哈利问道,听到自己声音像耳语,他并不感到奇怪。

克利切抬起他那丑陋的脑袋,用充血的大眼睛望着哈利。

"雷古勒斯少爷说过要克利切回家。"他说。

"我知道——可是你怎么摆脱阴尸的呢?"

克利切似乎听不懂。

"雷古勒斯少爷说过要克利切回家。"他重复道。

"我知道,可是——"

"哎呀,很明显是不是,哈利?"罗恩说,"他幻影移形了!"

"可是……你没法通过幻影显形进出那个岩洞,"哈利说,"不然邓布利多——"

"小精灵的魔法与巫师的魔法不同,是不是?"罗恩说,"我是说,他们可以在霍格沃茨幻影显形或移形,而我们不能。"

一阵静默,哈利回味着这句话。伏地魔怎么会犯这样的错误?他刚想到这里时,赫敏说话了,声音冰冷。

"当然啦,伏地魔对家养小精灵的行为是不屑一顾的,就像所有把小精灵当畜生的纯血统巫师那样……他永远不会想到小精灵也许具备他所没有的魔法。"

"家养小精灵的最高法律就是主人的命令,"克利切庄重地说,"主人叫克利切回家,克利切就回家了……"

"那么,你做了主人命令你做的事,不是吗?"赫敏温和地说,"一点也没有违反命令!"

CHAPTER TEN Kreacher's Tale

Kreacher shook his head, rocking as fast as ever.

'So what happened when you got back?' Harry asked. 'What did Regulus say when you told him what had happened?'

'Master Regulus was very worried, very worried,' croaked Kreacher. 'Master Regulus told Kreacher to stay hidden, and not to leave the house. And then ... it was a little while later ... Master Regulus came to find Kreacher in his cupboard one night, and Master Regulus was strange, not as he usually was, disturbed in his mind, Kreacher could tell ... and he asked Kreacher to take him to the cave, the cave where Kreacher had gone with the Dark Lord ...'

And so they had set off. Harry could visualise them quite clearly, the frightened old elf and the thin, dark Seeker who had so resembled Sirius ... Kreacher knew how to open the concealed entrance to the underground cavern, knew how to raise the tiny boat; this time it was his beloved Regulus who sailed with him to the island with its basin of poison ...

'And he made you drink the potion?' said Harry, disgusted.

But Kreacher shook his head and wept. Hermione's hands leapt to her mouth: she seemed to have understood something.

'M – Master Regulus took from his pocket a locket like the one the Dark Lord had,' said Kreacher, tears pouring down either side of his snout-like nose. 'And he told Kreacher to take it and, when the basin was empty, to switch the lockets ...'

Kreacher's sobs came in great rasps now; Harry had to concentrate hard to understand him.

'And he ordered – Kreacher to leave – without him. And he told Kreacher – to go home – and never to tell my mistress – what he had done – but to destroy – the first locket. And he drank – all the potion – and Kreacher swapped the lockets – and watched ... as Master Regulus ... was dragged beneath the water ... and ...'

'Oh, Kreacher!' wailed Hermione, who was crying. She dropped to her knees beside the elf and tried to hug him. At once he was on his feet, cringing away from her, quite obviously repulsed.

'The Mudblood touched Kreacher, he will not allow it, what would his mistress say?'

'I told you not to call her "Mudblood"!' snarled Harry, but the elf was already punishing himself: he fell to the ground and banged his forehead on the floor.

第10章 克利切的故事

克利切点点头，摇晃得更快了。

"那你回来之后发生了什么？"哈利问，"当你把事情告诉主人之后，雷古勒斯怎么说？"

"雷古勒斯少爷非常担心，非常担心。"克利切嘶声叫道，"雷古勒斯叫克利切躲起来，不要离开家门。然后……过了一阵子……一天夜里，雷古勒斯少爷到碗柜来找克利切。雷古勒斯少爷显得很奇怪，不像平常的样子，克利切看得出他心里很乱……少爷叫克利切带他到岩洞去，就是克利切跟黑魔王去过的那个岩洞……"

于是他们就出发了，哈利能清楚地想象出，一个惊恐万分的衰老的小精灵，和那个精瘦黝黑、与小天狼星如此相像的找球手……克利切知道怎样打开地下岩洞的秘密入口，知道怎样让小船浮上来，这次是跟他热爱的雷古勒斯一起驶向那盛有魔药的小岛……

"他让你喝了魔药？"哈利反感地问。

克利切摇摇头，痛哭失声。赫敏捂住了嘴巴：她似乎猜到了什么。

"雷——雷古勒斯少爷从口袋里掏出一个挂坠盒，跟黑魔王的那个一样。"克利切说，泪水顺着他的长鼻子两边哗哗地流淌，"他叫克利切拿着它，等石盆干了之后，把挂坠盒调换一下……"

克利切的抽泣变得粗重刺耳，哈利必须全神贯注才能听懂他的话。

"他命令——克利切离开——不要管他。他叫克利切——回家——不许对女主人说——他做的事——但是必须摧毁——第一个挂坠盒。然后他就喝了——喝干了魔药——克利切调换了挂坠盒——眼睁睁看着……雷古勒斯少爷……被拖到水下……然后……"

"哦，克利切！"赫敏哀叫道，她哭了，跪在小精灵身边，想拥抱他。小精灵马上站了起来，直往后躲，脸上带着明显的厌恶。

"泥巴种碰了克利切，克利切不允许，女主人会怎么说啊？"

"我说过不许叫她'泥巴种'！"哈利吼道，可是小精灵已经在惩罚自己了：他扑倒在地，把头往地板上撞。

CHAPTER TEN Kreacher's Tale

'Stop him – stop him!' Hermione cried. 'Oh, don't you see, now, how sick it is, the way they've got to obey?'

'Kreacher – stop, stop!' shouted Harry.

The elf lay on the floor, panting and shivering, green mucus glistening around his snout, a bruise already blooming on his pallid forehead where he had struck himself, his eyes swollen and bloodshot and swimming in tears. Harry had never seen anything so pitiful.

'So you brought the locket home,' he said relentlessly, for he was determined to know the full story. 'And you tried to destroy it?'

'Nothing Kreacher did made any mark upon it,' moaned the elf. 'Kreacher tried everything, everything he knew, but nothing, nothing would work ... so many powerful spells upon the casing, Kreacher was sure the way to destroy it was to get inside it, but it would not open ... Kreacher punished himself, he tried again, he punished himself, he tried again. Kreacher failed to obey orders, Kreacher could not destroy the locket! And his mistress was mad with grief, because Master Regulus had disappeared, and Kreacher could not tell her what had happened, no, because Master Regulus had f – f – forbidden him to tell any of the f – f – family what happened in the c – cave ...'

Kreacher began to sob so hard that there were no more coherent words. Tears flowed down Hermione's cheeks as she watched Kreacher, but she did not dare touch him again. Even Ron, who was no fan of Kreacher's, looked troubled. Harry sat back on his heels and shook his head, trying to clear it.

'I don't understand you, Kreacher,' he said finally. 'Voldemort tried to kill you, Regulus died to bring Voldemort down, but you were still happy to betray Sirius to Voldemort? You were happy to go to Narcissa and Bellatrix, and pass information to Voldemort through them ...'

'Harry, Kreacher doesn't think like that,' said Hermione, wiping her eyes on the back of her hand. 'He's a slave; house-elves are used to bad, even brutal treatment; what Voldemort did to Kreacher wasn't that far out of the common way. What do wizard wars mean to an elf like Kreacher? He's loyal to people who are kind to him, and Mrs Black must have been, and Regulus certainly was, so he served them willingly and parroted their beliefs. I know what you're going to say,' she went on, as Harry began to protest, 'that Regulus changed his mind ... but he doesn't seem to have explained that to Kreacher, does he? And I think I know why. Kreacher and Regulus's family

"拦住他——拦住他！"赫敏叫起来，"哦，你们现在还看不到这是多么残忍吗，他们只能服从！"

"克利切——停止，停止！"哈利高喊。

小精灵躺在地上，喘着气，浑身发抖，鼻子周围亮晶晶的全是绿色黏液，苍白的额头上已经肿起一个大包，眼睛红肿充血，泪汪汪的。哈利从没见过如此可怜的景象。

"那么，你把挂坠盒带回了家，"他狠狠心继续问，决心要了解全部经过，"试着摧毁它了吗？"

"克利切没法在它上面留下一点痕迹。"小精灵难过地说，"克利切试了所有的办法，所有的办法，可是没有一个，没有一个成功……盒子上有那么多强大的魔法，克利切相信只有从里面才能把它摧毁，可是它打不开……克利切惩罚自己，重新再试，又惩罚自己，重新再试。克利切没能执行命令，克利切摧毁不了挂坠盒！女主人悲伤得发了疯，因为雷古勒斯少爷失踪了，克利切不能告诉她发生了什么，不能，因为雷古勒斯少爷禁——禁止他对家——家里人说岩——岩洞里的事……"

克利切泣不成声，赫敏望着克利切，也泪流满面，可是不敢再碰他。就连对克利切毫无好感的罗恩也显得有些不安。哈利跪坐起来，甩甩头，让脑子清楚一些。

"我搞不懂你，克利切。"他开口道，"伏地魔想害死你，雷古勒斯又为打败伏地魔而死，可你却甘愿把小天狼星出卖给伏地魔？甘愿到纳西莎和贝拉特里克斯那里，给伏地魔通风报信……"

"哈利，克利切不是那么想的，"赫敏用手背擦着眼睛说，"他是个奴隶，家养小精灵受惯了粗鲁的，甚至残暴的待遇。伏地魔对克利切做的事情并没有那么骇人听闻。巫师间的战争对克利切这样的小精灵有什么意义呢？他只是忠于对他好的人，布莱克夫人想必对他不错，雷古勒斯当然也是，所以他心甘情愿为他们效命，并完全接受了他们的信仰。我知道你要说什么，"哈利正待争辩，她已经说道，"雷古勒斯思想转变了……但他似乎并未向克利切解释，是不是？我想我知道为什么。保持纯血统的老观念，克利切和雷古勒斯的家人都会更安全，

CHAPTER TEN Kreacher's Tale

were all safer if they kept to the old pure-blood line. Regulus was trying to protect them all.'

'Sirius —'

'Sirius was horrible to Kreacher, Harry, and it's no good looking like that, you know it's true. Kreacher had been alone for a long time when Sirius came to live here, and he was probably starving for a bit of affection. I'm sure "Miss Cissy" and "Miss Bella" were perfectly lovely to Kreacher when he turned up, so he did them a favour and told them everything they wanted to know. I've said all along that wizards would pay for how they treat house-elves. Well, Voldemort did ... and so did Sirius.'

Harry had no retort. As he watched Kreacher sobbing on the floor, he remembered what Dumbledore had said to him, mere hours after Sirius's death: *I do not think Sirius ever saw Kreacher as a being with feelings as acute as a human's ...*

'Kreacher,' said Harry, after a while, 'when you feel up to it, er ... please sit up.'

It was several minutes before Kreacher hiccoughed himself into silence. Then he pushed himself into a sitting position again, rubbing his knuckles into his eyes like a small child.

'Kreacher, I am going to ask you to do something,' said Harry. He glanced at Hermione for assistance: he wanted to give the order kindly, but at the same time, he could not pretend that it was not an order. However, the change in his tone seemed to have gained her approval: she smiled encouragingly.

'Kreacher, I want you, please, to go and find Mundungus Fletcher. We need to find out where the locket — where Master Regulus's locket is. It's really important. We want to finish the work Master Regulus started, we want to — er — ensure that he didn't die in vain.'

Kreacher dropped his fists and looked up at Harry.

'Find Mundungus Fletcher?' he croaked.

'And bring him here, to Grimmauld Place,' said Harry. 'Do you think you could do that for us?'

As Kreacher nodded and got to his feet, Harry had a sudden inspiration. He pulled out Hagrid's purse and took out the fake Horcrux, the substitute locket in which Regulus had placed the note to Voldemort.

第 10 章 克利切的故事

雷古勒斯是想保护他们。"

"小天狼星——"

"小天狼星对克利切态度很恶劣,哈利。那样看着我也没有用,你知道这是事实。小天狼星住到这里来时,克利切已经独自生活了很长时间,他也许正渴望一点温情,我相信'西茜小姐'和'贝拉小姐'对克利切相当亲切,于是他便愿意帮忙,说出了她们想知道的一切。我一直说巫师要为他们对待家养小精灵的方式付出代价,看,伏地魔付出了代价……还有小天狼星。"

哈利无言以对,看着克利切躺在地上哭泣,他想起邓布利多在小天狼星刚刚去世几小时后说的话:我认为小天狼星从没把克利切看作是跟人类拥有同样敏感情绪的一种生物……

"克利切,"过了一会儿哈利说道,"当你觉得可以的时候,嗯……请坐起来。"

好几分钟后,克利切才打着嗝儿安静下来。他撑着坐起身,像小孩子似的用拳头揉眼睛。

"克利切,我要请你做一件事。"哈利说,他望了望赫敏,希望得到支持。他想把命令说得和蔼些,但又不能假装这不是个命令。不过,他语气的变化似乎赢得了赫敏的赞许,她鼓励地微笑着。

"克利切,我要请你,去找到蒙顿格斯·弗莱奇。我们需要查明那个挂坠盒——雷古勒斯少爷的挂坠盒在哪儿。这真的很重要。我们想完成雷古勒斯少爷未完成的事。我们想——嗯——想确保他没有白死。"

克利切放下拳头,抬头望着哈利。

"找到蒙顿格斯·弗莱奇?"他嘶哑地说。

"把他带到格里莫广场来。"哈利说,"你觉得能为我们办这件事吗?"

克利切点点头,爬了起来。哈利灵机一动,掏出海格送的皮袋子,取出那个假魂器——那个冒牌的挂坠盒,里面有雷古勒斯给伏地魔的字条。

CHAPTER TEN Kreacher's Tale

'Kreacher, I'd, er, like you to have this,' he said, pressing the locket into the elf's hand. 'This belonged to Regulus and I'm sure he'd want you to have it as a token of gratitude for what you —'

'Overkill, mate,' said Ron, as the elf took one look at the locket, let out a howl of shock and misery and threw himself back on to the ground.

It took them nearly half an hour to calm down Kreacher, who was so overcome to be presented with a Black family heirloom for his very own that he was too weak at the knees to stand properly. When finally he was able to totter a few steps, they all accompanied him to his cupboard, watched him tuck up the locket safely in his dirty blankets, and assured him that they would make its protection their first priority while he was away. He then made two low bows to Harry and Ron, and even gave a funny little spasm in Hermione's direction that might have been an attempt at a respectful salute, before Disapparating with the usual loud *crack*.

第10章 克利切的故事

"克利切,我,呃,希望你收下这个,"他把挂坠盒塞进小精灵的手中,"这是雷古勒斯的,我相信他会愿意把它给你,以感谢你——"

"过头了,伙计。"罗恩说。小精灵一看到挂坠盒,发出一声又是吃惊又是痛苦的号叫,再次瘫倒在地。

他们花了近半个小时才使克利切平静下来,小精灵没想到自己竟能得到一件布莱克家族的遗物,激动得膝盖发软,站都站不住了。当他终于能蹒跚几步时,他们陪他走到碗柜前,看着他把挂坠盒仔细地藏在脏毯子里,并向他保证说,他离开期间他们一定会好好保护它。小精灵分别向哈利和罗恩低低地鞠了一躬,甚至朝赫敏滑稽地抽搐了一下,也许是试图行一个礼,随后便在熟悉的啪的一声中幻影移形了。

CHAPTER ELEVEN

The Bribe

If Kreacher could escape a lake full of Inferi, Harry was confident that the capture of Mundungus would take a few hours at most, and he prowled the house all morning in a state of high anticipation. However, Kreacher did not return that morning, or even that afternoon. By nightfall, Harry felt discouraged and anxious, and a supper composed largely of mouldy bread, upon which Hermione had tried a variety of unsuccessful Transfigurations, did nothing to help.

Kreacher did not return the following day, nor the day after that. However, two cloaked men had appeared in the square outside number twelve, and they remained there into the night, gazing in the direction of the house that they could not see.

'Death Eaters, for sure,' said Ron, as he, Harry and Hermione watched from the drawing-room windows. 'Reckon they know we're in here?'

'I don't think so,' said Hermione, though she looked frightened, 'or they'd have sent Snape in after us, wouldn't they?'

'D'you reckon he's been in here and had his tongue tied by Moody's curse?' asked Ron.

'Yes,' said Hermione, 'otherwise he'd have been able to tell that lot how to get in, wouldn't he? But they're probably watching to see whether we turn up. They know that Harry owns the house, after all.'

'How do they –?' began Harry.

'Wizarding wills are examined by the Ministry, remember? They'll know Sirius left you the place.'

The presence of the Death Eaters outside increased the ominous mood inside number twelve. They had not heard a word from anyone beyond Grimmauld Place since Mr Weasley's Patronus, and the strain was starting to

第 11 章

贿　赂

既然克利切能摆脱满湖的阴尸，那么哈利相信，克利切抓回蒙顿格斯至多也只要几小时。他一上午都满怀期待地在屋里走来走去。然而，克利切上午没有回来，下午也没有。到了傍晚，哈利感到灰心丧气，焦虑不安，而以发霉面包为主的晚饭也不能让人心情好一点儿，赫敏对它们试了许多变形的魔法，都没有成功。

克利切第二天、第三天也没有回来。倒是有两个穿斗篷的人出现在12号门外的广场上，一直待到夜间，盯着这所他们并不能看见的房子。

"肯定是食死徒。"罗恩说，他和哈利、赫敏一起从客厅窗口向外窥视，"你说他们知道我们在这儿吗？"

"我想不知道吧，"赫敏说，但她显得有些害怕，"要是知道就会派斯内普来抓我们了，是不是？"

"你说他是不是来过，中了穆迪的结舌咒？"罗恩问。

"是的，"赫敏说，"不然他就会告诉那帮人怎么进来了，对不对？但他们也许是在等我们现身，毕竟，他们知道哈利拥有这所房子。"

"他们怎么——"哈利说。

"巫师的遗嘱都要经魔法部检查，记得吗？他们会知道小天狼星把这所房子留给你了。"

外面的食死徒增加了12号宅子中的不祥气氛。从韦斯莱先生的守护神来过之后，他们没有听到格里莫广场以外任何人的音信，压抑感开始表现出来。罗恩烦躁不安，多了个恼人的习惯，爱玩衣袋里的那

CHAPTER ELEVEN   The Bribe

tell. Restless and irritable, Ron had developed an annoying habit of playing with the Deluminator in his pocket: this particularly infuriated Hermione, who was whiling away the wait for Kreacher by studying *The Tales of Beedle the Bard* and did not appreciate the way the lights kept flashing on and off.

'Will you stop it!' she cried on the third evening of Kreacher's absence, as all light was sucked from the drawing room yet again.

'Sorry, sorry!' said Ron, clicking the Deluminator and restoring the lights. 'I don't know I'm doing it!'

'Well, can't you find something useful to occupy yourself?'

'What, like reading kids' stories?'

'Dumbledore left me this book, Ron –'

'– and he left me the Deluminator, maybe I'm supposed to use it!'

Unable to stand the bickering, Harry slipped out of the room unnoticed by either of them. He headed downstairs towards the kitchen, which he kept visiting because he was sure that was where Kreacher was most likely to reappear. Halfway down the flight of stairs into the hall, however, he heard a tap on the front door, then metallic clicks and the grinding of the chain.

Every nerve in his body seemed to tauten: he pulled out his wand, moved into the shadows beside the decapitated elf-heads and waited. The door opened: he saw a glimpse of the lamplit square outside, and a cloaked figure edged into the hall and closed the door behind it. The intruder took a step forwards and Moody's voice asked, '*Severus Snape?*' Then the dust figure rose from the end of the hall and rushed him, raising its dead hand.

'It was not I who killed you, Albus,' said a quiet voice.

The jinx broke: the dust figure exploded again, and it was impossible to make out the newcomer through the dense grey cloud it left behind.

Harry pointed his wand into the middle of it.

'Don't move!'

He had forgotten the portrait of Mrs Black: at the sound of his yell the curtains hiding her flew open and she began to scream, '*Mudbloods and filth dishonouring my house –*'

Ron and Hermione came crashing down the stairs behind Harry, wands pointing, like his, at the unknown man now standing with his arms raised in the hall below.

'Hold your fire, it's me, Remus!'

第 11 章 贿　赂

个熄灯器，这让赫敏大为不满，她一边读《诗翁彼豆故事集》一边等克利切，很是讨厌灯光忽明忽暗。

"你别玩了行不行！"克利切离开后的第三个晚上，客厅的灯光又一次全部被吸走时，赫敏嚷道。

"对不起，对不起！"罗恩咔嗒一摁熄灯器，把灯点亮，"我没意识到自己在做什么！"

"你不能找点有用的事做做吗？"

"什么事？看童话书？"

"这本书是邓布利多留给我的，罗恩——"

"——他把熄灯器留给了我，也许我应该用用它！"

哈利受不了这种斗嘴，悄悄溜出了房间，下楼朝厨房走去。他经常去厨房，因为他相信克利切最有可能在那里出现。但走到通往门厅的楼梯中间时，他听见前门被敲了一下，接着是响亮的金属撞击声以及像链条发出的哗啦哗啦声。

哈利全身的每根神经都紧张起来，他拔出魔杖，躲进那些小精灵脑袋旁边的阴影里等待。门开了，他瞥见了外面路灯照亮的广场，一个穿斗篷的人影闪进门厅，关上了门。来人向前走了一步，穆迪的声音问道："西弗勒斯·斯内普？"那个土灰色的身影从门厅尽头升起来，举着枯槁的手向来人扑去。

"杀你的不是我，阿不思。"一个镇静的声音说道。

恶咒解除了，土灰色的身影又一次爆炸，灰尘弥漫，看不清来人。

哈利用魔杖指着灰尘中间。

"不许动！"

他忘记了布莱克夫人的肖像。他刚喊出声，帷幔马上掀开，那女人尖叫起来："泥巴种，脏货，玷污了我的房子——"

罗恩和赫敏急忙冲下楼，像哈利一样举着魔杖，对准那个不速之客，那人现在举起双手站在楼下门厅中。

"别开火，是我，莱姆斯！"

CHAPTER ELEVEN   The Bribe

'Oh, thank goodness,' said Hermione weakly, pointing her wand at Mrs Black instead; with a bang, the curtains swished shut again and silence fell. Ron, too, lowered his wand, but Harry did not.

'Show yourself!' he called back.

Lupin moved forwards into the lamplight, hands still held high in a gesture of surrender.

'I am Remus John Lupin, werewolf, sometimes known as Moony, one of the four creators of the Marauder's Map, married to Nymphadora, usually known as Tonks, and I taught you how to produce a Patronus, Harry, which takes the form of a stag.'

'Oh, all right,' said Harry, lowering his wand, 'but I had to check, didn't I?'

'Speaking as your ex-Defence Against the Dark Arts teacher, I quite agree that you had to check. Ron, Hermione, you shouldn't be quite so quick to lower your defences.'

They ran down the stairs towards him. Wrapped in a thick, black travelling cloak, he looked exhausted, but pleased to see them.

'No sign of Severus, then?' he asked.

'No,' said Harry. 'What's going on? Is everyone OK?'

'Yes,' said Lupin, 'but we're all being watched. There are a couple of Death Eaters in the square outside –'

'– we know –'

'– I had to Apparate very precisely on to the top step outside the front door to be sure that they would not see me. They can't know you're in here or I'm sure they'd have more people out there; they're staking out everywhere that's got any connection with you, Harry. Let's go downstairs, there's a lot to tell you and I want to know what happened after you left The Burrow.'

They descended into the kitchen, where Hermione pointed her wand at the grate. A fire sprang up instantly: it gave the illusion of cosiness to the stark stone walls and glistened off the long wooden table. Lupin pulled a few Butterbeers from beneath his travelling cloak and they sat down.

'I'd have been here three days ago but I needed to shake off the Death Eater tailing me,' said Lupin. 'So, you came straight here after the wedding?'

'No,' said Harry, 'only after we ran into a couple of Death Eaters in a café on Tottenham Court Road.'

Lupin slopped most of his Butterbeer down his front.

第11章 贿 赂

"哦,谢天谢地。"赫敏虚弱地说,把魔杖转向布莱克夫人,砰的一声,帷幔唰地拉上了,屋里安静下来。罗恩也垂下了魔杖,然而哈利没有。

"让我看见你!"他喊道。

卢平走进灯光中,仍然高举双手,做出投降的姿势。

"我是莱姆斯·约翰·卢平,狼人,有时被称作月亮脸,是活点地图的四位作者之一,太太是尼法朵拉,通常叫唐克斯。我教过你怎样召出守护神,哈利,它是一头牡鹿。"

"哦,没错,"哈利垂下了魔杖,"但我必须核查一下,是不是?"

"作为你的前任黑魔法防御术课教师,我完全同意必须核查。罗恩、赫敏,你们不应该这么快就放松警惕。"

他们向他奔过去。卢平穿着一件厚厚的黑色旅行斗篷,看上去疲惫不堪,但很高兴见到他们。

"没见到西弗勒斯?"他问。

"没有。"哈利说,"怎么样?大家都好吗?"

"都好!"卢平说,"但我们都受到了监视。外面广场上有两个食死徒——"

"——我们知道——"

"——我必须正好幻影显形到前门台阶顶上,才能确保他们不看到我。他们不可能知道你们在这儿,不然肯定会派更多的人来。他们在所有与你有联系的地方都设了岗哨,哈利。到楼下去吧,我有很多事情要告诉你们,也想知道你们离开陋居后发生了什么。"

他们下到厨房里,赫敏用魔杖指了指炉栅,火苗立刻蹿起,在冷硬的石墙上造成舒适的幻觉,把火光映在木质长桌上。卢平从旅行斗篷里掏出几瓶黄油啤酒,四人坐了下来。

"我本来三天前就要来的,可是得甩掉盯梢的食死徒。"卢平说,"那么,婚礼之后你们就直接来这儿了?"

"没有,"哈利说,"是在托腾汉宫路的咖啡馆遭遇两个食死徒之后才来的。"

卢平把大半瓶黄油啤酒洒到了胸前。

CHAPTER ELEVEN   The Bribe

'*What?*'

They explained what had happened; when they had finished, Lupin looked aghast.

'But how did they find you so quickly? It's impossible to track anyone who Apparates, unless you grab hold of them as they disappear!'

'And it doesn't seem likely they were just strolling down Tottenham Court Road at the time, does it?' said Harry.

'We wondered,' said Hermione tentatively, 'whether Harry could still have the Trace on him?'

'Impossible,' said Lupin. Ron looked smug, and Harry felt hugely relieved. 'Apart from anything else, they'd know for sure Harry was here if he still had the Trace on him, wouldn't they? But I can't see how they could have tracked you to Tottenham Court Road, that's worrying, really worrying.'

He looked disturbed, but as far as Harry was concerned, that question could wait.

'Tell us what happened after we left, we haven't heard a thing since Ron's dad told us the family were safe.'

'Well, Kingsley saved us,' said Lupin. 'Thanks to his warning most of the wedding guests were able to Disapparate before they arrived.'

'Were they Death Eaters or Ministry people?' interjected Hermione.

'A mixture; but to all intents and purposes they're the same thing now,' said Lupin. 'There were about a dozen of them, but they didn't know you were there, Harry. Arthur heard a rumour that they tried to torture your whereabouts out of Scrimgeour before they killed him; if it's true, he didn't give you away.'

Harry looked at Ron and Hermione; their expressions reflected the mingled shock and gratitude he felt. He had never liked Scrimgeour much, but if what Lupin said was true, the man's final act had been to try to protect Harry.

'The Death Eaters searched The Burrow from top to bottom,' Lupin went on. 'They found the ghoul, but didn't want to get too close – and then they interrogated those of us who remained for hours. They were trying to get information on you, Harry, but, of course, nobody apart from the Order knew that you had been there.

'At the same time that they were smashing up the wedding, more Death Eaters were forcing their way into every Order-connected house in the country. No deaths,' he added quickly, forestalling the question, 'but they were rough. They burned down Dedalus Diggle's house, but as you know he

第11章 贿 赂

"什么？"

他们说了事情的经过，讲完之后，卢平一脸惊骇。

"可是他们怎么会这么快就发现了你们呢？要跟踪幻影显形的人是不可能的，除非你在他消失时抓住他！"

"他们也不大可能恰好那个时候在托腾汉宫路散步，是不是？"哈利说。

"我们想过，"赫敏试探地说，"哈利是不是还带着踪丝？"

"不可能！"卢平说，罗恩露出得意之色，哈利大大松了口气，"首先，如果他还带着踪丝，他们就会确定他在这里，是不是？可是我想不通他们怎么会跟到了托腾汉宫路，这令人担心，真令人担心。"

他显得忧心忡忡，但在哈利看来，这个问题还可以放一放。

"说说我们走后发生的事吧，自从罗恩的爸爸说全家平安之后，我们什么消息也没有。"

"哦，金斯莱救了我们，"卢平说，"多亏他报信，大多数客人都在那帮人赶到之前幻影移形了。"

"那帮人是食死徒还是魔法部的？"赫敏插进来问。

"都有。他们现在实际上是一回事了。"卢平说，"有十来个人，但他们不知道你在场，哈利。亚瑟听到传言说，他们在杀死斯克林杰之前，曾经给他用刑拷问过你的下落，如果真有此事，他没有出卖你。"

哈利看了看罗恩和赫敏，他们俩的表情反映出跟他一样的震惊与感激。他从来都不怎么喜欢斯克林杰，但如果卢平说的是实情，那斯克林杰最后的行为却是竭力保护哈利。

"食死徒把陋居搜了个底朝天，"卢平接着说，"他们发现了食尸鬼，但不愿靠近——后来又把我们那些没走的审问了几小时。他们想得到你的消息，哈利，但是当然啦，除了凤凰社成员之外，没人知道你曾经在那里。

"在搅乱婚礼的同时，更多的食死徒闯进全国每一户与凤凰社有联系的家庭。没人死亡，"他不等他们询问就忙说，"可是那帮人很粗暴，

CHAPTER ELEVEN   The Bribe

wasn't there, and they used the Cruciatus Curse on Tonks's family. Again, trying to find out where you went after you visited them. They're all right – shaken, obviously, but otherwise OK.'

'The Death Eaters got through all those protective charms?' Harry asked, remembering how effective these had been on the night he had crashed in Tonks's parents' garden.

'What you've got to realise, Harry, is that the Death Eaters have got the full might of the Ministry on their side now,' said Lupin. 'They've got the power to perform brutal spells without fear of identification or arrest. They managed to penetrate every defensive spell we'd cast against them, and once inside, they were completely open about why they'd come.'

'And are they bothering to give an excuse for torturing Harry's whereabouts out of people?' asked Hermione, an edge to her voice.

'Well,' said Lupin. He hesitated, then pulled out a folded copy of the *Daily Prophet*.

'Here,' he said, pushing it across the table to Harry, 'you'll know sooner or later anyway. That's their pretext for going after you.'

Harry smoothed out the paper. A huge photograph of his own face filled the front page. He read the headline over it:

WANTED FOR QUESTIONING ABOUT THE DEATH OF ALBUS DUMBLEDORE

Ron and Hermione gave roars of outrage, but Harry said nothing. He pushed the newspaper away; he did not want to read any more: he knew what it would say. Nobody but those who had been on top of the Tower when Dumbledore died knew who had really killed him and, as Rita Skeeter had already told the wizarding world, Harry had been seen running from the place moments after Dumbledore had fallen.

'I'm sorry, Harry,' Lupin said.

'So Death Eaters have taken over the *Daily Prophet* too?' asked Hermione furiously.

Lupin nodded.

'But surely people realise what's going on?'

'The coup has been smooth and virtually silent,' said Lupin. 'The official version of Scrimgeour's murder is that he resigned; he has been replaced by Pius Thicknesse, who is under the Imperius Curse.'

第11章 贿　赂

烧掉了德达洛·迪歌的房子，但你们知道他不在那儿。他们还对唐克斯一家用了钻心咒，也是试图问出你去过他们家之后的下落。他们没事——看上去有些虚弱，但其他都还好。"

"食死徒突破了所有那些防护咒？"哈利问道，想起他坠落在唐克斯父母家花园的那天夜里，那些咒语曾是多么有效。

"你必须明白，哈利，食死徒现在有整个魔法部撑腰了，"卢平说，"他们可以使用残酷的魔法，而不用担心被发现和逮捕。他们突破了我们施的所有防护咒，进来之后，也毫不掩饰他们的来意。"

"他们这样酷刑拷问哈利的下落，给自己找了什么借口吗？"赫敏问，声音有些尖锐。

"嗯。"卢平犹豫了一下，掏出一张折叠的《预言家日报》。

"看看吧，"他说着，把报纸从桌面推给哈利，"反正你迟早会知道的。这就是他们搜捕你的借口。"

哈利展开报纸，一张他的大照片占满了头版。他看着照片上方的大标题：

通缉追查
阿不思·邓布利多死因

罗恩和赫敏气愤地叫了起来，但哈利没说话。他把报纸推到一边，不想再看。他知道里面会怎么说。除了当时在塔顶的人之外，没有人知道是谁杀死了邓布利多，而且丽塔·斯基特已经告诉魔法界，邓布利多坠楼后不久，便有人看到哈利逃离了现场。

"对不起，哈利。"卢平说。

"这么说，食死徒也控制了《预言家日报》？"赫敏愤怒地问。

卢平点点头。

"可是人们一定知道是怎么回事吧？"

"政变很平稳，几乎无声无息。"卢平说，"斯克林杰遇害的官方说法是他辞职了，接替他的是皮尔斯·辛克尼斯，被施了迷魂咒。"

CHAPTER ELEVEN The Bribe

'Why didn't Voldemort declare himself Minister for Magic?' asked Ron.

Lupin laughed.

'He doesn't need to, Ron. Effectively he is the Minister, but why should he sit behind a desk at the Ministry? His puppet, Thicknesse, is taking care of everyday business, leaving Voldemort free to extend his power beyond the Ministry.

'Naturally many people have deduced what has happened: there has been such a dramatic change in Ministry policy in the last few days, and many are whispering that Voldemort must be behind it. However, that is the point: they whisper. They daren't confide in each other, not knowing whom to trust; they are scared to speak out, in case their suspicions are true and their families are targeted. Yes, Voldemort is playing a very clever game. Declaring himself might have provoked open rebellion: remaining masked has created confusion, uncertainty and fear.'

'And this dramatic change in Ministry policy,' said Harry, 'involves warning the wizarding world against me instead of Voldemort?'

'That's certainly part of it,' said Lupin, 'and it is a masterstroke. Now that Dumbledore is dead, you – the Boy Who Lived – were sure to be the symbol and rallying point for any resistance to Voldemort. But by suggesting that you had a hand in the old hero's death, Voldemort has not only set a price upon your head, but sown doubt and fear amongst many who would have defended you.

'Meanwhile, the Ministry has started moving against Muggle-borns.'

Lupin pointed at the *Daily Prophet*.

'Look at page two.'

Hermione turned the pages with much the same expression of distaste she had worn when handling *Secrets of the Darkest Art*.

'"*Muggle-born Register*",' she read aloud. '"*The Ministry of Magic is undertaking a survey of so-called 'Muggle-borns', the better to understand how they came to possess magical secrets.*

'"*Recent research undertaken by the Department of Mysteries reveals that magic can only be passed from person to person when wizards reproduce. Where no proven wizarding ancestry exists, therefore, the so-called Muggle-born is likely to have obtained magical power by theft or force.*

'"*The Ministry is determined to root out such usurpers of magical power, and to this end has issued an invitation to every so-called Muggle-born to present themselves for interview by the newly appointed Muggle-born Registration Commission.*"'

第11章 贿 赂

"伏地魔为什么不自封为魔法部长呢?"罗恩问道。

卢平笑了。

"他用不着,罗恩。他实际上就是部长,何必要坐在部里的办公桌后面呢?他的傀儡辛克尼斯处理日常事务,让伏地魔得以把势力延伸到魔法部之外。

"许多人自然推测到了发生的事情:几天来魔法部的政策变化太大了,他们私下里说一定是伏地魔在幕后指使。但问题就在这里,他们只是私下里说,不敢互相交心,不知道谁可以相信。他们不敢畅所欲言,生怕万一怀疑的情况属实,家人会受到迫害。伏地魔这一着棋非常聪明。宣布篡位也许会引来公开的反抗,躲在幕后却能造成迷惑、猜疑和恐惧。"

"魔法部政策的显著变化,"哈利说,"也包括让魔法世界都来提防我而不是伏地魔吗?"

"这确实是其中的一部分,"卢平说,"这是一手绝招。邓布利多死后,你——大难不死的男孩——必然会成为反抗伏地魔的象征和号召。而通过暗示你与老英雄之死有干系,伏地魔不仅可以悬赏缉拿你,而且在许多本来可能维护你的人中间撒下了怀疑和恐惧的种子。

"与此同时,魔法部开始排查麻瓜的后代。"

卢平指着《预言家日报》。

"看第二版。"

赫敏翻开报纸,脸上带着看《尖端黑魔法揭秘》时一样厌恶的表情。

"麻瓜出身登记,"她念道,"魔法部正在对所谓'麻瓜出身'进行调查,以便了解他们是如何获得魔法秘密的。

"神秘事务司最新研究显示,魔法只能通过巫师的生育遗传。由此可见,如果没有验证确凿的巫师血统,所谓麻瓜出身的人就可能是通过盗窃或暴力而获取魔法能力的。

"魔法部决心根除这些盗用魔法能力者,为此邀请每一位所谓麻瓜出身的人到新任命的麻瓜出身登记委员会面谈。"

CHAPTER ELEVEN   The Bribe

'People won't let this happen,' said Ron.

'It is happening, Ron,' said Lupin. 'Muggle-borns are being rounded up as we speak.'

'But how are they supposed to have "stolen" magic?' said Ron. 'It's mental, if you could steal magic there wouldn't be any Squibs, would there?'

'I know,' said Lupin. 'Nevertheless, unless you can prove that you have at least one close wizarding relative, you are now deemed to have obtained your magical power illegally and must suffer the punishment.'

Ron glanced at Hermione, then said, 'What if pure-bloods and half-bloods swear a Muggle-born's part of their family? I'll tell everyone Hermione's my cousin –'

Hermione covered Ron's hand with hers and squeezed it.

'Thank you, Ron, but I couldn't let you –'

'You won't have a choice,' said Ron fiercely, gripping her hand back. 'I'll teach you my family tree so you can answer questions on it.'

Hermione gave a shaky laugh.

'Ron, as we're on the run with Harry Potter, the most wanted person in the country, I don't think it matters. If I was going back to school, it would be different. What's Voldemort planning for Hogwarts?' she asked Lupin.

'Attendance is now compulsory for every young witch and wizard,' he replied. 'That was announced yesterday. It's a change, because it was never obligatory before. Of course, nearly every witch and wizard in Britain has been educated at Hogwarts, but their parents had the right to teach them at home or send them abroad if they preferred. This way, Voldemort will have the whole wizarding population under his eye from a young age. And it's also another way of weeding out Muggle-borns, because students must be given Blood Status – meaning that they have proven to the Ministry that they are of wizard descent – before they are allowed to attend.'

Harry felt sickened and angry: at this moment excited eleven-year-olds would be poring over stacks of newly purchased spellbooks, unaware that they would never see Hogwarts, perhaps never see their families again, either.

'It's … it's …' he muttered, struggling to find words that did justice to the horror of his thoughts, but Lupin said quietly, 'I know.'

Lupin hesitated.

第11章 贿　赂

"人们不会允许这种事发生的。"罗恩说。

"它已经发生了，罗恩，"卢平说，"在我们说话的时候，就已经有麻瓜出身的人被抓了。"

"可是他们怎么可能'盗窃'魔法呢？"罗恩问，"真是神经病。要是能盗窃魔法的话，就不会有哑炮了，是不是？"

"我理解，"卢平说，"可是，你必须证明你至少有一位巫师血统的近亲，否则就会被认为是非法获得魔法能力的，就要受到惩罚。"

罗恩看了看赫敏，说道："如果纯血和混血的巫师发誓说某个麻瓜出身的人是自己的亲戚呢？我可以对所有的人说赫敏是我表姐——"

赫敏双手拉住罗恩的手，紧紧地握着。

"谢谢你，罗恩，可是我不能让你——"

"你没有选择，"罗恩激动地说，也紧攥着她的手，"我要教你熟悉我的家谱，这样你就不怕提问了。"

赫敏颤声笑了一下。

"罗恩，我想这已经不重要，因为我们在跟全国第一通缉犯哈利·波特一起逃亡。要是我回到学校，情况就不一样了。伏地魔对霍格沃茨有什么计划吗？"她问卢平。

"现在每个少年巫师都必须入学，"他答道，"昨天宣布的。这是一个变化，因为以前从来不是强制性的。当然，几乎所有英国巫师都在霍格沃茨上过学，但父母有权让子女在家自学或到国外留学。而现在这样，伏地魔就能把所有的巫师从小就置于他的监视之下。这也是清除麻瓜出身者的办法之一，因为学生必须持有血统证明——表明他们已向魔法部证明自己的巫师血统，才能获准入学。"

哈利感到恶心而愤怒：此刻有多少十一岁的孩子正在兴高采烈地翻看好多本新买的魔法书，却不知他们永远也见不到霍格沃茨，甚至永远也见不到自己的家人了。

"这……这……"他语塞了，找不到话能够表达他所感到的恐怖，但卢平轻声说："我知道。"

卢平迟疑了一下。

CHAPTER ELEVEN   The Bribe

'I'll understand if you can't confirm this, Harry, but the Order is under the impression that Dumbledore left you a mission.'

'He did,' Harry replied, 'and Ron and Hermione are in on it and they're coming with me.'

'Can you confide in me what the mission is?'

Harry looked into the prematurely lined face, framed in thick but greying hair, and wished that he could return a different answer.

'I can't, Remus, I'm sorry. If Dumbledore didn't tell you, I don't think I can.'

'I thought you'd say that,' said Lupin, looking disappointed. 'But I might still be of some use to you. You know what I am and what I can do. I could come with you to provide protection. There would be no need to tell me exactly what you were up to.'

Harry hesitated. It was a very tempting offer, though how they would be able to keep their mission secret from Lupin if he were with them all the time he could not imagine.

Hermione, however, looked puzzled.

'But what about Tonks?' she asked.

'What about her?' said Lupin.

'Well,' said Hermione, frowning, 'you're married! How does she feel about you going away with us?'

'Tonks will be perfectly safe,' said Lupin. 'She'll be at her parents' house.'

There was something strange in Lupin's tone; it was almost cold. There was also something odd in the idea of Tonks remaining hidden at her parents' house; she was, after all, a member of the Order and, as far as Harry knew, was likely to want to be in the thick of the action.

'Remus,' said Hermione tentatively, 'is everything all right ... you know ... between you and –'

'Everything is fine, thank you,' said Lupin pointedly.

Hermione turned pink. There was another pause, an awkward and embarrassed one, and then Lupin said, with an air of forcing himself to admit something unpleasant, 'Tonks is going to have a baby.'

'Oh, how wonderful!' squealed Hermione.

'Excellent!' said Ron enthusiastically.

'Congratulations,' said Harry.

Lupin gave an artificial smile that was more like a grimace, then said,

第11章 贿　赂

"如果你不能证实,我可以理解,哈利,但凤凰社得到的印象是邓布利多给你留下了一个使命。"

"是的,"哈利答道,"罗恩和赫敏也知道,他们要跟我一起去。"

"能不能告诉我这使命是什么?"

哈利望着那张过早刻上皱纹的脸庞,浓密但已花白的头发,希望自己能有别的回答。

"我不能,莱姆斯,对不起。如果邓布利多没有告诉你,我想我也不能说。"

"我猜到你会这么说,"卢平显得有些失望,"但我仍然可以对你有些用处。你知道我的身份和能耐。我可以与你们同行,提供保护。不用对我说你们在干什么。"

哈利犹豫着,这是个非常诱人的提议,虽然他想象不出,如果卢平整天跟着他们,还怎么能对他继续保密。

赫敏却显得有些疑惑。

"唐克斯呢?"她问。

"她怎么啦?"卢平说。

"哎呀,"赫敏皱眉道,"你们结婚了!你要跟我们走,她怎么想呢?"

"唐克斯会很安全的,"卢平说,"住在她父母家。"

卢平的语气有些奇怪,几乎有些冷淡。再说,唐克斯躲在她父母家里也有点不正常,她毕竟是凤凰社成员,据哈利所知,她可能希望投身于积极的行动中。

"莱姆斯,"赫敏试探地说,"一切都好吗……我是说……你和——"

"一切都好,谢谢你。"卢平刻板地说。

赫敏脸红了,又是一阵沉默,气氛拘束而尴尬,然后,卢平像强迫自己承认一件不愉快的事情那样说道:"唐克斯怀孕了。"

"哦,太好了!"赫敏尖叫道。

"真棒!"罗恩热情地说。

"恭喜呀。"哈利说。

卢平不自然地笑了笑,看上去像做了个鬼脸,又说:"那么……你

CHAPTER ELEVEN The Bribe

'So ... do you accept my offer? Will three become four? I cannot believe that Dumbledore would have disapproved, he appointed me your Defence Against the Dark Arts teacher, after all. And I must tell you that I believe that we are facing magic many of us have never encountered or imagined.'

Ron and Hermione both looked at Harry.

'Just – just to be clear,' he said. 'You want to leave Tonks at her parents' house and come away with us?'

'She'll be perfectly safe there, they'll look after her,' said Lupin. He spoke with a finality bordering on indifference. 'Harry, I'm sure James would have wanted me to stick with you.'

'Well,' said Harry slowly, 'I'm not. I'm pretty sure my father would have wanted to know why you aren't sticking with your own kid, actually.'

Lupin's face drained of colour. The temperature in the kitchen might have dropped ten degrees. Ron stared around the room as though he had been bidden to memorise it, while Hermione's eyes swivelled backwards and forwards from Harry to Lupin.

'You don't understand,' said Lupin at last.

'Explain, then,' said Harry.

Lupin swallowed.

'I – I made a grave mistake in marrying Tonks. I did it against my better judgement and I have regretted it very much ever since.'

'I see,' said Harry, 'so you're just going to dump her and the kid and run off with us?'

Lupin sprang to his feet: his chair toppled over backwards, and he glared at them so fiercely that Harry saw, for the first time ever, the shadow of the wolf upon his human face.

'Don't you understand what I've done to my wife and my unborn child? I should never have married her, I've made her an outcast!'

Lupin kicked aside the chair he had overturned.

'You have only ever seen me amongst the Order, or under Dumbledore's protection at Hogwarts! You don't know how most of the wizarding world sees creatures like me! When they know of my affliction, they can barely talk to me! Don't you see what I've done? Even her own family is disgusted by our marriage, what parents want their only daughter to marry a werewolf? And the child – the child –'

第11章 贿 赂

们接受我的提议吗？三个人可以变成四个人吗？我不相信邓布利多会反对。毕竟，他曾任命我做你们的黑魔法防御术课老师。我必须告诉你们，我相信此行要面对许多人从没见过也想象不到的邪恶魔法。"

罗恩和赫敏都望着哈利。

"嗯——我想问清楚。"他说，"你想把唐克斯留在她父母家，自己跟我们走？"

"她在那儿非常安全，他们会照料她的。"卢平说，语气坚决得近乎冷漠，"哈利，我相信詹姆也会希望我守护你。"

"嗯，"哈利缓缓地说，"我不这样想。我倒相信我父亲会希望知道你为什么不守护自己的孩子。"

卢平脸上失去了血色。厨房里的温度好像降低了十度。罗恩环顾着这个房间，好像有人命令他要把它记住似的，赫敏的目光在哈利和卢平之间来回移动。

"你不明白。"卢平终于说。

"那就解释一下吧。"哈利说。

卢平咽了口唾沫。

"我——我和唐克斯结婚是个严重的错误，我丧失了理智，事后一直非常后悔。"

"噢，"哈利说，"所以你就要抛弃她和孩子，跟我们跑掉？"

卢平跳了起来，椅子都翻倒了。他那样狂暴地瞪着他们，哈利第一次在他那张人脸上看到了狼的影子。

"你不明白我对我妻子和未出生的孩子做了什么吗？我根本不该和她结婚，我把她变成了被排斥的人！"

卢平一脚踢开被他弄翻的椅子。

"你们看到我都是在凤凰社里，或者是在霍格沃茨，在邓布利多的庇护之下！你们不知道大多数巫师怎样看待我的同类！知道我的情况之后，他们几乎都不肯跟我说话！你们没明白我做了什么吗？就连她的家人也排斥我们的婚姻，哪个父母愿意自己的独生女儿嫁给狼人呢？还有孩子——孩子——"

CHAPTER ELEVEN The Bribe

Lupin actually seized handfuls of his own hair; he looked quite deranged.

'My kind don't usually breed! It will be like me, I am convinced of it – how can I forgive myself, when I knowingly risked passing on my own condition to an innocent child? And if, by some miracle, it is not like me, then it will be better off, a hundred times so, without a father of whom it must always be ashamed!'

'Remus!' whispered Hermione, tears in her eyes. 'Don't say that – how could any child be ashamed of you?'

'Oh, I don't know, Hermione,' said Harry. 'I'd be pretty ashamed of him.'

Harry did not know where his rage was coming from, but it had propelled him to his feet too. Lupin looked as though Harry had hit him.

'If the new regime thinks Muggle-borns are bad,' Harry said, 'what will they do to a half-werewolf whose father's in the Order? My father died trying to protect my mother and me, and you reckon he'd tell you to abandon your kid to go on an adventure with us?'

'How – how dare you?' said Lupin. 'This is not about a desire for – for danger or personal glory – how dare you suggest such a –'

'I think you're feeling a bit of a daredevil,' Harry said. 'You fancy stepping into Sirius's shoes –'

'Harry, no!' Hermione begged him, but he continued to glare into Lupin's livid face.

'I'd never have believed this,' Harry said. 'The man who taught me to fight Dementors – a coward.'

Lupin drew his wand so fast that Harry had barely reached for his own; there was a loud bang and he felt himself flying backwards as if punched; as he slammed into the kitchen wall and slid to the floor, he glimpsed the tail of Lupin's cloak disappearing round the door.

'Remus, Remus, come back!' Hermione cried, but Lupin did not respond. A moment later they heard the front door slam.

'Harry!' wailed Hermione. 'How could you?'

'It was easy,' said Harry. He stood up; he could feel a lump swelling where his head had hit the wall. He was still so full of anger he was shaking.

'Don't look at me like that!' he snapped at Hermione.

'Don't you start on her!' snarled Ron.

第11章 贿　赂

卢平揪着自己的头发,他好像精神错乱了。

"我的同类通常是不生育的!孩子会跟我一样,我知道肯定会的——我怎么能原谅自己?明知自己的情况却仍然把它遗传给一个无辜的婴儿。即使奇迹发生,孩子不像我这样,那么没有一个永远让他感到羞耻的父亲岂不更好,好一百倍!"

"莱姆斯!"赫敏轻声说,热泪盈眶,"别这么说——怎么会有孩子为你感到羞耻呢?"

"哦,说不准,赫敏,"哈利说,"我就会为他感到羞耻。"

哈利不知自己哪来的火气,他也气得站了起来。卢平的表情好像哈利打了他一样。

"如果新政权认为麻瓜出身都是坏的,"哈利说,"他们又会怎样对待一个父亲是凤凰社成员的狼人混血儿呢?我父亲是为保护我母亲和我而死的,你觉得他会叫你抛弃你的孩子,去跟我们一起冒险吗?"

"你——你怎么敢?"卢平说,"这不是追求——不是追求冒险或个人出风头——你怎么敢说出这种——"

"我认为你觉得自己英勇无畏,"哈利说,"你幻想步小天狼星的后尘——"

"哈利,别说了!"赫敏恳求道,可是哈利继续瞪着卢平铁青的面孔。

"我真不能相信,"哈利说,"教我打败摄魂怪的人——是个懦夫。"

卢平拔魔杖的动作太快了,哈利刚来得及抓到自己的魔杖,就听砰的一声,同时感到自己像被猛击了一下,身子向后飞去,撞在厨房的墙上,然后滑落在地。他瞥见卢平的斗篷后摆消失在门口。

"莱姆斯,莱姆斯,回来!"赫敏叫道,但卢平没有回答。片刻后,他们听到前门重重地关上了。

"哈利!"赫敏哭着说,"你怎么能这样?"

"有什么不能的。"哈利说着站了起来,感到脑袋撞在墙上的地方正在肿起一个包。他仍然气得浑身发抖。

"别那样看着我!"他没好气地对赫敏说。

"你别又冲她来!"罗恩吼道。

CHAPTER ELEVEN The Bribe

'No – no – we mustn't fight!' said Hermione, launching herself between them.

'You shouldn't have said that stuff to Lupin,' Ron told Harry.

'He had it coming to him,' said Harry. Broken images were racing each other through his mind: Sirius falling through the Veil; Dumbledore suspended, broken, in mid-air; a flash of green light and his mother's voice, begging for mercy ...

'Parents,' said Harry, 'shouldn't leave their kids unless – unless they've got to.'

'Harry –' said Hermione, stretching out a consoling hand, but he shrugged it off and walked away, his eyes on the fire Hermione had conjured. He had once spoken to Lupin out of that fireplace, seeking reassurance about James, and Lupin had consoled him. Now Lupin's tortured, white face seemed to swim in the air before him. He felt a sickening surge of remorse. Neither Ron nor Hermione spoke, but Harry felt sure that they were looking at each other behind his back, communicating silently.

He turned round and caught them turning hurriedly away from each other.

'I know I shouldn't have called him a coward.'

'No, you shouldn't,' said Ron at once.

'But he's acting like one.'

'All the same ...' said Hermione.

'I know,' said Harry. 'But if it makes him go back to Tonks, it'll be worth it, won't it?'

He could not keep the plea out of his voice. Hermione looked sympathetic, Ron uncertain. Harry looked down at his feet, thinking of his father. Would James have backed Harry in what he had said to Lupin, or would he have been angry at how his son had treated his old friend?

The silent kitchen seemed to hum with the shock of the recent scene and with Ron and Hermione's unspoken reproaches. The *Daily Prophet* Lupin had brought was still lying on the table, Harry's own face staring up at the ceiling from the front page. He walked over to it and sat down, opened the paper at random and pretended to read. He could not take in the words, his mind was still too full of the encounter with Lupin. He was sure that Ron and Hermione had resumed their silent communications on the other side of the *Prophet*. He turned a page loudly, and Dumbledore's name leapt out at him. It was a moment or two before he took in the meaning of the photograph, which

第11章 贿　赂

"不要——不要——我们不能吵架！"赫敏冲到他们俩中间说。

"你不应该对卢平说那样的话。"罗恩责备哈利说。

"他自找的。"哈利说。破碎的画面在他脑海中快速闪过：小天狼星穿过帷幔倒下；伤残的邓布利多悬在空中；一道绿光和他母亲哀求的声音……

"身为父母，"哈利说，"不应该离开自己的孩子，除非——除非是迫不得已。"

"哈利——"赫敏伸出一只抚慰的手，但他一耸肩甩掉了，走到一边，盯着赫敏变出的火苗。他曾经通过那个壁炉和卢平说过话，希望能恢复对詹姆的信心，卢平给了他安慰。现在，卢平那痛苦、苍白的面容好像在他面前晃动，一阵悔恨涌上心头，他感到非常难受。罗恩和赫敏都没有说话，但哈利觉得他们肯定在他背后面面相觑，无声地交流。

他转过身，看见他们俩慌忙分开了对视的目光。

"我知道我不应该叫他懦夫。"

"你是不应该。"罗恩马上说。

"可他的行为像懦夫。"

"但是……"赫敏说。

"我知道，"哈利说，"但如果这能让他回到唐克斯身边，还是值得的，是不是？"

他无法消除语气中的恳求。赫敏露出同情的样子，罗恩则不置可否。哈利低头看着脚，想着自己的父亲。詹姆会支持哈利对卢平说那样的话吗，还是会因为儿子那样对待他的老朋友而生气呢？

寂静的厨房里似乎回响着刚才那一幕带来的震惊和罗恩、赫敏无言的谴责。卢平带来的《预言家日报》还搁在桌上，哈利的面孔在头版上呆望着天花板。他走过去坐下，随手翻开报纸，假装在读，可是读不进去，脑子里还满是和卢平冲突的场面。他能肯定罗恩和赫敏在报纸的另一面又开始了无声的交流。他很响地翻动报纸，邓布利多的名字跳入了眼帘。他好一会儿才看明白那张照片，是一张全家合影。照片下面写着：邓布利多一家，左起：阿不思、珀西瓦尔（抱着刚出

CHAPTER ELEVEN   The Bribe

showed a family group. Beneath the photograph were the words: *The Dumbledore family: left to right, Albus, Percival, holding newborn Ariana, Kendra and Aberforth.*

His attention caught, Harry examined the picture more carefully. Dumbledore's father, Percival, was a good-looking man with eyes that seemed to twinkle even in this faded old photograph. The baby, Ariana, was little longer than a loaf of bread and no more distinctive-looking. The mother, Kendra, had jet black hair pulled into a high bun. Her face had a carved quality about it. Despite the high-necked silk gown she wore, Harry thought of Native Americans as he studied her dark eyes, high cheekbones and straight nose. Albus and Aberforth wore matching lacy collared jackets and had identical, shoulder-length hairstyles. Albus looked several years older, but otherwise the two boys looked very alike, for this was before Albus's nose had been broken and before he started wearing glasses.

The family looked quite happy and normal, smiling serenely up out of the newspaper. Baby Ariana's arm waved vaguely out of her shawl. Harry looked above the picture and saw the headline:

EXCLUSIVE EXTRACT FROM THE UPCOMING BIOGRAPHY OF ALBUS DUMBLEDORE
by Rita Skeeter

Thinking that it could hardly make him feel any worse than he already did, Harry began to read:

> Proud and haughty, Kendra Dumbledore could not bear to remain in Mould-on-the-Wold after her husband Percival's well-publicised arrest and imprisonment in Azkaban. She therefore decided to uproot the family and relocate to Godric's Hollow, the village that was later to gain fame as the scene of Harry Potter's strange escape from You-Know-Who.
>
> Like Mould-on-the-Wold, Godric's Hollow was home to a number of wizarding families, but as Kendra knew none of them, she would be spared the curiosity about her husband's crime she had faced in her former village. By repeatedly rebuffing the friendly advances of her new wizarding neighbours, she soon ensured that her family was left well alone.

第11章 贿 赂

生的阿利安娜）、坎德拉和阿不福思。

这吸引了他的注意。哈利仔细盯着这张照片。邓布利多的父亲珀西瓦尔是个英俊的男子，一双眼睛在这张褪色的老照片上似乎仍闪着光芒。婴儿阿利安娜比一块面包大不了多少，也看不出更多的面部特征。母亲坎德拉乌黑的头发盘成一个高髻，五官有如刀刻一般。尽管她穿着高领缎袍，但那黑眼睛、高颧骨和挺直的鼻梁令哈利联想到了印第安人。阿不思和阿不福思穿着一式的花边领短上衣，留着一式的披肩发。阿不思看上去大几岁，但其他方面两个男孩显得非常相似，因为这是在阿不思鼻梁被打断和开始戴眼镜之前。

一家人看上去相当幸福美满，和普通家庭一样，安详地在报纸上微笑。婴儿阿利安娜的胳膊在襁褓外微微地挥舞着。哈利在照片的上方看到了一行标题：

独家摘录
——即将出版的邓布利多传记

丽塔·斯基特 著

哈利心想反正不可能让自己的情绪更糟了，便读了起来：

坎德拉·邓布利多个性自尊而高傲，在丈夫珀西瓦尔被逮捕并关入阿兹卡班之事公布于众后，无法忍受继续住在沃土原。于是她决定举家搬到戈德里克山谷，那个村子后来出了名，因为它就是哈利·波特奇迹般逃脱神秘人魔掌的地方。

像沃土原一样，戈德里克山谷也聚居了许多巫师家庭，但坎德拉一户也不认识，所以不会像在原来村子里那样总有人对她丈夫的罪行感到好奇。她多次拒绝新巫师邻居们的友好表示，很快就使自己一家与外界隔绝了。

CHAPTER ELEVEN   The Bribe

'Slammed the door in my face when I went round to welcome her with a batch of homemade cauldron cakes,' says Bathilda Bagshot. 'The first year they were there I only ever saw the two boys. Wouldn't have known there was a daughter if I hadn't been picking Plangentines by moonlight the winter after they moved in, and saw Kendra leading Ariana out into the back garden. Walked her round the lawn once, keeping a firm grip on her, then took her back inside. Didn't know what to make of it.'

It seems that Kendra thought the move to Godric's Hollow was the perfect opportunity to hide Ariana once and for all, something she had probably been planning for years. The timing was significant. Ariana was barely seven years old when she vanished from sight, and seven is the age by which most experts agree that magic will have revealed itself, if present. Nobody now alive remembers Ariana ever demonstrating even the slightest sign of magical ability. It seems clear, therefore, that Kendra made a decision to hide her daughter's existence rather than suffer the shame of admitting that she had produced a Squib. Moving away from the friends and neighbours who knew Ariana would, of course, make imprisoning her all the easier. The tiny number of people who henceforth knew of Ariana's existence could be counted upon to keep the secret, including her two brothers, who deflected awkward questions with the answer their mother had taught them: 'My sister is too frail for school.'

Next week: Albus Dumbledore at Hogwarts – the prizes and the pretence.

Harry had been wrong: what he had read had indeed made him feel worse. He looked back at the photograph of the apparently happy family. Was it true? How could he find out? He wanted to go to Godric's Hollow, even if Bathilda was in no fit state to talk to him; he wanted to visit the place where he and Dumbledore had both lost loved ones. He was in the process of lowering the newspaper, to ask Ron and Hermione's opinions, when a deafening *crack* echoed around the kitchen.

For the first time in three days, Harry had forgotten all about Kreacher. His immediate thought was that Lupin had burst back into the room and for a split second, he did not take in the mass of struggling limbs that had appeared out of thin air right beside his chair. He hurried to his feet as Kreacher disentangled himself and, bowing low to Harry, croaked, 'Kreacher

第11章 贿　赂

"我带了一批自己做的坩埚蛋糕过去欢迎她，她当着我的面关上了门。"巴希达·巴沙特说，"他们搬来的第一年，我只见过两个男孩。要不是冬天里有一次我在月光下摘悲啼果，看到坎德拉领着阿利安娜走进后花园，我根本不会知道她还有个女儿。她妈妈带她绕草坪走了一圈，一直紧紧抓着她，然后就领回屋里去了。搞不懂是怎么回事。"

坎德拉似乎认为搬到戈德里克山谷是隐藏阿利安娜的良机，这件事她或许已经筹划多年。时机很重要，阿利安娜消失时刚满七岁，许多专家认为七岁是魔法能力应该显露的年龄——如果确实有魔法能力的话。没有一位在世的人记得阿利安娜显示过丝毫的魔法能力。由此可见，坎德拉决定隐瞒女儿的存在，她羞于承认自己生了一个哑炮。当然，离开了认识阿利安娜的朋友和邻居，囚禁她就容易多了。此后知道阿利安娜存在的人屈指可数，都是能保守秘密的，其中包括她的两个哥哥，他们用母亲教的话挡住令人尴尬的问题："我妹妹身体太弱，上不了学。"

下星期内容：阿不思·邓布利多在霍格沃茨——获奖与假象。

哈利想错了：报上的内容实际上让他情绪更糟。他看着照片上貌似幸福的一家人。是真的吗？怎么才能知道？他想去戈德里克山谷，即使巴希达已经不能与他交谈，他也想去看看自己和邓布利多都曾经失去亲人的地方。他正要放下报纸问问罗恩和赫敏的想法，厨房里突然爆出一声震耳欲聋的巨响。

三天来第一次，哈利把克利切忘得干干净净，他的第一个念头是卢平冲回来了。一瞬间，哈利搞不清椅子旁边这团凭空出现的扭打着的胳膊和腿是怎么回事。他急忙站起身。克利切挣脱出来，低低地鞠了一躬，嘶哑地说："克利切把小偷蒙顿格斯·弗莱奇抓回来了，

CHAPTER ELEVEN   The Bribe

has returned with the thief Mundungus Fletcher, Master.'

Mundungus scrambled up and pulled out his wand; Hermione, however, was too quick for him.

'*Expelliarmus!*'

Mundungus's wand soared into the air and Hermione caught it. Wild-eyed, Mundungus dived for the stairs: Ron rugby-tackled him and Mundungus hit the stone floor with a muffled crunch.

'What?' he bellowed, writhing in his attempts to free himself from Ron's grip. 'Wha've I done? Setting a bleedin' 'ouse-elf on me, what are you playing at, wha've I done, lemme go, lemme go, or –'

'You're not in much of a position to make threats,' said Harry. He threw aside the newspaper, crossed the kitchen in a few strides and dropped to his knees beside Mundungus, who stopped struggling and looked terrified. Ron got up, panting, and watched as Harry pointed his wand deliberately at Mundungus's nose. Mundungus stank of stale sweat and tobacco smoke: his hair was matted and his robes stained.

'Kreacher apologises for the delay in bringing the thief, Master,' croaked the elf. 'Fletcher knows how to avoid capture, has many hidey-holes and accomplices. Nevertheless, Kreacher cornered the thief in the end.'

'You've done really well, Kreacher,' said Harry, and the elf bowed low.

'Right, we've got a few questions for you,' Harry told Mundungus, who shouted at once: 'I panicked, OK? I never wanted to come along, no offence, mate, but I never volunteered to die for you, an' that was bleedin' You-Know-Who come flying at me, anyone woulda got outta there, I said all along I didn't wanna do it –'

'For your information, none of the rest of us Disapparated,' said Hermione.

'Well, you're a bunch of bleedin' 'eroes, then, aren't you, but I never pretended I was up for killing meself –'

'We're not interested in why you ran out on Mad-Eye,' said Harry, moving his wand a little closer to Mundungus's baggy, bloodshot eyes. 'We already knew you were an unreliable bit of scum.'

'Well then, why the 'ell am I being 'unted down by 'ouse-elves? Or is this about them goblets again? I ain't got none of 'em left, or you could 'ave 'em –'

'It's not about the goblets either, although you're getting warmer,' said Harry. 'Shut up and listen.'

第11章 贿　赂

主人。"

蒙顿格斯挣扎着爬起来，抽出了魔杖。但赫敏比他更快。

"除你武器！"

蒙顿格斯的魔杖飞到空中，被赫敏接住。他疯狂地朝楼梯冲去，罗恩把他撂倒了。蒙顿格斯摔到石板地上，发出一声闷响。

"干吗？"他吼道，扭动身体想挣脱罗恩，"我干什么了？派一个该死的家养小精灵来抓我。你们搞什么鬼，我干什么了，放开我，放开我，不然——"

"你没有资格威胁谁了。"哈利说着把报纸扔到一边，几步走到厨房那头，跪在蒙顿格斯旁边。蒙顿格斯立刻停止了挣扎，表情惊恐。罗恩喘着气爬起来，哈利沉着地用魔杖指着蒙顿格斯的鼻子，这家伙散发着臭烘烘的汗味和烟味，头发纠结，袍子上污渍斑斑。

"克利切道歉，抓小偷回来迟了，主人。"小精灵嘶声说道，"弗莱奇善于躲避抓捕，有许多窝穴和同伙。不过，克利切最后还是堵住了这个小偷。"

"你做得很好，克利切。"哈利说。小精灵低低地鞠躬。

"好，我们有几个问题要问你。"哈利对蒙顿格斯说。这家伙立刻叫了起来："我吓坏了，行了吧？我从来就没想参加。别生气，伙计，可我从来没有自愿为你去死，当时是该死的神秘人朝我飞了过来啊，谁都会逃走的，我一直说我不想干——"

"告诉你吧，我们其他人没有一个幻影移形的。"赫敏说。

"嗯，你们是一帮他娘的英雄，是不是，可我从没假装说我打算搭上性命——"

"我们对你为什么丢下疯眼汉逃跑不感兴趣，"哈利把魔杖凑近蒙顿格斯那双肿胀充血的眼睛，"我们已经知道你是个靠不住的渣滓。"

"那为什么要派家养小精灵来抓我？难道又是那些杯子的事儿？我一个也没有了，不然你们可以拿去——"

"也不是那些杯子的事儿，不过有点靠谱了。"哈利说，"闭上嘴巴听着。"

CHAPTER ELEVEN The Bribe

It felt wonderful to have something to do, someone of whom he could demand some small portion of truth. Harry's wand was now so close to the bridge of Mundungus's nose that Mundungus had gone cross-eyed trying to keep it in view.

'When you cleaned out this house of anything valuable,' Harry began, but Mundungus interrupted him again.

'Sirius never cared about any of the junk –'

There was the sound of pattering feet, a blaze of shining copper, an echoing clang and a shriek of agony: Kreacher had taken a run at Mundungus and hit him over the head with a saucepan.

'Call 'im off, call 'im off, 'e should be locked up!' screamed Mundungus, cowering as Kreacher raised the heavy-bottomed pan again.

'Kreacher, no!' shouted Harry.

Kreacher's thin arms trembled with the weight of the pan, still held aloft.

'Perhaps just one more, Master Harry, for luck?'

Ron laughed.

'We need him conscious, Kreacher, but if he needs persuading you can do the honours,' said Harry.

'Thank you very much, Master,' said Kreacher with a bow, and he retreated a short distance, his great, pale eyes still fixed upon Mundungus with loathing.

'When you stripped this house of all the valuables you could find,' Harry began again, 'you took a bunch of stuff from the kitchen cupboard. There was a locket there.' Harry's mouth was suddenly dry: he could sense Ron and Hermione's tension and excitement too. 'What did you do with it?'

'Why?' asked Mundungus. 'Is it valuable?'

'You've still got it!' cried Hermione.

'No, he hasn't,' said Ron shrewdly. 'He's wondering whether he should have asked more money for it.'

'More?' said Mundungus. 'That wouldn't have been effing difficult ... bleedin' gave it away, di'n' I? No choice.'

'What do you mean?'

'I was selling in Diagon Alley an' she come up to me an' asks if I've got a

第11章 贿 赂

能有点事情做做,能从某人那里问出一点实情,感觉真不错。哈利的魔杖现在离蒙顿格斯的鼻梁如此之近,这家伙的两只眼睛都对上了,他紧盯着哈利的动作。

"当你掳走这所房子里值钱的东西时——"哈利说道,但蒙顿格斯又打断了他。

"小天狼星从来不在意那些垃圾——"

脚板啪啪作响,黄铜的光一闪,响亮的哐当一声,伴着痛苦的号叫:克利切冲过去用长柄锅狠狠敲了一下蒙顿格斯的脑袋。

"叫他住手,叫他住手,应该把他关起来!"蒙顿格斯畏缩着叫道,克利切又举起了那只厚底锅。

"克利切,不要!"哈利高喊道。

克利切的瘦胳膊在沉重的锅子下颤抖,仍然高高地举着。

"再来一下行吗,哈利少爷,讨个彩头?"

罗恩笑了。

"我们需要他神志清楚,克利切,但如果他需要劝导的话,可以由你来执行。"哈利说。

"非常感谢您,主人。"克利切鞠了一躬,退后几步,浅色的大眼睛仍然憎恶地盯着蒙顿格斯。

"当你把这所房子里你能找到的值钱东西掳取一空时,"哈利又说道,"你从厨房碗柜里拿走了一批东西,其中有一个挂坠盒。"哈利突然嘴巴发干,他也能感到罗恩、赫敏的紧张和兴奋,"你把它弄到哪儿去了?"

"怎么?"蒙顿格斯问,"它很值钱吗?"

"它还在你那儿!"赫敏叫道。

"不,不在了,"罗恩一针见血地说,"他在想当时是不是应该卖得更贵一点。"

"更贵?"蒙顿格斯说,"那倒一点也不难……该死的,我不是把它送掉了吗?没法子啊。"

"什么意思?"

"我在对角巷卖货,那女人走过来问我有没有经销魔法制品的执照,

CHAPTER ELEVEN The Bribe

licence for trading in magical artefacts. Bleedin' snoop. She was gonna fine me, but she took a fancy to the locket an' told me she'd take it and let me off that time an' to fink meself lucky.'

'Who was this woman?' asked Harry.

'I dunno, some Ministry hag.'

Mundungus considered for a moment, brow wrinkled.

'Little woman. Bow on top of 'er head.'

He frowned and then added, 'Looked like a toad.'

Harry dropped his wand: it hit Mundungus on the nose and shot red sparks into his eyebrows, which ignited.

'*Aguamenti!*' screamed Hermione, and a jet of water streamed from her wand, engulfing a spluttering and choking Mundungus.

Harry looked up and saw his own shock reflected in Ron and Hermione's faces. The scars on the back of his right hand seemed to be tingling again.

该死的搅屎棍,她本来要罚我款,忽然看上了挂坠盒,就说拿那个顶了,放过我这一回,还说算我走运。"

"那女人是谁?"哈利问。

"不知道,魔法部的老女妖。"

蒙顿格斯皱眉想了一会儿。

"小矮个,头顶戴个蝴蝶结。"

他紧蹙着眉头,又加了一句:"看上去像只癞蛤蟆。"

哈利的魔杖失手掉下,打中了蒙顿格斯的鼻子,红色火星喷到他的眉毛上,眉毛着了火。

"清水如泉!"赫敏高叫,一股清水从她杖尖流出,浇在蒙顿格斯脸上,但他已呛得连咳带喘。

哈利抬起头,在罗恩和赫敏的脸上也看到了自己的震惊。他右手手背上的伤疤似乎又刺痛起来。

CHAPTER TWELVE

Magic is Might

As August wore on, the square of unkempt grass in the middle of Grimmauld Place shrivelled in the sun until it was brittle and brown. The inhabitants of number twelve were never seen by anybody in the surrounding houses, and nor was number twelve itself. The Muggles who lived in Grimmauld Place had long since accepted the amusing mistake in the numbering that had caused number eleven to sit beside number thirteen.

And yet the square was now attracting a trickle of visitors who seemed to find the anomaly most intriguing. Barely a day passed without one or two people arriving in Grimmauld Place with no other purpose, or so it seemed, than to lean against the railings facing numbers eleven and thirteen, watching the join between the two houses. The lurkers were never the same two days running, although they all seemed to share a dislike for normal clothing. Most of the Londoners who passed them were used to eccentric dressers and took little notice, though occasionally one of them might glance back, wondering why anyone would wear such long cloaks in this heat.

The watchers seemed to be gleaning little satisfaction from their vigil. Occasionally one of them started forwards excitedly, as if they had seen something interesting at last, only to fall back looking disappointed.

On the first day of September there were more people lurking in the square than ever before. Half a dozen men in long cloaks stood silent and watchful, gazing as ever at houses eleven and thirteen, but the thing for which they were waiting still appeared elusive. As evening drew in, bringing with it an unexpected gust of chilly rain for the first time in weeks, there occurred one of those inexplicable moments when they appeared to have seen something interesting. The man with the twisted face pointed and his closest companion, a podgy, pallid man, started forwards, but a moment later they had relaxed into their previous state of inactivity, looking frustrated and disappointed.

第12章

魔法即强权

八月一天天过去了,格里莫广场中间那片荒草在阳光中枯萎,变脆变黄。12号的房客一直没有被周围人家发现,12号本身也不为人所知。格里莫广场的麻瓜住户早已习惯了11号紧挨着13号的可笑错误。

但广场现在吸引了一小批来客,他们好像对这个异常现象很感兴趣。几乎每天都有一两个人来到格里莫广场,没有别的目的(或貌似如此),只为倚在面向11号和13号的栏杆上,凝视两座房子的连接处。每天来的窥视者都与前一天的不同,不过他们似乎都不喜欢正常的服饰。路过这里的伦敦人大都看惯了奇装异服,所以并不留意,只是偶尔有人回头看一眼,奇怪怎么有人在这样的大热天还穿着长斗篷。

窥视者似乎未能从守望中得到什么满足。偶尔有个人兴奋地冲向前去,仿佛终于看到了什么有趣的东西,但又总是失望地退了回来。

九月的第一天,逗留在广场上的人比以前更多。六个穿着长斗篷的男人沉默警惕,像往常一样凝视着11号和13号房子,但他们等待的东西似乎仍无影踪。傍晚来临,意外地带来了几星期里第一场凉飕飕的阵雨。这时,那种神秘时刻又出现了,他们似乎看到了什么有趣的东西。一个歪脸男人指点着,那个离他最近的同伴——一个矮胖而苍白的男人跃向前去,但片刻之后,他们又恢复了先前的静止状态,显得懊丧而失望。

CHAPTER TWELVE   Magic is Might

Meanwhile, inside number twelve, Harry had just entered the hall. He had nearly lost his balance as he Apparated on to the top step just outside the front door, and thought that the Death Eaters might have caught a glimpse of his momentarily exposed elbow. Shutting the front door carefully behind him he pulled off the Invisibility Cloak, draped it over his arm and hurried along the gloomy hallway towards the door that led to the basement, a stolen copy of the *Daily Prophet* clutched in his hand.

The usual low whisper of '*Severus Snape?*' greeted him, the chill wind swept him and his tongue rolled up for a moment.

'I didn't kill you,' he said, once it had unrolled, then held his breath as the dusty jinx-figure exploded. He waited until he was halfway down the stairs to the kitchen, out of earshot of Mrs Black and clear of the dust cloud before calling, 'I've got news, and you won't like it.'

The kitchen was almost unrecognisable. Every surface now shone: copper pots and pans had been burnished to a rosy glow, the wooden table top gleamed, the goblets and plates already laid for dinner glinted in the light from a merrily blazing fire, on which a cauldron was simmering. Nothing in the room, however, was more dramatically different than the house-elf who now came hurrying towards Harry, dressed in a snowy-white towel, his ear hair as clean and fluffy as cotton wool, Regulus's locket bouncing on his thin chest.

'Shoes off, if you please, Master Harry, and hands washed before dinner,' croaked Kreacher, seizing the Invisibility Cloak and slouching off to hang it on a hook on the wall, beside a number of old-fashioned robes that had been freshly laundered.

'What's happened?' Ron asked apprehensively. He and Hermione had been poring over a sheaf of scribbled notes and hand-drawn maps that littered the end of the long kitchen table, but now they watched Harry as he strode towards them and threw down the newspaper on top of their scattered parchment.

A large picture of a familiar, hook-nosed, black-haired man stared up at them all, beneath a headline that read:

**SEVERUS SNAPE CONFIRMED
AS HOGWARTS HEADMASTER**

第12章 魔法即强权

与此同时,在12号房中,哈利刚刚走进门厅。他刚才幻影显形到前门外的台阶顶上时差点失去平衡,心想食死徒可能看到了他一时暴露在外的胳膊肘。他小心地关上前门,脱下隐形衣搭在手臂上,沿着昏暗的走廊匆匆朝通往地下室的门口走去,手里还捏着一份偷来的《预言家日报》。

迎接他的还是那个低低的声音:"西弗勒斯·斯内普?"一阵阴风刮过,哈利的舌头卷缩了片刻。

"我没有杀死你。"舌头一松开,他就说道,然后屏住呼吸,土灰色的身影爆炸了。他一直下到通往厨房的楼梯中部,远离了炸出的灰尘,确保布莱克夫人听不见他的声音时,他才叫道:"有新闻,你们肯定不会喜欢。"

厨房几乎认不出来了。现在所有东西的表面都焕然一新:铜制锅具擦出了玫瑰色光泽,木头桌面也擦得发亮,晚餐的杯碟已经摆好,在炉火的辉映下闪闪发光,欢乐的火苗上炖着一口大锅。但那快步迎向哈利的家养小精灵的变化比屋里的变化更大,他裹着一条雪白的毛巾,耳朵里的毛像棉絮一般洁白蓬松,雷古勒斯的挂坠盒在他瘦瘦的胸脯上跳动。

"请脱鞋,哈利少爷,洗过手再用晚餐。"克利切用低沉沙哑的声音说,一边抓住隐形衣,疲惫地走过去把它挂到墙上,旁边还挂着好多件新洗的老式袍子。

"有什么情况?"罗恩担心地问。他和赫敏刚才在研究一沓笔记和手绘地图,厨房长桌的一头都摊满了,但现在两人都看着哈利。哈利大步走过去,把报纸丢在他们的那堆散乱的羊皮纸上。

报纸上是一张大照片,一个熟悉的鹰钩鼻、黑头发的男子瞪着他们。上面的标题是:

西弗勒斯·斯内普
接任霍格沃茨校长

CHAPTER TWELVE Magic is Might

'No!' said Ron and Hermione loudly.

Hermione was quickest; she snatched up the newspaper and began to read the accompanying story out loud.

'"*Severus Snape, long-standing Potions master at Hogwarts School of Witchcraft and Wizardry, was today appointed Headmaster in the most important of several staffing changes at the ancient school. Following the resignation of the previous Muggle Studies teacher, Alecto Carrow will take over the post while her brother, Amycus, fills the position of Defence Against the Dark Arts professor.*

'"*"I welcome the opportunity to uphold our finest wizarding traditions and values –*"' Like committing murder and cutting off people's ears, I suppose! Snape, Headmaster! Snape in Dumbledore's study – Merlin's pants!' she shrieked, making both Harry and Ron jump. She leapt up from the table and hurtled from the room, shouting as she went, 'I'll be back in a minute!'

'"Merlin's pants"?' repeated Ron, looking amused. 'She must be upset.' He pulled the newspaper towards him and perused the article about Snape.

'The other teachers won't stand for this. McGonagall and Flitwick and Sprout all know the truth, they know how Dumbledore died. They won't accept Snape as Headmaster. And who are these Carrows?'

'Death Eaters,' said Harry. 'There are pictures of them inside. They were at the top of the Tower when Snape killed Dumbledore, so it's all friends together. And,' Harry went on bitterly, drawing up a chair, 'I can't see that the other teachers have got any choice but to stay. If the Ministry and Voldemort are behind Snape, it'll be a choice between staying and teaching, or a nice few years in Azkaban – and that's if they're lucky. I reckon they'll stay to try and protect the students.'

Kreacher came bustling to the table with a large tureen in his hands, and ladled out soup into pristine bowls, whistling between his teeth as he did so.

'Thanks, Kreacher,' said Harry, flipping over the *Prophet* so as not to have to look at Snape's face. 'Well, at least we know exactly where Snape is, now.'

He began to spoon soup into his mouth. The quality of Kreacher's cooking had improved dramatically ever since he had been given Regulus's locket: today's French onion was as good as Harry had ever tasted.

'There are still a load of Death Eaters watching the house,' he told Ron as he ate, 'more than usual. It's like they're hoping we'll march out carrying our school trunks and head off for the Hogwarts Express.'

第12章 魔法即强权

"不可能!"罗恩和赫敏同时叫道。

赫敏动作最快,她抓起报纸大声念了起来。

"'西弗勒斯·斯内普,霍格沃茨魔法学校的资深魔药课教师,今日被任命为校长,该决定系这所古老学校的几项人事变动中最重要的一项。原麻瓜研究课教师已经辞职,将由阿莱克托·卡罗接任,其兄阿米库斯将出任黑魔法防御术课教师。

"我很高兴有机会维护我们最优秀的魔法传统和价值观——就是杀人和割耳朵吧,我想!斯内普,校长!斯内普坐在邓布利多的办公室里——梅林的裤子啊!"她尖声大叫,把哈利和罗恩都吓了一大跳。她从桌边蹦起来,冲出厨房,嘴里喊着:"我马上回来!"

"'梅林的裤子'?"罗恩似乎觉得好笑,"她准是气糊涂了。"他把报纸拉到面前,细看关于斯内普的文章。

"其他教师不会容忍的,麦格、弗立维和斯普劳特都知道真相,知道邓布利多是怎么死的。他们不会同意斯内普做校长。卡罗兄妹是什么人呀?"

"食死徒,"哈利说,"报纸里面有照片。斯内普杀死邓布利多时他们也在塔顶,所以都是狐朋狗党。而且,"哈利拉过一把椅子,激愤地说,"我看其他教师除了留下任教之外别无选择。如果魔法部和伏地魔都是斯内普的靠山,那么不是留下任教,就是到阿兹卡班蹲几年——这还算是运气好的。我估计他们会留下来设法保护学生。"

克利切端着大汤碗匆匆走到桌旁,把汤舀进洁净的小碗里,一边吹着口哨。

"谢谢,克利切。"哈利说着合上报纸,他不想看到斯内普的面孔,"至少我们现在知道斯内普在哪儿了。"

他开始用勺子喝汤,自从得到雷古勒斯的挂坠盒之后,克利切的厨艺大大提高,今天的法式洋葱汤堪称哈利尝过的最好口味。

"仍然有好多食死徒在监视这幢房子,"他边吃边告诉罗恩,"比平时多,好像指望我们拖着箱子出去乘坐霍格沃茨特快列车似的。"

CHAPTER TWELVE   Magic is Might

Ron glanced at his watch.

'I've been thinking about that all day. It left nearly six hours ago. Weird, not being on it, isn't it?'

In his mind's eye Harry seemed to see the scarlet steam engine as he and Ron had once followed it by air, shimmering between fields and hills, a rippling scarlet caterpillar. He was sure Ginny, Neville and Luna were sitting together at this moment, perhaps wondering where he, Ron and Hermione were, or debating how best to undermine Snape's new regime.

'They nearly saw me coming back in, just now,' Harry said. 'I landed badly on the top step, and the Cloak slipped.'

'I do that every time. Oh, here she is,' Ron added, craning round in his seat to watch Hermione re-entering the kitchen. 'And what in the name of Merlin's most baggy Y-fronts was that about?'

'I remembered this,' Hermione panted.

She was carrying a large, framed picture, which she now lowered to the floor before seizing her small, beaded bag from the kitchen dresser. Opening it, she proceeded to force the painting inside, and despite the fact that it was patently too large to fit inside the tiny bag, within a few seconds it had vanished, like so much else, into the bag's capacious depths.

'Phineas Nigellus,' Hermione explained as she threw the bag on to the kitchen table with the usual sonorous, clanking crash.

'Sorry?' said Ron, but Harry understood. The painted image of Phineas Nigellus Black was able to flit between his portrait in Grimmauld Place and the one that hung in the Headmaster's office at Hogwarts: the circular tower-top room where Snape was no doubt sitting right now, in triumphant possession of Dumbledore's collection of delicate, silver magical instruments, the stone Pensieve, the Sorting Hat and, unless it had been moved elsewhere, the sword of Gryffindor.

'Snape could send Phineas Nigellus to look inside this house for him,' Hermione explained to Ron as she resumed her seat. 'But let him try it now, all Phineas Nigellus will be able to see is the inside of my handbag.'

'Good thinking!' said Ron, looking impressed.

'Thank you,' smiled Hermione, pulling her soup towards her. 'So, Harry, what else happened today?'

'Nothing,' said Harry. 'Watched the Ministry entrance for seven hours. No

第12章　魔法即强权

罗恩看了看表。

"我一整天都在想这事。它六小时前就开走了，不在车上感觉怪怪的，是不是？"

哈利仿佛看到了那列深红色的蒸汽机车，跟他和罗恩在空中追随它的那次一样，闪闪发光地穿行在田野山岭之间，像一条蠕动的红色毛虫。他相信金妮、纳威和卢娜此刻正坐在一起，也许在猜测他、罗恩和赫敏在什么地方，或是在争论怎样才能破坏斯内普的新政权。

"刚才他们差点看见我回来。"哈利说，"我在台阶顶上没站稳，隐形衣滑开了。"

"我每次都这样。哦，她来了。"罗恩扭过头去看赫敏走进厨房，"梅林最肥的三角短裤啊，这到底是怎么回事？"

"我想起了这个。"赫敏气喘吁吁地说。

她抱来个大相框，放到地上，从厨房柜子里抓过她的串珠小包，打开来把画往里塞。虽然相框明显太大，但几秒钟后它竟也像那么多东西一样，消失在小包宽敞无比的肚囊里了。

"菲尼亚斯·奈杰勒斯。"赫敏解释道，把小包扔在厨房桌子上，发出平常那种响亮沉重的撞击声。

"什么？"罗恩说，可是哈利懂了。菲尼亚斯·奈杰勒斯·布莱克的肖像能在格里莫广场和霍格沃茨校长办公室的两个相框间来去自由，斯内普现在肯定已坐在塔楼顶上那个圆形的房间里，得意地占据了邓布利多那些精致的银色魔法仪器、石头冥想盆、分院帽，还有格兰芬多的宝剑——如果它未被转移的话。

"斯内普可以派菲尼亚斯·奈杰勒斯到这所房子里来打探情况。"赫敏向罗恩解释着，坐了下来，"现在让他打探去吧，菲尼亚斯·奈杰勒斯只能看到我手提包里的东西。"

"这招儿高啊！"罗恩钦佩地说。

"谢谢。"赫敏微微一笑，把汤碗拉到面前，"哈利，今天还有什么情况？"

"没什么了，"哈利说，"在魔法部门口侦察了七个小时，没发现那

CHAPTER TWELVE   Magic is Might

sign of her. Saw your dad, though, Ron. He looks fine.'

Ron nodded his appreciation of this news. They had agreed that it was far too dangerous to try to communicate with Mr Weasley while he walked in and out of the Ministry, because he was always surrounded by other Ministry workers. It was, however, reassuring to catch these glimpses of him, even if he did look very strained and anxious.

'Dad always told us most Ministry people use the Floo Network to get to work,' Ron said. 'That's why we haven't seen Umbridge, she'd never walk, she'd think she's too important.'

'And what about that funny old witch and that little wizard in the navy robes?' Hermione asked.

'Oh, yeah, the bloke from Magical Maintenance,' said Ron.

'How do you know he works for Magical Maintenance?' Hermione asked, her soup spoon suspended in mid-air.

'Dad said everyone from Magical Maintenance wears navy blue robes.'

'But you never told us that!'

Hermione dropped her spoon and pulled towards her the sheaf of notes and maps that she and Ron had been examining when Harry had entered the kitchen.

'There's nothing in here about navy blue robes, nothing!' she said, flipping feverishly through the pages.

'Well, does it really matter?'

'Ron, it *all* matters! If we're going to get into the Ministry and not give ourselves away when they're *bound* to be on the lookout for intruders, every little detail matters! We've been over and over this, I mean, what's the point of all these reconnaissance trips if you aren't even bothering to tell us –'

'Blimey, Hermione, I forget one little thing –'

'You do realise, don't you, that there's probably no more dangerous place in the whole world for us to be right now than the Ministry of –'

'I think we should do it tomorrow,' said Harry.

Hermione stopped dead, her jaw hanging; Ron choked a little over his soup.

'Tomorrow?' repeated Hermione. 'You aren't serious, Harry?'

'I am,' said Harry. 'I don't think we're going to be much better prepared than we are now even if we skulk around the Ministry entrance for another month. The longer we put it off, the further away that locket could be. There's already a good chance Umbridge has chucked it away; the thing doesn't open.'

第12章 魔法即强权

女人,但见到了你爸爸,罗恩,他看上去挺好的。"

罗恩点点头对这个消息表示感谢。他们一致认为在韦斯莱先生进出魔法部时跟他联络太危险了,因为他身边总是围着部里的其他人员。不过,能够看到他也是一种安慰,尽管他看上去十分紧张和焦虑。

"爸爸常说部里大多数人都用飞路网上班,"罗恩说,"所以我们没有看到乌姆里奇,她不会走路的,她那么趾高气扬。"

"那个可笑的老女巫和那个穿藏青色袍子的小个子男巫呢?"赫敏问。

"哦,对了,就是魔法维修保养处的那家伙。"罗恩说。

"你怎么知道他在魔法维修保养处工作?"赫敏问,汤勺举在半空。

"爸爸说魔法维修保养处的人都穿藏青色袍子。"

"可你没跟我们说过!"

赫敏放下汤勺,把哈利进来时她和罗恩正在研究的那沓笔记和地图拉到面前。

"这里没提到藏青色袍子,压根儿没提!"她焦急地翻着那些纸片说。

"好啦,真的有关系吗?"

"罗恩,这些都有关系!魔法部现在肯定是戒备森严,如果我们要溜进部里而不被人发现,每个小细节都很重要!我们已经重复了很多遍,可是,侦察这么多趟有什么用,如果你都没告诉我们——"

"我的天哪,赫敏,我只忘记了一件小事——"

"你知不知道,现在对我们来讲,也许全世界再没有哪个地方比魔法部更危——"

"我想我们应该明天就去。"哈利说。

赫敏目瞪口呆。罗恩喝汤呛着了。

"明天?"赫敏问道,"你不是认真的吧,哈利?"

"没开玩笑,"哈利说,"我想,就算我们在魔法部门口再侦察一个月,也不会比现在的准备更充分多少。拖得越久就会离挂坠盒越远。很可能乌姆里奇已经把它扔掉了,那玩意儿打不开。"

CHAPTER TWELVE   Magic is Might

'Unless,' said Ron, 'she's found a way of opening it and she's now possessed.'

'Wouldn't make any difference to her, she was so evil in the first place,' Harry shrugged.

Hermione was biting her lip, deep in thought.

'We know everything important,' Harry went on, addressing Hermione. 'We know they've stopped Apparition in and out of the Ministry. We know only the most senior Ministry members are allowed to connect their homes to the Floo Network now, because Ron heard those two Unspeakables complaining about it. And we know roughly where Umbridge's office is, because of what you heard that bearded bloke saying to his mate –'

'"*I'll be up on Level One, Dolores wants to see me,*"' Hermione recited immediately.

'Exactly,' said Harry. 'And we know you get in using those funny coins, or tokens, or whatever they are, because I saw that witch borrowing one from her friend –'

'But we haven't got any!'

'If the plan works, we will have,' Harry continued calmly.

'I don't know, Harry, I don't know ... there are an awful lot of things that could go wrong, so much relies on chance ...'

'That'll be true even if we spend another three months preparing,' said Harry. 'It's time to act.'

He could tell from Ron and Hermione's faces that they were scared; he was not particularly confident himself, and yet he was sure the time had come to put their plan into operation.

They had spent the previous four weeks taking it in turns to don the Invisibility Cloak and spy on the official entrance to the Ministry, which Ron, thanks to Mr Weasley, had known since childhood. They had tailed Ministry workers on their way in, eavesdropped on their conversations and learned by careful observation which of them could be relied upon to appear, alone, at the same time every day. Occasionally, there had been a chance to sneak a *Daily Prophet* out of somebody's briefcase. Slowly, they had built up the sketchy maps and notes now stacked in front of Hermione.

'All right,' said Ron slowly, 'let's say we go for it tomorrow ... I think it should just be me and Harry.'

'Oh, don't start that again!' sighed Hermione. 'I thought we'd settled this.'

第12章 魔法即强权

"除非,"罗恩说,"她想办法打开了它,现在已经被它附身了。"

"对她来说没什么区别,她本来就够邪恶了。"哈利耸耸肩说。

赫敏咬着嘴唇,在那里沉思。

"我们知道了所有重要的情况,"哈利对赫敏继续说,"他们不再幻影显形出入魔法部,现在只有部里级别最高的人家里才能连接飞路网,这是罗恩听那两个缄默人抱怨时说的。我们大致知道乌姆里奇的办公室在哪儿,因为你听到那个山羊胡对他的同伴说——"

"'我要上一层,多洛雷斯想见我。'"赫敏马上背诵道。

"正是,"哈利说,"而且我们知道进门要用那些可笑的硬币,或是证明币,管它叫什么呢,我看到那个女巫向朋友借了一个——"

"可我们没有呀!"

"如果计划成功,我们就会有的。"哈利平静地说。

"怎么说呢,哈利,怎么说呢……有那么多环节可能出错,那么多地方都要靠运气……"

"即使我们再花三个月准备,也还是如此。"哈利说,"该采取行动了。"

从罗恩和赫敏的表情,哈利看出他们很害怕。他自己也不是那么有信心,然而他相信已经到了该实施计划的时候。

过去的四个星期里,他们轮流穿着隐形衣去魔法部门口侦察,由于韦斯莱先生的关系,罗恩自幼对那里很熟。他们跟踪进去上班的部里人员,偷听人家谈话,并通过仔细观察摸清了哪些人会在每天同一时间单独出现。偶尔有机会从某人公文包里偷一份《预言家日报》。一点一点地,他们积攒成了此刻堆在赫敏面前的草图和笔记。

"好吧,"罗恩慢吞吞地说,"假设我们明天就去……我想应该就哈利跟我两个人。"

"哦,别再提这个了!"赫敏叹着气说,"我想我们都已经说好了。"

CHAPTER TWELVE   Magic is Might

'It's one thing hanging around the entrances under the Cloak, but this is different, Hermione.' Ron jabbed a finger at a copy of the *Daily Prophet* dated ten days previously. 'You're on the list of Muggle-borns who didn't present themselves for interrogation!'

'And you're supposed to be dying of spattergroit at The Burrow! If anyone shouldn't go, it's Harry, he's got a ten thousand Galleon price on his head –'

'Fine, I'll stay here,' said Harry. 'Let me know if you ever defeat Voldemort, won't you?'

As Ron and Hermione laughed, pain shot through the scar on Harry's forehead. His hand jumped to it: he saw Hermione's eyes narrow, and he tried to pass off the movement by brushing his hair out of his eyes.

'Well, if all three of us go, we'll have to Disapparate separately,' Ron was saying. 'We can't all fit under the Cloak any more.'

Harry's scar was becoming more and more painful. He stood up. At once, Kreacher hurried forwards.

'Master has not finished his soup, would Master prefer the savoury stew, or else the treacle tart to which Master is so partial?'

'Thanks, Kreacher, but I'll be back in a minute – er – bathroom.'

Aware that Hermione was watching him suspiciously, Harry hurried up the stairs to the hall and then to the first landing, where he dashed into the bathroom and bolted the door again. Grunting with pain, he slumped over the black basin with its taps in the form of open-mouthed serpents and closed his eyes ...

He was gliding along a twilit street. The buildings on either side of him had high, timbered gables; they looked like gingerbread houses.

He approached one of them, then saw the whiteness of his own long-fingered hand against the door. He knocked. He felt a mounting excitement ...

The door opened: a laughing woman stood there. Her face fell as she looked into Harry's face, humour gone, terror replacing it ...

'Gregorovitch?' said a high, cold voice.

She shook her head: she was trying to close the door. A white hand held it steady, prevented her shutting him out ...

'I want Gregorovitch.'

'*Er wohnt hier nicht mehr!* ' she cried, shaking her head. 'He no live here! He no live here! I know him not!'

第12章 魔法即强权

"穿着隐形衣在门口侦察是一回事，可现在是另一回事，赫敏。"罗恩用手指戳着一份十天前的《预言家日报》，"你被列入了没去接受审查的麻瓜出身者名单！"

"而你应该在陋居身患散花痘，生命垂危！如果有谁不应该去，那就是哈利，他被悬赏一万加隆——"

"好吧，我留在这儿，"哈利说，"你们要是打败了伏地魔，给我送个信，好不好？"

罗恩和赫敏笑了起来，哈利额上的伤疤突然一阵剧痛，他本能地用手一捂，看到赫敏眯起了眼睛，赶忙捋了捋头发加以掩饰。

"如果三个人都去，就必须分头幻影移形，"罗恩说，"隐形衣已经盖不住我们三个了。"

哈利的伤疤越来越痛，他站起身，克利切立刻奔上前去。

"主人的汤没有喝完，主人是要美味的炖菜，还是要主人非常偏爱的糖浆水果馅饼？"

"谢谢，克利切，我马上就回来——呃——去趟卫生间。"

哈利感觉到赫敏在怀疑地盯着他，急忙上楼经过门厅，到了二楼的楼梯口，冲进卫生间，插上了门。他痛苦地呻吟着，趴到那个蛇嘴形状水龙头的黑盆上，紧闭双眼……

他在一条昏暗的巷子里飘行，两边的房屋都有高高的木板山墙，看上去像姜饼做的房子。

他走近一座房子，看到他自己苍白修长的手指伸到门上，他在敲门，内心越来越兴奋……

门开了：一个女人笑着站在那里，看到哈利的面孔，她一下变了脸色，笑容消失了，取而代之的是恐惧……

"格里戈维奇？"一个高亢、冷酷的声音问。

她摇摇头，想要关门。一只苍白的手牢牢抵住门，不让她把他关在外面……

"我找格里戈维奇。"

"他不住这儿了！"她摇着头喊道，"他不住这儿！他不住这儿！我不认识他！"

CHAPTER TWELVE   Magic is Might

Abandoning the attempt to close the door, she began to back away down the dark hall, and Harry followed, gliding towards her, and his long-fingered hand had drawn his wand.

'Where is he?'

'*Das weiß ich nicht!* He move! I know not, I know not!'

He raised the wand. She screamed. Two young children came running into the hall. She tried to shield them with her arms. There was a flash of green light –

'Harry! HARRY!'

He opened his eyes; he had sunk to the floor. Hermione was pounding on the door again.

'Harry, open up!'

He had shouted out, he knew it. He got up and unbolted the door; Hermione toppled inside at once, regained her balance and looked around suspiciously. Ron was right behind her, looking unnerved as he pointed his wand into the corners of the chilly bathroom.

'What were you doing?' asked Hermione sternly.

'What d'you think I was doing?' asked Harry, with feeble bravado.

'You were yelling your head off!' said Ron.

'Oh yeah ... I must've dozed off or –'

'Harry, please don't insult our intelligence,' said Hermione, taking deep breaths. 'We know your scar hurt downstairs, and you're white as a sheet.'

Harry sat down on the edge of the bath.

'Fine. I've just seen Voldemort murdering a woman. By now he's probably killed her whole family. And he didn't need to. It was Cedric all over again, they were just *there* ...'

'Harry, you aren't supposed to let this happen any more!' Hermione cried, her voice echoing through the bathroom. 'Dumbledore wanted you to use Occlumency! He thought the connection was dangerous – Voldemort can *use* it, Harry! What good is it to watch him kill and torture, how can it help?'

'Because it means I know what he's doing,' said Harry.

'So you're not even going to try to shut him out?'

'Hermione, I can't. You know I'm lousy at Occlumency, I never got the hang of it.'

第12章 魔法即强权

她放弃了关门，往黑暗的门厅里退去。哈利跟在后面，无声无息地向她飘过去，长长的手指已经抽出了魔杖。

"他在哪儿？"

"我不知道！他搬走了！我不知道，我不知道！"

他举起魔杖，女人尖叫起来，两个小孩跑进门厅。她张开双臂想保护他们，一道绿光——

"哈利！**哈利！**"

他睁开眼，发现自己已经倒在地上，赫敏又在捶门。

"哈利，开门！"

自己刚才喊出了声，他知道。他站起来打开门，赫敏一头栽了进来，恢复平衡之后怀疑地打量着四周。罗恩也跟了进来，紧张地用魔杖指着阴冷卫生间里的各个角落。

"你在干什么？"赫敏严厉地问。

"你认为我在干什么？"哈利虚张声势地反问。

"你在里面大喊大叫！"罗恩说。

"哦，是啊……我一定是睡着了，或者——"

"哈利，请不要侮辱我们的智商，"赫敏大口吸着气说，"我们在楼下就知道你的伤疤又疼了，而且你的脸跟纸一样白。"

哈利在浴缸边沿坐了下来。

"好吧，我刚才看到伏地魔杀死了一个女人。现在他可能已经杀死了她的全家。他不需要这么做，又像塞德里克那次一样，只是因为他们在场……"

"哈利，你不应该再让这样的事发生！"赫敏嚷道，回音响彻卫生间，"邓布利多要你学会大脑封闭术！他认为这种联系是危险的——伏地魔可以利用它，哈利！看他杀人和折磨人有什么好处，有什么用呢？"

"我能知道他在干什么。"哈利说。

"所以你根本不想努力切断这种联系？"

"赫敏，我做不到。你知道我大脑封闭术练得多差，一直找不到诀窍。"

CHAPTER TWELVE   Magic is Might

'You never really tried!' she said hotly. 'I don't get it, Harry – do you *like* having this special connection or relationship or what – whatever –'

She faltered under the look he gave her as he stood up.

'Like it?' he said quietly. 'Would *you* like it?'

'I – no – I'm sorry, Harry, I didn't mean –'

'I hate it, I hate the fact that he can get inside me, that I have to watch him when he's most dangerous. But I'm going to use it.'

'Dumbledore –'

'Forget Dumbledore. This is my choice, nobody else's. I want to know why he's after Gregorovitch.'

'Who?'

'He's a foreign wandmaker,' said Harry. 'He made Krum's wand and Krum reckons he's brilliant.'

'But according to you,' said Ron, 'Voldemort's got Ollivander locked up somewhere. If he's already got a wandmaker, what does he need another one for?'

'Maybe he agrees with Krum, maybe he thinks Gregorovitch is better … or else he thinks Gregorovitch will be able to explain what my wand did when he was chasing me, because Ollivander didn't know.'

Harry glanced into the cracked, dusty mirror and saw Ron and Hermione exchanging sceptical looks behind his back.

'Harry, you keep talking about what your wand did,' said Hermione, 'but *you* made it happen! Why are you so determined not to take responsibility for your own power?'

'Because I know it wasn't me! And so does Voldemort, Hermione! We both know what really happened!'

They glared at each other: Harry knew that he had not convinced Hermione and that she was marshalling counter-arguments, against both his theory on his wand and the fact that he was permitting himself to see into Voldemort's mind. To his relief, Ron intervened.

'Drop it,' he advised her. 'It's up to him. And if we're going to the Ministry tomorrow, don't you reckon we should go over the plan?'

第12章 魔法即强权

"你从来没有真正努力过!"赫敏激烈地说,"我不明白,哈利——你是不是喜欢有这种特殊的联系,或感应,或——管它叫什么——"

看到哈利的目光,她噘嚅了。哈利站了起来。

"喜欢?"他低声问,"你会喜欢吗?"

"我——不——对不起,哈利,我不是那个意思——"

"我讨厌这联系,我讨厌他闯进我的脑海,讨厌不得不在他最可怕的时候看到他,但是我要利用它。"

"邓布利多——"

"别提邓布利多。这是我的选择,不是其他人的。我想知道他为什么要找格里戈维奇。"

"谁?"

"一个制作魔杖的外国人,"哈利说,"他做了克鲁姆的魔杖,克鲁姆认为他手艺高超。"

"可是你说过,"罗恩说,"伏地魔把奥利凡德关在了什么地方。他既然已经有了一个会做魔杖的,为什么还要再找一个呢?"

"也许他与克鲁姆的看法一样,也许他认为格里戈维奇手艺更好……或者,上次他追我时我魔杖的所作所为,他认为只有格里戈维奇能够解释,而奥利凡德不知道。"

哈利朝灰蒙蒙的破镜子里望去,看到罗恩和赫敏在他背后交换着怀疑的眼神。

"哈利,你口口声声说你的魔杖做了什么,"赫敏说,"其实是你使它发生的!你为什么这样坚决不肯为你自己的能力负责呢?"

"因为我知道不是我!伏地魔也知道,赫敏!我和他都知道事实是什么样的!"

两人互相瞪着对方,哈利知道他并未说服赫敏,她脑子里正在搜集论据,要批驳他的魔杖理论,还要批驳他允许自己看到伏地魔的思想。令他庆幸的是,罗恩来调停了。

"算了,"他对赫敏说,"这是他的事。如果明天要去魔法部,你不觉得我们应该温习一下行动计划吗?"

CHAPTER TWELVE   Magic is Might

Reluctantly, as the other two could tell, Hermione let the matter rest, though Harry was quite sure she would attack again at the first opportunity. In the meantime, they returned to the basement kitchen, where Kreacher served them all stew and treacle tart.

They did not get to bed until late that night, after spending hours going over and over their plan until they could recite it, word-perfect, to each other. Harry, who was now sleeping in Sirius's room, lay in bed with his wandlight trained on the old photograph of his father, Sirius, Lupin and Pettigrew, and muttered the plan to himself for another ten minutes. As he extinguished his wand, however, he was thinking not of Polyjuice Potion, Puking Pastilles or the navy blue robes of Magical Maintenance; he thought of Gregorovitch the wandmaker, and how long he could hope to remain hidden while Voldemort sought him so determinedly.

Dawn seemed to follow midnight with indecent haste.

'You look terrible,' was Ron's greeting, as he entered the room to wake Harry.

'Not for long,' said Harry, yawning.

They found Hermione downstairs in the kitchen. She was being served coffee and hot rolls by Kreacher and wearing the slightly manic expression that Harry associated with exam revision.

'Robes,' she said under her breath, acknowledging their presence with a nervous nod and continuing to poke around in her beaded bag, 'Polyjuice Potion ... Invisibility Cloak ... Decoy Detonators ... you should each take a couple just in case ... Puking Pastilles, Nosebleed Nougat, Extendable Ears ...'

They gulped down their breakfast then set off upstairs, Kreacher bowing them out and promising to have a steak and kidney pie ready for them when they returned.

'Bless him,' said Ron fondly, 'and when you think I used to fantasise about cutting off his head and sticking it on the wall.'

They made their way on to the front step with immense caution: they could see a couple of puffy-eyed Death Eaters watching the house from across the misty square. Hermione Disapparated with Ron first, then came back for Harry.

After the usual brief spell of darkness and near suffocation, Harry found himself in the tiny alleyway where the first phase of their plan was scheduled to take place. It was as yet deserted, except for a couple of large bins; the first Ministry workers did not usually appear here until at least eight o'clock.

第12章 魔法即强权

赫敏放开了这个话题，哈利和罗恩看得出她很不情愿，哈利相信她一有机会还要开火。三个人回到地下室的厨房，克利切给他们端上了炖菜和糖浆水果馅饼。

他们一遍遍地温习行动计划，最后背得一字不差，直到深夜才上床睡觉。哈利现在睡在小天狼星的房间，他躺在床上，魔杖的光指着他父亲、小天狼星、卢平和小矮星的那张旧照片，他又叽里咕噜地把计划背了十分钟。但熄灭魔杖时，他想的不是复方汤剂、吐吐糖和魔法维修保养处的藏青色袍子，而是制作魔杖的格里戈维奇，伏地魔如此决意要找到他，不知道他还能躲多久。

黎明追着子夜来临了，似乎匆忙得乱了阵脚。

"你的脸色很难看。"罗恩进来叫醒哈利时说。

"很快就会好的。"哈利打着哈欠回答。

他们在楼下厨房里看到了赫敏，她对着克利切端上的咖啡和热面包卷，脸上是那种有点疯狂的表情，哈利马上联想到考前复习。

"袍子，"她喃喃自语，紧张地朝他们点了下头，继续在她的串珠小包里摸索，"复方汤剂……隐形衣……诱饵炸弹……你们每人要拿两个，以防万一……吐吐糖、鼻血牛轧糖、伸缩耳……"

他们大口吃完早饭，动身上楼，克利切鞠躬相送，并保证做好牛排腰子馅饼等他们回来。

"上帝保佑他，"罗恩感动地说，"想想吧，我还曾经幻想把他脑袋割下来，钉在墙上呢。"

他们小心翼翼地站到前门台阶顶上：可以看到两个肿眼睛的食死徒隔着雾蒙蒙的广场朝这边望。赫敏先跟罗恩幻影移形，然后又回来带哈利。

经过那短暂的黑暗和窒息般的感觉，哈利发现自己站在一条小巷子里，按照计划，行动的第一部分将在这里进行。巷子里空荡荡的，只有两个大垃圾箱。第一批魔法部工作人员至少要到八点才会出现。

CHAPTER TWELVE Magic is Might

'Right then,' said Hermione, checking her watch. 'She ought to be here in about five minutes. When I've Stunned her –'

'Hermione, we know,' said Ron sternly. 'And I thought we were supposed to open the door before she got here?'

Hermione squealed.

'I nearly forgot! Stand back –'

She pointed her wand at the padlocked and heavily graffitied fire door beside them, which burst open with a crash. The dark corridor behind it led, as they knew from their careful scouting trips, into an empty theatre. Hermione pulled the door back towards her, to make it look as though it was still closed.

'And now,' she said, turning back to face the other two in the alleyway, 'we put on the Cloak again –'

'– and we wait,' Ron finished, throwing it over Hermione's head like baize over a budgerigar and rolling his eyes at Harry.

Little more than a minute later, there was a tiny *pop* and a little Ministry witch with flyaway, grey hair Apparated feet from them, blinking a little in the sudden brightness; the sun had just come out from behind a cloud. She barely had time to enjoy the unexpected warmth, however, before Hermione's silent Stunning Spell hit her in the chest and she toppled over.

'Nicely done, Hermione,' said Ron, emerging from behind a bin beside the theatre door as Harry took off the Invisibility Cloak. Together they carried the little witch into the dark passageway that led backstage. Hermione plucked a few hairs from the witch's head and added them to a flask of muddy Polyjuice Potion she had taken from the beaded bag. Ron was rummaging through the little witch's handbag.

'She's Mafalda Hopkirk,' he said, reading a small card that identified their victim as an assistant in the Improper Use of Magic Office. 'You'd better take this, Hermione, and here are the tokens.'

He passed her several small golden coins, all embossed with the letters M.O.M., which he had taken from the witch's purse.

Hermione drank the Polyjuice Potion, which was now a pleasant heliotrope colour, and within seconds stood before them, the double of Mafalda Hopkirk. As she removed Mafalda's spectacles and put them on, Harry checked his watch.

第12章 魔法即强权

"好啦,"赫敏看看手表,"她再过五分钟就该到了,我把她击昏之后——"

"赫敏,我们知道了,"罗恩不高兴地说,"而且,我记得我们应该在她来之前把门打开吧?"

赫敏尖叫一声。

"我差点忘了!闪开——"

她用魔杖一指旁边那扇挂着铁锁、满是涂鸦的防火门,门砰的一声开了。他们通过多次仔细侦察知道,门后黑乎乎的走廊通向一个无人的剧院。赫敏把门拉上,使它看上去还像关着一样。

"现在,"她转过身,对着巷子里的两个同伴说,"我们重新披上隐形衣——"

"——等着。"罗恩接口说完,把隐形衣披到赫敏头上,像用羊毛毯盖住一只虎皮鹦鹉似的,一边朝哈利翻了个白眼。

一分多钟之后,他们听到噗的一声轻响,一个灰发飘飘的小个子魔法部女巫在他们面前几英尺处幻影显形,被突如其来的光亮照得有点睁不开眼睛。太阳刚从一片云后面露出来,可是,她还没来得及享受这意外的温暖,赫敏无声的昏迷咒已经击中她的胸口,她倒了下去。

"干得漂亮,赫敏。"罗恩赞道,从剧院门口的垃圾箱后钻了出来,哈利脱下隐形衣。三人一起把小个子女巫拖进通往后台的黑暗走廊。赫敏从女巫头上拔了几根头发,从串珠小包里拿出一瓶浑浊的复方汤剂,把头发加了进去。罗恩在女巫的手提包里翻找。

"她是马法尔达·霍普柯克。"他念着一张小卡片,被击昏的那人是禁止滥用魔法办公室的一名助理,"你最好拿着这个,赫敏,还有证明币。"

他递给赫敏几枚小小的金色硬币,都印着 M.O.M. 的凸纹字样,是在那个女巫的钱包里找到的。

复方汤剂已经变成了令人愉快的淡紫色,赫敏把它喝下去,几秒钟后就变成马法尔达·霍普柯克站在他们面前。她摘下马法尔达的眼镜戴上,哈利看了看表。

CHAPTER TWELVE   Magic is Might

'We're running late, Mr Magical Maintenance will be here any second.'

They hurried to close the door on the real Mafalda; Harry and Ron threw the Invisibility Cloak over themselves but Hermione remained in view, waiting. Seconds later there was another *pop*, and a small, ferrety-looking wizard appeared before them.

'Oh, hello, Mafalda.'

'Hello!' said Hermione in a quavery voice. 'How are you today?'

'Not so good, actually,' replied the little wizard, who looked thoroughly downcast.

As Hermione and the wizard headed for the main road, Harry and Ron crept along behind them.

'I'm sorry to hear you're under the weather,' said Hermione, talking firmly over the little wizard as he tried to expound upon his problems; it was essential to stop him reaching the street. 'Here, have a sweet.'

'Eh? Oh, no thanks –'

'I insist!' said Hermione aggressively, shaking the bag of pastilles in his face. Looking rather alarmed, the little wizard took one.

The effect was instantaneous. The moment the pastille touched his tongue, the little wizard started vomiting so hard that he did not even notice as Hermione yanked a handful of hairs from the top of his head.

'Oh dear!' she said, as he splattered the alley with sick. 'Perhaps you'd better take the day off!'

'No – no!' He choked and retched, trying to continue on his way despite being unable to walk straight. 'I must – today – must go –'

'But that's just silly!' said Hermione, alarmed. 'You can't go to work in this state – I think you ought to go to St Mungo's and get them to sort you out!'

The wizard had collapsed, heaving, on all fours, still trying to crawl towards the main street.

'You simply can't go to work like this!' cried Hermione.

At last he seemed to accept the truth of her words. Using a repulsed Hermione to claw his way back into a standing position, he turned on the spot and vanished, leaving nothing behind but the bag Ron had snatched from his hand as he went, and some flying chunks of vomit.

'Urgh,' said Hermione, holding up the skirts of her robe to avoid the puddles of sick. 'It would have made much less mess to Stun him too.'

第 12 章　魔法即强权

"我们有点晚了，魔法维修保养处先生就要来了。"

他们赶紧把真马法尔达关在门后，哈利和罗恩披上隐形衣，赫敏仍站在那里等候。几秒钟后，又是噗的一声，一个长得像白鼬的小个子男巫出现在他们面前。

"哦，你好，马法尔达。"

"你好！"赫敏用发颤的嗓音说，"你今天怎么样？"

"说实话，不大好。"小个子男巫答道，他看上去萎靡不振。

赫敏和男巫朝主街道走去，哈利和罗恩蹑手蹑脚地跟在后面。

"你身体不舒服，我很同情。"小个子男巫想解释他的情况，赫敏坚决地提高嗓门把他的话压了回去，她必须在他走到街上之前拦住他，"给，吃块糖吧。"

"呃？哦，不用了，谢谢——"

"一定要吃！"赫敏强硬地说，在他面前挥舞那包吐吐糖，小个子男巫似乎被吓着了，就拿了一块。

效果立竿见影。吐吐糖一碰到他的舌头，小个子男巫就剧烈地呕吐起来，甚至没有注意到赫敏从他头顶扯下了一撮头发。

"哦，天哪！"赫敏说，看到他在巷子里吐了一地，"你可能得休息一天了！"

"不——不！"他一边干呕，一边还在往前走，虽然路都走不直了，"我必须——今天——必须去——"

"可这样太愚蠢了！"赫敏惊恐地说，"你这个样子不能上班——我想你应该去圣芒戈医院查一查！"

男巫已经站不起来了，还在一边呕吐，一边试图往街上爬。

"你不能这样去上班！"赫敏喊道。

男巫终于似乎接受了她所讲的事实，抓着一脸嫌恶的赫敏勉强站起来，原地旋转消失了，只留下罗恩在最后一刻从他手中扯下的一个包，和一些飘飞的呕吐物。

"哟嗐，"赫敏拎起袍子下摆，避开吐在地上的那一摊东西，"还不如把他也击昏干净得多。"

CHAPTER TWELVE   Magic is Might

'Yeah,' said Ron, emerging from under the Cloak holding the wizard's bag, 'but I still think a whole pile of unconscious bodies would have drawn more attention. Keen on his job, though, isn't he? Chuck us the hair and the Potion, then.'

Within two minutes, Ron stood before them, as small and ferrety as the sick wizard, and wearing the navy blue robes that had been folded in his bag.

'Weird he wasn't wearing them today, wasn't it, seeing how much he wanted to go? Anyway, I'm Reg Cattermole, according to the label in the back.'

'Now wait here,' Hermione told Harry, who was still under the Invisibility Cloak, 'and we'll be back with some hairs for you.'

He had to wait ten minutes, but it seemed much longer to Harry, skulking alone in the sick-splattered alleyway, beside the door concealing the Stunned Mafalda. Finally, Ron and Hermione reappeared.

'We don't know who he is,' Hermione said, passing Harry several curly, black hairs, 'but he's gone home with a dreadful nosebleed! Here, he's pretty tall, you'll need bigger robes ...'

She pulled out a set of the old robes Kreacher had laundered for them, and Harry retired to take the Potion and change.

Once the painful transformation was complete, he was more than six feet tall and, from what he could tell from his well-muscled arms, powerfully built. He also had a beard. Stowing the Invisibility Cloak and his glasses inside his new robes, he rejoined the other two.

'Blimey, that's scary,' said Ron, looking up at Harry, who now towered over him.

'Take one of Mafalda's tokens,' Hermione told Harry, 'and let's go, it's nearly nine.'

They stepped out of the alleyway together. Fifty yards along the crowded pavement, there were spiked black railings flanking two flights of steps, one labelled Gentlemen, the other, Ladies.

'See you in a moment, then,' said Hermione nervously, and she tottered off down the steps to the ladies'. Harry and Ron joined a number of oddly dressed men descending into what appeared to be an ordinary underground public toilet, tiled in grimy black and white.

'Morning, Reg!' called another wizard in navy blue robes as he let himself into a cubicle by inserting his golden token into a slot in the door. 'Blooming pain in the bum, this, eh? Forcing us all to get to work this way! Who are they

第12章 魔法即强权

"是啊,"罗恩说,拿着男巫的包钻出隐形衣,"但我还是认为一堆昏迷的人更容易引起注意。他倒挺热爱工作的,是不是?把头发和汤剂扔过来吧。"

两分钟后,罗恩站在他们面前,个子矮小,长得像白鼬,跟那个生病的男巫一模一样,并且穿上了叠放在他包里的藏青色袍子。

"奇怪他今天为什么没穿,是不是,既然他那么想上班?管他呢,我是雷吉·卡特莫尔,衣服背后有名字。"

"在这儿等着,"赫敏对哈利说,此时哈利还披着隐形衣,"我们去给你找几根头发来。"

哈利等了十分钟,但是感觉过了好久,一个人躲在满地都是呕吐物的巷子里,旁边的门里藏着被击昏的马法尔达。终于,罗恩和赫敏回来了。

"不知道他是谁,"赫敏递给哈利几根黑色的鬈发说,"但他已经回家了,鼻血流得一塌糊涂!他挺高的,你得换件大袍子……"

她抽出一套克利切为他们洗干净的旧袍子,哈利走到一旁开始喝下汤剂、换衣服。

痛苦的变化完成后,他身高六英尺多,从胳膊上的肌肉可以看出体魄十分健壮,下巴上还留着胡须。他把隐形衣和眼镜塞进新换的袍子里,站到另外两人旁边。

"我的天,好吓人哪。"罗恩仰望着铁塔般屹立在他面前的哈利说。

"拿一个马法尔达的证明币。"赫敏跟哈利说,"我们走吧,快九点了。"

三个人一起走出小巷。沿着拥挤的人行道走了约五十米远,那儿有两道黑色尖头栅栏夹护的台阶,一边写着男,一边写着女。

"一会儿见。"赫敏紧张地说,摇摇摆摆地走下标着女字的台阶。哈利和罗恩随着一些衣着古怪的男人走下去,好像来到了一个普通的地下公厕,墙上贴着脏兮兮的黑白瓷砖。

"早上好,雷吉!"一个穿藏青色袍子的男巫叫道,把金色证明币塞入门上的一道狭缝,进了一个小隔间,"真他妈讨厌,是吧?非要我

CHAPTER TWELVE   Magic is Might

expecting to turn up, Harry Potter?'

The wizard roared with laughter at his own wit. Ron gave a forced chuckle.

'Yeah,' he said, 'stupid, isn't it?'

And he and Harry let themselves into adjoining cubicles.

To Harry's left and right came the sound of flushing. He crouched down and peered through the gap at the bottom of the cubicle, just in time to see a pair of booted feet climbing into the toilet next door. He looked left, and saw Ron blinking at him.

'We have to flush ourselves in?' he whispered.

'Looks like it,' Harry whispered back; his voice came out deep and gravelly.

They both stood up. Feeling exceptionally foolish, Harry clambered into the toilet.

He knew at once that he had done the right thing; though he appeared to be standing in water, his shoes, feet and robes remained quite dry. He reached up, pulled the chain, and next moment had zoomed down a short chute, emerging out of a fireplace into the Ministry of Magic.

He got up clumsily; there was a lot more of his body than he was accustomed to. The great Atrium seemed darker than Harry remembered it. Previously, a golden fountain had filled the centre of the hall, casting shimmering spots of light over the polished wooden floor and walls. Now a gigantic statue of black stone dominated the scene. It was rather frightening, this vast sculpture of a witch and a wizard sitting on ornately carved thrones, looking down at the Ministry workers toppling out of fireplaces below them. Engraved in foot-high letters at the base of the statue were the words:

MAGIC IS MIGHT

Harry received a heavy blow on the back of the legs: another wizard had just flown out of the fireplace behind him.

'Out of the way, can't y— oh, sorry, Runcorn!'

Clearly frightened, the balding wizard hurried away. Apparently the man whom Harry was impersonating, Runcorn, was intimidating.

'Psst!' said a voice, and he looked round to see a wispy little witch and the ferrety wizard from Magical Maintenance gesturing to him from over beside the statue. Harry hastened to join them.

们这样来上班！他们以为会有谁来，哈利·波特？"

那男巫为自己的俏皮话嘎嘎大笑，罗恩勉强笑了两声。

"嘿嘿，"他说，"够蠢的，是不是？"

他和哈利进了相邻的小隔间。

哈利的左右两边都响起冲水声，他猫腰从隔板底下的空隙看过去，刚好看到一双靴子爬进了隔壁的抽水马桶。他又看看左边，只见罗恩正惊愕地冲他眨着眼睛。

"要把自己冲进去？"罗恩小声问。

"看来是这样。"哈利小声回答，他的声音低沉而沙哑。

两人都直起身，哈利爬进抽水马桶，感觉荒谬透顶。

他立刻知道做对了，虽然好像站在水里，但他的鞋、脚和袍子都很干。他伸手一拉链绳，立即疾速地通过一条短短的滑道，从一个壁炉里冲出来，进入了魔法部。

他笨拙地爬起来，身子比平时庞大了许多，不太适应。大厅似乎比哈利记忆中的昏暗一些。原来大厅中央是一个金色喷泉，在光亮的木地板和墙壁上投射出点点光斑。而现在，一座巨大的黑色石像占据了中心位置。看着令人生畏。这样一座巨型石像，一个女巫和一个男巫坐在雕刻华美的宝座上，俯视着从壁炉里滚出来的魔法部工作人员。石像底部刻着几个一英尺高的大字：

魔法即强权

哈利的腿后面被重重地撞了一下：一名男巫刚从壁炉里飞出来。

"别挡道，行不——哦，对不起，伦考恩！"

谢顶的男巫显然很惶恐，急忙走开了。看来哈利现在冒充的这个人——伦考恩，是个狠角色。

"嘘！"又一个声音说。哈利回过头，看到一个纤小的女巫和魔法维修保养处那个白鼬似的男巫在雕像旁边向他招手，就赶紧走了过去。

CHAPTER TWELVE   Magic is Might

'You got in all right, then?' Hermione whispered to Harry.

'No, he's still stuck in the bog,' said Ron.

'Oh, very funny ... it's horrible, isn't it?' she said to Harry, who was staring up at the statue. 'Have you seen what they're sitting on?'

Harry looked more closely and realised that what he had thought were decoratively carved thrones were actually mounds of carved humans: hundreds and hundreds of naked bodies, men, women and children, all with rather stupid, ugly faces, twisted and pressed together to support the weight of the handsomely robed wizards.

'Muggles,' whispered Hermione. 'In their rightful place. Come on, let's get going.'

They joined the stream of witches and wizards moving towards the golden gates at the end of the hall, looking around as surreptitiously as possible, but there was no sign of the distinctive figure of Dolores Umbridge. They passed through the gates and into a smaller hall, where queues were forming in front of twenty golden grilles housing as many lifts. They had barely joined the nearest one when a voice said, 'Cattermole!'

They looked around: Harry's stomach turned over. One of the Death Eaters who had witnessed Dumbledore's death was striding towards them. The Ministry workers beside them fell silent, their eyes downcast; Harry could feel fear rippling through them. The man's scowling, slightly brutish face was somehow at odds with his magnificent, sweeping robes, which were embroidered with much gold thread. Someone in the crowd around the lifts called sycophantically, 'Morning, Yaxley!' Yaxley ignored them.

'I requested somebody from Magical Maintenance to sort out my office, Cattermole. It's still raining in there.'

Ron looked around as though hoping somebody else would intervene, but nobody spoke.

'Raining ... in your office? That's – that's not good, is it?'

Ron gave a nervous laugh. Yaxley's eyes widened.

'You think it's funny, Cattermole, do you?'

A pair of witches broke away from the queue for the lift and bustled off.

'No,' said Ron, 'no, of course –'

'You realise that I am on my way downstairs to interrogate your wife, Cattermole? In fact, I'm quite surprised you're not down there holding her hand while she waits. Already given her up as a bad job, have you? Probably

第12章 魔法即强权

"你顺利地进来了？"赫敏悄声问哈利。

"没有，他还卡在马桶里呢。"罗恩开玩笑说。

"哦，真滑稽……很恐怖，是不是？"赫敏说，看见哈利仍然盯着雕像，"你看到他们坐在什么上面了吗？"

哈利仔细一看，才发现他刚才以为雕刻华美的宝座，实际上是一堆石雕的人体，成百上千赤裸的人体：男人、女人和孩子，相貌都比较呆傻丑陋，肢体扭曲着挤压在一起，支撑着那两个俊美的、穿袍子的巫师。

"麻瓜，"赫敏轻声说，"在他们应该待的地方。快，我们走吧。"

他们汇入了男女巫师的人流，向大厅尽头的金色大门走去，一边尽可能不引人注意地扫视着四周，但没有见到多洛雷斯·乌姆里奇那特征鲜明的身影。他们穿过金色大门来到一个较小的厅里，看见人们在二十部升降梯的金色栅栏门前面排队。他们刚刚排进最近的队伍中，就有一个声音说道："卡特莫尔！"

他们回过头，哈利胃中一阵痉挛。邓布利多死时在场的一个食死徒迎面大步走来。旁边的魔法部人员都垂下眼睛，不再作声。哈利能感到恐惧正在他们中间弥漫。那人阴沉的、略显残暴的面孔，与他那身镶着金丝的华丽、飘逸的长袍不大相称，升降梯旁的队伍中有人讨好地叫道："早上好，亚克斯利！"他没有理睬。

"我叫魔法维修保养处的人去给我修办公室了，卡特莫尔，屋里一直在下雨。"

罗恩环顾四周，好像希望有人插话，但没人吭气。

"下雨……在您的办公室？那——那真糟糕，是不是？"

罗恩紧张地笑了一下，亚克斯利瞪圆了眼睛。

"你觉得很好玩，是吗，卡特莫尔？"

两个排队等升降梯的女巫匆匆逃走了。

"不，"罗恩说，"当然不是——"

"你知道我正要下楼去审讯你老婆吧，卡特莫尔？我倒觉得挺意外，你怎么没在那里握着她的手陪她等着？已经要跟她划清界限了吗，啊？

CHAPTER TWELVE   Magic is Might

wise. Be sure and marry a pure-blood next time.'

Hermione had let out a little squeak of horror. Yaxley looked at her. She coughed feebly and turned away.

'I – I –' stammered Ron.

'But if *my* wife were accused of being a Mudblood,' said Yaxley, '– not that any woman I married would ever be mistaken for such filth – and the Head of the Department of Magical Law Enforcement needed a job doing, I would make it my priority to do that job, Cattermole. Do you understand me?'

'Yes,' whispered Ron.

'Then attend to it, Cattermole, and if my office is not completely dry within an hour your wife's Blood Status will be in even graver doubt than it is now.'

The golden grille before them clattered open. With a nod and unpleasant smile to Harry, who was evidently expected to appreciate this treatment of Cattermole, Yaxley swept away towards another lift. Harry, Ron and Hermione entered theirs, but nobody followed them: it was as if they were infectious. The grilles shut with a clang and the lift began to move upwards.

'What am I going to do?' Ron asked the other two at once; he looked stricken. 'If I don't turn up, my wife – I mean, Cattermole's wife –'

'We'll come with you, we should stick together –' began Harry, but Ron shook his head feverishly.

'That's mental, we haven't got much time. You two find Umbridge, I'll go and sort out Yaxley's office – but how do I stop it raining?'

'Try *Finite Incantatem*,' said Hermione at once, 'that should stop the rain if it's a hex or curse; if it doesn't, something's gone wrong with an Atmospheric Charm, which will be more difficult to fix, so as an interim measure try *Impervius* to protect his belongings –'

'Say it again, slowly –' said Ron, searching his pockets desperately for a quill, but at that moment the lift juddered to a halt. A disembodied female voice said, 'Level Four, Department for the Regulation and Control of Magical Creatures, incorporating Beast, Being and Spirit Divisions, Goblin Liaison Office and Pest Advisory Bureau,' and the grilles slid open again, admitting a couple of wizards and several pale violet paper aeroplanes that fluttered around the lamp in the ceiling of the lift.

这可能是明智之举。下次记着找一个纯血统的。"

赫敏惊恐地轻轻叫了一声。亚克斯利看着她。她忙假装虚弱地咳嗽起来，移开了目光。

"我——我——"罗恩结结巴巴地说。

"我娶的女人绝不会与那些垃圾混为一谈，不过，假设我的老婆被指控为泥巴种，"亚克斯利说，"而魔法法律执行司的头儿有个活要做，我一定会把这活当作头等大事去办，卡特莫尔，你明白我的意思吗？"

"明白。"罗恩低声说。

"那就去办吧，卡特莫尔，如果我的办公室一小时后不能完全干透，你老婆的血统成分就会比现在更成问题了。"

他们面前的金色栅栏门哗啦一声打开，亚克斯利转身朝另一部升降梯走去，临走时朝哈利点了点头，还露出一个令人厌恶的笑容，显然以为哈利会对他这样教训卡特莫尔表示欣赏。哈利、罗恩和赫敏进了他们的升降梯，但没有别人进来，好像他们有传染病似的。栅栏门哐当关上，升降梯开始上升。

"我该怎么办？"罗恩马上问两个同伴，好像大难临头一般，"我要是不去，我的老婆——我是说，卡特莫尔的老婆——"

"我们跟你一起去，我们不要分开——"哈利说，但罗恩拼命摇头。

"那真是有病，我们可没多少时间。你们两个去找乌姆里奇，我去修亚克斯利的办公室——可是怎么让它不下雨呢？"

"试试咒立停，"赫敏马上说，"如果是恶咒或咒语造成的下雨，应该会停的。如果停不了，那就是气象咒出了问题，比较麻烦一点，你暂时先用防水防湿咒保护他的东西——"

"再说一遍，慢点儿——"罗恩一边说，一边着急地在口袋里找笔，但这时升降梯震颤着停住了。一个空洞的女声说道："第四层，神奇动物管理控制司，包含野兽、异类和幽灵办公室、妖精联络处和害虫咨询处。"栅栏门再次打开，放进来两个巫师，还有几架淡紫色的纸飞机，绕着升降梯顶部的灯光飞舞。

CHAPTER TWELVE   Magic is Might

'Morning Albert,' said a bushily whiskered man, smiling at Harry. He glanced over at Ron and Hermione as the lift creaked upwards once more; Hermione was now whispering frantic instructions to Ron. The wizard leaned towards Harry, leering, and muttered, 'Dirk Cresswell, eh? From Goblin Liaison? Nice one, Albert. I'm pretty confident I'll get his job, now!'

He winked. Harry smiled back, hoping that this would suffice. The lift stopped; the grilles opened once more.

'Level Two, Department of Magical Law Enforcement, including the Improper Use of Magic Office, Auror Headquarters and Wizengamot Administration Services,' said the disembodied witch's voice.

Harry saw Hermione give Ron a little push and he hurried out of the lift, followed by the other wizards, leaving Harry and Hermione alone. The moment the golden door had closed Hermione said, very fast, 'Actually, Harry, I think I'd better go after him, I don't think he knows what he's doing and if he gets caught the whole thing –'

'Level One, Minister for Magic and Support Staff.'

The golden grilles slid apart again and Hermione gasped. Four people stood before them, two of them deep in conversation: a long-haired wizard wearing magnificent robes of black and gold and a squat, toad-like witch wearing a velvet bow in her short hair and clutching a clipboard to her chest.

第 12 章　魔法即强权

"早上好，艾伯特。"一个大胡子男巫笑着对哈利说，然后瞟了罗恩、赫敏一眼。升降梯又吱嘎上升。赫敏在急急地小声给罗恩支着招，那个男巫凑到哈利跟前，冲着他坏笑，低声道："德克·克莱斯韦，嗯？妖精联络处的？干得好，艾伯特。现在，我很有把握会得到他的职位了！"

他眨眨眼睛，哈利微笑了一下，希望这能让对方满意。升降梯停了下来，栅栏门再次打开。

"第二层，魔法法律执行司，包含禁止滥用魔法办公室、傲罗指挥部和威森加摩管理机构。"那个空洞的女声说。

哈利看到赫敏轻轻推了罗恩一把，罗恩匆忙走出升降梯，另外两个巫师也都下了，升降梯里只剩下哈利和赫敏两个。金色栅栏门一关，赫敏就急促地说，"哈利，我想我最好跟着他去，我看他不知所措，如果他被抓住，整个计划——"

"第一层，魔法部长办公室及后勤处。"

金色栅栏门再次拉开，赫敏倒吸一口凉气。四个人站在他们面前，其中两个正在密切交谈：一个长发男巫身穿黑底绣金的华丽长袍，一个矮矮胖胖、长得像癞蛤蟆的女巫，短发上戴着天鹅绒蝴蝶结，胸前抱着个笔记板。

CHAPTER THIRTEEN

The Muggle-Born Registration Commission

'Ah, Mafalda!' said Umbridge, looking at Hermione. 'Travers sent you, did he?'

'Y – yes,' squeaked Hermione.

'Good, you'll do perfectly well.' Umbridge spoke to the wizard in black and gold. 'That's that problem solved, Minister, if Mafalda can be spared for record-keeping we shall be able to start straight away.' She consulted her clipboard. 'Ten people today and one of them the wife of a Ministry employee! Tut, tut ... even here, in the heart of the Ministry!' She stepped into the lift beside Hermione, as did the two wizards who had been listening to Umbridge's conversation with the Minister. 'We'll go straight down, Mafalda, you'll find everything you need in the courtroom. Good morning, Albert, aren't you getting out?'

'Yes, of course,' said Harry in Runcorn's deep voice.

Harry stepped out of the lift. The golden grilles clanged shut behind him. Glancing over his shoulder, Harry saw Hermione's anxious face sinking back out of sight, a tall wizard on either side of her, Umbridge's velvet hair-bow level with her shoulder.

'What brings you up here, Runcorn?' asked the new Minister for Magic. His long, black hair and beard were streaked with silver, and a great overhanging forehead shadowed his glinting eyes, putting Harry in mind of a crab looking out from beneath a rock.

'Needed a quick word with,' Harry hesitated for a fraction of a second, 'Arthur Weasley. Someone said he was up on Level One.'

'Ah,' said Pius Thicknesse. 'Has he been caught having contact with an Undesirable?'

第 13 章

麻瓜出身登记委员会

"啊,马法尔达!"乌姆里奇看着赫敏说,"是特拉弗斯让你来的吧?"

"是——是的,"赫敏细声说。

"好,你会干好的。"乌姆里奇转向那个穿绣金黑袍的男巫说,"这样一来问题就解决了,部长,既然马法尔达能来做记录,我们现在就可以开始。"她看看笔记板,"今天有十个人,其中一个还是魔法部雇员的妻子!啧,啧……就在这儿,魔法部的内部!"她走进升降梯,站在赫敏旁边,另外两个聆听乌姆里奇和部长对话的巫师也跟了进来。"我们直接下去,马法尔达,你要用的东西法庭里都有。早上好,艾伯特,你不出去吗?"

"出去,当然。"哈利用伦考恩那低沉的声音说。

哈利走出升降梯。金色栅栏门在他身后哐当关上。他回过头,看到赫敏焦虑的面孔又降了下去,一边一个高大的男巫,乌姆里奇的天鹅绒蝴蝶结齐到赫敏的肩膀。

"你来这儿有何贵干,伦考恩?"新任魔法部长问道,他黑色的长发和胡须中夹着缕缕银丝,大脑门的阴影遮着闪烁的双眼,使哈利想到一只螃蟹正从岩石底下往外张望。

"要找,"哈利犹豫了零点几秒,"要找亚瑟·韦斯莱说句话。有人说他在一层。"

"啊,"皮尔斯·辛克尼斯说,"有人撞见他跟不良分子说话吗?"

CHAPTER THIRTEEN   The Muggle-Born Registration Commission

'No,' said Harry, his throat dry. 'No, nothing like that.'

'Ah, well. It's only a matter of time,' said Thicknesse. 'If you ask me, the blood traitors are as bad as the Mudbloods. Good day, Runcorn.'

'Good day, Minister.'

Harry watched Thicknesse march away along the thickly carpeted corridor. The moment the Minister had passed out of sight, Harry tugged the Invisibility Cloak out from under his heavy, black cloak, threw it over himself and set off along the corridor in the opposite direction. Runcorn was so tall that Harry was forced to stoop to make sure his big feet were hidden.

Panic pulsed in the pit of his stomach. As he passed gleaming wooden door after gleaming wooden door, each bearing a small plaque with the owner's name and occupation upon it, the might of the Ministry, its complexity, its impenetrability, seemed to force themselves upon him so that the plan he had been carefully concocting with Ron and Hermione over the past four weeks seemed laughably childish. They had concentrated all their efforts on getting inside without being detected: they had not given a moment's thought to what they would do if they were forced to separate. Now Hermione was stuck in court proceedings, which would undoubtedly last hours: Ron was struggling to do magic that Harry was sure was beyond him, a woman's liberty possibly depending on the outcome, and he, Harry, was wandering around on the top floor when he knew perfectly well that his quarry had just gone down in the lift.

He stopped walking, leaned against a wall and tried to decide what to do. The silence pressed upon him: there was no bustling or talk or swift footsteps here; the purple-carpeted corridors were as hushed as though the *Muffliato* charm had been cast over the place.

Her office must be up here, Harry thought.

It seemed most unlikely that Umbridge would keep her jewellery in her office, but on the other hand it seemed foolish not to search it to make sure. He therefore set off along the corridor again, passing nobody but a frowning wizard who was murmuring instructions to a quill that floated in front of him, scribbling on a trail of parchment.

Now paying attention to the names on the doors, Harry turned a corner. Halfway along the next corridor he emerged into a wide, open space where a dozen witches and wizards sat in rows at small desks not unlike school desks, though much more highly polished and free from graffiti. Harry paused to watch

第13章 麻瓜出身登记委员会

"不,"哈利嗓子发干,"不,不是。"

"啊,哼,那只是时间问题。"辛克尼斯说,"要我说,纯血统的叛徒和泥巴种一样坏。再见,伦考恩。"

"再见,部长。"

哈利目送辛克尼斯在铺着厚地毯的过道里走远。部长刚一消失,哈利就从沉重的黑袍子底下掏出隐形衣,披到身上,朝相反的方向走去。伦考恩个子这么高,哈利不得不弯下身子,确保他的大脚不露出来。

恐惧一阵阵袭上心头,他经过一扇又一扇亮光光的木门,每扇门上都有一块小牌子,写着屋里人的姓名和职务。魔法部的威严、复杂和高深莫测似乎把他给镇住了,使他和罗恩、赫敏四个星期来精心筹划的行动方案显得像可笑的儿戏。他们把全部心思都放在了怎么混进来,却根本没有想过倘若彼此被迫分开怎么办。现在赫敏被困在法庭上,那无疑一拖就是几小时;罗恩在努力尝试一些魔法,而哈利知道它们是超出他能力之外的,但一个女人的自由可能就取决于他的表现;哈利呢,还在顶层游荡,明明知道自己要找的人刚乘升降梯下去了。

他停住脚步,靠在墙上,试图拿定主意该怎么办。寂静压迫着他:这里没有忙碌声、讲话声和匆匆的脚步声,铺着紫红地毯的过道里鸦雀无声,好像被施了闭耳塞听咒一样。

她的办公室一定在这儿,哈利想。

乌姆里奇把珠宝藏在办公室的可能性似乎不大,然而不搜一搜,确定一下,又似乎是愚蠢的。于是他又沿着过道走去,路上只看到一个眉头紧锁的男巫对着一支羽毛笔念念有词地说着什么,那笔悬在他面前的一卷羊皮纸上飞快地写字。

哈利开始注意看门上的名字,转过拐角走了一段后,过道通入一块宽敞的区域。十来个男女巫师坐在一排排小桌子前,那些桌子与课桌相似,只是光滑得多,没有乱涂的痕迹。哈利不由得停下来观看,因

CHAPTER THIRTEEN   The Muggle-Born Registration Commission

them, for the effect was quite mesmerising. They were all waving and twiddling their wands in unison, and squares of coloured paper were flying in every direction like little pink kites. After a few seconds, Harry realised that there was a rhythm to the proceedings, that the papers all formed the same pattern, and after a few more seconds he realised that what he was watching was the creation of pamphlets, that the paper squares were pages, which when assembled, folded and magicked into place, fell into neat stacks beside each witch or wizard.

Harry crept closer, although the workers were so intent on what they were doing that he doubted they would notice a carpet-muffled footstep, and he slid a completed pamphlet from the pile beside a young witch. He examined it beneath the Invisibility Cloak. Its pink cover was emblazoned with a golden title:

MUDBLOODS
and the Dangers They Pose
to a Peaceful Pure-Blood Society

Beneath the title was a picture of a red rose, with a simpering face in the middle of its petals, being strangled by a green weed with fangs and a scowl. There was no author's name upon the pamphlet, but again, the scars on the back of his right hand seemed to tingle as he examined it. Then the young witch beside him confirmed his suspicion as she said, still waving and twirling her wand, 'Will the old hag be interrogating Mudbloods all day, does anyone know?'

'Careful,' said the wizard beside her, glancing around nervously; one of his pages slipped and fell to the floor.

'What, has she got magic ears as well as an eye, now?'

The witch glanced towards the shining mahogany door facing the space full of pamphlet-makers; Harry looked too, and rage reared in him like a snake. Where there might have been a peephole on a Muggle front door, a large, round eye with a bright blue iris had been set into the wood; an eye that was shockingly familiar to anybody who had known Alastor Moody.

For a split second Harry forgot where he was and what he was doing there: he even forgot that he was invisible. He strode straight over to the door to examine the eye. It was not moving: it gazed blindly upwards, frozen. The plaque beneath it read:

为这景象有种催眠的效果。那些巫师动作一致地挥舞和转动魔杖，许多方形彩纸像粉红色的小风筝一样在空中向四面八方飞去。几秒钟后，哈利意识到这是一种有节奏的程序，彩纸的聚散也有一定规律。又过了几秒钟，他意识到自己在观看小册子的制作过程，那些方纸是一页页内容，聚拢折叠，用魔法订牢之后，整齐地摞在每个巫师身边。

哈利轻手轻脚地走近，其实，那些巫师工作得非常专心，他认为他们并不会注意到他因地毯而减弱的脚步声。他从一个年轻女巫身边偷偷取了一份装订好的小册子，拿到隐形衣里来看。粉红色的封面上印着醒目的金字标题：

泥巴种
对祥和的纯血统社会的威胁

下面画着一朵红玫瑰，被一根长着毒牙、一副凶相的绿草紧紧勒住，花瓣中央是一张傻笑的面孔。小册子上没有署名，但哈利右手手背的伤疤在这时又隐隐刺痛起来。这时身旁的女巫证实了他内心的怀疑，她一边挥舞和转动魔杖，一边说道："那老女妖一整天都要在那儿审问泥巴种吗？有谁知道？"

"当心。"她旁边的男巫不安地张望了一下说，他的一张纸滑落到地上。

"怎么，她不光有一只魔眼，现在又有了魔耳不成？"

女巫朝小册子制作者们对面的那扇油亮的红木门瞥了一眼。哈利也向那边看去，一股怒气像毒蛇一样在他胸中蹿起。在麻瓜门上安装门镜的地方，红木中嵌着一只大大的圆眼球，亮蓝色的虹膜，对任何认识阿拉斯托·穆迪的人来说，这个眼球都熟悉得触目惊心。

在那一瞬间，哈利忘记了自己是在哪儿，要来做什么，甚至忘记了他是隐形的。他大步走到门前去看那只眼睛，眼睛不再转动，只是呆滞地望着上方。下面的牌子上写着：

CHAPTER THIRTEEN — The Muggle-Born Registration Commission

Dolores Umbridge
Senior Undersecretary to the Minister

Below that, a slightly shinier new plaque read:

Head of the Muggle-born
Registration Commission

Harry looked back at the dozen pamphlet-makers: though they were intent upon their work, he could hardly suppose that they would not notice if the door of an empty office opened in front of them. He therefore withdrew from an inner pocket an odd object with little waving legs, and a rubber-bulbed horn for a body. Crouching down beneath the Cloak, he placed the Decoy Detonator on the ground.

It scuttled away at once through the legs of the witches and wizards in front of him. A few moments later, during which Harry waited with his hand upon the doorknob, there came a loud bang and a great deal of acrid, black smoke billowed from a corner. The young witch in the front row shrieked: pink pages flew everywhere as she and her fellows jumped up, looking around for the source of the commotion. Harry turned the doorknob, stepped into Umbridge's office and closed the door behind him.

He felt he had stepped back in time. The room was exactly like Umbridge's office at Hogwarts: lace draperies, doilies and dried flowers covered every available surface. The walls bore the same ornamental plates, each featuring a highly coloured, beribboned kitten, gambolling and frisking with sickening cuteness. The desk was covered with a flouncy, flowered cloth. Behind Mad-Eye's eye, a telescopic attachment enabled Umbridge to spy on the workers on the other side of the door. Harry took a look through it and saw that they were all still gathered round the Decoy Detonator. He wrenched the telescope out of the door, leaving a hole behind, pulled the magical eyeball out of it and placed it in his pocket. Then he turned to face the room again, raised his wand and murmured, '*Accio locket.*'

Nothing happened, but he had not expected it to; no doubt Umbridge knew all about protective charms and spells. He therefore hurried behind her desk and began pulling open the drawers. He saw quills and notebooks and

第 13 章 麻瓜出身登记委员会

多洛雷斯·乌姆里奇
魔法部高级副部长

底下还有一块亮一点的新牌子：

麻瓜出身登记委员会
主任

哈利回头看看那十几个做小册子的巫师，尽管他们都在埋头干活，但如果一间空办公室的门在他们面前打开，很难设想会没人注意到。于是他从衣服里面的口袋里掏出一个形状怪异的东西。它长着摆动的小腿，身体是个球形的橡皮喇叭。哈利在隐形衣里蹲下身，把诱饵炸弹搁到地板上。

诱饵炸弹立刻动起来，疾速地在那群巫师的小腿之间穿行。哈利把手扶在门把手上等着，少顷，便听到一声巨响，大量呛鼻的黑烟从一个角落里涌出。前排那个年轻女巫失声尖叫，她和同伴们都跳了起来，四处寻找混乱的来源，粉红色纸页飞得到处都是。哈利趁机转动门把手，踏进了乌姆里奇的办公室，把门在身后关上。

他感觉好像时光倒流了一样，这间屋子与乌姆里奇在霍格沃茨的办公室一模一样：花边帷帘、装饰布垫和干花覆盖了每一处能装饰到的表面，墙上还是那些花盘子，图案都是一只戴着蝴蝶结的色彩鲜艳的大猫，在那里欢跳嬉戏，嗲得令人恶心。桌上盖着一块有荷叶边和花卉装饰的桌布。疯眼汉的眼球后面连着一个望远镜似的装置，使乌姆里奇可以监视门外的员工。哈利凑上去看了一眼，见他们仍围在诱饵炸弹旁边。他把望远镜从门上扯下来，门上留下了一个洞。他拆下魔眼装进兜里，然后转身面向屋内，举起魔杖低声念道："挂坠盒飞来。"

没有动静，但他也没指望会有，乌姆里奇无疑对防护咒十分精通。他急忙走到办公桌后，拉开一个个抽屉，看到羽毛笔、笔记本和魔法

CHAPTER THIRTEEN   The Muggle-Born Registration Commission

Spellotape; enchanted paperclips that coiled snake-like from their drawer and had to be beaten back; a fussy little lace box full of spare hair-bows and clips; but no sign of a locket.

There was a filing cabinet behind the desk: Harry set to searching it. Like Filch's filing cabinets at Hogwarts, it was full of folders, each labelled with a name. It was not until Harry reached the bottommost drawer that he saw something to distract him from his search: Mr Weasley's file.

He pulled it out and opened it.

ARTHUR WEASLEY

Blood Status: **Pure-blood, but with unacceptable pro-Muggle leanings. Known menber of the Order of the Phoenix.**

Family: **Wife (pure-blood), seven children, two yongest at Hogwarts.**
NB: Youngest son currently at home, seriously ill, Ministry inspectors have confirmed.

Security Status: **TRACKED. All movements are being monitored.**

Strong likelihood Undesirable No. 1 will contact (has stayed with Weasley family previously).

'Undesirable Number One,' Harry muttered under his breath as he replaced Mr Weasley's folder and shut the drawer. He had an idea he knew who that was, and sure enough, as he straightened up and glanced around the office for fresh hiding places, he saw a poster of himself on the wall, with the words UNDESIRABLE NO. 1 emblazoned across his chest. A little pink note was stuck to it, with a picture of a kitten in the corner. Harry moved across to read it and saw that Umbridge had written '*To be punished*'.

Angrier than ever, he proceeded to grope in the bottoms of the vases and baskets of dried flowers, but was not at all surprised that the locket was not there. He gave the office one last sweeping look, and his heart skipped a beat. Dumbledore was staring at him from a small, rectangular mirror, propped up on a bookcase beside the desk.

Harry crossed the room at a run and snatched it up, but realised the moment he touched it that it was not a mirror at all. Dumbledore was smiling wistfully out of the front cover of a glossy book. Harry had not

胶带；施有魔法的回形针像蛇一样从抽屉里盘旋钻出，他不得不把它们打回去；还有一个考究的花边小盒子里装满蝴蝶结和发卡；然而就是不见挂坠盒。

桌子后面有个档案柜，哈利过去翻找。它像霍格沃茨管理员费尔奇的那些档案柜一样，装满了文件夹，每个上面都贴有名字。哈利一直搜到最底层抽屉，才看见一样让他分心的东西：韦斯莱先生的档案。

他把它抽出来打开。

亚瑟·韦斯莱

血统：纯血统，但有不可容忍的亲麻瓜倾向。
已知凤凰社成员。
家庭：妻子（纯血统）、七个子女，最小的两个尚在霍格沃茨。
注：小儿子目前重病在家，已由魔法部检查员证实。
安全状况：**跟踪**。一切行动受到监视。

头号不良分子很可能与其联络（曾在韦斯莱家居住）。

"头号不良分子。"哈利轻声嘀咕道，把韦斯莱先生的档案放回去，关上了抽屉。他心里知道指的是谁，果然，当他直起身，搜寻屋内还有什么藏东西的地方时，看到墙上有一幅自己的大肖像，胸口印着**头号不良分子**几个大字。画上还贴了张一角画着小猫的粉红色小笺。哈利走过去看，发现乌姆里奇在上面写了将受处罚几个字。

他更加怒火中烧，在装着干花的花瓶和篮子底部摸索，但没有摸到挂坠盒，他也并不感到意外。他最后扫视了一下这间办公室，突然心脏停跳了一下：桌边的书架上，邓布利多正从一面长方形的小镜子里望着他。

哈利冲过去抓起它，但刚一摸到就发现那不是镜子，邓布利多是在一本书的光亮封皮上沉思微笑。哈利一时没有注意到他帽子上的绿色花体字：阿不思·邓布利多的生平和谎言，也没看到他胸前还有更

CHAPTER THIRTEEN   The Muggle-Born Registration Commission

immediately noticed the curly, green writing across his hat: *The Life and Lies of Albus Dumbledore*, nor the slightly smaller writing across his chest: *by Rita Skeeter, bestselling author of* Armando Dippet: Master or Moron?

Harry opened the book at random and saw a full-page photograph of two teenage boys, both laughing immoderately with their arms around each other's shoulders. Dumbledore, now with elbow-length hair, had grown a tiny, wispy beard that recalled the one on Krum's chin that had so annoyed Ron. The boy who roared in silent amusement beside Dumbledore had a gleeful, wild look about him. His golden hair fell in curls to his shoulders. Harry wondered whether it was a young Doge, but before he could check the caption, the door of the office opened.

If Thicknesse had not been looking over his shoulder as he entered, Harry would not have had time to pull the Invisibility Cloak over himself. As it was, he thought Thicknesse might have caught a glimpse of movement, because for a moment or two he remained quite still, staring curiously at the place where Harry had just vanished. Perhaps deciding that all he had seen was Dumbledore scratching his nose on the front of the book, for Harry had hastily replaced it upon the shelf, Thicknesse finally walked to the desk and pointed his wand at the quill standing ready in the ink pot. It sprang out and began scribbling a note to Umbridge. Very slowly, hardly daring to breathe, Harry backed out of the office into the open area beyond.

The pamphlet-makers were still clustered round the remains of the Decoy Detonator, which continued to hoot feebly as it smoked. Harry hurried off up the corridor as the young witch said, 'I bet it sneaked up here from Experimental Charms, they're so careless, remember that poisonous duck?'

Speeding back towards the lifts, Harry reviewed his options. It had never been likely that the locket was here at the Ministry, and there was no hope of bewitching its whereabouts out of Umbridge while she was sitting in a crowded court. Their priority now had to be to leave the Ministry before they were exposed, and try again another day. The first thing to do was to find Ron, and then they could work out a way of extracting Hermione from the courtroom.

The lift was empty when it arrived. Harry jumped in and pulled off the Invisibility Cloak as it started its descent. To his enormous relief, when it rattled to a halt at Level Two a soaking wet and wild-eyed Ron got in.

'M – morning,' he stammered to Harry, as the lift set off again.

第13章　麻瓜出身登记委员会

小的字：出自丽塔·斯基特，畅销书《阿芒多·迪佩特：大师还是白痴？》的作者。

哈利随手把书翻开，看到一页照片，是两个十来岁的男孩，互相搭着肩膀，放肆地大笑。邓布利多头发已长及胳膊肘，还多了一绺淡淡的小胡子，让人想到克鲁姆下巴上让罗恩那么讨厌的细须。在邓布利多旁边无声大笑的那个少年给人一种快乐狂放的感觉，金色的鬈发垂到肩头。哈利猜想他是不是年轻时的多吉，但还没来得及看说明，办公室的门开了。

要不是辛克尼斯进来时扭头望了望外面，哈利都没有时间披上隐形衣。但是，他想辛克尼斯可能还是瞥见了一点动静，因为他有那么一会儿站着一动不动，惊奇地盯着哈利刚刚消失的地方。辛克尼斯或许断定刚才看到的是邓布利多在封面上挠鼻子（哈利已经匆忙把书放回了架子上），他终于走到桌前，用魔杖指着插在墨水瓶里的羽毛笔，它立刻跳出来，开始给乌姆里奇写一张便条。哈利屏住呼吸，慢慢退出办公室，回到那块宽敞的区域。

做小册子的巫师们还围在诱饵炸弹的残骸旁。它冒着烟，仍在微弱地呜呜叫着。哈利快步走入过道，听到年轻女巫说："我猜准是从实验咒语委员会爬过来的，他们那么粗心，还记得那只毒鸭子吗？"

哈利一边匆匆朝升降梯走去，一边考虑自己的选择。本来挂坠盒在魔法部的可能性就不大，而乌姆里奇坐在围满了人的法庭上，用魔法从她那里找到挂坠盒的下落也不会有什么希望。当务之急是在暴露之前撤出魔法部，改天再试。首先要找到罗恩，然后一起想办法把赫敏从法庭里弄出来。

升降梯来了，里面没人。哈利跳进去，在开始下降时扯下了隐形衣。令他万分庆幸的是，升降梯在二层吱嘎停下时，浑身湿透、两眼发直的罗恩跨了进来。

"早——早上好。"他结结巴巴地说，升降梯又开动了。

CHAPTER THIRTEEN The Muggle-Born Registration Commission

'Ron, it's me, Harry!'

'Harry! Blimey, I forgot what you looked like – why isn't Hermione with you?'

'She had to go down to the courtrooms with Umbridge, she couldn't refuse, and –'

But before Harry could finish the lift had stopped again: the doors opened and Mr Weasley walked inside, talking to an elderly witch whose blonde hair was teased so high it resembled an anthill.

'... I quite understand what you're saying, Wakanda, but I'm afraid I cannot be party to –'

Mr Weasley broke off; he had noticed Harry. It was very strange to have Mr Weasley glare at him with that much dislike. The lift doors closed and the four of them trundled downwards once more.

'Oh, hello, Reg,' said Mr Weasley, looking round at the sound of steady dripping from Ron's robes. 'Isn't your wife in for questioning today? Er – what's happened to you? Why are you so wet?'

'Yaxley's office is raining,' said Ron. He addressed Mr Weasley's shoulder, and Harry felt sure he was scared that his father might recognise him if they looked directly into each other's eyes. 'I couldn't stop it, so they've sent me to get Bernie – Pillsworth, I think they said –'

'Yes, a lot of offices have been raining lately,' said Mr Weasley. 'Did you try *meteolojinx recanto*? It worked for Bletchley.'

'*Meteolojinx recanto*?' whispered Ron. 'No, I didn't. Thanks, D– I mean, thanks, Arthur.'

The lift doors opened; the old witch with the anthill hair left and Ron darted past her out of sight. Harry made to follow him, but found his path blocked as Percy Weasley strode into the lift, his nose buried in some papers he was reading.

Not until the doors had clanged shut again did Percy realise he was in a lift with his father. He glanced up, saw Mr Weasley, turned radish red, and left the lift the moment the doors opened again. For the second time, Harry tried to get out, but this time found his way blocked by Mr Weasley's arm.

'One moment, Runcorn.'

The lift doors closed and as they clanked down another floor, Mr Weasley said, 'I hear you laid information about Dirk Cresswell.'

Harry had the impression that Mr Weasley's anger was no less because of

"罗恩，是我，哈利！"

"哈利！我的天哪，我忘了你长什么样了——赫敏怎么不在？"

"她跟乌姆里奇到楼下法庭去了，没法拒绝，而且——"

哈利还没说完，升降梯又停住了。门一开，韦斯莱先生走了进来，一边还在跟一个老女巫说话，她那金色的发髻高得像蚁丘。

"……我很理解你说的情况，瓦坎达，可是我恐怕不能参与——"

韦斯莱先生突然打住，因为他看到了哈利。被韦斯莱先生那样厌恶地瞪着，真是一种非常陌生的感受。升降梯的门关上了，四个人又呼噜噜地降下去。

"哦，你好，雷吉，"韦斯莱先生听到罗恩袍子不断滴水的声音，回过头来说，"你太太今天不是要出庭吗？我说——你怎么啦？身上这么湿？"

"亚克斯利的办公室在下雨，"罗恩对着韦斯莱先生的肩头说，哈利想他准是害怕如果目光相对，父亲会认出他来，"我止不住，他们让我去找伯尼——皮尔思沃斯，我想他们说——"

"是啊，最近好多办公室都在下雨，"韦斯莱先生说，"你试过云咒撤回吗？布莱奇用了挺灵的。"

"云咒撤回？"罗恩低声说，"没试过，谢谢，老——我是说，谢谢，亚瑟。"

门开了，顶着蚁丘的老女巫走出升降梯，罗恩从她旁边冲过去跑没影了，哈利想跟上他，却被挡住了去路，珀西·韦斯莱跨进升降梯，鼻子都快埋进他正在读的文件里了。

门哐当关上了，珀西才意识到他跟父亲乘了同一部升降梯。他抬起眼睛，看到韦斯莱先生，脸涨成了红萝卜，升降梯门一开就出去了。哈利又想下去，这次却被韦斯莱先生的胳膊挡住了去路。

"等一等，伦考恩。"

升降梯门关了，叮叮当当又下了一层，韦斯莱先生说："我听说你揭发了德克·克雷斯韦。"

哈利感觉韦斯莱先生的怒气因为碰到珀西而有增无减，他决定最

CHAPTER THIRTEEN The Muggle-Born Registration Commission

the brush with Percy. He decided his best chance was to act stupid.

'Sorry?' he said.

'Don't pretend, Runcorn,' said Mr Weasley fiercely. 'You tracked down the wizard who faked his family tree, didn't you?'

'I – so what if I did?' said Harry.

'So, Dirk Cresswell is ten times the wizard you are,' said Mr Weasley quietly, as the lift sank ever lower. 'And if he survives Azkaban, you'll have to answer to him, not to mention his wife, his sons and his friends –'

'Arthur,' Harry interrupted, 'you know you're being tracked, don't you?'

'Is that a threat, Runcorn?' said Mr Weasley loudly.

'No,' said Harry, 'it's a fact! They're watching your every move –'

The lift doors opened. They had reached the Atrium. Mr Weasley gave Harry a scathing look and swept from the lift. Harry stood there, shaken. He wished he was impersonating somebody other than Runcorn ... the lift doors clanged shut.

Harry pulled out the Invisibility Cloak and put it back on. He would try to extricate Hermione on his own while Ron was dealing with the raining office. When the doors opened, he stepped out into a torchlit stone passageway quite different from the wood-panelled and carpeted corridors above. As the lift rattled away again, Harry shivered slightly, looking towards the distant black door that marked the entrance to the Department of Mysteries.

He set off, his destination not the black door, but the doorway he remembered on the left-hand side, which opened on to the flight of stairs down to the court chambers. His mind grappled with possibilities as he crept down them: he still had a couple of Decoy Detonators, but perhaps it would be better to simply knock on the courtroom door, enter as Runcorn and ask for a quick word with Mafalda? Of course, he did not know whether Runcorn was sufficiently important to get away with this, and even if he managed it, Hermione's non-reappearance might trigger a search before they were clear of the Ministry ...

Lost in thought, he did not immediately register the unnatural chill that was creeping over him as if he were descending into fog. It was becoming colder and colder with every step he took: a cold that reached right down into his throat and tore at his lungs. And then he felt that stealing sense of despair, of hopelessness, filling him, expanding inside him ...

第13章 麻瓜出身登记委员会

安全的办法是装傻。

"您说什么?"他说。

"别装了,伦考恩,"韦斯莱先生愤然道,"你追捕了那个假造家谱的巫师,是不是?"

"我——是又怎么样?"哈利说。

"怎么样?德克·克雷斯韦作为巫师比你强十倍!"韦斯莱先生低声说,升降梯还在下降,"如果他能从阿兹卡班出来,会找你算账的,更别说他的妻儿和朋友——"

"亚瑟,"哈利打断了他,"你知不知道,你正在被跟踪?"

"这是威胁吗,伦考恩?"韦斯莱先生大声说。

"不,"哈利说,"这是事实!他们在监视你的每个行动——"

升降梯门开了,他们已经到了大厅。韦斯莱先生严厉地瞪了哈利一眼,拂袖而去。哈利呆立在原地,希望自己冒充的不是伦考恩……升降梯的门哐当关上了。

哈利掏出隐形衣重新披上,罗恩还在对付下雨的办公室,他得一个人想办法去把赫敏解救出来。升降梯的门打开后,他踏入了一条点着火把的石廊,与上层铺着地毯的镶着木板壁的过道截然不同。升降梯当啷当啷开走了,哈利微微打了个寒战,望着远处那扇标着神秘事务司入口的黑门。

他往前走去,目标不是黑门,而是他记忆中左侧的那个门口。那里有段楼梯通向下面的法庭。悄悄下楼时,他脑子里想象着各种可能:他还有两个诱饵炸弹,但也许不如直接敲门,以伦考恩的身份进去要求跟马法尔达说句话?当然,他不知道伦考恩是否有这么大的权力,即使能行,赫敏一直不回去也可能引起搜查,而他们还没来得及撤离魔法部……

想着心事,他没有立刻注意到一股异常的寒气悄悄袭来,使他好像坠入雾中那样,每一步都更冷一分。那寒气灌入他的喉咙,冰彻心肺。他感觉到那种绝望无助侵上心头,蔓延到全身……

CHAPTER THIRTEEN   The Muggle-Born Registration Commission

Dementors, he thought.

And as he reached the foot of the stairs and turned to his right, he saw a dreadful scene. The dark passage outside the courtrooms was packed with tall, black hooded figures, their faces completely hidden, their ragged breathing the only sound in the place. The petrified Muggle-borns brought in for questioning sat huddled and shivering on hard wooden benches. Most of them were hiding their faces in their hands, perhaps in an instinctive attempt to shield themselves from the Dementors' greedy mouths. Some were accompanied by families, others sat alone. The Dementors were gliding up and down in front of them, and the cold, and the hopelessness, and the despair of the place laid themselves upon Harry like a curse ...

Fight it, he told himself, but he knew that he could not conjure a Patronus here without revealing himself instantly. So he moved forwards, as silently as he could, and with every step he took numbness seemed to steal over his brain, but he forced himself to think of Hermione and of Ron, who needed him.

Moving through the towering, black figures was terrifying: the eyeless faces hidden beneath their hoods turned as he passed, and he felt sure that they sensed him, sensed, perhaps, a human presence that still had some hope, some resilience ...

And then, abruptly and shockingly amid the frozen silence, one of the dungeon doors on the left of the corridor was flung open and screams echoed out of it.

'No, no, I'm half-blood, I'm half-blood, I tell you! My father was a wizard, he *was*, look him up, Arkie Alderton, he's a well-known broomstick designer, look him up, I tell you – get your hands off me, get your hands off –'

'This is your final warning,' said Umbridge's soft voice, magically magnified so that it sounded clearly over the man's desperate screams. 'If you struggle, you will be subjected to the Dementor's kiss.'

The man's screams subsided, but dry sobs echoed through the corridor.

'Take him away,' said Umbridge.

Two Dementors appeared in the doorway of the courtroom, their rotting, scabbed hands clutching the upper arms of a wizard who appeared to be fainting. They glided away down the corridor with him and the darkness they trailed behind them swallowed him from sight.

'Next – Mary Cattermole,' called Umbridge.

摄魂怪,他想。

到了楼梯底部,向右一转,眼前是一幕恐怖的景象。法庭门外的昏暗走廊上,立满了戴着兜帽的高高黑影,面孔完全被遮住了,刺耳的呼吸声是那里唯一的声音。那些被传来出庭的麻瓜出身的巫师恐惧地挤在一堆,在硬木板凳上瑟瑟发抖。大多数人用手捂着脸,也许是本能地想挡开摄魂怪贪婪的大嘴。一些人有家人陪伴,另一些人独自坐着。摄魂怪在他们面前飘来飘去,那寒气,那无助和绝望,如魔咒一般向哈利逼来……

抵抗,他对自己说,但是他知道如果在这里召出守护神,肯定会立刻暴露自己。于是他尽可能悄无声息地往前走去,每走一步,脑子里的麻木便增加一分,但他强迫自己想着赫敏和罗恩,他们需要他。

在那些高大的黑影间穿行极其恐怖:当他走过时,一张张没有眼睛的面孔在兜帽下转过来,他确信它们能感觉到他,或许能感觉到一个人的躯体内仍然存有的一些希望,一些活力……

突然,在冰冻般的沉寂中,过道左边一间法庭的门开了,传出带着回音的高喊。

"不,不,我跟你说过我是混血,我是混血。我父亲是巫师,他是巫师,你们去查,阿基·阿尔德顿,他是出名的飞天扫帚设计师,你们去查呀。我告诉你——别碰我,别碰——"

"这是最后一次警告,"乌姆里奇软声软气地说,声音经过魔法放大,清楚地盖过了那男人绝望的叫喊,"你要是再抵抗,就会得到摄魂怪的亲吻。"

那男人的叫声低了下去,但抽噎声还在过道里回响。

"把他带走。"乌姆里奇说。

两个摄魂怪出现在法庭门口,腐烂结痂的大手抓着一个男巫的上臂,他似乎晕过去了。摄魂怪拖着他在过道里飘远,它们身后的黑暗将他吞没。

"下一个——玛丽·卡特莫尔。"乌姆里奇叫道。

CHAPTER THIRTEEN The Muggle-Born Registration Commission

A small woman stood up; she was trembling from head to foot. Her dark hair was smoothed back into a bun and she wore long, plain robes. Her face was completely bloodless. As she passed the Dementors, Harry saw her shudder.

He did it instinctively, without any sort of plan, because he hated the sight of her walking alone into the dungeon: as the door began to swing closed, he slipped into the courtroom behind her.

It was not the same room in which he had once been interrogated for improper use of magic. This one was much smaller, though the ceiling was quite as high; it gave the claustrophobic sense of being stuck at the bottom of a deep well.

There were more Dementors in here, casting their freezing aura over the place; they stood like faceless sentinels in the corners furthest from the high, raised platform. Here, behind a balustrade, sat Umbridge, with Yaxley on one side of her, and Hermione, quite as white-faced as Mrs Cattermole, on the other. At the foot of the platform a bright silver, long-haired cat prowled up and down, up and down, and Harry realised that it was there to protect the prosecutors from the despair that emanated from the Dementors: that was for the accused to feel, not the accusers.

'Sit down,' said Umbridge in her soft, silky voice.

Mrs Cattermole stumbled to the single seat in the middle of the floor beneath the raised platform. The moment she had sat down, chains clinked out of the arms of the chair and bound her there.

'You are Mary Elizabeth Cattermole?' asked Umbridge.

Mrs Cattermole gave a single, shaky nod.

'Married to Reginald Cattermole of the Magical Maintenance Department?'

Mrs Cattermole burst into tears.

'I don't know where he is, he was supposed to meet me here!'

Umbridge ignored her.

'Mother to Maisie, Ellie and Alfred Cattermole?'

Mrs Cattermole sobbed harder than ever.

'They're frightened, they think I might not come home –'

'Spare us,' spat Yaxley. 'The brats of Mudbloods do not stir our sympathies.'

Mrs Cattermole's sobs masked Harry's footsteps as he made his way carefully towards the steps that led up to the raised platform. The moment he had passed the place where the Patronus cat patrolled he felt the change in

第13章 麻瓜出身登记委员会

一个瘦小的女人浑身发抖着站了起来。她身穿朴素的长袍,黑发在脑后梳成一个圆髻,脸上全无血色。当这女人经过摄魂怪旁边时,哈利看到她哆嗦了一下。

他完全出于冲动,没有任何计划,只是不忍看到她一个人走进法庭:门开始关上时,他跟在她后面溜了进去。

这不是上次以滥用魔法为由审讯他的那个法庭,虽然天花板一样高,但比那间屋子小得多,有一种被困在深井底部那样的恐怖感。

这里有更多的摄魂怪,寒气笼罩了整个房间。它们像没有面孔的哨兵,站在离高高的审讯台最远的角落里。台上栏杆后面坐着乌姆里奇,她的一边是亚克斯利,另一边是脸色像卡特莫尔太太一样苍白的赫敏。一只银亮的长毛大猫在高台底部踱来踱去,哈利意识到它是在那里保护起诉人的,不让他们感受到摄魂怪所散发出来的绝望。绝望是让被告而不是让审讯者感受的。

"坐下。"乌姆里奇用她那甜腻的声音说。

卡特莫尔太太蹒跚地走到台下中央那把孤零零的椅子旁。她刚坐下,扶手便叮叮当当甩出锁链把她固定在那儿。

"你是玛丽·伊丽莎白·卡特莫尔?"乌姆里奇问。

卡特莫尔太太颤巍巍地点了一下头。

"魔法维修保养处雷吉纳尔德·卡特莫尔的妻子?"

卡特莫尔太太哭了起来。

"我不知道他在哪儿,他本来应该在这儿陪我的!"

乌姆里奇不予理睬。

"梅齐、埃莉和阿尔弗雷德·卡特莫尔的母亲?"

卡特莫尔太太哭得更厉害了。

"他们很害怕,担心我可能回不去了——"

"行了,"亚克斯利轻蔑地说,"泥巴种的崽子引不起我们的同情。"

卡特莫尔太太的抽泣掩盖了哈利的脚步声,他小心地朝通向高台的台阶走去。经过银猫守护神走动的地方时,他马上感到了温度的变化:这里温暖而舒适。他敢肯定这守护神是乌姆里奇的,它如此

CHAPTER THIRTEEN The Muggle-Born Registration Commission

temperature: it was warm and comfortable here. The Patronus, he was sure, was Umbridge's, and it glowed brightly because she was so happy here, in her element, upholding the twisted laws she had helped to write. Slowly and very carefully, he edged his way along the platform behind Umbridge, Yaxley and Hermione, taking a seat behind the latter. He was worried about making Hermione jump. He thought of casting the *Muffliato* charm upon Umbridge and Yaxley, but even murmuring the word might cause Hermione alarm. Then Umbridge raised her voice to address Mrs Cattermole, and Harry seized his chance.

'I'm behind you,' he whispered into Hermione's ear.

As he had expected, she jumped so violently she nearly overturned the bottle of ink with which she was supposed to be recording the interview, but both Umbridge and Yaxley were concentrating upon Mrs Cattermole, and this went unnoticed.

'A wand was taken from you upon your arrival at the Ministry today, Mrs Cattermole,' Umbridge was saying. 'Eight and three-quarter inches, cherry, unicorn hair core. Do you recognise that description?'

Mrs Cattermole nodded, mopping her eyes on her sleeve.

'Could you please tell us from which witch or wizard you took that wand?'

'T – took?' sobbed Mrs Cattermole. 'I didn't t – take it from anybody. I b – bought it when I was eleven years old. It – it – it – *chose* me.'

She cried harder than ever.

Umbridge laughed a soft, girlish laugh that made Harry want to attack her. She leaned forwards over the barrier, the better to observe her victim, and something gold swung forwards too, and dangled over the void: the locket.

Hermione had seen it, she let out a little squeak, but Umbridge and Yaxley, still intent upon their prey, were deaf to everything else.

'No,' said Umbridge, 'no, I don't think so, Mrs Cattermole. Wands only choose witches or wizards. You are not a witch. I have your responses to the questionnaire that was sent to you here – Mafalda, pass them to me.'

Umbridge held out a small hand: she looked so toad-like at that moment that Harry was quite surprised not to see webs between the stubby fingers. Hermione's hands were shaking with shock. She fumbled in a pile of documents balanced on the chair beside her, finally withdrawing a wad of parchment with Mrs Cattermole's name on it.

第13章 麻瓜出身登记委员会

明亮,是因为乌姆里奇在这儿很开心,得其所哉,维护着她参与制定的被扭曲的法律。哈利一点一点地、小心翼翼地在乌姆里奇、亚克斯利和赫敏的后面移动,最后在赫敏身后坐了下来。他担心把赫敏吓一跳,本来想对乌姆里奇和亚克斯利施闭耳塞听咒,但轻声念咒也有可能吓着赫敏。这时乌姆里奇提高嗓门对卡特莫尔太太说话了,哈利抓住了机会。

"我在你后面。"他对赫敏耳语道。

果然不出所料,赫敏猛地一怔,差点打翻了做记录用的墨水瓶。但乌姆里奇和亚克斯利的注意力都在卡特莫尔太太身上,没有察觉。

"你今天到魔法部时,被收走了一根魔杖,卡特莫尔太太,"乌姆里奇说,"八又四分之三英寸,樱桃木,独角兽毛做的杖芯。你确认这一描述吗?"

卡特莫尔太太点点头,用袖子擦着眼睛。

"能否告诉我们,你是从哪位巫师手里夺取这根魔杖的?"

"夺——夺取?"卡特莫尔太太哭泣道,"我没有从谁那里夺——夺取。它是我十一岁的时候买——买的,它——它——它选择了我。"

她哭得更凶了。

乌姆里奇发出一声小姑娘似的娇笑,哈利真想把她痛揍一顿。她身子前倾,为了越过障碍更好地审视她的猎物,一个金色的东西也随之荡到胸前,悬在那里:挂坠盒。

赫敏看见了,轻轻尖叫一声,但乌姆里奇和亚克斯利仍然一心盯着猎物,听不见别的声音。

"不,"乌姆里奇说,"不,我不这么认为,卡特莫尔太太。魔杖只选择巫师,而你不是巫师。我这里有上次发给你的问卷调查表——马法尔达,拿过来。"

乌姆里奇伸出一只小手,她看上去那么像癞蛤蟆,哈利一时很惊讶那短粗的手指之间怎么没有蹼。赫敏的手因为震惊而发抖,她在身边椅子上的一堆文件中摸索了一阵,终于抽出了一卷有卡特莫尔太太名字的羊皮纸。

CHAPTER THIRTEEN The Muggle-Born Registration Commission

'That's – that's pretty, Dolores,' she said, pointing at the pendant gleaming in the ruffled folds of Umbridge's blouse.

'What?' snapped Umbridge, glancing down. 'Oh yes – an old family heirloom,' she said, patting the locket lying on her large bosom. 'The "S" stands for Selwyn ... I am related to the Selwyns ... indeed, there are few pure-blood families to whom I am not related ... a pity,' she continued, in a louder voice, flicking through Mrs Cattermole's questionnaire, 'that the same cannot be said for you. Parents' professions: greengrocers.'

Yaxley laughed jeeringly. Below, the fluffy silver cat patrolled up and down, and the Dementors stood waiting in the corners.

It was Umbridge's lie that brought the blood surging into Harry's brain and obliterated his sense of caution; that the locket she had taken as a bribe from a petty criminal was being used to bolster her own pure-blood credentials. He raised his wand, not even troubling to keep it concealed beneath the Invisibility Cloak, and said, '*Stupefy!*'

There was a flash of red light; Umbridge crumpled and her forehead hit the edge of the balustrade: Mrs Cattermole's papers slid off her lap on to the floor and, down below, the prowling silver cat vanished. Ice-cold air hit them like an oncoming wind: Yaxley, confused, looked around for the source of the trouble and saw Harry's disembodied hand and wand pointing at him. He tried to draw his own wand, but too late.

'*Stupefy!*'

Yaxley slid to the ground to lie curled on the floor.

'Harry!'

'Hermione, if you think I was going to sit here and let her pretend –'

'Harry, Mrs Cattermole!'

Harry whirled round, throwing off the Invisibility Cloak; down below, the Dementors had moved out of their corners; they were gliding towards the woman chained to the chair: whether because the Patronus had vanished or because they sensed that their masters were no longer in control, they seemed to have abandoned restraint. Mrs Cattermole let out a terrible scream of fear as a slimy, scabbed hand grasped her chin and forced her face back.

'*EXPECTO PATRONUM!*'

The silver stag soared from the tip of Harry's wand and leapt towards the Dementors, which fell back and melted into the dark shadows again. The

"那个——那个很漂亮，多洛雷斯。"她指着乌姆里奇上衣褶裥里的那个闪闪发光的坠子。

"什么？"乌姆里奇厉声说，低头看了一眼，"哦，是啊——一件古老的传家宝。"她拍拍贴在她那丰满胸脯上的挂坠盒说，"'S'是塞尔温的缩写……我与塞尔温家族有亲戚关系……实际上，很少有纯血统的家庭跟我没有亲戚关系……可惜，"她翻着卡特莫尔太太的问卷调查表，提高了嗓门说，"你就不能这样说了。父母职业：蔬菜商。"

亚克斯利不屑地大笑。台下，毛茸茸的银猫踱来踱去，摄魂怪立在屋角等候。

乌姆里奇的谎言使哈利血液直冲头顶，忘却了谨慎。她从一个不法小贩那里受贿得来的挂坠盒，现在却拿来证明自己的纯血统身份。哈利甚至没有考虑要继续藏在隐形衣下面，他举起魔杖，喝道："昏昏倒地！"

红光一闪，乌姆里奇倒了下去，脑袋撞到栏杆边沿，卡特莫尔太太的文件从她腿上滑到了地上，那只来回走动的银猫消失了，冰冷的空气像风一样袭来。亚克斯利莫名其妙，扭头寻找骚乱的来源。他看见一只没有身子的手正拿魔杖指着他，赶紧去拔自己的魔杖，但为时已晚。

"昏昏倒地！"

亚克斯利滑到地上，蜷成一团。

"哈利！"

"赫敏，如果你觉得我会坐在这里看着她假装——"

"哈利，卡特莫尔太太！"

哈利急忙转过身，甩掉了隐形衣。台下，摄魂怪已经从角落里出来，正朝捆在椅子上的女人飘去。不知是因为守护神消失，还是因为感觉到主人已经对场面失去控制，它们似乎变得肆无忌惮。卡特莫尔太太恐怖地尖叫起来，一只黏糊糊的、结痂的大手捏住了她的下巴，把她的脸向后扳去。

"呼神护卫！"

银色的牡鹿从哈利的杖尖升起，向摄魂怪跃去，它们纷纷后退，又融进了黑影之中。银鹿在屋里一圈圈地慢跑，它的光芒比那只猫更强、

stag's light, more powerful and more warming than the cat's protection, filled the whole dungeon as it cantered round and round the room.

'Get the Horcrux,' Harry told Hermione.

He ran back down the steps, stuffing the Invisibility Cloak back into his bag, and approached Mrs Cattermole.

'You?' she whispered, gazing into his face. 'But – but Reg said you were the one who submitted my name for questioning!'

'Did I?' muttered Harry, tugging at the chains binding her arms. 'Well, I've had a change of heart. *Diffindo!* ' Nothing happened. 'Hermione, how do I get rid of these chains?'

'Wait, I'm trying something up here –'

'Hermione, we're surrounded by Dementors!'

'I know that, Harry, but if she wakes up and the locket's gone – I need to duplicate it ... *Geminio!* There ... that should fool her ...'

Hermione came running downstairs.

'Let's see ... *Relashio!* '

The chains clinked and withdrew into the arms of the chair. Mrs Cattermole looked just as frightened as ever before.

'I don't understand,' she whispered.

'You're going to leave here with us,' said Harry, pulling her to her feet. 'Go home, grab your children and get out, get out of the country if you've got to. Disguise yourselves and run. You've seen how it is, you won't get anything like a fair hearing here.'

'Harry,' said Hermione, 'how are we going to get out of here with all those Dementors outside the door?'

'Patronuses,' said Harry, pointing his wand at his own: the stag slowed and walked, still gleaming brightly, towards the door. 'As many as we can muster; do yours, Hermione.'

'*Expec – expecto patronum*,' said Hermione. Nothing happened.

'It's the only spell she ever has trouble with,' Harry told a completely bemused Mrs Cattermole. 'Bit unfortunate, really ... come on, Hermione ...'

'*Expecto patronum!* '

A silver otter burst from the end of Hermione's wand and swam gracefully through the air to join the stag.

更温暖，充满了整个法庭。

"拿上魂器。"哈利对赫敏说。

他一边把隐形衣塞进包里，一边跑下台阶，来到了卡特莫尔太太身边。

"你？"卡特莫尔太太望着他的脸，低声说，"可是——可是雷吉说是你把我的名字报上去审查的！"

"是吗？"哈利嘟囔道，一边扯动她手臂上的锁链，"哦，我改主意了。四分五裂！"没有反应。"赫敏，怎么去掉这些锁链？"

"等等，我正在做一件事——"

"赫敏，我们周围都是摄魂怪！"

"我知道，哈利，可是如果她醒来发现挂坠盒没了——我必须复制一个……复制成双！好了……这样她应该看不出来了……"

赫敏冲下台阶。

"我看看……力松劲泄！"

锁链叮叮当当缩进了椅子扶手里。卡特莫尔太太看上去还是非常害怕。

"我不明白。"她喃喃道。

"你得跟我们离开这儿，"哈利说着把她拉了起来，"回家带上你的孩子们逃走吧，实在不行就逃出国去，化了装逃。你看到了现在是什么情况，你在这儿是得不到公道的。"

"哈利，"赫敏说，"门口那么多摄魂怪，我们怎么出去？"

"守护神。"哈利说，用魔杖指着自己的守护神：银色的牡鹿放慢脚步，依然明亮地闪耀着，向门口走去，"越多越好，把你的也召出来，赫敏。"

"呼神——呼神护卫。"赫敏说，什么也没出现。

"这是唯一对她有点困难的魔咒，"哈利对完全惊呆了的卡特莫尔太太说，"有点不幸……加油，赫敏……"

"呼神护卫！"

一只银色水獭从赫敏的魔杖尖里跳了出来，在空中优雅地游向银色的牡鹿。

CHAPTER THIRTEEN   The Muggle-Born Registration Commission

'C'mon,' said Harry, and he led Hermione and Mrs Cattermole to the door.

When the Patronuses glided out of the dungeon, there were cries of shock from the people waiting outside. Harry looked around; the Dementors were falling back on both sides of them, melding into the darkness, scattering before the silver creatures.

'It's been decided that you should all go home and go into hiding with your families,' Harry told the waiting Muggle-borns, who were dazzled by the light of the Patronuses, and still cowering slightly. 'Go abroad if you can. Just get well away from the Ministry. That's the – er – new official position. Now, if you'll just follow the Patronuses, you'll be able to leave from the Atrium.'

They managed to get up the stone steps without being intercepted, but as they approached the lifts Harry started to have misgivings. If they emerged into the Atrium with a silver stag, an otter soaring alongside it, and twenty or so people, half of them accused Muggle-borns, he could not help feeling that they would attract unwanted attention. He had just reached this unwelcome conclusion when the lift clanged to a halt in front of them.

'Reg!' screamed Mrs Cattermole, and she threw herself into Ron's arms. 'Runcorn let me out, he attacked Umbridge and Yaxley, and he's told all of us to leave the country, I think we'd better do it, Reg, I really do. Let's hurry home and fetch the children and – why are you so wet?'

'Water,' muttered Ron, disengaging himself. 'Harry, they know there are intruders inside the Ministry, something about a hole in Umbridge's office door, I reckon we've got five minutes if that –'

Hermione's Patronus vanished with a *pop* as she turned a horror-struck face to Harry.

'Harry, if we're trapped here –!'

'We won't be if we move fast,' said Harry. He addressed the silent group behind them, who were all gawping at him.

'Who's got wands?'

About half of them raised their hands.

'OK, all of you who haven't got wands need to attach yourself to somebody who has. We'll need to be fast – before they stop us. Come on.'

They managed to cram themselves into two lifts. Harry's Patronus stood sentinel before the golden grilles as they shut and the lifts began to rise.

"走。"哈利领着赫敏和卡特莫尔太太朝门口走去。

守护神飘出法庭时,等在外面的人群发出惊叫。哈利四下扫了一眼,两边的摄魂怪都在向后退却,融入黑暗中,被银色的灵物驱散了。

"现在决定了,你们都回家去,带着家人躲起来。"哈利对外面那些被守护神的光亮照花了眼,仍然有点畏缩的麻瓜出身的巫师说,"如果可能就到国外去,离魔法部远远的。这是——呃——新的官方立场。现在,只要跟随守护神,你们就能逃出大厅。"

他们一直走到石梯顶上都没有受到阻拦。但向升降梯走去时,哈利担心起来。要是他们跟着一头银色牡鹿和一只银色水獭走进大厅,还带着二十来个人,其中一半都是被指控的麻瓜出身的巫师,这无疑是太引人注目了。正当他得出这个不愉快的结论时,他们面前升降梯的门哐当一声开了。

"雷吉!"卡特莫尔太太叫了起来,扑进罗恩的怀里,"伦考恩把我放出来了,他击昏了乌姆里奇和亚克斯利,还叫我们大家都逃出国去。我想我们应该这么做,雷吉,真的。赶快回家带上孩子——你怎么搞得这么湿?"

"水,"罗恩嘟囔着,挣脱出来,"哈利,他们知道有人闯进魔法部了,好像乌姆里奇办公室门上有个洞。那样的话,我想我们还有五分钟——"

赫敏的守护神噗地消失了,她大惊失色地转向哈利。

"哈利,要是我们被困在这儿——!"

"只要行动迅速就不会。"哈利说。他转向身后那群目瞪口呆地望着他的人。

"谁有魔杖?"

约有一半人举手。

"好,没有魔杖的找个有魔杖的跟着。我们动作要快——抢在被他们堵住之前。上吧。"

大家挤进两部升降梯,哈利的守护神在金色的栅栏门前守着,门关上了,升降梯开始上升。

CHAPTER THIRTEEN   The Muggle-Born Registration Commission

'Level Eight,' said the witch's cool voice, 'Atrium.'

Harry knew at once that they were in trouble. The Atrium was full of people moving from fireplace to fireplace, sealing them off.

'Harry!' squeaked Hermione. 'What are we going to –?'

'STOP!' Harry thundered, and the powerful voice of Runcorn echoed through the Atrium: the wizards sealing the fireplaces froze. 'Follow me,' he whispered to the group of terrified Muggle-borns, who moved forwards in a huddle, shepherded by Ron and Hermione.

'What's up, Albert?' said the same balding wizard who had followed Harry out of the fireplace earlier. He looked nervous.

'This lot need to leave before you seal the exits,' said Harry, with all the authority he could muster.

The group of wizards in front of him looked at one another.

'We've been told to seal all exits and not let anyone –'

'*Are you contradicting me?*' Harry blustered. 'Would you like me to have your family tree examined, like I had Dirk Cresswell's?'

'Sorry!' gasped the balding wizard, backing away. 'I didn't mean nothing, Albert, but I thought ... I thought they were in for questioning and ...'

'Their blood is pure,' said Harry, and his deep voice echoed impressively through the hall. 'Purer than many of yours, I daresay. Off you go,' he boomed to the Muggle-borns, who scurried forwards into the fireplaces and began to vanish in pairs. The Ministry wizards hung back, some looking confused, others scared and resentful. Then –

'Mary!'

Mrs Cattermole looked over her shoulder. The real Reg Cattermole, no longer vomiting, but pale and wan, had just come running out of a lift.

'R – Reg?'

She looked from her husband to Ron, who swore loudly.

The balding wizard gaped, his head turning ludicrously from one Reg Cattermole to the other.

'Hey – what's going on? What is this?'

'Seal the exit! SEAL IT!'

"第八层,"女巫冷漠的声音说,"正厅。"

哈利立刻知道有麻烦了。正厅里有许多人,在那些壁炉前面走来走去,正在封闭壁炉。

"哈利!"赫敏尖叫道,"我们怎么——?"

"**住手**!"哈利大喝一声,伦考恩有力的声音在正厅中回响,那些封锁壁炉的巫师们都愣住了。"跟我来。"他低声对那些惊恐的麻瓜出身的巫师们说,这群人由罗恩和赫敏领着往前拥去。

"怎么啦,艾伯特?"先前跟着哈利滚出壁炉的那个秃顶男巫问道,他看上去很紧张。

"这些人要在你们封闭出口前离开。"哈利竭力用最威严的语调说。

他面前那帮巫师面面相觑。

"我们奉命封闭所有出口,不许任何人——"

"你在违抗我吗?"哈利气势汹汹地说,"是不是要我调查一下你的家谱,像德克·克莱斯韦那样?"

"对不起!"秃顶男巫吃了一惊,朝后退去,"我没别的意思,艾伯特,只是我想……我想他们是受审讯的……"

"他们的血统很纯正,"哈利说,他低沉的嗓音在大厅中回响,很有震慑力,"我敢说比你们中的许多人都要纯正。走吧。"他高声对那些麻瓜出身的巫师们说,他们急忙钻进壁炉,一对对地消失了。魔法部的巫师迟疑地留在后面,有的一脸困惑,有的惊恐不满。突然——

"玛丽!"

卡特莫尔太太回过头,真正的雷吉·卡特莫尔刚从一部升降梯里跑出来,已经停止了呕吐,但脸色仍然苍白憔悴。

"雷——雷吉?"

她看看丈夫又看看罗恩,后者大声诅咒了一句。

秃顶男巫张大了嘴巴,脑袋在两个雷吉·卡特莫尔之间可笑地转来转去。

"嘿——这是怎么回事?"

"封闭出口!**封闭**!"

CHAPTER THIRTEEN   The Muggle-Born Registration Commission

Yaxley had burst out of another lift and was running towards the group beside the fireplaces into which all of the Muggle-borns but Mrs Cattermole had now vanished. As the balding wizard lifted his wand, Harry raised an enormous fist and punched him, sending him flying through the air.

'He's been helping Muggle-borns escape, Yaxley!' Harry shouted.

The balding wizard's colleagues set up an uproar, under cover of which Ron grabbed Mrs Cattermole, pulled her into the still open fireplace and disappeared. Confused, Yaxley looked from Harry to the punched wizard, while the real Reg Cattermole screamed, 'My wife! Who was that with my wife? What's going on?'

Harry saw Yaxley's head turn, saw an inkling of the truth dawn in that brutish face.

'Come on!' Harry shouted at Hermione; he seized her hand and they jumped into the fireplace together as Yaxley's curse sailed over Harry's head. They spun for a few seconds before shooting up out of a toilet into a cubicle. Harry flung open the door; Ron was standing there beside the sinks, still wrestling with Mrs Cattermole.

'Reg, I don't understand –'

'Let go, I'm not your husband, you've got to go home!'

There was a noise in the cubicle behind them; Harry looked around; Yaxley had just appeared.

'LET'S GO!' Harry yelled. He seized Hermione by the hand and Ron by the arm and turned on the spot.

Darkness engulfed them along with the sensation of compressing bands, but something was wrong ... Hermione's hand seemed to be sliding out of his grip ...

He wondered whether he was going to suffocate, he could not breathe or see and the only solid things in the world were Ron's arm and Hermione's fingers, which were slowly slipping away ...

And then he saw the door of number twelve, Grimmauld Place, with its serpent doorknocker, but before he could draw breath there was a scream and a flash of purple light; Hermione's hand was suddenly vice-like upon his and everything went dark again.

第13章 麻瓜出身登记委员会

亚克斯利从另一部升降梯里冲出来，奔向壁炉旁的人群。这时，那些麻瓜出身的巫师除了卡特莫尔太太之外全都已经从壁炉消失了。秃顶男巫刚举起魔杖，哈利就抡起硕大的拳头，一拳把他打飞出去。

"他在帮麻瓜出身的巫师逃跑，亚克斯利！"哈利喊道。

秃顶男巫的同伴们一片哗然，罗恩趁乱拽住卡特莫尔太太，把她拉进仍然敞开的壁炉里消失了。亚克斯利迷惑地看看哈利，又看看那挨打的男巫，这时真的雷吉·卡特莫尔高叫道："我太太！跟我太太在一起的那个人是谁？发生了什么事？"

哈利看到亚克斯利转过头来，凶悍的脸上现出一丝醒悟的神情。

"快走！"哈利大声对赫敏说，抓住她的手，两人一起跳进壁炉，亚克斯利的咒语从哈利头顶飞过。他们旋转了几秒钟，从抽水马桶中喷射出来。哈利打开小隔间的门，见罗恩站在水池旁，还跟卡特莫尔太太扭在一起。

"雷吉，我不明白——"

"放开，我不是你丈夫，你必须回家去！"

身后的小隔间里轰隆一响，哈利回过头，亚克斯利刚好跳了出来。

"**我们走！**"哈利高喊，抓住赫敏的手和罗恩的胳膊，疾速旋转。

黑暗吞没了他们，还有那种被带子束紧的感觉，可是有点儿不对劲……赫敏的手似乎要从他手中滑脱……

他怀疑自己要窒息了，他无法呼吸，也看不见，世界上唯一实在的东西就是罗恩的手臂和赫敏的手指，可是她的手指正在慢慢滑落……

然后他看到了格里莫广场12号的大门和那蛇形的门环，但他还没来得及透一口气，就听到一声尖叫，一道紫光一闪，赫敏的手突然变得像钳子一般抓住他，一切重又没入黑暗。

CHAPTER FOURTEEN

The Thief

Harry opened his eyes and was dazzled by gold and green; he had no idea what had happened, he only knew that he was lying on what seemed to be leaves and twigs. Struggling to draw breath into lungs that felt flattened, he blinked and realised that the gaudy glare was sunlight streaming through a canopy of leaves far above him. Then an object twitched close to his face. He pushed himself on to his hands and knees, ready to face some small, fierce creature, but saw that the object was Ron's foot. Looking around, Harry saw that they and Hermione were lying on a forest floor, apparently alone.

Harry's first thought was of the Forbidden Forest, and for a moment, even though he knew how foolish and dangerous it would be for them to appear in the grounds of Hogwarts, his heart leapt at the thought of sneaking through the trees to Hagrid's hut. However, in the few moments it took for Ron to give a low groan and Harry to start crawling towards him, he realised that this was not the Forbidden Forest: the trees looked younger, they were more widely spaced, the ground clearer.

He met Hermione, also on her hands and knees, at Ron's head. The moment his eyes fell upon Ron, all other concerns fled Harry's mind, for blood drenched the whole of Ron's left side and his face stood out, greyish white, against the leaf-strewn earth. The Polyjuice Potion was wearing off now: Ron was halfway between Cattermole and himself in appearance, his hair turning redder and redder as his face drained of the little colour it had left.

'What's happened to him?'

'Splinched,' said Hermione, her fingers already busy at Ron's sleeve, where the blood was wettest and darkest.

Harry watched, horrified, as she tore open Ron's shirt. He had always thought of Splinching as something comical, but this ... his insides crawled

第14章

小　偷

　　哈利睁开眼睛，看到一片炫目的金色和绿色。他不知道发生了什么，只知道自己似乎是躺在树叶和细树枝间。他艰难地吸气，肺像被压瘪了一样。他眨眨眼睛，意识到那耀眼的色彩是透过高高的树冠洒下的阳光。一个东西在他脸旁抽动了一下，他用手撑地跪了起来，以为会看到某种凶猛的小动物，却原来是罗恩的脚。哈利环顾四周，发现他们和赫敏都躺在森林中的地面上，周围应该没有别人。

　　哈利首先想到的是禁林，有一瞬间，虽然知道他们三人出现在霍格沃茨是多么愚蠢、多么危险，但想到从树林间偷偷溜进海格的小屋，他的心仍然兴奋得怦怦跳起来。这时罗恩低低地呻吟了一声，哈利向他爬过去，很快发现这里不是禁林：树木看上去年轻一些，间距较大，地面也更空旷。

　　他在罗恩脑袋旁边碰到了赫敏，她也手撑地面跪着。哈利一看见罗恩，就把一切都忘光了，因为罗恩的左半身都浸在血里，枕在泥土和落叶上的脸像死灰一样白。复方汤剂的药性正在消失。罗恩的模样介于卡特莫尔和他自己之间，脸上仅有的一点血色退去的同时，头发却越来越红了。

　　"他怎么了？"

　　"分体了。"赫敏说，她的手已经忙着摸索罗恩的袖子，那儿的血渍最湿，颜色最深。

　　哈利惊恐地看着她撕开罗恩的衬衫，他一直以为分体是滑稽的事

CHAPTER FOURTEEN The Thief

unpleasantly as Hermione laid bare Ron's upper arm, where a great chunk of flesh was missing, scooped cleanly away as though by a knife.

'Harry, quickly, in my bag, there's a small bottle labelled *Essence of Dittany* –'

'Bag – right –'

Harry sped to the place where Hermione had landed, seized the tiny beaded bag and thrust his hand inside it. At once, object after object began presenting itself to his touch: he felt the leather spines of books, woolly sleeves of jumpers, heels of shoes –

'*Quickly!*'

He grabbed his wand from the ground and pointed it into the depths of the magical bag.

'*Accio dittany!*'

A small brown bottle zoomed out of the bag; he caught it and hastened back to Hermione and Ron, whose eyes were now half closed, strips of white eyeball all that was visible between his lids.

'He's fainted,' said Hermione, who was also rather pale; she no longer looked like Mafalda, though her hair was still grey in places. 'Unstopper it for me, Harry, my hands are shaking.'

Harry wrenched the stopper off the little bottle, Hermione took it and poured three drops of the potion on the bleeding wound. Greenish smoke billowed upwards and when it had cleared, Harry saw that the bleeding had stopped. The wound now looked several days old; new skin stretched over what had just been open flesh.

'Wow,' said Harry.

'It's all I feel safe doing,' said Hermione shakily. 'There are spells that would put him completely right, but I daren't try in case I do them wrong and cause more damage ... he's lost so much blood already ...'

'How did he get hurt? I mean,' Harry shook his head, trying to clear it, to make sense of whatever had just taken place, 'why are we here? I thought we were going back to Grimmauld Place?'

Hermione took a deep breath. She looked close to tears.

'Harry, I don't think we're going to be able to go back there.'

'What d'you –?'

'As we Disapparated, Yaxley caught hold of me, and I couldn't get rid of him, he was too strong, and he was still holding on when we arrived at Grimmauld Place, and then – well, I think he must have seen the door, and thought we were stopping there, so he slackened his grip and I managed to

情，可这次……赫敏袒露出罗恩的上臂，他的五脏不舒服地搅动起来，那里少了一大块肉，好像被刀子剜走的一般……

"哈利，快，在我包里，有一个小瓶子上面写着白鲜香精——"

"包里——好——"

哈利冲到赫敏降落的地方，抓起那个串珠小包，把手插了进去。立刻，他的手碰到了一件件东西：皮面的书脊、羊毛衫的袖子、鞋跟——

"快啊！"

他从地上抓起魔杖，指着魔法小包里面。

"白鲜飞来！"

一个棕色小瓶从包里飞了出来，他一把抓住，急忙跑回赫敏和罗恩身边。罗恩双眼半睁半闭，上下眼睑间只露出一点眼白。

"他晕过去了。"赫敏也面色苍白，她已不再像马法尔达，尽管头发还有几处发灰，"帮我打开，哈利，我的手在抖。"

哈利揪下瓶塞，赫敏接过瓶子，在流血的伤口上倒了三滴药液。绿烟滚滚升起，当它散去之后，哈利看到血已经止住，伤口看上去好像已经长了几天，刚才暴露着的血肉上面覆了一层新皮。

"哇。"哈利说。

"我只敢做这么多，"赫敏颤抖着说，"有些魔咒可以让他完全恢复，但我不敢用，怕做错了，造成更大的伤害……他已经流了这么多血……"

"他怎么会受伤呢？我是说，"哈利摇摇头，试图理清思路，弄明白所发生的事情，"我们怎么会在这儿？不是回格里莫广场的吗？"

赫敏深深吸了口气，看上去快要哭了。

"哈利，我想我们回不去了。"

"什么——？"

"我们幻影移形时，亚克斯利抓住了我，我甩不掉他，他力气太大了。到格里莫广场时，他还抓着不放，然后——我想他一定看见了那个门，猜到我们要停在那里，所以他手松了一些，我甩开了他，把你们带到

CHAPTER FOURTEEN   The Thief

shake him off and I brought us here instead!'

'But then, where's he? Hang on ... you don't mean he's at Grimmauld Place? He can't get in there?'

Her eyes sparkled with unshed tears as she nodded.

'Harry, I think he can. I – I forced him to let go with a Revulsion Jinx, but I'd already taken him inside the Fidelius Charm's protection. Since Dumbledore died, we're Secret Keepers, so I've given him the secret, haven't I?'

There was no pretending; Harry was sure she was right. It was a serious blow. If Yaxley could now get inside the house, there was no way that they could return. Even now, he could be bringing other Death Eaters in there by Apparition. Gloomy and oppressive though the house was, it had been their one safe refuge: even, now that Kreacher was so much happier and friendlier, a kind of home. With a twinge of regret that had nothing to do with food, Harry imagined the house-elf busying himself over the steak and kidney pie that Harry, Ron and Hermione would never eat.

'Harry, I'm sorry, I'm so sorry!'

'Don't be stupid, it wasn't your fault! If anything, it was mine ...'

Harry put his hand in his pocket and drew out Mad-Eye's eye. Hermione recoiled, looking horrified.

'Umbridge had stuck it to her office door, to spy on people. I couldn't leave it there ... but that's how they knew there were intruders.'

Before Hermione could answer, Ron groaned and opened his eyes. He was still grey and his face glistened with sweat.

'How d'you feel?' Hermione whispered.

'Lousy,' croaked Ron, wincing as he felt his injured arm. 'Where are we?'

'In the woods where they held the Quidditch World cup,' said Hermione. 'I wanted somewhere enclosed, undercover, and this was –'

'– the first place you thought of,' Harry finished for her, glancing around at the apparently deserted glade. He could not help remembering what had happened the last time they had Apparated to the first place Hermione had thought of; how Death Eaters had found them within minutes. Had it been Legilimency? Did Voldemort or his henchmen know, even now, where Hermione had taken them?

第14章 小 偷

这儿来了！"

"可是，他在哪儿？等一等……你不会是说他在格里莫广场吧？他进不去吧？"

赫敏眼眶里闪着泪光，摇了摇头。

"哈利，我想他能。我——我用抽离咒迫使他放手，可是我已经把他带进了赤胆忠心咒的保护范围。邓布利多死后，我们就是保密人了，所以我泄了密，是不是？"

无须掩饰，哈利知道她说的是事实，这是个沉重的打击。如果亚克斯利已经能进那所房子，他们确实是回不去了。现在亚克斯利可能正用幻影显形把其他食死徒带到那里。那所房子虽然阴暗压抑，却曾是他们安全的庇护所，现在克利切已经开心友好得多，那里甚至有几分像家了。想到那家养小精灵还在忙着做哈利、罗恩和赫敏再也吃不到的牛排腰子馅饼，哈利心中一阵难过，但不是为了美食。

"哈利，对不起，对不起！"

"别傻了，这不是你的错！如果要怪的话，应该怪我……"

哈利把手伸进口袋里，掏出了疯眼汉的魔眼，赫敏惊恐地向后退去。

"乌姆里奇把它安在她办公室的门上，监视别人。我不能把它留在那儿……可他们就是这样发现有人混进去的。"

赫敏还没搭腔，罗恩呻吟了一声，睁开眼睛。他依然面色发灰，脸上汗津津的。

"你感觉怎么样？"赫敏轻声问。

"糟透了。"罗恩沙哑地说，摸摸受伤的胳膊，疼得缩了一下，"我们在哪儿？"

"举行魁地奇世界杯的树林里。"赫敏说，"我当时想找个隔绝、隐蔽的地方，这是——"

"——你想到的第一个地方。"哈利替她说完，望望这片似乎无人的林间空地，不禁想起上次他们幻影显形到赫敏想到的第一个地方时发生的事。食死徒是怎么在几分钟内就发现他们的？是摄神取念吗？伏地魔或其党羽是否现在就已知道赫敏把他们带到了哪儿？

CHAPTER FOURTEEN   The Thief

'D'you reckon we should move on?' Ron asked Harry, and Harry could tell, by the look on Ron's face, that he was thinking the same.

'I dunno.'

Ron still looked pale and clammy. He had made no attempt to sit up and it looked as though he was too weak to do so. The prospect of moving him was daunting.

'Let's stay here for now,' Harry said.

Looking relieved, Hermione sprang to her feet.

'Where are you going?' asked Ron.

'If we're staying, we should put some protective enchantments around the place,' she replied, and raising her wand, she began to walk in a wide circle around Harry and Ron, murmuring incantations as she went. Harry saw little disturbances in the surrounding air: it was as if Hermione had cast a heat haze upon their clearing.

'*Salvio hexia* ... *Protego totalum* ... *Repello Muggletum* ... *Muffliato* ... You could get out the tent, Harry ...'

'Tent?'

'In the bag!'

'In the ... of course,' said Harry.

He did not bother to grope inside it this time, but used another Summoning Charm The tent emerged in a lumpy mass of canvas, rope and poles. Harry recognised it, partly because of the smell of cats, as the same tent in which they had slept on the night of the Quidditch World cup.

'I thought this belonged to that bloke Perkins at the Ministry?' he asked, starting to disentangle the tent pegs.

'Apparently he didn't want it back, his lumbago's so bad,' said Hermione, now performing complicated figure of eight movements with her wand, 'so Ron's dad said I could borrow it. *Erecto!* ' she added, pointing her wand at the misshapen canvas, which in one fluid motion rose into the air and settled, fully constructed, on to the ground before Harry, out of whose startled hands a tent peg soared, to land with a final thud at the end of a guy rope.

'*Cave inimicum*,' Hermione finished with a skyward flourish. 'That's as much as I can do. At the very least, we should know they're coming, I can't guarantee it will keep out Vol–'

'Don't say the name!' Ron cut across her, his voice harsh.

第14章 小　偷

"你觉得我们应该转移吗？"罗恩问。哈利从罗恩的表情看出他也在这么想。

"我不知道。"

罗恩依然面色苍白，满脸汗湿。他没有尝试坐起来，似乎没有力气这么做。带他转移难度太大了。

"暂时先待在这儿吧。"哈利说。

赫敏如释重负，跳了起来。

"你去哪儿？"罗恩问。

"如果要待在这儿，就得在周围设一些防护魔法。"赫敏答道，举着魔杖，开始在哈利和罗恩旁边绕着一个大圈走动，嘴里念念有词。哈利看到周围的空气在轻微颤动，仿佛赫敏在空地上方变出了一股热气。

"平安镇守……统统加护……麻瓜驱逐……闭耳塞听……你可以把帐篷拿出来，哈利……"

"帐篷？"

"在包里！"

"在……当然。"哈利说。

这次他没再费劲去摸，而是又用了个召唤咒。一堆帆布、绳子和杆子飞了出来，大概是因为散发着一股猫味吧，哈利认出这就是他们在魁地奇世界杯那一夜睡的帐篷。

"这不是魔法部那个珀金斯老头儿的吗？"他问，一边开始解开帐篷的钉子。

"他显然不想把它要回去了，他的腰痛那么严重。"赫敏说，此刻她正用魔杖画着复杂的八字形花样，"罗恩的爸爸说可以借给我。竖立成形！"她指着乱糟糟的帆布说。那堆东西立刻升到空中，一眨眼的工夫便全部搭好落在哈利面前的地上，最后一枚钉子从惊讶的哈利手中飞出，噗地钉入支索末端。

"降敌陷阱。"赫敏最后朝天挥舞了一下魔杖，"我只能做到这样了。至少，如果他们来了，我们应该能发觉，可我没法保证这能挡住伏——"

"别说名字！"罗恩厉声打断了她。

CHAPTER FOURTEEN The Thief

Harry and Hermione looked at each other.

'I'm sorry,' Ron said, moaning a little as he raised himself to look at them, 'but it feels like a – a jinx, or something. Can't we call him You-Know-Who – please?'

'Dumbledore said fear of a name –' began Harry.

'In case you hadn't noticed, mate, calling You-Know-Who by his name didn't do Dumbledore much good in the end,' Ron snapped back. 'Just – just show You-Know-Who some respect, will you?'

'*Respect?* ' Harry repeated, but Hermione shot him a warning look; apparently he was not to argue with Ron while the latter was in such a weakened condition.

Harry and Hermione half carried, half dragged Ron through the entrance of the tent. The interior was exactly as Harry remembered it: a small flat, complete with bathroom and tiny kitchen. He shoved aside an old armchair and lowered Ron carefully on to the lower berth of a bunk bed. Even this very short journey had turned Ron whiter still, and once they had settled him on the mattress, he closed his eyes again and did not speak for a while.

'I'll make some tea,' said Hermione breathlessly, pulling kettle and mugs from the depths of her bag and heading towards the kitchen.

Harry found the hot drink as welcome as the Firewhisky had been on the night that Mad-Eye had died; it seemed to burn away a little of the fear fluttering in his chest. After a minute or two, Ron broke the silence.

'What d'you reckon happened to the Cattermoles?'

'With any luck, they'll have got away,' said Hermione, clutching her hot mug for comfort. 'As long as Mr Cattermole had his wits about him, he'll have transported Mrs Cattermole by Side-Along-Apparition and they'll be fleeing the country right now with their children. That's what Harry told her to do.'

'Blimey, I hope they escaped,' said Ron, leaning back on his pillows. The tea seemed to be doing him good; a little of his colour had returned. 'I didn't get the feeling Reg Cattermole was all that quick-witted, though, the way everyone was talking to me when I was him. God, I hope they made it ... if they both end up in Azkaban because of us ...'

Harry looked over at Hermione and the question he had been about to ask – about whether Mrs Cattermole's lack of a wand would prevent her Apparating alongside her husband – died in his throat. Hermione was watching Ron fret over the fate of the Cattermoles, and there was such tenderness in her expression that Harry felt almost as if he had surprised her

第14章 小 偷

哈利和赫敏面面相觑。

"对不起,"罗恩撑起身子看着他们,轻轻呻吟了一声,"那让我感觉像一个——一个恶咒什么的。我们不能叫他神秘人吗,拜托?"

"邓布利多说,对一个名字的恐惧——"哈利说。

"提醒一下,伙计,直呼神秘人的名字并没有给邓布利多带来什么好下场。"罗恩抢白道,"就——就对神秘人表示一点尊重,行不行?"

"尊重?"哈利重复道,赫敏警告地瞥了哈利一眼,显然,在罗恩这样虚弱的情况下,不该与他争论。

哈利和赫敏连拖带抱地把罗恩弄进帐篷。里面和哈利记忆中的一样:一个小套间,配有卫生间和小小的厨房。他推开一把旧扶手椅,小心地把罗恩放到一张双层床的下铺。这短短的路程也已经让罗恩的脸色更加苍白,一被安放到床垫上,他就又闭上眼睛,好一会儿没说话。

"我去煮点茶。"赫敏气喘吁吁地说,从她的小包里掏出水壶和杯子,进厨房去了。

哈利觉得这热茶像疯眼汉牺牲当夜的火焰威士忌一样及时,似乎把他心头悸动的恐惧烫去了一点。过了一两分钟,罗恩打破了沉默。

"你们说卡特莫尔夫妇怎么样了?"

"运气好的话,他们已经逃走了。"赫敏说,紧紧地捧着热茶杯寻求安慰,"只要卡特莫尔先生头脑还清醒,就会用随从显形把他太太带走。他们现在可能正带着孩子逃往国外呢,哈利叫她这么做的。"

"我的天,但愿他们逃走了。"罗恩靠回枕头上说道,热茶似乎让他精神好了些,脸上也恢复了一点血色,"可是,我并不觉得雷吉·卡特莫尔的脑子有那么好使,我冒充他时所有的人对我说话都是那态度。上帝啊,我真希望他们逃走了……要是两个人都因为我们而进了阿兹卡班……"

哈利望望赫敏,到嘴边的问题——卡特莫尔太太没有魔杖会不会妨碍她随丈夫显形——又咽了下去。赫敏注视着为卡特莫尔夫妇的命运而忧心忡忡的罗恩,她的表情如此温柔,哈利觉得就好像看到她在

CHAPTER FOURTEEN The Thief

in the act of kissing him.

'So, have you got it?' Harry asked her, partly to remind her that he was there.

'Got – got what?' she said, with a little start.

'What did we just go through all that for? The locket! Where's the locket?'

'*You got it?* ' shouted Ron, raising himself a little higher on his pillows. 'No one tells me anything! Blimey, you could have mentioned it!'

'Well, we were running for our lives from the Death Eaters, weren't we?' said Hermione. 'Here.'

And she pulled the locket out of the pocket of her robes and handed it to Ron.

It was as large as a chicken's egg. An ornate letter 'S', inlaid with many small green stones, glinted dully in the diffused light shining through the tent's canvas roof.

'There isn't any chance someone's destroyed it since Kreacher had it?' asked Ron hopefully. 'I mean, are we sure it's still a Horcrux?'

'I think so,' said Hermione, taking it back from him and looking at it closely. 'There'd be some sign of damage if it had been magically destroyed.'

She passed it to Harry, who turned it over in his fingers. The thing looked perfect, pristine. He remembered the mangled remains of the diary, and how the stone in the Horcrux-ring had been cracked open when Dumbledore destroyed it.

'I reckon Kreacher's right,' said Harry. 'We're going to have to work out how to open this thing before we can destroy it.'

Sudden awareness of what he was holding, of what lived behind the little golden doors, hit Harry as he spoke. Even after all their efforts to find it, he felt a violent urge to fling the locket from him. Mastering himself again, he tried to prise the locket apart with his fingers, then attempted the charm Hermione had used to open Regulus's bedroom door. Neither worked. He handed the locket back to Ron and Hermione, each of whom did their best, but were no more successful at opening it than he had been.

'Can you feel it, though?' Ron asked in a hushed voice, as he held it tight in his clenched fist.

'What d'you mean?'

Ron passed the Horcrux to Harry. After a moment or two, Harry thought he knew what Ron meant. Was it his own blood pulsing through his veins that he could feel, or was it something beating inside the locket, like a tiny metal heart?

第14章 小　偷

亲吻罗恩一样。

"哎，你拿到没有？"哈利问她，一半是为了提醒她别忘了他的存在。

"拿到——拿到什么？"她有点吃惊。

"我们冒这么大风险干什么去了？挂坠盒啊！挂坠盒在哪儿？"

"你们拿到了？"罗恩大叫，身子从枕头上抬起了一点，"没人跟我说过！我的天哪，你们也该提一下啊！"

"好啦，我们不是要从食死徒手里逃生吗？"赫敏说，"在这儿呢。"

她从袍子口袋里掏出挂坠盒，递给了罗恩。

挂坠盒有鸡蛋那么大，一个华丽的"S"，由多颗小绿宝石嵌成，在帆布帐篷顶透下的微明中闪着暗淡的光芒。

"会不会在克利切之后已经有人把它摧毁了？"罗恩心存侥幸地问，"我是说，能确定它还是魂器吗？"

"我想还是。"赫敏说，把它拿在手里细细查看，"如果用魔法破坏过，上面会有痕迹的。"

她把挂坠盒递给哈利，哈利拿在手上翻来覆去地端详，这玩意儿看上去完好无损、一尘不染。他想到那本残缺不全的日记，还有戒指魂器被邓布利多摧毁时，宝石上出现的裂缝。

"我想克利切说得对，"哈利说，"我们必须想办法打开这个东西，才能把它摧毁。"

说话时，哈利突然意识到他拿着的是什么，那两扇小金门后面藏着的是什么。虽然费尽周折才找到这个挂坠盒，他却有一种强烈的冲动，想把它马上抛掉。他克制住自己，试图用手掰开挂坠盒，然后又试了赫敏打开雷古勒斯卧室房门时用的咒语，都没有用。他又把挂坠盒交给罗恩和赫敏，他们各自使出浑身解数，也都跟他一样不成功。

"可你感觉到了吗？"罗恩把挂坠盒紧紧地捏在手中，小声问。

"什么呀？"

罗恩把魂器递给哈利。过了片刻，哈利明白了罗恩的意思。他感觉到的是自己的脉动，还是挂坠盒中有东西在跳动，像一颗小小的金属心脏？

CHAPTER FOURTEEN   The Thief

'What are we going to do with it?' Hermione asked.

'Keep it safe 'til we work out how to destroy it,' Harry replied, and, little though he wanted to, he hung the chain around his own neck, dropping the locket out of sight beneath his robes, where it rested against his chest beside the pouch Hagrid had given him.

'I think we should take it in turns to keep watch outside the tent,' he added to Hermione, standing up and stretching. 'And we'll need to think about some food, as well. You stay there,' he added sharply, as Ron attempted to sit up and turned a nasty shade of green.

With the Sneakoscope Hermione had given Harry for his birthday set carefully upon the table in the tent, Harry and Hermione spent the rest of the day sharing the role of lookout. However, the Sneakoscope remained silent and still upon its point all day, and whether because of the protective enchantments and Muggle-Repelling Charms Hermione had spread around them, or because people rarely ventured this way, their patch of wood remained deserted apart from occasional birds and squirrels. Evening brought no change; Harry lit his wand as he swapped places with Hermione at ten o'clock, and looked out upon a deserted scene, noting the bats fluttering high above him across the single patch of starry sky visible from their protected clearing.

He felt hungry now, and a little light-headed. Hermione had not packed any food in her magical bag, as she had assumed that they would be returning to Grimmauld Place that night, so they had had nothing to eat except some wild mushrooms that Hermione had collected from amongst the nearest trees and stewed in a billycan. After a couple of mouthfuls, Ron had pushed his portion away, looking queasy; Harry had only persevered so as not to hurt Hermione's feelings.

The surrounding silence was broken by odd rustlings and what sounded like crackings of twigs: Harry thought that they were caused by animals rather than people, yet he kept his wand held tight at the ready. His insides, already uncomfortable due to their inadequate helping of rubbery mushrooms, tingled with unease.

He had thought that he would feel elated if they managed to steal back the Horcrux, but somehow he did not; all he felt as he sat looking out at the darkness, of which his wand lit only a tiny part, was worry about what would happen next. It was as though he had been hurtling towards this point for weeks, months, maybe even years, but now he had come to an abrupt halt, run out of road.

第14章 小 偷

"我们拿它怎么办呢?"赫敏问。

"妥善保管,直到想出摧毁它的办法。"哈利答道。尽管满不情愿,他还是把链子挂到了自己的脖子上,让挂坠盒落到袍子里面,贴胸挂在海格给他的那个袋子旁边。

"我想我们应该轮流在帐篷外面放哨,"他接着对赫敏说,站起来伸了个懒腰,"而且也需要想想吃饭问题。你待在这儿。"他又坚决地说,因为罗恩挣扎着要坐起来,脸色都发绿了。

哈利生日时赫敏送给他的窥镜被仔细安在帐篷里的桌子上,哈利和赫敏在一天中轮流承担放哨的任务。不过,窥镜一整天都毫无动静,不知是因为赫敏在周围施的防护魔法和麻瓜驱逐咒,还是人们很少到这里来,他们那片树林里始终寂静无人,只有小鸟和松鼠偶尔经过。晚上也没有变化。十点钟,哈利点亮魔杖,跟赫敏换了班,守望着一片空寂,看着蝙蝠在高处盘旋飞舞,掠过宿营地上方那一小块繁星点点的夜空。

他觉得饿了,还有一点头晕。赫敏没有往她的魔法小包里装任何食物,因为她以为晚上要回格里莫广场。他们没什么可吃的,只有一些赫敏从附近的树丛中摘来,放在马口铁罐里煮熟的野蘑菇。吃了两口之后,罗恩就推开了他的那份,显出有点想吐的样子。哈利也只是为了不伤害赫敏的感情才勉强吃了下去。

周围的寂静被奇怪的沙沙声和细枝折断似的声音打破,哈利想那是由动物而不是人引起的,但还是紧握魔杖保持戒备。他吃了那点橡皮似的、不够充饥的蘑菇,肚子已经不大舒服,现在更是因为紧张而烧灼起来。

他本来以为偷回魂器之后自己会欢欣鼓舞,但不知为什么,他没有这种感觉。坐在那里,望着只被他魔杖照亮了一小片的茫茫黑暗,他感到的只是对未来的担忧,就好像他几个星期、几个月甚至几年都在朝着这个目标冲刺,而现在猛然刹住脚步,无路可走了。

CHAPTER FOURTEEN The Thief

There were other Horcruxes out there somewhere, but he did not have the faintest idea where they could be. He did not even know what all of them were. Meanwhile, he was at a loss to know how to destroy the only one that they had found, the Horcrux that currently lay against the bare flesh of his chest. Curiously, it had not taken heat from his body, but lay so cold against his skin it might just have emerged from icy water. From time to time, Harry thought, or perhaps imagined, that he could feel the tiny heartbeat ticking irregularly alongside his own.

Nameless forebodings crept up on him as he sat there in the dark: he tried to resist them, push them away, yet they came at him relentlessly. *Neither can live while the other survives.* Ron and Hermione, now talking softly behind him in the tent, could walk away if they wanted to: he could not. And it seemed to Harry as he sat there trying to master his own fear and exhaustion, that the Horcrux against his chest was ticking away the time he had left ... *Stupid idea*, he told himself, *don't think that* ...

His scar was starting to prickle again. He was afraid that he was making it happen by having these thoughts, and tried to direct them into another channel. He thought of poor Kreacher, who had expected them home and had received Yaxley instead. Would the elf keep silent or would he tell the Death Eater everything he knew? Harry wanted to believe that Kreacher had changed towards him in the past month, that he would be loyal now, but who knew what would happen? What if the Death Eaters tortured the elf? Sick images swarmed into Harry's head and he tried to push these away too, for there was nothing he could do for Kreacher: he and Hermione had already decided against trying to summon him; what if someone from the Ministry came too? They could not count on elfish Apparition being free from the same flaw that had taken Yaxley to Grimmauld Place on the hem of Hermione's sleeve.

Harry's scar was burning now. He thought that there was so much they did not know: Lupin had been right about magic they had never encountered or imagined. Why hadn't Dumbledore explained more? Had he thought that there would be time; that he would live for years, for centuries, perhaps, like his friend Nicolas Flamel? If so, he had been wrong ... Snape had seen to that ... Snape, the sleeping snake, who had struck at the top of the Tower ...

And Dumbledore had fallen ... fallen ...

'*Give it to me, Gregorovitch.*'

第14章 小　偷

还有几个魂器没有找到,他根本不知道它们可能藏在哪儿,甚至不知道它们分别是什么。而且,他也不知道怎样才能摧毁找到的唯一一个、现在紧贴在他胸口的这个魂器。奇怪的是,它没有吸收他的体温,而是冰凉地贴在他的皮肤上,简直像刚从冰水里捞出来的一样。有时哈利觉得,也许是想象——他能感觉到一个小小的心脏在自己的心脏旁边不规则地跳动。

坐在黑暗中,无数不祥的预感爬上心头。他试图抵御,把它们驱走,但它们还是无情地袭来。两个人不能都活着。罗恩和赫敏在他身后的帐篷里轻声说话,他们如果愿意可以随时离开,而他不能。坐在那里努力克服自己的恐惧和疲劳时,哈利感到压在胸口的魂器在滴滴答答,倒数他剩下的时间……愚蠢的念头,他对自己说,别那样想……

伤疤又刺痛起来,他担心是自己的胡思乱想造成的,便试图把思绪引往别处。他想到了可怜的克利切,在家盼着他们回去,不料看到的却是亚克斯利。小精灵会守口如瓶吗?还是会把知道的一切告诉那个食死徒?哈利愿意相信克利切在这一个月里已经被他感化,现在能够保持忠诚了,可是谁又知道会发生什么呢?如果食死徒折磨小精灵呢?可怕的画面涌入哈利脑海,他又努力推开它们,因为他无法为克利切做什么。哈利和赫敏已经商定不召唤小精灵,因为,万一魔法部的人跟来怎么办?亚克斯利就是拽着赫敏的袖子跟到了格里莫广场,他们不能保证小精灵的幻影显形没有类似的缺陷。

哈利的伤疤现在火烧火燎地痛。他想到还有那么多他们不知道的事,卢平说得对,那么多从没见过的和想象不到的魔法。邓布利多为什么不多说一点呢?难道他以为有的是时间,以为他能活许多年,许多个世纪,像他的朋友尼克·勒梅一样?如果那样的话,他想错了……斯内普已经下手……斯内普,那条潜伏的毒蛇,在塔楼顶上发起了攻击……

邓布利多坠落下去……坠落下去……

"把它交给我,格里戈维奇。"

CHAPTER FOURTEEN   The Thief

Harry's voice was high, clear and cold: his wand held in front of him by a long-fingered, white hand. The man at whom he was pointing was suspended upside-down in mid-air, though there were no ropes holding him; he swung there, invisibly and eerily bound, his limbs wrapped about him, his terrified face, on a level with Harry's, ruddy due to the blood that had rushed to his head. He had pure white hair and a thick, bushy beard: a trussed-up Father Christmas.

'I have it not, I have it no more! It was, many years ago, stolen from me!'

'Do not lie to Lord Voldemort, Gregorovitch. He knows ... he always knows.'

The hanging man's pupils were wide, dilated with fear, and they seemed to swell, bigger and bigger until their blackness swallowed Harry whole –

And now Harry was hurrying along a dark corridor in stout little Gregorovitch's wake as he held a lantern aloft: Gregorovitch burst into the room at the end of the passage and his lantern illuminated what looked like a workshop; wood-shavings and gold gleamed in the swinging pool of light, and there on the window ledge sat perched, like a giant bird, a young man with golden hair. In the split second that the lantern's light illuminated him, Harry saw the delight upon his handsome face, then the intruder shot a Stunning Spell from his wand and jumped neatly backwards out of the window with a crow of laughter.

And Harry was hurtling back out of those wide, tunnel-like pupils and Gregorovitch's face was stricken with terror.

'*Who was the thief, Gregorovitch?*' said the high, cold voice.

'*I do not know, I never knew, a young man – no – please – PLEASE!*'

A scream that went on and on and then a burst of green light –

'*Harry!*'

He opened his eyes, panting, his forehead throbbing. He had passed out against the side of the tent; had slid sideways down the canvas and was sprawled on the ground. He looked up at Hermione, whose bushy hair obscured the tiny patch of sky visible through the dark branches high above them.

'Dream,' he said, sitting up quickly and attempting to meet Hermione's glower with a look of innocence. 'Must've dozed off, sorry.'

'I *know* it was your scar! I can tell by the look on your face! You were looking into Vol–'

第14章 小　偷

哈利的声音高亢、清晰而冷酷。他的魔杖举在面前，握在一只苍白修长的手里。被魔杖指着的人倒吊在空中，被无形的绳子绑着，荡来荡去，看上去很怪异，他的胳膊紧紧地捆在身体两旁，恐惧的面孔与哈利的脸一样高，因为充血而涨得通红。他头发雪白，还有一把蓬松的大胡子：一个被绑着的圣诞老人。

"我没有，没有了！许多年以前，被偷走了！"

"别对伏地魔说谎，格里戈维奇，他知道……他永远知道。"

由于恐惧，被吊着的人瞳孔放大了。它们似乎在变得越来越大，像两个黑洞，最后把哈利整个人吸了进去——

现在哈利跟在身材矮胖、举着灯笼的格里戈维奇后面，沿着一条黑暗的走廊疾行。格里戈维奇冲进走廊尽头的房间。灯光映照下，这里像是个工作间，木屑和金子在晃动的光圈中闪烁，窗台上栖着一个金发少年，姿态像一只大鸟。在灯笼的光晕照到他的一刹那，哈利看到那张英俊的脸上充满喜悦，然后这位不速之客用魔杖射出一个昏迷咒，飞身跃出窗外，留下一串朗朗的笑声。

哈利从那宽敞的、隧道般的瞳孔中疾速退出，格里戈维奇的脸上现出极度的恐惧。

"那个小偷是谁，格里戈维奇？"高亢、冷酷的声音问。

"我不知道，我一直不知道，一个年轻人——不——求求你——**求求你**！"

一声凄厉的、久久不绝的尖叫，接着是一道绿光——

"哈利！"

他睁开眼睛，喘着气，额头突突地跳疼。他刚才靠在帐篷上失去了知觉，顺着帆布歪着滑下去，现在躺在地上。他抬眼望着赫敏，她浓密的头发遮住了高高的黑色树梢间的一小块天空。

"做梦了，"他赶快坐起来，试图用无辜的表情面对赫敏的瞪视，"准是打了个盹儿，对不起。"

"我知道是你的伤疤！从你的表情就能看出来！你刚才看到了伏——"

CHAPTER FOURTEEN The Thief

'Don't say his name!' came Ron's angry voice from the depths of the tent.

'*Fine,*' retorted Hermione. '*You-Know-Who's* mind, then!'

'I didn't mean it to happen!' Harry said. 'It was a dream! Can you control what you dream about, Hermione?'

'If you just learned to apply Occlumency –'

But Harry was not interested in being told off; he wanted to discuss what he had just seen.

'He's found Gregorovitch, Hermione, and I think he's killed him, but before he killed him he read Gregorovitch's mind and I saw –'

'I think I'd better take over the watch if you're so tired you're falling asleep,' said Hermione coldly.

'I can finish the watch!'

'No, you're obviously exhausted. Go and lie down.'

She dropped down in the mouth of the tent, looking stubborn. Angry, but wishing to avoid a row, Harry ducked back inside.

Ron's still pale face was poking out from the lower bunk; Harry climbed into the one above him, lay down and looked up at the dark canvas ceiling. After several moments, Ron spoke in a voice so low that it would not carry to Hermione, huddled in the entrance.

'What's You-Know-Who doing?'

Harry screwed up his eyes in the effort to remember every detail, then whispered into the darkness.

'He found Gregorovitch. He had him tied up, he was torturing him.'

'How's Gregorovitch supposed to make him a new wand if he's tied up?'

'I dunno ... it's weird, isn't it?'

Harry closed his eyes, thinking of all he had seen and heard. The more he recalled, the less sense it made ... Voldemort had said nothing about Harry's wand, nothing about the twin cores, nothing about Gregorovitch making a new and more powerful wand to beat Harry's ...

'He wanted something from Gregorovitch,' Harry said, eyes still closed tight. 'He asked him to hand it over, but Gregorovitch said it had been stolen from him ... and then ... then ...'

He remembered how he, as Voldemort, had seemed to hurtle through Gregorovitch's eyes, into his memories ...

第14章 小　偷

"别说他的名字！"罗恩恼火的声音从帐篷深处传来。

"好吧，"赫敏没好气地说，"看到了神秘人的思想！"

"我不是有意的！"哈利说，"是一个梦！你能控制自己做什么梦吗，赫敏？"

"如果你学会用大脑封闭术——"

但哈利不想听训斥，他想讨论刚才看到的事情。

"他找到了格里戈维奇，赫敏，我想他已经杀死了他，但在此之前，他看到了格里戈维奇的思想，我看见——"

"我想还是由我来放哨吧，如果你都累得睡着了的话。"赫敏冷冷地说。

"我能值完这班！"

"不行，你显然累坏了，进去躺着吧。"

赫敏一屁股坐在帐篷口，看来是铁了心。哈利很窝火，但不想吵架，就低头钻进了帐篷。

罗恩仍然苍白的脸从下铺伸出来，哈利爬到他的上铺，躺下来望着黑漆漆的帆布顶棚。过了一阵，罗恩说话了，声音低得传不到蜷缩在门口的赫敏那里。

"神秘人在干什么？"

哈利眯起眼睛，努力回忆每个细节，然后小声对着黑暗说道：

"他找到了格里戈维奇，把老头儿捆在那里拷问。"

"格里戈维奇被捆了起来，还怎么给他做魔杖啊？"

"我不知道……挺怪的，是不是？"

哈利闭上眼睛，想着他的所见所闻，越想越觉得讲不通……伏地魔根本没有提到哈利的魔杖，没有提到孪生杖芯，也没有提到让格里戈维奇做一根更强大的新魔杖来打败哈利……

"他想要格里戈维奇交出一样东西，"哈利说，依然紧闭双眼，"可是格里戈维奇说被偷走了……然后……然后……"

他想起自己，身为伏地魔，似乎穿过格里戈维奇的瞳孔，飞进了他的记忆。

CHAPTER FOURTEEN The Thief

'He read Gregorovitch's mind, and I saw this young bloke perched on a window sill, and he fired a curse at Gregorovitch and jumped out of sight. He stole it, he stole whatever You-Know-Who's after. And I ... I think I've seen him somewhere ...'

Harry wished he could have another glimpse of the laughing boy's face. The theft had happened many years ago, according to Gregorovitch. Why did the young thief look familiar?

The noises of the surrounding woods were muffled inside the tent; all Harry could hear was Ron's breathing. After a while, Ron whispered, 'Couldn't you see what the thief was holding?'

'No ... it must've been something small.'

'Harry?'

The wooden slats of Ron's bunk creaked as he repositioned himself in bed.

'Harry, you don't reckon You-Know-Who's after something else to turn into a Horcrux?'

'I don't know,' said Harry slowly. 'Maybe. But wouldn't it be dangerous for him to make another one? Didn't Hermione say he had pushed his soul to the limit already?'

'Yeah, but maybe he doesn't know that.'

'Yeah ... maybe,' said Harry.

He had been sure that Voldemort had been looking for a way round the problem of the twin cores, sure that Voldemort sought a solution from the old wandmaker ... and yet he had killed him, apparently without asking him a single question about wandlore.

What was Voldemort trying to find? Why, with the Ministry of Magic and the wizarding world at his feet, was he far away, intent on the pursuit of an object that Gregorovitch had once owned, and which had been stolen by the unknown thief?

Harry could still see the blond-haired youth's face, it was merry, wild; there was a Fred and George-ish air of triumphant trickery about him. He had soared from the window sill like a bird, and Harry had seen him before, but he could not think where ...

With Gregorovitch dead, it was the merry-faced thief who was in danger now, and it was on him that Harry's thoughts dwelled, as Ron's snores began to rumble from the lower bunk and as he himself drifted slowly into sleep once more.

第14章 小　偷

"神秘人看到了格里戈维奇的思想，我看见一个少年坐在窗台上，他朝格里戈维奇发了一个咒语，就跳出去不见了。他偷走了那件东西，他偷走了神秘人要找的东西。而且，我……我想我在哪儿见过他……"

哈利希望能再看一眼那个大笑的少年的面孔。根据格里戈维奇的记忆，这次失窃发生在许多年以前。为什么那个年轻的小偷看上去很面熟呢？

在帐篷里，周围林中的声响减弱了许多，哈利只听到罗恩的呼吸声。过了一会儿，罗恩轻声问："你没看到小偷拿着什么吗？"

"没有……肯定是件小东西。"

"哈利？"

罗恩的床板嘎吱作响，他在床上换了个姿势。

"哈利，你认为神秘人会不会在寻找做魂器的东西？"

"不知道，"哈利缓缓地说，"也许吧。但是再做一个对他来说不是很危险吗？赫敏不是说过他已经把他的灵魂摧残到极限了吗？"

"是啊，但也许他自己不知道。"

"嗯……也许。"哈利说。

他本来认定伏地魔是在找克服孪生杖芯的办法，认定伏地魔想从老魔杖师傅那里找到答案……可是他却把老头儿杀了，好像没有问过任何关于魔杖的问题。

伏地魔想找什么呢？咳，当魔法部和整个巫师界都被他踩在脚下时，他却要到遥远的地方，苦苦寻觅一件格里戈维奇曾经拥有，而被那个不知名的小偷盗走的东西，这是为什么呢？

哈利还能看到那个金发少年的脸，快乐狂放，有一种弗雷德和乔治式的、恶作剧成功的得意神态。他像大鸟一般从窗台上飞了出去，哈利曾经见过他，却想不起是在哪儿……

格里戈维奇已经死了，现在有危险的就是那个神采飞扬的小偷了。当罗恩的鼾声从下铺响起，哈利自己的意识也再次渐渐模糊时，他还在想着那个小偷。

CHAPTER FIFTEEN

The Goblin's Revenge

Early next morning, before the other two were awake, Harry left the tent to search the woods around them for the oldest, most gnarled and resilient-looking tree he could find. There in its shadow he buried Mad-Eye Moody's eye and marked the spot by gouging a small cross in the bark with his wand. It was not much, but Harry felt that Mad-Eye would have much preferred this to being stuck on Dolores Umbridge's door. Then he returned to the tent to wait for the others to wake, and discuss what they were going to do next.

Harry and Hermione felt that it was best not to stay anywhere too long, and Ron agreed, with the sole proviso that their next move took them within reach of a bacon sandwich. Hermione therefore removed the enchantments she had placed around the clearing, while Harry and Ron obliterated all the marks and impressions on the ground that might show they had camped there. Then they Disapparated to the outskirts of a small market town.

Once they had pitched the tent in the shelter of a small copse of trees, and surrounded it with freshly cast defensive enchantments, Harry venture out under the Invisibility Cloak to find sustenance. This, however, did not go as planned. He had barely entered the town when an unnatural chill, a descending mist and a sudden darkening of the skies made him freeze where he stood.

'But you can make a brilliant Patronus!' protested Ron, when Harry arrived back at the tent empty-handed, out of breath, and mouthing the single word 'Dementors'.

'I couldn't ... make one,' he panted, clutching the stitch in his side. 'Wouldn't ... come.'

Their expressions of consternation and disappointment made Harry feel ashamed. It had been a nightmarish experience, seeing the Dementors gliding out of the mist in the distance and realising, as the paralysing cold choked his lungs and a distant screaming filled his ears, that he was not

第 15 章

妖精的报复

第二天一大早，在另外两人醒来之前，哈利走出帐篷，在周围的林子里找到一棵最苍老虬曲、看上去最坚韧的大树，把疯眼汉穆迪的魔眼埋在树下，用魔杖在树皮上刻了个小十字作为记号。这不算什么，但哈利想疯眼汉会觉得比安在乌姆里奇的门上好得多。他回到帐篷里，等两个伙伴醒来讨论下一步怎么办。

哈利和赫敏认为最好不要在一个地方待太久，罗恩也同意，只提出到了下一个宿营地必须吃到熏咸肉三明治。于是赫敏解除了她在空地上设的防护魔法，哈利和罗恩消去了地上他们宿营过的痕迹，三人幻影移形到了一个小集镇的外围。

他们在一小片幽僻的矮林子里搭好帐篷，又在周围设了新的防护魔法之后，哈利便披着隐形衣去找吃的。但此行并不顺利，他刚进集镇，就感到一阵不正常的寒意，弥漫的雾气和突然的天昏地暗使他僵立在那里。

"但你可以召出非常棒的守护神啊！"当哈利空着手回到帐篷里，气喘吁吁地用口形说出"摄魂怪"时，罗恩不甘心地说。

"我……不行，"他上气不接下气，捂着肋部说，"召不……出来。"

他们震惊和失望的表情让哈利感到羞耻。那是一种噩梦般的感受，眼看着摄魂怪从远处雾中飘出，令人麻木的寒气使他肺部窒息，缥缈的尖叫灌进他的耳朵，却意识到他无法保护自己。哈利用了全部的意志力才拔起腿来，逃出了那个地方，那些没有眼睛的摄魂怪还在麻瓜

CHAPTER FIFTEEN The Goblin's Revenge

going to be able to protect himself. It had taken all Harry's will power to uproot himself from the spot and run, leaving the eyeless Dementors to glide amongst the Muggles who might not be able to see them, but would assuredly feel the despair they cast wherever they went.

'So we still haven't got any food.'

'Shut up, Ron,' snapped Hermione. 'Harry, what happened? Why do you think you couldn't make your Patronus? You managed perfectly yesterday!'

'I don't know.'

He sat low in one of Perkins's old armchairs, feeling more humiliated by the moment. He was afraid that something had gone wrong inside him. Yesterday seemed a long time ago: today he might have been thirteen years old again, the only one who collapsed on the Hogwarts Express.

Ron kicked a chair leg.

'What?' he snarled at Hermione. 'I'm starving! All I've had since I bled half to death is a couple of toadstools!'

'You go and fight your way through the Dementors, then,' said Harry, stung.

'I would, but my arm's in a sling, in case you hadn't noticed!'

'That's convenient.'

'And what's that supposed to –?'

'Of course!' cried Hermione, clapping a hand to her forehead and startling both of them into silence. 'Harry, give me the locket! Come on,' she said impatiently, clicking her fingers at him when he did not react, 'the Horcrux, Harry, you're still wearing it!'

She held out her hands and Harry lifted the golden chain over his head. The moment it parted contact with Harry's skin he felt free and oddly light. He had not even realised that he was clammy, or that there was a heavy weight pressing on his stomach, until both sensations lifted.

'Better?' asked Hermione.

'Yeah, loads better!'

'Harry,' she said, crouching down in front of him and using the kind of voice he associated with visiting the very sick, 'you don't think you've been possessed, do you?'

'What? No!' he said defensively. 'I remember everything we've done while I've been wearing it. I wouldn't know what I'd done if I'd been possessed, would I? Ginny told me there were times when she couldn't remember anything.'

第15章 妖精的报复

中间飘行,麻瓜或许看不见它们,但一定也会感觉到它们所到之处散发的绝望。

"这么说我们还是没有吃的。"

"别说了,罗恩。"赫敏厉声说,"哈利,怎么回事?你为什么召不出守护神?你昨天还做得很好啊!"

"我不知道。"

他矮身坐在珀金斯的旧扶手椅上,此刻感觉更加羞耻。他担心自己内心出了什么问题,昨天好像已是很久以前:今天他似乎又回到了十三岁,是唯一一个在霍格沃茨特快列车上昏倒的学生。

罗恩踢了一下椅子腿。

"怎么回事啊?"他对赫敏吼道,"我饿死了!我从差点失血而死到现在,只吃了几块毒蘑菇!"

"那你去抵抗摄魂怪啊。"哈利受了刺激,说道。

"我是想去,可是我胳膊还吊着呢,你可能没注意到!"

"很巧嘛。"

"你这是什么——?"

"对了!"赫敏一拍额头,叫了起来,两人都惊讶地沉默了,"哈利,给我那个挂坠盒!快,"见哈利没有反应,她朝他打着响指,急躁地说,"那个魂器,哈利,你还戴着它呢!"

她伸出双手,哈利把金链子从脑袋上脱下来。那玩意儿一离开他的皮肤,哈利立刻感觉到了自由和出奇的轻松,这才意识到自己刚才已被冷汗黏湿,胃里像压着一块巨石。

"好些了吗?"赫敏问。

"嗯,好多了!"

"哈利,"赫敏在他面前蹲下来,用令他联想到探望危重病人的语气说,"你没有被附身吧?"

"什么?没有!"他辩白道,"我戴着它时做过的事情我都记得,如果被附身了,我是不会记得的,对不对?金妮告诉我说,有些时候她什么都不记得。"

CHAPTER FIFTEEN The Goblin's Revenge

'Hm,' said Hermione, looking down at the heavy locket. 'Well, maybe we ought not to wear it. We can just keep it in the tent.'

'We are not leaving that Horcrux lying around,' Harry stated firmly. 'If we lose it, if it gets stolen –'

'Oh, all right, all right,' said Hermione, and she placed it around her own neck and tucked it out of sight down the front of her shirt. 'But we'll take turns wearing it, so nobody keeps it on too long.'

'Great,' said Ron irritably, 'and now we've sorted that out, can we please get some food?'

'Fine, but we'll go somewhere else to find it,' said Hermione, with half a glance at Harry. 'There's no point staying where we know Dementors are swooping around.'

In the end they settled down for the night in a far-flung field belonging to a lonely farm, from which they had managed to obtain eggs and bread.

'It's not stealing, is it?' asked Hermione in a troubled voice, as they devoured scrambled eggs on toast. 'Not if I left some money under the chicken coop?'

Ron rolled his eyes and said, with his cheeks bulging, ''Er-my-nee, 'oo worry 'oo much. 'Elax!'

And, indeed, it was much easier to relax when they were comfortably well fed: the argument about the Dementors was forgotten in laughter that night, and Harry felt cheerful, even hopeful, as he took the first of the three night watches.

This was their first encounter with the fact that a full stomach meant good spirits; an empty one, bickering and gloom. Harry was the least surprised by this, because he had suffered periods of near starvation at the Dursleys'. Hermione bore up reasonably well on those nights when they managed to scavenge nothing but berries or stale biscuits, her temper perhaps a little shorter than usual and her silences rather dour. Ron, however, had always been used to three delicious meals a day, courtesy of his mother or of the Hogwarts house-elves, and hunger made him both unreasonable and irascible. Whenever lack of food coincided with Ron's turn to wear the Horcrux, he became downright unpleasant.

'So where next?' was his constant refrain. He did not seem to have any ideas himself, but expected Harry and Hermione to come up with plans while he sat and brooded over the low food supplies. Accordingly, Harry and Hermione spent fruitless hours trying to decide where they might find

第15章 妖精的报复

"唔,"赫敏低头看着那个沉甸甸的挂坠盒,"也许我们不应该戴着它,可以把它留在帐篷里。"

"我们不能把魂器随便乱放,"哈利坚决地说,"要是弄丢了,要是被偷走——"

"哦,好吧,好吧,"赫敏说着,把它挂到自己的脖子上,塞进衬衫领子里,"但我们要轮流戴它,谁都不要戴得太久。"

"太好了。"罗恩烦躁地说,"现在问题解决了,能不能搞点吃的啦?"

"好啊,但要到别的地方去找。"赫敏往哈利那边瞟了瞟说,"明知有摄魂怪出没还待在这儿是不明智的。"

最后他们停在一片广阔的田野里过夜,并从那家孤零零的农场搞到了鸡蛋和面包。

"这不是偷,对吧?"三人狼吞虎咽地吃着烤面包夹炒鸡蛋时,赫敏不安地问,"我在鸡笼下面塞了点钱。"

罗恩翻翻白眼,鼓着腮帮子说:"赫—敏—,你—想得—太—多—了,放—松—点儿!"

舒舒服服吃饱之后,确实容易放松。关于摄魂怪的争吵在笑声中被遗忘了。晚上分三班放哨,哈利值第一班时,心情很愉快,甚至是乐观的。

这是他们第一次体会到饱肚子会带来好心情,而空肚子会引起争吵和沮丧。哈利对此最不意外,因为他在德思礼家多次尝过忍饥挨饿的滋味。在那些只能找到浆果或陈饼干的夜晚,赫敏风度还不错,虽然脾气或许比平时急躁一些,沉默时脸色也阴沉一些。罗恩却是习惯了一日三餐都能享用妈妈或霍格沃茨家养小精灵提供的可口饭菜,饥饿使他失去了理智,暴躁易怒。每当缺少吃的又赶上佩戴魂器时,他就变得简直令人讨厌了。

"下面去哪儿?"成了他的口头禅,他自己似乎一点主意也没有,全指望哈利、赫敏拿出计划,而他只坐在那里为食物不足而闷闷不乐。哈利和赫敏长时间地合计去哪儿可能找到其他魂器,讨论如何摧毁已

CHAPTER FIFTEEN   The Goblin's Revenge

the other Horcruxes, and how to destroy the one they had already got, their conversations becoming increasingly repetitive, as they had no new information.

As Dumbledore had told Harry that he believed Voldemort had hidden the Horcruxes in places important to him, they kept reciting, in a sort of dreary litany, those locations they knew that Voldemort had lived in or visited. The orphanage where he had been born and raised, Hogwarts, where he had been educated, Borgin and Burkes, where he had worked after leaving school, then Albania, where he had spent his years of exile: these formed the basis of their speculations.

'Yeah, let's go to Albania. Shouldn't take more than an afternoon to search an entire country,' said Ron sarcastically.

'There can't be anything there. He'd already made five of his Horcruxes before he went into exile, and Dumbledore was certain the snake is the sixth,' said Hermione. 'We know the snake's not in Albania, it's usually with Vol–'

'*Didn't I ask you to stop saying that?*'

'Fine! The snake is usually with *You-Know-Who* – happy?'

'Not particularly.'

'I can't see him hiding anything at Borgin and Burkes,' said Harry, who had made this point many times before, but said it again simply to break the nasty silence. 'Borgin and Burke were experts on Dark objects, they would've recognised a Horcrux straight away.'

Ron yawned pointedly. Repressing a strong urge to throw something at him, Harry ploughed on, 'I still reckon he might have hidden something at Hogwarts.'

Hermione sighed.

'But Dumbledore would have found it, Harry!'

Harry repeated the argument he kept bringing out in favour of this theory.

'Dumbledore said in front of me that he never assumed he knew all of Hogwarts' secrets. I'm telling you, if there was one place Vol–'

'Oi!'

'YOU-KNOW-WHO, then!' Harry shouted, goaded past endurance. 'If there was one place that was really important to You-Know-Who, it was Hogwarts!'

'Oh, come on,' scoffed Ron. 'His *school?*'

经找到的这一个,但毫无结果。因为得不到新的信息,他们的对话越来越重复单调。

邓布利多对哈利说过,伏地魔可能把魂器藏在对他有重要意义的地方。于是,他们枯燥地反复念叨他们听说过的伏地魔曾经居住或访问的地点。他出生和度过童年的孤儿院,他就读的霍格沃茨,他离校后工作过的博金-博克,还有他流亡多年的阿尔巴尼亚,这些构成了他们推想的依据。

"是啊,去阿尔巴尼亚吧,搜索整个国家只要花一下午。"罗恩讽刺地说。

"那儿不会有什么。他流亡前已经制作了五个魂器,邓布利多断定那条蛇是第六个。"赫敏说,"我们知道那条蛇不在阿尔巴尼亚,它一般都跟伏——"

"我没告诉你不要说那个名字吗?"

"好吧!那条蛇一般都跟神秘人在一起——满意了吧?"

"不大满意。"

"我看他不会在博金-博克藏什么东西。"哈利说,他已经多次表达过这一观点,但又说了一遍,只为打破那不愉快的沉默,"博金和博克都是黑魔法专家,他们一眼就会看出魂器的。"

罗恩有意打了个哈欠,哈利忍住想朝他扔东西的强烈冲动,勉强说下去:"我仍然觉得他可能在霍格沃茨藏了东西。"

赫敏叹了口气。

"但邓布利多会发现的呀,哈利!"

哈利又搬出他为支持这个论点而反复提起的说法。

"邓布利多当面对我说,他从不认为自己知道霍格沃茨的所有秘密,如果有一个地方是伏——"

"喂!"

"好吧,**神秘人**!"哈利吼道,被刺激得忍无可忍,"如果有一个地方真正对神秘人有重要意义,那就是霍格沃茨!"

"哦,得了,"罗恩嘲笑道,"他的学校?"

CHAPTER FIFTEEN   The Goblin's Revenge

'Yeah, his school! It was his first real home, the place that meant he was special, it meant everything to him, and even after he left –'

'This is You-Know-Who we're talking about, right? Not you?' enquired Ron. He was tugging at the chain of the Horcrux around his neck: Harry was visited by a desire to seize it and throttle him.

'You told us that You-Know-Who asked Dumbledore to give him a job after he left,' said Hermione.

'That's right,' said Harry.

'And Dumbledore thought he only wanted to come back to try and find something, probably another founder's object, to make into another Horcrux?'

'Yeah,' said Harry.

'But he didn't get the job, did he?' said Hermione. 'So he never got the chance to find a founder's object there and hide it in the school!'

'OK, then,' said Harry, defeated. 'Forget Hogwarts.'

Without any other leads, they travelled into London and, hidden beneath the Invisibility Cloak, searched for the orphanage in which Voldemort had been raised. Hermione stole into a library and discovered from their records that the place had been demolished many years before. They visited its site and found a towerblock of offices.

'We could try digging in the foundations?' Hermione suggested half-heartedly.

'He wouldn't have hidden a Horcrux here,' Harry said. He had known it all along: the orphanage had been the place Voldemort had been determined to escape from; he would never have hidden a part of his soul there. Dumbledore had shown Harry that Voldemort sought grandeur or mystique in his hiding places; this dismal, grey corner of London was as far removed as you could imagine from Hogwarts, or the Ministry or a building like Gringotts, the wizarding bank, with its golden doors and marble floors.

Even without any new ideas, they continued to move through the countryside, pitching the tent in a different place each night for security. Every morning they made sure that they had removed all clues to their presence, then set off to find another lonely and secluded spot, travelling by Apparition to more woods, to the shadowy crevices of cliffs, to purple moors, gorse-covered mountainsides and, once, a sheltered and pebbly cove. Every twelve hours or so, they passed the Horcrux between them as though they were playing some perverse, slow-motion game of pass the parcel, where they dreaded the music stopping because the reward was twelve hours of

第15章 妖精的报复

"对,他的学校!这是他第一个真正的家,一个表明他很特殊的地方,对他来说意味着一切,即使在他离开之后——"

"我们说的是神秘人,对吗?不是在说你吧?"罗恩问道,他在拉扯脖子上魂器的链子。哈利那一刻真想抓住那链子把他勒死。

"你告诉过我们,神秘人离校后曾请求邓布利多给他一份工作。"赫敏说。

"不错。"哈利说。

"邓布利多认为他只是想回来找什么东西,也许是另一个创始人的遗物,用来制作新的魂器,对吗?"

"对。"哈利说。

"可是他没有得到那份工作,是不是?"赫敏说,"所以他没有机会找到创始人的遗物,再把它藏在学校!"

"好吧,那么,"哈利认输地说,"忘掉霍格沃茨吧。"

没有别的线索,他们去了伦敦,披着隐形衣寻找伏地魔住过的那所孤儿院。赫敏溜进一个图书馆,从资料中发现那所孤儿院多年前就拆毁了。他们到原址转了转,发现那里已是办公大楼。

"我们可以试试到地基里挖一挖?"赫敏热情不高地说。

"他不会把魂器藏在这里的。"哈利说。他早就知道:孤儿院是伏地魔决心要逃离的地方,他绝不会把自己灵魂的一部分藏在那儿。邓布利多曾提示哈利,伏地魔选择藏身之处时追求庄严或神秘的气氛。伦敦的这个阴郁灰暗的角落,与霍格沃茨、魔法部或古灵阁巫师银行的金色大门和大理石地面,可以说有天壤之别。

尽管没有新的主意,他们仍然在野外流浪。为安全起见,他们每天晚上都在不同的地方宿营,早晨消去留下的所有痕迹,然后出发去寻找另一个偏僻隐蔽的地方,幻影显形到森林、幽暗的崖缝、紫色的沼地、开满金雀花的山坡,还有一次到了一个隐蔽的卵石小湾。他们轮流佩戴魂器,大约每十二小时一换,好像在玩一种邪恶的、慢动作的击鼓传花游戏,每个人都害怕鼓声停止,因为带来的惩罚是十二个

CHAPTER FIFTEEN The Goblin's Revenge

increased fear and anxiety.

Harry's scar kept prickling. It happened most often, he noticed, when he was wearing the Horcrux. Sometimes he could not stop himself reacting to the pain.

'What? What did you see?' demanded Ron, whenever he noticed Harry wince.

'A face,' muttered Harry, every time. 'The same face. The thief who stole from Gregorovitch.'

And Ron would turn away, making no effort to hide his disappointment. Harry knew that Ron was hoping to hear news of his family, or of the rest of the Order of the Phoenix, but after all, he, Harry, was not a television aerial; he could only see what Voldemort was thinking at the time, not tune in to whatever took his fancy. Apparently Voldemort was dwelling endlessly on the unknown youth with the gleeful face, whose name and whereabouts, Harry felt sure, Voldemort knew no better than he did. As Harry's scar continued to burn and the merry, blond-haired boy swam tantalisingly in his memory, he learned to suppress any sign of pain or discomfort, for the other two showed nothing but impatience at the mention of the thief. He could not entirely blame them, when they were so desperate for a lead on the Horcruxes.

As the days stretched into weeks, Harry began to suspect that Ron and Hermione were having conversations without, and about, him. Several times they stopped talking abruptly when Harry entered the tent, and twice he came accidentally upon them, huddled a little distance away, heads together and talking fast; both times they fell silent when they realised he was approaching them and hastened to appear busy collecting wood or water.

Harry could not help wondering whether they had only agreed to come on what now felt like a pointless and rambling journey because they thought he had some secret plan that they would learn in due course. Ron was making no effort to hide his bad mood, and Harry was starting to fear that Hermione, too, was disappointed by his poor leadership. In desperation he tried to think of further Horcrux locations, but the only one that continued to occur to him was Hogwarts, and as neither of the others thought this at all likely, he stopped suggesting it.

Autumn rolled over the countryside as they moved through it: they were now pitching the tent on mulches of fallen leaves. Natural mists joined those cast by the Dementors; wind and rain added to their troubles. The fact that Hermione was getting better at identifying edible fungi could not altogether compensate for their continuing isolation, the lack of other people's company,

第15章 妖精的报复

小时更强烈的恐惧和焦虑。

哈利的伤疤经常刺痛。他注意到，当他佩戴魂器时，伤疤痛的次数最多，有时痛得他禁不住有所反应。

"什么？你看见了什么？"每当看到哈利皱紧眉头，罗恩就问。

"一张面孔，"哈利每次都喃喃地说道，"同一张面孔。格里戈维奇家的那个小偷。"

罗恩便转过头去，并不掩饰他的失望。哈利知道罗恩希望听到他家人的消息，或是凤凰社其他成员的消息。可他哈利毕竟不是电视天线，他只能看到伏地魔此时在想什么，而无法做到想调什么频道就能如愿。显然伏地魔在无休止地想着那个神采飞扬的无名少年，想他叫什么，在什么地方。哈利确信伏地魔并不比自己知道得更多。哈利的伤疤继续灼痛，那个快乐的金发少年在他记忆中晃来晃去，让他干着急。他学会了掩饰疼痛或不适，因为两个同伴在他提起那个小偷时表现出的只有不耐烦。他不能完全怪他们，毕竟大家都迫切希望得到一点魂器的线索。

从几天挨到了几星期，哈利开始疑心罗恩和赫敏在背后议论他。有几次，他们俩在哈利走进帐篷时突然停止了交谈。还有两次，他碰见他们俩在不远处紧挨着，脑袋凑在一起，急速地窃窃私语，发现他走近，两人都急忙住口，装作拾柴或打水。

哈利不禁怀疑，他们当初之所以同意参加这一行动，是以为他有什么秘密计划，会在适当的时候透露给他们，而现在感觉这行动像是漫无目标的流浪。罗恩毫不掩饰他的坏情绪，哈利开始担心赫敏也对他的领导能力感到失望。绝望中，他试图猜想其他魂器的地点，可是唯一一个老是想到的地方就是霍格沃茨，而他们俩都认为这根本不可能，他也就不再提了。

秋色在郊外蔓延，他们继续流浪。现在他们把帐篷搭在了满地落叶上。自然的雾气与摄魂怪带来的冷雾混在一起；风雨也给他们增添了困难。赫敏识别食用菌的本领提高了，但这并不能抵消其他方面的消极因素：长期孤独，没有其他人陪伴，而且完全不知道反伏地魔的

CHAPTER FIFTEEN   The Goblin's Revenge

or their total ignorance of what was going on in the war against Voldemort.

'My mother,' said Ron one night, as they sat in the tent on a riverbank in Wales, 'can make good food appear out of thin air.'

He prodded moodily at the lumps of charred, grey fish on his plate. Harry glanced automatically at Ron's neck and saw, as he had expected, the golden chain of the Horcrux glinting there. He managed to fight down the impulse to swear at Ron, whose attitude would, he knew, improve slightly when the time came to take off the locket.

'Your mother can't produce food out of thin air,' said Hermione. 'No one can. Food is the first of the five Principal Exceptions to Gamp's Law of Elemental Transfigur–'

'Oh, speak English, can't you?' Ron said, prising a fishbone out from between his teeth.

'It's impossible to make good food out of nothing! You can Summon it if you know where it is, you can transform it, you can increase the quantity if you've already got some –'

'– well, don't bother increasing this, it's disgusting,' said Ron.

'Harry caught the fish and I did my best with it! I notice I'm always the one who ends up sorting out the food; because I'm a *girl*, I suppose!'

'No, it's because you're supposed to be the best at magic!' shot back Ron.

Hermione jumped up and bits of roast pike slid off her tin plate on to the floor.

'*You* can do the cooking tomorrow, Ron, *you* can find the ingredients and try and charm them into something worth eating, and I'll sit here and pull faces and moan and you can see how you –'

'Shut up!' said Harry, leaping to his feet and holding up both hands. 'Shut up *now*!'

Hermione looked outraged.

'How can you side with him, he hardly ever does the cook–'

'Hermione, be quiet, I can hear someone!'

He was listening hard, his hands still raised, warning them not to talk. Then, over the rush and gush of the dark river beside them, he heard voices again. He looked round at the Sneakoscope. It was not moving.

'You cast the *Muffliato* charm over us, right?' he whispered to Hermione.

'I did everything,' she whispered back, '*Muffliato*, Muggle-Repelling and Disillusionment Charms, all of it. They shouldn't be able to hear or see us, whoever they are.'

第15章 妖精的报复

斗争进展如何。

"我妈妈,"一天晚上,坐在威尔士一处河岸边的帐篷里,罗恩说道,"能凭空变出美味佳肴。"

他忧郁地戳着盘中那几块烧焦的、灰不溜秋的鱼肉。哈利不由得瞟了一眼罗恩的脖子,果然看到魂器的金链子在那里闪烁,便压下了想骂他几句的冲动,知道挂坠盒拿掉后他的态度会稍有好转。

"你妈妈不能凭空变出食物,"赫敏说,"谁也不能。食物是'甘普基本变形法则'的五大例外中的第一项——"

"哦,说大白话,行不行?"罗恩说,从牙缝中剔出一根鱼刺。

"不可能凭空变出美味佳肴!如果你知道食物在哪儿,可以把它召来;如果你已经有了一些,可以给它变形,也可以使它增多——"

"——哦,这个就不用增多了,真难吃。"罗恩说。

"哈利抓的鱼,我尽了最大努力!我发现最后总是我去弄吃的,大概因为我是女孩吧!"

"不,因为据说你是最精通魔法的!"罗恩反唇相讥。

赫敏蹦了起来,几小块烤梭子鱼从她的锡盘里滑到地上。

"你明天负责做饭好了,罗恩,你可以去找原料,想办法把它们变成能够下咽的东西,我坐在这儿拉长了脸发牢骚,你可以看到你——"

"住口!"哈利举着双手跳起来说,"马上住口!"

赫敏看上去很愤慨。

"你怎么可以站在他那边,他几乎从来不做饭——"

"赫敏,安静,我听到有人!"

哈利仔细聆听,双手仍然举着,警告他们不要说话。少顷,在旁边黑暗中河水的哗哗声里,他再次听到了说话声。他回头看看窥镜,窥镜一动不动。

"你在我们周围施了闭耳塞听咒,是不是?"他小声问赫敏。

"我什么都用上了,"赫敏小声回答,"闭耳塞听、麻瓜驱逐咒和幻身咒,一股脑儿全用上了。不管是什么人,应该不会听到或看到我们。"

CHAPTER FIFTEEN   The Goblin's Revenge

Heavy scuffing and scraping noises, plus the sound of dislodged stones and twigs, told them that several people were clambering down the steep, wooded slope that descended to the narrow bank where they had pitched the tent. They drew their wands, waiting. The enchantments they had cast around themselves ought to be sufficient, in the near total darkness, to shield them from the notice of Muggles and normal witches and wizards. If these were Death Eaters, then perhaps their defences were about to be tested by Dark Magic for the first time.

The voices became louder but no more intelligible as the group of men reached the bank. Harry estimated that their owners were less than twenty feet away, but the cascading river made it impossible to tell for sure. Hermione snatched up the beaded bag and started to rummage; after a moment she drew out three Extendable Ears and threw one each to Harry and Ron, who hastily inserted the ends of the flesh-coloured strings into their ears and fed the other ends out of the tent entrance.

Within seconds Harry heard a weary, male voice.

'There ought to be a few salmon in here, or d'you reckon it's too early in the season? *Accio salmon!*'

There were several distinct splashes and then the slapping sounds of fish against flesh. Somebody grunted appreciatively. Harry pressed the Extendable Ear deeper into his own: over the murmur of the river he could make out more voices, but they were not speaking English or any human language he had ever heard. It was a rough and unmelodious tongue, a string of rattling, guttural noises, and there seemed to be two speakers, one with a slightly lower, slower voice than the other.

A fire danced into life on the other side of the canvas; large shadows passed between tent and flames. The delicious smell of baking salmon wafted tantalisingly in their direction. Then came the clinking of cutlery on plates, and the first man spoke again.

'Here, Griphook, Gornuk.'

Goblins! Hermione mouthed at Harry, who nodded.

'Thank you,' said the goblins together in English.

'So, you three have been on the run, how long?' asked a new, mellow and pleasant voice; it was vaguely familiar to Harry, who pictured a roundbellied, cheerful-faced man.

'Six weeks ... seven ... I forget,' said the tired man. 'Met up with Griphook in the first couple of days and joined forces with Gornuk not

第15章 妖精的报复

沉重的脚步声和摩擦声,还有石头和树枝掉落的声音,告诉他们有几个人正在攀下陡峭多树的山坡,渐渐接近坡下搭着帐篷的狭窄河岸。他们抽出魔杖等待着。在几乎一片漆黑中,防护魔法应该足以挡住麻瓜和一般巫师的注意。如果来的是食死徒,这防护屏障可能就要第一次经受黑魔法的检验。

声音大了一些,还是听不清楚,因为那帮人到了河边。哈利估计说话者离他们不到二十英尺,但在奔流的河水声中不能确定。赫敏抓过串珠小包翻找起来,一会儿便掏出三个伸缩耳,扔给哈利和罗恩一人一个。他们急忙将那肉色的细绳一头塞进耳中,另一头送到帐篷外。

几秒钟后哈利就听到了一个疲惫的男声。

"这儿应该有一些鲑鱼,你说是不是季节还太早?鲑鱼飞来!"

几处泼剌剌的溅水声,接着是鱼撞到皮肤上的啪唧声。有人赞赏地嘟囔着。哈利把伸缩耳往自己耳朵里塞得更深一点,在潺潺的水声中他又听到了一些说话声,但说的不是英语,也不是他听过的任何人类语言。那是一种粗哑刺耳的说话声,一连串嘎嘎的喉音,听起来好像有两个人,一个声音稍微低一些、慢一些。

帐篷的一面帆布外有火焰跳动起来,庞大的黑影在帐篷与火焰之间晃动。烤鲑鱼的香味诱人地飘来,然后传来了盘子上刀叉的叮当声,第一个男声又说话了。

"给,拉环、戈努克。"

妖精!赫敏对哈利做着口型说,哈利点点头。

"谢谢。"两个妖精一齐用英语说。

"这么说,你们三个一直在逃亡,有多久了?"另一个醇厚悦耳的声音说,哈利觉得似乎有点耳熟,他想象出一个大肚子、慈眉善目的男人。

"六个……七个星期……我忘了。"那个疲惫的男声说,"头两天遇到了拉环,不久之后又跟戈努克会合。很高兴有个伴。"片刻的沉默,

CHAPTER FIFTEEN The Goblin's Revenge

long after. Nice to have a bit of company.' There was a pause, while knives scraped plates and tin mugs were picked up and replaced on the ground. 'What made you leave, Ted?' continued the man.

'Knew they were coming for me,' replied mellow-voiced Ted, and Harry suddenly knew who he was: Tonks's father. 'Heard Death Eaters were in the area last week and decided I'd better run for it. Refused to register as a Muggle-born on principle, see, so I knew it was a matter of time, knew I'd have to leave in the end. My wife should be OK, she's pure-blood. And then I met Dean here, what, a few days ago, son?'

'Yeah,' said another voice, and Harry, Ron and Hermione stared at each other, silent but beside themselves with excitement, sure they recognised the voice of Dean Thomas, their fellow Gryffindor.

'Muggle-born, eh?' asked the first man.

'Not sure,' said Dean. 'My dad left my mum when I was a kid. I've got no proof he was a wizard, though.'

There was silence for a while, except for the sounds of munching; then Ted spoke again.

'I've got to say, Dirk, I'm surprised to run into you. Pleased, but surprised. Word was you'd been caught.'

'I was,' said Dirk. 'I was halfway to Azkaban when I made a break for it, Stunned Dawlish and nicked his broom. It was easier than you'd think; I don't reckon he's quite right at the moment. Might be Confunded. If so, I'd like to shake the hand of the witch or wizard who did it, probably saved my life.'

There was another pause, in which the fire crackled and the river rushed on. Then Ted said, 'And where do you two fit in? I, er, had the impression the goblins were for You-Know-Who, on the whole.'

'You had a false impression,' said the higher-voiced of the goblins. 'We take no sides. This is a wizards' war.'

'How come you're in hiding, then?'

'I deemed it prudent,' said the deeper-voiced goblin. 'Having refused what I considered an impertinent request, I could see that my personal safety was in jeopardy.'

'What did they ask you to do?' asked Ted.

第15章 妖精的报复

刀刮盘子的声音，锡杯子被拿起又放回地上。"你怎么出来了，泰德？"那人又问。

"知道他们要来找我。"声音醇厚的泰德答道。哈利突然知道他是谁了：唐克斯的父亲。"听说上星期这个地区有食死徒出现，我决定还是逃走吧。我出于原则拒绝参加麻瓜出身登记，所以，我知道这是迟早的事，终归非走不可。我太太应该没事，她是纯血统。后来我在这儿碰到了迪安，是几天前吧，孩子？"

"是。"又一个声音说。哈利、罗恩和赫敏对视了一下，没有出声但都兴奋极了，他们听出那声音分明是迪安·托马斯，他们在格兰芬多学院的同学。

"麻瓜出身，嗯？"第一个男声问。

"搞不清。"迪安说，"我很小的时候，我爸就离开了我妈，我没有证据证明我爸是巫师。"

一阵沉默，只听到咀嚼的声音，然后泰德又说话了。

"我不得不说，德克，遇见你让我感到意外。很高兴，但也很意外。传闻说你已经被捕了。"

"是的，"德克说，"我在被押往阿兹卡班的路上逃了出来。击昏了德力士，偷了他的飞天扫帚。比想象的容易。我看他当时不大正常，也许被施了混淆咒，如果是那样，我真想跟那位施咒的巫师握握手，等于救了我一命呢。"

又是一阵沉默，火堆噼啪作响，河水汩汩流淌。然后泰德说："那么，你们两个又是怎么回事？我——呃——我印象中妖精大体上是支持神秘人的呀。"

"你的印象是错误的，"声音较高的那个妖精说，"我们并不偏向哪一边，这是巫师的战争。"

"那你们为什么要躲藏呢？"

"我认为躲藏是明智的，"声音较低沉的那个妖精说，"在拒绝了我认为无礼的要求后，我可以想见我的人身安全处于危险之中。"

"他们要你做什么？"泰德问。

CHAPTER FIFTEEN   The Goblin's Revenge

'Duties ill-befitting the dignity of my race,' replied the goblin, his voice rougher and less human as he said it. 'I am not a house-elf.'

'What about you, Griphook?'

'Similar reasons,' said the higher-voiced goblin. 'Gringotts is no longer under the sole control of my race. I recognise no wizarding master.'

He added something under his breath in Gobbledegook and Gornuk laughed.

'What's the joke?' asked Dean.

'He said,' replied Dirk, 'that there are things wizards don't recognise, either.'

There was a short pause.

'I don't get it,' said Dean.

'I had my small revenge before I left,' said Griphook in English.

'Good man – goblin, I should say,' amended Ted hastily. 'Didn't manage to lock a Death Eater up in one of the old high-security vaults, I suppose?'

'If I had, the sword would not have helped him break out,' replied Griphook. Gornuk laughed again and even Dirk gave a dry chuckle.

'Dean and I are still missing something here,' said Ted.

'So is Severus Snape, though he does not know it,' said Griphook, and the two goblins roared with malicious laughter.

Inside the tent Harry's breathing was shallow with excitement: he and Hermione stared at each other, listening as hard as they could.

'Didn't you hear about that, Ted?' asked Dirk. 'About the kids who tried to steal Gryffindor's sword out of Snape's office at Hogwarts?'

An electric current seemed to course through Harry, jangling his every nerve as he stood rooted to the spot.

'Never heard a word,' said Ted. 'Not in the *Prophet*, was it?'

'Hardly,' chortled Dirk. 'Griphook here told me, he heard about it from Bill Weasley who works for the bank. One of the kids who tried to take the sword was Bill's younger sister.'

Harry glanced towards Hermione and Ron, both of whom were clutching the Extendable Ears as tightly as lifelines.

第15章 妖精的报复

"与我的种族尊严不相称的事情,"那妖精答道,声音变得更加粗犷,不像人声,"我不是家养小精灵。"

"你呢,拉环?"

"类似的原因。"声音较高的妖精说,"古灵阁不再由我的种族单独控制。我不承认巫师是我的主人。"

他小声用妖精语言叽咕了几句,戈努克大笑起来。

"有什么好笑的?"迪安问。

"他说,"德克答道,"有些事情巫师还蒙在鼓里呢。"

片刻的沉默。

"我不明白。"迪安说。

"我离开前施了一个小小的报复。"拉环用英语说。

"真是好汉——好妖精,我应该说。"泰德连忙更正道,"没有把一个食死徒锁在超级保险的古老金库里吧?"

"即使我锁了,那把剑也不会帮他逃出来。"拉环答道。戈努克又笑起来,德克也干巴巴地笑了两声。

"迪安和我还是有些糊涂。"泰德说。

"西弗勒斯·斯内普也是,但他还不知道。"拉环说,两个妖精恶意地放声狂笑。

帐篷里,哈利的呼吸兴奋而短促。他和赫敏瞪大眼睛对视着,竭力仔细聆听。

"你没有听说吗,泰德?"德克问道,"霍格沃茨那些孩子试图把格兰芬多的宝剑从斯内普办公室偷出去。"

似乎有一股电流传遍了哈利全身,刺激着他的每一根神经。他像生了根一样伫立在原地。

"一个字也没听说,"泰德说,"《预言家日报》上没有提吧?"

"不会有的,"德克高声笑道,"是拉环告诉我的。他又是听在银行工作的比尔·韦斯莱说的。偷宝剑的孩子中有一个是比尔的妹妹。"

哈利瞥了一眼赫敏和罗恩,他们俩都紧紧捏着伸缩耳,像抓着救命稻草一般。

CHAPTER FIFTEEN The Goblin's Revenge

'She and a couple of friends got into Snape's office and smashed open the glass case where he was apparently keeping the sword. Snape caught them as they were trying to smuggle it down the staircase.'

'Ah, God bless 'em,' said Ted. 'What did they think, that they'd be able to use the sword on You-Know-Who? Or on Snape himself?'

'Well, whatever they thought they were going to do with it, Snape decided the sword wasn't safe where it was,' said Dirk. 'Couple of days later, once he'd got the say so from You-Know-Who, I imagine, he sent it down to London to be kept in Gringotts instead.'

The goblins started to laugh again.

'I'm still not seeing the joke,' said Ted.

'It's a fake,' rasped Griphook.

'The sword of Gryffindor!'

'Oh, yes. It is a copy – an excellent copy, it is true – but it was wizard-made. The original was forged centuries ago by goblins and had certain properties only goblin-made armour possesses. Wherever the genuine sword of Gryffindor is, it is not in a vault at Gringotts Bank.'

'I see,' said Ted. 'And I take it you didn't bother telling the Death Eaters this?'

'I saw no reason to trouble them with the information,' said Griphook smugly, and now Ted and Dean joined in Gornuk and Dirk's laughter.

Inside the tent, Harry closed his eyes, willing someone to ask the question he needed answered, and after a minute that seemed ten, Dean obliged; he was (Harry remembered with a jolt) an ex-boyfriend of Ginny's too.

'What happened to Ginny and the others? The ones who tried to steal it?'

'Oh, they were punished, and cruelly,' said Griphook indifferently.

'They're OK, though?' asked Ted quickly. 'I mean, the Weasleys don't need any more of their kids injured, do they?'

'They suffered no serious injury, as far as I am aware,' said Griphook.

'Lucky for them,' said Ted. 'With Snape's track record, I suppose we should just be glad they're still alive.'

'You believe that story, then, do you, Ted?' asked Dirk. 'You believe Snape killed Dumbledore?'

第15章 妖精的报复

"那小姑娘和几个朋友一起溜进斯内普的办公室,砸开了好像是放着宝剑的那个玻璃匣子,正在偷偷把宝剑拿下楼时,被斯内普抓住了。"

"啊,上帝保佑他们。"泰德说,"这帮孩子是怎么想的,以为他们能用这把宝剑去对付神秘人?或对付斯内普本人?"

"哦,不管他们想用它干什么,斯内普断定这把剑放在那里不安全了。"德克说,"几天之后,我想是得到了神秘人的许可,他把它运到伦敦,存在了古灵阁。"

两个妖精又大笑起来。

"我还是看不出有什么好笑的。"泰德说。

"那是赝品。"拉环刺耳地说。

"格兰芬多的宝剑!"

"哦,是的,是仿制品——仿制得非常好,这点不假——但它是巫师制造的。真品是许多世纪以前由妖精铸造的,有一些只有妖精造的武器才具备的特性。不管真正的格兰芬多宝剑在哪儿,反正不在古灵阁银行的金库里。"

"我明白了。"泰德说,"我想你没有去把这告诉食死徒吧?"

"我认为没有必要用这个消息去困扰他们。"拉环洋洋自得地说。

现在泰德和迪安也跟着戈努克和德克大笑起来。

帐篷里,哈利闭起眼睛,希望有人问起他想知道的问题。过了一分钟,他感觉像过了十分钟,迪安满足了他的愿望。他(哈利猛然想起)以前也是金妮的男友。

"金妮和其他人怎么样了?那帮偷宝剑的学生?"

"哦,他们受到了惩罚,残酷的惩罚。"拉环冷淡地说。

"他们没事吧?"泰德马上问,"我想,韦斯莱家可不能再有孩子受伤了,是不是?"

"据我所知,他们没有受什么重伤。"拉环说。

"真幸运。"泰德说,"以斯内普的一贯作风,我认为那帮孩子能活下来就不错了。"

"那么你也相信那个说法了,泰德?"德克问,"你相信是斯内普杀死了邓布利多?"

CHAPTER FIFTEEN   The Goblin's Revenge

'"Course I do,' said Ted. 'You're not going to sit there and tell me you think Potter had anything to do with it?'

'Hard to know what to believe these days,' muttered Dirk.

'I know Harry Potter,' said Dean. 'And I reckon he's the real thing – the Chosen One, or whatever you want to call it.'

'Yeah, there's a lot would like to believe he's that, son,' said Dirk, 'me included. But where is he? Run for it, by the looks of things. You'd think, if he knew anything we don't, or had anything special going for him, he'd be out there now fighting, rallying resistance, instead of hiding. And you know, the *Prophet* made a pretty good case against him –'

'The *Prophet*?' scoffed Ted. 'You deserve to be lied to if you're still reading that muck, Dirk. You want the facts, try *The Quibbler*.'

There was a sudden explosion of choking and retching, plus a good deal of thumping; by the sound of it, Dirk had swallowed a fishbone. At last he spluttered, '*The Quibbler?* That lunatic rag of Xeno Lovegood's?'

'It's not so lunatic these days,' said Ted. 'You want to give it a look. Xeno is printing all the stuff the *Prophet*'s ignoring, not a single mention of Crumple-Horned Snorkacks in the last issue. How long they'll let him get away with it, mind, I don't know. But Xeno says, front page of every issue, that any wizard who's against You-Know-Who ought to make helping Harry Potter their number one priority.'

'Hard to help a boy who's vanished off the face of the earth,' said Dirk.

'Listen, the fact that they haven't caught him yet's one hell of an achievement,' said Ted. 'I'd take tips from him gladly. It's what we're trying to do, stay free, isn't it?'

'Yeah, well, you've got a point there,' said Dirk heavily. 'With the whole of the Ministry and all their informers looking for him, I'd have expected him to be caught by now. Mind, who's to say they haven't already caught and killed him without publicising it?'

'Ah, don't say that, Dirk,' murmured Ted.

There was a long pause filled with more clattering of knives and forks. When they spoke again, it was to discuss whether they ought to sleep on the bank or retreat back up the wooded slope. Deciding the trees would give better cover, they extinguished their fire, then clambered back up the incline, their voices fading away.

第15章 妖精的报复

"我当然相信,"泰德说,"你不会坐在那儿告诉我,你认为波特与这事儿有关系吧?"

"这些日子很难知道该相信什么。"德克咕哝道。

"我认识哈利·波特,"迪安说,"我认为他是真正的——救世之星,或随便你想用什么词。"

"是啊,很多人都愿意相信他是,孩子,"德克说,"包括我在内。可是他在哪儿呢?看样子是跑了。照理说,如果他知道一些我们不知道的事情,或者有什么特殊的能耐,现在就应该挺身而出,率领大家反抗,而不是销声匿迹。你知道,《预言家日报》对他的一些揭露挺有道理——"

"《预言家日报》?"泰德嗤之以鼻,"如果你还在读那种垃圾,被欺骗也是活该,德克。你要想知道事实,去看《唱唱反调》吧。"

突然爆发出一阵咳嗽声和吐东西的声音,还有重重的拍击声,听起来好像德克吞下了一根鱼刺。最后他呛着说:"《唱唱反调》?谢诺·洛夫古德的那份疯话连篇的破小报?"

"现在不那么疯话连篇了。"泰德说,"你应该看一看。谢诺发表的是《预言家日报》忽略的一切,上期报纸上一个字没提到弯角鼾兽。注意,他们能容忍他多久,我不知道。但是谢诺在每期的头版都说,反对神秘人的巫师都应该把帮助哈利·波特摆在第一位。"

"要帮助一个从地球上消失的男孩,难哪。"德克说。

"听我说,他们迄今为止还没有抓到他,这本身就是了不起的成绩。"泰德说,"我倒很乐意听听他的诀窍。这正是我们努力在做的——不让自己被抓住,不是吗?"

"是啊,嗯,你这话倒是有道理,"德克沉重地说,"整个魔法部和他们的眼线都在寻找他,我以为他已经被抓到了呢。不过,谁知道他们会不会已经逮捕和杀害了他,只是秘而不宣呢?"

"啊,别那么说,德克。"泰德喃喃道。

长时间的沉默,刀叉叮当作响。当说话声再次响起时,他们开始讨论该睡在河岸上,还是该退回到树多的山坡上。他们认为树荫下更隐蔽些,便把火熄灭了,往坡上爬去,说话声渐渐减弱,听不见了。

CHAPTER FIFTEEN   The Goblin's Revenge

Harry, Ron and Hermione reeled in the Extendable Ears. Harry, who had found the need to remain silent increasingly difficult the longer they eavesdropped, now found himself unable to say more than, 'Ginny – the sword –'

'I know!' said Hermione.

She lunged for the tiny beaded bag, this time sinking her arm in it right up to the armpit.

'Here ... we ... are ...' she said between gritted teeth, and she pulled at something that was evidently in the depths of the bag. Slowly, the edge of an ornate picture frame came into sight. Harry hurried to help her. As they lifted the empty portrait of Phineas Nigellus free of Hermione's bag, she kept her wand pointing at it, ready to cast a spell at any moment.

'If somebody swapped the real sword for the fake while it was in Dumbledore's office,' she panted, as they propped the painting against the side of the tent, 'Phineas Nigellus would have seen it happen, he hangs right beside the case!'

'Unless he was asleep,' said Harry, but he still held his breath as Hermione knelt down in front of the empty canvas, her wand directed at its centre, cleared her throat, then said, 'Er – Phineas? Phineas Nigellus?'

Nothing happened.

'Phineas Nigellus?' said Hermione again. 'Professor Black? Please could we talk to you? Please?'

'"Please" always helps,' said a cold, snide voice, and Phineas Nigellus slid into his portrait. At once, Hermione cried, '*Obscuro!*'

A black blindfold appeared over Phineas Nigellus's clever, dark eyes, causing him to bump into the frame and shriek with pain.

'What – how dare – what are you –?'

'I'm very sorry, Professor Black,' said Hermione, 'but it's a necessary precaution!'

'Remove this foul addition at once! Remove it, I say! You are ruining a great work of art! Where am I? What is going on?'

'Never mind where we are,' said Harry, and Phineas Nigellus froze, abandoning his attempts to peel off the painted blindfold.

'Can that possibly be the voice of the elusive Mr Potter?'

'Maybe,' said Harry, knowing that this would keep Phineas Nigellus's

第15章 妖精的报复

哈利、罗恩和赫敏收起伸缩耳。哈利刚才偷听的时间越长，越觉得忍不住要说话，可现在却发现自己只会说："金妮——那把剑——"

"我知道！"赫敏说。

她冲过去抓起串珠小包，这次整个胳膊都伸了进去，直到胳肢窝。

"找……到……了……"她咬着牙说，用力拽着一个显然压在深处的东西。慢慢地，一个华丽相框的边缘露了出来。哈利急忙过去帮她，两个人把菲尼亚斯·奈杰勒斯的空肖像拖出赫敏的小包时，她一直用魔杖指着它，准备随时施出咒语。

"如果有人在邓布利多办公室里用赝品跟真宝剑调包，"他们把相框靠在帐篷壁上时，赫敏喘着气说，"菲尼亚斯·奈杰勒斯会看到的，他就挂在宝剑匣子旁边！"

"除非他睡着了。"哈利说，他仍然屏着呼吸，赫敏跪在空画布面前，用魔杖指着它的中心，清了清嗓子说，"呃——菲尼亚斯？菲尼亚斯·奈杰勒斯？"

没有动静。

"菲尼亚斯·奈杰勒斯？"赫敏又说，"布莱克教授？能请您跟我们谈谈吗？劳驾？"

"'请'总是有用的。"一个冷冰冰的、讥讽的声音说，菲尼亚斯·奈杰勒斯溜进肖像中。赫敏马上叫道："掩目蔽视！"

一块黑眼罩蒙住了菲尼亚斯·奈杰勒斯那双机敏的黑眼睛，他撞到相框上，痛得嗷嗷叫。

"什么——你们怎么敢——搞什么——？"

"我很抱歉，布莱克教授，"赫敏说，"但这是必要的防备！"

"马上去掉这块脏东西！马上去掉，我说！你们在毁掉一幅伟大的艺术品！我在哪儿？怎么回事？"

"别管我们在哪儿。"哈利说，菲尼亚斯·奈杰勒斯呆住了，不再拉扯那块画上去的眼罩。

"莫非是那位行踪不定的波特同学的声音？"

"也许。"哈利说，知道这会让菲尼亚斯·奈杰勒斯保持兴趣，"我

CHAPTER FIFTEEN   The Goblin's Revenge

interest. 'We've got a couple of questions to ask you – about the sword of Gryffindor.'

'Ah,' said Phineas Nigellus, now turning his head this way and that in an effort to catch sight of Harry, 'yes. That silly girl acted most unwisely there –'

'Shut up about my sister,' said Ron roughly. Phineas Nigellus raised supercilious eyebrows.

'Who else is here?' he asked, turning his head from side to side. 'Your tone displeases me! The girl and her friends were foolhardy in the extreme. Thieving from the Headmaster!'

'They weren't thieving,' said Harry. 'That sword isn't Snape's.'

'It belongs to Professor Snape's school,' said Phineas Nigellus. 'Exactly what claim did the Weasley girl have upon it? She deserved her punishment, as did the idiot Longbottom and the Lovegood oddity!'

'Neville is not an idiot and Luna is not an oddity!' said Hermione.

'Where am I?' repeated Phineas Nigellus, starting to wrestle with the blindfold again. 'Where have you brought me? Why have you removed me from the house of my forebears?'

'Never mind that! How did Snape punish Ginny, Neville and Luna?' asked Harry urgently.

'*Professor* Snape sent them into the Forbidden Forest, to do some work for the oaf, Hagrid.'

'Hagrid's not an oaf!' said Hermione shrilly.

'And Snape might've thought that was a punishment,' said Harry, 'but Ginny, Neville and Luna probably had a good laugh with Hagrid. The Forbidden Forest ... they've faced plenty worse than the Forbidden Forest, big deal!'

He felt relieved; he had been imagining horrors, the Cruciatus Curse at the very least.

'What we really wanted to know, Professor Black, is whether anyone else has, um, taken out the sword at all? Maybe it's been taken away for cleaning or – or something?'

Phineas Nigellus paused again in his struggles to free his eyes and sniggered.

'*Muggle-borns*,' he said. 'Goblin-made armour does not require cleaning, simple girl. Goblins' silver repels mundane dirt, imbibing only that which strengthens it.'

'Don't call Hermione simple,' said Harry.

第15章 妖精的报复

们有几个问题想问您,关于格兰芬多的宝剑。"

"啊,"菲尼亚斯·奈杰勒斯现在把头歪过来扭过去,企图看到哈利,"是的,那个傻丫头此举极不明智——"

"不许这么说我妹妹。"罗恩粗声说。菲尼亚斯·奈杰勒斯扬起高傲的眉毛。

"还有谁在这儿?"他问,脑袋转来转去,"你的口气让我不快!那个丫头和她的朋友们愚蠢透顶,偷校长的东西!"

"他们不是偷,"哈利说,"那把剑不是斯内普的。"

"可它属于斯内普教授的学校,"菲尼亚斯·奈杰勒斯说,"韦斯莱家的丫头有什么权利拿走它?她活该受到惩罚,还有那个白痴隆巴顿和怪物洛夫古德!"

"纳威不是白痴,卢娜也不是怪物!"赫敏说。

"我在哪儿?"菲尼亚斯·奈杰勒斯再次问道,又开始拉扯眼罩,"你们把我弄到了什么地方?为什么把我从我祖先的宅子里搬走?"

"别管那个!斯内普是怎么惩罚金妮、纳威和卢娜的?"哈利迫不及待地问。

"斯内普教授罚他们到禁林里,给那个呆子海格干活。"

"海格不是呆子!"赫敏尖厉地说。

"斯内普也许以为那是惩罚,"哈利说,"但金妮、纳威和卢娜可能跟海格一起开怀大笑呢。禁林……他们经过了多少比禁林更可怕的考验啊,这没什么大不了的!"

他觉得松了口气,他刚才想象得很恐怖,以为至少是钻心咒。

"布莱克教授,我们其实是想知道,有没有人——嗯,把那把剑拿出来过?也许它曾经被拿出去擦拭——什么的?"

菲尼亚斯·奈杰勒斯又停下了解放自己眼睛的努力,哂笑起来。

"你这个麻瓜出身的人,"他说,"妖精造的武器是不需要擦拭的,头脑简单的丫头。妖精的银器能排斥灰尘,只吸收能强化它的东西。"

"不许说赫敏头脑简单。"哈利说。

CHAPTER FIFTEEN   The Goblin's Revenge

'I grow weary of contradiction,' said Phineas Nigellus. 'Perhaps it is time for me to return to the Headmaster's office?'

Still blindfolded, he began groping the side of his frame, trying to feel his way out of his picture and back into the one at Hogwarts. Harry had a sudden inspiration.

'Dumbledore! Can't you bring us Dumbledore?'

'I beg your pardon?' asked Phineas Nigellus.

'Professor Dumbledore's portrait – couldn't you bring him along, here, into yours?'

Phineas Nigellus turned his face in the direction of Harry's voice.

'Evidently it is not only Muggle-borns who are ignorant, Potter. The portraits of Hogwarts may commune with each other, but they cannot travel outside the castle except to visit a painting of themselves hanging elsewhere. Dumbledore cannot come here with me, and after the treatment I have received at your hands, I can assure you that I shall not be making a return visit!'

Slightly crestfallen, Harry watched Phineas redouble his attempts to leave his frame.

'Professor Black,' said Hermione, 'couldn't you just tell us, *please*, when was the last time the sword was taken out of its case? Before Ginny took it out, I mean?'

Phineas snorted impatiently.

'I believe that the last time I saw the sword of Gryffindor leave its case was when Professor Dumbledore used it to break open a ring.'

Hermione whipped round to look at Harry. Neither of them dared say more in front of Phineas Nigellus, who had at last managed to locate the exit.

'Well, goodnight to you,' he said, a little waspishly, and he began to move out of sight again. Only the edge of his hat brim remained in view when Harry gave a sudden shout.

'Wait! Have you told Snape you saw this?'

Phineas Nigellus stuck his blindfolded head back into the picture.

'Professor Snape has more important things on his mind than the many eccentricities of Albus Dumbledore. *Goodbye*, Potter!'

And with that, he vanished completely, leaving behind him nothing but his murky backdrop.

'Harry!' Hermione cried.

'I know!' Harry shouted. Unable to contain himself, he punched the air:

第 15 章 妖精的报复

"我对反驳感到厌倦，"菲尼亚斯·奈杰勒斯说，"也许我该回校长办公室去了？"

仍然蒙着眼睛的他开始在画框侧面摸索，想摸着走出肖像，回到霍格沃茨的那一幅里去。哈利突然灵机一动。

"邓布利多！您能把邓布利多带来吗？"

"什么？"菲尼亚斯·奈杰勒斯问。

"邓布利多教授的肖像——您能把他带来吗，带到您的肖像里？"

菲尼亚斯·奈杰勒斯把脸转向哈利发声的方向。

"显然，无知的不只是麻瓜出身的人，波特。霍格沃茨的肖像可以互相交谈，但不能离开城堡，除非是去访问他们自己在别处的肖像。邓布利多不能跟我来此，而且，在你们手中受到这种待遇之后，我可以向你们保证，本人也不会再来造访！"

哈利有点沮丧，看着菲尼亚斯加倍努力要离开相框。

"布莱克教授，"赫敏说，"劳驾，能不能请您告诉我们，那把剑上一次从匣子里取出是什么时候？我是说，在金妮把它取出之前？"

菲尼亚斯不耐烦地哼了一声。

"我相信，上一次我看见格兰芬多的宝剑离开匣子，是邓布利多用它劈开了一枚戒指。"

赫敏猛然转身望着哈利。当着菲尼亚斯·奈杰勒斯的面，他们都不敢多说。菲尼亚斯终于摸到了出口。

"好吧，祝你们晚安。"他有点暴躁地说，开始退出。当画面上只看得见一点帽檐时，哈利突然大叫一声。

"等等！你把这告诉斯内普了吗？"

菲尼亚斯·奈杰勒斯把蒙着眼罩的脑袋又探进相框。

"斯内普教授有更重要的事去操心，无暇考虑阿不思·邓布利多的种种怪癖行为。再见，波特！"

说完，他彻底消失了，只留下一片混沌的背景。

"哈利！"赫敏叫道。

"我知道！"哈利高声说。他无法抑制自己，向空中猛击了一拳：

CHAPTER FIFTEEN The Goblin's Revenge

it was more than he had dared to hope for. He strode up and down the tent, feeling that he could have run a mile; he did not even feel hungry any more. Hermione was squashing Phineas Nigellus's portrait back into the beaded bag; when she had fastened the clasp, she threw the bag aside and raised a shining face to Harry.

'The sword can destroy Horcruxes! Goblin-made blades imbibe only that which strengthens them – Harry, that sword's impregnated with Basilisk venom!'

'And Dumbledore didn't give it to me because he still needed it, he wanted to use it on the locket –'

'– and he must have realised they wouldn't let you have it if he put it in his will –'

'– so he made a copy –'

'– and put a fake in the glass case –'

'– and he left the real one ... where?'

They gazed at each other; Harry felt that the answer was dangling invisibly in the air above them, tantalisingly close. Why hadn't Dumbledore told him? Or had he, in fact, told Harry, but Harry had not realised it at the time?

'Think!' whispered Hermione. 'Think! Where would he have left it?'

'Not at Hogwarts,' said Harry, resuming his pacing.

'Somewhere in Hogsmeade?' suggested Hermione.

'The Shrieking Shack?' said Harry. 'Nobody ever goes in there.'

'But Snape knows how to get in, wouldn't that be a bit risky?'

'Dumbledore trusted Snape,' Harry reminded her.

'Not enough to tell him that he had swapped the swords,' said Hermione.

'Yeah, you're right!' said Harry; and he felt even more cheered at the thought that Dumbledore had had some reservations, however faint, about Snape's trustworthiness. 'So, would he have hidden the sword well away from Hogsmeade, then? What d'you reckon, Ron? Ron?'

Harry looked around. For one bewildered moment he thought that Ron had left the tent, then realised that Ron was lying in the shadow of a lower bunk, looking stony.

'Oh, remembered me, have you?' he said.

'What?'

第15章 妖精的报复

这超过了他敢于期望的最好情况。他在帐篷里大步走来走去,感觉自己能一口气跑上一英里,甚至都不觉得饿了。赫敏正在把菲尼亚斯·奈杰勒斯的肖像塞回串珠小包,扣好搭扣之后,她把小包扔到一边,抬起发亮的面孔望着哈利。

"那把剑能摧毁魂器!妖精造的刀刃只吸收能强化它的东西——哈利,那把剑浸透了蛇怪的毒液!"

"邓布利多没有把它交给我,是因为他还需要它,想用它摧毁挂坠盒——"

"——他一定想到了,如果把宝剑写进了遗嘱,他们就不会让你得到它——"

"——所以他仿制了一把——"

"——然后把真的那把放在……哪儿呢?"

他们瞪着对方,哈利感到答案就悬在他们头顶的空气中,那么近,却就是够不到。为什么邓布利多没有告诉他呢?或者其实告诉过,但哈利当时没意识到?

"想想!"赫敏小声说,"想想!他会把它放在哪儿?"

"不在霍格沃茨。"哈利说,又踱起步来。

"在霍格莫德的什么地方?"赫敏猜道。

"尖叫棚屋?"哈利说,"没人到那儿去。"

"可是斯内普知道怎么进去,那不是有点冒险吗?"

"邓布利多信任斯内普。"哈利提醒她。

"没有信任到告诉他宝剑已经调包。"赫敏说。

"是啊,你说得对!"哈利说,想到邓布利多对斯内普的信任有所保留,他感到更加快慰,不管那保留是多么微不足道,"那么,他会不会把宝剑藏在远离霍格莫德的地方呢?你怎么想,罗恩?罗恩?"

哈利回过头,他一时迷惑,以为罗恩已经离开帐篷,随后才发现罗恩躺在下铺的阴影中,像石头一般。

"哦,想起我来啦?"他说。

"什么?"

CHAPTER FIFTEEN   The Goblin's Revenge

Ron snorted as he stared up at the underside of the upper bunk.

'You two carry on. Don't let me spoil your fun.'

Perplexed, Harry looked to Hermione for help, but she shook her head, apparently as nonplussed as he was.

'What's the problem?' asked Harry.

'Problem? There's no problem,' said Ron, still refusing to look at Harry. 'Not according to you, anyway.'

There were several *plunks* on the canvas over their heads. It had started to rain.

'Well, you've obviously got a problem,' said Harry. 'Spit it out, will you?'

Ron swung his long legs off the bed and sat up. He looked mean, unlike himself.

'All right, I'll spit it out. Don't expect me to skip up and down the tent because there's some other damn thing we've got to find. Just add it to the list of stuff you don't know.'

'I don't know?' repeated Harry. '*I* don't know?'

Plunk, plunk, plunk: the rain was falling harder and heavier; it pattered on the leaf-strewn bank all around them and into the river chattering through the dark. Dread doused Harry's jubilation: Ron was saying exactly what he had suspected and feared him to be thinking.

'It's not like I'm not having the time of my life here,' said Ron, 'you know, with my arm mangled and nothing to eat and freezing my backside off every night. I just hoped, you know, after we'd been running round a few weeks, we'd have achieved something.'

'Ron,' Hermione said, but in such a quiet voice that Ron could pretend not to have heard it over the loud tattoo the rain was now beating on the tent.

'I thought you knew what you'd signed up for,' said Harry.

'Yeah, I thought I did too.'

'So what part of it isn't living up to your expectations?' asked Harry. Anger was coming to his defence now. 'Did you think we'd be staying in five star hotels? Finding a Horcrux every other day? Did you think you'd be back to Mummy by Christmas?'

'We thought you knew what you were doing!' shouted Ron, standing up; and his words pierced Harry like scalding knives. 'We thought Dumbledore had told you what to do, we thought you had a real plan!'

罗恩哼了一声,盯着上铺的床板。

"你们两个接着聊啊,别让我搅了你们的兴致。"

哈利迷惑不解,求助地看看赫敏。但她摇了摇头,显然也和他一样不知所措。

"出了什么问题?"哈利问。

"问题?没有问题,"罗恩说,仍然不肯看哈利,"至少在你看来。"

头顶的帆布啪嗒啪嗒响了几声,下雨了。

"好吧,你显然有问题。"哈利说,"一吐为快,好不好?"

罗恩把长腿荡下床沿,坐了起来。他看上去很刻薄,简直有点不像他了。

"好,我就一吐为快。别指望我在帐篷里欢呼雀跃,不就是又多了一个该死的东西要找吗。直接把它加到你不知道的东西里去好了。"

"我不知道?"哈利说,"我不知道?"

啪嗒,啪嗒,啪嗒:雨越来越急,越来越大。打在周围落叶覆盖的河岸上,打在黑暗中潺潺的河水上。恐惧浇灭了哈利的欢乐:罗恩说的正是哈利怀疑并害怕他会有的想法。

"我在这儿确实过得有点儿终生难忘,"罗恩说,"你知道,胳膊残了,没东西吃,每天夜里后背都要冻掉。你知道,我只是希望在四处奔波了几个星期后,我们能够有一点成绩。"

"罗恩。"赫敏说,但声音如此之低,在噼里啪啦敲在帐篷上的雨声中,罗恩可以假装没有听到。

"我还以为你知道参加的是什么行动呢。"哈利说。

"是啊,我也以为我知道。"

"那么,哪个部分没有符合你的期望呢?"哈利问,恼怒使他开始自卫,"你以为我们会住在五星级酒店里?隔一天就找到一个魂器?你以为圣诞节就能回到妈咪身边吗?"

"我们以为你知道自己在干什么!"罗恩嚷道,站了起来。他的话像滚烫的刀子刺进哈利心中。"我们以为邓布利多告诉过你要干什么,我们以为你有一个像样的计划!"

CHAPTER FIFTEEN The Goblin's Revenge

'Ron!' said Hermione, this time clearly audible over the rain thundering on the tent roof, but again, he ignored her.

'Well, sorry to let you down,' said Harry, his voice quite calm even though he felt hollow, inadequate. 'I've been straight with you from the start, I told you everything Dumbledore told me. And in case you haven't noticed, we've found one Horcrux –'

'Yeah, and we're about as near getting rid of it as we are to finding the rest of them – nowhere effing near, in other words!'

'Take off the locket, Ron,' Hermione said, her voice unusually high. 'Please take it off. You wouldn't be talking like this if you hadn't been wearing it all day.'

'Yeah, he would,' said Harry, who did not want excuses made for Ron. 'D'you think I haven't noticed the two of you whispering behind my back? D'you think I didn't guess you were thinking this stuff?'

'Harry, we weren't –'

'Don't lie!' Ron hurled at her. 'You said it too, you said you were disappointed, you said you'd thought he had a bit more to go on than –'

'I didn't say it like that – Harry, I didn't!' she cried.

The rain was pounding the tent, tears were pouring down Hermione's face, and the excitement of a few minutes before had vanished as if it had never been, a short-lived firework that had flared and died, leaving everything dark, wet and cold. The sword of Gryffindor was hidden they knew not where, and they were three teenagers in a tent whose only achievement was not, yet, to be dead.

'So why are you still here?' Harry asked Ron.

'Search me,' said Ron.

'Go home then,' said Harry.

'Yeah, maybe I will!' shouted Ron, and he took several steps towards Harry, who did not back away. 'Didn't you hear what they said about my sister? But you don't give a rat's fart, do you, it's only the Forbidden Forest, Harry *I've-Faced-Worse* Potter doesn't care what happens to her in here, well, I do, all right, giant spiders and mental stuff –'

'I was only saying – she was with the others, they were with Hagrid –'

'– yeah, I get it, you don't care! And what about the rest of my family, "The Weasleys don't need another kid injured", did you hear that?'

第15章 妖精的报复

"罗恩！"赫敏说,这次在帐篷顶上哗哗的雨声中听得很清楚,但罗恩还是没有睬她。

"好吧,对不起,让你们失望了。"哈利说,声音相当平静,其实他感到空洞、底气不足,"我从一开始就对你们直言相告,跟你们讲了邓布利多告诉过我的一切。也许你没注意到,我们已经找到了一个魂器——"

"是啊,我们要毁灭它容易着呢,就跟找到其他几个魂器一样容易——他妈的遥不可及,换句话说。"

"摘下挂坠盒,罗恩,"赫敏说,嗓音高得不正常,"请你把它摘下来。你要不是戴了它一天,是不会说这种话的。"

"不,他会的。"哈利说,他不想为罗恩开脱,"你以为我没有注意到你们两个背着我嘀嘀咕咕吗?你以为我猜不到你们在想这些吗?"

"哈利,我们没有——"

"别撒谎!"罗恩冲她吼道,"你也说了,你说你感到失望,你说你本来以为他有更多的线索——"

"我没有那样说——哈利,我没有!"赫敏哭了。

雨水狂敲着帐篷,泪水从赫敏脸上流下。几分钟前的兴奋消失得无影无踪,好像从未有过一样,如同烟花一般绚丽片刻便熄灭了,留下的是黑暗、潮湿和寒冷。格兰芬多的宝剑不知藏在什么地方,他们只是躲在帐篷里的三个少年,唯一的成绩就是还没死掉。

"那你为什么还在这儿?"哈利问罗恩。

"我不知道。"罗恩说。

"那就回家吧。"哈利说。

"是啊,也许我应该回家了!"罗恩嚷着,朝哈利走了几步,哈利没有后退,"你没听到他们说我妹妹的事吗?但你根本不在乎,是吧,不过是禁林嘛,'我经历过更可怕的'——大英雄哈利·波特才不在乎我妹妹在那儿遇到了什么呢,可我在乎,巨蜘蛛和让人发疯的东西——"

"我只是说——她跟同伴们在一起,跟海格在一起——"

"——是啊,我听懂了,你不在乎!还有我的家人呢,'韦斯莱家可不能再有孩子受伤了',你听到了吗?"

CHAPTER FIFTEEN The Goblin's Revenge

'Yeah, I –'

'Not bothered what it meant, though?'

'Ron!' said Hermione, forcing her way between them, 'I don't think it means anything new has happened, anything we don't know about; think, Ron, Bill's already scarred, plenty of people must have seen that George has lost an ear by now, and you're supposed to be on your deathbed with spattergroit, I'm sure that's all he meant –'

'Oh, you're sure, are you? Right then, well, I won't bother myself about them. It's all right for you two, isn't it, with your parents safely out of the way –'

'My parents are *dead*!' Harry bellowed.

'And mine could be going the same way!' yelled Ron.

'Then GO!' roared Harry. 'Go back to them, pretend you've got over your spattergroit and Mummy'll be able to feed you up and –'

Ron made a sudden movement: Harry reacted, but before either wand was clear of its owner's pocket, Hermione had raised her own.

'*Protego!*' she cried, and an invisible shield expanded between her and Harry on the one side and Ron on the other; all of them were forced backwards a few steps by the strength of the spell and Harry and Ron glared from either side of the transparent barrier as though they were seeing each other clearly for the first time. Harry felt a corrosive hatred towards Ron: something had broken between them.

'Leave the Horcrux,' Harry said.

Ron wrenched the chain from over his head and cast the locket into a nearby chair. He turned to Hermione.

'What are you doing?'

'What do you mean?'

'Are you staying, or what?'

'I ...' She looked anguished. 'Yes – yes, I'm staying. Ron, we said we'd go with Harry, we said we'd help –'

'I get it. You choose him.'

'Ron, no – please – come back, come back!'

She was impeded by her own Shield Charm; by the time she had removed it, he had already stormed into the night. Harry stood quite still and silent,

"听到了，我——"

"没去想那意味着什么吧？"

"罗恩！"赫敏挤到他们中间，"我认为那并不意味着出了什么新的事，我们不知道的事。想一想吧，罗恩，比尔已经留下伤疤，现在许多人一定已看到乔治少了一只耳朵，你又得了散花痘重病不起，我相信指的就是这些——"

"哦，你相信，是吗？好吧，我就不用去想他们了。你们两个觉得没关系，是不是，反正你们的父母都在安全的地方——"

"我的父母死了！"哈利吼道。

"我的父母也可能是同样下场！"罗恩喊了起来。

"那就*走吧*！"哈利咆哮道，"回到他们那儿去，假装你的散花痘好了，妈咪会把你喂得饱饱的——"

罗恩突然动手，哈利迅速反应，但两人的魔杖还没拔出口袋，赫敏已经举起了她的。

"盔甲护身！"她叫道。一道无形的坚壁立刻形成，她和哈利在一边，罗恩在另一边。三人都被魔咒的力量震得倒退了几步。哈利和罗恩隔着透明的屏障怒目而视，好像第一次看清对方一样。哈利对罗恩感到一种带腐蚀性的憎恨：他们之间有某种东西断裂了。

"把魂器留下。"哈利说。

罗恩从头上扯下链子，把挂坠盒丢在旁边的一把椅子上，然后转向赫敏。

"你打算干什么？"

"你说什么？"

"你是留下，还是怎么着？"

"我……"赫敏显得很痛苦，"是——是的，我要留下。罗恩，我们说过要跟哈利一起，我们说过要帮——"

"我明白了，你选择了他。"

"罗恩，不——求求你——回来，回来！"

她被自己施的铁甲咒挡住了，等到把它除去，罗恩已经冲进了夜幕中。哈利呆呆地、默默地站在那儿，听着赫敏在哭泣，在树林中呼

CHAPTER FIFTEEN The Goblin's Revenge

listening to her sobbing and calling Ron's name amongst the trees.

After a few minutes she returned, her sopping hair plastered to her face.

'He's g – g – gone! Disapparated!'

She threw herself into a chair, curled up and started to cry.

Harry felt dazed. He stooped, picked up the Horcrux and placed it around his own neck. He dragged blankets off Ron's bunk and threw them over Hermione. Then he climbed on to his own bed and stared up at the dark canvas roof, listening to the pounding of the rain.

唤罗恩的名字。

几分钟后她回来了,头发湿漉漉地贴在脸上。

"他——他——他走了!幻影移形了!"

她扑通坐在椅子上,蜷着身子哭了起来。

哈利心中一片茫然。他俯身捡起魂器,挂在自己的脖子上,又拽下罗恩铺上的毯子,给赫敏披上,然后爬上自己的床铺,盯着黑漆漆的帆布帐篷顶,听着滂沱的雨声。

CHAPTER SIXTEEN

Godric's Hollow

When Harry woke the following day, it was several seconds before he remembered what had happened. Then he hoped, childishly, that it had been a dream, that Ron was still there and had never left. Yet by turning his head on his pillow he could see Ron's deserted bunk. It was like a dead body in the way it seemed to draw his eyes. Harry jumped down from his own bed, keeping his eyes averted from Ron's. Hermione, who was already busy in the kitchen, did not wish Harry good morning, but turned her face away quickly as he went by.

He's gone, Harry told himself. *He's gone*. He had to keep thinking it as he washed and dressed, as though repetition would dull the shock of it. *He's gone and he's not coming back*. And that was the simple truth of it, Harry knew, because their protective enchantments meant that it would be impossible, once they vacated this spot, for Ron to find them again.

He and Hermione ate breakfast in silence. Hermione's eyes were puffy and red; she looked as if she had not slept. They packed up their things, Hermione dawdling. Harry knew why she wanted to spin out their time on the riverbank; several times he saw her look up eagerly and he was sure she had deluded herself into thinking that she heard footsteps through the heavy rain, but no red-haired figure appeared between the trees. Every time Harry imitated her, looked round (for he could not help hoping a little himself) and saw nothing but rain-swept woods, another little parcel of fury exploded inside him. He could hear Ron saying '*We thought you knew what you were doing!*', and he resumed packing with a hard knot in the pit of his stomach.

The muddy river beside them was rising rapidly and would soon spill over on to their bank. They had lingered a good hour after they would usually have departed their campsite. Finally, having entirely repacked the beaded bag three times, Hermione seemed unable to find any more reasons to delay: she and Harry grasped hands and Disapparated, reappearing on a

第 16 章

戈德里克山谷

第二天哈利醒来时,过了几秒钟才想起发生了什么事。他天真地希望那是个梦,希望罗恩还在这儿,没有离开。可是他转过头,看到的是罗恩的空床,像横在路上的尸体那样吸引着他的目光。哈利从自己床上跳下来,不去看罗恩的床铺。赫敏已经在厨房里忙碌,哈利走过时,她没有跟他说早上好,而是急忙扭过头去。

他走了,哈利对自己说。他走了。洗脸穿衣时,他止不住一直这么想,好像重复这句话会使打击减轻一些似的。他走了,不回来了。这是简单的事实,哈利知道,因为他们的防护魔法意味着,只要他们一离开这个地方,罗恩就再也无法找到他们。

他和赫敏在沉默中吃完了早饭。赫敏两眼红肿,看来一夜未睡。两人收拾行装时,赫敏磨磨蹭蹭。哈利知道她为什么希望在河边拖延时间。有几次发现她热切地抬起头,他相信她是自己欺骗自己,以为在大雨中听到了脚步声。然而,并没有红头发的身影出现在树林中。每次哈利像她那样四下张望(他自己也忍不住抱有一点希望),却只看到被雨水冲刷的树林,心中便有一小股怒火在喷发。他能听到罗恩说:"我们以为你知道自己在干什么!"于是他继续收拾行装,心窝里像堵着一个硬疙瘩。

混浊的河水迅速上涨,很快就会漫上他们这片堤岸。两人比正常应该离开营地的时间多逗留了一个小时。终于,把串珠小包打开又重装三次之后,赫敏似乎再也找不出拖延的理由了,她和哈利手拉手幻

CHAPTER SIXTEEN Godric's Hollow

windswept, heather-covered hillside.

The instant they arrived Hermione dropped Harry's hand and walked away from him, finally sitting down on a large rock, her face on her knees, shaking with what he knew were sobs. He watched her, supposing that he ought to go and comfort her, but something kept him rooted to the spot. Everything inside him felt cold and tight: again he saw the contemptuous expression on Ron's face. Harry strode off through the heather, walking in a large circle with the distraught Hermione at its centre, casting the spells she usually performed to ensure their protection.

They did not discuss Ron at all over the next few days. Harry was determined never to mention his name again, and Hermione seemed to know that it was no use forcing the issue, although sometimes at night when she thought he was sleeping, he would hear her crying. Meanwhile, Harry had started bringing out the Marauder's Map and examining it by wandlight. He was waiting for the moment when Ron's labelled dot would reappear in the corridors of Hogwarts, proving that he had returned to the comfortable castle, protected by his status of pure-blood. However, Ron did not appear on the map, and after a while Harry found himself taking it out simply to stare at Ginny's name in the girls' dormitory, wondering whether the intensity with which he gazed at it might break into her sleep, that she would somehow know he was thinking about her, hoping that she was all right.

By day, they devoted themselves to trying to determine the possible locations of Gryffindor's sword, but the more they talked about the places in which Dumbledore might have hidden it, the more desperate and far-fetched their speculation became. Cudgel his brains though he might, Harry could not remember Dumbledore ever mentioning a place in which he might hide something. There were moments when he did not know whether he was angrier with Ron or with Dumbledore. *We thought you knew what you were doing ... we thought Dumbledore had told you what to do ... we thought you had a real plan!*

He could not hide it from himself: Ron had been right. Dumbledore had left him with virtually nothing. They had discovered one Horcrux, but they had no means of destroying it: the others were as unattainable as they had ever been. Hopelessness threatened to engulf him. He was staggered, now, to think of his own presumption in accepting his friends' offers to accompany him on this meandering, pointless journey. He knew nothing, he had no ideas, and he was constantly, painfully on the alert for any indication that Hermione, too, was about to tell him that she had had enough, that she was leaving.

第16章 戈德里克山谷

影移形,出现在一片石楠丛生、狂风呼啸的山坡上。

一到地方,赫敏就松开哈利的手,从他身边走开,最后坐到一块大石头上,脸埋在膝头,身体发抖。哈利知道她在哭。他望着她,觉得应该去安慰她,但不知什么东西使他定在了原地。他从内到外都冷冰冰、紧绷绷的:仿佛又看到了罗恩脸上轻蔑的表情。哈利在石楠丛中大步走动,以情绪紊乱的赫敏为圆心绕着大圈,一边施着赫敏往常为保护他们安全而施的魔咒。

他们接下来几天都没有谈到罗恩。哈利决心不再提起他的名字,赫敏似乎知道硬要提起也没有用。但有时在夜里,当她以为哈利睡着了的时候,哈利能听到她在偷偷地哭泣。而哈利则开始拿出活点地图,用魔杖照着细看。他在等待标着罗恩的黑点出现在霍格沃茨走廊上,证明他回到了舒适的城堡里,受到他纯血统身份的保护。然而,罗恩没有在地图上出现。过了一段时间,哈利发现自己拿出地图只是为了盯着女生宿舍里金妮的名字,不知道自己热切的目光能不能进入她的梦境,让她感应到他在想念她,愿她一切都好。

白天,他们冥思苦想格兰芬多的宝剑可能在哪里,讨论邓布利多会选择什么地方来藏它。可是越讨论,他们的猜测就越绝望牵强。哈利无论怎么敲脑袋,也想不起邓布利多提过藏东西的地方。有时候他不知道是罗恩还是邓布利多更让他生气。我们以为你知道自己在干什么……我们以为邓布利多告诉过你要干什么……我们以为你有一个像样的计划!

他无法对自己隐瞒:罗恩是对的,邓布利多留给他的几乎是零。他们发现了一个魂器,但没有办法摧毁它,另外几个魂器和以前一样无从寻觅。绝望似乎要将他吞没。哈利现在想想都吃惊,他竟然那么自以为是,让两个朋友来陪自己开始这场漫无目标的旅行。他什么都不知道,也没有主意,他一直痛苦地提防着任何一丝迹象,怕赫敏也会来跟他说她受够了,要走了。

CHAPTER SIXTEEN   Godric's Hollow

They were spending many evenings in near silence, and Hermione took to bringing out Phineas Nigellus's portrait and propping it up in a chair, as though he might fill part of the gaping hole left by Ron's departure. Despite his previous assertion that he would never visit them again, Phineas Nigellus did not seem able to resist the chance to find out more about what Harry was up to, and consented to reappear, blindfolded, every few days or so. Harry was even glad to see him, because he was company, albeit of a snide and taunting kind. They relished any news about what was happening at Hogwarts, though Phineas Nigellus was not an ideal informer. He venerated Snape, the first Slytherin Headmaster since he himself had controlled the school, and they had to be careful not to criticise, or ask impertinent questions about Snape, or Phineas Nigellus would instantly leave his painting.

However, he did let drop certain snippets. Snape seemed to be facing a constant, low-level of mutiny from a hard core of students. Ginny had been banned from going into Hogsmeade. Snape had reinstated Umbridge's old decree forbidding gatherings of three or more students, or any unofficial student societies.

From all of these things, Harry deduced that Ginny, and probably Neville and Luna along with her, had been doing their best to continue Dumbledore's Army. This scant news made Harry want to see Ginny so badly it felt like stomach ache; but it also made him think of Ron again, and of Dumbledore, and of Hogwarts itself, which he missed nearly as much as his ex-girlfriend. Indeed, as Phineas Nigellus talked about Snape's crackdown, Harry experienced a split second of madness when he imagined simply going back to school to join the destabilisation of Snape's regime: being fed, and having a soft bed, and other people being in charge seemed the most wonderful prospect in the world at that moment. But then he remembered that he was Undesirable Number One, that there was a ten thousand Galleon price on his head, and that to walk into Hogwarts these days was just as dangerous as walking into the Ministry of Magic. Indeed, Phineas Nigellus inadvertently emphasised this fact by slipping in leading questions about Harry and Hermione's whereabouts. Hermione shoved him back inside the beaded bag every time he did this, and Phineas Nigellus invariably refused to reappear for several days after these unceremonious goodbyes.

The weather grew colder and colder. They did not dare remain in any one area too long, so rather than staying in the south of England, where a hard

第 16 章 戈德里克山谷

许多个夜晚，他们几乎都是在沉默中度过的，赫敏常把菲尼亚斯·奈杰勒斯的肖像拿出来，支在椅子上，仿佛他能填补罗恩出走留下的巨大空洞似的。菲尼亚斯·奈杰勒斯尽管上次扬言决不再来，却似乎无法抗拒打探哈利情况的机会，所以同意每隔几天蒙着眼睛出现一次。哈利甚至挺高兴见到他，毕竟是个伴儿，虽然是喜欢讥诮讽刺的那种。他们喜欢听发生在霍格沃茨的各种新闻，但菲尼亚斯·奈杰勒斯不是个理想的报告员。他崇敬斯内普——那是自从他本人掌管学校之后第一位斯莱特林出身的校长。哈利他们要小心，不能批评斯内普或提出对他不敬的问题，否则菲尼亚斯·奈杰勒斯就会马上离开画像。

不过，他还是透露了一些片段。斯内普要对付一帮死硬派学生持续不断的低调反抗。金妮被禁止进入霍格莫德。斯内普恢复了乌姆里奇的旧规定，禁止三人以上的学生集会以及任何非正式的学生社团。

从这一切中，哈利推测金妮，可能还有纳威和卢娜跟她一起，在尽力维持邓布利多军。零星的消息使哈利如此渴望见到金妮，几乎想到了胃痛的程度，同时也让他想到了罗恩，想到了邓布利多，想到了霍格沃茨，他对学校的思念几乎和对前女友的思念一样强烈。真的，当菲尼亚斯·奈杰勒斯讲述斯内普的镇压措施时，哈利有过一刹那的疯狂，想象着干脆回学校去参加给斯内普捣乱的行动：有饱饭吃，有软和的床铺睡，有别人在负责，似乎是世界上最美妙的生活。但他随即想起自己是头号不良分子，被悬赏一万金加隆通缉，如今走进霍格沃茨就像走进魔法部一样危险。菲尼亚斯·奈杰勒斯无意间强调了这一事实，他常用诱导性的问题探听哈利和赫敏在什么地方。每当这种时候，赫敏便把他塞回串珠小包。在这样粗暴的送行之后，菲尼亚斯·奈杰勒斯总是几天都不肯露面。

天气越来越冷。因为不敢在一个地区待得太久，他们没有留在英国南部（那儿最坏也就是地面结霜而已），而是继续在国内四处迁徙：

CHAPTER SIXTEEN   Godric's Hollow

ground frost was the worst of their worries, they continued to meander up and down the country, braving a mountainside, where sleet pounded the tent, a wide flat marsh, where the tent was flooded with chill water, and a tiny island in the middle of a Scottish loch, where snow half buried the tent in the night.

They had already spotted Christmas trees twinkling from several sitting-room windows, before there came an evening when Harry resolved to suggest, again, what seemed to him the only unexplored avenue left to them. They had just eaten an unusually good meal: Hermione had been to a supermarket under the Invisibility Cloak (scrupulously dropping the money into an open till as she left) and Harry thought that she might be more persuadable than usual on a stomach full of spaghetti Bolognese and tinned pears. He had also had the foresight to suggest that they take a few hours' break from wearing the Horcrux, which was hanging over the end of the bunk beside him.

'Hermione?'

'Hm?' She was curled up in one of the sagging armchairs with *The Tales of Beedle the Bard*. He could not imagine how much more she could get out of the book, which was not, after all, very long; but evidently she was still deciphering something in it, because *Spellman's Syllabary* lay open on the arm of the chair.

Harry cleared his throat. He felt exactly as he had done on the occasion, several years previously, when he had asked Professor McGonagall whether he could go into Hogsmeade, despite the fact that he had not persuaded the Dursleys to sign his permission slip.

'Hermione, I've been thinking, and –'

'Harry, could you help me with something?'

Apparently she had not been listening to him. She leaned forwards and held out *The Tales of Beedle the Bard*.

'Look at that symbol,' she said, pointing to the top of a page. Above what Harry assumed was the title of the story (being unable to read runes, he could not be sure), there was a picture of what looked like a triangular eye, its pupil crossed with a vertical line.

'I never took Ancient Runes, Hermione.'

'I know that, but it isn't a rune and it's not in the syllabary, either. All along I thought it was a picture of an eye, but I don't think it is! It's been inked in, look, somebody's drawn it there, it isn't really part of the book. Think, have you ever seen it before?'

第16章 戈德里克山谷

在寒冷的半山腰,冻雨敲打着帐篷;在广阔平整的沼泽地,冷水灌进帐篷里;在苏格兰的湖心小岛,夜间积雪埋住了半个帐篷。

他们已经从几家客厅窗口看到圣诞树在闪耀,一天晚上,哈利终于决心再次提起在他看来是唯一一条还未探索的路。刚吃完一顿难得的美餐(赫敏穿着隐形衣去了超市,还细心地往收银台抽屉里丢了些钱),肚子里填满了意大利细面条和梨罐头,哈利猜想赫敏这时也许会比平时更容易说动一些。而且他已周密地预先提议歇几个小时不戴魂器,它现在正挂在他身边的床头。

"赫敏?"

"嗯?"赫敏正蜷在一把凹陷的扶手椅里,读《诗翁彼豆故事集》。哈利想象不出她还能从那本书里读出什么新鲜东西,书毕竟不是很厚。但她显然还在破译着什么,因为《魔法字音表》摊在椅子扶手上。

哈利清了清嗓子,感觉就好像几年前,他没能得到德思礼夫妇签字允许,却要问麦格教授他能不能去霍格莫德一样。

"赫敏,我一直在想——"

"哈利,你能帮我个忙吗?"

显然赫敏没有听他说话。她身体前倾,举着那本《诗翁彼豆故事集》。

"看那个符号。"她指着一页的顶端。在估计是故事标题的文字上面(哈利看不懂如尼文,所以不能确定),有一个图形,看上去像只三角眼,瞳孔中间有一道竖线。

"我没上过如尼文课,赫敏。"

"我知道。可那不是如尼文,字音表里也没有。我一直以为是一只眼睛的图案,但现在觉得不是!它是墨水做的记号,看,是有人画上去的,不是书里的内容。想想,你有没有见过它?"

'No ... no, wait a moment.' Harry looked closer. 'Isn't it the same symbol Luna's dad was wearing round his neck?'

'Well, that's what I thought too!'

'Then it's Grindelwald's mark.'

She stared at him, open-mouthed.

'*What?*'

'Krum told me ...'

He recounted the story that Viktor Krum had told him at the wedding. Hermione looked astonished.

'*Grindelwald's mark?*'

She looked from Harry to the weird symbol and back again. 'I've never heard that Grindelwald had a mark. There's no mention of it in anything I've ever read about him.'

'Well, like I say, Krum reckoned that symbol was carved on a wall at Durmstrang, and Grindelwald put it there.'

She fell back into the old armchair, frowning.

'That's very odd. If it's a symbol of Dark Magic, what's it doing in a book of children's stories?'

'Yeah, it is weird,' said Harry. 'And you'd think Scrimgeour would have recognised it. He was Minister, he ought to have been expert on Dark stuff.'

'I know ... perhaps he thought it was an eye, just like I did. All the other stories have little pictures over the titles.'

She did not speak, but continued to pore over the strange mark. Harry tried again.

'Hermione?'

'Hm?'

'I've been thinking. I – I want to go to Godric's Hollow.'

She looked up at him but her eyes were unfocused and he was sure she was still thinking about the mysterious mark on the book.

'Yes,' she said. 'Yes, I've been wondering that too. I really think we'll have to.'

第16章 戈德里克山谷

"没有……不，等等。"哈利又仔细看了看，"这不是和卢娜爸爸脖子上戴的一样吗？"

"嗯，我也是这么想的！"

"那就是格林德沃的标志。"

她瞪着他，张大了嘴巴。

"什么？"

"克鲁姆告诉过我……"

他复述了威克多尔·克鲁姆在婚礼上跟他讲的故事。赫敏显得很吃惊。

"格林德沃的标志？"

她来回地看着哈利和那个奇怪的符号，"我从没听说过格林德沃有个标志。我读过的有关资料中都没有提到。"

"我说了，克鲁姆认为那符号刻在德姆斯特朗的墙上，是格林德沃刻上去的。"

赫敏靠到旧扶手椅上，皱起眉头。

"那非常蹊跷。如果它是黑魔法的符号，又怎么会在一本儿童故事书里呢？"

"是啊，挺奇怪的。"哈利说，"而且按理斯克林杰会认出它啊。他身为部长，应该是识别黑魔法的专家。"

"我知道……也许他以为这是一只眼睛，就像我刚才那样。其他故事的标题上面都有小图案。"

她不再说话，继续研究那个奇怪的标志。哈利又试了一次。

"赫敏？"

"唔？"

"我一直在想。我——我想去戈德里克山谷。"

她抬头望着他，但眼睛没有聚焦，哈利断定她还在想着书上那个神秘标志。

"是啊，"她说，"是啊，我也在考虑这个事。我真的认为我们应该去。"

CHAPTER SIXTEEN   Godric's Hollow

'Did you hear me right?' he asked.

'Of course I did. You want to go to Godric's Hollow. I agree, I think we should. I mean, I can't think of anywhere else it could be, either. It'll be dangerous, but the more I think about it, the more likely it seems it's there.'

'Er – *what's* there?' asked Harry.

At that, she looked just as bewildered as he felt.

'Well, the sword, Harry! Dumbledore must have known you'd want to go back there, and I mean, Godric's Hollow is Godric Gryffindor's birthplace –'

'Really? Gryffindor came from Godric's Hollow?'

'Harry, did you ever even open *A History of Magic*?'

'Erm,' he said, smiling for what felt like the first time in months: the muscles in his face felt oddly stiff. 'I might've opened it, you know, when I bought it ... just the once ...'

'Well, as the village is named after him, I'd have thought you might have made the connection,' said Hermione. She sounded much more like her old self than she had done of late; Harry half expected her to announce that she was off to the library. 'There's a bit about the village in *A History of Magic*, wait ...'

She opened the beaded bag and rummaged for a while, finally extracting her copy of their old school textbook, *A History of Magic* by Bathilda Bagshot, which she thumbed through until finding the page she wanted.

'"*Upon the signature of the International Statute of Secrecy in 1689, wizards went into hiding for good. It was natural, perhaps, that they formed their own small communities within a community. Many small villages and hamlets attracted several magical families, who banded together for mutual support and protection. The villages of Tinworth in Cornwall, Upper Flagley in Yorkshire and Ottery St Catchpole on the south coast of England were notable homes to knots of wizarding families who lived alongside tolerant and sometimes Confunded Muggles. Most celebrated of these half-magical dwelling places is, perhaps, Godric's Hollow, the West Country village where the great wizard Godric Gryffindor was born, and where Bowman Wright, wizarding smith, forged the first Golden Snitch. The graveyard is full of the names of ancient magical families, and this accounts, no doubt, for the stories of hauntings that have dogged the little church for many centuries.*"

第16章 戈德里克山谷

"你听清我的话了吗？"他问。

"当然。你想去戈德里克山谷。我同意。我认为我们应该去。我是说，我想不出还有什么地方能找到它。去的话会很危险，但我越想越觉得它可能在那儿。"

"呃——什么可能在那儿？"哈利问。

这下，她看上去像哈利刚才一样困惑。

"那把剑啊，哈利！邓布利多一定知道你会想回那儿看看，何况，戈德里克山谷是戈德里克·格兰芬多的出生地——"

"是吗？格兰芬多出生在戈德里克山谷？"

"哈利，你到底有没有翻开过《魔法史》啊？"

"嗯，"哈利笑了，好像是几个月来第一次微笑，面部肌肉发僵，感觉怪怪的，"我也许翻开过，刚买的时候……就那一次……"

"那个村子是以他的名字命名的，我还以为你也许能联系起来呢。"赫敏说，相较她最近的表现，这话大大接近于她往日的风格，哈利几乎等着她宣布要去图书馆了，"《魔法史》中提到过一点那个村子，等等……"

她打开串珠小包，摸了一会儿，终于抽出她的旧课本：巴希达·巴沙特的《魔法史》，翻到了她想找的那一页。

《国际保密法》一六八九年签署生效之后，巫师们永久性地转入隐蔽。也许是自然而然地，他们在社区内部形成了自己的小社区。许多小村庄吸引了几户巫师家庭，这几家便团结起来，互相帮助，互相保护。康沃尔郡的丁沃斯、约克郡的上弗莱格利、英格兰南海岸的奥特里·圣卡奇波尔，都有巫师家庭聚居，在宽容的、有时是被施了混淆咒的麻瓜中间生活。在此类半巫师聚居地中，最著名的也许是戈德里克山谷。这个西南部的村庄是伟大的巫师戈德里克·格兰芬多的出生地，也是巫师金匠鲍曼·赖特打造第一个金色飞贼的地方。墓地上刻满古老巫师家族的姓氏，这无疑也是小教堂许多世纪以来鬼故事不断的原因。

'You and your parents aren't mentioned,' Hermione said, closing the book, 'because Professor Bagshot doesn't cover anything later than the end of the nineteenth century. But you see? Godric's Hollow, Godric Gryffindor, Gryffindor's sword; don't you think Dumbledore would have expected you to make the connection?'

'Oh, yeah ...'

Harry did not want to admit that he had not been thinking about the sword at all when he suggested they go to Godric's Hollow. For him, the lure of the village lay in his parents' graves, the house where he had narrowly escaped death, and in the person of Bathilda Bagshot.

'Remember what Muriel said?' he asked eventually.

'Who?'

'You know,' he hesitated: he did not want to say Ron's name. 'Ginny's great aunt. At the wedding. The one who said you had skinny ankles.'

'Oh,' said Hermione.

It was a sticky moment: Harry knew that she had sensed Ron's name in the offing. He rushed on: 'She said Bathilda Bagshot still lives in Godric's Hollow.'

'Bathilda Bagshot,' murmured Hermione, running her index finger over Bathilda's embossed name on the front cover of *A History of Magic*. 'Well, I suppose –'

She gasped so dramatically that Harry's insides turned over; he drew his wand, looking round at the entrance, half expecting to see a hand forcing its way through the entrance flap, but there was nothing there.

'What?' he said, half angry, half relieved. 'What did you do that for? I thought you'd seen a Death Eater unzipping the tent, at least –'

'Harry, *what if Bathilda's got the sword?* What if Dumbledore entrusted it to her?'

Harry considered this possibility. Bathilda would be an extremely old woman by now, and according to Muriel, she was 'gaga'. Was it likely that Dumbledore would have hidden the sword of Gryffindor with her? If so, Harry felt that Dumbledore had left a great deal to chance: Dumbledore had never revealed that he had replaced the sword with a fake, nor had he so much as mentioned a friendship with Bathilda. Now, however, was not the moment to cast doubt on Hermione's theory, not when she was so surprisingly willing to fall in with Harry's dearest wish.

第16章 戈德里克山谷

"没有提到你和你的父母,"赫敏合上书说,"因为巴沙特教授只写到十九世纪末。可是你看到没有?戈德里克山谷、戈德里克·格兰芬多、格兰芬多的宝剑,你不认为邓布利多会希望你这样联想吗?"

"哦,是啊……"

哈利不想承认,他在提议去戈德里克山谷时其实并没想到宝剑,对他来说,那个村子的吸引力在于他父母的坟墓、他大难不死的房子,还有巴希达·巴沙特这个人。

"记得穆丽尔的话吗?"他最后问道。

"谁?"

"你知道,"他犹豫了一下,不想说罗恩的名字,"金妮的姨婆,在婚礼上,就是说你踝骨太突出的那个。"

"哦。"赫敏说。

这是一个尴尬的时刻:哈利知道赫敏感觉到了罗恩的名字差点出现。他急忙说下去:"她说巴希达·巴沙特还住在戈德里克山谷。"

"巴希达·巴沙特,"赫敏喃喃地说道,食指轻轻抚摸着《魔法史》封面上凸印的作者名字,"嗯,我想——"

她猛地倒吸一口冷气,哈利心里翻腾起来。他拔出魔杖,回头朝帐篷口看去,以为会看到一只手正从门帘上伸进来,然而什么也没有。

"什么呀?"他说,既恼火,又松了口气,"你干吗那样?我还以为你看到食死徒在拉帐篷门呢,至少——"

"哈利,要是巴希达手里有那把剑呢?要是邓布利多把剑托付给了她呢?"

哈利考虑了一下这种可能性。巴希达现在应该是年岁很老的老太太了,而且据穆丽尔说,她还老"糊涂了"。邓布利多会不会把格兰芬多的宝剑藏在她那儿?如果真是那样,哈利觉得未免太冒险了。邓布利多从未透露过他把宝剑调了包,甚至都没有提过跟巴希达的交情。但现在不是怀疑赫敏推理的时候,她正出乎意料地赞同哈利最热切的愿望。

CHAPTER SIXTEEN   Godric's Hollow

'Yeah, he might've done! So, are we going to go to Godric's Hollow?'

'Yes, but we'll have to think it through carefully, Harry.' She was sitting up now, and Harry could tell that the prospect of having a plan again had lifted her mood as much as his. 'We'll need to practise Disapparating together under the Invisibility Cloak, for a start, and perhaps Disillusionment Charms would be sensible too, unless you think we should go the whole hog and use Polyjuice Potion? In that case we'll need to collect hair from somebody. I actually think we'd better do that, Harry, the thicker our disguises the better ...'

Harry let her talk, nodding and agreeing whenever there was a pause, but his mind had left the conversation. For the first time since he had discovered that the sword in Gringotts was a fake, he felt excited.

He was about to go home, about to return to the place where he had had a family. It was in Godric's Hollow that, but for Voldemort, he would have grown up and spent every school holiday. He could have invited friends to his house ... he might even have had brothers and sisters ... it would have been his mother who had made his seventeenth birthday cake. The life he had lost had hardly ever seemed so real to him as at this moment when he knew he was about to see the place where it had been taken from him. After Hermione had gone to bed that night, Harry quietly extracted his rucksack from her beaded bag, and from inside it, the photograph album Hagrid had given him so long ago. For the first time in months, he perused the old pictures of his parents, smiling and waving up at him from the images, which were all he had left of them now.

Harry would gladly have set out for Godric's Hollow the following day, but Hermione had other ideas. Convinced as she was that Voldemort would expect Harry to return to the scene of his parents' deaths, she was determined that they would set off only after they had ensured that they had the best disguises possible. It was therefore a full week later – once they had surreptitiously obtained hairs from innocent Muggles who were Christmas shopping, and had practised Apparating and Disapparating while underneath the Invisibility Cloak together – that Hermione agreed to make the journey.

They were to Apparate to the village under cover of darkness, so it was late afternoon when they finally swallowed Polyjuice Potion, Harry transforming into a balding, middle-aged Muggle man, Hermione into his small and rather mousy wife. The beaded bag containing all of their possessions (apart from the Horcrux, which Harry was wearing around his neck) was tucked into an inside pocket of Hermione's buttoned-up coat. Harry lowered the Invisibility Cloak over them, then they turned into the suffocating darkness once again.

第16章 戈德里克山谷

"是啊，有可能！那么，我们去戈德里克山谷吗？"

"去，但必须考虑周密，哈利。"赫敏现在坐正了，哈利看出，又能够有一个计划，使她的心情像他的一样振奋了许多，"首先，我们得练习披着隐形衣一起幻影移形，幻身咒可能也用得上，要么你主张一路都用复方汤剂？那样就得搞到别人的头发。哎，我觉得我们最好去搞一些，哈利，伪装越多越好……"

哈利任她说下去，每当她停顿时便点头附和，但他的心思已经离开谈话，从发现古灵阁那把剑是赝品之后，他第一次兴奋起来。

他要回家了，要回到他有过一个家的地方。如果没有伏地魔的话，他会在戈德里克山谷长大，度过每个假期。他会邀请朋友到家里玩……甚至可能有弟弟妹妹……给他做十七岁生日蛋糕的就会是他的妈妈。想到即将要去访问这一切都被夺走的地方，他所失去的生活从未像此刻这样真切。那天夜里赫敏上床睡觉之后，哈利悄悄从串珠小包里取出他的背包，翻出海格很久以前送给他的那本相册。几个月来，他第一次端详着父母的旧照片，他们在向他微笑招手，他就只剩下这么一点纪念了。

哈利很想第二天就去戈德里克山谷，但赫敏另有主张。她相信伏地魔料到哈利会去父母逝世的地方凭吊，坚持要确保伪装最充分之后再出发。所以，整整过了一个星期——他们从圣诞节前购物的麻瓜身上偷到了头发，又一起在隐形衣下反复练习了幻影显形和移形——赫敏才同意启程。

他们要在黑暗掩护下幻影显形到那个村子，所以黄昏时分两人才喝下复方汤剂，哈利变成了一位秃顶的中年麻瓜，赫敏变成了他那瘦瘦小小，有点像老鼠的妻子。她穿了件扣得严严实实的外衣，串珠小包塞在外衣内侧的口袋里，装着他们全部的家当（除了哈利戴在脖子上的魂器）。哈利把隐形衣披到两人身上，然后便一起旋转着进入了令人窒息的黑暗。

CHAPTER SIXTEEN Godric's Hollow

Heart beating in his throat, Harry opened his eyes. They were standing hand in hand in a snowy lane under a dark blue sky in which the night's first stars were already glimmering feebly. Cottages stood on either side of the narrow road, Christmas decorations twinkling in their windows. A short way ahead of them, a glow of golden streetlights indicated the centre of the village.

'All this snow!' Hermione whispered beneath the Cloak. 'Why didn't we think of snow? After all our precautions, we'll leave prints! We'll just have to get rid of them – you go in front, I'll do it –'

Harry did not want to enter the village like a pantomime horse, trying to keep themselves concealed while magically covering their traces.

'Let's take off the Cloak,' said Harry, and when she looked frightened, 'oh, come on, we don't look like us and there's no one around.'

He stowed the Cloak under his jacket and they made their way forwards unhampered, the icy air stinging their faces as they passed more cottages: any one of them might have been the one in which James and Lily had once lived, or where Bathilda lived now. Harry gazed at the front doors, their snow-burdened roofs and their front porches, wondering whether he remembered any of them, knowing deep inside that it was impossible, that he had been little over a year old when he had left this place forever. He was not even sure whether he would be able to see the cottage at all; he did not know what happened when the subjects of a Fidelius Charm died. Then the little lane along which they were walking curved to the left and the heart of the village, a small square, was revealed to them.

Strung all around with coloured lights, there was what looked like a war memorial in the middle, partly obscured by a windblown Christmas tree. There were several shops, a post office, a pub and a little church whose stained-glass windows were glowing jewel bright across the square.

The snow here had become impacted: it was hard and slippery where people had trodden on it all day. Villagers were criss-crossing in front of them, their figures briefly illuminated by street lamps. They heard a snatch of laughter and pop music as the pub door opened and closed; then they heard a carol start up inside the little church.

'Harry, I think it's Christmas Eve!' said Hermione.

'Is it?'

He had lost track of the date; they had not seen a newspaper for weeks.

第16章 戈德里克山谷

心跳到了喉咙口,哈利睁开双眼。他们俩手拉手站在一条积雪的小巷,头上是深蓝色的苍穹,第一批星星已经闪烁着微光。一些房子立在窄巷两旁,窗户里的圣诞装饰闪闪发亮。前方不远处,金色的街灯显示出那里是村子的中心。

"这么多雪!"赫敏在隐形衣下悄声说,"我们怎么没想到雪呢?千算万算,还是会留下脚印!必须把它们销掉——你走前面,我来——"

哈利不愿意像哑剧中双人扮的假马那样进村,身上蒙着东西,边走边用魔法掩去足迹。

"脱掉隐形衣吧。"哈利说,看到赫敏显出害怕的样子,他又说,"哦,没事的,我们变了形,周围又没人。"

他把隐形衣塞进外衣里面,两人没有羁绊地朝前走去。冰冷的空气像针扎在面颊上,沿途经过更多的房子:每一座都可能是詹姆和莉莉曾经住过的,或是巴希达现在住着的。哈利望着那些前门、积雪的屋顶和门廊,自问是否还能记起一二,而内心深处知道这是不可能的,自己才一岁多一点儿就永久地离开了这儿。他甚至不知道还能不能看到那所房子,不知道被施了赤胆忠心咒的人死后会发生什么情况。小巷向左一拐,村子的中心——一个小广场呈现在他们眼前。

广场中央有一个战争纪念碑状的建筑,半掩在被风吹得有些零落的圣诞树后面,周围张挂着彩灯。这里有几家店铺、一个邮局、一家酒吧,还有一座小教堂,彩绘玻璃在广场对面放射着珠宝般的光辉。

地上的雪都压实了:被人们踩了一天的地方硬邦邦、滑溜溜的。村民们在他们面前交叉往来,被街灯短暂地照亮。酒吧门开关时传出片断的笑声和流行音乐声,小教堂里有人唱起了颂歌。

"哈利,我想今天是圣诞前夜!"赫敏说。

"是吗?"

他已经忘记了日期,两人都好几个星期没看报纸了。

CHAPTER SIXTEEN   Godric's Hollow

'I'm sure it is,' said Hermione, her eyes upon the church. 'They ... they'll be in there, won't they? Your mum and dad? I can see the graveyard behind it.'

Harry felt a thrill of something that was beyond excitement, more like fear. Now that he was so near, he wondered whether he wanted to see, after all. Perhaps Hermione knew how he was feeling, because she reached for his hand and took the lead for the first time, pulling him forwards. Halfway across the square, however, she stopped dead.

'Harry, look!'

She was pointing at the war memorial. As they had passed it, it had transformed. Instead of an obelisk covered in names, there was a statue of three people: a man with untidy hair and glasses, a woman with long hair and a kind, pretty face, and a baby boy sitting in his mother's arms. Snow lay upon all their heads, like fluffy, white caps.

Harry drew closer, gazing up into his parents' faces. He had never imagined that there would be a statue ... how strange it was to see himself represented in stone, a happy baby without a scar on his forehead ...

'C'mon,' said Harry, when he had looked his fill, and they turned again towards the church. As they crossed the road, he glanced over his shoulder; the statue had turned back into the war memorial.

The singing grew louder as they approached the church. It made Harry's throat constrict, it reminded him so forcefully of Hogwarts, of Peeves bellowing rude versions of carols from inside suits of armour, of the Great Hall's twelve Christmas trees, of Dumbledore wearing a bonnet he had won in a cracker, of Ron in a hand-knitted sweater ...

There was a kissing gate at the entrance to the graveyard. Hermione pushed it open as quietly as possible and they edged through it. On either side of the slippery path to the church doors the snow lay deep and untouched. They moved off through the snow, carving deep trenches behind them as they walked round the building, keeping to the shadows beneath the brilliant windows.

Behind the church, row upon row of snowy tombstones protruded from a blanket of pale blue that was flecked with dazzling red, gold and green wherever the reflections from the stained glass hit the snow. Keeping his hand closed tightly on the wand in his jacket pocket, Harry moved towards the nearest grave.

'Look at this, it's an Abbott, could be some long lost relation of Hannah's!'

第16章 戈德里克山谷

"我可以肯定。"赫敏说，眼睛望着教堂，"他们……他们会在那儿，是不是？你的爸爸妈妈？我能看到教堂后面的墓地。"

哈利感到一阵战栗，那不只是激动，更像是恐惧。现在距离这么近，他倒不知道自己究竟想不想看了。也许赫敏了解他的感受，她拉起他的手，第一次在前领路，拉着他往前走。但走到广场中间时，她突然停住了。

"哈利，看！"

她指着那块纪念碑。在他们走过时，纪念碑起了变化，不再是一块刻满名字的方尖石碑，而是变成了三个人的雕像：一个头发蓬乱、戴着眼镜的男人，一个长头发、容貌美丽善良的女人，还有一个坐在妈妈怀中的男婴。雪花落在他们三个人的头顶，像松软的白绒帽。

哈利走到近前，凝望着他父母的面庞。他从没想过会有一座雕塑……多么奇怪，看到石刻的自己，一个快乐的婴儿，头上没有伤疤……

"走吧。"瞻仰够了之后，哈利说道。两人继续朝教堂走去，过街时他回头看了看，雕像又变成了战争纪念碑。

走近教堂，歌声越来越响，哈利嗓子眼里发紧，他如此强烈地想到了霍格沃茨，想到了皮皮鬼从盔甲里胡乱吼唱圣诞颂歌，想到了大礼堂里的十二棵圣诞树，想到了邓布利多戴着拉彩包爆竹赢得的女帽，想到了罗恩穿着手织毛衣……

墓地入口有一道窄门。赫敏尽可能轻轻地推开它，两人钻了进去。通向教堂门口的小径滑溜溜的，两边积雪很深，未经踩踏。他们从雪地上穿过去，小心地贴着明亮窗户下的阴影绕向屋后，身后留下深深的沟印。

教堂后面，一排排积雪的墓碑伫立在浅蓝色的银毯上，耀眼的红色、金色和绿色光斑点缀其间，是彩绘玻璃在雪地上的投影。哈利用手在衣袋里握紧魔杖，朝最近的墓碑走去。

"看这个，姓艾博，说不定是汉娜失散的亲戚！"

CHAPTER SIXTEEN   Godric's Hollow

'Keep your voice down,' Hermione begged him.

They waded deeper and deeper into the graveyard, gouging dark tracks into the snow behind them, stooping to peer at the words on old headstones, every now and then squinting into the surrounding darkness to make absolutely sure that they were unaccompanied.

'Harry, here!'

Hermione was two rows of tombstones away; he had to wade back to her, his heart positively banging in his chest.

'Is it –?'

'No, but look!'

She pointed to the dark stone. Harry stooped down and saw, upon the frozen, lichen-spotted granite, the words *Kendra Dumbledore* and, a short way below her dates of birth and death, *and her daughter Ariana*. There was also a quotation:

> *Where your treasure is,*
> *there will your heart be also.*

So Rita Skeeter and Muriel had got some of their facts right. The Dumbledore family had indeed lived here, and part of it had died here.

Seeing the grave was worse than hearing about it. Harry could not help thinking that he and Dumbledore both had deep roots in this graveyard, and that Dumbledore ought to have told him so; yet he had never thought to share the connection. They could have visited the place together; for a moment Harry imagined coming here with Dumbledore, of what a bond that would have been, of how much it would have meant to him. But it seemed that to Dumbledore, the fact that their families lay side by side in the same graveyard had been an unimportant coincidence, irrelevant, perhaps, to the job he wanted Harry to do.

Hermione was looking at Harry, and he was glad that his face was hidden in shadow. He read the words on the tombstone again. *Where your treasure is, there will your heart be also.* He did not understand what these words meant. Surely Dumbledore had chosen them, as the eldest member of the family once his mother had died.

'Are you sure he never mentioned –?' Hermione began.

第16章 戈德里克山谷

"小点声。"赫敏恳求道。

两人踏着雪往墓地深处走去,雪地上留下深深的黑色踪迹。他们弯腰细看古老墓碑上的铭文,时而向周围的黑暗处张望,确定没有旁人。

"哈利,这儿!"

赫敏在两排墓碑之外,哈利只好费力地返回去,心脏怦怦地撞击着胸口。

"是不是——"

"不是,但你看!"

赫敏指着黑乎乎的碑石,哈利弯下腰,看到在结冰的、地衣斑驳的花岗石上,刻着坎德拉·邓布利多,生卒日期底下是及女儿阿利安娜。还有一句格言:

> 珍宝在何处,
> 心也在何处

那么,丽塔·斯基特和穆丽尔说对了几分事实。邓布利多一家确实在这儿住过,还有人在这儿去世。

看到这坟墓比听说它时还要难过,哈利不禁心潮起伏,他和邓布利多都有深深的根埋在这片墓地中。邓布利多本该告诉他这一点,却从来没想点破这层关系。他们本可以一起造访这个地方,一瞬间哈利想象着跟邓布利多同来这里,那将是怎样的一种交情,那将对他有多么大的意义。然而对于邓布利多而言,他们的亲人躺在同一块墓地上,似乎只是一个不重要的巧合,或许与他要哈利做的事情毫不相干。

赫敏望着哈利,哈利庆幸自己的脸在暗处。他又读了读墓碑上的字。珍宝在何处,心也在何处。但他不明白这话的意思。这一定是邓布利多选的碑文,母亲去世后他就成了一家之主。

"你确定他从没提过——?"赫敏问。

'No,' said Harry curtly, then, 'let's keep looking,' and he turned away, wishing he had not seen the stone: he did not want his excited trepidation tainted with resentment.

'Here!' cried Hermione again a few moments later, from out of the darkness. 'Oh, no, sorry! I thought it said Potter.'

She was rubbing at a crumbling, mossy stone, gazing down at it, a little frown on her face.

'Harry, come back a moment.'

He did not want to be sidetracked again, and only grudgingly made his way back through the snow towards her.

'What?'

'Look at this!'

The grave was extremely old, weathered so that Harry could hardly make out the name. Hermione showed him the symbol beneath it.

'Harry, that's the mark in the book!'

He peered at the place she indicated: the stone was so worn that it was hard to make out what was engraved there, though there did seem to be a triangular mark beneath the nearly illegible name.

'Yeah ... it could be ...'

Hermione lit her wand and pointed it at the name on the headstone.

'It says Ig – Ignotus, I think ...'

'I'm going to keep looking for my parents, all right?' Harry told her, a slight edge to his voice, and he set off again, leaving her crouched beside the old grave.

Every now and then he recognised a surname that, like Abbott, he had met at Hogwarts. Sometimes there were several generations of the same wizarding family represented in the graveyard: Harry could tell from the dates that it had either died out, or the current members had moved away from Godric's Hollow. Deeper and deeper amongst the graves he went, and every time he reached a new headstone he felt a little lurch of apprehension and anticipation.

The darkness and the silence seemed to become, all of a sudden, much deeper. Harry looked around, worried, thinking of Dementors, then realised that the carols had finished, that the chatter and flurry of church-goers were fading away as they made their way back into the square. Somebody inside the church had just turned off the lights.

Then Hermione's voice came out of the blackness for the third time, sharp and clear from a few yards away.

第16章　戈德里克山谷

"没有。"哈利简短地说,"接着找吧。"他转身走开,希望自己没有看到那块石碑。他不想让自己紧张激动的心情被怨恨沾染。

"这儿!"过了一会儿赫敏又在黑暗中叫起来,"哦,不是,对不起!我还以为是波特呢。"

她擦着一块残破的、长满青苔的石碑,低头辨认,微微皱着眉头。

"哈利,回来一下。"

他不想再被打岔,老大不情愿地踏着雪向她走去。

"什么呀?"

"看这个!"

这块墓碑极其古老,已经风化,哈利几乎看不清上面的名字。赫敏指着名字下面的符号。

"哈利,这是书里的那个标志!"

他仔细看去,石碑风化得太厉害,看不清刻着什么,但那几乎无法辨认的名字下面,好像确实有个三角形记号。

"嗯……有可能……"

赫敏点亮魔杖,指着墓碑上的名字。

"伊格——伊格诺图斯,我猜……"

"我接着去找我的父母,好吗?"哈利对她说,声音有一点尖刻,然后便走开了,留下赫敏蹲在古老的墓碑旁。

哈利时不时地认出一个像艾博那样,在霍格沃茨见到过的姓氏。有时同一巫师家族的几代人都列在墓碑上。哈利从年代上看出,这些家庭有的死绝了,有的后代离开了戈德里克山谷。他在墓地中越走越远,每次走近一块墓碑,都感到一阵既害怕又期待的激动。

黑暗和寂静似乎突然加深了许多。哈利担心地环顾四周,想到了摄魂怪,然后意识到颂歌结束了,杂乱的人声渐渐远去,做礼拜的人们散入广场中。教堂里有人刚把灯熄灭。

赫敏的声音第三次从黑暗中传来,尖锐清晰,在几米之外。

'Harry, they're here ... right here.'

And he knew by her tone that it was his mother and father this time: he moved towards her feeling as if something heavy were pressing on his chest, the same sensation he had had right after Dumbledore had died, a grief that had actually weighed on his heart and lungs.

The headstone was only two rows behind Kendra and Ariana's. It was made of white marble, just like Dumbledore's tomb, and this made it easy to read, as it seemed to shine in the dark. Harry did not need to kneel or even approach very close to it to make out the words engraved upon it.

JAMES POTTER,
born 27 March 1960, died 31 October 1981

LILY POTTER,
born 30 January 1960, died 31 October 1981

The last enemy that shall be destroyed is death.

Harry read the words slowly, as though he would have only one chance to take in their meaning, and he read the last of them aloud.

'"*The last enemy that shall be destroyed is death*" ...' A horrible thought came to him, and with it a kind of panic. 'Isn't that a Death Eater idea? Why is that there?'

'It doesn't mean defeating death in the way the Death Eaters mean it, Harry,' said Hermione, her voice gentle. 'It means ... you know ... living beyond death. Living after death.'

But they were not living, thought Harry: they were gone. The empty words could not disguise the fact that his parents' mouldering remains lay beneath snow and stone, indifferent, unknowing. And tears came before he could stop them, boiling hot then instantly freezing on his face, and what was the point in wiping them off, or pretending? He let them fall, his lips pressed hard together, looking down at the thick snow hiding from his eyes the place where the last of Lily and James lay, bones now, surely, or dust, not knowing or caring that their living son stood so near, his heart still beating, alive

第 16 章 戈德里克山谷

"哈利,在这儿……这边。"

哈利从她的语调中听出,这次是他的父母。他朝赫敏走去,感觉有个东西沉甸甸地压在胸口,就像邓布利多死后他感到的那样,一种真正压迫心肺的悲痛。

墓碑与坎德拉和阿利安娜的只隔了两排,它像邓布利多的坟墓一样是白色大理石的,文字比较容易辨读,因为它似乎在黑暗中闪闪发亮。哈利不用跪下,甚至不用走得很近,就能看清上面的铭文。

詹姆·波特

生于 1960 年 3 月 27 日

卒于 1981 年 10 月 31 日

莉莉·波特

生于 1960 年 1 月 30 日

卒于 1981 年 10 月 31 日

最后一个要消灭的敌人是死亡

哈利慢慢地读着这些文字,仿佛只有一次机会读懂它们的含义。他把最后一行念了出来。

"最后一个要消灭的敌人是死亡……"一个可怕的念头突然涌入脑海,伴随而来的是一阵恐慌,"这不是食死徒的想法吗?怎么会在这儿?"

"它指的不是食死徒那种打败死亡的方式,哈利。"赫敏声音温柔地说,"它指的是……你知道……生命超越死亡,虽死犹生。"

可是他们没有生命,哈利想:他们不在了。空洞的文字掩饰不了这个现实,他父母腐烂的尸骸躺在冰雪和石头下面,冷冰冰的,没有知觉。泪水一下子涌了出来,滚烫滚烫,顷刻间冻在脸上,擦拭和掩饰又有什么意义?他任凭泪水纵横,紧闭双唇,低头看着厚厚的积雪,那下面掩盖着莉莉和詹姆的遗体,现在想必只剩下骨殖与泥土,不知道、

CHAPTER SIXTEEN   Godric's Hollow

because of their sacrifice and close to wishing, at this moment, that he was sleeping under the snow with them.

Hermione had taken his hand again and was gripping it tightly. He could not look at her, but returned the pressure, now taking deep, sharp gulps of the night air, trying to steady himself, trying to regain control. He should have brought something to give them, and he had not thought of it, and every plant in the graveyard was leafless and frozen. But Hermione raised her wand, moved it in a circle through the air and a wreath of Christmas roses blossomed before them. Harry caught it and laid it on his parents' grave.

As soon as he stood up, he wanted to leave: he did not think he could stand another moment there. He put his arm around Hermione's shoulders, and she put hers around his waist, and they turned in silence and walked away through the snow, past Dumbledore's mother and sister, back towards the dark church and the out-of-sight kissing gate.

第16章 戈德里克山谷

也不关心他们留在世上的儿子就站在这么近的地方。他的心脏仍在有力地跳动,是他们的牺牲换来的,但他此刻几乎希望自己和他们一起长眠在白雪下面。

赫敏又拉住了他的手,紧紧地握着。他不能看她,但用力回握着,深深地大口吸进夜晚的凉气,努力使自己平静下来。他应该带点什么给他们的,来时没有想到,墓地上的植物都光秃秃的,结了冰。赫敏举起魔杖,在空中画了一个圈,一个圣诞玫瑰花环盛开在他们面前。哈利接过来,摆在父母的坟上。

一站起来,他就想走,觉得再多待一会儿都受不了。他把胳膊搭在赫敏的肩上,她搂着他的腰,两人默默地转身穿过雪地,经过邓布利多的母亲和妹妹的坟墓,朝黑暗的教堂和视线之外的窄门走去。

CHAPTER SEVENTEEN

Bathilda's Secret

'Harry, stop.'

'What's wrong?'

They had only just reached the grave of the unknown Abbott.

'There's someone there. Someone watching us. I can tell. There, over by the bushes.'

They stood quite still, holding on to each other, gazing at the dense black boundary of the graveyard. Harry could not see anything.

'Are you sure?'

'I saw something move, I could have sworn I did ...'

She broke from him to free her wand arm.

'We look like Muggles,' Harry pointed out.

'Muggles who've just been laying flowers on your parents' grave! Harry, I'm sure there's someone over there!'

Harry thought of *A History of Magic*; the graveyard was supposed to be haunted: what if –? But then he heard a rustle and saw a little eddy of dislodged snow in the bush to which Hermione had pointed. Ghosts could not move snow.

'It's a cat,' said Harry, after a second or two, 'or a bird. If it was a Death Eater, we'd be dead by now. But let's get out of here, and we can put the Cloak back on.'

They glanced back repeatedly as they made their way out of the graveyard. Harry, who did not feel as sanguine as he had pretended when reassuring Hermione, was glad to reach the gate and the slippery pavement. They pulled the Invisibility Cloak back over themselves. The pub was fuller than before: many voices inside it were now singing the carol that they had heard as they approached the church. For a moment Harry considered

第 17 章

巴希达的秘密

"哈利,停下。"

"怎么啦?"

他们刚走到那位不知名的艾博的墓前。

"有人在那儿,有人在看着我们,我能感觉到。那儿,灌木丛旁边。"

他们一动不动地站着,搂在一起,盯着黑森森的墓地边缘。哈利什么也没看见。

"你确定?"

"我看到有东西在动,我可以发誓……"

赫敏挣脱开哈利,腾出握着魔杖的手臂。

"我们外表跟麻瓜一样。"哈利指出。

"刚刚在你父母坟前放了鲜花的麻瓜!哈利,我相信那儿有人!"

哈利想到了《魔法史》,那上面说这片墓地闹鬼:要是——?这时他听到一阵窸窣声,并看见赫敏所指的灌木丛间有一小团雪花的旋涡,鬼是不能让雪移动的。

"是猫,"一两秒钟后,哈利说,"或是小鸟。如果是食死徒的话,我们现在已经死了。不过,还是离开这里吧,然后我们可以穿上隐形衣。"

两人不住地回头看着,往墓地外走去。哈利其实并不像安慰赫敏时假装的那样乐观,走到门口,踏上了滑溜溜的石板路,他才感到松了口气。两人披上了隐形衣。酒吧里的客人比先前多了,许多声音在

CHAPTER SEVENTEEN   Bathilda's Secret

suggesting they take refuge inside it, but before he could say anything Hermione murmured, 'Let's go this way,' and pulled him down the dark street leading out of the village in the opposite direction from which they had entered. Harry could make out the point where the cottages ended and the lane turned into open country again. They walked as quickly as they dared, past more windows sparkling with multicoloured lights, the outlines of Christmas trees dark through the curtains.

'How are we going to find Bathilda's house?' asked Hermione, who was shivering a little and kept glancing back over her shoulder. 'Harry? What do you think? Harry?'

She tugged at his arm, but Harry was not paying attention. He was looking towards the dark mass that stood at the very end of this row of houses. Next moment he had sped up, dragging Hermione along with him; she slipped a little on the ice.

'Harry –'

'Look … look at it, Hermione …'

'I don't … oh!'

He could see it; the Fidelius Charm must have died with James and Lily. The hedge had grown wild in the sixteen years since Hagrid had taken Harry from the rubble that lay scattered amongst the waist-high grass. Most of the cottage was still standing, though entirely covered in dark ivy and snow, but the right side of the top floor had been blown apart; that, Harry was sure, was where the curse had backfired. He and Hermione stood at the gate, gazing up at the wreck of what must once have been a cottage just like those that flanked it.

'I wonder why nobody's ever rebuilt it?' whispered Hermione.

'Maybe you can't rebuild it?' Harry replied. 'Maybe it's like the injuries from Dark Magic and you can't repair the damage?'

He slipped a hand from beneath the Cloak and grasped the snowy and thickly rusted gate, not wishing to open it, but simply to hold some part of the house.

'You're not going to go inside? It looks unsafe, it might – oh, Harry, look!'

His touch on the gate seemed to have done it. A sign had risen out of the ground in front of them, up through the tangles of nettles and weeds, like some bizarre, fast-growing flower, and in golden letters upon the wood it said:

第 17 章 巴希达的秘密

唱他们之前在教堂附近听到的颂歌。哈利想提议进去躲一躲,但没等他说话,赫敏就悄声说"走这边",拉着他走上了一条黑暗的街道。它通往村外,与他们进来的路正好相反。哈利能看到房屋消失、小街又转为旷野的地方。他们步子快到不敢再快,经过了更多彩灯闪烁的窗口,窗帘后现出圣诞树的剪影。

"怎么能找到巴希达的房子呢?"赫敏问,她有点哆嗦,时常回头张望,"哈利?你怎么想?哈利?"

她拽了拽哈利的胳膊,但哈利没有注意。他正望着这排房子尽头的一团黑影,接着他加快脚步,拖着赫敏走过去,赫敏在冰上滑了一下。

"哈利——"

"看……看哪,赫敏……"

"我没……哦!"

他看到了。赤胆忠心咒一定是随詹姆和莉莉的死亡而失效了。在海格把哈利从废墟中抱走后的十六年中,树篱已经长得乱七八糟,瓦砾埋藏在齐腰深的荒草间。房子的大部分还立在那里,完全被深黑的常春藤和积雪覆盖,但顶层房间的右侧已被炸毁,哈利想那一定就是咒语弹回的地方。他和赫敏站在门口瞻仰这座废墟,它以前想必和两边的房子一样。

"为什么没有人重修它呢?"赫敏小声说。

"也许没法重修吧?"哈利答道,"也许就像黑魔法造成的那种损害,不能修复?"

他从隐形衣下伸出一只手,抓住了锈得厉害的、积雪的铁门,不想打开,只想握住房子的一部分。

"你不会要进去吧?看上去不安全,也许——哦,哈利,看!"

好像是他的手放在门上引起的:一块木牌从他们前面的地上升起,从杂乱的荨麻和野草中钻出,就像某种奇异的、迅速长大的花朵。牌子上的金字写道:

CHAPTER SEVENTEEN   Bathilda's Secret

> On this spot, on the night of 31 October 1981,
> Lily and James Potter lost their lives.
> Their son, Harry, remains the only wizard
> ever to have survived the Killing Curse.
> This house, invisible to Muggles, has been
> lift in its ruined state as a monument to the
> Potters and as a reminder of the violence
> that tore apart their family.

And all round these neatly lettered words scribbles had been added by other witches and wizards who had come to see the place where the Boy Who Lived had escaped. Some had merely signed their names in Everlasting Ink; others had carved their initials into the wood, still others had left messages. The most recent of these, shining brightly over sixteen years' worth of magical graffiti, all said similar things.

Good luck, Harry, wherever you are.
If you read this, Harry, we're all behind you!
Long live Harry Potter

'They shouldn't have written on the sign!' said Hermione, indignant.

But Harry beamed at her.

'It's brilliant. I'm glad they did. I ...'

He broke off. A heavily muffled figure was hobbling up the lane towards them, silhouetted by the bright lights in the distant square. Harry thought, though it was hard to judge, that the figure was a woman. She was moving slowly, possibly frightened of slipping on the snowy ground. Her stoop, her stoutness, her shuffling gait all gave an impression of extreme age. They watched in silence as she drew nearer. Harry was waiting to see whether she would turn into any of the cottages she was passing, but he knew, instinctively, that she would not. At last she came to a halt a few yards from them, and simply stood there in the middle of the frozen road, facing them.

He did not need Hermione's pinch to his arm. There was next to no

第 17 章 巴希达的秘密

1981 年 10 月 31 日夜里，
莉莉和詹姆·波特在这里牺牲
他们的儿子哈利是唯一一位
中了杀戮咒而幸存的巫师。
这所麻瓜看不见的房屋被原样保留，
以此废墟纪念波特夫妇，
并警示造成他们家破人亡的暴力。

在这些工整的字迹旁边，写满了各种题字，都是来瞻仰"大难不死的男孩"死里逃生之处的巫师写上去的。有的只是用永不褪色的墨水写下了自己的名字，有的在木牌上刻下了名字的首字母，还有的写了留言。最近的那些留言亮闪闪地覆盖了十六年的魔法涂鸦，内容大致相同。

祝你好运，哈利，无论你在哪里。
希望你能读到，哈利，我们都支持你！
哈利·波特万岁。

"他们不应该写在牌子上！"赫敏不满地说。

但哈利朝她粲然一笑。

"很好啊，我很高兴他们这么做，我……"

他顿住了，一个裹得严严实实的人影从小街上蹒跚走来，被远处广场的灯光映出黑色的轮廓。虽然很难判断，但哈利觉得那是个女人。她走得很慢，也许是怕在雪地上滑倒。那佝偻的身子、臃肿的体态、蹒跚的步伐，都给人以年纪很老的印象。他们默默地看着她走近，哈利等着看她是否会拐进路旁哪所小房子里，但又本能地知道不会。最后，她在几米远外停住了，就那样站在冰冻的街道中央，面朝着他们。

不需要赫敏掐他的胳膊，哈利知道这女人是麻瓜的可能性几乎为

CHAPTER SEVENTEEN Bathilda's Secret

chance that this woman was a Muggle: she was standing there gazing at a house that ought to have been completely invisible to her, if she was not a witch. Even assuming that she *was* a witch, however, it was odd behaviour to come out on a night this cold, simply to look at an old ruin. By all the rules of normal magic, meanwhile, she ought not to be able to see Hermione and him at all. Nevertheless, Harry had the strangest feeling that she knew that they were there, and also who they were. Just as he had reached this uneasy conclusion, she raised a gloved hand and beckoned.

Hermione moved closer to him under the Cloak, her arm pressed against his.

'How does she know?'

He shook his head. The woman beckoned again, more vigorously. Harry could think of many reasons not to obey the summons, and yet his suspicions about her identity were growing stronger every moment that they stood facing each other in the deserted street.

Was it possible that she had been waiting for them all these long months? That Dumbledore had told her to wait, and that Harry would come in the end? Was it not likely that it was she who had moved in the shadows in the graveyard and had followed them to this spot? Even her ability to sense them suggested some Dumbledore-ish power that he had never encountered before.

Finally Harry spoke, causing Hermione to gasp and jump.

'Are you Bathilda?'

The muffled figure nodded and beckoned again.

Beneath the Cloak, Harry and Hermione looked at each other. Harry raised his eyebrows; Hermione gave a tiny, nervous nod.

They stepped towards the woman and, at once, she turned and hobbled off back the way they had come. Leading them past several houses, she turned in at a gate. They followed her up the front path through a garden nearly as overgrown as the one they had just left. She fumbled for a moment with a key at the front door, then opened it and stepped back to let them pass.

She smelled bad, or perhaps it was her house: Harry wrinkled his nose as they sidled past her and pulled off the Cloak. Now that he was beside her, he realised how tiny she was; bowed down with age, she came barely level with his chest. She closed the door behind them, her knuckles blue and mottled against the peeling paint, then turned and peered into Harry's face. Her eyes were thick with cataracts and sunken into folds of transparent skin, and

第17章 巴希达的秘密

零:她站在那儿凝视着一座只有巫师才能看见的房子。但就算她是女巫,这也够奇怪的,在这么寒冷的夜晚跑出来,就为看一座老屋的废墟。而且,按照魔法常规来说,她应该根本就看不到他和赫敏。不过,哈利有一种非常奇怪的感觉,好像她知道他们在这儿,而且知道他们是谁。正当他得出这一令人不安的结论时,女人举起一只戴手套的手,招了一下。

赫敏在隐形衣下向哈利靠了靠,手臂紧贴着他的手臂。

"她怎么知道?"

他摇摇头。女人又更起劲地招了招手。哈利能想出许多理由不听从这召唤,但双方在空荡荡的街道上对视时,他对她身份的怀疑越来越强烈了。

她会不会这几个月一直在等待他们的到来?是不是邓布利多叫她在这里等候,说哈利总有一天会来?会不会就是她在墓地里暗中窥视,又尾随到此?而且她能感觉到他们,这一点也令哈利想起某种他从未领略过的、邓布利多式的法力。

终于,哈利说话了,赫敏惊得一跳。

"你是巴希达吗?"

那个裹得严严实实的人影点点头,又招了招手。

隐形衣下面,哈利和赫敏对视了一下,哈利扬起眉毛,赫敏紧张地微微点了点头。

两人朝那女人走去,她立刻转过身,蹒跚地沿着来路往回走,经过几座房子之后,拐进了一个门口。他们跟着她走入小径,穿过一个几乎跟刚才那个一样荒芜的花园。她拿着钥匙在前门上摸索了一会儿,打开了门,退到一旁让他们进去。

她身上的味道很难闻,也许是她的屋子有怪味儿:他们侧身进门,脱下隐形衣时,哈利皱起了鼻子。他站到她的近旁,发现她是那么矮小,老得都佝偻了,刚刚到他胸口。她关上门,青紫带斑的指节衬在剥落的油漆上,然后她转身注视着哈利的面庞,眼睛深陷在透明的皮肤皱褶中,里面是厚厚的白内障。她的脸上布满支离破碎的血管和老人斑。

CHAPTER SEVENTEEN Bathilda's Secret

her whole face was dotted with broken veins and liver spots. He wondered whether she could make him out at all; even if she could, it was the balding Muggle whose identity he had stolen that she would see.

The odour of old age, of dust, of unwashed clothes and stale food intensified as she unwound a moth-eaten, black shawl, revealing a head of scant white hair through which the scalp showed clearly.

'Bathilda?' Harry repeated.

She nodded again. Harry became aware of the locket against his skin; the thing inside it that sometimes ticked or beat had woken; he could feel it pulsing through the cold gold. Did it know, could it sense, that the thing that would destroy it was near?

Bathilda shuffled past them, pushing Hermione aside as though she had not seen her, and vanished into what seemed to be a sitting room.

'Harry, I'm not sure about this,' breathed Hermione.

'Look at the size of her; I think we could overpower her if we had to,' said Harry. 'Listen, I should have told you, I knew she wasn't all there. Muriel called her "gaga".'

'Come!' called Bathilda from the next room.

Hermione jumped and clutched Harry's arm.

'It's OK,' said Harry reassuringly, and he led the way into the sitting room.

Bathilda was tottering around the place lighting candles, but it was still very dark, not to mention extremely dirty. Thick dust crunched beneath their feet and Harry's nose detected, underneath the dank and mildewed smell, something worse, like meat gone bad. He wondered when was the last time anyone had been inside Bathilda's house to check whether she was coping. She seemed to have forgotten that she could do magic too, for she lit the candles clumsily by hand, her trailing lace cuff in constant danger of catching fire.

'Let me do that,' offered Harry, and he took the matches from her. She stood watching him as he finished lighting the candle stubs that stood on saucers around the room, perched precariously on stacks of books and on side tables crammed with cracked and mouldy cups.

The last surface on which Harry spotted a candle was a bow-fronted chest of drawers on which there stood a large number of photographs. When the flame danced into life, its reflection wavered on their dusty glass and silver. He saw a few tiny movements from the pictures. As Bathilda fumbled

第17章 巴希达的秘密

哈利怀疑老太太能不能看得清,就算能,也只会看见他冒充的那个秃顶麻瓜。

她解开虫蛀的黑头巾,露出一个白发稀疏、头皮清晰可见的脑袋,老年人身上的陈腐味、灰尘味、脏衣服味和变质食品味更加浓烈了。

"巴希达?"哈利又问。

她再次点点头。哈利感觉到挂坠盒贴在他的皮肤上,里面那个有时滴滴答答或轻轻跳动的东西醒来了,他能感到它在冰冷的金壳里面搏动。它是否知道,是否能感觉到,那个能够摧毁它的东西就在附近?

巴希达蹒跚地从他们身边走过,仿佛没看见似的把赫敏挤到一边,走进了一间好像是起居室的屋子。

"哈利,我没有把握。"赫敏悄声说。

"看她的个头,万一不行,我想我们能制服她。"哈利说,"对了,我应该告诉你的,我知道她不大正常,穆丽尔说她老'糊涂'了。"

"过来!"巴希达在隔壁喊道。

赫敏惊跳了一下,抓住哈利的胳膊。

"没事儿。"哈利安慰道,带头走进了起居室。

巴希达蹒跚地走来走去点蜡烛,但屋里仍然很昏暗,更不用说有多脏了。厚厚的灰尘在他们脚下噗噗作响,哈利的鼻子在霉湿的气味下闻到了更恶心的东西,好像是腐肉。他想,不知道上一次是何时有人走进巴希达的屋子,看看她是否还活着。她似乎已经忘记自己会魔法了,在那里笨拙地用手点蜡烛,袖子上的花边随时都有着火的危险。

"我来吧。"哈利说,从她手里接过了火柴。她站在那儿看着他点完屋里各处的蜡烛,它们竖在小碟子里,危险地顶在书堆上或放满发霉的破杯子的小桌上。

哈利看到最后一个放蜡烛的地方,是一个弓形的五斗橱,上面摆着好多照片。火苗跳跃起来后,火光在灰蒙蒙的玻璃和银框中闪动。他看到照片中隐隐有东西在动。巴希达摸索着搬木头生火时,哈利轻轻

CHAPTER SEVENTEEN Bathilda's Secret

with logs for the fire, he muttered, '*Tergeo.*' The dust vanished from the photographs, and he saw at once that half a dozen were missing from the largest and most ornate frames. He wondered whether Bathilda or somebody else had removed them. Then the sight of a photograph near the back of the collection caught his eye, and he snatched it up.

It was the golden-haired, merry-faced thief, the young man who had perched on Gregorovitch's window sill, smiling lazily up at Harry out of the silver frame. And it came to Harry, instantly, where he had seen the boy before: *in The Life and Lies of Albus Dumbledore*, arm in arm with the teenage Dumbledore, and that must be where all the missing photographs were: in Rita's book.

'Mrs – Miss – Bagshot?' he said, and his voice shook slightly. 'Who is this?'

Bathilda was standing in the middle of the room watching Hermione light the fire for her.

'Miss Bagshot?' Harry repeated, and he advanced, with the picture in his hands, as the flames burst into life in the fireplace. Bathilda looked up at his voice and the Horcrux beat faster upon his chest.

'Who is this person?' Harry asked her, pushing the picture forwards.

She peered at it solemnly, then up at Harry.

'Do you know who this is?' he repeated, in a much slower and louder voice than usual. 'This man? Do you know him? What's he called?'

Bathilda merely looked vague. Harry felt an awful frustration. How had Rita Skeeter unlocked Bathilda's memories?

'Who is this man?' he repeated loudly.

'Harry, what are you doing?' asked Hermione.

'This picture, Hermione, it's the thief, the thief who stole from Gregorovitch! Please!' he said to Bathilda. 'Who is this?'

But she only stared at him.

'Why did you ask us to come with you, Mrs – Miss – Bagshot?' asked Hermione, raising her own voice. 'Was there something you wanted to tell us?'

Giving no sign that she had heard Hermione, Bathilda now shuffled a few steps closer to Harry. With a little jerk of her head, she looked back into the hall.

'You want us to leave?' he asked.

She repeated the gesture, this time pointing first at him, then at herself, then at the ceiling.

'Oh, right ... Hermione, I think she wants me to go upstairs with her.'

第17章 巴希达的秘密

说了声:"旋风扫净。"灰尘从照片上消失了,他立刻看出少了六张照片,都是最大、最华丽的相框中的,不知道是巴希达还是别人把它们拿走了。这时,靠后面的一张照片吸引了他的目光,他把它拿了起来。

是那个神采飞扬的金发小偷,那个栖在格里戈维奇窗台上的少年,在银相框中懒洋洋地冲着哈利微笑。哈利立刻想起他在哪儿见过这个少年:他在《邓布利多的生平和谎言》中,跟少年邓布利多挽着手臂。另外几张失踪的照片一定也都在那儿:在丽塔的书里。

"巴沙特夫人——女士?"他问道,声音微微颤抖,"这是谁?"

巴希达站在屋子中央,看着赫敏帮她生火。

"巴沙特女士?"哈利又叫了一声,捧着相框走过去,壁炉中腾起火焰。巴希达听到他的声音抬起头,魂器在他胸口跳得更快了。

"这个人是谁?"哈利问她,把照片递上前去。

她严肃地看了一会儿,然后抬头望着哈利。

"您知道这是谁吗?"哈利又问,声音比平时缓慢、响亮得多,"这个人?您认识他吗?他叫什么名字?"

巴希达表情茫然。哈利感到十分沮丧,丽塔·斯基特是怎样打开巴希达的记忆的呢?

"这个人是谁?"他再次大声问道。

"哈利,你在干吗?"赫敏问。

"这张照片,赫敏,是那个小偷,格里戈维奇家的小偷!请告诉我们!"他对巴希达说,"这个人是谁?"

巴希达只是木然地盯着他。

"您为什么叫我们到这儿来,巴沙特夫人——女士?"赫敏问道,也提高了嗓门,"您想告诉我们什么吗?"

巴希达好像没听见赫敏说话,蹒跚地朝哈利走了几步,头微微一摆,望着外面的过道。

"您想要我们出去?"哈利问。

巴希达重复着那个动作,指指哈利,再指指自己,然后指着天花板。

"哦,好的……赫敏,我想她是要我跟她上楼。"

CHAPTER SEVENTEEN Bathilda's Secret

'All right,' said Hermione, 'let's go.'

But when Hermione moved, Bathilda shook her head with surprising vigour, once more pointing first at Harry, then to herself.

'She wants me to go with her, alone.'

'Why?' asked Hermione, and her voice rang out sharp and clear in the candlelit room; the old lady shook her head a little at the loud noise.

'Maybe Dumbledore told her to give the sword to me, and only to me?'

'Do you really think she knows who you are?'

'Yes,' said Harry, looking down into the milky eyes fixed upon his own, 'I think she does.'

'Well, OK then, but be quick, Harry.'

'Lead the way,' Harry told Bathilda.

She seemed to understand, because she shuffled round him towards the door. Harry glanced back at Hermione with a reassuring smile, but he was not sure she had seen it; she stood hugging herself in the midst of the candlelit squalor, looking towards the bookcase. As Harry walked out of the room, unseen by both Hermione and Bathilda, he slipped the silver-framed photograph of the unknown thief inside his jacket.

The stairs were steep and narrow: Harry was half tempted to place his hands on stout Bathilda's backside to ensure that she did not topple over backwards on top of him, which seemed only too likely. Slowly, wheezing a little, she climbed to the upper landing, turned immediately right and led him into a low-ceilinged bedroom.

It was pitch black and smelled horrible: Harry had just made out a chamber pot protruding from under the bed before Bathilda closed the door and even that was swallowed by the darkness.

'*Lumos*,' said Harry, and his wand ignited. He gave a start: Bathilda had moved close to him in those few seconds of darkness, and he had not heard her approach.

'You are Potter?' she whispered.

'Yes, I am.'

She nodded slowly, solemnly. Harry felt the Horcrux beating fast, faster than his own heart: it was an unpleasant, agitating sensation.

'Have you got anything for me?' Harry asked, but she seemed distracted by his lit wand-tip.

第17章 巴希达的秘密

"好吧,"赫敏说,"我们走。"

但是赫敏刚一动,巴希达就出乎意料地使劲摇头,又指指哈利,指指自己。

"她想要我一个人跟她去。"

"为什么?"赫敏问,声音尖锐清晰,回荡在烛光摇曳的房间里。老太太听到这么响的声音轻轻摇了摇头。

"也许邓布利多叫她把宝剑交给我,只能给我?"

"你真的认为她知道你是谁吗?"

"是的,"哈利说,低头凝视着那双盯着他的混浊的眼睛,"我想她知道。"

"好吧,但要快点,哈利。"

"带路吧。"哈利对巴希达说。

她似乎听懂了,蹒跚地绕过哈利朝门口走去。哈利回头安慰地朝赫敏笑了一下,但不知道她看到没有。赫敏抱着手臂站在烛光中的脏屋子里,望着书架。赫敏和巴希达都没看见,哈利走出房间时,把那个不知名小偷的银相框塞进了外衣里面。

楼梯又陡又窄:哈利几乎想用手顶住臃肿的巴希达的后背,以防她朝后倒下来压到自己,这看上去太有可能了。她有点呼哧带喘,慢慢地爬到了楼梯顶上,马上向右一转,把哈利带进了一间低矮的卧室。

里面漆黑一片,气味很难闻。哈利刚模糊地看出床下突出来一只尿壶,巴希达就关上了门,连那一点点视觉也被黑暗吞没了。

"荧光闪烁。"哈利说,魔杖点亮了,他吓了一跳:在那几秒钟的黑暗中,巴希达已经走到他身边,他都没有听见。

"你是波特?"巴希达悄声问。

"是的。"

她缓缓地、庄严地点了点头。哈利感到魂器在急速跳动,比他自己的心跳还快,那是一种不舒服的、令人焦躁的感觉。

"您有东西要给我吗?"哈利问,但巴希达似乎被他杖尖的亮光分了神。

CHAPTER SEVENTEEN   Bathilda's Secret

'Have you got anything for me?' he repeated.

Then she closed her eyes and several things happened at once: Harry's scar prickled painfully; the Horcrux twitched so that the front of his sweater actually moved; the dark, fetid room dissolved momentarily. He felt a leap of joy and spoke in a high, cold voice: *hold him!*

Harry swayed where he stood: the dark, foul-smelling room seemed to close around him again; he did not know what had just happened.

'Have you got anything for me?' he asked for a third time, much louder.

'Over here,' she whispered, pointing to the corner. Harry raised his wand and saw the outline of a cluttered dressing table beneath the curtained window.

This time she did not lead him. Harry edged between her and the unmade bed, his wand raised. He did not want to look away from her.

'What is it?' he asked as he reached the dressing table, which was heaped high with what looked and smelled like dirty laundry.

'There,' she said, pointing at the shapeless mass.

And in the instant that he looked away, his eyes raking the tangled mess for a sword hilt, a ruby, she moved weirdly: he saw it out of the corner of his eye; panic made him turn and horror paralysed him as he saw the old body collapsing and the great snake pouring from the place where her neck had been.

The snake struck as he raised his wand: the force of the bite to his forearm sent the wand spinning up towards the ceiling, its light swung dizzyingly around the room and was extinguished: then a powerful blow from the tail to his midriff knocked the breath out of him: he fell backwards on to the dressing table, into the mound of filthy clothing –

He rolled sideways, narrowly avoiding the snake's tail, which thrashed down upon the table where he had been a second earlier: fragments of the glass surface rained upon him as he hit the floor. From below, he heard Hermione call, 'Harry?'

He could not get enough breath into his lungs to call back: then a heavy smooth mass smashed him to the floor and he felt it slide over him, powerful, muscular –

'No!' he gasped, pinned to the floor.

'*Yes*,' whispered the voice. '*Yesss … hold you … hold you …*'

"您有东西要给我吗？"他再问。

巴希达闭上眼睛，几件事情同时发生了：哈利的伤疤针扎一般的痛；魂器颤动着，连他胸前的毛衣都跟着动了起来；黑暗腐臭的房间暂时消失，他感到一阵欣喜，用高亢、冷酷的声音说：看住他！

哈利在原地摇晃了一下：黑暗腐臭的房间似乎又围在了他身边，他不明白刚才发生了什么事。

"您有东西要给我吗？"他第三次问道，声音响多了。

"这边。"巴希达指着角落里小声说。哈利举起魔杖，依稀看见拉着窗帘的窗子底下有一张乱糟糟的梳妆台。

这次巴希达没有领他过去。哈利举着魔杖，侧身移到她和没整理的床铺之间，他不想让目光离开她。

"这是什么？"他问，一边移到梳妆台边，那上面堆得高高的，看着和闻着都像是脏衣服。

"那儿。"巴希达指着那乱糟糟的一堆说。

就在他移开目光，在那堆东西里搜寻一把剑柄和一颗红宝石的一刹那，巴希达古怪地动了动：他从眼角的余光看到了，惊恐地转过身来，吓得浑身瘫软。他看到那衰老的身躯倒了下去，一条大蛇从原来是她脖子的地方喷射出来。

他举起魔杖时，大蛇发起了袭击，在他前臂上猛咬一口，魔杖打着跟头飞向天花板，荧光令人眩晕地在四壁旋转着，熄灭了。紧接着，蛇尾在他腹部重重一扫，击得他透不过气。他向后倒在梳妆台上，摔进臭烘烘的脏衣服堆里——

他往旁边一滚，勉强躲过了扫来的蛇尾，蛇尾啪地打在桌上他一秒钟前所在的位置。哈利滚落在地上，碎玻璃溅了一身，听到楼下赫敏在叫："哈利？"

他肺里吸不进足够的空气来回答，冷不防一个沉重而光滑的东西又将他撞倒在地，他感到蛇从身上滑过，强大，有力——

"不！"他喘息着，被压在地上。

"是，"那声音低低地说，"是……看住你……看住你……"

CHAPTER SEVENTEEN Bathilda's Secret

'*Accio ... Accio wand ...*'

But nothing happened and he needed his hands to try to force the snake from him as it coiled itself around his torso, squeezing the air from him, pressing the Horcrux hard into his chest, a circle of ice that throbbed with life, inches from his own frantic heart, and his brain was flooding with cold, white light, all thought obliterated, his own breath drowned, distant footsteps, everything going ...

A metal heart was banging outside his chest, and now he was flying, flying with triumph in his heart, without need of broomstick or Thestral ...

He was abruptly awake in the sour-smelling darkness; Nagini had released him. He scrambled up and saw the snake outlined against the landing light: it struck, and Hermione dived aside with a shriek: her deflected curse hit the curtained window, which shattered. Frozen air filled the room as Harry ducked to avoid another shower of broken glass and his foot slipped on a pencil-like something – his wand –

He bent and snatched it up, but now the room was full of the snake, its tail thrashing; Hermione was nowhere to be seen and for a moment Harry thought the worst, but then there was a loud bang and a flash of red light and the snake flew into the air, smacking Harry hard in the face as it went, coil after heavy coil rising up to the ceiling. Harry raised his wand, but as he did so his scar seared more painfully, more powerfully than it had done in years.

'He's coming! *Hermione, he's coming!*'

As he yelled, the snake fell, hissing wildly. Everything was chaos: it smashed shelves from the wall and splintered china flew everywhere as Harry jumped over the bed and seized the dark shape he knew to be Hermione –

She shrieked with pain as he pulled her back across the bed: the snake reared again, but Harry knew that worse than the snake was coming, was perhaps already at the gate, his head was going to split open with the pain from his scar –

The snake lunged as he took a running leap, dragging Hermione with him; as it struck, Hermione screamed, '*Confringo!*' and her spell flew around the room, exploding the wardrobe mirror and ricocheting back at them, bouncing from floor to ceiling; Harry felt the heat of it sear the back of his hand. Glass cut his cheek as, pulling Hermione with him, he leapt from bed

第17章 巴希达的秘密

"魔杖……魔杖飞来……"

可是不起作用。他需要用双手把缠到他身上的大蛇推开，它正挤出他肺里的空气，把魂器紧紧压进他的胸膛，如同一个搏动的冰圈，离他自己狂跳的心脏只有几寸。他的大脑中顿时涌现出一片白色的冷光，所有思维都变成了空白，他的呼吸被淹没了，远处的脚步声，一切都消失了……

一颗金属的心脏在他的胸腔外撞击，此刻他在飞，心中带着胜利的喜悦，不需要飞天扫帚和夜骐……

哈利突然在一股酸腐味的黑暗中醒来，纳吉尼已经把他松开。他急忙爬起来，看到大蛇的轮廓映在楼梯口的微光中：它发起了袭击，赫敏尖叫着往旁边一躲，她的咒语打偏了，把挂着窗帘的窗户击得粉碎，冰冷的空气灌入房中。哈利又闪身躲避阵雨般的碎玻璃，脚踩到了一根铅笔似的东西——他的魔杖——

他弯腰把魔杖捡了起来，但现在大蛇充满了整个房间，不住抽打着尾巴。赫敏不见了，哈利一瞬间想到了最坏的情况，但突然砰的一声，红光一闪，大蛇飞到空中，重重地撞在哈利的脸上，一圈一圈沉重的蛇身升向天花板。哈利举起魔杖，但这时伤疤灼痛得更厉害了，好多年都没有这么痛过。

"他来了！赫敏，他来了！"

当哈利大叫时，大蛇落了下来，疯狂地发出咝咝声。一片混乱：它打翻了墙上的架子，破碎的瓷器四处乱飞，哈利从床上跳过去，抓住了他知道是赫敏的那个黑影——

赫敏痛得尖叫，被哈利拉回到床这边，大蛇又立了起来，但哈利知道比蛇更可怕的就要来了，也许已经在大门口，他的伤疤痛得脑袋像要裂开——

大蛇猛扑过来，哈利拉着赫敏一个箭步冲出去。在它袭来时，赫敏尖叫一声："霹雳爆炸！"她的咒语绕着屋子疾飞，炸毁了穿衣镜，在地面和天花板之间蹦跳着朝他们反弹回来，哈利感到咒语的热气烫伤了他的手背。他不顾碎玻璃扎破了面颊，拉着赫敏，从床边跃到梳

CHAPTER SEVENTEEN   Bathilda's Secret

to broken dressing table and then straight out of the smashed window into nothingness, her scream reverberating through the night as they twisted in mid-air ...

And then his scar burst open and he was Voldemort and he was running across the fetid bedroom, his long, white hands clutching at the window sill as he glimpsed the bald man and the little woman twist and vanish, and he screamed with rage, a scream that mingled with the girl's, that echoed across the dark gardens over the church bells ringing in Christmas Day ...

And his scream was Harry's scream, his pain was Harry's pain ... that it could happen here, where it had happened before ... here, within sight of that house where he had come so close to knowing what it was to die ... to die ... the pain was so terrible ... ripped from his body ... but if he had no body, why did his head hurt so badly, if he was dead, how could he feel so unbearably, didn't pain cease with death, didn't it go ...

The night wet and windy, two children dressed as pumpkins waddling across the square, and the shop windows covered in paper spiders, all the tawdry Muggle trappings of a world in which they did not believe ... and he was gliding along, that sense of purpose and power and rightness in him that he always knew on these occasions ... not anger ... that was for weaker souls than he ... but triumph, yes ... he had waited for this, he had hoped for it ...

'Nice costume, Mister!'

He saw the small boy's smile falter as he ran near enough to see beneath the hood of the cloak, saw the fear cloud his painted face: then the child turned and ran away ... beneath the robe he fingered the handle of his wand ... one simple movement and the child would never reach his mother ... but unnecessary, quite unnecessary ...

And along a new and darker street he moved, and now his destination was in sight at last, the Fidelius Charm broken, though they did not know it yet ... and he made less noise than the dead leaves slithering along the pavement as he drew level with the dark hedge, and stared over it ...

They had not drawn the curtains, he saw them quite clearly in their little sitting room, the tall, black-haired man in his glasses, making puffs of coloured smoke erupt from his wand for the amusement of the small black-haired boy in his blue pyjamas. The child was laughing and trying to catch the smoke, to grab it in his small fist ...

A door opened and the mother entered, saying words he could not hear, her long, dark red hair falling over her face. Now the father scooped up the son and handed him to the mother. He threw his wand down upon the sofa and stretched, yawning ...

第 17 章 巴希达的秘密

妆台前，直接从打破的窗户跳入虚空，赫敏的尖叫在夜幕中回响，两人在半空中旋转……

这时哈利的伤疤炸裂了，他是伏地魔，疾步奔过臭烘烘的卧室，细长苍白的手指抓着窗台。他看到那个秃顶男人和小女人旋转着消失，他狂怒地高喊，他的喊声与那女孩的混在一起，回荡在黑暗的花园中，盖过了教堂传来的圣诞节钟声……

他的喊声是哈利的喊声，他的痛苦是哈利的痛苦……竟然会发生在这儿，在已经发生过一次的地方……这儿，能看到那所房子，他曾在那里尝到了死亡的滋味……死亡……那痛苦如此可怕……从自己的身体中撕裂出来……可是，如果他没有身体，为什么头会痛得这么厉害，如果他死了，为什么还会觉得不堪忍受，痛苦不是会随死亡而消失吗，难道没有……

夜晚潮湿多风，两个打扮成南瓜的小孩摇摇摆摆走过广场，商店橱窗上爬满了纸蜘蛛，都是些俗气的麻瓜饰品，装点出一个他们并不相信的世界……他飘然而行，怀着他在这种场合总是油然而生的那种目的感、权力感和正确感……不是愤怒……愤怒是那些比他软弱的灵魂才有的……而是胜利，是的……他一直等着这一刻，盼着这一刻……

"化装得很漂亮，先生！"

一个小男孩跑过来朝斗篷兜帽下一看，笑容迟疑起来，恐惧笼罩了涂着油彩的面孔。那孩子转身跑开……袍子下他的手抓住了魔杖……只要稍稍一动，那孩子就再也跑不到妈妈那儿了……但是没有必要，完全没有必要……

他走在一条新的、更加昏暗的街道上，目的地终于出现在眼前，赤胆忠心咒已经破了，但他们还不知道……他发出的声音比路面上滑动的枯叶还轻，他悄悄走到黑乎乎的树篱前，向里面望去……

他们没有拉上窗帘，他清楚地看到他们正在小小的客厅里，高个子、戴眼镜的黑发男子，在用魔杖喷出一股股彩色的烟雾，逗那穿蓝睡衣的黑发小男孩开心。孩子咯咯地笑着去抓烟雾，捏在小拳头里……

一扇门开了，母亲走进来，说着他听不见的话，她那深红色的长发垂在脸旁。父亲把儿子抱起来交给母亲，然后把魔杖扔到沙发上，伸了个懒腰，打着哈欠……

CHAPTER SEVENTEEN Bathilda's Secret

The gate creaked a little as he pushed it open, but James Potter did not hear. His white hand pulled out the wand beneath his cloak and pointed it at the door, which burst open.

He was over the threshold as James came sprinting into the hall. It was easy, too easy, he had not even picked up his wand ...

'Lily, take Harry and go! It's him! Go! Run! I'll hold him off —'

Hold him off, without a wand in his hand! ... He laughed before casting the curse ...

'Avada Kedavra!'

The green light filled the cramped hallway, it lit the pram pushed against the wall, it made the banisters glare like lightning rods, and James Potter fell like a marionette whose strings were cut ...

He could hear her screaming from the upper floor, trapped, but as long as she was sensible she, at least, had nothing to fear ... he climbed the steps, listening with faint amusement to her attempts to barricade herself in ... she had no wand upon her either ... how stupid they were, and how trusting, thinking that their safety lay in friends, that weapons could be discarded even for moments ...

He forced the door open, cast aside the chair and boxes hastily piled against it with one lazy wave of his wand ... and there she stood, the child in her arms. At the sight of him, she dropped her son into the cot behind her and threw her arms wide, as if this would help, as if in shielding him from sight she hoped to be chosen instead ...

'Not Harry, not Harry, please not Harry!'

'Stand aside, you silly girl ... stand aside, now ...'

'Not Harry, please no, take me, kill me instead —'

'This is my last warning —'

'Not Harry! Please ... have mercy ... have mercy ... Not Harry! Not Harry! Please — I'll do anything —'

'Stand aside — stand aside, girl —'

He could have forced her away from the cot, but it seemed more prudent to finish them all ...

The green light flashed around the room and she dropped like her husband. The child had not cried all this time: he could stand, clutching the bars of his cot, and he looked up into the intruder's face with a kind of bright interest, perhaps thinking that it was his father who hid beneath the cloak, making more pretty lights, and his mother would pop up any moment, laughing —

第17章 巴希达的秘密

大门轻轻一响,被他推开了,但詹姆·波特没有听到。苍白的手从斗篷下抽出魔杖,指着房门,门砰然打开。

他跨过门槛时,詹姆冲进门厅,真轻松,太轻松了,詹姆甚至没有捡起魔杖……

"莉莉,带着哈利快走!是他!快走!跑!我来挡住他——"

挡住他,手中都没有魔杖!……他哈哈大笑,然后施出魔咒……

"阿瓦达索命!"

绿光充斥了狭窄的门厅,照亮了靠在墙边的婴儿车,楼梯栏杆像避雷针一样亮得刺眼,詹姆·波特像断了线的木偶一样倒了下去……

他听见女人在楼上尖叫,她已无路可逃,但只要她还有点头脑,至少她自己是不用害怕的……他爬上楼梯,听到她试图用东西把自己挡起来,觉得有点好笑……她也没拿魔杖……他们多么愚蠢,多么轻信啊,以为可以把自己的安全托付给朋友,以为可以把武器丢掉哪怕是一小会儿……

他撞开门,懒洋洋地一挥魔杖,就把她匆忙堆在门后的椅子和箱子抛到一边……她站在那儿,怀里抱着那个孩子。一看到他,她就把儿子放进身后的婴儿床里,张开双臂,好像这有什么用似的,好像指望只要把孩子挡住,他就能转而选择她似的……

"别杀哈利,别杀哈利,求求你,别杀哈利!"

"闪开,愚蠢的女人……闪开……"

"别杀哈利,求求你,杀我吧,杀我吧——"

"我最后一次警告——"

"别杀哈利!求求你……发发慈悲……发发慈悲……别杀哈利!别杀哈利!求求你——我什么都可以做——"

"闪开——闪开,女人——"

他本来可以把她从婴儿床旁推走,但斩尽杀绝似乎更保险一些……

绿光在房间里闪过,她像她丈夫一样倒下。那孩子一直没有哭:他能站立了,抓着婴儿床的围栏,兴趣盎然地仰望着闯入者的面孔,也许以为是爸爸藏在斗篷里面,变出更多漂亮的焰火,而妈妈随时会笑着跳起来——

CHAPTER SEVENTEEN   Bathilda's Secret

He pointed the wand very carefully into the boy's face: he wanted to see it happen, the destruction of this one, inexplicable danger. The child began to cry: it had seen that he was not James. He did not like it crying, he had never been able to stomach the small ones' whining in the orphanage –

'Avada Kedavra!'

And then he broke: he was nothing, nothing but pain and terror, and he must hide himself, not here in the rubble of the ruined house, where the child was trapped and screaming, but far away ... far away ...

'No,' he moaned.

The snake rustled on the filthy, cluttered floor, and he had killed the boy, and yet he was the boy ...

'No ...'

And now he stood at the broken window of Bathilda's house, immersed in memories of his greatest loss, and at his feet the great snake slithered over broken china and glass ... he looked down, and saw something ... something incredible ...

'No ...'

'Harry, it's all right, you're all right!'

He stooped down and picked up the smashed photograph. There he was, the unknown thief, the thief he was seeking ...

'No ... I dropped it ... I dropped it ...'

'Harry, it's OK, wake up, wake up!'

He was Harry ... Harry, not Voldemort ... and the thing that was rustling was not a snake ...

He opened his eyes.

'Harry,' Hermione whispered. 'Do you feel all – all right?'

'Yes,' he lied.

He was in the tent, lying on one of the lower bunks beneath a heap of blankets. He could tell that it was almost dawn by the stillness and the quality of the cold, flat light beyond the canvas ceiling. He was drenched in sweat; he could feel it on the sheets and blankets.

'We got away.'

'Yes,' said Hermione. 'I had to use a Hover Charm to get you into your bunk, I couldn't lift you. You've been ... well, you haven't been quite ...'

第17章 巴希达的秘密

他非常仔细地把魔杖指在小男孩的脸上,他想亲眼看着它发生,看着摧毁这个无法解释的隐患。孩子哭了起来,已经明白他不是詹姆。他不喜欢这哭声,他一向无法忍受孤儿院那帮小孩子的哭哭啼啼——

"阿瓦达索命!"

然后他碎裂了:他什么也不是,只有痛苦和恐惧,他必须躲藏起来,不能躲在这座房子的废墟中,那孩子还困在里面哭喊,必须躲得远远的……远远的……

"不。"他呻吟道。

蛇在肮脏杂乱的地板上沙沙滑行,他杀死了那个男孩,可他就是那个男孩……

"不……"

现在他站在巴希达家被打破的窗户前,沉浸在对自己那次最大失败的回忆中,在他脚边,大蛇从碎瓷器和玻璃片上滑过……他低下头,看到了一件东西……一件不可思议的东西……

"不……"

"哈利,没事,你没事!"

他俯身捡起那张破碎的照片,是他——那个不知名的小偷,他一直在找的那个小偷……

"不……我把它丢了……我把它丢了……"

"哈利,没事,醒醒,醒醒!"

他是哈利……哈利,不是伏地魔……那沙沙作响的东西也不是蛇……

他睁开眼睛。

"哈利,"赫敏小声说,"你觉得还——还好吗?"

"还好。"他没说真话。

他在帐篷里,躺在一张下铺上,盖着一堆毯子。从周围的寂静和帆布顶篷上淡淡的冷光,他知道天快要破晓了。他浑身浸透了汗水,在床单和毯子上能摸出来。

"我们逃出来了。"

"是的,"赫敏说,"我用了一个悬停咒才把你弄到床上,我搬不动你。你刚才……嗯,你刚才不大……"

CHAPTER SEVENTEEN Bathilda's Secret

There were purple shadows under her brown eyes and he noticed a small sponge in her hand: she had been wiping his face.

'You've been ill,' she finished. 'Quite ill.'

'How long ago did we leave?'

'Hours ago. It's nearly morning.'

'And I've been ... what, unconscious?'

'Not exactly,' said Hermione uncomfortably. 'You've been shouting and moaning and ... things,' she added, in a tone that made Harry feel uneasy. What had he done? Screamed curses like Voldemort; cried like the baby in the cot?

'I couldn't get the Horcrux off you,' Hermione said, and he knew she wanted to change the subject. 'It was stuck, stuck to your chest. You've got a mark; I'm sorry, I had to use a Severing Charm to get it away. The snake bit you, too, but I've cleaned the wound and put some dittany on it ...'

He pulled the sweaty T-shirt he was wearing away from himself and looked down. There was a scarlet oval over his heart where the locket had burned him. He could also see the half-healed puncture marks to his forearm.

'Where've you put the Horcrux?'

'In my bag. I think we should keep it off for a while.'

He lay back on his pillows and looked into her pinched, grey face.

'We shouldn't have gone to Godric's Hollow. It's my fault, it's all my fault, Hermione, I'm sorry.'

'It's not your fault. I wanted to go too; I really thought Dumbledore might have left the sword there for you.'

'Yeah, well ... we got that wrong, didn't we?'

'What happened, Harry? What happened when she took you upstairs? Was the snake hiding somewhere? Did it just come out and kill her and attack you?'

'No,' he said. '*She* was the snake ... or the snake was her ... all along.'

'W – what?'

He closed his eyes. He could still smell Bathilda's house on him: it made the whole thing horribly vivid.

'Bathilda must've been dead a while. The snake was ... was inside her. You-Know-Who put it there in Godric's Hollow, to wait. You were right. He knew I'd go back.'

第17章 巴希达的秘密

她褐色的眼睛下有紫色的阴影,哈利看到她手中有块小海绵:她刚才在给他擦脸。

"你病了,"她最后说,"病得很厉害。"

"我们逃出来多久了?"

"好几个钟头了,现在都快早晨了。"

"我一直……怎么,昏迷不醒?"

"不完全是,"赫敏不自然地说,"你一会儿大叫,一会儿呻吟,还有……诸如此类的。"她用让哈利觉得不安的语气补充道。他做了什么?像伏地魔那样高喊咒语?像婴儿床里的婴儿那样哭泣?

"我没法把魂器从你身上摘下来,"赫敏说,哈利知道她想转移话题,"它粘上了,粘在你的胸口。给你留下了一个印记,对不起,我不得不用了个切割咒才把它弄了下来。你还被蛇咬了,但我已经清洗了伤口,加了一些白鲜香精……"

哈利扯下身上汗湿的T恤,低头看去。心口上有一个深红的椭圆形,是挂坠盒烙下的痕迹。他还看到前臂上那个已经愈合一半的洞眼。

"你把魂器放在哪儿了?"

"在我包里。我想我们应该把它收起来一段时间。"

哈利躺到枕头上,望着她憔悴、灰暗的面孔。

"我们不该去戈德里克山谷,是我的错,都是我的错,赫敏,对不起。"

"不是你的错,我也想去,我真的以为邓布利多会把剑留在那儿等你去取。"

"是啊,唉……我们猜错了,是不是?"

"发生了什么事,哈利?她带你上楼之后发生了什么?那条蛇是藏在什么地方的吗?它是不是蹿出来咬死了她,又来袭击你?"

"不,"他说,"她就是那条蛇……或者那条蛇就是她……一直都是。"

"什——什么?"

哈利闭上眼睛,闻到自己身上还有巴希达房子里的气味,这使得整个事件真切得可怕。

"巴希达大概是死掉有一段时间了。那条蛇在……在她身体里。神秘人把它留在戈德里克山谷等着。你说得对,他知道我会回来。"

CHAPTER SEVENTEEN Bathilda's Secret

'The snake was *inside* her?'

He opened his eyes again: Hermione looked revolted, nauseated.

'Lupin said there would be magic we'd never imagined,' Harry said. 'She didn't want to talk in front of you, because it was Parseltongue, all Parseltongue, and I didn't realise, but of course, I could understand her. Once we were up in the room, the snake sent a message to You-Know-Who, I heard it happen inside my head, I felt him get excited, he said to keep me there ... and then ...'

He remembered the snake coming out of Bathilda's neck: Hermione did not need to know the details.

'... she changed, changed into the snake, and attacked.'

He looked down at the puncture marks.

'It wasn't supposed to kill me, just keep me there 'til You-Know-Who came.'

If he had only managed to kill the snake, it would have been worth it, all of it ... Sick at heart, he sat up and threw back the covers.

'Harry, no, I'm sure you ought to rest!'

'You're the one who needs sleep. No offence, but you look terrible. I'm fine. I'll keep watch for a while. Where's my wand?'

She did not answer, she merely looked at him.

'Where's my wand, Hermione?'

She was biting her lip, and tears swam in her eyes.

'Harry ...'

'*Where's my wand?*'

She reached down beside the bed and held it out to him.

The holly and phoenix wand was nearly severed in two. One fragile strand of phoenix feather kept both pieces hanging together. The wood had splintered apart completely. Harry took it into his hands as though it was a living thing that had suffered a terrible injury. He could not think properly: everything was a blur of panic and fear. Then he held out the wand to Hermione.

'Mend it. Please.'

'Harry, I don't think, when it's broken like this —'

'Please, Hermione, try!'

第17章 巴希达的秘密

"那条蛇在她身体里？"

他又睁开了眼睛：赫敏好像恶心得要吐了。

"卢平说过会有我们想象不到的魔法。"哈利说，"刚才巴希达不想在你面前说话，因为是蛇佬腔，都是蛇佬腔，我没有意识到。但是当然啦，我听得懂。我们一到楼上那个房间，那条蛇就给神秘人报了信，我在脑子里听到的，我感到神秘人兴奋起来，他说要把我看在那儿……然后……"

他想起那条蛇从巴希达的脖子里蹿出来，赫敏不需要知道这些细节。

"……她变了，变成了那条蛇，发起攻击。"

他低头看着手臂上的洞眼。

"它不会杀死我，只是要把我看住，等神秘人到来。"

他要是能杀死那条蛇，也算是值了，一切没有白费……他心中十分沮丧，坐起来掀开了毯子。

"哈利，不行，你需要休息！"

"是你需要去睡觉。你听了别见怪，你脸色真难看。我没事了，我来放一会儿哨。我的魔杖呢？"

赫敏没有回答，只是望着他。

"我的魔杖呢，赫敏？"

她咬着嘴唇，泪水在眼眶中打转。

"哈利……"

"我的魔杖呢？"

她伸手到床边，捡起来递给了他。

冬青木和凤凰尾羽魔杖几乎断成了两截。一根脆弱的凤凰羽毛把两截连在一起，木头已经完全断裂。哈利把它捧到手中，好像捧着一个受了重伤的生命一样。他无法思考，脑子里一片慌乱和恐惧。然后他把魔杖递给了赫敏。

"修好它，求求你。"

"哈利，我想不行，断成这样了——"

"求求你，赫敏，试一试！"

'*R – Reparo.*'

The dangling half of the wand resealed itself. Harry held it up.

'*Lumos!*'

The wand sparked feebly, then went out. Harry pointed it at Hermione.

'*Expelliarmus!*'

Hermione's wand gave a little jerk, but did not leave her hand. The feeble attempt at magic was too much for Harry's wand, which split into two again. He stared at it, aghast, unable to take in what he was seeing ... the wand that had survived so much ...

'Harry,' Hermione whispered, so quietly he could hardly hear her. 'I'm so, so sorry. I think it was me. As we were leaving, you know, the snake was coming for us, and so I cast a Blasting Curse, and it rebounded everywhere, and it must have – must have hit –'

'It was an accident,' said Harry mechanically. He felt empty, stunned. 'We'll – we'll find a way to repair it.'

'Harry, I don't think we're going to be able to,' said Hermione, the tears trickling down her face. 'Remember ... remember Ron? When he broke his wand, crashing the car? It was never the same again, he had to get a new one.'

Harry thought of Ollivander, kidnapped and held hostage by Voldemort, of Gregorovitch, who was dead. How was he supposed to find himself a new wand?

'Well,' he said, in a falsely matter-of-fact voice, 'well, I'll just borrow yours for now, then. While I keep watch.'

Her face glazed with tears, Hermione handed over her wand, and he left her sitting beside his bed, desiring nothing more than to get away from her.

第17章 巴希达的秘密

"恢——恢复如初。"

晃晃荡荡耷拉着的半截魔杖接好了。哈利把它举起来。

"荧光闪烁！"

魔杖微弱地一亮，又熄灭了。哈利用它指着赫敏。

"除你武器！"

赫敏的魔杖歪了一下，但没有脱手。这无力的尝试已经让哈利的魔杖不能承受，又断成了两截。哈利看着它，吓呆了，不能理解眼前的一幕……这根身经百战的魔杖……

"哈利，"赫敏说，声音轻得他几乎听不到，"我非常，非常抱歉。我想是我弄的。你知道，我们逃走的时候，大蛇正扑过来，所以我施了个爆炸咒，它到处反弹，一定是——一定是打到了——"

"是个意外，"哈利机械地说，他感到心里空落落的，脑袋发蒙，"我们——我们会有办法修好它的。"

"哈利，我想没有办法了。"赫敏说，眼泪流了下来，"记得……记得罗恩吗？他的魔杖在车祸中折断后，就再也没有恢复原样，不得不另买了一根。"

哈利想到了奥利凡德，被伏地魔绑架扣押着，想到了格里戈维奇，已经死了。他如何才能找到一根新魔杖呢？

"哦，"他装出一副平平常常的口气说，"好吧，那我就暂时借你的用一下吧。我去放哨。"

赫敏满脸是泪，递过她的魔杖。哈利留下她一个人坐在床边，他此刻只想离开她。

CHAPTER EIGHTEEN

The Life and Lies of Albus Dumbledore

The sun was coming up: the pure, colourless vastness of the sky stretched over him, indifferent to him and his suffering. Harry sat down in the tent entrance and took a deep breath of clean air. Simply to be alive to watch the sun rise over the sparkling snowy hillside ought to have been the greatest treasure on earth, yet he could not appreciate it: his senses had been spiked by the calamity of losing his wand. He looked out over a valley blanketed in snow, distant church bells chiming through the glittering silence.

Without realising it, he was digging his fingers into his arms as if he were trying to resist physical pain. He had spilled his own blood more times than he could count; he had lost all the bones in his right arm once; this journey had already given him scars to his chest and forearm to join those on his hand and forehead, but never, until this moment, had he felt himself to be fatally weakened, vulnerable and naked, as though the best part of his magical power had been torn from him. He knew exactly what Hermione would say if he expressed any of this: the wand is only as good as the wizard. But she was wrong, his case was different. She had not felt the wand spin like the needle of a compass and shoot golden flames at his enemy. He had lost the protection of the twin cores, and only now that it was gone did he realise how much he had been counting upon it.

He pulled the pieces of the broken wand out of his pocket and, without looking at them, tucked them away in Hagrid's pouch around his neck. The pouch was now too full of broken and useless objects to take any more. Harry's hand brushed the old Snitch through the Mokeskin and for a moment he had to fight the temptation to pull it out and throw it away. Impenetrable, unhelpful, useless like everything else Dumbledore had left behind –

第 18 章

阿不思·邓布利多的生平和谎言

阳正在升起，纯净无色、广袤无垠的天空高悬在头上，对哈利的痛苦无动于衷。他在帐篷口坐下来，深深吸了一口清澈的空气。能活着观看太阳在亮晶晶的、积雪的山坡上升起，这本身应该就是世上最大的财富了吧。然而他却无心欣赏，他的感官被失去魔杖的灾难击伤了。他眺望着白雪皑皑的山谷，远处教堂的钟声穿透了晶光闪烁的寂静。

不知不觉地，他的手指掐进了手臂里，像在抵御剧烈的疼痛。他曾无数次流血；曾有一次失去了右胳膊中所有的骨头；这次旅行已经给他胸口和前臂留下了伤疤，再加上手背和额头上原有的伤疤。可是，直到这一刻之前，他从没感到自己曾被致命地削弱，变得赤裸裸的，易受伤害，仿佛他的魔法能力被剥夺到所剩无几了。他知道如果流露这样的想法，赫敏会怎么说：魔杖再好也好不过巫师。但她错了，他的情况不同。她没有感受过那魔杖像指南针般地旋转，向他的敌人发射金色火焰。他失去了孪生杖芯的保护，现在它不在了，他才意识到自己是多么依赖它。

哈利把那两截魔杖从口袋里掏出来，没有再看一眼，就塞进了脖子上海格送的皮袋。皮袋里已经装满了残破无用的东西，装不下别的了。哈利的手隔着驴皮触到了旧飞贼，有一刻差点忍不住把它掏出来扔掉。无法破解，帮不上忙，没有用处，像邓布利多留下的其他东西一样——

CHAPTER EIGHTEEN The Life and Lies of Albus Dumbledore

And his fury at Dumbledore broke over him now like lava, scorching him inside, wiping out every other feeling. Out of sheer desperation they had talked themselves into believing that Godric's Hollow held answers, and convinced themselves that they were supposed to go back, that it was all part of some secret path laid out for them by Dumbledore; but there was no map, no plan. Dumbledore had left them to grope in the darkness, to wrestle with unknown and undreamed of terrors alone and unaided: nothing was explained, nothing was given freely, they had no sword, and now, Harry had no wand. And he had dropped the photograph of the thief, and it would surely be easy, now, for Voldemort to find out who he was ... Voldemort had all the information now ...

'Harry?'

Hermione looked frightened that he might curse her with her own wand. Her face streaked with tears, she crouched down beside him, two cups of tea trembling in her hands and something bulky under her arm.

'Thanks,' he said, taking one of the cups.

'Do you mind if I talk to you?'

'No,' he said, because he did not want to hurt her feelings.

'Harry, you wanted to know who that man in the picture was. Well ... I've got the book.'

Timidly she pushed it on to his lap, a pristine copy of *The Life and Lies of Albus Dumbledore*.

'Where – how –?'

'It was in Bathilda's sitting room, just lying there ... this note was sticking out of the top of it.'

Hermione read the few lines of spiky, acid-green writing aloud.

'"*Dear Batty, Thanks for your help. Here's a copy of the book, hope you like it. You said everything, even if you don't remember it. Rita.*" I think it must have arrived while the real Bathilda was alive, but perhaps she wasn't in any fit state to read it?'

'No, she probably wasn't.'

Harry looked down upon Dumbledore's face and experienced a surge of savage pleasure: now he would know all the things that Dumbledore had never thought it worth telling him, whether Dumbledore wanted him to, or not.

'You're still really angry at me, aren't you?' said Hermione; he looked up to see fresh tears leaking out of her eyes, and knew that his anger must have shown in his face.

第18章 阿不思·邓布利多的生平和谎言

对邓布利多的愤怒像岩浆一样喷发出来，灼烫着哈利的内心，湮灭了所有其他感情。他们纯粹是出于绝望，才说服自己相信了戈德里克山谷藏有答案，相信这都是邓布利多安排的秘密行动路线，示意他们去那里；然而没有地图，没有计划。邓布利多让他们在黑暗中摸索，独自对付未知的、想象不到的恐怖，孤立无援。什么都没解释，什么都没直接提供，他们没有宝剑，现在，哈利又失去了魔杖。他还丢掉了那个小偷的照片，现在伏地魔一定很容易搞清他是谁了……伏地魔拥有了所有的信息……

"哈利？"

赫敏好像害怕哈利用她的魔杖给她施咒似的。她脸上挂着泪痕，在哈利身边蹲下，手里哆哆嗦嗦地端着两杯茶，胳膊下还夹着个大东西。

"谢谢。"哈利说，接过了一只杯子。

"跟你说说话可以吗？"

"可以。"他说，因为不想伤害她的感情。

"哈利，你想知道照片中那个人是谁吗，嗯……我有这本书。"

她怯怯地把书推到哈利的膝上，一本崭新的《阿不思·邓布利多的生平和谎言》。

"在哪儿——怎么——？"

"在巴希达的起居室里，就搁在那儿……顶上露出来这张纸条。"

赫敏读出了那几行绿得刺眼的尖体字。

"亲爱的巴蒂，多谢您的帮助，奉上一本新书，希望您喜欢。您说出了一切，尽管您现在已经不记得了。丽塔。我想这大概是真的巴希达还活着时收到的，但也许她已经不能阅读了。"

"是啊，也许吧。"

哈利低头看着邓布利多的脸，感到一阵残忍的快意：邓布利多一直认为不值得告诉他的一切，现在他可以知道了，无论邓布利多想不想让他知道。

"你还很生我的气，是不是？"赫敏问。哈利抬起头，见她眼里又淌出泪水，知道他的愤怒一定表现在脸上。

CHAPTER EIGHTEEN   The Life and Lies of Albus Dumbledore

'No,' he said quietly. 'No, Hermione, I know it was an accident. You were trying to get us out of there alive, and you were incredible. I'd be dead if you hadn't been there to help me.'

He tried to return her watery smile, then turned his attention to the book. Its spine was stiff; it had clearly never been opened before. He riffled through the pages, looking for photographs. He came across the one he sought almost at once, the young Dumbledore and his handsome companion, roaring with laughter at some long forgotten joke. Harry dropped his eyes to the caption.

Albus Dumbledore, shortly after his mother's death, with his friend Gellert Grindelwald.

Harry gaped at the last word for several long moments. Grindelwald. His friend, Grindelwald. He looked sideways at Hermione, who was still contemplating the name as though she could not believe her eyes. Slowly, she looked up at Harry.

'*Grindelwald?*'

Ignoring the remainder of the photographs, Harry searched the pages around them for a recurrence of that fatal name. He soon discovered it, and read greedily, but became lost: it was necessary to go further back to make sense of it all, and eventually he found himself at the start of a chapter entitled 'The Greater Good'. Together, he and Hermione started to read:

Now approaching his eighteenth birthday, Dumbledore left Hogwarts in a blaze of glory – Head Boy, Prefect, Winner of the Barnabus Finkley Prize for Exceptional Spell-Casting, British Youth Representative to the Wizengamot, Gold Medal-Winner for Ground-Breaking Contribution to the International Alchemical Conference in Cairo. Dumbledore intended, next, to take a Grand Tour with Elphias 'Dogbreath' Doge, the dim-witted but devoted sidekick he had picked up at school.

The two young men were staying at the Leaky Cauldron in London, preparing to depart for Greece the following morning, when an owl arrived bearing news of Dumbledore's mother's death. 'Dogbreath' Doge, who refused to be interviewed for this book, has given the public his own sentimental version of what happened next. He represents Kendra's death as a tragic blow, and Dumbledore's decision to give up his expedition as an act of noble self-sacrifice.

Certainly, Dumbledore returned to Godric's Hollow at once, supposedly to 'care' for his younger brother and sister. But how much care did he actually give them?

第18章 阿不思·邓布利多的生平和谎言

"不，"他轻轻地说，"不，赫敏。我知道这是意外。你想让我们活着逃出来，你很了不起。要不是你在那儿帮我，我已经死了。"

他努力回应赫敏含泪的微笑，然后把注意力转到书上。书脊坚硬，显然还没有打开过。他在书里寻找照片，几乎一下子就翻到了要找的那张，少年邓布利多和他那英俊的同伴，因为某个久已遗忘的笑话而开怀大笑。哈利的目光落到照片说明上。

阿不思·邓布利多，在其母去世后不久，与朋友盖勒特·格林德沃在一起。

哈利瞪着那个名字愣了许久。格林德沃，邓布利多的朋友格林德沃。他瞥向身边的赫敏，她还在看着那个名字，仿佛不能相信自己的眼睛。慢慢地，她抬起头望着哈利。

"格林德沃？"

哈利顾不上看其他照片，只在前后书页中寻找那个致命的名字。他很快便找到了，贪婪地读起来，但一头雾水，必须再往前读才能弄懂。最后，他发现自己翻到了一章的开头，标题是更伟大的利益。他和赫敏一起读了起来：

临近十八岁生日时，邓布利多带着耀眼的光环离开了霍格沃茨——男生学生会主席、级长、巴纳布斯·芬克利优异施咒手法奖、威森加摩不列颠青少年代表、开罗国际炼金术大会开拓性贡献金奖。接下来，邓布利多打算与"狗狗"埃非亚斯·多吉——他在学校结识的那个智商不高但忠心耿耿的老朋友一起周游欧洲。

两个年轻人住在伦敦的破釜酒吧，准备第二天一早动身去希腊，一只猫头鹰带来了邓布利多母亲的死讯。至于此后发生的事情，"狗狗"多吉已向公众提供了他的煽情描述（但他拒绝接受本书采访），其中把坎德拉之死说成一个悲剧性的打击，把邓布利多决定放弃旅行说成高尚的自我牺牲。

当然，邓布利多立刻回到了戈德里克山谷，据说是为了"照顾"弟弟妹妹，但他到底给了他们多少照顾呢？

CHAPTER EIGHTEEN   The Life and Lies of Albus Dumbledore

'He were a headcase, that Aberforth,' says Enid Smeek, whose family lived on the outskirts of Godric's Hollow at that time. 'Ran wild. 'Course, with his mum and dad gone you'd have felt sorry for him, only he kept chucking goat dung at my head. I don't think Albus was fussed about him, I never saw them together, anyway.'

So what was Albus doing, if not comforting his wild young brother? The answer, it seems, is ensuring the continued imprisonment of his sister. For, though her first gaoler had died, there was no change in the pitiful condition of Ariana Dumbledore. Her very existence continued to be known only to those few outsiders who, like 'Dogbreath' Doge, could be counted upon to believe in the story of her 'ill-health'.

Another such easily satisfied friend of the family was Bathilda Bagshot, the celebrated magical historian who has lived in Godric's Hollow for many years. Kendra, of course, had rebuffed Bathilda when she first attempted to welcome the family to the village. Several years later, however, the author sent an owl to Albus at Hogwarts, having been favourably impressed by his paper on Trans-Species Transformation in Transfiguration Today. *This initial contact led to acquaintance with the entire Dumbledore family. At the time of Kendra's death, Bathilda was the only person in Godric's Hollow who was on speaking terms with Dumbledore's mother.*

Unfortunately, the brilliance that Bathilda exhibited earlier in her life has now dimmed. 'The fire's lit, but the cauldron's empty,' as Ivor Dillonsby put it to me, or, in Enid Smeek's slightly earthier phrase, 'She's nutty as squirrel poo.' Nevertheless, a combination of tried and tested reporting techniques enabled me to extract enough nuggets of hard fact to string together the whole scandalous story.

Like the rest of the wizarding world, Bathilda puts Kendra's premature death down to a 'backfiring charm', a story repeated by Albus and Aberforth in later years. Bathilda also parrots the family line on Ariana, calling her 'frail' and 'delicate'. On one subject, however, Bathilda is well worth the effort I put into procuring Veritaserum, for she, and she alone, knows the full story of the best-kept secret of Albus Dumbledore's life. Now revealed for the first time, it calls into question everything that his admirers believed of Dumbledore: his supposed hatred of the Dark Arts, his opposition to the oppression of Muggles, even his devotion to his own family.

The very same summer that Dumbledore went home to Godric's Hollow, now an orphan

第18章 阿不思·邓布利多的生平和谎言

"真够呛,那个阿不福思,"艾妮·斯米克说,她家当时住在戈德里克山谷边缘,"像个野孩子。当然,父母都不在了,本来是怪可怜见的,可他总往我头上扔羊屎。我没觉得阿不思关心过他,反正从没见过他们在一块。"

那么,如果不是在安慰他那顽劣的弟弟,阿不思在干什么呢?答案似乎是:在确保继续囚禁他的妹妹。因为,在第一任看守死后,阿利安娜·邓布利多可怜的处境并没有改变。她的存在仍然只有几个外人知道,他们像"狗狗"多吉一样,能够相信她"身体不好"的说法。

另一个这样容易满足的朋友是巴希达·巴沙特,著名魔法史专家,在戈德里克山谷住了许多年。当然,她第一次来对这家人表示欢迎时,曾被坎德拉拒之门外。但几年之后,这位作家派猫头鹰给在霍格沃茨的阿不思送了封信,表示很欣赏他在《今日变形术》上发表的那篇关于跨物种变形的论文。这初次的接触发展成与邓布利多全家的交情。坎德拉去世之前,巴希达是戈德里克山谷唯一能与邓布利多的母亲说上话的人。

不幸的是,巴希达早年显示出的智慧光辉如今已经黯淡。"火还点着,锅已空了。"伊凡·迪隆斯比对我这样说。或者用艾妮·斯米克的稍稍平实一些的话说:"她的脑子像松鼠屎一样松。"不过,利用多种可靠的、经过考验的采访技巧,我还是挖到了足够的事实金块,串起了这个不光彩的故事。

像整个巫师界一样,巴希达把坎德拉早逝的原因归结为咒语走火,这是阿不思和阿不福思多年来一口咬定的版本。巴希达还重复着那家人关于阿利安娜的说法,称她"体弱多病"。但在有一点上,巴希达完全对得起我辛辛苦苦搞来的吐真剂,因为她知道,也只有她知道阿不思·邓布利多一生中最不为人知晓的秘密。现在首次披露,它使崇拜者们对他们所相信的邓布利多的一切都产生了疑问:包括他对黑魔法所谓的憎恶,他反对压迫麻瓜的立场,甚至包括他对家人的关爱。

就在邓布利多作为孤儿和一家之主回到戈德里克山谷的那个

533

CHAPTER EIGHTEEN The Life and Lies of Albus Dumbledore

and head of the family, Bathilda Bagshot agreed to accept into her home her great nephew, Gellert Grindelwald.

The name of Grindelwald is justly famous: in a list of Most Dangerous Dark Wizards of All Time, he would miss out on the top spot only because You-Know-Who arrived, a generation later, to steal his crown. As Grindelwald never extended his campaign of terror to Britain, however, the details of his rise to power are not widely known here.

Educated at Durmstrang, a school famous even then for its unfortunate tolerance of the Dark Arts, Grindelwald showed himself quite as precociously brilliant as Dumbledore. Rather than channel his abilities into the attainment of awards and prizes, however, Gellert Grindelwald devoted himself to other pursuits. At sixteen years old, even Durmstrang felt it could no longer turn a blind eye to the twisted experiments of Gellert Grindelwald, and he was expelled.

Hitherto, all that has been known of Grindelwald's next movements is that he 'travelled abroad for some months'. It can now be revealed that Grindelwald chose to visit his great aunt in Godric's Hollow, and that there, intensely shocking though it will be for many to hear it, he struck up a close friendship with none other than Albus Dumbledore.

'He seemed a charming boy to me,' babbles Bathilda, 'whatever he became later. Naturally, I introduced him to poor Albus, who was missing the company of lads his own age. The boys took to each other at once.'

They certainly did. Bathilda shows me a letter, kept by her, that Albus Dumbledore sent Gellert Grindelwald in the dead of night.

'Yes, even after they'd spent all day in discussion – both such brilliant young boys, they got on like a cauldron on fire – I'd sometimes hear an owl tapping at Gellert's bedroom window, delivering a letter from Albus! An idea would have struck him, and he had to let Gellert know immediately!'

And what ideas they were. Profoundly shocking though Albus Dumbledore's fans will find it, here are the thoughts of their seventeen-year-old hero, as relayed to his new best friend (a copy of the original letter may be seen on page 463):

> *Gellert –*
> *Your point about wizard dominance being FOR THE MUGGLES' OWN GOOD – this, I think, is the crucial point. Yes, we have been given power and,*

第18章 阿不思·邓布利多的生平和谎言

夏天,巴希达·巴沙特同意在家里接待她的侄孙盖勒特·格林德沃。

格林德沃的名字自然是十分显赫的:在古今最危险的黑巫师名录上,他若未能名列榜首,只是因为晚一辈的神秘人后来居上,夺取了王冠。但是由于格林德沃从未将他的恐怖活动延伸到英国,他崛起的详情在此地并不广为人知。

格林德沃就读于德姆斯特朗,一所当时就不幸以宽容黑魔法而闻名的学校,他像邓布利多一样表现出早熟的才华。盖勒特·格林德沃没有把他的才能引向获奖,而是投入了其他追求。格林德沃十六岁时,就连德姆斯特朗也感到无法再对他的邪门试验睁一只眼闭一只眼,他被学校开除了。

迄今为止,对于格林德沃下一段经历的说法都是"到国外游历数月"。现在可以看到,格林德沃是选择到戈德里克山谷的姑婆家去了,并且在那儿结交了一位密友,也许很多人听了会大跌眼镜,这个密友不是别人,正是阿不思·邓布利多。

"他当时在我印象中是个可爱的男孩,"巴希达絮絮叨叨地说,"不管后来如何。自然,我把他介绍给了可怜阿不思,那孩子正缺少同龄的伙伴。两个男孩子一下就成了好朋友。"

的确如此。巴希达给我看了她保存的一封信,是阿不思·邓布利多在深夜送给盖勒特·格林德沃的。

"是啊,即使在聊了一天之后还要写信——两个才华横溢的少年,他们就像火和锅一样投缘。我有时听到猫头鹰在敲盖勒特的卧室窗户,送来阿不思的信!有时他突然有了灵感,就要马上让盖勒特知道!"

那是怎样的灵感啊。尽管阿不思·邓布利多的崇拜者们会深感震惊,但以下就是他们十七岁的英雄传递给他那位新密友的想法(原信复印件在第463页)。

盖勒特——

你提到巫师统治是为了**麻瓜自身的利益**——我认为这是关键的一点。是的,我们被赋予能力,是的,这能力赋予我们统治的权力,

CHAPTER EIGHTEEN   The Life and Lies of Albus Dumbledore

yes, that power gives us the right to rule, but it also gives us responsibilities over the ruled. We must stress this point, it will be the foundation stone upon which we build. Where we are opposed, as we surely will be, this must be the basis of all our counter-arguments. We seize control FOR THE GREATER GOOD. And from this it follows that where we meet resistance, we must use only the force that is necessary and no more. (This was your mistake at Durmstrang! But I do not complain, because if you had not been expelled, we would never have met.)

Albus

Astonished and appalled though his many admirers will be, this letter constitutes proof that Albus Dumbledore once dreamed of overthrowing the Statute of Secrecy, and establishing wizard rule over Muggles. What a blow, for those who have always portrayed Dumbledore as the Muggle-borns' greatest champion! How hollow those speeches promoting Muggle rights seem, in the light of this damning new evidence! How despicable does Albus Dumbledore appear, busy plotting his rise to power when he should have been mourning his mother, and caring for his sister!

No doubt those determined to keep Dumbledore on his crumbling pedestal will bleat that he did not, after all, put his plans into action, that he must have suffered a change of heart, that he came to his senses. However, the truth seems altogether more shocking.

Barely two months into their great new friendship, Dumbledore and Grindelwald parted, never to see each other again until they met for their legendary duel (for more, see chapter 22). What caused this abrupt rupture? Had Dumbledore come to his senses? Had he told Grindelwald he wanted no more part in his plans? Alas, no.

'It was poor little Ariana dying, I think, that did it,' says Bathilda. 'It came as an awful shock. Gellert was there in the house when it happened, and he came back to my house all of a dither, told me he wanted to go home the next day. Terribly distressed, you know. So I arranged a Portkey and that was the last I saw of him.

'Albus was beside himself at Ariana's death. It was so dreadful for those two brothers. They had lost everybody except each other. No wonder tempers ran a little high. Aberforth blamed Albus, you know, as people will under these dreadful circumstances. But Aberforth always talked a little madly, poor boy. All the same, breaking Albus's nose at the funeral

第18章 阿不思·邓布利多的生平和谎言

但它同时包含了对被统治者的责任。我们必须强调这一点，并以此作为事业的基石。遭到反对时（反对是必然会有的），它必须成为我们所有论辩的基础。我们争取统治是为了**更伟大的利益**。因此，如果遇到抵抗，我们只能使用必要的武力，而不能过当。（这就是你在德姆斯特朗犯的错误！但我不该抱怨，因为你要是没被开除，你我就无缘见面了。）

阿不思

许多崇拜者可能会感到惊骇和难以置信，但这封信证明阿不思·邓布利多曾经幻想推翻《保密法》，建立巫师对麻瓜的统治。对于那些一直宣传邓布利多最维护麻瓜出身权益的人来说，这将是多么大的打击！在这个逃避不了的新证据面前，那些维护麻瓜权利的演说显得多么空洞！而阿不思·邓布利多又是多么令人不齿，在本应哀悼亡母、照顾妹妹的时候，他却忙着谋划自己争夺权力！

无疑，那些决意把邓布利多留在残破的碑座上的人会无力地辩解，他毕竟没有把计划付诸实践，他准是经历过思想转变，醒悟过来了。然而，事实似乎更令人震惊。

这段重要的新友谊开始了刚刚两个月，邓布利多和格林德沃便分开了，一直没有再见面，直到两人之间的那场传奇的决斗（参见第22章）。是什么造成了这突然的决裂呢？是邓布利多醒悟了吗？他是否告诉过格林德沃他不想继续参与那计划了？可惜，非也。

"是可怜的小阿利安娜之死引起的，我想。"巴希达说，"此事发生得非常突然，盖勒特当时在他们家。那天他失魂落魄地回到我屋里，跟我说他明天就想回家。盖勒特心情糟透了。于是我弄了个门钥匙把他送走，那是我最后一次见到他。

"阿利安娜死后，阿不思像发了狂一样。兄弟俩失去了所有的亲人，只剩下他们两个，这真是人间惨剧。也难怪他们的火气会大一些。阿不福思怪罪阿不思，你知道，人在这种可怕的情况下经常会如此。不过阿不福思说话总是有一点疯狂，可怜的孩子。

CHAPTER EIGHTEEN   The Life and Lies of Albus Dumbledore

was not decent. It would have destroyed Kendra to see her sons fighting like that, across her daughter's body. A shame Gellert could not have stayed for the funeral ... he would have been a comfort to Albus, at least ...'

This dreadful coffin-side brawl, known only to those few who attended Ariana Dumbledore's funeral, raises several questions. Why, exactly, did Aberforth Dumbledore blame Albus for his sister's death? Was it, as 'Batty' pretends, a mere effusion of grief? Or could there have been some more concrete reason for his fury? Grindelwald, expelled from Durmstrang for near-fatal attacks upon fellow students, fled the country hours after the girl's death and Albus (out of shame, or fear?) never saw him again, not until forced to do so by the pleas of the wizarding world.

Neither Dumbledore nor Grindelwald ever seems to have referred to this brief boyhood friendship in later life. However, there can be no doubt that Dumbledore delayed, for some five years of turmoil, fatalities and disappearances, his attack upon Gellert Grindelwald. Was it lingering affection for the man, or fear of exposure as his once best friend, that caused Dumbledore to hesitate? Was it only reluctantly that Dumbledore set out to capture the man he was once so delighted he had met?

And how did the mysterious Ariana die? Was she the inadvertent victim of some Dark rite? Did she stumble across something she ought not to have done, as the two young men sat practising for their attempt at glory and domination? Is it possible that Ariana Dumbledore was the first person to die 'for the greater good'?

The chapter ended here and Harry looked up. Hermione had reached the bottom of the page before him. She tugged the book out of Harry's hands, looking a little alarmed by his expression, and closed it without looking at it, as though hiding something indecent.

'Harry –'

But he shook his head. Some inner certainty had crashed down inside him; it was exactly as he had felt after Ron left. He had trusted Dumbledore, believed him the embodiment of goodness and wisdom. All was ashes: how much more could he lose? Ron, Dumbledore, the phoenix wand ...

'Harry.' She seemed to have heard his thoughts. 'Listen to me. It – it doesn't make very nice reading –'

第18章 阿不思·邓布利多的生平和谎言

但在葬礼上打断阿不思的鼻子也太过分了。坎德拉要是看到两个儿子在女儿遗骨旁大打出手,准会伤心欲绝。可惜盖勒特没能留下来参加葬礼……他对阿不思会是一个安慰,至少……"

这场棺材旁的可怕争斗,只有少数参加阿利安娜·邓布利多的葬礼的人知道。它提出了几个问题。阿不福思·邓布利多究竟为何把妹妹的死怪罪于阿不思呢?是不是真如"巴蒂"所说,只是悲伤过度?他的愤怒会不会有一些更具体的原因呢?曾因袭击同学险出人命而被学校开除的格林德沃,在那女孩死亡后没过几个小时就逃离英国,而阿不思(出于羞耻还是恐惧?)再也没见过他,后来在魔法界多次呼吁之下才被迫与之相会。

邓布利多和格林德沃日后似乎都没有提及这段短暂的少年友谊。然而,邓布利多无疑推迟了大约五年才去挑战盖勒特·格林德沃,世上因此而多了五年的动荡、伤亡和失踪事件。邓布利多为何踌躇不前,是念旧,还是害怕被揭露出昔日的密友关系?邓布利多是否很不情愿去捉拿那个他曾经相见恨晚的人?

神秘的阿利安娜又是怎么死的?她是否无意中成了某种黑魔仪式的牺牲品?还是当两位年轻男士坐在那里排练如何名扬四海、统治天下时,小姑娘撞见了她不该看到的东西?阿利安娜·邓布利多会不会是"为了更伟大的利益"而牺牲的第一人?

这章到此结束,哈利抬起头来。赫敏比他先读到末尾,似乎有点被他的表情吓着了,将书从哈利手中夺过去,看都没看就合上了,像藏起什么恶心的东西。

"哈利——"

但他摇了摇头。内心的某种信念崩塌了,正像罗恩离开后他感觉到的那样。他一直相信邓布利多,相信他是美德和智慧的化身。一切化为灰烬:他还能失去什么?罗恩、邓布利多、凤凰尾羽魔杖……

"哈利,"赫敏似乎听到了他的想法,"听我说,这——这读起来不大愉快——"

CHAPTER EIGHTEEN   The Life and Lies of Albus Dumbledore

'– yeah, you could say that –'

'– but don't forget, Harry, this is Rita Skeeter writing.'

'You did read that letter to Grindelwald, didn't you?'

'Yes, I – I did.' She hesitated, looking upset, cradling her tea in her cold hands. 'I think that's the worst bit. I know Bathilda thought it was all just talk, but "For the Greater Good" became Grindelwald's slogan, his justification for all the atrocities he committed later. And ... from that ... it looks like Dumbledore gave him the idea. They say "For the Greater Good" was even carved over the entrance to Nurmengard.'

'What's Nurmengard?'

'The prison Grindelwald had built to hold his opponents. He ended up in there himself, once Dumbledore had caught him. Anyway, it's – it's an awful thought that Dumbledore's ideas helped Grindelwald rise to power. But on the other hand, even Rita can't pretend that they knew each other for more than a few months one summer when they were both really young, and –'

'I thought you'd say that,' said Harry. He did not want to let his anger spill out at her, but it was hard to keep his voice steady. 'I thought you'd say "they were young". They were the same age as we are now. And here we are, risking our lives to fight the Dark Arts, and there he was, in a huddle with his new best friend, plotting their rise to power over the Muggles.'

His temper would not remain in check much longer: he stood up and walked around, trying to work some of it off.

'I'm not trying to defend what Dumbledore wrote,' said Hermione. 'All that "right to rule" rubbish, it's "Magic is Might" all over again. But Harry, his mother had just died, he was stuck alone in the house –'

'Alone? He wasn't alone! He had his brother and sister for company, his Squib sister he was keeping locked up –'

'I don't believe it,' said Hermione. She stood up too. 'Whatever was wrong with that girl, I don't think she was a Squib. The Dumbledore we knew would never, ever have allowed –'

'The Dumbledore we thought we knew didn't want to conquer Muggles by force!' Harry shouted, his voice echoing across the empty hilltop, and several blackbirds rose into the air, squawking and spiralling against the pearly sky.

第18章 阿不思·邓布利多的生平和谎言

"——是啊,可以这么说——"

"——可是别忘了,哈利,这是丽塔·斯基特写的。"

"你读了给格林德沃的那封信吗?"

"嗯,我——我读了。"她欲言又止,好像心里很乱,把茶杯捧在冰冷的手里,"我想那是最糟糕的一点。我知道巴希达认为那只是说说而已,但'为了更伟大的利益'成了格林德沃的口号,成了他为后来所有暴行辩护的理由。而……从这里……看起来像是邓布利多给了他这个主意。据说'为了更伟大的利益'还刻在纽蒙迦德的入口上方呢。"

"纽蒙迦德是什么?"

"是格林德沃建造的监狱,用来关押反对他的人。后来他被邓布利多抓住之后,自己也被关进去了。不管怎么说,是邓布利多的主意帮助了格林德沃称霸,想起来挺可怕的。可是另一方面,他们的交往只是那年夏天的几个月而已,当时两人都还年少,就连丽塔也无法编造更多——"

"我猜到你会这么说。"哈利说。他不想把自己的愤怒发泄到赫敏头上,但很难使声音保持平静,"我猜到你会说'还年少',可他们跟你我现在一样大。我们在这儿冒着生命危险抵抗黑魔法,而他呢,跟他的新密友凑在一起,谋划着要统治麻瓜。"

他的怒气再也压不住了。他站起身走来走去,努力使怒气消除一些。

"我不是想为邓布利多写的东西辩护,"赫敏说,"那一套'统治权'之类的鬼话,简直又是'魔法即强权'。可是哈利,他母亲刚去世,他一个人待在那所房子里——"

"一个人?他不是一个人!还有弟弟和妹妹,一直被他关着的哑炮妹妹——"

"我不相信,"赫敏说,她也站了起来,"无论那女孩有什么问题,我不认为她是哑炮。我们了解的邓布利多绝不会允许——"

"我们自以为了解的邓布利多不想用武力征服麻瓜!"哈利喊道,声音在空旷的山头回响,几只乌鸦飞起,咕咕叫着在珍珠色的天空下盘旋。

CHAPTER EIGHTEEN The Life and Lies of Albus Dumbledore

'He changed, Harry, he changed! It's as simple as that! Maybe he did believe these things when he was seventeen, but the whole of the rest of his life was devoted to fighting the Dark Arts! Dumbledore was the one who stopped Grindelwald, the one who always voted for Muggle protection and Muggle-born rights, who fought You-Know-Who from the start and who died trying to bring him down!'

Rita's book lay on the ground between them, so that the face of Albus Dumbledore smiled dolefully at both.

'Harry, I'm sorry, but I think the real reason you're so angry is that Dumbledore never told you any of this himself.'

'Maybe I am!' Harry bellowed, and he flung his arms over his head, hardly knowing whether he was trying to hold in his anger or protect himself from the weight of his own disillusionment. 'Look what he asked from me, Hermione! Risk your life, Harry! And again! And again! And don't expect me to explain everything, just trust me blindly, trust that I know what I'm doing, trust me even though I don't trust you! Never the whole truth! Never!'

His voice cracked with the strain, and they stood looking at each other in the whiteness and the emptiness, and Harry felt they were as insignificant as insects beneath that wide sky.

'He loved you,' Hermione whispered. 'I know he loved you.'

Harry dropped his arms.

'I don't know who he loved, Hermione, but it was never me. This isn't love, the mess he's left me in. He shared a damn sight more of what he was really thinking with Gellert Grindelwald than he ever shared with me.'

Harry picked up Hermione's wand, which he had dropped in the snow, and sat back down in the entrance of the tent.

'Thanks for the tea. I'll finish the watch. You get back in the warm.'

She hesitated, but recognised the dismissal. She picked up the book and then walked back past him into the tent, but as she did so, she brushed the top of his head lightly with her hand. He closed his eyes at her touch, and hated himself for wishing that what she said was true: that Dumbledore had really cared.

第18章 阿不思·邓布利多的生平和谎言

"他转变了,哈利,他转变了!就是这么简单!也许他十七岁时是相信过这些东西,但他后来毕生都与黑魔法做斗争。是邓布利多阻止了格林德沃,是他始终支持保护麻瓜和麻瓜出身者的权益,是他从一开始就在抵抗神秘人,并且最终为打败神秘人而死!"

丽塔的书躺在他们之间的地上,阿不思·邓布利多的脸苦笑地看着两个人。

"哈利,对不起,我觉得你这么生气的真正原因是,邓布利多从来没有亲口告诉过你这些。"

"也许吧!"哈利吼道,猛然把双臂挡到头上,不知是想控制怒气,还是想抵挡失望的重压,"看看他要我做什么,赫敏!冒生命危险,哈利!一次又一次!别指望我解释一切,只要盲目地相信我,相信我自有把握,相信我,尽管我并不相信你!从来不让你知道全部真相!从来不!"

他激动得声音都变了,两人站在一片白色的空地上对视,哈利感到他们就像苍茫天宇下的昆虫一样渺小。

"他爱你,"赫敏小声说,"我知道他爱你。"

哈利放下了手臂。

"我不知道他爱谁,赫敏,但绝不是我。他留给我的这个烂摊子,这不是爱。他对盖勒特·格林德沃吐露的真实想法,都比告诉我的多得多。"

哈利捡起他掉在雪地上的赫敏的魔杖,坐回到帐篷口。

"谢谢你的茶,我接着放哨,你回去暖和暖和吧。"

赫敏犹豫着,但看出了这是逐客令。她捡起书走进帐篷,但经过哈利身边时用手轻轻抚了抚他的头顶。哈利闭上眼睛,恨自己内心深处还希望她说的是真的:邓布利多真的关心过他。

CHAPTER NINETEEN

The Silver Doe

It was snowing by the time Hermione took over the watch at midnight. Harry's dreams were confused and disturbing: Nagini wove in and out of them, first through a gigantic, cracked ring, then through a wreath of Christmas roses. He woke repeatedly, panicky, convinced that somebody had called out to him in the distance, imagining that the wind whipping around the tent was footsteps or voices.

Finally, he got up in the darkness and joined Hermione, who was huddled in the entrance to the tent reading *A History of Magic* by the light of her wand. The snow was still falling thickly and she greeted with relief his suggestion of packing up early and moving on.

'We'll go somewhere more sheltered,' she agreed, shivering as she pulled on a sweatshirt over her pyjamas. 'I kept thinking I could hear people moving outside. I even thought I saw somebody once or twice.'

Harry paused in the act of pulling on a jumper and glanced at the silent, motionless Sneakoscope on the table.

'I'm sure I imagined it,' said Hermione, looking nervous, 'the snow in the dark, it plays tricks on your eyes … but perhaps we ought to Disapparate under the Invisibility Cloak, just in case?'

Half an hour later, with the tent packed, Harry wearing the Horcrux and Hermione clutching the beaded bag, they Disapparated. The usual tightness engulfed them; Harry's feet parted company with the snowy ground then slammed hard on to what felt like frozen earth covered with leaves.

'Where are we?' he asked, peering around at a fresh mass of trees as Hermione opened the beaded bag and began tugging out tent poles.

'The Forest of Dean,' she said. 'I came camping here once, with my mum and dad.'

第 19 章

银色的牝鹿

午夜赫敏来换班时,外面下起了雪。哈利的梦境混乱而不安:纳吉尼游进游出,先是钻过一个巨大的、有裂缝的戒指,然后又钻过一个圣诞玫瑰花环。他一次次惊恐地醒来,相信刚才有人在远处叫他的名字,把风吹打帐篷的声音想象成脚步声或说话声。

终于,他在黑暗中爬起来,走到赫敏身边。她正蜷缩在帐篷口,借着魔杖的光亮看《魔法史》。大雪还在纷纷扬扬地下着,听到哈利提议早点收拾东西转移,她欣然同意。

"是得换个更隐蔽的地方。"她赞同道,一边哆嗦着在睡衣上加了一件运动衫,"我总觉得听到有人在外面走动,有一两次好像还看到了人影。"

正在穿套头衫的哈利停了下来,看了看桌上静悄悄的、纹丝不动的窥镜。

"我相信是幻觉,"赫敏说,显得有点紧张,"黑暗中的雪,容易让人的眼睛产生错觉……但也许我们应该披着隐形衣幻影移形,以防万一,对吗?"

半小时后,帐篷收好了,哈利戴着魂器,赫敏抓着串珠小包,一同幻影移形。熟悉的窒息感吞没了他们,哈利的双脚离开了雪地,然后重重地落在地面上,脚下好像是一片覆满落叶的冻土。

"我们在哪儿?"他问,一边打量着这片陌生的林子。赫敏已经打开串珠小包,开始把帐篷杆抽出来。

"迪安森林,"她说,"我来这儿露营过一次,跟爸爸妈妈一起。"

CHAPTER NINETEEN   The Silver Doe

Here, too, snow lay on the trees all around and it was bitterly cold, but they were at least protected from the wind. They spent most of the day inside the tent, huddled for warmth round the useful bright blue flames that Hermione was so adept at producing, and which could be scooped up and carried around in a jar. Harry felt as though he was recuperating from some brief but severe illness, an impression reinforced by Hermione's solicitousness. That afternoon fresh flakes drifted down upon them, so that even their sheltered clearing had a fresh dusting of powdery snow.

After two nights of little sleep, Harry's senses seemed more alert than usual. Their escape from Godric's Hollow had been so narrow that Voldemort seemed somehow closer than before, more threatening. As darkness drew in again, Harry refused Hermione's offer to keep watch and told her to go to bed.

Harry moved an old cushion into the tent mouth and sat down, wearing all the sweaters he owned but, even so, still shivery. The darkness deepened with the passing hours until it was virtually impenetrable. He was on the point of taking out the Marauder's Map, so as to watch Ginny's dot for a while, before he remembered that it was the Christmas holidays and that she would be back at The Burrow.

Every tiny movement seemed magnified in the vastness of the forest. Harry knew that it must be full of living creatures, but he wished they would all remain still and silent so that he could separate their innocent scurryings and prowlings from noises that might proclaim other, sinister, movements. He remembered the sound of a cloak slithering over dead leaves many years ago, and at once thought he heard it again before mentally shaking himself. Their protective enchantments had worked for weeks; why should they break now? And yet he could not throw off the feeling that something was different tonight.

Several times he jerked upright, his neck aching because he had fallen asleep, slumped at an awkward angle against the side of the tent. The night reached such a depth of velvety blackness that he might have been suspended in limbo between Disapparition and Apparition. He had just held up a hand in front of his face to see whether he could make out his fingers when it happened.

A bright silver light appeared right ahead of him, moving through the trees. Whatever the source, it was moving soundlessly. The light seemed simply to drift towards him.

He jumped to his feet, his voice frozen in his throat, and raised Hermione's wand. He screwed up his eyes as the light became blinding, the trees in front of it pitch black in silhouette, and still the thing came closer ...

第 19 章　银色的牝鹿

这儿同样冷得够呛，树木也是银装素裹，但至少能挡风。他们大部分时间都躲在帐篷里，蜷在赫敏擅长营造的那些明亮的蓝色火苗旁边取暖。这些火苗非常有用，可以舀起来放在瓶子里随身携带。哈利觉得自己像经历了一场短暂但严重的疾病后在休养康复，赫敏的关怀强化了这种感觉。下午天空中又飘下雪花，连他们所在的这片有遮挡的空地上也撒了一层晶粉。

哈利两夜没怎么睡觉，感官似乎更加警觉了。戈德里克山谷的死里逃生是那么惊险，伏地魔似乎比以前更近，威胁更大了。夜幕再次降临，赫敏提出由自己来放哨，哈利拒绝了，叫她去睡觉。

哈利搬了个旧垫子坐在帐篷口，身上穿着他所有的毛衣，还是冷得直打哆嗦。黑暗越来越浓，浓得几乎无法穿透。他正要取出活点地图看一会儿金妮的黑点，才想起今天是圣诞节，她应该在陋居。

在大森林里，每个细微的动静似乎都被放大了。哈利知道林子里一定有许多动物，但他希望它们都保持安静，免得他把它们无害的奔跑和蹑行声跟其他预示危险的声音混在一起。他想起多年前斗篷在枯叶上滑动的声音，立刻觉得又听到了似的，赶紧抖擞起精神。防护魔法这么多星期来一直有效，现在怎么会不灵呢？然而他有一种感觉甩不掉：今晚似乎有些异常。

哈利几次猛然坐起，脖子僵硬发痛，因为他不知不觉歪靠在帐篷壁上睡着了。夜色更加深沉，是一种天鹅绒般的浓黑，他仿佛悬在幻影移形和幻影显形之间的境界。他正要把一只手举到面前，试试能否看到五指时，奇事发生了。

一点明亮的银光出现在他的正前方，在树林间穿行。不知道光源是什么，但它的移动无声无息，那银光简直就像在向他飘来。

他跳了起来，举起赫敏的魔杖，声音在嗓子里冻结了。他眯起眼睛，因为那银光已非常耀眼，前面的树丛都成了漆黑的剪影，而那东西还在靠近……

CHAPTER NINETEEN The Silver Doe

And then the source of the light stepped out from behind an oak. It was a silver-white doe, moon-bright and dazzling, picking her way over the ground, still silent, and leaving no hoof prints in the fine powdering of snow. She stepped towards him, her beautiful head with its wide, long-lashed eyes held high.

Harry stared at the creature, filled with wonder, not at her strangeness, but at her inexplicable familiarity. He felt that he had been waiting for her to come, but that he had forgotten, until this moment, that they had arranged to meet. His impulse to shout for Hermione, which had been so strong a moment ago, had gone. He knew, he would have staked his life on it, that she had come for him, and him alone.

They gazed at each other for several long moments and then she turned and walked away.

'No,' he said, and his voice was cracked with lack of use. 'Come back!'

She continued to step deliberately through the trees, and soon her brightness was striped by their thick, black trunks. For one trembling second he hesitated. Caution murmured: it could be a trick, a lure, a trap. But instinct, overwhelming instinct, told him that this was not Dark Magic. He set off in pursuit.

Snow crunched beneath his feet, but the doe made no noise as she passed through the trees, for she was nothing but light. Deeper and deeper into the forest she led him, and Harry walked quickly, sure that when she stopped, she would allow him to approach her properly. And then she would speak, and the voice would tell him what he needed to know.

At last, she came to a halt. She turned her beautiful head towards him once more, and he broke into a run, a question burning in him, but as he opened his lips to ask it, she vanished.

Though the darkness had swallowed her whole, her burnished image was still imprinted on his retinas; it obscured his vision, brightening when he lowered his eyelids, disorientating him. Now fear came: her presence had meant safety.

'*Lumos!*' he whispered, and the wand-tip ignited.

The imprint of the doe faded away with every blink of his eyes as he stood there, listening to the sounds of the forest, to distant crackles of twigs, soft swishes of snow. Was he about to be attacked? Had she enticed him into an ambush? Was he imagining that somebody stood beyond the reach of the wandlight, watching him?

第19章 银色的牝鹿

然后那光源从一棵橡树后面飘了出来，是一头银白色的牝鹿，月光般皎洁明亮，优雅地轻踏地面，依然无声无息，细软的白雪上没有留下丝毫蹄印。它朝哈利走来，高昂着美丽的头，大眼睛，长睫毛。

哈利盯着这个灵物，心中充满惊讶，不是因为它的奇异，而是因为它那无法解释的熟悉和亲切。他觉得自己一直在等它，只是一度忘记了，现在才想起他们的约会。他想喊赫敏的冲动刚才还那样强烈，现在一下子消失了。他知道，并可以用生命打赌，它是来找他的，是专门来找他的。

他们对视了良久，然后它转身离去。

"不，"他说，嗓子因为长时间不用而沙哑，"回来！"

牝鹿继续从容不迫地在树林中穿行，很快，明亮的身体便被又粗又黑的树干掩映出一条条阴影。在紧张战栗的一秒钟里，哈利犹豫着，警钟轻轻敲响：这可能是一个诡计，一个诱饵。但是本能，不可抗拒的本能，告诉他这不是黑魔法。他追了上去。

雪在哈利脚下嘎吱作响，但牝鹿无声无息地在林中穿行，因为它只是光。它领着哈利往森林里越走越深。哈利走得很快，相信等牝鹿停下时，会让他好好走近它的，然后它还会说话，那声音将说出他需要知道的东西。

终于，牝鹿停了下来，再次把美丽的头转向哈利。哈利急忙奔过去，一个问题在他心中燃烧，但就在他张嘴要问时，牝鹿消失了。

黑暗已将牝鹿整个吞没，但它明亮的形象仍印在哈利的视网膜上，模糊了他的视线。他垂下眼帘时，那形象变得更加明亮，让他辨不清方向。现在，恐惧袭上了他的心头：本来牝鹿的存在意味着安全。

"荧光闪烁！"他轻声说，杖尖发出亮光。

牝鹿的形象随着哈利的每一次眨眼而渐渐消失。他站在那儿，听着森林里的各种声音，远处树枝的折断声，夜雪轻柔的沙沙声。他会受到袭击吗？牝鹿会不会把他引进了一个埋伏圈？好像有人站在魔杖照不到的地方看着他，是他的幻觉吗？

CHAPTER NINETEEN The Silver Doe

He held the wand higher. Nobody ran out at him, no flash of green light burst from behind a tree. Why, then, had she led him to this spot?

Something gleamed in the light of the wand and Harry spun about, but all that was there was a small, frozen pool, its cracked, black surface glittering as he raised the wand higher to examine it.

He moved forwards rather cautiously and looked down. The ice reflected his distorted shadow, and the beam of wandlight, but deep below the thick, misty grey carapace, something else glinted. A great silver cross ...

His heart skipped into his mouth: he dropped to his knees at the pool's edge and angled the wand so as to flood the bottom of the pool with as much light as possible. A glint of deep red ... it was a sword with glittering rubies in its hilt ... the sword of Gryffindor was lying at the bottom of the forest pool.

Barely breathing, he stared down at it. How was this possible? How could it have come to be lying in a forest pool, this close to the place where they were camping? Had some unknown magic drawn Hermione to this spot, or was the doe, which he had taken to be a Patronus, some kind of guardian of the pool? Or had the sword been put into the pool after they had arrived, precisely because they were here? In which case, where was the person who had wanted to pass it to Harry? Again he directed the wand at the surrounding trees and bushes, searching for a human outline, for the glint of an eye, but he could not see anyone there. All the same, a little more fear leavened his exhilaration as he returned his attention to the sword reposing upon the bottom of the frozen pool.

He pointed the wand at the silvery shape and murmured, '*Accio sword.*'

It did not stir. He had not expected it to. If it had been that easy, the sword would have lain on the ground for him to pick up, not in the depths of a frozen pool. He set off around the circle of ice, thinking hard about the last time the sword had delivered itself to him. He had been in terrible danger, then, and had asked for help.

'Help,' he murmured, but the sword remained upon the pool bottom, indifferent, motionless.

What was it, Harry asked himself (walking again), that Dumbledore had told him the last time he had retrieved the sword? *Only a true Gryffindor could have pulled that out of the Hat.* And what were the qualities that defined a Gryffindor? A small voice inside Harry's head answered him: *their daring, nerve and chivalry set Gryffindors apart.*

第19章 银色的牝鹿

哈利把魔杖举高了一些，没有人朝他冲过来，没有绿光从树后射出。那牝鹿为什么把他带到这儿来呢？

什么东西在魔杖的荧光中一闪，哈利猛然转身，原来只是一个结冰的小池塘。他举高魔杖细看，破裂的黑色表面闪闪发光。

他小心地走上前俯视，冰面映出他变形的影子和魔杖的亮光。但那厚厚的、朦胧的灰色冰盖下还有一个东西在闪亮，一个银色的大十字……

他的心跳到了喉咙口：他在池塘边跪了下来，将魔杖倾斜，让光尽可能照到池底。深红色的光芒一闪……是一把剑，柄上的红宝石闪闪发光……格兰芬多的宝剑躺在森林中的池底。

他几乎停止了呼吸，低头盯着宝剑。这怎么可能呢？它怎么会躺在森林中的池塘里，离他们宿营的地方这么近？难道是什么未知的魔法把赫敏吸引到这里的吗？或者牝鹿是在守卫这个池塘（他本来觉得它是个守护神）？或者宝剑是在他们来了之后才特意被放进池塘的？要是这样，想把宝剑交给哈利的人又是谁呢？他再次用魔杖指着周围的树丛，搜索着一个人影或一只闪烁的眼睛，但没有发现任何人。不过，这一丝新添的恐惧加深了他的兴奋，他把注意力转到了静静躺在冰下池底的那把宝剑上。

他用魔杖指着银色的剑身，轻声念道："宝剑飞来！"

宝剑一动不动，他并没指望它会飞来。要是那么容易的话，宝剑就会躺在地上等他来捡，而不会在结冰的池塘深处了。他开始绕着圆形冰面走动，努力回忆着上次宝剑自动落入他手中的情形，当时他处境危急，正在求救。

"救救我。"他轻声说，但宝剑还是躺在池底，冷冰冰地纹丝不动。

哈利问自己（他又开始走动），上次他拿到宝剑之后邓布利多是怎么说的？"只有真正的格兰芬多人，才能把它从帽子里抽出来。"什么是格兰芬多人特有的品质呢？哈利脑子里有个小声音答道：他们的胆识、气魄和侠义，使格兰芬多出类拔萃。

CHAPTER NINETEEN The Silver Doe

Harry stopped walking and let out a long sigh, his smoky breath dispersing rapidly upon the frozen air. He knew what he had to do. If he was honest with himself, he had thought it might come to this from the moment he had spotted the sword through the ice.

He glanced around at the surrounding trees again, but was convinced, now, that nobody was going to attack him. They had had their chance as he walked alone through the forest, had had plenty of opportunity as he examined the pool. The only reason to delay at this point was because the immediate prospect was so deeply uninviting.

With fumbling fingers Harry started to remove his many layers of clothing. Where 'chivalry' entered into this, he thought ruefully, he was not entirely sure, unless it counted as chivalrous that he was not calling for Hermione to do it in his stead.

An owl hooted somewhere as he stripped off, and he thought with a pang of Hedwig. He was shivering now, his teeth chattering horribly, and yet he continued to strip off until at last he stood there in his underwear, barefooted in the snow. He placed the pouch containing his wand, his mother's letter, the shard of Sirius's mirror and the old Snitch on top of his clothes, then he pointed Hermione's wand at the ice.

'*Diffindo.*'

It cracked with a sound like a bullet in the silence: the surface of the pool broke and chunks of dark ice rocked on the ruffled water. As far as Harry could judge, it was not deep, but to retrieve the sword he would have to submerge himself completely.

Contemplating the task ahead would not make it easier or the water warmer. He stepped to the pool's edge and placed Hermione's wand on the ground, still lit. Then, trying not to imagine how much colder he was about to become or how violently he would soon be shivering, he jumped.

Every pore of his body screamed in protest: the very air in his lungs seemed to freeze solid as he was submerged to his shoulders in the frozen water. He could hardly breathe; trembling so violently the water lapped over the edges of the pool, he felt for the blade with his numb feet. He only wanted to dive once.

Harry put off the moment of total submersion from second to second, gasping and shaking, until he told himself that it must be done, gathered all his courage and dived.

第19章 银色的牝鹿

哈利停住脚步，发出一声长长的叹息，呼出的水雾迅速在寒冷的空气中散开。他知道该干什么，坦白地说，他从看见宝剑躺在冰下的那一刻起就料到是这样了。

他又扫视了一下周围的林子，但现在已确信没有人会来袭击他。要是有人想袭击他的话，在他独自穿过森林时就可以下手，在他察看池塘时也有许多机会。此刻的拖延只有一个原因：要做的事情太不愉快了。

哈利开始用不听使唤的手脱去一层层衣服。这里面有什么可被称作"侠义"的吗，他郁闷地想，除非没叫赫敏来替他做这件事也能算"侠义"。

脱衣服时，不知何处有一只猫头鹰叫了起来，他心痛地想起了海德薇。他现在瑟瑟发抖，牙齿咯咯打战，但还是继续脱着，最后身上只剩下内衣内裤，光脚站在雪地里。他把装着自己的魔杖、妈妈的信、小天狼星的镜子碎片和旧飞贼的袋子放到衣服堆上，然后用赫敏的魔杖指着冰面。

"四分五裂。"

一声爆响像子弹划破寂静：冰面裂开了，灰黑色的大冰块在水面上随波晃动。哈利判断，水并不深，但要拿到宝剑，他必须完全没入水中。

想得再多也不会使面前的任务变得容易，也不会让水温变暖。哈利走到池塘边，把赫敏的魔杖放在地上，仍让它亮着。然后，他竭力不去想自己会有多冷，也不去想自己很快会哆嗦成什么样子，一下跳了进去。

他身上的每个毛孔都在尖叫抗议，肺里的空气似乎都冻结了，刺骨的冰水没到了肩膀。他几乎无法呼吸，浑身哆嗦得那么厉害，水都被晃得打到了岸上。他用麻木的双脚寻找剑身，只想潜下去一次。

哈利喘息着、哆嗦着，一秒一秒地推迟着全身浸没的那一刻。最后他对自己说不做不行了，便鼓起全部勇气潜入了水中。

CHAPTER NINETEEN The Silver Doe

The cold was agony: it attacked him like fire. His brain itself seemed to have frozen as he pushed through the dark water to the bottom and reached out, groping for the sword. His fingers closed around the hilt; he pulled it upwards.

Then something closed tight around his neck. He thought of water weeds, though nothing had brushed him as he dived, and raised his empty hand to free himself. It was not weed: the chain of the Horcrux had tightened and was slowly constricting his wind pipe.

Harry kicked out wildly, trying to push himself back to the surface, but merely propelled himself into the rocky side of the pool. Thrashing, suffocating, he scrabbled at the strangling chain, his frozen fingers unable to loosen it, and now little lights were popping inside his head, and he was going to drown, there was nothing left, nothing he could do, and the arms that closed around his chest were surely Death's ...

Choking and retching, soaking and colder than he had ever been in his life, he came to, face down in the snow. Somewhere close by, another person was panting and coughing and staggering around. Hermione had come again, as she had come when the snake attacked ... yet it did not sound like her, not with those deep coughs, not judging by the weight of the footsteps ...

Harry had no strength to lift his head and see his saviour's identity. All he could do was raise a shaking hand to his throat and feel the place where the locket had cut tightly into his flesh. It was gone: someone had cut him free. Then a panting voice spoke from over his head.

'Are – you – *mental?*'

Nothing but the shock of hearing that voice could have given Harry the strength to get up. Shivering violently, he staggered to his feet. There before him stood Ron, fully dressed but drenched to the skin, his hair plastered to his face, the sword of Gryffindor in one hand and the Horcrux dangling from its broken chain in the other.

'Why the *hell*,' panted Ron, holding up the Horcrux, which swung backwards and forwards on its shortened chain in some parody of hypnosis, 'didn't you take this thing off before you dived?'

Harry could not answer. The silver doe was nothing, nothing compared with Ron's reappearance, he could not believe it. Shuddering with cold, he caught up the pile of clothes still lying at the water's edge and began to pull them on. As he dragged sweater after sweater over his head, Harry stared

第19章 银色的牝鹿

钻心透髓的冷,像火一样煎熬着他。脑子似乎都冻僵了,他在黑暗的冰水中潜到池底,伸出双臂摸索宝剑。他的手指抓到了剑柄,把它往上拔。

忽然,什么东西箍紧了他的脖子。他想到了水草,尽管下潜时他并没碰到什么东西。他抬起没拿宝剑的那只手想把它扯掉,发现并不是水草:魂器的链子收紧了,正在慢慢勒住他的气管。

哈利拼命踢蹬,想把自己推上水面,却只是撞到了池塘的石壁上。他扑打着,呼吸困难,用力扒住越勒越紧的链子,但冻僵的手指怎么也扒不开它。他脑子里开始冒出金星,想着,要淹死了,没希望了,已经无能为力了,抱住他的这双手臂一定是死神的……

他脸埋在雪地里苏醒过来,咳嗽着,干呕着,浑身湿透,从来没有这么冷过。不远处,另一个人在喘气,咳嗽,摇摇晃晃地走动。又是赫敏及时赶到了,就像大蛇袭来时那样……然而听声音不像是她,听那低沉的咳嗽声,那沉重的脚步声……

哈利没有力气抬起头看看救他的是谁。他能做的只是将颤抖的手举到喉咙口,摸一摸刚才挂坠盒紧紧勒进他肉里的地方。挂坠盒没了:有人帮他割断了。这时,一个气喘吁吁的声音在头顶上响起。

"你——你——你有病啊?"

也只有听到这个声音时的震惊能让哈利有力气爬起来。他剧烈地哆嗦着,摇摇晃晃地站起身。他的面前站着罗恩,穿着衣服,但像个落汤鸡,头发贴在脸上,一手拿着格兰芬多的宝剑,一手握着被割断的金链子,魂器还挂在上面。

"真见鬼,"罗恩喘着气举起魂器,它在截短的链子上荡来荡去,有点像模仿催眠术表演,"你跳下去时怎么没把这东西摘下来?"

哈利无法回答。与罗恩重新出现相比,银色的牝鹿已无关紧要,真的无关紧要。他真不敢相信。他冷得瑟瑟发抖,抓起仍然搁在水边的那堆衣服,一件接一件地套到头上,一边盯着罗恩,隐约担心每次

CHAPTER NINETEEN   The Silver Doe

at Ron, half expecting him to have disappeared every time he lost sight of him, and yet he had to be real: he had just dived into the pool, he had saved Harry's life.

'It was y – you?' Harry said at last, his teeth chattering, his voice weaker than usual due to his near-strangulation.

'Well, yeah,' said Ron, looking slightly confused.

'Y – you cast that doe?'

'What? No, of course not! I thought it was you doing it!'

'My Patronus is a stag.'

'Oh yeah. I thought it looked different. No antlers.'

Harry put Hagrid's pouch back around his neck, pulled on a final sweater, stooped to pick up Hermione's wand and faced Ron again.

'How come you're here?'

Apparently Ron had hoped that this point would come up later, if at all.

'Well, I've – you know – I've come back. If –' He cleared his throat. 'You know. You still want me.'

There was a pause, in which the subject of Ron's departure seemed to rise like a wall between them. Yet he was here. He had returned. He had just saved Harry's life.

Ron looked down at his hands. He seemed momentarily surprised to see the things he was holding.

'Oh yeah; I got it out,' he said, rather unnecessarily, holding up the sword for Harry's inspection. 'That's why you jumped in, right?'

'Yeah,' said Harry. 'But I don't understand. How did you get here? How did you find us?'

'Long story,' said Ron. 'I've been looking for you for hours, it's a big forest, isn't it? And I was just thinking I'd have to kip under a tree and wait for morning when I saw that deer coming, and you following.'

'You didn't see anyone else?'

'No,' said Ron. 'I –'

But he hesitated, glancing at two trees growing close together some yards away.

'– I did think I saw something move over there, but I was running to the pool at the time, because you'd gone in and you hadn't come up, so I wasn't going to make a detour to – hey!'

第 19 章 银色的牝鹿

一看不见他就会消失。但罗恩应该是真的：他刚才跳进池塘救了自己的命。

"是——是你？"哈利终于说道，牙齿咯咯打架，声音因为刚才差点被勒死而比平时微弱。

"嗯，是啊。"罗恩说，显得有点困惑。

"你——你召出了那头牝鹿？"

"什么？不是，当然不是！我还以为是你呢！"

"我的守护神是牡鹿。"

"哦，对了，我是觉着长得不大一样，没有角。"

哈利把海格送的皮袋子挂到脖子上，套上最后一件毛衣，弯腰捡起赫敏的魔杖，重新看着罗恩。

"你怎么会在这儿？"

显然，罗恩希望这个问题晚一点提出，或根本不提出。

"嗯，我——你知道——我回来了，如果——"他清了清嗓子，"怎么说呢，如果你们还要我的话。"

一阵沉默，罗恩出走的话题如同一道墙挡在两人之间。但他在这儿，他回来了，他刚刚救了哈利的命。

罗恩低头看看手里的东西，一时似乎很惊讶。

"哦，对了，我把它捞出来了。"他不必要地说，一边把宝剑举给哈利检查，"你就是为这个跳下去的，是吧？"

"是的，"哈利说，"但我不明白，你怎么会到这儿来？你是怎么找到我们的？"

"说来话长。"罗恩说，"我找了你们好几个小时，这森林真大，是不是？我正想在树底下睡一觉，等天亮再说，就看见那头鹿跑了过来，你在后面跟着。"

"你有没有看到别人？"

"没有，"罗恩说，"我——"

他犹豫了，望着几米外两棵挨在一起的树。

"——我好像是看到那边有东西在动，但我正在往池塘边跑，因为你跳下去了，没有上来，所以我不想绕道——嘿！"

CHAPTER NINETEEN   The Silver Doe

Harry was already hurrying to the place Ron had indicated. The two oaks grew close together; there was a gap of only a few inches between the trunks at eye-level, an ideal place to see, but not be seen. The ground around the roots, however, was free of snow and Harry could see no sign of footprints. He walked back to where Ron stood waiting, still holding the sword and the Horcrux.

'Anything there?' Ron asked.

'No,' said Harry.

'So how did the sword get in that pool?'

'Whoever cast the Patronus must have put it there.'

They both looked at the ornate silver sword, its rubied hilt glinting a little in the light from Hermione's wand.

'You reckon this is the real one?' asked Ron.

'One way to find out, isn't there?' said Harry.

The Horcrux was still swinging from Ron's hand. The locket was twitching slightly. Harry knew that the thing inside it was agitated again. It had sensed the presence of the sword and had tried to kill Harry rather than let him possess it. Now was not the time for long discussions; now was the moment to destroy the locket once and for all. Harry looked around, holding Hermione's wand high, and saw the place: a flattish rock lying in the shadow of a sycamore tree.

'Come here,' he said, and he led the way, brushed snow from the rock's surface and held out his hand for the Horcrux. When Ron offered the sword, however, Harry shook his head.

'No, you should do it.'

'Me?' said Ron, looking shocked. 'Why?'

'Because you got the sword out of the pool. I think it's supposed to be you.'

He was not being kind or generous. As certainly as he had known that the doe was benign, he knew that Ron had to be the one to wield the sword. Dumbledore had at least taught Harry something about certain kinds of magic, of the incalculable power of certain acts.

'I'm going to open it,' said Harry, 'and you stab it. Straight away, OK? Because whatever's in there will put up a fight. The bit of Riddle in the diary tried to kill me.'

'How are you going to open it?' asked Ron. He looked terrified.

'I'm going to ask it to open, using Parseltongue,' said Harry. The answer

第19章 银色的牝鹿

哈利已经往罗恩指的地方奔去。两棵橡树长得紧挨在一起，在眼睛那么高的地方有个仅仅几英寸的空隙，是个可以偷窥而不被发现的好地方。但树根周围没有雪，哈利没看见脚印。他走回原地，罗恩站在那儿等着，手里仍然握着宝剑和魂器。

"那儿有东西吗？"罗恩问。

"没有。"哈利说。

"宝剑怎么会在池塘里呢？"

"肯定是召出守护神的那位把它放进去的。"

两人看着精美的银剑，嵌着红宝石的剑柄在赫敏魔杖的荧光中微微闪亮。

"你觉得这把是真的吗？"罗恩问。

"有个办法知道，是不是？"哈利说。

魂器仍在罗恩手中晃荡，挂坠盒微微颤动。哈利知道里面的东西又焦躁不安了，它刚才感到宝剑近在咫尺，便试图勒死哈利，不让他拿到宝剑。现在不是长谈的时候，应该马上彻底摧毁挂坠盒。哈利高举着赫敏的魔杖环顾四周，找到了地方：在一棵悬铃木的树荫下，有一块平坦的大石头。

"跟我来。"他率先走过去，拂去石头上的积雪，伸手拿过魂器。但当罗恩把宝剑也递过去时，哈利摇了摇头。

"不，应该由你来做。"

"我？"罗恩惊愕地说，"为什么？"

"因为是你把宝剑从池塘里捞上来的。我想应该由你来。"

他不是大方或谦让。就像刚才相信牝鹿是无害的一样，他确信必须由罗恩来使这把剑。邓布利多至少教哈利认识到某些类型的魔法，认识到某些行为有不可估量的神力。

"我来打开，"哈利说，"你来刺。一打开就刺，行吗？因为里面的东西会反抗的，日记中的里德尔就曾想杀死我。"

"你怎么打开呢？"罗恩神情惊恐地问。

"我来叫它打开，用蛇佬腔。"哈利说，这答案如此自然地脱口而出，

came so readily to his lips that he thought that he had always known it, deep down: perhaps it had taken his recent encounter with Nagini to make him realise it. He looked at the serpentine 'S', inlaid with glittering green stones: it was easy to visualise it as a minuscule snake, curled upon the cold rock.

'No!' said Ron, 'no, don't open it! I'm serious!'

'Why not?' asked Harry. 'Let's get rid of the damn thing, it's been months –'

'I can't, Harry, I'm serious – you do it –'

'But why?'

'Because that thing's bad for me!' said Ron, backing away from the locket on the rock. 'I can't handle it! I'm not making excuses, Harry, for what I was like, but it affects me worse than it affected you and Hermione, it made me think stuff, stuff I was thinking anyway, but it made everything worse, I can't explain it, and then I'd take it off and I'd get my head on straight again, and then I'd have to put the effing thing back on – I can't do it, Harry!'

He had backed away, the sword dragging at his side, shaking his head.

'You can do it,' said Harry, 'you can! You've just got the sword, I know it's supposed to be you who uses it. Please, just get rid of it, Ron.'

The sound of his name seemed to act like a stimulant. Ron swallowed, then, still breathing hard through his long nose, moved back towards the rock.

'Tell me when,' he croaked.

'On three,' said Harry, looking back down at the locket and narrowing his eyes, concentrating on the letter 'S', imagining a serpent, while the contents of the locket rattled like a trapped cockroach. It would have been easy to pity it, except that the cut around Harry's neck still burned.

'One ... two ... three ... *open*.'

The last word came as a hiss and a snarl and the golden doors of the locket swung wide with a little click.

Behind both of the glass windows within blinked a living eye, dark and handsome as Tom Riddle's eyes had been before he turned them scarlet and slit-pupilled.

'Stab,' said Harry, holding the locket steady on the rock.

Ron raised the sword in his shaking hands: the point dangled over the frantically swivelling eyes, and Harry gripped the locket tightly, bracing himself, already imagining blood pouring from the empty windows.

第19章 银色的牝鹿

他觉得好像内心深处一直就知道：也许是最近遭遇了纳吉尼才让他意识到的。他看着那个蛇形的"S"，由闪闪发光的绿宝石嵌成，很容易把它想象成一条小蛇，盘在冰冷的石头上。

"不！"罗恩说，"不，别打开它！真的！"

"为什么不？"哈利问，"我们赶快除掉这该死的东西，已经好几个月——"

"我不行，哈利，真的——你来吧——"

"可是为什么呢？"

"因为这东西对我有害！"罗恩望着石头上的挂坠盒，直往后退，"我对付不了它！我不是在为自己找借口，哈利，但这玩意儿对我的影响比对你和赫敏要大，它让我产生了一些念头，那些念头我原来也有，但它使一切变得更糟。我无法解释，每当把它拿下来，我就会清醒过来，可是接着我又得戴上这该死的东西——我不行，哈利！"

他已经拖着宝剑退到远处，连连摇头。

"你能做到，"哈利说，"你能行的！你刚才捞上了宝剑，我知道应该由你来用它。拜托，除掉它吧，罗恩。"

听到自己的名字好像是一种激励，罗恩咽了口唾沫，走回大石头跟前，长长的鼻子仍然呼吸粗重。

"告诉我什么时候。"他用低沉沙哑的声音说。

"数到三。"哈利低头看着挂坠盒，眯起眼睛盯住字母"S"，想象着一条蛇，而此时挂坠盒里的东西像笼中的蟑螂一样窸窣作响。几乎很容易对它产生怜悯，只是哈利脖子上的伤痕还在火辣辣地痛。

"一……二……三……开。"

最后一个词是一声嘶嘶的咆哮，挂坠盒的小金盖咔嗒一声弹开了。

两扇小玻璃窗后各有一只活的眼睛在眨，黑亮有神，像汤姆·里德尔的，在他的眼球变成红色、瞳孔变成一条线之前。

"刺啊！"哈利说，一边把挂坠盒牢牢地按在石头上。

罗恩用颤抖的双手举起宝剑，剑尖悬在两只疯狂转动的眼睛上面。哈利紧紧地抓着挂坠盒，做好准备，已经想象着鲜血从空了的小窗里喷出来。

CHAPTER NINETEEN The Silver Doe

Then a voice hissed from out of the Horcrux.

'*I have seen your heart, and it is mine.*'

'Don't listen to it!' Harry said harshly. 'Stab it!'

'*I have seen your dreams, Ronald Weasley, and I have seen your fears. All you desire is possible, but all that you dread is also possible ...*'

'Stab!' shouted Harry; his voice echoed off the surrounding trees, the sword point trembled, and Ron gazed down into Riddle's eyes.

'*Least loved, always, by the mother who craved a daughter ... least loved, now, by the girl who prefers your friend ... second best, always, eternally overshadowed ...*'

'Ron, stab it now!' Harry bellowed: he could feel the locket quivering in his grip and was scared of what was coming. Ron raised the sword still higher, and as he did so, Riddle's eyes gleamed scarlet.

Out of the locket's two windows, out of the eyes, there bloomed, like two grotesque bubbles, the heads of Harry and Hermione, weirdly distorted.

Ron yelled in shock and backed away as the figures blossomed out of the locket, first chests, then waists, then legs, until they stood in the locket, side by side like trees with a common root, swaying over Ron and the real Harry, who had snatched his fingers away from the locket as it burned, suddenly, white-hot.

'Ron!' he shouted, but the Riddle-Harry was now speaking with Voldemort's voice and Ron was gazing, mesmerised, into its face.

'*Why return? We were better without you, happier without you, glad of your absence ... we laughed at your stupidity, your cowardice, your presumption –*'

'*Presumption!*' echoed the Riddle-Hermione, who was more beautiful and yet more terrible than the real Hermione: she swayed, cackling, before Ron, who looked horrified yet transfixed, the sword hanging pointlessly at his side. '*Who could look at you, who would ever look at you, beside Harry Potter? What have you ever done, compared with the Chosen One? What are you, compared with the Boy Who Lived?*'

'Ron, stab it, STAB IT!' Harry yelled, but Ron did not move: his eyes were wide, and the Riddle-Harry and the Riddle-Hermione were reflected in them, their hair swirling like flames, their eyes shining red, their voices lifted in an evil duet.

'*Your mother confessed,*' sneered Riddle-Harry, while Riddle-Hermione jeered, '*that she would have preferred me as a son, would be glad to exchange ...*'

第19章　银色的牝鹿

这时一个声音从魂器中嘶嘶响起。

"我看到了你的心，它是我的。"

"别听它的！"哈利厉声说，"快刺！"

"我看到了你的梦想，罗恩·韦斯莱，我也看到了你的恐惧。你渴望的都可能发生，但你惧怕的也都可能发生……"

"快刺！"哈利高喊，树林中响着回声。剑尖颤抖着，罗恩盯着里德尔的眼睛。

"一直最不受宠爱，妈妈一直想要女儿……现在也最不受宠爱，那女孩更倾心于你的朋友……总是屈居第二，永远相形见绌……"

"罗恩，赶快刺它！"哈利吼道，他能感到挂坠盒在他手中颤动，很害怕会发生什么。罗恩把宝剑举得更高，里德尔的眼睛变红了。

从挂坠盒的两扇小窗里，从那对眼睛里，冒出了两个怪诞的肥皂泡似的东西，是哈利和赫敏的脑袋，离奇地变了形。

罗恩惊叫一声，倒退几步，两个人形从挂坠盒里升起，胸部，腰部，双腿，最后像两棵同根的树一样站在挂坠盒里，在罗恩和真哈利上方摇摆。哈利已经把手从挂坠盒上缩回，因为它突然变得炽热无比。

"罗恩！"他喊道，但现在里德尔－哈利用伏地魔的声音说起话来，罗恩像被催眠了一般盯着那张面孔。

"干吗回来？没有你我们更好，更快乐，很高兴你不在……我们嘲笑你的愚蠢、你的懦弱、你的自以为是——"

"自以为是！"里德尔－赫敏重复道，她比真赫敏漂亮，但很可怕：她在罗恩面前摇摆，大笑。罗恩似乎惊恐万分但又无法动弹，宝剑无力地垂在身边。"谁会看你啊，有哈利·波特在旁边，谁会看你一眼？跟'救世之星'比起来，你做过什么？跟'大难不死的男孩'比起来，你算什么？"

"罗恩，刺它，刺它！"哈利大喊，但罗恩没有动，他眼睛睁得大大的，里面映出里德尔－哈利和里德尔－赫敏，他们的头发像火焰一般旋舞，眼睛里发着红光，声音升高成邪恶的二重唱。

"你妈妈承认过，"里德尔－哈利讥讽地说，里德尔－赫敏大声嘲笑，"她更喜欢要我当儿子，她很愿意换一换……"

CHAPTER NINETEEN   The Silver Doe

'*Who wouldn't prefer him, what woman would take you? You are nothing, nothing, nothing to him,*' crooned Riddle-Hermione, and she stretched like a snake and entwined herself around Riddle-Harry, wrapping him in a close embrace: their lips met.

On the ground in front of them, Ron's face filled with anguish: he raised the sword high, his arms shaking.

'Do it, Ron!' Harry yelled.

Ron looked towards him and Harry thought he saw a trace of scarlet in his eyes.

'Ron –?'

The sword flashed, plunged: Harry threw himself out of the way, there was a clang of metal and a long, drawn-out scream. Harry whirled round, slipping in the snow, wand held ready to defend himself: but there was nothing to fight.

The monstrous versions of himself and Hermione were gone: there was only Ron, standing there with the sword held slackly in his hand, looking down at the shattered remains of the locket on the flat rock.

Slowly, Harry walked back to him, hardly knowing what to say or do. Ron was breathing heavily. His eyes were no longer red at all, but their normal blue; they were also wet.

Harry stooped, pretending he had not seen, and picked up the broken Horcrux. Ron had pierced the glass in both windows: Riddle's eyes were gone, and the stained silk lining of the locket was smoking slightly. The thing that had lived in the Horcrux had vanished; torturing Ron had been its final act.

The sword clanged as Ron dropped it. He had sunk to his knees, his head in his arms. He was shaking, but not, Harry realised, from cold. Harry crammed the broken locket into his pocket, knelt down beside Ron and placed a hand, cautiously, on his shoulder. He took it as a good sign that Ron did not throw it off.

'After you left,' he said in a low voice, grateful for the fact that Ron's face was hidden, 'she cried for a week. Probably longer, only she didn't want me to see. There were loads of nights when we never even spoke to each other. With you gone ...'

He could not finish; it was only now that Ron was here again that Harry fully realised how much his absence had cost them.

'She's like my sister,' he went on. 'I love her like a sister and I reckon she

第19章 银色的牝鹿

"谁会不更喜欢他呢,哪个女人会选择你呢?跟他比起来,你什么都不是,什么都不是。"里德尔-赫敏轻唱道,身子变得像蛇一样长,缠住里德尔-哈利,与他紧紧拥抱,嘴唇相接。

在他们前面,罗恩的脸上充满痛苦,他高高地举着宝剑,手臂在发抖。

"刺呀,罗恩!"哈利叫道。

罗恩朝他望了望,哈利仿佛看到罗恩眼里有一丝红色。

"罗恩——?"

剑光一闪,宝剑突然刺出,哈利纵身闪开,金属声当啷一响,接着是一声长长的尖叫。哈利急速转身,在雪地上滑了一下,举起魔杖准备自卫,却并没有东西要抵挡。

他自己和赫敏的恐怖幻影不见了,只有罗恩站在那儿,无力地提着宝剑,低头看着平坦的石头上挂坠盒的碎片。

哈利慢慢走回他身边,不知该说些什么,做些什么。罗恩呼吸粗重,眼睛一点也不红,还是原来那样的蓝色,微微有点湿润。

哈利假装没看见,弯腰捡起破碎的魂器。罗恩把两扇小窗的玻璃都刺破了,里德尔的眼睛不见了,挂坠盒满是污痕的彩色丝绸内衬冒出缕缕青烟。活在魂器中的那个东西消失了,折磨罗恩是它的最后一个行为。

宝剑当啷一声从罗恩手里掉下,他跪倒在地,抱着脑袋。他在发抖,哈利知道那不是因为寒冷。哈利把破挂坠盒塞进口袋,跪到罗恩身边,谨慎地把一只手放到他的肩上。没有被甩掉,他觉得是个好兆头。

"你走后,"他低声说,暗自庆幸罗恩的脸被挡住了,"她哭了一个星期,也许更久,只是她不想让我看见。有好些个夜晚,我们都不说话。你不在……"

他说不下去了,现在罗恩回来了,哈利才完全意识到,对他们来说,没有了他是多么大的缺憾。

"她就像我的姐妹,"他继续说,"我像爱姐妹一样爱她,我相信她

CHAPTER NINETEEN The Silver Doe

feels the same way about me. It's always been like that. I thought you knew.'

Ron did not respond, but turned his face away from Harry and wiped his nose noisily on his sleeve. Harry got to his feet again and walked to where Ron's enormous rucksack lay, yards away, discarded as Ron had run towards the pool to save Harry from drowning. He hoisted it on to his own back and walked back to Ron, who clambered to his feet as Harry approached, eyes bloodshot but otherwise composed.

'I'm sorry,' he said in a thick voice. 'I'm sorry I left. I know I was a – a –'

He looked around at the darkness, as if hoping a bad enough word would swoop down upon him and claim him.

'You've sort of made up for it tonight,' said Harry. 'Getting the sword. Finishing off the Horcrux. Saving my life.'

'That makes me sound a lot cooler than I was,' Ron mumbled.

'Stuff like that always sounds cooler than it really was,' said Harry. 'I've been trying to tell you that for years.'

Simultaneously they walked forwards and hugged, Harry gripping the still sopping back of Ron's jacket.

'And now,' said Harry, as they broke apart, 'all we've got to do is find the tent again.'

But it was not difficult. Though the walk through the dark forest with the doe had seemed lengthy, with Ron by his side the journey back seemed to take a surprisingly short time. Harry could not wait to wake Hermione, and it was with quickening excitement that he entered the tent, Ron lagging a little behind him.

It was gloriously warm after the pool and the forest, the only illumination the bluebell flames still shimmering in a bowl on the floor. Hermione was fast asleep, curled up under her blankets, and did not move until Harry had said her name several times.

'*Hermione!*'

She stirred, then sat up quickly, pushing her hair out of her face.

'What's wrong? Harry? Are you all right?'

'It's OK, everything's fine. More than fine. I'm great. There's someone here.'

'What do you mean? Who –?'

She saw Ron, who stood there holding the sword and dripping on to the threadbare carpet. Harry backed into a shadowy corner, slipped off Ron's rucksack and attempted to blend in with the canvas.

第 19 章　银色的牝鹿

对我也是这样。一直都是这样，我以为你知道。"

罗恩没有回答，而是扭过脸去，响亮地用衣袖擦了擦鼻子。哈利起身走向几米外罗恩的那只巨大背包，那是罗恩奔向池塘去救他时丢下的。哈利把它扛到背上，走回罗恩身边。罗恩也爬了起来，眼睛充血，但还平静。

"对不起，"他瓮声瓮气地说，"对不起，我不该离开。我知道我是个——是个——"

他在黑暗中环顾四周，仿佛希望一个足够恶毒的词会扑下来认领他。

"你今晚差不多都补偿了，"哈利说，"捞出宝剑，消灭魂器，还救了我的命。"

"听起来比我本人伟大得多。"罗恩嘟囔道。

"这样的事听起来总是比实际伟大得多，"哈利说，"我这些年一直想告诉你这一点。"

两人同时走上前，抱在一起，哈利抓着罗恩背上仍然潮湿的衣服。

"现在，"他们分开之后哈利说，"我们要做的就是找到帐篷了。"

找到帐篷并不难。虽然跟着牝鹿在黑森林里走的路似乎很长，但有罗恩在身边，回去时用的时间短得令人惊讶。哈利迫不及待地要叫醒赫敏。他兴奋地走进帐篷，罗恩有点迟疑地跟在后面。

与池塘和森林里比起来，这里暖和极了。唯一的光源是那些蓝铃花般的火苗，还在地上的一只碗里闪闪发光。赫敏蜷在毯子里睡得正香，哈利叫了好几遍她才醒过来。

"赫敏！"

她动了一下，迅速坐起来，拨开脸上的头发。

"怎么啦，哈利？你没事吧？"

"没事，一切都好，不只是好，简直是棒极了，这儿有个人。"

"你说什么？谁——？"

她看到了提着剑站在那儿、往破地毯上滴水的罗恩。哈利退到角落的阴影中，取下罗恩的背包，努力与帐篷的帆布墙融为一体。

CHAPTER NINETEEN   The Silver Doe

Hermione slid out of her bunk and moved like a sleepwalker towards Ron, her eyes upon his pale face. She stopped right in front of him, her lips slightly parted, her eyes wide. Ron gave a weak, hopeful smile and half raised his arms.

Hermione launched herself forwards and started punching every inch of him that she could reach.

'Ouch – ow – gerroff! What the –? Hermione – OW!'

'You – complete – *arse* – Ronald – Weasley!'

She punctuated every word with a blow: Ron backed away, shielding his head as Hermione advanced.

'You – crawl – back – here – after – weeks – and – weeks – oh, *where's my wand?*'

She looked as though ready to wrestle it out of Harry's hands and he reacted instinctively.

'*Protego!*'

The invisible shield erupted between Ron and Hermione: the force of it knocked her backwards on to the floor. Spitting hair out of her mouth, she leapt up again.

'Hermione!' said Harry. 'Calm –'

'I will not calm down!' she screamed. Never before had he seen her lose control like this; she looked quite demented.

'Give me back my wand! *Give it back to me!*'

'Hermione, will you please –'

'Don't you tell me what to do, Harry Potter!' she screeched. 'Don't you dare! Give it back now! And YOU!'

She was pointing at Ron in dire accusation: it was like a malediction and Harry could not blame Ron for retreating several steps.

'I came running after you! I called you! I begged you to come back!'

'I know,' Ron said. 'Hermione, I'm sorry, I'm really –'

'Oh, you're *sorry*!'

She laughed, a high-pitched, out-of-control sound; Ron looked at Harry for help, but Harry merely grimaced his helplessness.

'You come back after weeks – *weeks* – and you think it's all going to be all right if you just say *sorry*?'

第19章 银色的牝鹿

赫敏下了床,梦游似的朝罗恩走去,眼睛盯着他苍白的面孔。她停在罗恩面前,嘴唇微张,双眼圆睁。罗恩怀着期待无力地笑了一下,半张开手臂。

赫敏往前一冲,开始痛打罗恩身上每一寸她够得到的地方。

"哎哟——嗷——放开!干吗——?赫敏——嗷!"

"你这个——大——混蛋——罗恩——韦斯莱!"

她每说一个词都加上一拳。罗恩护着脑袋往后躲,赫敏紧追向前。

"你——爬回——来了?——这么多——这么多——星期——之后——哦,我的魔杖呢?"

她好像要把魔杖从哈利手里夺过去,哈利本能地做出反应。

"盔甲护身!"

无形的坚壁立时将罗恩和赫敏隔开了,那股冲力把赫敏撞得仰面摔倒。她吐着嘴里的头发,又跳了起来。

"赫敏!"哈利说,"冷静——"

"我不会冷静!"她尖叫着。哈利从未见过她如此失控,简直像疯了一样。

"把魔杖还给我!还给我!"

"赫敏,请你——"

"别来指挥我,哈利·波特!"她厉声喊道,"我警告你!快还给我!还有你!"

她控诉一般狠狠指着罗恩,好像要下恶咒,哈利觉得不能怪罗恩连退了几步。

"我跑出去追你!我喊你!哀求你回来!"

"我知道,"罗恩说,"赫敏,对不起,我真的——"

"哦,你对不起!"

她大笑起来,那是一种尖厉的、歇斯底里的声音。罗恩求助地看看哈利,但哈利只是苦着脸表示无可奈何。

"你过了这么多星期才回来——这么多星期——你以为说一声对不起就没事了?"

CHAPTER NINETEEN The Silver Doe

'Well, what else can I say?' Ron shouted, and Harry was glad that Ron was fighting back.

'Oh, I don't know!' yelled Hermione, with awful sarcasm. 'Rack your brains, Ron, that should only take a couple of seconds –'

'Hermione,' interjected Harry, who considered this a low blow, 'he just saved my –'

'I don't care!' she screamed. 'I don't care what he's done! Weeks and weeks, we could have been *dead* for all he knew –'

'I knew you weren't dead!' bellowed Ron, drowning her voice for the first time, and approaching as close as he could with the Shield Charm between them. 'Harry's all over the *Prophet*, all over the radio, they're looking for you everywhere, all these rumours and mental stories, I knew I'd hear straight off if you were dead, you don't know what it's been like –'

'What it's been like for *you*?'

Her voice was now so shrill only bats would be able to hear it soon, but she had reached a level of indignation that rendered her temporarily speechless, and Ron seized his opportunity.

'I wanted to come back the minute I'd Disapparated, but I walked straight into a gang of Snatchers, Hermione, and I couldn't go anywhere!'

'A gang of what?' asked Harry, as Hermione threw herself down into a chair with her arms and legs crossed so tightly it seemed unlikely that she would unravel them for several years.

'Snatchers,' said Ron. 'They're everywhere, gangs trying to earn gold by rounding up Muggle-borns and blood traitors, there's a reward from the Ministry for everyone captured. I was on my own and I look like I might be school age, they got really excited, thought I was a Muggle-born in hiding. I had to talk fast to get out of being dragged to the Ministry.'

'What did you say to them?'

'Told them I was Stan Shunpike. First person I could think of.'

'And they believed that?'

'They weren't the brightest. One of them was definitely part troll, the smell off him ...'

Ron glanced at Hermione, clearly hopeful she might soften at this small instance of humour, but her expression remained stony above her tightly knotted limbs.

第19章 银色的牝鹿

"那我还能说什么?"罗恩喊道,哈利很高兴罗恩开始反抗了。

"哦,我不知道!"赫敏高叫道,带着辛辣的讽刺,"绞尽你的脑汁吧,罗恩,那只需要两秒钟——"

"赫敏,"哈利插嘴道,他认为这是很不厚道的攻击,"他刚才救了我的——"

"我不管!"她尖叫道,"我不管他做了什么!这么多星期,我们说不定都死了——"

"我知道你们没死!"罗恩吼了起来,第一次压过了赫敏的声音,并且隔着铁甲咒尽可能靠上前,"《预言家日报》上成天讲哈利,广播里也是,他们到处找你,有好多谣言和荒谬的故事,我知道你们要是死了我马上就会听说,你们不知道——"

"不知道你是怎么过的?"

赫敏的声音现在这么尖,很快就只有蝙蝠才能听见了。但她已经气愤到了一时说不出话的程度,罗恩抓住了机会。

"我刚一幻影移形就想回来,可是我落在了一群搜捕队员中间,赫敏,根本走不掉!"

"一群什么?"哈利问道。赫敏一屁股坐到椅子上,紧紧抱着胳膊,交叉着双腿,看样子几年都不会松开。

"搜捕队员,"罗恩说,"到处都是,一帮想靠搜捕麻瓜出身的巫师和纯血统的叛徒赚取金子的家伙。每抓到一个人,魔法部都有赏。我独自一人,看上去又像上学的年龄,他们可兴奋了,以为我是逃出来的麻瓜出身的人。我赶紧好说歹说,才没有被拖进魔法部。"

"你是怎么对他们说的?"

"我说我是斯坦·桑帕克,那是我能想到的第一个人。"

"他们相信了?"

"那帮人不怎么聪明。有一个肯定有巨怪血统,身上那味儿……"

罗恩瞥了一眼赫敏,显然希望这个小幽默能使她情绪缓和一些,但是赫敏仍然四肢紧紧地缠结在一起,表情像石板一块。

CHAPTER NINETEEN The Silver Doe

'Anyway, they had a row about whether I was Stan or not. It was a bit pathetic to be honest, but there were still five of them and only one of me and they'd taken my wand. Then two of them got into a fight and while the others were distracted I managed to hit the one holding me in the stomach, grabbed his wand, Disarmed the bloke holding mine and Disapparated. I didn't do it so well, Splinched myself again –' Ron held up his right hand to show two missing fingernails; Hermione raised her eyebrows coldly '– and I came out miles from where you were. By the time I got back to that bit of riverbank where we'd been … you'd gone.'

'Gosh, what a gripping story,' Hermione said, in the lofty voice she adopted when wishing to wound. 'You must have been simply terrified. Meanwhile, we went to Godric's Hollow and, let's think, what happened there, Harry? Oh yes, You-Know-Who's snake turned up, it nearly killed both of us and then You-Know-Who himself arrived and missed us by about a second.'

'What?' Ron said, gaping from her to Harry, but Hermione ignored him.

'Imagine losing fingernails, Harry! That really puts our sufferings into perspective, doesn't it?'

'Hermione,' said Harry quietly, 'Ron just saved my life.'

She appeared not to have heard him.

'One thing I would like to know, though,' she said, fixing her eyes on a spot a foot over Ron's head. 'How exactly did you find us tonight? That's important. Once we know, we'll be able to make sure we're not visited by anyone else we don't want to see.'

Ron glared at her, then pulled a small silver object from his jeans pocket.

'This.'

She had to look at Ron to see what he was showing them.

'The Deluminator?' she asked, so surprised she forgot to look cold and fierce.

'It doesn't just turn the lights on and off,' said Ron. 'I don't know how it works or why it happened then and not any other time, because I've been wanting to come back ever since I left. But I was listening to the radio, really early on Christmas morning, and I heard … I heard you.'

He was looking at Hermione.

'You heard me on the radio?' she asked incredulously.

第 19 章　银色的牝鹿

"总之，他们为我是不是斯坦争吵了起来，说实在的真有点可怜。但他们毕竟是五个对我一个，还抢走了我的魔杖。后来有两个人打了起来，趁其他人分神的时候，我一拳打在抓我的那人肚子上，夺过他的魔杖，对拿我魔杖的家伙使了个缴械咒，就幻影移形了。我做得不大好，又分体了——"罗恩举起右手，少了两个指甲。赫敏冷冷地扬起眉毛。"——显形的地方离你们好远。等我回到原来的河边时……你们已经走了。"

"哎呀，多么惊心动魄的故事，"赫敏说，用了她想伤害别人时惯用的那种高傲语气，"你一定吓坏了吧。而我们去了戈德里克山谷。让我想想，那儿发生了什么，哈利？哦，对了，神秘人的蛇蹿了出来，差点把我们咬死，然后神秘人亲自赶到，只差一秒钟就抓住我们了。"

"什么？"罗恩张大了嘴巴，望望赫敏又望望哈利，但赫敏没有睬他。

"想想看，丢了指甲，哈利！这真能衬出我们遭的罪多么渺小，是不是？"

"赫敏，"哈利低声说，"罗恩刚才救了我的命。"

她好像没有听见。

"不过，我倒想知道一点，"她说，眼睛盯着罗恩头顶上一英尺的地方，"你今晚是怎么找到我们的？这很重要。知道了这个，可以保证以后不再会有我们不想见到的人来打搅。"

罗恩瞪着她，然后从牛仔裤口袋里掏出一个银色的小东西。

"这个。"

为了看到他拿出的东西，赫敏不得不看了罗恩一眼。

"熄灯器？"她问，惊讶得忘记了摆出冷漠、凶狠的样子。

"它不只是能点灯熄灯，"罗恩说，"我也不知道它怎么会这样，我也不知道为什么偏偏在那一次而不是在其他时候，因为我自从离开之后一直都想回来的呀。那天我在听广播，是圣诞节的一大早，我听到……我听到了你的声音。"

他看着赫敏。

"你在广播里听到了我的声音？"赫敏不相信地问。

CHAPTER NINETEEN The Silver Doe

'No, I heard you coming out of my pocket. Your voice,' he held up the Deluminator again, 'came out of this.'

'And what exactly did I say?' asked Hermione, her tone somewhere between scepticism and curiosity.

'My name. "Ron." And you said ... something about a wand ...'

Hermione turned a fiery shade of scarlet. Harry remembered: it had been the first time Ron's name had been said aloud by either of them since the day he had left; Hermione had mentioned it when talking about repairing Harry's wand.

'So I took it out,' Ron went on, looking at the Deluminator, 'and it didn't seem different, or anything, but I was sure I'd heard you. So I clicked it. And the light went out in my room, but another light appeared right outside the window.'

Ron raised his empty hand and pointed in front of him, his eyes focused on something neither Harry nor Hermione could see.

'It was a ball of light, kind of pulsing, and bluish, like that light you get around a Portkey, you know?'

'Yeah,' said Harry and Hermione together, automatically.

'I knew this was it,' said Ron. 'I grabbed my stuff and packed it, then I put on my rucksack and went out into the garden.

'The little ball of light was hovering there, waiting for me, and when I came out it bobbed along a bit and I followed it behind the shed and then it ... well, it went inside me.'

'Sorry?' said Harry, sure he had not heard correctly.

'It sort of floated towards me,' said Ron, illustrating the movement with his free index finger, 'right to my chest, and then – it just went straight through. It was here,' he touched a point close to his heart, 'I could feel it, it was hot. And once it was inside me I knew what I was supposed to do, I knew it would take me where I needed to go. So I Disapparated and came out on the side of a hill. There was snow everywhere ...'

'We were there,' said Harry. 'We spent two nights there, and the second night I kept thinking I could hear someone moving around in the dark and calling out!'

'Yeah, well, that would've been me,' said Ron. 'Your protective spells work, anyway, because I couldn't see you and I couldn't hear you. I was sure you were around, though, so in the end I got in my sleeping bag and waited for one of you to appear. I thought you'd have to show yourselves when you packed up the tent.'

"不,我听到你在我的口袋里。你的声音,"他又举起熄灯器,"是从这个里面发出来的。"

"我究竟在说什么?"赫敏问,语调介于怀疑和好奇之间。

"我的名字,'罗恩'。你说到……什么魔杖……"

赫敏脸色变得赤红,哈利想起来了:那是罗恩走后他们第一次说出他的名字。赫敏在说修复哈利的魔杖时提到了他。

"于是我把它拿了出来,"罗恩看着熄灯器继续说,"它看上去没有什么异样,但我很确定我听到了你的声音,所以就摁了一下,我屋里的灯熄灭了,但另一个灯出现在窗外。"

罗恩举起空着的那只手指向前方,眼睛盯着哈利和赫敏都看不见的东西。

"那是一个光球,好像在搏动,蓝莹莹的,就像门钥匙周围的那种光,你们知道吧?"

"嗯。"哈利、赫敏一起不由自主地说。

"我知道这就是了,"罗恩说,"于是赶紧收拾东西,背上背包走进了花园。

"那个小光球停在空中等着我,我出来后,它上下浮动着飘了一段,我跟着它走到小屋后面,然后它……嗯,它飘进了我的身体里。"

"什么?"哈利以为自己没听清。

"它向我飘了过来,"罗恩用食指演示着说,"一直飘到我胸口,然后——它就进去了。在这儿,"他指着心脏附近的一点,"我能感觉到它,热乎乎的。它一进入我体内,我就知道该做什么了,它会带我去我必须去的地方。于是我幻影移形,来到了一个山坡上,到处都是雪……"

"我们去过那儿,"哈利说,"在那儿待了两夜,第二夜我总觉得有人在黑暗中走动、呼喊!"

"嗯,那应该就是我。"罗恩说,"至少,你们的防护咒是有效的,因为我看不见也听不见你们。但我相信你们就在附近,所以最后就钻进了睡袋,等你们哪一个出现。我想你们收帐篷时总会现身的。"

CHAPTER NINETEEN The Silver Doe

'No, actually,' said Hermione. 'We've been Disapparating under the Invisibility Cloak as an extra precaution. And we left really early, because, as Harry says, we'd heard somebody blundering around.'

'Well, I stayed on that hill all day,' said Ron. 'I kept hoping you'd appear. But when it started to get dark I knew I must have missed you, so I clicked the Deluminator again, the blue light came out and went inside me, and I Disapparated and arrived here, in these woods. I still couldn't see you, so I just had to hope one of you would show yourselves in the end – and Harry did. Well, I saw the doe first, obviously.'

'You saw the what?' said Hermione sharply.

They explained what had happened, and as the story of the silver doe and the sword in the pool unfolded, Hermione frowned from one to the other of them, concentrating so hard she forgot to keep her limbs locked together.

'But it must have been a Patronus!' she said. 'Couldn't you see who was casting it? Didn't you see anyone? And it led you to the sword! I can't believe this! Then what happened?'

Ron explained how he had watched Harry jump into the pool and had waited for him to resurface; how he had realised that something was wrong, dived in and saved Harry, then returned for the sword. He got as far as the opening of the locket, then hesitated, and Harry cut in.

'– and Ron stabbed it with the sword.'

'And ... and it went? Just like that?' she whispered.

'Well, it – it screamed,' said Harry, with half a glance at Ron. 'Here.'

He threw the locket into her lap; gingerly she picked it up and examined its punctured windows.

Deciding that it was at last safe to do so, Harry removed the Shield Charm with a wave of Hermione's wand and turned to Ron.

'Did you just say you got away from the Snatchers with a spare wand?'

'What?' said Ron, who had been watching Hermione examining the locket. 'Oh – oh yeah.'

He tugged open a buckle on his rucksack and pulled a short, dark wand out of its pocket. 'Here. I figured it's always handy to have a back-up.'

'You were right,' said Harry, holding out his hand. 'Mine's broken.'

'You're kidding?' Ron said, but at that moment Hermione got to her feet, and he looked apprehensive again.

第 19 章 银色的牝鹿

"其实不会,"赫敏说,"为了更加保险,我们都是在隐形衣下幻影移形。而且我们走得很早,因为正如哈利说的,我们听到有人在周围东碰西撞。"

"我在那座山上待了一整天,"罗恩说,"一直希望你们会出现。天黑时,我知道大概错过了,就又摁了一下熄灯器,蓝光出现了,又飘进了我的体内,我幻影移形到了这片林子里。还是看不到你们,我只能希望你们哪一个会出现——哈利出现了。哦,我显然是先看到了那头牝鹿。"

"你看到了什么?"赫敏尖声问。

他们俩讲述了刚才的奇遇。随着银色的牝鹿和池底宝剑故事的展开,赫敏皱着眉头来回看着他们俩,专心得忘记了缠紧四肢。

"但那一定是个守护神!"她说,"你们没看见是谁把它召出来的吗?没看见有人吗?它把你们领到了宝剑那里!真是难以置信!那后来呢?"

罗恩讲了自己看到哈利跳进池塘,想等他上来,然后意识到出了问题,急忙跳下去救上哈利,又回去捞出那把剑。他一直讲到打开挂坠盒,然后就犹豫了,于是哈利插了进来。

"——罗恩用宝剑刺穿了它。"

"然后……然后它就死了?就这样?"赫敏轻声问。

"哦,它——它尖叫来着。"哈利瞥了瞥罗恩说,"给。"

他把挂坠盒丢到赫敏膝上,赫敏小心翼翼地拿起来,细细查看着被刺破的小窗口。

哈利断定终于安全了,一挥赫敏的魔杖,解除了铁甲咒,又转向罗恩。

"你刚才说,你从搜捕队那儿逃走时还赚了根魔杖?"

"什么?"正在看赫敏检查挂坠盒的罗恩说,"哦——是啊。"

他扯开背包的一个扣带,从口袋里抽出一根短而黑的魔杖。"在这儿呢。我想有根备用总是好的。"

"你说得对,"哈利伸出手说,"我的断了。"

"你开玩笑吧?"罗恩说,但这时赫敏站起身,他又惶恐不安起来。

CHAPTER NINETEEN   The Silver Doe

Hermione put the vanquished Horcrux into the beaded bag, then climbed back into her bed and settled down without another word.

Ron passed Harry the new wand.

'About the best you could hope for, I think,' murmured Harry.

'Yeah,' said Ron. 'Could've been worse. Remember those birds she set on me?'

'I still haven't ruled it out,' came Hermione's muffled voice from beneath her blankets, but Harry saw Ron smiling slightly as he pulled his maroon pyjamas out of his rucksack.

第 19 章 银色的牝鹿

赫敏把被征服的魂器放进了串珠小包,爬回自己的床上,一言不发地躺下了。

罗恩把新魔杖递给了哈利。

"这就算是最好的情况了,我想。"哈利悄声道。

"是啊,"罗恩说,"还不算最糟,还记得她放出来啄我的那些鸟吗?"

"我还没有排除这个可能。"赫敏闷闷的声音从毯子下传来,但哈利看到罗恩露出一丝微笑,从背包里抽出了他的暗紫红色睡衣。

WIZARDING WORLD